Edward Bulwer Lytton

Bulwer's Plays

Vol. 1

Edward Bulwer Lytton

Bulwer's Plays
Vol. 1

ISBN/EAN: 9783337335137

Printed in Europe, USA, Canada, Australia, Japan

Cover: Foto ©Andreas Hilbeck / pixelio.de

More available books at **www.hansebooks.com**

DE WITT'S ACTING EDITION.

BULWER'S PLAYS:

BEING THE

COMPLETE DRAMATIC WORKS

OF

LORD LYTTON,

(SIR EDWARD LYTTON BULWER, BART.)

COMPRISING

THE LADY OF LYONS.	THE RIGHTFUL HEIR.
MONEY.	WALPOLE.
RICHELIEU.	NOT SO BAD AS WE SEEM.

THE DUCHESS DE LA VALLIÈRE.

FROM THE ORIGINAL TEXT, AS PRODUCED UNDER THE SUPERVISION OF THE AUTHOR AND MR. MACREADY.

AN ENTIRELY NEW ACTING EDITION.

WITH ADDITIONAL STAGE DIRECTIONS, ACCURATELY MARKED—FULL CAST OF CHARACTERS—SYNOPSIS OF SCENERY—COSTUMES—BILL FOR PRO-GRAMMES—STORY OF THE PLAY, AND REMARKS.

EDITED

By JOHN M. KINGDOM,

Author of "*Marcoretti,*" "*The Fountain of Beauty,*" "*A Life's Vengeance,*" "*Tancred,*" *etc.*

NEW YORK:

ROBERT M. DE WITT, PUBLISHER,

No. 33 Rose Street.

(BETWEEN DUANE AND FRANKFORT STREETS.)

THE LADY OF LYONS.

CAST OF CHARACTERS.

	Theatre Royal, Covent Garden, London, 1838.	Old Park Theatre, May 14, 1838.
Claude Melnotte	Mr. Macready.	Mr. Edwin Forrest.
Colonel Damas	Mr. Bartley.	Mr. Placide.
Beauseant	Mr. Elton.	Mr. Richings.
Glavis	Mr. Meadows.	Mr. Wm. Wheatley.
Mons. Deschappelles	Mr. Strickland.	Mr. Clarke.
Landlord	Mr. Yarnold.	
Gaspar	Mr. Diddear.	
Captain Gervais (1st Officer)	Mr. Howe.	
Captain Dupont (2d Officer)	Mr. Pritchard.	
Major Desmoulins (3d Officer)	Mr. Roberts.	
Notary	Mr. Harris.	
Servant	Mr. Bender.	
Pauline	Miss Helen Faucit.	Mrs. Richardson.
Madame Deschappelles	Mrs. Clifford.	Mrs. Wheatley.
Widow Melnotte	Mrs. Griffiths.	Miss Cushman.
Janet	Mrs. East.	
Marian	Miss Garrick.	

TIME IN REPRESENTATION—THREE HOURS.

SCENERY.

The scene is laid in France, in the city of Lyons and the neighborhood, during the period of 1795 to 1798

ACT I., Scene I.—Room in the house of M. Deschappelles at Lyons.
Garden scene background.
——.. | Window. | ..——
4th Groove.   4th Groove.

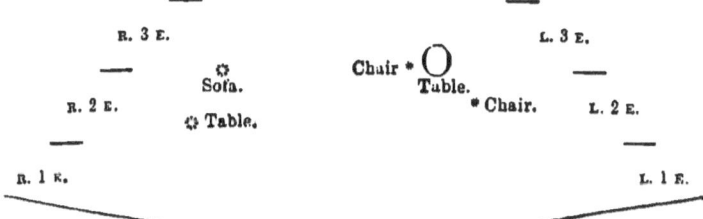

The flats in the 4th grooves represent one side of a handsomely furnished room; in the centre a large window, open, beyond which are beautiful gardens. The wings correspond with the room. A rich sofa placed in an oblique direction, R. C. Near R. 2 E. a small table, R. H. of sofa, with notes, letters, and bouquet of flowers in vase upon it. Rich table and chairs, L. C.

Scene II.—Exterior of a small village inn, in the 2d grooves. The left half of the scene represents a portion of the inn; casement and practicable door; above it is painted the sign of the inn, "The Golden Lion;" the right half of the scene represents open country, with the city of Lyons in the distance; a working moon to be used in *Act III.* but not in this scene.

Scene III.—Interior of the WIDOW MELNOTTE's cottage.

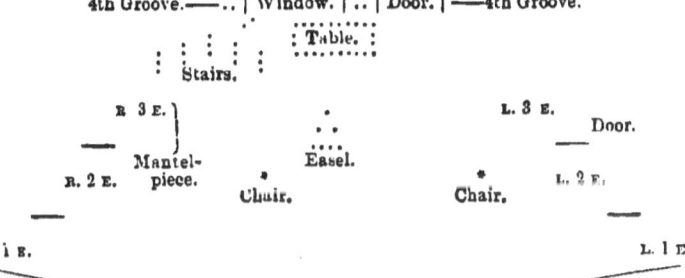

In the 4th grooves the flat represents one side of a neat and homely cottage. It, U. E. a flight of stairs, projecting some distance on the stage, leading to the upper rooms. Door L. F. Practicable lattice window, C. F., with curtains drawn back. Door L. H., between 2 E. and 3 E. Painter's easel with pictures upon it, brushes, etc., placed C., in a slanting direction towards the window, covered by a curtain. Chairs L. C. and R. C.—plain oaken chairs. Mantel-piece R. H., between 2 E. and 3 E., and over it, fencing foils, crossed. Flowers on the mantel-piece and at the window, through which flower garden is seen; underneath the window an oaken table with guitar and portfolio upon it. Everything has a neat and clean appearance.

ACT II., Scene I.—The gardens of M. DESCHAPPELLES' house at Lyons. The flats placed in the 4th grooves represent beautiful gardens. Wings R. H., to correspond. From L. S. E. up to the flats a portion of the house is shown, and another portion in continuation, L. H. F., with entrance ways L. 3 E. and L. U. E.

ACT III., Scene I.—Exterior of the Golden Lion Inn. Same as Scene II., Act I., only that it is now evening and the moon rises during the progress of the business of the Scene.

Scene II.—Interior of the WIDOW MELNOTTE's cottage, as before.

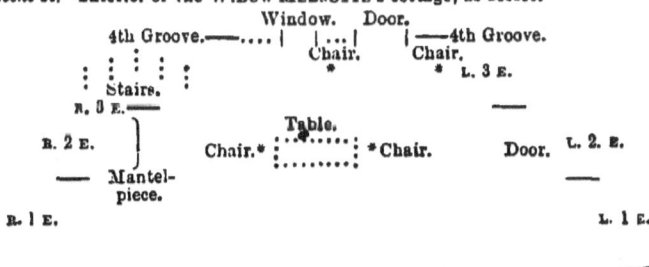

In the 4th grooves one side of the apartment as before, but the window curtains are drawn. A chair between the door and window, another L. H. U. E. A table C., with cloth, plates, etc., spread for supper. Candlestick and lighted candle. A chair on either side, R. C. and L. C.

ACT IV., Scene I.—Same as the last, but the cloth and supper things have been removed and in their place writing materials; the candle remains.

ACT V., Scene I.—A street in Lyons. The old French style of houses, in 2d grooves

Scene II.—Room in the house of M. DESCHAPPELLES—as before, but not so richly furnished.

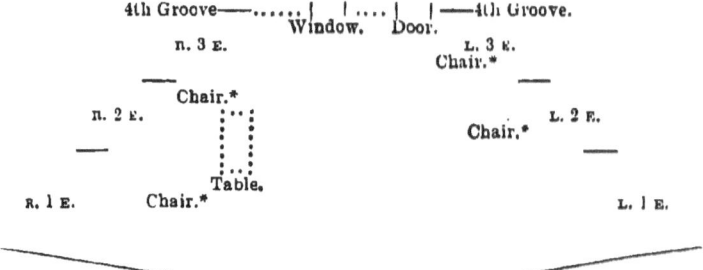

In the 4th grooves the scene represents the side of the apartment. Window, C. F.,
garden beyond. D. L. F. A table and chairs R. C., with writing materials upon it.
Chairs L. 2 E. and L. U. E.

COSTUMES.

CLAUDE MELNOTTE.—*Act I.*—Loose blouse, blue, with waist belt, cap, and loose,
light trousers, and shoes—but all of good quality. *Act II.*—Dark green coat
with broad facings, broad black braid across breast and cuffs; knee breeches,
dark silk stockings, shoes and buckles, black hat, turned up with a side loop.
Act III.—Same with the addition of a cloak. *Act V.*—Blue military coat with
broad tails, broad lappels faced with white and trimmed with lace, and also
cuffs, epaulettes; white small clothes and knee boots fitting to leg, belt and tri-
colored sash, and sword, three-cornered hat with tri-colored knot. Moustache;
complexion bronzed, and military cloak.
COLONEL DAMAS.—*Act I.*—Blue coat and vest, trimmed with lace, broad lappels and
cuffs, dark pantaloons and tight boots; tri-colored knot on three-cornered hat.
Act V.—Similar dress to CLAUDE'S, with the exception of the cloak.
BEAUSEANT.—*Act I.*—Dark claret-colored coat, reaching to the knee, broad lappels
and facings braided, and also on the cuffs; pantaloons and high boots, after the
Hessian style, fitting close to the leg; three-cornered hat with tri-color. *Act V.*
—Similar kind of coat, white knee-breeches, stockings, and shoes with buckles;
three-cornered hat and rosette.
GLAVIS.—*Act I.*—Similar to BEAUSEANT'S, but not quite so good in appearance.
MONS. DESCHAPPELLES.—*Act I.*—Dark gray surtout coat, reaching to the knees,
broad lappels, silk facings and braid, as also on cuffs, knee-breeches, three-cor-
nered hat and rosette. *Act V.*—A similar dress, but rather mean in appearance.
LANDLORD.—Blue blouse, loose breeches, and gaiters, white apron, and half sleeves,
white, from wrist to elbow.
GASPAR.—Coarse blouse or short jacket, wide trousers, shoes, and cap of liberty.
CAPT. GERVAIS.
CAPT. DUPONT.   } Similar dresses to COL. DAMAS, but not so heavily orna-
MAJOR DESMOULINS.   } mented or rich looking.
NOTARY.—Black stuff gown, fastened round the waist and reaching nearly to the feet,
skull cap with broad top, black pantaloons, stockings and shoes.
SERVANTS.—Similar to GASPER.
PAULINE.—*Act I.*—Rich silk dress (any color), high waisted, arms bare, lace shawl
or scarf over shoulders, rose in hair, which is worn plain, small bonnet. *Act II.*
—Similar costume, but of different material. *Act V.*—Plain dark dress, meaner
in appearance than before, edged with white trimmings, neck and sleeves.

MADAME DESCHAPPELLES.—*Act I.*—Rich green silk dress, trimmed with lace, small bonnet, black lace scarf. *Act V.*—Plain black dress, moderately trimmed with lace.

WIDOW MELNOTTE.—Plain brown stuff dress, neat white cap and apron, shoes with buckles

JANET. } Dresses of plain materials, white caps and aprons, blue stockings and
MARIAN. } shoes.

PROPERTIES.

ACT I., *Scene 1.*—Rich sofa; two tables; three or four chairs; bouquet of flowers, in vase; letters and notes. *Scene 2.*—A bill of fare. *Scene 3.*—An old-fashioned oaken table; portfolio; guitar; painter's easel; brushes and palette; painting on it of a female bust, covered by a curtain; two or three vases of flowers in the latticed window and on the mantel-piece; two old-fashioned chairs; rifle for CLAUDE; letters for GASPAR and BEAUSEANT's servant.

ACT II., *Scene 1.*—Fan for MAD. DESCHAPPELLES; diamond ring and snuff-box for CLAUDE; letters; two swords.

ACT III., *Scene 1.*—Purse with money for BEAUSEANT. *Scene 2.*—Old-fashioned oak table; four chairs; tablecloth, plates, etc.; candle and candlestick.

ACT IV., *Scene 1.*—Same as last scene, except that the cloth and plates have been removed; writing materials; pistol for BEAUSEANT; folded paper for CLAUDE.

ACT V., *Scene 1.*—Snuff-box for DESCHAPELLES. *Scene 2.*—Table, not very rich-looking, and four chairs; folded paper for M. DESCHAPELLES; marriage contract, papers and bag for NOTARY; writing materials; bundle of banknotes for BEAUSEANT; pocket-book and notes for CLAUDE.

STORY OF THE PLAY.

IN the year 1795 there resided in the quaint old city of Lyons in France a wealthy family by the name of Deschappelles. The husband had amassed a large fortune as a silk manufacturer, and had passed through the early part of the Revolution without sustaining any noticeable loss. Madame Deschappelles, as frequently the case, was the ruler of the house; and the success of her husband in amassing wealth had put into her head very high and aristocratic notions far beyond her position, and certainly not in keeping with the Republican spirit of the times. They had but one child, Pauline, a girl of such surpassing and attractive loveliness, that old and young —rich and poor—all paid homage to her as the Beauty of Lyons. For her, Madame Deschappelles was fully determined a brilliant marriage should be brought about. It was true that the aristocracy of France had been cleared out, the Revolution had reduced every one to a common level, only one degree of rank was known, that of "citizen," but the designing mother conceived it to be possible to catch some foreign prince or nobleman who might be travelling *incog.*; no matter how it was to be brought about, nothing less than a prince was to possess the hand of the rich and beautiful Lady of Lyons,

Amongst the numerous suitors, who had made an offer of his heart and fortune, and had been rejected, was a Mons. Beauseant, who, if his deceased father had not been deprived of his title, would have been a Marquis, but as he was not one, he fell below Madame Deschappelles' standard of perfection, and in spite of the temptation of his great wealth, his offer was refused. It is at this point the play commences.

Smarting severely under the indignity he considered he had suffered by receiving a refusal from a merchant's daughter, and the ridicule he would be exposed to throughout the city when it became known, he resolves to be revenged, to seek some plan to humble her pride severely ; an opportunity soon presents itself.

On journeying from Lyons to his chateau, he meets with one of his friends, M. Glavis, to whom, whilst baiting his horses at the Golden Lion Inn, a few miles from the city, he reveals all that has taken place and his intentions. As he is doing so, he is interrupted by loud shouts of " Long live the Prince." This cry of " Prince," when royalty and nobility no longer existed, astonishes him, and he calls out the landlord of the inn to give an explanation. From this source he finds that the so called prince is the pride of the village—Claude Melnotte—the only son of a deceased gardener, who had left him pretty well off, with a mother who doated upon him. Upon the father's death, a great change was observed in Claude. He threw up his trade, took to reading and studying much, hired a professor from Lyons, and soon became an accomplished scholar, a skillful fencer, a musician, and an artist. Handsome, strong, and brave, the lads of the village swore by him and the girls prayed for him. They called him " Prince " because he was at the head of them all, had a proud bearing, wore fine clothes, and, in fact, as they said, " looked like a prince." Beauseant further learned that it was reported and believed, Claude Melnotte was madly in love with the Beauty of Lyons—the seeds of the passion having been first planted when he worked with his father in M. Deschappelles' garden ; and that upon his father's death, it was the ambitious hope of winning her had induced him to seek the education and accomplishments which he had so successfully done. It was believed, however, that the Beauty of Lyons had never seen him, to know of, or to encourage, his love.

The idea at once strikes Beauseant that here are the means of revenge. He will induce Claude to pass himself off as a foreign prince, travelling quietly for pleasure, provide him with money, jewels, horses, carriages, servants ; introduce him as such to the Deschappelles family, make him propose to Pauline, and, by working upon the ambitious pride of her mother, bring about a marriage ; then strip him of his borrowed plumes and crush the haughty beauty. Accordingly he sends a letter to Claude requesting him to come to the inn.

After his success in winning the rifle prizes at the village festival, Claude returns to his mother's cottage, elated with joy, but his mind is still occupied with the grand desire of his existence—to be worthier to love Pauline. In vain does his loving mother point out the absurdity of his hopes. Useless—day and night he thinks and dreams of her ; every morning he sends her the choicest flowers he can pick ; he has painted her image from memory ; nay, more, that morning he has gone to the fullest extent ; he has set forth his worship in poetry, signed his own name, and sent the verses to her by a trusty messenger. Alas ! a fearful blow awaits him. His messenger returns not only bringing back the letter which had been thrown at his feet, but also the galling news that he had been driven from the door with kicks and blows. Crushed and bewildered, Claude's every hope seems blasted, when Beauseant's letter is brought in. It promises success (the writer telling him he knows his secret), upon condition that he will undertake to bear his bride to his mother's cottage on the wedding night. Is revenge or love the stronger ? Half frenzied as he is, he goes with the messenger and the compact is made.

By well contrived means, he is introduced into the family of the Deschappelles as the Prince of Como, travelling incognito, for fear of the interference of the Republican government, and by his presumed rank but real attraction and accomplishments, very soon secures the love of Pauline and the consent of her parents to a union.

His conduct, however, does not please Colonel Damas, a rough and ready soldier, and cousin to Pauline ; he suspects there is some deception, and to test him, addresses him in Italian, a language which Claude is, unfortunately, not master of ; he evades it as best he can, but only to convince the Colonel of the correctness of his suspicions, and he determines to insult him and force him to fight. With the infatuated mother and daughter, Claude is more successful ; they do not see any absolute reason why an Italian Prince is bound to speak or understand his native tongue.

He further enchants Pauline, by the description he gives, not of his own palace on the lake of Como, but of a palace of eternal love and summer, joy and happiness — one of the most exquisite pieces of poetry ever written.

Beauseant now claims from him the fulfillment of the bond ; he hesitates. Beauseant points out to him, that Damas suspects him, the police will be set to work, arrest will follow, he will be sent to jail as a swindler, and Pauline will despise and execrate him. He consents, and is left alone—Damas returns, and insists, now that the ladies are not there, upon crossing swords with him. Excitedly, Claude accepts the offer, after a few passes disarms the Colonel, and generously returns him his sword. Delighted with his skill and gentlemanly bearing, the officer promises that if Claude should ever want his assistance or friendship, be he a prince or not, he shall have it.

Immediately, upon quitting Claude, Beauseant finds means to float a story that the republican authorities are looking after the prince ; consequently an immediate marriage is absolutely necessary ; this is agreed to and it takes place.

By a strange chance, the carriage conveying Claude and his bride to his mother's cottage, according to the bond with Beauseant, breaks down, near the Golden Lion Inn, and they are obliged to alight and seek shelter there. They are exposed to the half-suppressed smiles and ridicule of the landlord and his servants, who, of course, recognize Claude, though not openly ; all of which is a great mystery to Pauline, and the more so, when Claude induces her to continue the journey on foot, as she believes him to be strange to the place : but the climax is reached, and her agony intensified, when she is led into the humble dwelling of the Widow Melnotte.

Light breaks upon her—the veil is lifted from her eyes : she has been deceived— all is revealed—and in bitter language she reproaches him for his conduct.

In a speech of most beautiful pathos and faultless construction, Claude pictures to her the story of his love, his hopes and sufferings, and lays at her feet his husband's rights, declaring that a marriage so brought about is null and void, according to the laws of France—that under his aged mother's care she shall, that night, sleep in peace and safety, and in the morning he will restore her to her father, pure and unsullied as he had received her.

With broken-heart and fevered brain, he writes to M. Deschappelles, and in the morning awaits patiently his arrival. Beauseant takes the opportunity to call, to gloat over the misery he has created, and in the excitement of his triumph, goes so far as to insult Pauline, but the strong arm of her husband hurls him off, and he retreats with threats of renewed vengeance.

M. Deschappelles arrives, and Claude, after a brief explanation, places in his hands a full confession of the fraud that has been practiced, and his consent to a divorce — that pure and spotless he yields her back, and in a distant land he intends to mourn his sin, and pray for peace and forgiveness. Here comes forth a fine burst of maternal love ; in sorrow or in guilt, the widow will not disown her son : for no divorce can part them. This noble feeling arouses the woman and the wife in Pauline, and throwing herself into Claude's arms, she implores him to take her to his bosom. Her parents threaten to discard and disinherit her—Claude is inexorable ; he refuses firmly. Colonel Damas is charmed with his noble bearing, he tells him he is leaving that day to join the Army of Italy, and offers to take him. It is done ; fame or death are before him ; with a bitter struggle, Claude Melnotte sets out for the army.

Two years and a half elapse. Time has worked changes with all. M. Deschappelles has suffered such heavy reverses that he stands upon the brink of ruin. Beauseant, aware of this, offers to help him in return for Pauline's hand ; to save her father from destruction she consents to the marriage.

Claude, under the assumed name of Morier, has passed safely through the campaign, and returns wealthy, renowned, and with the rank of Colonel. Damas learns of the intended marriage, and he suggests that Claude, who, with his altered appearance, through hard service and change of dress, is not likely to be recognized, should be present at the signing of the contract of marriage—to take a last farewell; to this he agrees. Damas introduces him as his most particular friend and as a bosom comrade of Claude. Pauline eagerly appeals to him to bear to Claude her undying love, and tells him of the reason that she is making the sacrifice of all earthly happiness. Beauseant produces the roll of notes he is ready to hand over upon the signing of the contract. Pauline is about to do so, when Claude, seizing the contract, tears it into pieces, at the same time throwing to the merchant twice the proffered amount.

Beauseant retires defeated and angered; with the others all is happiness. Claude has blotted the stain from his name and redeemed his honor ; Pauline has regained her husband ; the merchant is restored to his high position ; and even Madam Deschappelles admits :

"A Colonel and a hero ! Well, that's something !"

REMARKS.

As "good wine needs no bush" so any panegryic upon the brilliant writings of Lord Lytton (but who will always be better known and spoken of as " Bulwer"— Sir Edward Lytton Bulwer)—is perfectly unnecessary. The hold that his works have taken in America is very great, and his reputation is daily increasing.

For a long time yet across the Atlantic, will live the name and works of James Fenimore Cooper, and equally so on this side rise those of Bulwer.

Nor is this to be wondered at, when the most glowing enconiums possible have been passed upon him in every circle. *Blackwood's Magazine* said of him :

" To Bulwer, the author of ' Pelham,' ' The Caxtons ' and ' My Novel,' we assign the highest place among modern writers of fiction. There is always power in the creation of his fancy; he is always polished, witty, learned. Since the days of Scott were ended, there is, in our own opinion, no pinacle so high as that on which we hang our wreath to Bulwer."

And the great American author, Edgar A. Poe, spoke of him thus :

" Who is there uniting the imagination, the passion, the humor, the energy, the knowledge of the heart, the artist-like eye, the originality, the fancy, and the learning of Bulwer ? In a vivid wit—in profundity and a gothic massiveness of thought —in style—in a calm certainty of definitiveness of purpose—in industry, and, above all, in the power of controlling and regulating by volition his illimitable faculties of mind, he is unequalled."

Such are specimens of the universal opinion entertained of the author of " The Lady of Lyons" " Richelieu " and " Money," Plays which will retain their position on the stage for years and years to come, and which will be published in this series, in the order named :

The period chosen for the incidents of the present play, is some years after the commencement of the Revolution in France. Arising chiefly from oppressive taxation, a spirit of discontent had long been growing up amongst the middle and lower classes against the sovereign power and the aristocracy. Political intrigues and crafty, remorseless schemes fed and fanned the flame which spread throughout the country with fearful and terrible rapidity. Many of the people and their leaders lost their heads by wild and ferocious delirium; the royal family and hundreds of the nobility and gentry lost theirs by the guillotine. And so, in' one continual scene of tumult, riot, debauchery and blood, year after year had passed on—now one party ruling, and now another, until at the period when the play commences, the governing power consisted of a body of men, or deputies, chosen from the people— and termed " The Directory "—all of them " Citizens," the only term recognized— all degrees of nobility and rank having been abolished.

The author's good judgment is most felicitously shown in selecting France and this period for the action of his play. Its emotional style is precisely of the nature to be found in that country, and the events then in progress enabled him to send his hero into the army and raise him naturally, and with a rapidity that was then not at all uncommon, to honor and wealth, instead of resorting to the old stagey devices of "unexpected fortune," "death of a wealthy uncle in India," and other reasons *ad libitum* and *ad nauseam*. Any and every position was open to a daring and successful soldier. Napoleon Bonaparte progressed from an artillery lieutenant to First Consul and Emperor; Claude Melnotte was more modest in his ambition, he was content to stop at Colonel.

Though very beautiful, in many respects, the play is undoubtedly to some extent faulty and forced in construction, yet, at the same time, the quickness of action, telling points, and beauty of language, rivet and please an audience and push aside any imperfections.

It is a curious fact, but fact it is, that very few good poets or novelists make good playwrights, their works require more excision and reforming than those written direct for the stage by practical dramatic hands. The Lady of Lyons, as acted, differs much from the dramatic poem as originally published.

Upon the first production of this play, at Covent Garden Theatre Royal, London, in 1838, it had the advantage of being most effectively cast—and probably never since have all the parts been so well and evenly filled. It must, however, be remembered, that the author knew what the company could do, and had them in mind when he wrote the play. Every person engaged, rose afterwards to a leading position in the profession. Mr. Macready, the representative of the hero of the play, was in every respect admirably adapted to the part. Educated for the bar, he quitted that profession for the stage, and combining a fine appearance with high intellect, an excellent voice and good elocution, he was all that the author could desire. He continued his successful career for many years, and held his position against all comers. Mr. Elton made one of the best *Beauseants* ever seen upon the stage. He steadily increased his laurels, and at the time of his lamented death (he was lost at sea) he occupied a position in the gallery of public favorites. Mr. Diddear made a hit in the small but telling part of Gaspar, and afterwards led a good career.

Claude Melnotte is a fine drawn character. It depictures well high ambition, ardent love, and at the same time a deep sense of true nobility and honor. His pride, his consciousness of possessing sterling merit worthy of the best of women, are for the moment crushed by the insulting treatment to his messenger, and the scornful rejection of his verses. It is at this opportune moment for evil, that the tempter comes, and he falls an easy victim to Beauseant's artful plans. But the principles of reason and honor revive; his eyes open to the discovery of the cruel fraud he has committed, and the grievous wrong and sacrifice he was about to cause for his own selfish ends. In true and pure nobility of spirit, he restores Pauline to her parents; lost to him forever unless he should succeed in the path of glory. This character has always been a great favorite with leading actors. Macready was followed by Charles Kean, Phelps, Creswick, James Anderson, and a host of others, by all of whom it was well rendered, and last, though by no means least, Barry Sullivan, who may be considered at the present period, the best Claude Melnotte on the English stage. The celebrated French actor, M. Fechter, also appeared in it, and in a version upon which he exercised his high talents and skill, by making various little practical alterations, he met with very great success, as he does in most of his parts.

Pauline is a sweet but somewhat curious type of woman. She has a warm, loving and sensitive heart, much injured by the lofty aspirations and vanity instilled into her by her flattering and ambitious mother. Not only by his presumed rank, but by his warm and passionate love and glowing language, Claude has won her affections, and though the fearful discovery of his deceit crushes them for the time, the true woman speaks forth and remains firm to the end. She is willing to give her hand to save her father from ruin, but, heart and soul, her love is Claude's.

Miss Helen Faucit was everything that could be desired to realize the author's picture. Young, beautiful, and accomplished, she made a great hit, and for many years afterwards held firm ground in public favor. Her intellect, beauty, talent and purity, won for her, as a husband, an accomplished scholar, gentleman, and lawyer (Mr. Theodore Martin), and there has, perhaps, never been a finer scene than when she took her farewell of the stage.

In Colonel Damas we have a well-drawn specimen of an honest and blunt soldier. He openly expresses his disapprobation of the scheming high notions of his relatives, and with the keenness of a well-trained soldier, he sees through the duplicity of Claude. But, rough as he is, he is open to conviction, and the skill and gallant bearing of his adversary win his admiration, his assistance and friendship. It is a capital part, giving ample scope for a good actor to make it a most effective one.

The Widow Melnotte is a neat little genial part. It is very touching when well played—the forcible points of maternal love are strongly and judiciously shown.

M. Deschappelles is simply a man of business; little sentiment or affection enters into his mind; his wife " rules the roost," and he looks after the money.

Madame Deschappelles is an excellent specimen of a vain, ambitious woman, whose only heaven seems to be " princes " or " lords." To the shrine of one or the other she is ready to sacrifice her daughter, and has carefully schooled her thoughts in that direction.

Beauseant is a crafty, self-inflated, and designing man; without principle, and presuming upon his father's former aristocratic position and his own wealth, he thinks, like many of a similar class in the present day, that they are sufficient to ensure success in everything he may undertake, and compliance with all his wishes —without the slightest regard to the claims of merit and the principles of honesty and integrity.

Even the landlord of the inn is a very neat little part, and can be made much of in the hands of a careful actor. Touching upon this, I remember an anecdote told me in England by the late William Searle, who occupied a very fair position in his profession. He was well educated, but like many young men at that time starting in the profession, he had, in travelling through the country, very much trouble to make both ends meet when business was not good—very often to slip away at nights and leave his lodgings unpaid. Upon one occasion, the company he was with was broken up. He sought, of course, a new engagement; he was but little known, and after a few words with the manager of another company, the question was abruptly put to him, " Can you do the Landlord in the Lady of Lyons ?"

To which he promptly and wittily replied, " I should say so, undoubtedly; I have done a good many landlords in my time, and never once failed."

He was engaged.

Now let us cross the water and come home. The eminent and great actor, Edwin Forrest, had appeared in London, in October, 1836, at the Theatre Royal, Drury Lane, as Spartacus in Dr. Bird's tragedy of the Gladiator, and achieved a decided success. He was intensely pleased with the production of the Lady of Lyons—his keen intellect and high genius at once saw and appreciated the beauty of the conception, and that its success here was as certain as in England. He returned to New York, and produced it at the Old Park Theatre, May 14, 1838, himself, of course, playing the hero. All the genius, energy, ability, and talent of this truly great actor were concentrated on the part; and from all the authorities I have looked at, it was a grand success, and I have little doubt his rendering of the character was equal to that of Macready's. Throughout the play he appears to have been well supported by an attractive and efficient Pauline, as also by an excellent Damas, Beauseant, and Madame Deschappelles. Taken altogether, it must have been cast almost as effectively as upon its first production. So successful was it, that the first three nights' takings are said to have realized $4,200. Mr. Forrest made this all through his life a favorite character, following it afterwards with Bulwer's succeeding plays of *Money* and *Richelieu*.

Mr. G. V. Brooke was another fine delineator of the character: indeed, it was almost the last he played in England previous to his departure for Australia in the unfortunate steamer, the *London*, which was wrecked in the Bay of Biscay, Jan. 11, 1866, when he and nearly all on board perished.

Mr. F. B. Conway, so recently deceased, also played the character at the Broadway Theatre, with considerable success. He had been educated in England previously in an excellent school, having had much experience in Dublin with Miss Helen Faucit (the original Pauline), and in London with the accomplished, beautiful, and versatile actress, Madame Vestris.

Mr. Thomas Placide, who played Colonel Damas, was a gentleman of much experience, having made his first appearance at the Park Theatre in 1823, and afterwards he visited England; his performance of the part is well recorded.

Mr. Richings, who filled the character of Beauseant, was an old stager at the Park Theatre, having first appeared there upon his arrival from England in Sept., 1821, as Harry Bertram, in "Guy Mannering." He continued a great favorite in the city until 1839, when he left for Philadelphia. He rendered the character of the rejected suitor in a style quite equal to the original.

Mrs. Wheatley's Madame Descheppelles is recorded as a finished piece of acting. She was one of the best representatives of old women upon the American stage. Possessed of remarkable study, she mastered the most difficult compositions with astounding rapidity, and her vivid and life-like acting was of a character that once seen could never be forgotten. Indeed, from all accounts, her Madame Deschappelles was a perfect gem.

One of the sweetest Paulines was Miss Laura Addison. She made a great hit in England, and first appeared at the Broadway Theatre, New York, in Sept., 1851. Twelve months afterwards she died on board the steamer *Oregon*, on her passage from Albany to New York, and her sudden demise created a great sensation. She was buried in the Marble Cemetery, Second street, New York; foul play was suspected, but a post-mortem examination showed that congestion of the brain was the cause of her death.

It is impossible to give anything like a list of those who have taken the leading characters. As Claude, besides those previously named, we have seen Charles Dillon, J. C. Freer, D. W. Osbaldiston, Watkins Burroughs, T. C. King, George Vandenhoff, Herman Vezin, E. L. Davenport, and a host of others.

As Pauline, Miss Elsworthy, Miss Vincent, Mrs. C. Dillon, Kate Saxon, Kate Reignolds, Mrs. H. Vezin (formerly Mrs. Charles Young), Mrs. Mowatt, Mrs. J. B. Booth, and Mrs. Sinclair Forrest, etc., etc.

Wherever and whenever produced, and even with the drawback of an inferior cast, the intrinsic merits of the three plays are such that they have been and always will be successful. It is to me quite certain that not one jot of their brilliancy and effect has been lost by their transfer to the American boards.   J. M. K.

BILL FOR PROGRAMMES, Etc.

The events of this Play take place at the city of Lyons, in France. Period, 1795 to 1798.

ACT I.

SCENE I.—ROOM IN THE HOUSE OF MONS. DESCHAPPELLES.

The Beauty of Lyons—The Mysterious Flowers—An Offer of Marriage— The Refusal.

SCENE II.—EXTERIOR OF "THE GOLDEN LION INN," WITH DISTANT VIEW OF THE CITY OF LYONS.

The Rejected Suitor—Plans for Revenge—The Story of Claude Melnotte, the Gardener's Son—His Love for the Beauty of Lyons--The Letter and the Trap.

SCENE III.—INTERIOR OF THE WIDOW MELNOTTE'S COTTAGE.

Claude Melnotte, the " Prince " of Riflemen—A Story of Ambition—An Artist's Love and a Painter's Idol—The Poetry of Love—Indignity and Disgrace - The Scheme of Revenge begins to Work—The Letter and the Snare—The Bird Caught.

ACT II.

SCENE I.—THE GARDENS OF MONS. DESCHAPPELLES' HOUSE, AT LYONS.

The Plot Succeeds—The Gardener's Son Changed into a Prince—Free Gifts —A Dream of Love and Fairyland—Darkness Approaches—A Forced Marriage with the Beauty of Lyons—A Duel and a Generous Adversary —Threatened Arrest and a Hasty Marriage—" Woo, Wed, and bear her Home," so runs the Bond.

ACT III.

SCENE I.—EXTERIOR OF "THE GOLDEN LION INN." MOONLIGHT.

The Mask falling off—Departure of the Pretended Prince and his Bride for Home.

SCENE II.—INTERIOR OF THE WIDOW MELNOTTE'S COTTAGE.

Humble Preparations for a Wedding Supper—Surprise and Explanations— The Fraud Detected—A Thrilling Story of Love—A Bride but no Wife.

ACT IV.

SCENE I.—INTERIOR OF THE WIDOW MELNOTTE'S COTTAGE. MORNING.

Claude's noble Sacrifice and Devotion—A Mother's holy Love—Triumph of the Rejected Suitor—A Libertine's Attack—A Husband to the Rescue— The Last Embrace— The Fraud Confessed—Claude Consents to a Divorce —Devotion of the Beauty of Lyons—" Too late ! I achieve Rank and Fame, or fall upon the Field !"—Departure of Claude for the Army of Italy.

TWO YEARS AND A HALF ELAPSE.

ACT V.

Scene I.—A STREET IN LYONS.

*Return from the War—The Mysterious Colonel—Honor, Fame and Fortune
—Divorce of the Beauty of Lyons—A Plan for the Last Look of Love.*

Scene II.—ROOM IN THE HOUSE OF MONS. DESCHAPELLES.

*Preparations for the Marriage of Pauline and the Rejected Suitor—A
Daughter's Heart Sold to Save a Ruined Father—The Mysterious Colo-
nel Again—" He is a Friend of Claude Melnotte "—Story of a Woman's
Love—Pauline's Confession—" Tell him I love him, but a father calls
upon his child to save him. We shall meet again in heaven!"—The
Stakes are Doubled and Claude wins the Race—A Wife Regained—A
Parent's Honor Saved—Unity of Love and Pride—Happy Re-union of
Claude Melnotte and*

THE LADY OF LYONS.

EXPLANATION OF THE STAGE DIRECTIONS.

The Actor is supposed to face the Audience.

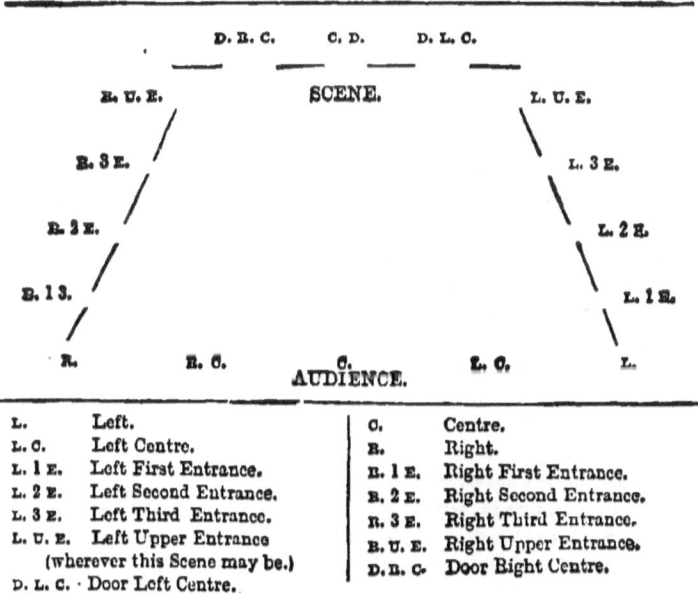

L.	Left.	c.	Centre.
L. C.	Left Centre.	R.	Right.
L. 1 E.	Left First Entrance.	R. 1 E.	Right First Entrance.
L. 2 E.	Left Second Entrance.	R. 2 E.	Right Second Entrance.
L. 3 E.	Left Third Entrance.	R. 3 E.	Right Third Entrance.
L. U. E.	Left Upper Entrance	R. U. E.	Right Upper Entrance.
	(wherever this Scene may be.)	D. R. C.	Door Right Centre.
D. L. C.	Door Left Centre.		

AUTHOR'S PREFACE.

AN indistinct recollection of the very pretty little tale, called "The Bellows-Mender," suggested the plot of this Drama. The incidents are, however, greatly altered from those of the tale, and the characters entirely recast.

Having long had a wish to illustrate certain periods of French history, so, in the selection of the date in which the scenes of this play are laid, I saw that the era of the Republic was that in which the incidents were rendered most probable, in which the probationary career of the hero could well be made sufficiently rapid for dramatic effect, and in which the character of the time itself was depicted by the agencies necessary to the conduct of the narrative. For during the early years of the first and most brilliant successes of the French Republic, in the general ferment of society, and the brief equalization of ranks, Claude's high-placed love, his ardent feelings, his unsettled principles (the struggle between which makes the passion of this drama), his ambition, and his career, were phenomena that characterized the age, and in which the spirit of the nation went along with the extravagance of the individual.

The play itself was composed with a twofold object. In the first place, sympathizing with the enterprise of Mr. Macready, as Manager of Covent Garden, and believing that many of the higher interests of the Drama were involved in the success or failure of an enterprise equally hazardous and disinterested, I felt, if I may so presume to express myself, something of the Brotherhood of Art, and it was only for Mr. Macready to think it possible that I might serve him in order to induce me to make the attempt.

Secondly, in that attempt I was mainly anxious to see whether or not, after the comparative failure on the stage of "The Duchess de la Valliere," certain critics had truly declared that it was not in my power to attain the art of dramatic construction and theatrical effect. I felt, indeed, that it was in this that a writer, accustomed to the narrative class of composition, would have the most both to learn and unlearn. Accordingly, it was to the development of the plot and the arrangement of the incidents that I directed my chief attention — and I sought to throw whatever belongs to poetry less into the diction and the "felicity of words" than into the construction of the story, the creation of the characters, and the spirit of the pervading sentiment.

The authorship of the play was neither avowed nor suspected until the play had established itself in public favor. The announcement of my name was the signal for attacks, chiefly political, to which it is now needless to refer. When a work has outlived for some time the earlier hostilities of criticism, there comes a new race of critics to which a writer may, for the most part, calmly trust for a fair consideration, whether of the faults or the merits of his performance.

THE LADY OF LYONS;

OR, LOVE AND PRIDE.

ACT I.

SCENE I.—*A room in the house of* M. Deschappelles, *at Lyons.* Pauline *reclining on a sofa,* R.; Marian, *her maid, fanning her,* R. *Flowers and notes on a table beside the sofa;* Madame Deschappelles *seated at a table,* L. C. *The gardens are seen from the open window.*

Mme. Deschap. Marian, put that rose a little more to the left (Marian *alters the position of a rose in* Pauline's *hair*) Ah, so! that improves the hair—the *tournure*, the *je ne sais quoi!* You are certainly very handsome, child!—quite my style—I don't wonder that you make such a sensation!—old, young, rich, and poor do homage to the Beauty of Lyons! Ah, we live again in our children—especially when they have our eyes and complexion!

Pauline (*languidly*) Dear mother, you spoil your Pauline. (*aside*) I wish I knew who sent me these flowers.

Mme. Deschap. No, child. If I praise you, it is only to inspire you with a proper ambition. You are born to make a great marriage. Beauty is valuable or worthless according as you invest the property to the best advantage. Marian, go and order the carriage!

[*Exit* Marian, R. 3 E.

Pauline. Who *can* it be that sends me, every day, these beautiful flowers? How sweet they are!

Enter Servant, L. 2 E.

Servant. Monsieur Beauseant, madam.

Mme. Deschap. Let him enter. (*Exit* Servant) Pauline, this is another offer!—I know it is! Your father should engage an additional clerk to keep the account book of your conquests.

Enter Beauseant, L. 2 E.

Beauseant. Ah, ladies, how fortunate I am to find you at home. (*aside*) How lovely she looks! It is a great sacrifice I make in marrying into a family in trade!—they will be eternally grateful! (*aloud*) Madam, you will permit me a word with your charming daughter? (*approaches* Pauline, *who rises disdainfully*) Mademoiselle, I have ventured to wait upon you, in a hope that you must long since have divined. Last night, when you outshone all the beauty of Lyons, you completed your conquest over me. You know that my fortune is not exceeded by any

estate in the province—you know that, but for the Revolution, which
has defrauded me of my titles, I should be noble. May I, then, trust
that you will not reject my alliance? I offer you my hand and heart.

PAULINE (*aside*). He has the air of a man who confers a favor. (*aloud*)
Sir, you are very condescending—I thank you humbly; but, being duly
sensible of my own demerits, you must allow me to decline the honor
you propose. (*curtsies, and turns away*.)

BEAU. (c.). Decline! impossible!—you are not serious. Madam,
suffer me to appeal to *you*. I am a suitor for your daughter's hand—
the settlements shall be worthy her beauty and my station. May I wait
on M. Deschappelles?

MME. DESCHAP. M. Deschappelles never interferes in the domestic
arrangements—you are very obliging. If you were still a marquis, or
if my daughter were intended to marry a commoner, why, perhaps, we
might give you the preference.

BEAU. A commoner!—we are all commoners in France now.

MME. DESCHAP. In France, yes; but there is a nobility still left in the
other countries in Europe. We are quite aware of your good qualities,
and don't doubt that you will find some lady more suitable to your pretensions. We shall be always happy to see you as an acquaintance, M.
Beauseant!—My dear child, the carriage will be here presently. (*goes to*
PAULINE.)

BEAU. Say no more, madam!—say no more! (*aside*) Refused! and
by a merchant's daughter!—refused! It will be all over Lyons before
sunset! I will go and bury myself in my chateau, study philosophy,
and turn woman-hater! Refused! They ought to be sent to a mad-
house! (*aloud*) Ladies, I have the honor to wish you a very good morning.   [*Exit,* L. 2 E.

MME. DESCHAP. How forward these men are!—I think, child, we
kept up our dignity. Any girl, however inexperienced, knows how to
accept an offer, but it requires a vast deal of address to refuse one with
proper condescension and disdain. I used to practise it at school with
the dancing-master.

Enter DAMAS, L 2 E.

DAMAS (c.). Good morning, cousin Deschappelles. Well, Pauline,
are you recovered from last night's ball? So many triumphs must be
very fatiguing. Even M. Glavis sighed most piteously when you departed; but that might be the effect of the supper.

PAULINE. M. Glavis, indeed!

MME. DESCHAP. M. Glavis?—as if my daughter would think of M.
Glavis!

DAMAS. Hey-day! why not? His father left him a very pretty fortune, and his birth is higher than yours, cousin Deschappelles. But
perhaps you are looking to M. Beauseant—his father was a marquis before the Revolution.

PAULINE. M. Beauseant! Cousin, you delight in tormenting me!

MME. DESCHAP. Don't mind him, Pauline! Cousin Damas, you have
no susceptibility of feeling—there is a certain indelicacy in all your
ideas. M. Beauseant knows already that he is no match for my daughter!

DAMAS. Pooh! pooh! one would think you intended your daughter
to marry a prince!

MME. DESCHAP. Well, and if I did?—what then? Many a foreign
prince——

DAMAS (*interrupting her*). Foreign prince!—foreign fiddlestick!—you
ought to be ashamed of such nonsense at your time of life. (*crosses* R.)

MME. DESCHAP. My time of life! That is an expression never applied to any lady till she is sixty-nine and three-quarters, and only then by the clergyman of the parish!

Enter SERVANT, L. 2 E.

SERVANT. Madam, the carriage is at the door.   [*Exit,* L. 2 E.

MME. DESCHAP. Come, child, put on your bonnet—you really have a very thoroughbred air—not at all like your poor father. (*fondly*) Ah, you little coquette! when a young lady is always making mischief, it is a sure sign that she takes after her mother!

PAULINE. Good day, cousin Damas—and a better humor to you. (*going back to the table, and taking the flowers*) Who *could* have sent me these flowers?   [*Exeunt* PAULINE *and* MADAME DESCHAPPELLES, L. 2 E.

DAMAS. That would be an excellent girl if her head had not been turned. I fear she is now become incorrigible! Zounds, what a lucky fellow I am to be still a bachelor! They may talk of the devotion of the sex—but the most faithful attachment in life is that of a woman in love—with herself.   [*Exit,* L. 2 E.

SCENE II.—*The exterior of a small village inn—sign " The Golden Lion "—a few leagues from Lyons, which is seen at a distance.*

BEAU. (*behind the scenes,* R.). Yes, you may bait the horses; we shall rest here an hour.

Enter BEAUSEANT *and* GLAVIS, R.

GLAVIS. Really, my dear Beauseant, consider that I have promised to spend a day or two with you at your chateau—that I am quite at your mercy for my entertainment—and yet you are as silent and as gloomy as a mute at a funeral, or an Englishman at a party of pleasure.

BEAU. Bear with me!—the fact is, that I am miserable.

GLA. You, the richest and gayest bachelor in Lyons?

BEAU. It is because I am a bachelor that I am miserable. Thou knowest Pauline—the only daughter of the rich merchant, M. Deschappelles?

GLA. Know her?—who does not?—as pretty as Venus, and as proud as Juno.

BEAU. Her taste is worse than her pride. (*drawing himself up*) Know, Glavis, she has actually refused *me!*

GLA. (*aside*). So she has me!—very consoling! In all cases of heartache the application of another man's disappointment draws out the pain and allays the irritation. (*aloud*) Refused you! and wherefore!

BEAU. I know not, unless it be because the Revolution swept away my father's title of Marquis—and she will not marry a commoner. Now, as we have no noblemen left in France—as we are all citizens and equals, she can only hope that, in spite of the war, some English Milord or German Count will risk his life, by coming to Lyons, that this *fille du Roturier* may condescend to accept him. Refused me, and with scorn! By Heaven, I'll not submit to it tamely; I'm in a perfect fever of mortification and rage. Refuse *me,* indeed! (*crosses* R.)

GLA. Be comforted, my dear fellow—I will tell you a secret. For the same reason she refused ME!

BEAU. You!—that's a very different matter! But give me your hand, Glavis—we'll think of some plan to humble her. *Mille diables!* I should like to see her married to a strolling player! (*crosses* L.)

Enter LANDLORD *from the Inn,* L. D. *in* F.

LANDLORD. Your servant, citizen Beauseant—servant, sir. Perhaps you will take dinner before you proceed to your chateau; our larder is most plentifully supplied.

BEAU. I have no appetite.

GLA. Nor I. Still it is bad travelling on an empty stomach. What have you got? (*takes the bill of fare from the* LANDLORD, *who has crossed* c. *Shout without:* "Long live the Prince!—long live the Prince!")

BEAU. The Prince!—what Prince is that? I thought we had no princes left in France.

LAND. Ha, ha! the lads always call him Prince. He has just won the prize in the shooting match, and they are taking him home in triumph.

BEAU. Him! and who's Mr. Him?

LAND. Who should he be but the pride of the village, Claude Melnotte? Of course you have heard of Claude Melnotte?

GLA (*giving back the bill of fare*). Never had that honor. Soup—ragout of hare—roast chicken, and, in short, all you have!

BEAU. The son of old Melnotte, the gardener?

LAND. Exactly so—a wonderful young man.

BEAU. How wonderful? Are his cabbages better than other people's?

LAND. Nay, he don't garden any more; his father left him well off. He's only a genius.

GLA. A what?

LAND. A genius!—a man who can do every thing in life except anything that's useful—that's a genius.

BEAU. You raise my curiosity—proceed.

LAND. Well, then, about four years ago, old Melnotte died, and left his son well to do in the world. We then all observed that a great change came over young Claude; he took to reading and Latin, and hired a professor from Lyons, who had so much in his head that he was forced to wear a great full-bottom wig to cover it. Then he took a fencing-master, and a dancing-master, and a music-master; and then he learned to paint; and at last it was said that young Claude was to go to Paris, and set up for a painter. The lads laughed at him at first; but he is a stout fellow, is Claude, and as brave as a lion, and soon taught them to laugh the wrong side of their mouths; and now all the boys swear by him, and all the girls pray for him.

BEAU. A promising youth, certainly! And why do they call him Prince?

LAND. Partly because he is at the head of them all, and partly because he has such a proud way with him, and wears such fine clothes—and, in short, looks like a prince.

BEAU. And what could have turned the foolish fellow's brain? The Revolution, I suppose?

LAND. Yes—the revolution that turns us all topsy-turvy—the revolution of Love.

BEAU. Romantic young Corydon! And with whom is he in love?

LAND. Why—but it is a secret, gentlemen.

BEAU. Oh, certainly.

LAND. Why, then, I hear from his mother, good soul, that it is no less a person than the Beauty of Lyons, Pauline Deschappelles.

BEAU *and* GLA. Ha, ha! Capital! (BEAUSEANT *crosses to* GLAVIS.)

LAND. You may laugh, but it is as true as I stand here.

BEAU. And what does the Beauty of Lyons say to his suit?

LAND. Lord, sir, she never even condescended to look at him, though when he was a boy he worked in her father's garden.

BEAU. Are you sure of that?

LAND. His mother says that Mademoiselle does not know him by sight.

BEAU. (*taking* GLAVIS *aside*). I have hit it—I have it—here is our revenge! Here is a prince for our damsel. Do you take me?

GLA. Deuce take me if I do!

BEAU. Blockhead!—it's as clear as a map. What if we could make this elegant clown pass himself off as a foreign prince?—lend him money, clothes, equipage for the purpose?—make him propose to Pauline?—marry Pauline? Would it not be delicious?

GLA. Ha, ha! Excellent! But how shall we support the necessary expenses of his highness?

BEAU. Pshaw! Revenge is worth a much larger sacrifice than a few hundred louis; as for details, my valet is the trustiest fellow in the world, and shall have the appointment of his highness's establishment. Let's go to him at once, and see if he be really this Admirable Crichton.

GLA. With all my heart; but the dinner?

BEAU. Always thinking of dinner! Hark ye, landlord; how far is it to young Melnotte's cottage? I should like to see such a prodigy.

LAND. Turn down the lane—then strike across the common—and you will see his mother's cottage.   [*Exit*, D. F.

BEAU. True, he lives with his mother. (*aside*) We will not trust to an old woman's discretion; better send for him hither. I'll just step in and write him a note. Come, Glavis.

GLA. Yes; Beauseant, Glavis & Co., manufacturers of princes, wholesale and retail—an uncommonly genteel line of business. But why so grave?

BEAU. You think only of the sport—I of the revenge.

[*Exeunt within the inn*, D. *in* F.

SCENE III.—*The interior of* MELNOTTE'S *cottage; flowers placed here and there; a guitar on an oaken table, with a portfolio, etc.; a picture on an easel, covered by a curtain; fencing-foils crossed over the mantel-piece; an attempt at refinement in spite of the homeliness of the furniture, etc.; a staircase to the right conducts to the upper story;* D. L. F.; *practicable window*, C. F.

The WIDOW *descends the stairs during the shouts.*

(*Shout without, distant*, L. U. E.). " Long live Claude Melnotte!" " Long live the Prince!"

WIDOW MELNOTTE. Hark! there's my dear son—carried off the prize, I'm sure; and now he'll want to treat them all. (*shouts nearer*, " Long live the Prince.")

CLAUDE MELNOTTE (*without*, L.). What! you will not come in, my friends? Well, well—there's a trifle to make merry elsewhere. Good day to you all—good day! (*Shouts*, " Hurrah! Long live Prince Claude!")

Enter CLAUDE MELNOTTE, L. D. *in* F., *with a rifle in his hand. He goes to the* WIDOW, *and kisses her.*

MEL. Give me joy, dear mother—I've won the prize—never missed one shot! Is it not handsome, this gun?

WIDOW. Humph! Well, what is it worth, Claude?

MEL. Worth! What is a ribband worth to a soldier? Worth! everything! Glory is priceless!"

WIDOW. Leave glory to great folks. Ah, Claude, Claude! castles in the air cost a vast deal to keep up. How is all this to end? What good does it do thee to learn Latin, and sing songs, and play on the guitar, and fence, and dance, and paint pictures? All very fine; but what does it bring in?

- MEL. Wealth! wealth, my mother! Wealth to the mind—wealth to the heart—high thoughts—bright dreams—the hope of fame—the ambition to be worthier to love Pauline.

WIDOW. My poor son!—the young lady will never think of thee.

MEL. Do the stars think of us? Yet if the prisoner see them shine into his dungeon, wouldst thou bid him turn away from *their* lustre? Even so from this low cell, poverty, I lift my eyes to Pauline and forget my chains. (*puts down his gun and cap near the staircase,* R. U. E., *the* WIDOW *takes a chair and sits* R. C. *Goes to the picture and draws aside the curtain*) See, this is her image—painted from memory. Oh, how the canvas wrongs her! (*takes up the brush and throws it aside*) I shall never be a painter. I can paint no likeness but one, and that is above all art. I would turn soldier—France needs soldiers!—but to leave the air that Pauline breathes! What is the hour?—so late? (*takes a chair and sits,* L. C.) I will tell thee a secret, mother. Thou knowest that for the last six weeks I have sent every day the rarest flowers to Pauline?—she wears them. I have seen them on her breast. Ah, and then the whole universe seemed filled with odors! I have now grown more bold—I have poured worship into poetry—I have sent the verses to Pauline—I have signed them with my own name. My messenger ought to be back by this time. I bade him wait for the answer.

WIDOW. And what answer do you expect, Claude?

MEL. (*rises*). That which the Queen of Navarre sent to the poor troubadour: "Let me see the Oracle that can tell nations I am beautiful!" She will admit me. I shall hear her speak—I shall meet her eyes—I shall read upon her cheek the sweet thoughts that translate themselves into blushes. Then,—then, oh, then—she may forget that I am the peasant's son! (*crosses to* L.)

WIDOW. Nay, if she will but hear thee talk, Claude.

MEL. I foresee it all. She will tell me that desert is the true rank. She will give me a badge—a flower—a glove! Oh, rapture! (*crosses* R.) I shall join the Armies of the Republic—I shall rise—I shall win a name that beauty will not blush to hear. I shall return with the right to say to her, "See, how love does not level the proud, but raises the humble!" Oh, how my heart swells within me! Oh, what glorious prophets of the future are youth and hope! (*knock at the* D. *in* F.) Who's there?

GASPAR (*without*). Gaspar.

MEL. Come in. (*the* WIDOW *opens the door.*)

Enter GASPAR, D. *in* F.

MEL. Welcome, Gaspar. welcome. Where is the letter? Why do you turn away; man? Where is the letter? (GASPAR *gives him one*) This! This is mine, the one I entrusted to thee. Didst thou not leave it?

GALPAR. Yes, I left it.

MEL. My own verses returned to me. Nothing else!

GASPAR. Thou wilt be proud to hear how thy messenger was honored. For thy sake, Melnotte, I have borne that which no Frenchman can bear without disgrace.

MEL. Disgrace, Gaspar! Disgrace?

GASPAR. I gave thy letter to the porter, who passed it from lackey to lackey till it reached the lady it was meant for.

MEL. It reached her, then—you are sure of that! It reached her—well, well '

GASPAR. It reached her, and was returned to me with blows. Dost hear, Melnotte ? with blows ! Death ! are we slaves still, that we are to be thus dealt with, we peasants ?

MEL. With blows ? No, Gaspar, no; not blows.

GASPAR. I could show thee the marks if it were not so deep a shame to bear them. The lackey who tossed thy letter into the mire swore that his lady and her mother never were so insulted. What could thy letter contain, Claude ?

MEL. (looking over the letter). Not a line that a serf might not have written to an Empress. No, not one.

GASPAR. They promise thee the same greeting they gave me, if thou wilt pass that way. Shall we endure this, Claude ?

MEL. (wringing GASPAR's hand). Forgive me, the fault is mine ; I have brought this on thee; I will not forget it ; thou shalt be avenged. The heartless insolence !

GASPAR. Thou art moved, Melnotte; think not of me; I would go through fire and water to serve thee ; but—a blow ! It is not the bruise that galls—it is the blush, Melnotte. (going)

MEL. Say, what message ? How insulted ? Wherefore ? What the offence ?

GASPAR. Did you not write to Pauline Deschappelles, the daughter of the rich merchant ?

MEL. Well ?

GASPAR. And are you not a peasant—a gardener's son ? that was the offence. Sleep on it, Melnotte. Blows to a French citizen ; blows !
[Exit, D. in F.

WIDOW. Now you are cured, Claude.

MEL. (tearing the letter). So do I scatter her image to the winds—I will stop her in the open streets—I will insult her—I will beat her menial ruffians—I will——(turns suddenly to WIDOW) Mother, am I hump-backed—deformed—hideous ?

WIDOW. You !

MEL. A coward—a thief—a liar ?

WIDOW. You !

MEL. Or a dull fool—a vain, drivelling, brainless idiot ?

WIDOW. No, no.

MEL. What am I then—worse than all these ? Why, I am a peasant. What has a peasant to do with love ? Vain revolutions, why lavish your cruelty on the great ? Oh, that we—we, the hewers of wood and drawers of water—had been swept away, so that the proud might learn what the world would be without us ! (paces the stage excitedly. Knock at the D. in F.)

Enter SERVANT *from the Inn,* D. *in* F.

SERVANT. A letter for Citizen Melnotte.

MEL. A letter ! from her perhaps—who sent thee ?

SERV. (R.). Why, Monsieur—I mean Citizen Beauseant, who stops to dine at the Golden Lion, on his way to his chateau.

MEL. Beauseant ! (reads) " Young man, I know thy secret—thou lovest above thy station ; if thou hast wit, courage, and discretion, I can secure to thee the realization of thy most sanguine hopes ; and the sole condition I ask in return is, that thou shalt be steadfast to thine own ends. I shall demand from thee a solemn oath to marry her whom thou

lovest; to bear her to thine home on thy wedding night. I am serious—
if thou wouldst learn more, lose not a moment, but follow the bearer of
this letter to thy friend and patron, CHARLES BEAUSEANT." Can I believe my eyes? Are our own passions the sorcerers that raise up for
us spirits of good or evil? I will go instantly. [*Exit* SERVANT, D. *in* F.

WIDOW. What is this, Claude?

MEL. "Marry her whom thou lovest"—"bear her to thine own
home." Oh, revenge and love; which of you is the stronger? (*gazing
on the picture*) Sweet face, thou smilest on me from the canvas; weak
fool that I am, do I then love her still? No, it is the vision of my own
romance that I have worshipped; it is the reality to which I bring scorn
for scorn. Adieu, mother! I will return anon. (*Exit* WIDOW *up the
staircase*) My brain reels—the earth swims before me. (*looks again at the
letter*) "Marry her whom thou lovest." No, it is *not* a mockery; I do
not dream !   [*Exit*, D. *in* F.

                              CURTAIN.

                        ———————

                          ACT II.

SCENE. I.—*The gardens of* M. DESCHAPPELLES' *house at Lyons—the house
                  seen at the back of the stage.*

        Enter BEAUSEANT *and* GLAVIS *from the house*, L. S. E.

BEAU. Well, what think you of my plot? Has it not succeeded to a
miracle? The instant that I introduced his Highness the Prince of Como
to the pompous mother and the scornful daughter, it was all over with
them; he came—he saw—he conquered; and, though it is not many
days since he arrived, they have already promised him the hand of Pauline.

GLA. It is lucky, though, that you told them his highness travelled
incognito, for fear the Directory (who are not very fond of princes)
should lay him by the heels; for he has a wonderful wish to keep up
his rank, and scatters our gold about with as much coolness as if he
were watering his own flower-pots.

BEAU. True, he is damnably extravagant; I think the sly dog does it
out of malice. However, it must be owned that he reflects credit on his
loyal subjects, and makes a very pretty figure in his fine clothes, with
my diamond snuff-box.

GLA. And my diamond ring! But do you think he will be firm to
the last? I fancy I see symptoms of relenting; he will never keep up
his rank if he once lets out his conscience.

BEAU. His oath binds him! he cannot retract without being for-
sworn, and those low fellows are always superstitious! But, as it is, I
tremble lest he be discovered; that bluff Colonel Damas (Madame Deschappelles' cousin) evidently suspects him; we must make haste and
conclude the farce; I have thought of a plan to end it this very day.

GLA. This very day! Poor Pauline! her dream will soon be over.

BEAU. Yes, this day they shall be married; this evening, according
to his oath, he shall carry his bride to the Golden Lion, and then pomp,
equipage, retinue, and title all shall vanish at once; and her Highness
the Princess shall find that she has refused the son of a Marquis, to
marry the son of a gardener. Oh, Pauline! once so loved, now hated,

yet still not relinquished, thou shalt drain the cup to the dregs—thou shalt know what it is to be humbled ! (*they go* L.)

Enter from the house, L. S. E., MELNOTTE, *as the Prince of Como, leading in* PAULINE ; MADAME DESCHAPPELLES, *fanning herself ;* and COLONEL DAMAS. BEAUSEANT *and* GLAVIS *bow respectfully.* PAULINE *and* MELNOTTE *walk apart.*

MME DESCHAP. Good morning, gentlemen ; really I am so fatigued with laughter ; the dear Prince is so entertaining. What wit he has ! Any one may see that he has spent his whole life in courts.

DAMAS (R.). And what the deuce do you know about courts, cousin Deschappelles ? You women regard men just as you buy books—you never care about what is in them, but how they are bound and lettered. 'Sdeath, I don't think you would even look at your Bible if it had not a title to it.

MME. DESCHAP. (R. C.). How coarse you are, cousin Damas ! quite the manners of a barrack—you don't deserve to be one of our family ; really, we must drop your acquaintance when Pauline marries. I cannot patronize any relations that would discredit my future son-in-law, Prince of Como.

MEL. (C., *advancing*). These are beautiful gardens, madam.

MME. DESCHAP. Does your highness really think so ?

MEL. They are laid out in the best taste ; who planned them ? (BEAUSEANT *and* GLAVIS *retire.*)

MME. DESCHAP. A gardener named Melnotte, your highness—an honest man who knew his station. I can't say as much for his son—a presuming fellow, who—ha, ha ! actually wrote verses—such doggerel !—to my daughter.

PAULINE. Yes, how you would have laughed at them, Prince ! *you* who write such beautiful verses !

MEL. This Melnotte must be a monstrous impudent person !

DAMAS. Is he good-looking ?

MME DESCHAP. I never notice such *canaille*—an ugly, mean-looking clown, if I remember right.

DAMAS. Yet I heard your porter say he was wonderfully like his highness.

MEL. (*taking snuff*). You are complimentary.

MME. DESCHAP. For shame, cousin Damas ! like the Prince, indeed !

PAULINE. Like you ! Ah, mother, like our beautiful Prince ! I'll never speak to you again, cousin Damas. (PAULINE, MADAME DESCHAPPLES, *and* DAMAS *retire,* R. BEAUSEANT *and* GLAVIS *advance,* L.)

MEL. (*aside*). Humph—rank is a great beautifier ! I never passed for an Apollo while I was a peasant ; if I am so handsome as a prince, what should I be as an emperor ! (*aloud*) Monsieur Beauseant, will you honor me ? (*offers snuff.*)

BEAU. No, your highness ; I have no small vices.

MEL. Nay, if it were a vice, you'd be sure to have it, Monsieur Beauseant. (MADAME DESCHAPPELLES *and* PAULINE *advance,* R. C.)

MME. DESCHAP. Ha ! ha ! how very severe—what wit !

BEAU. (*in a rage, and aside*). Curse his impertinence.

MME. DESCHAP. (C.). What a superb snuff-box !

PAULINE (R. C.). And what a beautiful ring !

MEL. You like the box—a trifle—interesting perhaps from associations —a present from Louis XIV. to my great-great-grandmother. Honor me by accepting it.

BEAU. (*plucking him by the sleeve*). How—what the devil ! my box—

are you mad ? It is worth five hundred louis. (MADAME DESCHAPPLLES *shows the box to* DAMAS.)

MEL. (*unheeding him, and turning to* PAULINE). And you like this ring ? Ah, it has, indeed, a lustre since your eyes have shone on it. (*placing it on her finger*) Henceforth hold me, sweet enchantress, the Slave of the Ring.

GLA. (*pulling him*). Stay, stay—what are you about ! My maiden aunt's legacy—a diamond of the first water. You shall be hanged for swindling, sir.

MEL. (*pretending not to hear*). It is curious, this ring ; it is the one with which my grandfather, the Doge of Venice, married the Adriatic ! (MADAME *and* PAULINE *examine the ring, and retire, R.*)

MEL. (*to* BEAUSEANT *and* GLAVIS). Fie, gentlemen ! princes must be generous. (*turns to* DAMAS, *who is* R. C., *and who watches them closely*) These kind friends have my interest so much at heart, that they are as careful of my property as if it were their own.

BEAU. *and* GLA. (*confusedly*). Ha ! ha ! very good joke that. (*appear to remonstrate with* MELNOTTE *in dumb show.*)

DAMAS. What's all that whispering ? I am sure there is some juggle here ; hang me, if I think he is an Italian after all. Gad, I'll try him. Servitore umillissimo, Eccellenza.* (CLAUDE *looks at* BEAUSEANT *for information.*)

MEL. Hum—what does he mean, I wonder ?

DAMAS. Godo di vedervi in buona salute.†

MEL. Hem—hem ! (*crosses, R.*)

DAMAS. Fa bel tempo—che si dice di nuovo ?‡

MEL. Well, sir, what's all that gibberish ?

DAMAS. Oh, oh ! only Italian, your highness—the Prince of Como does not understand his own language !

MEL. Not as you pronounce it ; who the deuce could ? (*goes up, c.*)

MME. DESCHAP. Ha ! ha ! cousin Damas, never pretend to what you don't know. (*goes to* MELNOTTE.)

PAULINE. Ha ! ha ! cousin Damas ; *you* speak Italian, indeed ! (*makes a mocking gesture at him, and joins* MELNOTTE *and* MADAME DESCHAPPELLES.)

BEAU. (*to* GLAVIS). Clever dog ! how ready !

GLA. (L.) Ready, yes ; with my diamond ring ! Damn his readiness. (*they retire a few paces.*)

DAMAS. Laugh at me ! laugh at a colonel in the French Army !—the fellow's an impostor ; I know he is. I 'll see if he understands fighting as well as he does Italian. (*goes up to him, and touches him upon the shoulder.* MELNOTTE *bows to the* LADIES *and comes forward*) Sir, you are a jackanapes ! Can you construe that ?

MEL. No, sir ; I never construe affronts in the presence of ladies ; byand by I shall be happy to take a lesson—or give one.

DAMAS. I'll find the occasion, never fear !

MME. DESCHAP. Where are you going, cousin ?

DAMAS. To correct my Italian. [*Exit into house,* L. S. E.

BEAU. (*to* GLAVIS). Let us after, and pacify him ; he evidently suspects something. (*going.*)

GLA. Yes !—but my diamond ring !

BEAU. And my box ! We are over-taxed fellow-subjects ! we must stop the supplies, and dethrone the prince.

GLA. Prince !—he ought to be heir-apparent to King Stork.

---

* Your Excellency's most humble servant.   † I am glad to see you in good health.
‡ Fine weather. What news is there ?

Exeunt BEAUSEANT *and* GLAVIS *into house*, L. S E.　*The* LADIES *and* MELNOTTE *advance.*

MME. DESCHAP. (R). Dare I ask your highness to forgive my cousin's insufferable vulgarity ?

PAULINE (L.). Oh, yes !—you will forgive his manner for the sake of his heart.

MEL. (C.). And the sake of his cousin. Ah, madam, there is one comfort in rank—we are so sure of our position that we are not easily affronted. Besides, M. Damas has bought the right of indulgence from his friends by never showing it to his enemies.

PAUL. Ah ! he is indeed as brave in action as he is rude in speech. He rose from the ranks to his present grade, and in two years !

MEL. In two years !—two years, did you say ?

MME. DESCHAP. (*aside*). I don't like leaving girls alone with their lovers; but, with a prince, it would be so ill-bred to be prudish.

[*Exit into house*, L. S. E.

MEL. You can be proud of your connection with one who owes his position to merit—not birth.

PAULINE. Why, yes ; but still——

MEL. Still what, Pauline?

PAULINE. There is something glorious in the heritage of command. A man who has ancestors is like a representative of the past.

MEL. True ; but, like other representatives, nine times out of ten he is a silent member. Ah, Pauline ! not to the past, but to the future, looks true nobility, and finds its blazon in posterity.

PAULINE. You say this to please me, who have no ancestors; but you, prince, must be proud of so illustrious a race !

MEL. No, no ! I would not, were I fifty times a prince, be a pensioner on the dead ! I honor birth and ancestry when they are regarded as the incentives to exertion, not the title-deeds to sloth ! I honor the laurels that overshadow the graves of our fathers—it is our fathers I emulate, when I desire that beneath the evergreen I myself have planted my own ashes may repose ! Dearest ! couldst thou but see with my eyes !

PAULINE. I cannot forego pride when I look on thee, and think that thou lovest me. Sweet Prince, tell me again of thy palace by the lake of Como ; it is so pleasant to hear of thy splendors since thou didst swear to me that they would be desolate without Pauline; and when thou describest them, it is with a mocking lip and a noble scorn, as if custom had made thee disdain greatness.

MEL. Nay, dearest, nay. if thou wouldst have me paint
　　　The home to which, could love fulfill its prayers,
　　　This hand would lead thee, listen !*　A deep vale
　　　Shut out by Alpine hills from the rude world ;
　　　Near a clear lake, margin'd by fruits of gold
　　　And whispering myrtles ; glassing softest skies,
　　　As cloudless, save with rare and roseate shadows
　　　As I would have thy fate !

---

* The reader will observe that Melnotte evades the request of Pauline. He proceeds to describe a home. which he does not say he possesses, but to which he would lead her, " *could love fulfill its prayers.*" This caution is intended as a reply to a sagacious critic who censures the description because it is not an exact and prosaic inventory of the characteristics of the Lake of Como ! When Melnotte, for instance, talks of birds " that syllable the name of Pauline " (by the way, a literal translation from an Italian poet), he is not thinking of ornithology, but probably of the " Arabian Nights." He is venting the extravagant but natural enthusiasm of the poet and the lover.

PAULINE.   My own dear love !

CLAUDE *and* PAULINE *pace the stage during this speech, and at the end* MEL-
NOTTE *stands* L.

MEL. A palace lifting to eternal summer
Its marble walls, from out a glossy bower
Of coolest foliage, musical with birds,
Whose songs should syllable thy name! At noon
We'd sit beneath the arching vines, and wonder
Why Earth could be unhappy, while the Heavens
Still left us youth and love! We'd have no friends
That were not lovers ; no ambition, save
To excel them all in love ; we'd read no books
That were not tales of love—that we might smile
To think how poorly eloquence of words
Translates the poetry of hearts like ours !
And when night came, amidst the breathless Heavens,
We'd guess what star should be our home when love
Becomes immortal ; while the perfumed light
Stole through the mist of alabaster lamps,
And every air was heavy with the sighs
Of orange groves and music from sweet lutes,
And murmurs of low fountains that gush forth
I' the midst of roses !—Dost thou like the picture ?
PAULINE. Oh, as the bee upon the flower, I hang
Upon the honey of thy eloquent tongue !
Am I not blest ? And if I love too wildly,
Who would not love thee like Pauline ?
MEL. (*bitterly*).   Oh, false one !
It is the *prince* thou lovest, not the *man ;*
If in the stead of luxury, pomp, and power,
I had painted poverty, and toil, and care,
Thou hadst found no honey on my tongue ; Pauline,
That is not love ! (*crosses* R.)
PAULINE.   `   Thou wrong'st me, cruel Prince !
At first, in truth, I might not have been won,
Save through the weakness of a flatter'd pride ;
But *now*—oh ! trust me—couldst thou fall from power
And sink——
MEL.   As low as that poor gardener's son
Who dared to lift his eyes to thee ?
PAULINE.   Even then,
Methinks thou wouldst be only made more dear
By the sweet thought that I could prove how deep
Is woman's love ! We are like the insects, caught
By the poor glittering of a garish flame ;
But, oh, the wings once scorch'd, the brightest star
Lures us no more ; and by the fatal light
We cling till death ! (*embrace.*)
MEL. Angel !
         (*aside*). O conscience ! conscience !
It must not be—her love hath grown a torture   `
Worse than her hate. I will at once to Beauseant,
And — ha ! he comes. Sweet love, one moment leave me.
I have business with these gentlemen—I—I
Will forthwith join you.

Enter BEAUSEANT *and* GLAVIS ; *they bow to* PAULINE, *and remain up stage.*

PAULINE. Do not tarry long ! [*Exit into house,* L. S. E.

BEAUSEANT *and* GLAVIS *advance.*

MEL. (c.). Release me from my oath—I will not marry her !
BEAU. Then thou art perjured. (GLAVIS *stands* L.)
MEL. No, I was not in my senses when I swore to thee to marry her !
I was blind to all but her scorn—deaf to all but my passion and my
rage ! Give me back my poverty and my honor.
BEAU. It is too late—you must marry her ! and this day. I have a
story already coined, and sure to pass current. This Damas suspects
thee—he will set the police to work—thou wilt be detected—Pauline
will despise and execrate thee. Thou wilt be sent to the common jail
as a swindler.
MEL. Fiend ! (*crosses to* R.)
BEAU. And in the heat of the girl's resentment (you know of what resentment is capable), and the parents' shame, she will be induced to
marry the first that offers—even perhaps your humble servant.
MEL. You ! No ; that were worse—for thou hast no mercy ! I will
marry her—I will keep my oath. Quick, then, with the damnable invention thou art hatching—quick, if thou wouldst not have me strangle
thee or myself. (*retires,* R)
GLA. What a tiger ! Too fierce for a prince—he ought to have been
the Grand Turk.
BEAU. Enough—I will use dispatch ; be prepared.
[*Exeunt* BEAUSEANT *and* GLAVIS *into house,* L. S. E. MELNOTTE *advances,* R.

Enter DAMAS, *from the house,* L. S. E., *with two swords.*

DAMAS. Now, then, sir, the ladies are no longer your excuse. I have
brought you a couple of dictionaries ; let us see if your highness can find
out the Latin for *bilbo.*
MEL. Away, sir ! I am in no humor for jesting.
DAMAS. I see you understand something of the grammar ; you decline the noun-substantive "small-sword " with great ease ; but that
won't do—you must take a lesson in *parsing.*
MEL. Fool ! (*crosses,* L.)
DAMAS. Sir, as sons take after their mother, so the man who calls me
a fool insults the lady who bore me ; there's no escape for you—fight
you shall, or——
MEL. (L.). Oh, enough ! enough—take your ground. (*they fight* ; DA-
MAS *is disarmed.* MELNOTTE *takes up the sword and returns it to* DAMAS
respectfully) A just punishment to the brave soldier who robs the State
of its best property—the sole right to his valor and his life.
DAMAS (R.). Sir, you fence exceedingly well ; you must be a man of
honor—I don't care a jot whether you are a prince ; but a man who has
carte and tierce at his finger's ends must be a gentleman.
MEL. (*aside*). Gentleman ! Ay, I was a gentleman before I turned
conspirator ; for honest men are the gentlemen of Nature ! (*aloud*) Colonel, they tell me you rose from the ranks.
DAMAS. I did.
MEL. And in two years !
DAMAS. It is true ; that's no wonder in our army at present. Why,
the oldest general in the service is scarcely thirty, and we have some of
two-and-twenty.

MEL Two-and-twenty!

DAMAS. Yes; in the French Army, now-a-days, promotion is not a matter of purchase. We are all heroes, because we may be all generals. We have no fear of the cypress, because we may all hope for the laurel.

MEL. A general at two-and-twenty! (*turning to* DAMAS) Sir, I may ask you a favor one of these days.

DAMAS. Sir, I shall be proud to grant it. (MELNOTTE *retires*) It is astonishing how much I like a man after I have fought with him. (*hides the swords,* R.)

Enter MADAME DESCHAPPELLES *and* BEAUSEANT, *from house,* L. S. E.
BEAUSEANT *crosses behind to* R.

MME DESCHAP. Oh, prince—prince! What do I hear? You must fly—you must quit us!

MEL. I!

BEAU. Yes, prince; read this letter, just received from my friend at Paris, one of the Directory; they suspect you of designs against the Republic; they are very suspicious of princes, and your family take part with the Austrians. Knowing that I introduced your highness at Lyons, my friend writes to me to say that you must quit the town immediately, or you will be arrested—thrown into prison, perhaps guillotined! Fly! I will order horses to your carriage instantly. Fly to Marseilles; there you can take ship to Leghorn.

MME. DESCHAP. And what's to become of Pauline? Am I not to be a mother to a princess, after all?

Enter PAULINE *and* MONSIEUR DESCHAPPELLES, *from house,* L. S. E.

PAULINE (*throwing herself into* MELNOTTE's *arms*). You must leave us. Leave Pauline!

BEAU. Not a moment is to be wasted.

M. DESCHAP. (C.). I will go to the magistrates, and inquire——

BEAU. Then he is lost; the magistrates, hearing he is suspected, will order his arrest.

MME. DESCHAP. And I shall not be a princess-dowager!

BEAU. Why not? There is only one thing to be done—send for the priest—let the marriage take place at once, and the prince carry home a bride. (*crosses to* L.)

MEL. Impossible! (*aside*) Villain!

MME. DESCHAP. What, lose my child?

BEAU. And gain a princess!

MME. DESCHAP. Oh, Monsieur Beauseant, you are so very kind, it must be so—we ought not to be selfish, my daughter's happiness at stake. She will go away, too, in a carriage and six!

PAULINE. Thou art here still—I cannot part from thee, my heart will break.

MEL. But you will not consent to this hasty union?—thou wilt not wed an outcast—a fugitive?

PAULINE. Ah! if thou art in danger, who should share it but Pauline?

MEL. (*aside*). Distraction! If the earth could swallow me!

M. DESCHAP. Gently! gently! The settlements—the contracts—my daughter's dowry!

MEL. The dowry! I am not base enough for that; no, not one farthing!

BEAU. (*to* MADAME). Noble fellow! Really your husband is too mercantile in these matters. Monsieur Deschappelles, you hear his highness? we can arrange the settlements by proxy 'tis the way with people of quality.

M. Deschap. But——

Mme. Deschap. Hold your tongue! Don't expose yourself.

Beau. I will bring the priest in a trice. Go in all of you and prepare: the carriage shall be at the door before the ceremony is over.

Mme. Deschap. Be sure there are six horses, Beauseant! You are very good to have forgiven us for refusing you; but you see—a prince.

Deau. And such a prince! Madame, I cannot blush at the success of so illustrious a rival. (*aside*) Now will I follow them to the village, enjoy my triumph, and to-morrow, in the hour of thy shame and grief, I think, proud girl, thou wilt prefer even these arms to those of the gardener's son.   [*Exit, L. S. E.*

Mme. Deschap. Come, Monsieur Deschappelles, give your arm to her highness that is to be.

M. Deschap. I don't like doing business in such a hurry; 'tis not the way with the house of Deschappelles and Co.

Mme. Deschap. There, now, you fancy you are in the counting-house, don't you? (*pushes him to* Pauline.)

Mel. Stay, stay, Pauline—one word. Have you no scruple, no fear? Speak—it is not yet too late.

Pauline. When I loved thee, thy fate became mine. Triumph or danger—joy or sorrow—I am by thy side.

Damas. Well, well, Prince, thou art a lucky man to be so loved. She is a good little girl in spite of her foibles—make her as happy as if she were not to be a princess. Come, sir, I wish you joy—young—tender—lovely—zounds! I envy you. (*slapping him on the shoulder.*)

Mel. (*who has stood apart in gloomy abstraction*).

Do you? Wise judges we are of each other.
" Woo, wed, and bear her home!" So runs the bond
To which I sold myself—and then—what then?
Away—I will not look beyond the hour.
You envy me—I thank you—you may read
My joy upon my brow—I thank you, sir!
If hearts had audible language, you would hear
What mine would answer when you talk of *envy* !
    [*Exeunt into house, L. C. E.*

CURTAIN.

ACT III.

SCENE I.—*The exterior of the Golden Lion—time, twilight. The moon rises during the scene.*

Enter Landlord *and his* Daughter *from the Inn, L. D. F.*

Land. Ha—ha—ha! Well, I never shall get over it. Our Claude is a prince with a vengeance now. His carriage breaks down at my inn—ha—ha!

Janet. And what airs the young lady gives herself! " Is this the best room you have, young woman?" with such a toss of the head.

Land. Well, get in, Janet; get in and see to the supper ; the servants must sup before they go back.   [*Exeunt, L. D. F.*

Enter BEAUSEANT *and* GLAVIS, L. H.

BEAU. You see our princess is lodged at last—one stage more, and she'll be at her journey's end—the beautiful pa'ace at the foot of the Alps—ha—ha !

GLA. Faith, I pity the poor Pauline—especially if she's going to sup at the Golden Lion. (*makes a wry face*) I shall never forget that cursed ragout.

Enter MELNOTTE *from the Inn*, L. D. F.

BEAU. Your servant, my Prince ; you reigned most worthily. I condole with you on your abdication. I am afraid that your highness's retinue are not very faithful servants. I think they will quit you in the moment of your fall—'tis the fate of greatness. But you are welcome to your fine clothes—also the diamond snuff-box, which Louis XIV. gave to your great-great-grandmother.

GLA. And the ring, with which your grandfather the Doge of Venice married the Adriatic.

MEL. I have kept my oath, gentlemen—say, have I kept my oath ?

BEAU. Most religiously.

MEL. Then you have done with me and mine—away with you.

BEAU. How, knave ?

MEL. Look you, our bond is over. Proud conquerors that we are, we have won the victory over a simple girl, compromised her honor—embittered her life—blasted, in their very blossoms, all the flowers of her youth. This is your triumph—it is my shame ! (*turns to* BEAUSEANT) Enjoy thy triumph, but not in my sight. I *was* her betrayer—I *am* her protector ! Cross but her path—one word of scorn, one look of insult—nay, but one quiver of that mocking lip, and I will teach thee that bitter word thou hast graven eternally in this heart—*Repentance !*

BEAU. His highness is most grandiloquent.

MEL. Highness me no more ! Beware ! Remorse has made me a new being. Away with you ! There is danger in me. Away !

GLA. (*aside*). He's an awkward fellow to deal with; come away, Beauseant !

BEAU. I know the respect due to rank. Adieu, my Prince. Any commands at Lyons ? Yet hold—I promised you 200 louis on your wedding-day; here they are.

MEL. (*dashing the purse to the ground*). I gave you revenge, I did not sell it. Take up your silver, Judas; take it. Ay, it is fit you should learn to stoop.

BEAU. You will beg my pardon for this some day. (*aside to* GLAVIS) Come to my chateau—I shall return hither to-morrow, to learn how Pauline likes her new dignity.

MEL. Are you not gone yet ?

BEAU. Your highness's most obedient, most faithful——

GLA. And most humble servants. Ha—ha !

[*Exeunt* BEAUSEANT *and* GLAVIS, R.

MEL. Thank Heaven I had no weapon, or I should have slain them. Wretch ! what can I say ? Where turn ? On all sides mockery—the very boors within—(*laughter from the Inn*) 'Sdeath, if even in this short absence the exposure should have chanced. I will call her. We will go hence. I have already sent one I can trust to my mother's house. There, at least, none can insult her agony—gloat upon her shame ! There alone must she learn what a villain she has sworn to love.

As he turns to the door, PAULINE *enters from the Inn,* L. D. F.

PAULINE. Ah! my lord, what a place! I never saw such rude people. I think the very sight of a prince, though he travels *incognito*, turns their honest heads. What a pity the carriage should break down in such a spot! You are not well—the drops stand on your brow—your hand is feverish.

MEL. Nay, it is but a passing spasm; the air——

PAULINE. Is not the soft air of your native south. (*pause*)
　　　How pale he is!—indeed thou art not well.
　　　Where are our people? I will call them. (*going.*)

MEL. 　　　　　　　　　　　　　　　Hold!
　　　I—I am well.

PAULINE. 　　　　　　Thou art! Ah! now I know it.
　　　Thou fanciest, my kind lord—I know thou dost—
　　　Thou fanciest these rude walls, these rustic gossips,
　　　Brick'd floors, sour wine, coarse viands, vex Pauline;
　　　And so they might, but thou art by my side,
　　　And I forget all else.

Enter LANDLORD *from* D. F., *the* SERVANTS *peeping and laughing over his shoulder.*

LAND. 　　　　　　　My lord—your highness—
　　　Will your most noble excellency choose——

MEL. Begone, sir! 　　　　　　　　[*Exit* LANDLORD, *laughing.*

PAULINE. 　　　　　　How could they have learn'd thy rank?
　　　One's servants are so vain; nay, let it not
　　　Chafe thee, sweet Prince!—a few short days and we
　　　Shall see thy palace by its lake of silver,
　　　And—nay, nay, spendthrift, is thy wealth of smiles
　　　Already drain'd, or dost thou play the miser?

MEL. (R. C.). Thine eyes would call up smiles in deserts, fair one.
　　　Let us escape these rustics; close at hand
　　　There is a cot, where I have bid prepare
　　　Our evening lodgment—a rude, homely roof,
　　　But honest, where our welcome will not be
　　　Made torture by the vulgar eyes and tongues
　　　That are as death to Love! A heavenly night!
　　　The wooing air and the soft moon invite us.
　　　Wilt walk? I pray thee, now—I know the path,
　　　Ay, every inch of it!

PAULINE. 　　　　　　　　What, *thou!* methought
　　　Thou wert a stranger in these parts? Ah, truant,
　　　Some village beauty lured thee!—thou art now
　　　Grown constant?

MEL. 　　　　　　　Trust me.

PAULINE. 　　　　　　　　　Princes are so changeful!

MEL. Come, dearest, come.

PAULINE. 　　　　　　Shall I not call our people
　　　To light us?

MEL. 　　　　　Heaven will lend its stars for torches!
　　　It is not far.

PAULINE. 　　　　The night breeze chills me.

MEL. 　　　　　　　　　　　　　　　Nay,
　　　Let me thus mantle thee; (*throws his cloak over her*) it is not cold.

PAULINE. Never beneath thy smile!

MEL. (*aside*). 　　　　　　　　O Heaven! forgive me!
　　　　　　　　　　　　　　　　　　[*Exeunt*, B.

SCENE II.—MELNOTTE's *cottage—*WIDOW *bustling about—a table spread
for supper.*

WIDOW   So, I think that looks very neat. He sent me a line, so blotted that I can scarcely read it, to say he would be here almost immediately. She must have loved him well indeed to have forgotten his birth;
for though he was introduced to her in disguise, he is too honorable not
to have revealed to her the artifice; which her love only could forgive.
Well, I do not wonder at it; for though my son is not a prince, he
ought to be one, and that's almost as good. (*knock at* D. *in* F.) Ah! here
they are.

Enter MELNOTTE *and* PAULINE *from* D. *in* F.; *he places his cloak and hat on
a chair.*

WIDOW. Oh, my boy—the pride of my heart!—welcome, welcome. I
beg pardon, ma'am, but I do love him so! (MELNOTTE *comes down* L.)
PAULINE (R.). Good woman, I really—why, Prince, what is this!—
does the old lady know you? Oh, I guess you have done her some service. Another proof of your kind heart; is it not?
MEL. (L.). Of my kind heart, ay!
PAULINE. So you know the Prince?
WIDOW. Know him, madam? Ah, I begin to fear it is you who know
him not!
PAULINE (*cross's to* MELNOTTE). Can we stay here, my lord? I think
there's something very wild about her. (MELNOTTE *passes her round to* L.)
MEL. Madam, I—no, I cannot tell her; what a coward is a man who
has lost his honor! Speak to her—speak to her—(*to his mother*) tell her
that—O Heaven, that I were dead! (*crosses* R.)
PAULINE. How confused he looks!—this strange place!—this woman
—what can it mean?—I half suspect—who are you, madam?—who are
you? can't you speak? are you struck dumb?
WIDOW (C). Claude, you have not deceived her? Ah, shame upon
you! I thought that, before you went to the altar, she was to have
known all.
PAULINE. All! what! My blood freezes in my veins!
WIDOW. Poor lady—dare I tell her, Claude? (MELNOTTE *makes a
sign of assent*) Know you not, then, madam, that this young man is of
poor though honest parents? Know you not that you are wedded to
my son, Claude Melnotte?
PAULINE. Your son! hold—hold! do not speak to me. (*approaches*
MELNOTTE, *and lays her hand on his arm*) Is this a jest? is it? I know
it is, only speak—one word—one look—one smile. I cannot believe—I
who loved thee so—I cannot believe that thou art such a—No, I will
not wrong thee by a harsh word! Speak.
MEL. Leave us. (*crosses to the* WIDOW *and sinks into a chair*) Have pity
on her, on me; leave us!
WIDOW. Oh, Claude, that I should live to see thee bowed by shame!
thee of whom I was so proud!   [*Exit,* D. L. H.
PAULINE. Her son—her son! (MELNOTTE *rises, brings forward the chair,
motions* PAULINE *to be seated; she proudly declines.*)
MEL. Now, lady, hear me.
PAULINE.   Hear thee!
      Ay, speak—her son! have fiends a parent? speak,
      That thou mayst silence curses—speak!
MEL.   No, curse me;
      Thy curse would blast me less than thy forgiveness.

PAULINE (*laughing wildly*). "This is thy palace, where the perfume I
    light
  Steals through the mist of alabaster lamps,
  And every air is heavy with the sighs
  Of orange groves, and music from sweet lutes,
  And murmurs of low fountains, that gush forth
  I' the midst of roses!"   Dost thou like the picture? (*crosses*, L.)
  This is my bridal home, and *thou* my bridegroom.
  O fool—O dupe—O wretch!   I see it all.
  The by-word and the jeer of every tongue
  In Lyons.   Hast thou in thy heart one touch
  Of human kindness? if thou hast, why, kill me,
  And save thy wife from madness. (*crosses*, R.) No, it cannot—
  It cannot be; this is some horrid dream!
  I shall wake soon. (*touching him*) Art flesh? art man? or but
  The shadows seen in sleep!   It is too real.
  What have I done to thee? how sinn'd against thee,
  That thou shouldst crush me thus?

MEL.   Pauline, by pride
  Angels have fallen ere thy time; by pride—
  That sole alloy of thy most lovely mould—
  The evil spirit of a bitter love,
  And a revengeful heart, had power upon thee.
  From my first years my soul was fill'd with thee;
  I saw thee midst the flow'rs the lowly boy
  Tended, unmark'd by thee—a spirit of bloom,
  And joy, and freshness, as if Spring itself
  Were made a living thing, and wore thy shape!
  I saw thee, and the passionate heart of man
  Enter'd the breast of the wild-dreaming boy.
  And from that hour I grew—what to the last
  I shall be—thine adorer!   Well, this love,
  Vain, frantic, guilty, if thou wilt, became
  A fountain of ambition and bright hope;
  I thought of tales that by the winter hearth
  Old gossips tell—how maidens sprung from kings,
  Have stoop'd from their high sphere; how love, like death,
  Levels all ranks, and lays the shepherd's crook
  Beside the sceptre.
  My father died; and I, the peasant born,
  Was my own lord.   Then did I seek to rise
  Out of the prison of my mean estate;
  And, with such jewels as the exploring mind
  Brings from the caves of knowledge, buy my ransom
  From those twin jailers of the daring heart—
  Low birth and iron fortune.   For thee I grew
  A midnight student o'er the dreams of sages.
  For thee I sought to borrow from each grace,
  And every muse, such attributes as lend
  Ideal charms to love.   I thought of thee,
  And passion taught me poesy—of thee.
  And on the painter's canvas grew the life
  Of beauty!   Art became the shadow
  Of the dear starlight of thy haunting eyes!
  Men call'd me vain—some mad—I heeded not;
  But still toil'd on—hoped on—for it was sweet,
  If not to win, to feel more worthy thee?

PAULINE. Why do I cease to hate him!
MEL. At last, in one mad hour, I dared to pour
      The thoughts that burst their channels into song,
      And sent them to thee—such a tribute, lady,
      As beauty rarely scorns, even from the meanest.
      The name—appended by the burning heart
      That long'd to show its idol what bright things
      It had created—yea, the enthusiast's name,
      That should have been thy triumph, was thy scorn;
      That very hour—when passion, turn'd to wrath,
      Resembled hatred most—when thy disdain
      Made my whole soul a chaos—in that hour
      The tempters found me a revengeful tool
      For their revenge! Thou hadst trampled on the worm—
      It turned and stung thee! (*throws himself into chair*, L. C.)
PAULINE.   Love, sir, hath no sting.
      What was the slight of a poor powerless girl
      To the deep wrong of this most vile revenge?
      Oh, how I loved this man!—a serf—a slave!
MEL. Hold, lady! (*starts up*) No, not a slave! Despair is free
      I will not tell thee of the throes—the struggles—
      The anguish—the remorse. No, let it pass!
      And let me come to such most poor atonement
      Yet in my power. Pauline!——
      (*approaching her with great emotion, and about to take her hand.*
PAULINE.   No, touch me not!
      I know my fate. You are, by law, my tyrant;
      And I—O Heaven!—a peasant's wife! I'll work—
      Toil—drudge—do what thou wilt—but touch me not!
      Let my wrongs make me sacred!
MEL.   Do not fear me.
      Thou dost not know me, madam; at the altar
      My vengeance ceased—my guilty oath expired!
      Henceforth, no image of some marble saint,
      Niched in cathedral aisles, is hallowed more
      From the rude hand of sacrilegious wrong.
      I am thy husband—nay, thou need'st not shudder!—
      Here, at thy feet, I lay a husband's rights.
      A marriage thus unholy—unfulfill'd—
      A bond of fraud—is, by the laws of France,
      Made void and null. To-night sleep—sleep in peace
      To-morrow, pure and virgin as this morn
      I bore thee, bathed in blushes, from the shrine,
      Thy father's arms shall take thee to thy home.
      The law shall do thee justice, and restore
      Thy right to bless another with thy love.
      And when thou art happy, and hast half forgot
      Him who so loved—so wrong'd thee, think at least
      Heaven left some remnant of the angel still
      In that poor peasant's nature! (*goes to* D. L. H. *and calls*) Ho! my
            mother!

            Enter WIDOW, D. L. H.

      Conduct this lady (she is not my wife;
      She is our guest—our honor'd guest, my mother)
      To the poor chamber, where the sleep of virtue

Never, beneath my father's honest roof,
E'en villains dared to mar! Now, lady, now,
I think thou wilt believe me. (*takes her hand and leads her to the*
    WIDOW) Go, my mother!
WIDOW. She is not thy wife! (*on the stairs.*)
MEL.   Hush, hush! for mercy's sake!
    Speak not, but go.

WIDOW *ascends the stairs.* R. U. E.   PAULINE *follows, weeping—turns to look*
    back.

MEL. (*throws himself upon his knees beside the chair*, C.). All angels bless
    and guard her!

                        CURTAIN.

ACT IV.

SCENE I.—*The cottage as before—*MELNOTTE *seated before a table—writing*
    implements, etc. (*Day breaking; he rises and goes to the foot of the*
    staircase, and listens.)

MEL. Hush, hush!—she sleeps at last!—thank Heaven, for a while
she forgets even that I live! Her sobs, which have gone to my heart
the whole, long, desolate night, have ceased!—all calm—all still! (*sits*
and writes) I will go now; I will send this letter to Pauline's father;
when he arrives I will place in his hands my own consent to the divorce,
and then, O France! my country! accept among thy protectors, thy de-
fenders—the Peasant's Son! Our country is less proud than custom,
and does not refuse the blood, the heart, the right hand of the poor
man.
            Enter WIDOW, *down the staircase,* R. U. E.

WIDOW. My son, thou hast acted ill; but sin brings its own punishment. In the hour of thy remorse, it is not for a mother to reproach
thee.
    MEL. What is past is past. There is a future left to all men, who
have the virtue to repent, and the energy to atone. Thou shalt be
proud of thy son yet. Meanwhile, remember this poor lady has been
grievously injured. For the sake of thy son's conscience, respect, hon-
or, bear with her. If she weep, console—if she chide, be silent. 'Tis
but a little while more—I shall send an express fast as horse can speed
to her father. Farewell! I shall return shortly.
    WIDOW. It is the only course left to thee—thou wert led astray, but
thou art not hardened. Thy heart is right still, as ever it was when, in
thy most ambitious hopes, thou wert never ashamed of thy poor mother.
    MEL. Ashamed of thee! No, if I yet endure, yet live, yet hope—it is
only because I would not die till I have redeemed the noble heritage I
have lost—the heritage I took unstained from thee and my dead father
—a proud conscience and an honest name. I shall win them back yet
—Heaven bless you!   [*Exit,* D. *in* F.
    WIDOW. My dear Claude! How my heart bleeds for him. (*the* WIDOW
draws back the window curtains, removes the candle from the table, and goes
off, D. L. H.)

PAULINE looks down from the stairs, and, after a pause, descends.

PAULINE. Not here!—he spares me that pain at least ; so far he is considerate—yet the place seems still more desolate without him. Oh, that I could hate him—the gardener's son!—and yet how nobly he—no —no—no, I will not be so mean a thing as to forgive him !

Re-enter WIDOW, D. L. H.

WIDOW. Good morning, madam ; I would have waited on you if I had known you were stirring.

PAULINE. It is no matter, ma'am—your son's wife ought to wait on herself.

WIDOW. My son's wife—let not that thought vex you, madam—he tells me that you will have your divorce. And I hope I shall live to see him smile again. There are maidens in this village, young and fair, ma'am, who may yet console him.

PAULINE. I dare say—they are very welcome—and when the divorce is got—he will marry again. I am sure I hope so. (*weeps.*)

WIDOW. He could have married the richest girl in the province, if he had pleased it ; but his head was turned. poor child ! he could think of nothing but you. (*weeps.*)

PAULINE. Don't weep, *mother.*

WIDOW. Ah, he has behaved very ill, I know, but love is so head-strong in the young.

PAULINE. So, as you were saying—go on.

WIDOW. Oh, I cannot excuse him, ma'am—he was not in his right senses.

PAULINE. But he always—always (*sobbing*) loved—loved me then ?

WIDOW. He thought of nothing else. See here—he learnt to paint ·that he might take your likeness. (*uncovers the picture*) But that's all over now—I trust you have cured him of his folly—but, dear heart, you have had no breakfast !

PAULINE. I can't take anything—don't trouble yourself. Oh, if he were but a poor gentleman, even a merchant ; but a gardener's son— and what a home ! Oh, no, it is too dreadful. (PAULINE *sits L. of the table.* BEAUSEANT *opens the lattice and looks in, F.*)

BEAU. So—so—the coast is clear ! I saw Claude in the lane—I sha'l have an excellent opportunity. (*shuts the lattice and knocks at the D. in F.*)

PAULINE (*starting*). Can it be my father ? he has not sent for him yet. No, he cannot be in such a hurry to get rid of me.

WIDOW. It is not time for your father to arrive yet ; it must be some neighbor.

PAULINE. Don't admit any one.

WIDOW opens the D. in F., BEAUSEANT pushes her aside, and enters.

Ha ! Heavens ! that hateful Beauseant ! This is indeed bitter !

BEAU. Good morning, madam ! O, widow, your son begs you will have the goodness to go to him in the village—he wants to speak to you on particular business ; you'll find him at the inn, or the grocer's shop, or the baker's, or at some other friend's of your family—make haste.

PAULINE. Don't leave me, mother—don't leave me !

BEAU. (*with great respect*). Be not alarmed, madam. Believe me your friend—your servant

PAULINE. Sir, I have no fear of you, even in this house ! Go, madam, if your son wishes it; I will not contradict his commands whilst, at least, he has still the right to be obeyed.

WIDOW. I don't understand this; however, I shan't be long gone.
[*Exit*, D. *in* F.

PAULINE. Sir, I divine the object of your visit—you wish to exult in the humiliation of one who humbled you. Be it so; I am prepared to endure all—even your presence!

BEAU. You mistake me, madam—Pauline, you mistake me! I come to lay my fortune at your feet. You must already be disenchanted with this impostor; these walls are not worthy to be hallowed by your beauty! Shall that form be clasped in the arms of a base-born peasant? Beloved, beautiful Pauline! fly with me—my carriage waits without—I will bear you to a home more meet for your reception. Wealth, luxury, station—all shall yet be yours. I forget your past disdain—I remember only your beauty, and my unconquerable love!

PAULINE. Sir! leave this house—it is humble; but a husband's roof, however lowly, is, in the eyes of God and man, the temple of a wife's honor! Know that I would rather starve—yes—with him who has betrayed me, than accept your lawful hand, even were you the prince whose name he bore. Go.

BEAU. What, is not your pride humbled yet?

PAULINE. Sir, what was pride in prosperity in affliction becomes virtue.

BEAU. Look round; these rugged floors—these homely walls—this wretched struggle of poverty for comfort—think of this! and contrast with such a picture the refinement, the luxury, the pomp, that the wealthiest gentleman of Lyons offers to the loveliest lady. Ah, hear me.

PAULINE. Oh! my father—why did I leave you?—why am I thus friendless? Sir, you see before you a betrayed, injured, miserable woman—respect her anguish!

BEAU. No, let me rather thus console it; let me snatch from those lips one breath of that fragrance which never should be wasted on the low churl thy husband.

PAULINE. Help! Claude!—Claude! Have I no protector?

BEAU. Be silent! (MELNOTTE *appears at the* D. F. *Seeing* BEAUSEANT, *he pauses at the threshold*. BEAUSEANT *shows pistol*) See, I do not come unprepared even for violence. I will brave all things—thy husband and all his race—for thy sake. Thus, then, I clasp thee! (MELNOTTE *rushes forward*.)

MEL. (*dashing him to the other end of the stage*). Pauline—look up, Pauline! thou art safe.

BEAU. Dare you insult a man of my birth, ruffian? (*levelling his pistol*.)

PAULINE. Oh, spare him—spare my husband! Beauseant—Claude—no—no—(*faints*)

MEL. Miserable trickster! shame upon you! brave devices to terrify a woman! Coward!—you tremble—you have outraged the laws—you know that your weapon is harmless—you have the courage of the mountebank, not the bravo! Pauline, there is no danger.

BEAU. I wish thou wert a gentleman—as it is, thou art beneath me. Good day, and a happy honeymoon. (*aside*) I will not die till I am avenged!   [*Exit*, D. *in* F.

MEL. I hold her in these arms—the last embrace!
Never, ah! never more, shall this dear head
Be pillow'd on the heart that should have sheltered
And has betrayed! Soft—soft! one kiss—poor wretch!
No scorn on that pale lip forbids me now!
One kiss—so ends all record of my crime!

It is the seal upon the tomb of hope,
By which, like some lost, sorrowing angel, sits
Sad memory ever more ;—she breathes—she moves—
She wakes to scorn, to hate, but not to shudder
Beneath the touch of my abhorred love. (*places her in a chair*)
There—we are strangers now !

PAULINE.   All gone—all calm—
Is *every* thing a dream? thou art safe, unhurt—
I do not love thee ; but—but I am a woman,
And—and—no blood is spilt ?

MEL. (R.).   No, lady, no ;
My guilt hath not deserved so rich a blessing
As even danger in thy cause.

Enter WIDOW, *from* D. *in* F. ; *comes down* C.

WIDOW. My son, I have been everywhere in search of you ; why did
you send for me ?

MEL. I did not send for you.

WIDOW. No! but I must tell you that your express has returned.

MEL. So soon ! impossible !

WIDOW. Yes, he met the lady's father and mother on the road ; they
were going into the country on a visit. Your messenger says that Monsieur Deschappelles turned almost white with anger when he read your
letter. They will be here almost immediately. Oh, Claude, Claude !
what will they do to you ? How I tremble ! Ah, madam ! do not let
them injure him—if you knew how he doated on you !

PAULINE. Injure him ! no, ma'am, be not afraid. (*the* WIDOW *goes up
to the widow*) My father ! how shall I meet him ? how go back to Lyons ?
the scoff of the whole city ! Cruel, cruel Claude. (*in great agitation*) Sir,
you have acted most treacherously.

MEL. I know it, madam.

PAULINE (*aside*). If he would but ask me to forgive him ! (*aloud*) I
never can forgive you, sir.

MEL. I never dared to hope it.

PAULINE. But you are my husband now, and I have sworn to—to love
you, sir.

MEL. That was under a false belief, madam. Heaven and the laws
will release you from your vow.

PAULINE. He will drive me mad ! if he were but less proud—if he
would but ask me to remain—hark, hark—I hear the wheels of the carriage—sir—Claude, they are coming ; have you no word to say ere it is
too late ? Quick—speak !

MEL. I can only congratulate you on your release. Behold your parents !

Enter MONSIEUR *and* MADAME DESCHAPPELLES *and* COLONEL DAMAS, D.
in F.

M. DESCHAP. My child ! my child ! (*goes to* PAULINE.)

MME. DESCHAP. Oh, my poor Pauline ! what a villainous hovel this is !
Old woman, get me a chair—I shall faint—I certainly shall. What will
the world say ? Child, you have been a fool. (*sits* L. C.) A mother's
heart is easily broken.

DAMAS (R.). Ha, ha ! most noble Prince—I am sorry to see a man of
your quality in such a condition ; I am afraid your highness will go to
the House of Correction.

MEL. (R. C.). Taunt on, sir; I spared *you* when you were unarmed—I am unarmed now. A man who has no excuse for crime is indeed defenceless!

DAMAS. There's something fine in the rascal, after all! (*retires and crosses behind to* L.)

M. DESCHAP. (L. C.). Where is the impostor? Are you this shameless traitor? Can you brave the presence of that girl's father?

MEL. Strike me, if it please you—you *are* her father.

PAULINE. Sir—sir, for my sake!—whatever his guilt, he has acted nobly in atonement.

MME. DESCHAP. Nobly! Are you mad, girl? I have no patience with you—to disgrace all your family thus! Nobly! Oh, you abominable, hardened, pitiful, mean, ugly villain! (*crosses to* MELNOTTE *and back again to* L.)

DAMAS (L.). Ugly! Why, he was beautiful yesterday!

PAULINE. Madame, this is his roof, and he is my husband. Respect your daughter, or let blame fall alone on her.

MME. DESCHAP. You—you! Oh, I'm choking (*retires and sits* L. U. E.)

M. DESCHAP. Sir, it were idle to waste reproach upon a conscience like yours—you renounce all pretensions to the person of this lady?

MEL. I do. (*gives a paper*) Here is my consent to a divorce—my full confession of the fraud which annuls the marriage. Your daughter has been foully wronged—I grant it, sir; but her own lips will tell you that, from the hour in which she crossed this threshold, I returned to my own station, and respected hers. Pure and inviolate, as when yestermorn you laid your hand upon her head and blessed her, I yield her back to you. For myself—I deliver you for ever from my presence. An outcast and a criminal, I seek some distant land, where I may mourn my sin, and pray for your daughter's peace. Farewell—farewell to you all, forever!

WIDOW. Claude, Claude, you would not leave your poor old mother? *She* does not disown you in your sorrow—no, not even in your guilt. No divorce can separate a mother from her son. (*embraces* CLAUDE.)

PAULINE. This poor widow teaches me my duty. No, mother—no, for you are now *my* mother also—nor should any law, human or divine, separate the wife from her husband's sorrows. Claude—Claude—all is forgotten—forgiven—I am thine forever! (*throws herself passionately into his arms.*)

MME. DESCHAP. What do I hear? Come away, or never see my face again.

M. DESCHAP. Pauline, *we* never betrayed you—do you forsake us for him?

PAULINE (*going back to her father*). Oh, no—but you will forgive him, too; we will live together—he shall be your son!

M. DESCHAP. Never! Cling to him and forsake your parents! His home shall be yours—his fortune yours—his fate yours; the wealth I have acquired by honest industry shall never enrich a dishonest man.

PAULINE. And you would have a wife enjoy luxury while a husband toils! Claude, take me; thou canst not give me wealth, titles, station—but thou canst give me a true heart. I will work for thee, tend thee, bear with thee, and never, never shall these lips reproach thee for the past. (*clasps her arms around him.*)

MEL. This is the heaviest blow of all. What a heart I have wronged! Do not fear me, sir; I am not all hardened—I will not rob her of a holier love than mine. Pauline!—angel of love and mercy—your memory shall lead me back to virtue. The husband of a being so beautiful in her noble and sublime tenderness may be poor—may be low-born;—

(there is no guilt in the decrees of Providence!)—but he should be one who can look thee in the face without a blush—to whom thy love does not bring remorse—who can fold thee to his heart, and say,—" *Here* there is no deceit!"—I am not that man! (*returns her to* DESCHAPPELLES.)

DAMAS (*who has been watching* MELNOTTE, *comes down*, R.). Thou art a noble fellow, notwithstanding; and wouldst make an excellent soldier. Serve in my regiment. I have had a letter from the Directory—our young general takes the command of the army in Italy—I am to join him at Marseilles—I will depart this day, if thou wilt go with me.

MEL. It is the favor I would have asked thee, if I dared. Place me where a foe is most dreaded—wherever France most needs a life!

DAMAS. There shall not be a forlorn hope without thee!

MEL. There is my hand! Mother, your blessing. (*goes to the* WIDOW, R.) I shall see you again—a better man than a prince—a man who has bought the right to high thoughts by brave deeds. And thou!—thou! so wildly worshipped, so guiltily betrayed—all is not yet lost—for thy memory, at least, must be mine till death! If I live, the name of him thou hast once loved shall not rest dishonored—if I fall, amidst the carnage and the roar of battle, my soul will fly back to thee, and love shall share with death my last sigh! More—more would I speak to thee—to pray—to bless! But no—when I am less unworthy I will utter it to Heaven! I cannot trust myself to—(*turning to* DESCHAPPELLES) Your pardon, sir—they are my last words—farewell!

[*Exeunt* MELNOTTE *and* DAMAS, D. *in* F.

PAULINE (*starting from her father's arms*). Claude—Claude—my husband! (*she falls;* DESCHAPPELLES *and* MADAME *raise her. The* WIDOW *stands at the door watching the departure of* CLAUDE.)

CURTAIN.

___

ACT V.

(*Two years and a half from the date of Act IV.*)

SCENE I.—*A street in Lyons.*

Enter CAPT. GERVAIS, LIEUT. DUPONT, *and* MAJOR DESMOULINS, L.

CAPT. GERVAIS. This Lyons is a fine city! your birth-place, I think?

LIEUT. DUPONT. Yes—it is just two years and a half since I left it under the command of the brave Colonel Damas; here we are returned—he a General, I a Lieutenant.

MAJOR DESMOULINS. Ay, promotion is rapid in the French army. Now the war in Italy is over, I hope he will find employment for our regiment elsewhere.

CAPT. G. Well, I hope so, too. Here comes the General.

Enter GENERAL DAMAS, L.

DAMAS. Good day, gentlemen, good day; so here we are in Lyons, improved since we left it. It is a pleasure to grow old when the years that bring decay to ourselves ripen the prosperity of our country.

CAPT. G. And cover our gray hairs with the laurel wreath, General.

DAMAS. I hope you will amuse yourselves during our stay at Lyons.

CAPT. G. I shall make the best use of my time, General; but I have little appetite for sight-seeing without Morier; his fine taste and extensive information qualify him for a professional cicerone; by the way, General, this is the anniversary of the glorious day in which the Colonel so distinguished himself.

DAMAS. Ah, poor Morier! he deserves all his honors.

LIEUT. D. That he does indeed, General. Pray, can you tell us who this Morier really is?

DAMAS. Is!—why, a colonel in the French army.

MAJOR D. True; but what was he at first?

DAMAS. At first? Why, a baby in long clothes, I suppose.

CAPT. G. Ha, ha! Ever facetious, General. Who were his parents? Who were his ancestors?

DAMAS. Brave deeds are the ancestors of brave men.

LIEUT. D. (aside). The General is sore upon this point; you will only chafe him. (aloud) Any commands, General?

DAMAS. None. Good day to you.

[Exeunt MAJOR DESMOULINS and LIEUT. DUPONT, R.

DAMAS. Our comrades are very inquisitive. Poor Morier is the subject of a vast deal of curiosity.

CAPT. G. Say interest, rather, General. His constant melancholy, the loneliness of his habits—his daring valor, his brilliant rise in the profession—your friendship, and the favors of the commander-in-chief—all tend to make him as much the matter of gossip as of admiration. But where is he, General? I have missed him all the morning.

DAMAS. Why, Captain, I'll let you into a secret. My young friend has come with me to Lyons in hopes of finding a miracle.

CAPT. G. A miracle!

DAMAS. Yes, a miracle! in other words, a constant woman.

CAPT. G. Oh, an affair of love!

DAMAS. Exactly so. No sooner did he enter Lyons than he waved his hand to me, threw himself from his horse, and is now, I warrant, asking every one who can know anything about the matter, whether a certain lady is still true to a certain gentleman!

CAPT. G. Success to him!—and of that success there can be no doubt. The gallant Colonel Morier, the hero of Lodi, might make his choice out of the proudest families in France.

DAMAS. Oh, if pride be a recommendation, the lady and her mother are most handsomely endowed. By the way, Captain, if you should chance to meet with Morier, tell him he will find me at the hotel.

CAPT. G. I will, General.   [Exit, R.

DAMAS. Now will I go to the Deschappelles, and make a report to my young Colonel. Ha! by Mars, Bacchus, Apollo, Virorum, here comes Monsieur Beauseant!

Enter BEAUSEANT, R.

Good morning, Monsieur Beauseant! How fares it with you?

BEAU. (aside). Damas! that is unfortunate!—if the Italian campaign should have filled his pockets, he may seek to baffle me in the moment of my victory. (aloud) Your servant, General—for such, I think, is your new distinction. Just arrived in Lyons?

DAMAS. Not an hour ago. Well, how go on the Deschappelles? Have they forgiven you in that affair of young Melnotte? You had some hand in that notable device—eh?

BEAU. Why, less than you think for! The fellow imposed upon me. I have set it all right now. What has become of him? He could not have joined the army, after all. There is no such name in the books.

DAMAS. I know nothing about Melnotte. As you say, I never heard the name in the Grand Army. .

BEAU. Hem! You are not married, General?

DAMAS. Do I look like a married man, sir? No, thank Heaven! My profession is to make widows, not wives.

BEAU. You must have gained much booty in Italy? Pauline will be your heiress—eh?

DAMAS. Booty! Not I. Heiress to what? Two trunks and a port-manteau—four horses—three swords—two suits of regimentals, and six pairs of white leather inexpressibles! A pretty fortune for a young lady!

BEAU. (*aside*). Then all is safe! (*aloud*) Ha! ha! Is that really all your capital, General Damas? Why, I thought Italy had been a second Mexico to you soldiers.

DAMAS. All a toss-up, sir. I was not one of the lucky ones! My friend Morier, indeed, saved something handsome. But our command-er-in-chief took care of him, and Morier is a thrifty, economical dog—not like the rest of us soldiers, who spend our money as carelessly as if it were our blood.

BEAU. Well, it is no matter. I do not want fortune with Pauline. And you must know, General Damas, that your fair cousin has at length consented to reward my long and ardent attachment.

DAMAS. You! the devil! Why, she is already married! There is no divorce!

BEAU. True; but this very day she is formally to authorize the ne-cessary proceedings—this very day she is to sign the contract that is to make her mine within one week from the day on which her present il-legal marriage is annulled.

DAMAS. You tell me wonders! Wonders! No; I believe anything of women!

BEAU. I must wish you good morning!

As he is going L., *enter* DESCHAPPELLES, L.

M. DESCHAP. Oh, Beauseant! well met. Let us come to the notary at once.

DAMAS (*to* DESCHAPPELLES). Why, cousin!

M. DESCHAP. Damas, welcome to Lyons! Pray call on us; my wife will be delighted to see you.

DAMAS. Your wife—blessed for her condescension! But (*taking him aside*) what do I hear? Is it possible that your daughter has consented to a divorce?—that she will marry Monsieur Beauseant!

M. DESCHAP. Certainly! What have you to say against it? A gen-tleman of birth, fortune, character. We are not so proud as we were; even my wife has had enough of nobility and princes!

DAMAS. But Pauline loved that young man so tenderly!

M. DESCHAP. (*taking snuff*). That was two years and a half ago!

DAMAS. Very true. Poor Melnotte!

M. DESCHAP. But do not talk of that impostor; I hope he is dead or has left the country. Nay, even were he in Lyons at this moment, he ought to rejoice that, in an honorable and suitable alliance, my daugh-ter may forget her sufferings and his crime.

DAMAS. Nay, if it be all settled, I have no more to say. Monsieur Beauseant informs me that the contract is to be signed this very day.

M. DESCHAP. It is; at one o'clock precisely. Will you be one of the witnesses?

DAMAS. I? No; that is to say—yes, certainly—at one o'clock I will wait on you.

M. Deschap. Till then, adieu—come, Beauseant.

　　　　[*Exeunt* Beauseant *and* Deschappelles, L.

Damas. The man who sets his heart upon a woman
　Is a chameleon, and doth feed on air ;
　From air he takes his colors—holds his life—
　Changes with every wind—grows lean or fat,
　Rosy with hope, or green with jealousy,
　Or pallid with despair—just as the gale
　Varies from north to south—from heat to cold !
　O, woman ! woman ! thou shouldst have few sins
　Of thine own to answer for ! Thou art the author
　Of such a book of follies in man,
　That it would need the tears of all the angels
　To blot the record out !

　　　　Enter Melnotte, *pale and agitated,* R.

　I need not tell thee ! Thou hast heard——
Mel.　　　　　　　　　　　　　　The worst !
　I have ! (*crosses,* L.)
Damas.　　　　　　Be cheer'd ; others are fair as she is !
Mel. Others ! The world is crumbled at my feet !
　She *was* my world ; fill'd up the whole of being—
　Smiled in the sunshine—walk'd the glorious earth—
　Sate in my heart—was the sweet life of life.
　The past was hers ; I dreamt not of a future
　That did not wear her shape ! Mem'ry and Hope
　Alike are gone. Pauline is faithless !
Damas. Hope yet.
Mel.　　　　　　Hope, yes !—one hope is left me still !—
　A soldier's grave ! (*after a pause*) But am I not deceived ?
　I went but by the rumor of the town ;
　Rumor is false—I was too hasty ! Damas,
　Whom hast thou seen ? ·
Damas.　　　　　　Thy rival and her father.
　Arm thyself for the truth. He heeds not——
Mel.　　　　　　　　　　　　　She
　Will never know how deeply she was loved.
Damas.　　　　　　　　　　Be a man !
Mel. I am a man !—it is the sting of woe
　Like mine that tells us we are men !
Damas.　　　　　　　　　The false one
　Did not deserve thee.
Mel.　　　　　　Hush ! No word against her !
　Why should she keep, through years and silent absence,
　The holy tablets of her virgin faith
　True to a traitor's name ! Oh, blame her not ;
　It were a sharper grief to think her worthless
　Than to be what I am ! To-day—to-day !
　They said " To-day !" This day, so wildly welcomed—
　This day, my soul had singled out of time
　And mark'd for bliss ! This day ! oh, could I see her,
　See her once more unknown ; but hear her voice.
Damas. Easily done ! Come with me to her house ;
　Your dress—your cloak—mustache—the bronzed hues
　Of time and toil—the name you bear—belief
　In your absence, all will ward away suspicion.

Keep in the shade. Ay, I would have you come.
There may be hope! Pauline is yet so young,
They may have forced her to these second bridals
Out of mistaken love.

MEL.　　　　　　　　　　No, bid me not hope!
Bid me not hope! I could not bear again
To fall from such a heaven! Oh, Damas,
There's no such thing as courage in a man ;
The veriest slave that ever crawled from danger
Might spurn me now. When first I lost her, Damas,
I bore it, did I not ? I still had hope,
And now I—I—(*bursts into an agony of grief*)

DAMAS.　　　　　　　What, comrade! all the women
That ever smiled destruction on brave hearts
Were not worth tears like these!

MEL. (*crossing to* R).　　　　　'Tis past—forget it.
I am prepared ; life has no further ills !

DAMAS. Come, Melnotte, rouse thyself ;
One effort more. Again thou'lt see her.

MEL.　　　　　　　　　　　　　　　　See her !

DAMAS. Time wanes ; come, ere it yet be too late.

MEL.　　　　　　　　　　　　　　"*Too late !*"
Lead on. One last look more, and then——

DAMAS.　　　　　　　　　　　　Forget her !

MEL. Forget her! yes—for death remembers not ! [*Exeunt,* L.

SCENE II.—*A room in the house of* M. DESCHAPPELLES ; *not so richly
furnished as in the First Act ;* PAULINE *seated, in great dejection, at a
table,* R.

PAULINE. It is so, then. I must be false to Love,
Or sacrifice a father! Oh, my Claude,
My lover, and my husband! Have I lived
To pray that thou mayest find some fairer boon
Than the deep faith of this devoted heart—
Nourish'd till now—now broken ?

Enter MONSIEUR. DESCHAPPELLES, L.

M. DESCHAP.　　　　　　　　　My dear child,
How shall I thank—how bless thee ? Thou hast saved,
I will not say my fortune—I could bear
Reverse, and shrink not—but that prouder wealth
Which merchants value most—my name, my credit—
The hard-won honors of a toilsome life ;
These thou hast saved, my child !

PAULINE.　　　　　　　　　Is there no hope ?
No hope but this ?

M. DESCHAP.　　　　　None. If, without the sum
Which Beauseant offers for thy hand, this day
Sinks to the west—to-morrow brings our ruin !
And hundreds, mingled in that ruin, curse
The bankrupt merchant! and the insolvent herd
We feasted and made merry, cry in scorn,
"How pride has fallen ! Lo, the bankrupt merchant!"
My daughter, thou hast saved us

PAULINE.　　　　　　　　　And I am lost !

M. DESCHAP. Come, let us hope that Beauseant's love——
PAULINE.   His love !
    Talk not of love. Love has no thought of self !
    Love buys not with the ruthless usurer's gold
    The loathsome prostitution of a hand
    Without a heart ! Love sacrifices all things
    To bless the thing it loves ! *He* knows not love.
    Father, his love is hate—his hope revenge !
    My tears, my anguish, my remorse for falsehood—
    These are the joys that he wrings from our despair !
M. DESCHAP. If thou deem'st thus, reject him. Shame and ruin
    Were better than thy misery ; think no more on't.
    My sand is well-nigh run—what boots it when
    The glass is broken ? We'll annul the contract ;
    And if to-morrow in the prisoner's cell
    These aged limbs are laid, why still, my child,
    I'll think thou art spared ; and wait the Liberal Hour
    That lays the beggar by the side of kings !
PAULINE. No—no—forgive me ! You, my honored father—
    You, who so loved, so cherish'd me, whose lips
    Never knew one harsh word ! I'm not ungrateful ;
    I am but human—hush ! *Now*, call the bridegroom.
    You see I am prepared—no tears—all calm ;
    But, father, *talk no more of love !*
M DESCHAP.   My child,
    'Tis but one struggle ; he is young, rich, noble ;
    Thy state will rank first 'mid the dames of Lyons ;
    And when this heart can shelter thee no more,
    Thy youth will not be guardianless.
PAULINE.   I have set
    My foot upon the ploughshare. (M DESCHAP. *retires*) I will pass
    The fiery ordeal. (*aside*) Merciful Heaven support me !
    And on the absent wanderer shed the light
    Of happier stars—lost evermore to me ?

Enter, C. L., MADAME DESCHAPPLLES, BEAUSEANT, GLAVIS, *and* NOTARY,
    who confers with M. DESCHAPPELLES, *and then sits at table*, R.

MME DESCHAP. Why, Pauline, you are quite in *deshabille*—you ought
to be more alive to the importance of this joyful occasion. We had once
looked higher, it is true ; but you see, after all, Monsieur Beauseant's
father *was* a Marquis, and that's a great comfort. Pedigree and join-
ture—you have them both in Monsieur Beauseant. A young lady dec-
orously brought up should only have two considerations in her choice
of a husband ; first, is his birth honorable ? secondly, will his death be
advantageous ? All other trifling details should be left to parental anxiety.
    BEAU. (L. C., *approaching and waving aside* MADAME). Ah, Pauline !
let me hope that you are reconciled to an event which confers such rapture upon me.
    PAULINE. I am reconciled to my doom.
    BEAU. Doom is a harsh word, sweet lady.
    PAULINE (*aside*). This man must have some mercy—his heart cannot
be marble. (*aloud*) Oh, sir, be just—be generous ! Seize a noble triumph—a great revenge ! Save the father, and spare the child !
    BEAU. (*aside*). Joy—joy alike to my hatred and my passion ! The
haughty Pauline is at last my suppliant. (*aloud*) You ask from me what

I have not the sublime virtue to grant—a virtue reserved only for the gardener's son! I cannot forego my hopes in the moment of their fulfilment! I adhere to the contract—your father's ruin or your hand.

PAULINE. Then all is over. Sir, I have decided. (*the clock strikes one.* BEAUSEANT *retires to* L. *of table and sits examining the papers.*)

Enter DAMAS *and* MELNOTTE, L. C.

DAMAS. Your servant, cousin Deschappelles. Let me introduce Colonel Morier.

MME. DESCHAP. (*curtseying very low*). What, the celebrated hero? This is, indeed, an honor! (*she crosses; seems to converse with* MELNOTTE, *who bows as she returns to the table,* R.; MELNOTTE *throws himself into a chair,* L. U. E.)

DAMAS (*to* PAULINE). My little cousin, I congratulate you. What, no smile—no blush? You are going to be divorced from poor Melnotte, and marry this rich gentleman. You ought to be excessively happy!

PAULINE. Happy!

DAMAS. Why, how pale you are, child! Poor Pauline! Hist—confide in me! Do they force you to this?

PAULINE. No.

DAMAS. You act with your own free consent?

PAULINE. My own consent—yes.

DAMAS. Then you are the most—I will not say what you are.

PAULINE. You think ill of me—be it so—yet if you know all——

DAMAS. There is some mystery—speak out, Pauline.

PAULINE (*suddenly*). Oh, perhaps you can save me! you are our relation—our friend. My father is on the verge of bankruptcy—this day he requires a large sum to meet demands that cannot be denied; that sum Beauseant will advance—this hand the condition of the barter. Save me if you have the means—save me! You will be repaid above!

DAMAS (*aside*). I recant. Women are not so bad after all! (*aloud*) Humph, child! I cannot help you—I am too poor.

PAULINE. The last plank to which I clung is shivered.

DAMAS. Hold—you see my friend Morier; Melnotte is his most intimate friend—fought in the same fields—slept in the same tent. Have you any message to send to Melnotte? any word to soften this blow? (*she bows;* DAMAS *goes to* MELNOTTE, *who rises and comes forward,* L. C.)

PAULINE. He knows Melnotte—he will see him—he will bear to him my last farewell. (*approaches* MELNOTTE; *he bows to her, and overcome by his emotion, turns toward* L.) He has a stern air—he turns away from me—he despises me! Sir, one word, I beseech you!

MEL. (*aside*). Her voice again. How the old time comes o'er me!

DAMAS (*to* MADAME). Don't interrupt them. He is going to tell her what a rascal young Melnotte is; he knows him well, I promise you.

MME. DESCHAP. So considerate in you, cousin Damas!

DAMAS *approaches* DESCHAPPELLES; *converses apart with him in dumb show—*DESCHAPPELLES *shows him a paper, which he inspects and takes.*

PAULINE. Thrice have I sought to speak; my courage fails me.
    Sir, is it true that you have known—nay, are
    The friend of—Melnotte?

MEL.   Lady, yes! Myself
    And misery know the man!

PAULINE.   And you will see him,
    And you will bear to him—ay—word for word,

All that this heart, which breaks in parting from him,
Would send, oro still for ever !

MEL. Lady, speak on !

PAULINE. Tell him, for years I never nursed a thought
That was not his; that on his wandering way,
Daily and nightly, pour'd a mourner's prayers;
Tell him e'en now that I would rather share
His lowliest lot—walk by his side, an outcast—
Work for him, beg with him—live upon the light
Of one kind smile from him—than wear the crown
The Bourbon lost :

MEL. (aside). Am I already mad ?
(aloud) You love him thus, and yet desert him ?

PAULINE. Say, that if his eyes
Could read this heart—its struggles, its temptations—
His love itself would pardon that desertion !
Look on that poor old man—he is my father;
He stands upon the verge of an abyss !—
He calls his child to save him ! Shall I shrink
From him who gave me birth ?—withhold my hand,
And see a parent perish ? Tell him this,
And say—that we shall meet again in heaven !

MEL. Night is past—joy cometh with the morrow !
(goes to DAMAS, who is L.) What is this' riddle?—what is the
nature of this sacrifice ?

BEAU. (at the table) The papers are prepared—we only need
Your hand and seal.

MEL. Stay, lady—one word more.
Were but your duty with your faith united,
Would you still share the low-born peasant's lot ?

PAULINE. Would I ? Ah, better death with I him love
Than all the pomp—which is but as the flowers
That crown the victim ! (turning away) I am ready.
(MELNOTTE goes to DAMAS, who has taken the paper from the table.)

DAMAS (showing paper). There—
This is the schedule—this the total.

BEAU. (to DESCHAPPELLEL, showing notes). These
Are yours the instant she has sign'd ; you are
Still the great house of Lyons !

The NOTARY is about to hand the contract to PAULINE, when MELNOTTE seizes
it and tears it.

BEAU. (going L.). Are you mad ?

M. DESCHAP. (L. C.). How, sir. What means this insult ?

MEL. (C.) Peace, old man !
I have a prior claim. Before the face
Of man and Heaven I urge it; I outbid
Yon sordid huckster for your priceless jewel. (giving a pocket-book)
There is the sum twice told ! Blush not to take it ;
There's not a coin that is not bought and hallow'd
In the cause of nations with a soldier's blood !

BEAU. Torments and death !

PAULINE. That voice ! Thou art——

MEL. Thy husband !
(PAULINE rushes into his arms)
Look up ! Look up, Pauline—for I can bear

Thine eyes! The stain is blotted from my name.
I have redeem'd mine honor. I can call
On France to sanction thy divine forgiveness!
Oh, joy!—oh, rapture! By the midnight watchfires
Thus have I seen thee! thus foretold'this hour!
And 'midst the roar of battle, thus have heard
The beating of thy heart against my own!
  (*places* PAULINE *in a chair—the* NOTARY *goes off*, L. C.)
BEAU. Fool'd, duped, and triumph'd over in the hour
Of mine own victory! Curses on ye both!
May thorns be planted in the marriage-bed!
And love grow sour'd and blacken'd into hate—
Such as the hate that gnaws me!
DAMAS.   Curse away!
And let me tell thee, Beauseant, a wise proverb
The Arabs have: "Curses are like young chickens,
(*solemnly*) And still come home to roost!"
BEAU.   Their happiness
Maddens my soul! I am powerless and revengeless!
(*to* MADAME) I wish you joy! Ha! ha! the gardener's son!
             [*Exit*, L. C.
 (PAULINE *rises and comes forward*, R. C. CLAUDE *grasps* DAMAS' *hand*.)
PAULINE.   Oh!
My father, you are saved—and by my husband!
Ah! blessed hour! (*she embraces* MELNOTTE.)
MEL.   Yet you weep still, Pauline!
PAULINE. But on thy breast—*these* tears are sweet and holy!
M. DESCHAP. You have won love and honor nobly, sir!
  Take her—be happy both!
MME. DESCHAP.   I'm all astonished!
Who, then, is Colonel Morier?
DAMAS.   You behold him!
MEL. Morier no more after this happy day! (*crosses*, R. C.)
I would not bear again my father's name
Till I could deem it spotless! The hour's come!
Heaven smiled on conscience! As the soldier rose
From rank to rank, how sacred was the fame
That cancell'd crime, and raised him nearer thee!
MME. DESCHAP. A colonel and a hero! Well, that's something!
He's wondrously improved! (*crosses to him*) I wish you joy, sir!
MEL. Ah! the same love that tempts us into sin,
If it be true love, works out its redemption!
And he who seeks repentance for the past
Should woo the Angel Virtue in the future.

  MADAME DESCHAPPELLES. MELNOTTE. PAULINE.
    R. C.   C.   L. C.
M. DESCHAPPELLES.   DAMAS.
  R.   . L.

      CURTAIN.

+ MONEY.

ORIGINAL CAST OF CHARACTERS.

	Theatre Royal, Haymarket, Dec. 8, 1840.	Old Park Theatre, New York, Feb. 1, 1841.
Alfred Evelyn	Mr. MACREADY.	Mr. HIELD.
Sir John Vesey	Mr. STRICKLAND.	Mr. CHIPPENDALE.
Lord Glossmore	Mr. F. VINING.	Mr. C. W. CLARKE.
Sir Frederick Blount	Mr. WALTER LACY	Mr. A. ANDERSON.
Benjamin Stout	Mr. D. REECE.	Mr. GUNN.
Graves	Mr. B. WEBSTER.	Mr. FISHER.
Captain Dudley Smooth	Mr. WRENCH.	Mr. NICKERSON.
Sharp	Mr. WALDRON.	Mr. BEDFORD.
Old Member	Mr. WILMOTT.	
Toke	Mr. OXBERRY.	
MacFinch	Mr. GOUGH.	
Crimson (a Portrait Painter)	Mr. GALLOT.	
MacStucco	Mr. MATTHEWS.	
Patent (a Coachmaker)	Mr. CLARKE.	
Frantz (a Tailor)	Mr. O. SMITH.	
Tabouret (an Upholsterer)	Mr. HOWE.	
Grab (a Publisher)	Mr. CAULFIELD.	
Clara Douglas	Miss H. FAUCIT.	Mrs. MAEDER.
Lady Franklin	Mrs. GLOVER.	Mrs. VERNON.
Georgina	Miss P. HORTON.	Mrs. CHIPPENDALE.

Officer, Club Members, Flat, Green, Waiters at Club, Pages, Servants.

TIME IN REPRESENTATION—THREE HOURS AND A HALF.

SCENERY.

ACT I.—Scene 1.—A Drawing-room in SIR JOHN VESEY's house.

....Drawing-room beyond....

4th grooves.——......... | Folding doors. | ....——4th grooves.

```
        · Chair.*              Chair.*    * Chair.
                  Chair.*  Chairs.
R. 3 E.——       ( )   *    *   Chair.*            ——L. 3 E.
          Table.                       Chair.*
                                              ( )
       Chair.*                       Table.   * Chair.
R. 2 E.——                                    ——E. 2 E.

                                              ....
    Chair.*                       Chair.*  :  : Writing
                                              :  : Table.
                                              ....
R. 1 E.——                                    ——L. 1 E.
```

A handsomely furnished, carpeted apartment. Folding doors open, showing another handsome room beyond. R. H., handsome table, upon which are newspapers, books, etc. L. H., another table, smaller, and near there a secretary writing-table, with a dozen chairs placed in the positions indicated.

ACT II—Scene 1.—An Ante-room in Evelyn's house. Small table R. H. Writ-ing-desk and materials L. H. Chairs R. H and L. H. Door L. C. F.

Scene 2.—Drawing-room in Sir John Vesey's house, as before. Portfolio and drawings upon the side table.

ACT III.—Scene 1.—Drawing-room in Sir John Vesey's house, as before. The scene so arranged as to allow the next scene to close in.

Scene 2.—Boudoir in Sir John Vesey's house. The flats in the second groove rep-resent a handsome apartment. Two chairs are brought on by the Page.

Scene 3.—Grand saloon at Evelyn's club house.

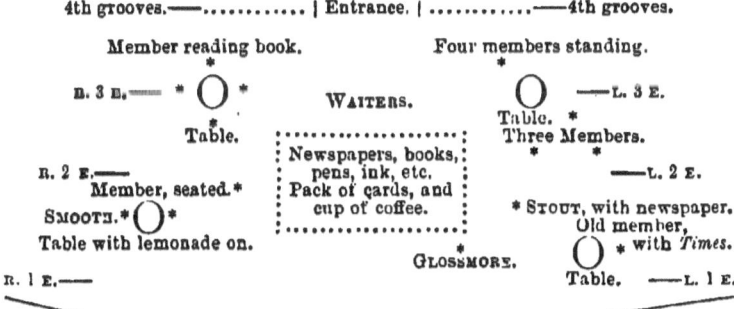

An elegantly furnished saloon with tables and chairs, and the other articles placed as shown in the diagram.

ACT IV.—Scene 1.—An ante-room in Evelyn's, as before.

Scene 2.—A splendid saloon in Evelyn's mansion.

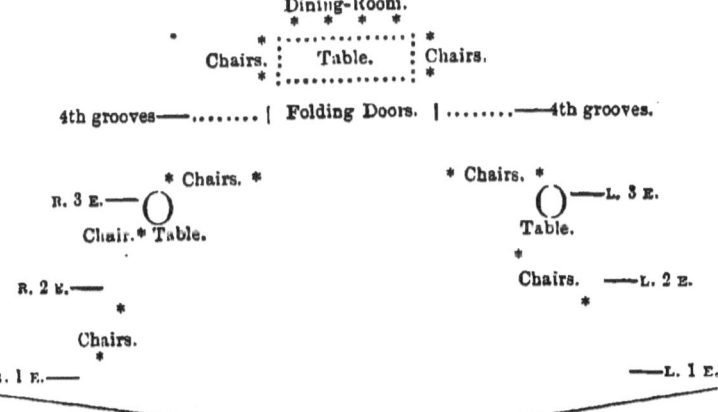

A magnificently furnished saloon, with paintings, etc. Two tables, R. H. and L. H., with candelabra. Chairs placed in the positions indicated. Folding doors C. F. Beyond them the interior of the dining-room, with chairs arranged for the guests—table spread for dinner. Candelebra, etc.

ACT V.—Scene 1.—Room at Evelyn's club house. Handsomely furnished. Tables R. H. and L. H. Cloth and breakfast pieces on the table L. H. Doors C. F. Two chairs at each table. Papers, etc., on table R. H.

Scene 2.—Drawing-room in Sir John Vesey's house, as before.

Scene 3.—Saloon in Evelyn's mansion, as before.

COSTUMES.

So far as the costumes of this play are concerned, there is nothing so very particular in the text, as in the previous plays, to rigidly compel an adherence to the one style of the one particular period.

At the time the play was produced there was a very peculiar style of fashion prevailing in London. The Count D'Orsay was the leader, the model in fact. He was at that time considered one of the most elegant and accomplished gentlemen; indeed, he might be termed the "Beau Brummell" of the period. It was the "D'Orsay hat," the "D'Orsay coat," the "D'Orsay vest," and "D'Orsay boots;" in fact, everything in a fashionable West-end store bore the title.

As this play was originally played, the above style of costume was adopted; but there is no actual necessity for it, and the costumes now given are expressly compiled for this edition of the work—observing a medium course between the past and present; but they may be altered, according to the manager's views, to the leading fashions prevailing at the time when the play is produced.

ALFRED EVELYN.—1*st Dress:* Frock coat and vest, black ; dark trousers ; black necktie ; boots. 2*d Dress:* Dark-blue frock coat ; fancy mixture trousers and vest ; patent-leather boots ; neck scarf ; riding gloves and hat. In *Act IV.*, a handsome dressing-gown, silk-lined, etc. ; and then in *Scene* 2, black dress-coat, white vest, black trousers, plain black necktie, patent-leather boots. *Act V.:* The same, or a similar dress, to the one secondly described.

SIR JOHN VESEY.—Black dress-coat and trousers, white vest and cravat, pair of gold-mounted eyeglasses, with black silk ribbon ; hair white.

LORD GLOSSMORE.—Black frock coat and trousers, fancy vest, patent-leather boots, scarf, and kid gloves. In *Act IV.*, usual dress for a fashionable dinner-party.

SIR FREDERICK BLOUNT —In the 1*st Act*, a plain black suit—handsome garments of any color, but made in the highest fashion and of the very best quality—rich silk handkerchiefs, and very fine light-colored overcoat, etc.*

STOUT.—Blue cloth coat with broad tails ; velvet vest, white cravat, and stand-up collar ; Oxford gray trousers, cloth boots, large red handkerchief, white hat with black band, afterwards removed.

GRAVES.—Body coat, vest, trousers, and gloves all black. In *Act III.*, a colored silk handkerchief.

CAPTAIN DUDLEY SMOOTH.—1*st Dress:* Dark fashionable morning or lounging coat, vest, and trousers. 2*d Dress:* Frock coat and fancy colored vest and trousers, patent-leather boots. 3*d Dress:* Usual dress for a fasionable dinner-party.

SHARP.—Plain black body coat, vest, and trousers ; white cravat, shoes.

OLD MEMBER.—Blue colored body coat with gilt buttons, fancy colored vest, nankeen trousers, shoes and cloth gaiters, white scarf, and high collar.

CLARA DOUGLAS.—1*st Dress:* Plain black walking dress with sleeves, and the hair plain. 2*d Dress:* Fancy muslin dress, ornamented, but not too much, accompanied by rich gold bracelets, etc. 3*d Dress:* A rich dark velvet walking costume, and handsome ornaments.

LADY FRANKLIN.—A very rich and gay colored silk dress, with lace shawl, etc. In *Act IV.*, handsome evening dress, the sleeves being short. In *Act V.*, a handsome morning costume, bonnet and lace shawl.

GEORGINA.—White muslin dress trimmed fancifully with black ribbons, jet ornaments on the breast and the wrists of the long sleeves ; neck-chain of jet. In *Act II.*, similar dress varied by fancy ribbons and gold ornaments. In *Act IV.*, change for dress for a fashionable dinner-party. In *Act V.*, silk dress, fashionably cut blue mantle and trimmings ; hat and feather.

SERVANTS.—Those belonging to SIR JOHN VESEY and ALFRED EVELYN: Plain black body coat, vest, and knee-breeches, white stockings and shoes. Those at the Club House : Puce colored body coats, with large brass buttons, velvet plush vests and knee-breeches, white neckties and stockings, shoes, and hair powdered.

---

* All actors whom I have seen play this part made it the medium for the display of the richest and most fashionable clothing.

PROPERTIES.

ACT I., Scene 1.—Two rich tables and covers; newspapers, books; twelve chairs; carpet; a secretaire writing table; writing materials; black-edged letter; watch; purse; banknote; wine; decanters; glasses; cake; will; letter;

ACT II., Scene 1.—Three drawings; bundle with new coat; writing desk and materials; table; chairs; book and parchment; piece of gold coin; letter. *Scene 2.*—As in Act I., with the addition of portfolio, drawings; a portrait; letter, as in last.

ACT III., Scene 1.—Same furniture, etc., as in Act I., Scene 1, except there need not be so many chairs; writing materials; letter. *Scene 2.*—Two chairs. *Scene 3.*—Five tables; twelve chairs; newspapers; books; writing materials; playing cards; coffee cups; large round snuff-box; two salvers; glasses; letter; note; pocket-book; wax lights in candelabras on the tables; lemonade and glasses.

ACT IV., Scene 1.—Two tables; two chairs; writing materials; pocket-book; checks. *Scene 2.*—Two tables with candelabra, etc.; nine chairs; painting; letter; paper for Sheriff's officer; table in dining-room at back; chairs round it; dinner service spread; candelabra and lights.

ACT V., Scene 1.—Two tables; four chairs; table cloth and breakfast things; glasses and wine; letter; bill; salver; large and small watches. *Scene 2.*—Bell pull and bell without. *Scene 3.*—Same as Act IV., Scene 2. Letter, salver, writing materials on table.

EXPLANATION OF THE STAGE DIRECTIONS.

The Actor is supposed to face the Audience.

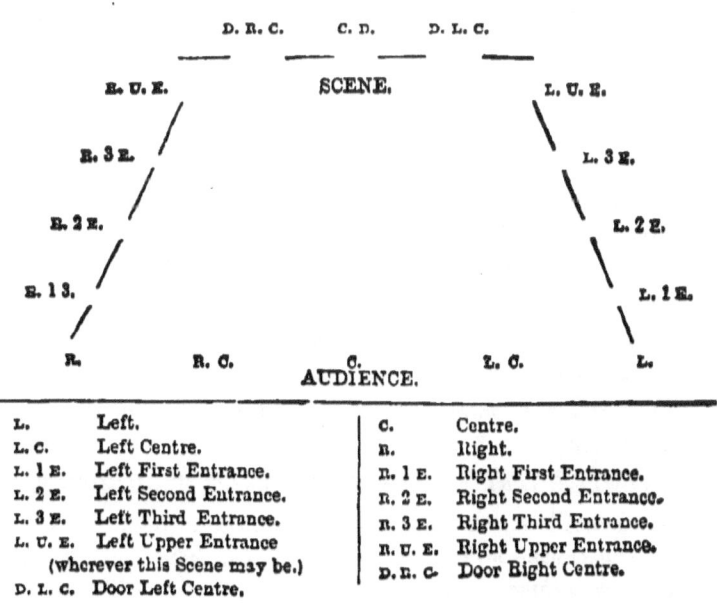

L.	Left.		C.	Centre.
L. C.	Left Centre.		R.	Right.
L. 1 E.	Left First Entrance.		R. 1 E.	Right First Entrance.
L. 2 E.	Left Second Entrance.		R. 2 E.	Right Second Entrance.
L. 3 E.	Left Third Entrance.		R. 3 E.	Right Third Entrance.
L. U. E.	Left Upper Entrance		R. U. E.	Right Upper Entrance.
	(wherever this Scene may be.)		D. R. C.	Door Right Centre.
D. L. C.	Door Left Centre.			

BILL FOR PROGRAMMES, Etc.

The events of this play take place in London. Period, the present century.

ACT I.

Scene I.—DRAWING-ROOM IN SIR JOHN VESEY'S HOUSE.

The Scheming Baronet and his Daughter—Death of a Rich Indian Cousin —The Poor Secretary and the Poor Ward—The Story of Evelyn's Love —Offer of Hand and Heart—Clara's Rejection—A Tale of Sorrow— The Reading of the Will—" I leave all the residue of my fortune to ——Alfred Evelyn."

ACT II.

Scene I.—AN ANTE-ROOM IN EVELYN'S NEW MANSION.

The Troubles of Riches - Specimen of a Political Economist—Election Prospects—Bribery and Corruption—A Game of Battledore and Shuttlecock—The Story of Evelyn's Life and Struggles—The Mysterious Letter—" Who sent it ? Clara or Georgina ?"

Scene II.—DRAWING-ROOM AT SIR JOHN VESEY'S.

Mr. Graves and his " Sainted Maria"—A Dangerous Widow—The Baronet's Cunning—An Artful Trick to Entrap Evelyn—The Portait—The Bait Caught—The Letter was from Georgina—She Sent her Savings to Relieve Distress—The Offer of Hand and Fortune to Georgina—Evelyn is Accepted—Clara's Agony—" With my whole heart I say it—be happy !"

ACT III.

Scene I.—DRAWING-ROOMS IN SIR JOHN VESEY'S HOUSE.

Clouds in the Horizon—Extravagance and Gambling—Rocks Ahead—Clara's Departure from England—The Warning Voice of Love, as a Sister— " Let us part friends ! " — Suspicions of Truth—Graves' Story of Georgina's Flirtations—A Trap Set for the Trapper.

Scene II.—BOUDOIR IN SIR JOHN VESEY'S HOUSE.

A Widower and Widow in Love—The Temptations of a Charming Woman —A Cure for Melancholy—Dancing and a Sweet Voice—Unpleasant Interruption.

Scene III.—GRAND SALOON AT EVELYN'S CLUB HOUSE.

A Gentleman and a Gambler—Captain DEADLY Smooth's Good Luck—Plot and Counterplot—Infatuation in Gaming—Loss after Loss—Evelyn's Ruin Approaching.

ACT IV.

Scene I.—ANTE-ROOM IN EVELYN'S HOUSE.

Morning Calls—Debt Against Debt—Novel Mode of Payment by Increasing —Not Quite Sharp Enough.

Scene II.—SPLENDID SALOON IN EVELYN'S HOUSE.

The Plot Thickens—Evelyn is Drifting Wrong—Suggestions for Assistance—" Will Georgina help me?—£10,000 for a time will save me" —An Answer Deferred—Unpleasant Duns and a Sherriff's Officer— Failure of Evelyn's Bankers—Clamorous Creditors—Pleasure Against Charity—Desertion of Friends as the Money goes Down!

ACT V.

Scene I.—A ROOM AT THE CLUB.

More News of the Downfall—A Friend in the Scheme—Georgina's Old Love —The Eccentric Baronet--Political Intrigues—The Mine is Opening.

Scene II.—DRAWING-ROOMS IN SIR JOHN VESEY'S HOUSE.

A Devoted Heart—A Woman in Distress—The Old Love Revived—If he Can be Saved he Shall—Departure of Clara to see Evelyn.

Scene III.—SPLENDID SALOON IN EVELYN'S HOUSE.'

Money Works Wonders—A Change from Respect to Infamy—'Tis the way of the World—£10,000 placed at Evelyn's Bankers—Saved— " 'Tis Georgina's act—the die is cast!"—Lovers Alone—The Story of Clara's Life—The Reasons for Rejection—Hope for the Future— Too Late!—Evelyn Elected a Member of Parliament—The Mine is Sprung—Startling News—Georgina Marries Sir Frederick Blount! " Who, then, sent the money to my bankers?"—The Mystery Solved —The Letter Explained—Clara Douglas!—Acceptance of Evelyn —The Scheme at an End—He was Never Ruined—Only a Plot to Show the Value of

MONEY.

THE STORY OF THE PLAY.

IN the centre of the most fashionable part of London there resided, at the commencement of the play, Sir John Vesey, Barouet, ex-Member of Parliament, etc., Fellow of ever so many societies, and President of ever so many Corporations; in fact, a man surrounded by all the attributes of wealth and high political and social position. Outwardly well polished, he had naturally a large and influential circle of admiring friends and cringing flatterers; wealth and position, like honey, attract many flies—and an artifice he resorted to of getting it mooted about that he was hoarding up his money, gradually acquired him the name of "Stingy Jack," and stimulated a belief, in some persons, and confirmed the opinion of others, that he really was a most highly honorable and wealthy gentleman, though somewhat eccentric, and that his only daughter, Georgina, was a rich heiress.

The fact, however, was just the reverse. He had been, and was, playing a very deep game indeed ; he was in every respect an unprincipled and unsubstantial man, —a living specimen, though more advanced in years, of Dickens' ever to be remembered character, Montague Tigg, *alias* Tigg Montague.

The members of Sir John Vesey's household were Georgina, his daughter ; Lady Franklin, his half-sister and a widow ; Clara Douglas, a poor orphan cousin and his ward, and Alfred Evelyn, another poor cousin, who acted as his private secretary.

As to Sir John himself—his father for services rendered in the army obtained a title, but expended all available means in keeping it up, consequently the only fortune he could leave his son was the title. But this worthy son was not to be so easily foiled. On the strength of his parent's services, he obtained a pension of £400 a year, which was quite sufficient trading capital for a man of Sir John's adventurous disposition and tactics. On £400 he took credit for £800 ; upon which credit he married a woman with £10,000, and increased his credit to £40,000. Then it was that he worked his artful scheme and paid a highly respectable but impoverished gentleman so much per week to mix in society and constantly allude to him as "Stingy Jack," upon the principle that if a man of position is called "stingy" he is presumed to be "rich," and to be presumed "rich," is to be universally respected.

Working the wires thus, he had been elected a member of Parliament, and remained so until a fitting opportunity arrived, when he resigned his seat in favor of a member of the Government, who, in return, gave him a sinecure appointment, bringing in about £2,000 a year; all of which, and more raised upon the strength of it, he expended annually in keeping up appearances, in the hopes of bringing about a wealthy match for his daughter.

Of Georgina little can be said, except that she was quite obedient to her father's wishes, though at the same time a little artful and self-willed. Her mother died young, and therefore the male parental guidance had its effect in moulding her to his views.

Lady Franklin was generous, kind, wealthy, and middled-aged—without any family, and therefore her half-brother had induced her to take off his hands the burden of his ward. Clara Douglas was an orphan of his cousin ; her mother died young, and her father at his death left her to the care of Sir John as her guardian, but having no wealth, that was all he did leave him, and therefore to a man of Sir John's temperament it was by no means an agreeable bequest. It was not long, however, before he found a way to transfer the charge to Lady Franklin.

Alfred Evelyn was left fatherless when a boy and his mother sacrificed everything she could to give him education. From school he proceeded to college, where he became a "sizar."[*]

---

[*] "Sizar" is a term used in the University of Cambridge, in England, to denote a body of students, next below the pensioners, who eat at the public table free of expense, after the fellows of the college have taken their meals. In former times they had to wait at table during the meal hours, but this custom has been done

One day, a young lord struck him, he returned the insult by horsewhipping his assailant. The then great difference between rich and poor was too strong for the affair to be passed over, so poor Evelyn was expelled the college and all his ambitious hopes blasted. Coming to London, he toiled and toiled to the best of his ability to earn a scanty subsistence for himself and mother, and so long as she lived he labored strenuously and successfully, but with her death, ambition seemed to expire also. As a last resource, he consented to become the ill-paid secretary and hanger-on to his cousin, Sir John Vesey; but there was a magnet in the house which attracted him; he loved Clara Douglas, and to be near that loadstone he sank his pride.

He prepared Sir John's speeches, wrote his pamphlets, made up his calculations, composed epitaphs, condensed the debates in Parliament, and even executed various orders for the ladies, in bringing home dresses, novels, music, securing boxes at the opera, etc.,—all done probably upon a salary less than was paid to Sir John's coachman. Such, then, were the constituent elements of the Baronet's household at the opening of the play.

Sir John has just received a letter from Mr. Graves, an eccentric, but well-meaning middle-aged gentleman, who never ceases to express, with a melancholy air, the loss he experienced by the death of his late wife; whom he invariably terms, with uplifted eyes, his " Sainted Maria," though very probably, if the truth were known, she had led him anything but a happy life, and her departure from this world was more of a blessing than a misfortune ; at least, so many persons said, and more believed.

Mr. Graves informs Sir John that a Mr. Mordaunt, to whom Georgina is the nearest relation, is dead ; that, having been appointed executor, and having since his wife's death lived only in apartments, he proposes to read the will that day at Sir John's house, and will come with Mr. Sharp, the lawyer, for that purpose.

This is great news to Sir John—Mr. Mordaunt was reputed to be worth half a million sterling ; Georgina is the nearest relation—there could surely be nothing therefore to prevent her coming in for the bulk of his fortune.

Lady Franklin and Clara arrive ; to the surprise of the worldly-minded Sir John, his half sister is not in mourning, but poor Clara is, explaining in the genuine feeling of her nature, that although only a third cousin of the deceased, he had once assisted her father, and the quiet mourning robes she had obtained were all the respect and gratitude she could show.

There are other distant relatives interested in the will; Mr. Stout, a political economist, Lord Glossmore, a sort of butterfly nobleman : and Sir Frederick Blount, a foppish baronet, who, as Lady Franklin facetiously observes, " objects to the letter r as being too wough and therefore dwops its acquaintance."

Alfred Evelyn, in the meantime, has arrived, and sits at the table absorbed in reading ; so, when the conversation flags, a general attack is made upon him to know if he has executed various commissions, and what has delayed him. He takes the opportunity to explain to Sir John, that his prolonged absence has been occasioned by his having gone to visit a poor woman who was his nurse, and his mother's last friend ; that she is very sick, nay, dying, that she owes six months rent, and he appeals to Sir John for assistance. It is refused ; but Georgina overhears it, and her first impulse is to assist him, but then she might not have the fortune, her allowance is very little, and she must purchase a pair of earrings she has seen ; she, however, inquires the address of the nurse. Upon this point the play hinges. Evelyn is misled by her unsolicited generosity, and gives it, and as Georgina reads it aloud, Clara silently takes a note of it, places all her little money in an envelope—but how to direct it ? Evelyn would know her handwriting, and that must not be, so she appeals to Lady Franklin, who promises that he shall not know

away with some years. The term so applied to them was probably derived from this ancient occupation, as the food they had to supply when so engaged was called " size." It may well be imagined how naturally a spirit like Evelyn's recoiled at the position.

it, that her ward shall direct it, and she will herself furnish the money, as it is more than Clara can spare.

Sir Frederick Blount arrives, and in his stupid, foppish way, addresses many very ridiculous observations to Clara, which produces some excellent by-play and sarcastic remarks from Evelyn, who, though apparently sitting at the table reading, is watching with a keen and jealous eye every movement of the idol of his affections. Sir Frederick being called away, they are left alone, and in the most exquisite and perfect language, he tells the story of his love. But what is his horror and dismay to meet a calm, yet firm, refusal! Clara sees that, poor as they are, it would only be a marriage of privation and of penury—a life of days that dread the morrow—her love is his—she can submit to suffer alone, but bring him into it also, she cannot.

Mr. Graves and Mr. Sharp the lawyer arrive, and the reading of the will commences. Much disappointment, but more amusement, is created by the peculiarity and smallness of the bequests ; the largest being one of £10,000 to Georgina Vesey. ● " What can the old fool have done with his money ?" exclaims Sir John, losing all control. The climax soon comes ; the deceased bequeaths the entire residue of his immense fortune to the only relative who never fawned upon him, and who, having known privation, may the better employ wealth—Alfred Evelyn ! Congratulations on every side are unbounded, but the voice of her he loves is silent.

Evelyn is speedily installed in the first style of position ; his patronage is sought by every one ; tradesmen, electors, artists, and every rank of persons—but this does not prevent his dispensing charity with a liberal hand, for which he secures the services of Mr. Sharp.

To Graves he tells the story of his life and love, and further, that in the letter which the lawyer gave him after the reading of the will, there was a request from Mr. Mordaunt—but not imposing any condition—asking as a favor, if he had formed no other attachment, to choose as his wife, either Georgina or Clara, who was the daughter of a dear friend of the deceased. He still loves Clara, but her rejection overcomes him ; besides, he has obtained the letter, written in a disguised hand, sending money to, and saving his nurse. His heart yearns to believe that it was Clara's doing, but he cannot conceive how she should know the address, besides the amount was too much for her to send. He also tells Graves, that determined to be revenged upon Clara for refusing him, he has bribed Sharp, the lawyer, to say that the letter he gave him contained a codicil to the will, bequeathing Clara £20,000 ; so that she will be no longer a dependent, and that she will owe her release from almost beggary and insult, unknowingly, to the poor scholar whom she had rejected. With this joyous and noble feeling he determines to visit Lady Franklin, and see if he can possibly ascertain by whom the money was sent to his nurse.

Consequent upon her unlooked-for wealth, Clara is now admired by all, even by Sir Frederick. Lady Franklin always assures her she believes Evelyn still loves her, and begs permission to tell him who sent the money to the nurse, otherwise he might imagine it came from Georgina. Sir John Vesey happens to overhear this remark, and determines to improve upon it, to secure Evelyn for his daughter. Clara makes Lady Franklin promise never to reveal the secret—most reluctantly she obeys.

Sir John questions his daughter ; she had taken down the address, intending to, but did not, send the money. That is quite enough ground for Sir John to work upon.

A new character now comes upon the scene, Captain Dudley Smooth, but who, in consequence of his fashionable manners and abilities, unusual success at the gaming table, and skill as a duellist, had acquired the name of " Deadly " Smooth, and he is of course soon one of the friends of the wealthy Evelyn.

Sir Frederick Blount also seeks Evelyn's aid to promote his suit with Clara, telling him that he finds Georgina had a prior attachment, which prior attachment was no other than Evelyn himself, and therefore he must give her up and try his luck with Clara. Evelyn agrees to help him, and urges his merits in a bantering tone. Observing Sir Frederick's attentions, Georgina determines to flirt with Evelyn, and

Sir John seizes the opportunity to introduce to his notice a portfolio of her drawings; turning them over one after another until up comes a portrait of—Alfred Evelyn !

He is astonished and confused. Can she really love him ? A thought strikes him—carelessly he asks her if she has yet purchased a guitar she spoke of some months since. Now is the time for the master stroke, so taking him aside, Sir John hints that she had applied the money in charity; that she did not wish it known, and had employed some one else to direct the letter. The blow is well struck, the shaft strikes home; such benevolence, and such love as to draw his portrait ; Clara had refused him, how could he do otherwise than offer to Georgina ? He frankly tells her of his love for another, deep and true, but *vain;* that he cannot give her a first love, but he does offer her esteem, gratitude, hand and fortune.

It is accepted. Poor Clara overhears all, and sinks on her chair fainting; he rushes to her side, and she rallies sufficiently to exclaim, " With my whole heart I say it—be happy—Alfred Evelyn !"

The time for the wedding is somewhat delayed, much to Sir John's annoyance, and Georgina complains that Evelyn's visits are not so frequent, nor his manners so cheerful as they used to be—indeed, her former admirer, Sir Frederick, was far more attentive and amusing. Sir John does not half like the way Evelyn is going on. Fine houses in London, and in the country balls, banquets, expensive pictures, horses, liberal charities, everything tending to diminish rapidly the largest fortune. In addition to which, it is reported, he has taken to gambling, and is nearly always in company with Captain *Deadly* Smooth, against whose arts, no young man of fortune had been known to stand long.

Sir John determines that it is absolutely necessary to bring about an early settlement, and to further this, he thinks it best to get Clara away. He speaks to her upon the subject, and she consents to leave England rather than cloud his daughter's hopes, and to that effect promises to write a letter. As she is finishing it, Evelyn calls to see Georgina, who is out, and, as they are alone, Clara tells him of her intended departure.

In a scene of the most choice and beautiful language, replete with exquisite pathos, she breathes her thanks for past kindness, and now, that he is betrothed to another, her love—as a sister—dictates to her to remonstrate with him upon his parade, and luxuries, and follies. But he tells her that this casting aside of his high qualities, this dalliance with a loftier fate, was her own work. It is impossible adequately to describe the pure and beautiful language of this scene—the skillful mingling of love and reproaches—and the bitter parting—as friends!

As he is recovering from the blow, Graves meets him, and tells him that he knows for a fact, Sir Frederick has proposed to Clara and been refused ; nay, more, that Georgina is not in love with him, but only with his fortune ; and that she plays affection with him in the afternoon, after she has practiced with Sir Frederick in the morning. And further, that Sir John is vastly alarmed at his gambling propensities, and his connection with Captain Smooth, so much so, that he intends visiting the club that evening to watch him.

A light breaks upon Evelyn, and he assures Graves that if these stories are true, the duper shall be duped, and he will extricate himself ; to this end, he determines to shape his plans.

One of the liveliest scenes in the play here follows between Lady Franklin, who is really in love with the solemn and melancholy Graves. She so talks and works upon his feelings, that he gradually relaxes his staid demeanor, and actually joins her in a dance, her own sweet, merry voice supplying the music. In the midst of their meriment they are interrupted and confused by the sudden entrance of Sir John, Blount and Georgina. It is the finest piece of comedy ever put upon the stage, and affords scope for excellent acting.

We are now introduced to the club. Evelyn arrives, and requests Smooth to play with him, and he loses game after game. Watching his opportunity, he takes the Captain aside and acquaints him with a plot he has formed to test the truth of his suspicions of the intentions of Georgina and her father—into this scheme, Smooth readily enters, and returning to the table, they renew their play. Sir John arrives, and watches with the most intense excitement, game after game lost, with constantly increasing stakes. In apparent agony, Evelyn rises from the table, declaring that the work is ruinous, and he will play no more. All the members crowd round the Captain to ascertain the extent of his winnings; the only answer they get is an offer to purchase from one of them a furnished house which he has to sell for £15,000, which, from his manner, he leads them to believe, is a mere trifle. They catch the bait, and at once imagine he must have won double and treble that sum. Sir John's consternation is fearful, but the more so when he sees Evelyn, apparently under the influence of too much wine, take hold of Smooth's arm, and declare they must now make a night of it.

In the morning, Glossmore and Sir Frederick call upon Evelyn to settle some small accounts with him. He still carries on the deception, and not only excuses paying them, but works a trick between them, by which he secures a further check from each, and makes a present to one of a horse he buys on credit from the other. He goes further than this; not only does he borrow £500 from Sir John, but he also tells him that he has sold out of the funds sufficient money to pay the balance for the purchase of an estate; that the money is laying at his bankers, but he cannot touch it for any other purpose, or the estate will be lost, and the deposit money he has paid forefeited. He alludes, therefore, to Georgina's £10,000 legacy, and managing cleverly to get Sir John out of the way, he speaks to her upon the subject. He tells her of his position, that they may probably have to retrench and live in the country, and suggests that she should lend him the £10,000 for a few weeks to meet some pressing claims; without confidence there can be no joy in wedlock. She hesitates, then promises he shall hear from her.

Smooth, Glossmore and others now arrive, and, still carrying on the deception, he appears most servile and cringing to the Captain. In a well constructed scene, he calls the attention of all to his unexpected accession to wealth twelve months since, and claims their good opinion for the way in which he has acted—they all outwardly approve, but inwardly they earnestly wish they had back their various loans. Their nervous excitement is increased by news being brought that the bankers with whom he banked have suspended payment, and they very much doubt his assurance that he had not much money there. This is followed by several tradesmen applying for their bills, and then by the entry of a sheriff's officer to serve him with a summons. All this is too overpowering—Sir John vehemently demands his £500, and the others join chorus. Graves is overcome; he tells Evelyn to go into dinner, and he will settle with the officer. Delighted at this generosity, Lady Franklin ingenuously exclaims, "I love you for that!" and poor Graves loses his usual solemnity in the pleasure he experiences at this avowal.

Again Evelyn appeals to Georgina; he shall hear to-morrow; but Sir John can restrain himself no longer, and he commands her, as his "poor, injured, innocent child," to take the arm of Sir Frederick Blount. The doors are thrown open, and Evelyn invites all his friends to the dinner prepared for them; but in doing so, he appeals to them, in mockery, to lend him £10 for his poor old nurse. This is too much, and he then bitterly reminds them that in the morning they lent him hundreds for pleasure, but now they refuse him a trifle for charity, and he commands them to go. Smooth alone remains, and being joined by Graves, the three repair to the table "to fill a bumper to the brave hearts that never desert us!"

Events now approach a climax. Graves and Lady Franklin have become more intimate and confidential. He tells her he is certain that Evelyn still loves Clara, but doubts if she cares for him. Lady Franklin, on the other hand, assures him that ever since she has heard of Evelyn's distress, she has been breaking her heart for him.

Clara arrives, having been to her bankers, for what purpose she declines to say; but she says she has heard that £10,000 would relieve Evelyn, and probably Georgina would lend him the amount. Graves much doubts such generosity in a woman, but be hints that he knew of greater generosity in a man, who, rejected in poverty, by one as poor as himself, when he became rich, through a well invented codicil, had made the woman rich. A light dawns upon Clara, she will see Evelyn and know the truth.

Evelyn's scheme has thus far succeeded. Upon Graves offering to aid him all he can, he is so pleased that he reveals his true position, and assures him that scarcely a month's income of his large fortune has been touched; it was merely a ruse to see whether a woman's love was given to "man" or "money." If Georgina should prove by her answer her confidence and generosity, then, though his heart should break, he would marry her; on the other hand, should she decline, there would be hope for explanations with Clara.

A letter is brought in, and upon opening it, he finds a notice that £10,000 has been paid into the bank to his account. This decides the matter—the die is cast, and Georgina wins. Lady Franklin arrives with Clara, and compelling Graves to withdraw, leaves her and Evelyn together.

In brilliant and telling language, the true and noble sentiments of Clara are revealed; explanation upon explanation follows, and the ardent love of both is powerfully and touchingly portrayed; but it is too late! Evelyn, still believing that it is Georgina who has assisted him, asserts, that by every tie of faith, gratitude, loyalty and love, he is bound to another! Sir John hurries in, stating that he has an offer from Georgina to advance the money, and is astounded when Evelyn tells him the amount has been already paid into his bankers. Then Sharp arrives with the news that Evelyn has been elected a Member of Parliament, and he also informs Sir John that the loss by the failure of the bank was only £200 or so, and that Evelyn has always been living within his income. This is indeed good news, and Sir John is in ecstasies, when his daughter and Sir Frederick arrive; but before he can speak, Evelyn addresses her, desiring to know if she has assisted and trusted him purely and sincerely. She cannot comprehend him, and tells him, that following the principles she once heard uttered, "what is money without happiness?" she had, that morning, promised her hand to Sir Frederick Blount! Utterly astounded, Evelyn produces the letter—Lady Franklin reads it—the money had been paid in by "a friend, to Alfred Evelyn;" the same name used in sending the money to the old nurse, and she at once proclaims both as Clara's acts. In an ecstacy of delight, Evelyn offers love and fortune; this time he is not rejected. The solemn Graves forgets his "sainted Maria," and joins hands with Lady Franklin, and all but Sir John realize the combination of happiness and—MONEY!

.

REMARKS.

IN introducing the third, in the new series of Bulwer's plays, it is a labor of love. The recollections of its excellent production, and of witnessing it afterwards upon almost every occasion of its reproduction in London, bring to mind old associations that are agreeable, yet saddening; for many of those who filled the parts, and whose company was ever welcome, both on and off the stage, are now no more.

Of all Bulwer's plays, this is, undoubtedly the best—it is more than fine—it is a splendid comedy, so telling, and so true to life in all the principles, and in the delineation of characters with which a wayfarer through the world constantly meets. It makes such a powerful appeal, in presenting the spectacle of a man endowed with intellect, education, and gentlemanly bearing, occupying a subordinate position, but expected to be of the greatest usefulness upon all occasions, at the same time receiving less pay than the tall footman of the establishment, and considerable fewer perquisites than the favorite butler; a position from which he is only released by a most unexpected stroke of fortune.

The conception and the execution of the plot are, in my opinion, perfect. All the

observations touching upon falsity, pride, deceptive appearances, worldly scheming, pure affection, hypocrisy, are painted and well drawn, so admirably depictured,
that they cannot fail to tell.

Upon reference to the remarks and dates in the previous plays, it will be found
that only about eleven months elapsed between the production of the Lady of Lyons
and Richelieu, whereas, between that play and this, nearly double that period
passed away, and certain it is, that the author made good use of it, by producing a
work, both in plot and language, very far surpassing all his previous efforts, and
giving to the world one of the finest comedies, if not *the* finest, in the English language.

He had again the good luck to be supported by the highest professional material
available for carrying out his ideas, and it can be stated, from personal knowledge
of all the ladies and gentlemen engaged in the play, that the characters were well
suited to the actors, and the actors to the characters; consequently, nothing could
be more felicitous or so likely to ensure success, as the result proved. Again he had
for his hero, Alfred Evelyn, Mr. Macready, the hero of his previous plays, and for
his heroine, Clara Douglas, Miss Helen Faucit, who had contributed so largely to
previous successes.

As was noticed in the remarks to the Lady of Lyons and Richelieu, those plays
had the benefit of being supported by actors, all of whom afterwards attained leading positions in the profession ; so was it with this play. On its first production
there was a concentration of talent, blooming, half blooming, and about to bloom,
that ensured a proper rendering of a meritorious play.

It will be observed, that the scene of triumph was changed from the Theatre
Royal, Covent Garden, to the Theatre Royal, Haymarket, London; and that of the
ladies and gentlemen who had played in the author's previous productions, only
four had parts in this, viz: Miss H. Faucit, Mr. Macready, Mr. F. Vining, and
Mr. Howe. But the others were a little host. Mr. Walter Lacy, one of the finest,
and most gentlemanly actors on the stage ; Mr. B. Webster, a great actor, and for
many years lessee of the Haymarket, Adelphi, and Princess' Theatres, in London,
where he is still playing, at an advanced age, and who is celebrated for having
brought out, at the Adelphi Theatre, in conjunction with Madame Celeste, a very
large number of first class dramas—" The Hop Pickers,"—" The Harvest Home,"
—" The Green Bushes," and farces innumerable. Mr. Wrench and Mr. Oxberry,
low comedians of the first class; the latter, a gentleman of much intellect and education, as his " Dramatic Budget " will testify.

Mr. O. Smith, who for many years played the " villain " in all domestic dramas,
with unqualified success, so good was his make up, and so well adapted for such
character, his cool, deep voice. Mrs. Glover, a most amiable and accomplished lady,
who was for many years a stock member of the Haymarket Company, and as
famous in London, for her admirable delineation of ladies of middle and more
advanced age, as Mrs. Wheately was in this country. Lastly, Miss P. Horton, who
was afterwards, for many years without a rival, as the chief burlesque and extrava-
ganza actress in London. She married Mr. T. G Reed, a celebrated musical direc-
tor and composer, and together they carried on for many years a beautiful little
theatre in Regent street, London, where they produced a number of musical
pieces of the highest class; it was like a handsome drawing-room, and was known
as " The Gallery of Illustration."

Poor Mrs. Glover met with a melancholy end. Upon the occasion of her farewell
benefit in London, July 12th, 1850, she was so overcome by the reception given to
her, and the emotions at quitting forever the scene of so many triumphs, and of
long standing associations—for the Haymarket Company was termed " the happy
family "—season after season for many years rarely witnessing any change amongst
the members—that she sudden y became speechless, and three days afterwards, July
15th, 1850, she expired.

Of Mr. O. Smith's popularity and fame, for his deep voice and demoniacal laugh, I
may mention a little incident. Some years since, I produced in London an extrav-

aganza called "The Three Princes," and I am happy to say it met with the greatest possible success. I introduced in it an allusion to his voice. The evil genius of the piece threatens utter annihilation to one of the princes, to which the reply came:

> "Destroy me, kin and kith!
> You speak exactly like the Adelphi Smith!"

and so well and so widely known was the actor and his voice, that during a run of nearly two hundred nights, the allusion and imitation never once failed to bring forth a hearty laugh.

With reference to the character of Sir John Vesey, it is interesting to observe that "truth is stranger than fiction." He says, in the first scene, "If you have no merit or money of your own, you must trade on the merits and money of other people." In a recent great law case in England, "The Tichborne Case," the trial of which lasted nearly twelve months, an old pocket book was produced in evidence, in which the claimant to the title and estates (afterwards sentenced to fourteen years imprisonment for perjury and forgery) had written "some people has plenty of money and no brains, and some people has plenty of brains and no money," therefore, he held it was the duty of the latter to prey upon the former. He was evidently a vulgar disciple of the Sir John Vesey school, of which there are specimens to be met with everywhere.

Mr. Macready was followed in the character of Alfred Evelyn, by all those who had followed him in the Lady of Lyons; Charles Kean, Phelps, Anderson, Creswick, and a host of others previously mentioned, who were as successful in this as in the previous plays.

As before stated, Money was first produced in America at the Old Park Theatre, New York, Feb. 1st, 1841, with an excellent cast.

Mr. Hield, who played the hero, was a gentlemanly and intellectual actor; he made a great hit, and for many years afterwards repeated the character with continued success.

Mr. Chippendale as Sir John Vesey, and Mrs. Chippendale as Georgina, were also most successful, whilst Mrs. Maeder as Clara Douglas, and Mrs. Vernon as the warm hearted Lady Franklin, added greatly to the triumph of the play.

It was afterwards produced at the Chatham Theatre, situated on Chatham street between Roosevelt and James streets, and at the Broadway, which was situated on Broadway between Pearl street and Anthony (now Worth) street, with the following cast:

	Chatham Theatre, Sept. 4, 1843.	Broadway Theatre, Nov. 4, 1847.
Alfred Evelyn	Mr. Hield.	Mr. G. Vandenhoff.
Sir John Vesey	Mr. Greene.	Mr. H. Wallack.
Lord Glossmore	Mr. Booth, Jr.	Mr. Fredericks.
Sir Frederick Blount	Mr. Field.	Mr. Lester.
Stout	Mr. Collins.	Mr. E. Shaw.
Graves	Mr. Burton.	Mr. Vache.
Captain Dudley Smooth	Mr. Stevens.	Mr. Dawson.
Clara Douglas	Mrs. G. Jones.	Miss F. Wallack.
Lady Franklin	Mrs. Rivers.	Mrs. Winstanley.
Georgina	Miss Kirby.	Mrs. Sergeant.

And also on September 16, 1857, at Burton's New Theatre, when Mr. Murdoch played Alfred Evelyn, Mr. Burton, Graves, and Mrs. W. H. Smith, Lady Franklin.

But perhaps as fine and almost as good a representation of the comedy was that produced at Wallack's Theatre, New York, Jan. 17, 1874, with the following excellent cast:

Alfred Evelyn..Mr. Lester Wallack.
Sir John Vesey...Mr. J. W. Carroll.
Lord Glossmore...Mr. J. W. Ferguson.
Sir Frederick Blount.....................................Mr. W. R. Floyd.
Benjamin Stout...Mr. John Brougham.
Graves...Mr. Harry Beckett.
Captain Dudley Smooth....................................Mr. J. B. Polk.
Mr. Sharp..Mr. G. F. Browne.
Old Member...Mr. T. C. Mills.
Clara Douglas..Miss Jeffreys Lewis.
Lady Franklin..Madame Ponisi.
Georgina...Miss Dora Goldthwaite.

Having been present upon innumerable occasions of the representations of this play, and witnessed the performance of nearly all the Alfred Evelyns on the London boards, I have no hesitation in saying I never, as a whole, saw the play better mounted or acted. The Alfred Evelyn of Mr. Lester Wallack will bear comparison with any ; if we could only have the pleasure of making him a few years younger it would enhance the beauty of the performance; but one could afford to put aside that little drawback; it was fully compensated for by the'fine delivery of the text, and the intellect and bearing of one of nature's nobleman, such as Alfred Evelyn is supposed to be, and the actor is.

Mr. John Brougham's *Stout,* Mr. Harry Beckett's *Graves,* Mr. W. R. Floyd's *Sir Frederick Blount,* were all most admirably rendered. Miss Jeffreys Lewis made an excellent *Clara Douglas,* and as *Lady Franklin,* Madame Ponisi well sustained her reputation, whilst Miss Dora Goldthwaite as *Georgina* was all that was needed. Indeed all engaged were good. As I have said in my former remarks, so I say of this play—not one jot of brilliancy and effect has been lost in transferring it to the American boards.   J. M. K.

MONEY.

ACT I.

SCENE I.—*A drawing-room in* SIR JOHN VESEY'S *house ; folding doors* C., *which open on another drawing-room. To the right a table, with the Morning Post newspaper, books, etc. ; to the left, a sofa and writing table. The furniture tasteful and costly.*

SIR JOHN *and* GEORGINA *discovered*, R. C.

SIR JOHN (*reading a letter edged with black*). Yes, he says at two precisely. "Dear Sir John, as since the death of my sainted Maria,"—Hum !—that's his wife ; she made him a martyr, and now he makes her a saint !

GEOR. Well, as since her death ?—

SIR J. (*reading*). " I have been living in chambers, where I cannot so well invite ladies, you will allow me to bring Mr. Sharp, the lawyer, to read the will of the late Mr. Mordaunt (to which I am appointed executor) at your house—your daughter being the nearest relation. I shall be with you at two precisely.—Henry Graves."

GEOR. And you really think I shall be uncle Mordaunt's heiress ? And that the fortune he made in India is half a million ?

SIR J. Ay! I have no doubt you will be the richest heiress in England. But sit down, my dear Georgy—my dear girl. (GEORGINA *sits* R. H. *of table*, SIR JOHN L. H.) Upon this happy—I mean melancholy—occasion, I feel that I may trust you with a secret. You see this fine house —our fine servants—our fine plate—our fine dinners ; every one thinks Sir John Vesey a rich man.

GEOR. And are you not, papa ?

SIR J. Not a bit of it—all humbug, child—all humbug, upon my soul ! There are two rules in life—FIRST, men are not valued for what they *are*, but what they *seem* to be. SECONDLY, if you have no merit or money of your own, you must trade on the merits and money of other people. My father got the title by services in the army, and died penniless. On the strength of his services I got a pension of £400 a year ; on the strength of £400 a year I took credit for £800 ; on the strength of £800 a year I married your mother with £10,000 ; on the strength of £10,000 I took credit for £40,000, and paid Dicky Gossip three guineas a week to go about everywhere calling me " Stingy Jack !"

GEOR. Ha! ha! A disagreeable nickname.

SIR J. But a valuable reputation. When a man is called stingy, it is as much as calling him rich ; and when a man's called rich, why he's a man ·universally respected. On the strength of my respectability I wheedled a constituency, changed my politics, resigned my seat to a minister, who, to a man of such stake in the country, could offer nothing

less in return than a patent office of £2,000 a year. That's the way to
succeed in life. Humbug, my dear—all humbug, upon my soul!

GEOR. I must say that you——

SIR J. Know the world, to be sure. Now, for your fortune—as I
spend more than my income, I can have nothing to leave you; yet, even
without counting your uncle, you have always passed for an heiress on
the credit of your expectations from the savings of "Stingy Jack."
Apropos of a husband; you know we thought of Sir Frederick Blount.

GEOR. Ah, papa, he is charming.

SIR J. Hem! He *was so*, my dear, before we knew your poor uncle
was dead ; but an heiress such as you will be should look out for a duke.
Where the deuce is Evelyn this morning ? (*rises, puts back the chair, goes
to* L. *table, marks the letter and puts it in his pocket.*)

GEOR. I've not seen him, papa. What a strange character he is—so
sarcastic ; and yet he can be agreeable. (*puts back her chair and then
goes* R.)

SIR J. A humorist—a cynic ! One never knows how to take him. My
private secretary—a poor cousin, has not got a shilling, and yet, hang
me, if he does not keep us all at a sort of a distance.

GEOR. But why do you take him to live with us, papa, since there's
no good to be got by it ?

SIR J. There you are wrong ; he has a great deal of talent; prepares
my speeches, writes my pamphlets, looks up my calculations. Besides,
he *is* our cousin—he has no salary ; kindness to a poor relation always
tells well in the world ; and benevolence is a useful virtue—particularly
when you can have it for nothing. With our other cousin, Clara, it was
different; her father thought fit to leave me her guardian, though she
had not a penny—a mere useless encumbrance ; so, you see, I got my
half-sister, Lady Franklin, to take her off my hands.

GEOR. How much longer is Lady Franklin's visit to be ? (*at table* R.,
takes up paper, reads until she speaks to EVELYN.)

SIR J. I don't know, my dear ; the longer the better—for her husband left her a good deal of money at her own disposal. Ah, here she
comes !

Enter LADY FRANKLIN *and* CLARA, C. R.

My dear sister, we were just loud in your praises. But how's this—not
in mourning ?

LADY F. Why should I go in mourning for a man I never saw ?

SIR J. Still there may be a legacy.

LADY F. Then there'll be less cause for affliction ! Ha, ha! my dear
Sir John, I'm one of those who think feelings a kind of property, and
never take credit for them upon false pretences. (*crosses to table* L., *sits.*)

SIR J. (*aside,* L.). Very silly woman ! (*aloud*) But, Clara, I see you are
more attentive to the proper decorum ; yet you are very, *very*, VERY dis-
tantly connected with the deceased—a third cousin, I think ?

CLARA. Mr. Mordaunt once assisted my father, and these poor robes
are all the gratitude I can show him. (*goes to* L. *table and sits.*)

SIR J. (*aside*). Gratitude ! humph ! I am afraid the minx has got expectations.

LADY F. So, Mr. Graves is the executor—the will is addressed to
him ? The same Mr. Graves who is always in black, always lamenting
his ill-fortune and his sainted Maria, who led him the life of a dog ?

SIR J. The very same. His liveries are black—his carriage is black
—he always rides a black galloway—and faith, if he ever marry again,
I think he will show his respect to the sainted Maria by marrying a
black woman.

LADY F. Ha! ha! we shall see. (*aside*) Poor Graves, I always liked him; he made an excellent husband. (*down* c.)

Enter EVELRN, c. L., *seats himself* L. *of* R. *table, and takes up a book unobserved.*

SIR J. What a crowd of relations this will brings to light! Mr. Stout, the Political Economist—Lord Glossmore——

LADY F. Whose grandfather kept a pawnbroker's shop, and who, accordingly, entertains the profoundest contempt for everything popular, *parvenu,* and plebeian.

SIR J. Sir Frederick Blount——

LADY F. Sir Fwedewick Blount, who objects to the letter *r* as being too *wough*, and therefore *dwops* its acquaintance; one of the new class of prudent young gentlemen, who, not having spirits and constitution for the hearty excesses of their predecessors, intrench themselves in the dignity of a lady-like languor. A man of fashion in the last century was riotous and thoughtless—in this he is tranquil and egotistical. He never does anything that is silly, or says anything that is wise. I beg your pardon, my dear; I believe Sir Frederick is an admirer of yours, provided, on reflection, he does not see "what harm it could do him" to fall in love with your beauty and expectations. Then, too, our poor cousin the scholar—(CLARA *touches* LADY FRANKLIN, *and points to* EVELYN. *All turn and look at him*) Oh, Mr. Evelyn, there you are! (*resumes her seat.*)

SIR J. (*going up to* EVELYN, R. c.). Evelyn—the very person I wanted; where have you been all day? Have you seen to those papers?—have you written my epitaph on poor Mordaunt?—Latin, you know?—have you reported my speech at Exeter Hall?—have you looked out the debates on the Customs?—and—oh, have you mended up all the old pens in the study?

GEOR. (R. *of* R. *table*). And have you brought me the black floss silk? —have you been to Storr's for my ring?—and, as we cannot go out on this melancholy occasion, did you call at Hookham's for the last H. B. and the Comic Annual?

LADY F. (*rises and goes to* EVELYN). And did you see what was really the matter with my bay horse?—did you get me the opera-box?—did you buy my little Charley his peg-top?

EVELYN (*always reading*). Certainly, Paley is right upon that point; for, put the syllogism thus—(*looking up*) Ma'am—sir—Miss Vesey—you want something of me?—Paley observes, that to assist even the undeserving tends to the better regulation of our charitable feelings.—No apologies—I am quite at your service. (*shuts the book and comes forward.*)

SIR J. Now he's in one of his humors!

LADY F. (*down* R.). You allow him strange liberties, Sir John.

EVE. (c.). You will be the less surprised at that, madam, when I inform you that Sir John allows me nothing else. I am now about to draw on his benevolence.

LADY F. I beg your pardon, sir, and like your spirit. Sir John, I'm in the way, I see; for I know your benevolence is so delicate that you never allow any one to detect it!   [*Retires and goes off,* c. L.

EVE. I could not do your commissions to-day—I have been to visit a poor woman, who was my nurse and my mother's last friend. She is very poor—*very*—sick—dying—and she owes six months' rent!

SIR J. (L). You know I should be most happy to do anything for yourself. But the nurse—(*aside*) Some people's nurses are always ill! (*aloud*) There are so many impostors about! We'll talk of it to-morrow.

(EVELYN *goes to the table*, L.) This mournful occasion takes up all of my attention. (*looking at his watch*) Bless me ! so late! I've letters to write, and—none of the pens are mended !   [*Exit*, R.

GEOR. (*taking out her purse*, R.). I think I will give it to him—and yet if I don't get the fortune. after all !—Papa allows me so little !—then I *must* have those earrings. (*puts up the purse*) Mr. Evelyn, what is the address of your nurse ?

EVE. (*writes at* L. *table, and gives it—aside*). She has a good heart with all her foibles ! (*aloud*) Ah ! Miss Vesey, if that poor woman had not closed the eyes of my lost mother, Alfred Evelyn would not have been this beggar to your father.

GEOR (*reading*). " Mrs. Staunton, 14 Amos street, Pentonville."

(CLARA, *at the table, writes down the address as she hears* GEORGINA *read it.*)

GEOR. I will certainly attend to it—(*aside*) if I get the fortune. (EVELYN *goes up* R.)

SIR J. (*calling, without*). Georgy, I say !

GEOR. Yes, papa!   [*Exit*, R.

EVELYN *has seated himself again at the table—to the right,—and leans his face on his hands.*

CLARA. His noble spirit bowed to this ! Ah, at least here I may give him comfort. (*sits down to write*) But he will recognize my hand.

Re-enter LADY FRANKLIN, C.

LADY F. (*looking over her shoulder*). What bill are you paying. Clara ?—putting up a bank-note ?

CLARA. Hush !—O, Lady Franklin, you are the kindest of human beings. This is for a poor person—I would not have her know whence it came, or she would refuse it ! Would you ?—No—No—he knows *her* handwriting also !

LADY F. Will I—what ?—give the money myself ?—with pleasure ! Poor Clara—why, this covers all your savings—and I am so rich !

CLARA. Nay, I would wish to do all myself ! It is a pride—a duty—it is a joy ; and I have so few joys ! But hush !—this way. (*they retire into the inner room and converse in dumb show.*)

EVE. (*seated*). And thus must I grind out my life for ever ! I am ambitious, and Poverty drags me down ; I have learning, and Poverty makes me the drudge of fools ! I love, and Poverty stands like a spectre before the altar ! But no, no—if, as I believe, I am but loved again, I will—will—what ?—turn opium eater, and dream of the Eden I may never enter ? (LADY FRANKLIN *and* CLARA *advance*, C.)

CLARA. But you must be sure that Evelyn never knows that I sent this money to his nurse.

LADY F. (*to* CLARA). Never fear—I will get my maid to copy and direct this—she writes well, and *her* hand will never be discovered. I will have it done and sent instantly.   [*Exit*, R.

CLARA *advances to the front of stage, and seats herself*, R. C. ; EVELYN *reading*. *Enter* SIR FREDERICK BLOUNT, C. L. ; *he comes down*, L. C.

BLOUNT. No one in the woom !—Oh, Miss Douglas ! Pway don't let me disturb you. Where is Miss Vesey—Georgina ? (*taking* CLARA'S *chair as she rises.*)

EVE. (*looking up, gives* CLARA *a chair, and reseats himself. Aside*) Insolent puppy !

CLARA. Shall I tell her you are here, Sir Frederick?

BLOUNT. Not for the world. Vewy pwetty girl this companion! (*sits L. C.*)

CLARA. What did you think of the Panorama the other day, Cousin Evelyn?

EVE. (*reading*).
> "I cannot talk with civet in the room,
> A fine puss gentleman that's all perfume!"

Rather good lines these.

BLOUNT. Sir!

EVE. (*offering the book*). Don't you think so?—Cowper.

BLOUNT. (*declining the book*). Cowper!

EVE. Cowper.

BLOUNT (*shrugging his shoulders, to* CLARA). Stwange person, Mr. Evelyn!—quite a chawacter!—Indeed the Panowama gives you no idea of Naples—a delightful place. I make it a wule to go there evewy second year—I'm vewy fond of twavelling. You'd like Wome (Rome)—bad inns, but vewy fine wuins; gives you quite a taste for that sort of thing!

EVE. (*reading*).
> "How much a dunce that has been sent to roam
> Excels a dunce that has been kept at home!"

BLOUNT. Sir?

EVE. Cowper.

BLOUNT (*aside*). That fellow Cowper says vewy odd things! Humph! it is beneath me to quawwell. (*aloud*) It will not take long to wead the will, I suppose.—I am his nearest male welation. He was vewy eccentwic. (*draws his chair nearer*) By the way, Miss Douglas, did you wemark my cuwicle? It is bwinging cuwicles into fashion. I should be most happy if you will allow me to dwive you out. Nay—nay—I should, upon my word. (*trying to take her hand.*)

EVE (*starting up*). A wasp!—a wasp!—just going to settle. Take care of the wasp, Miss Douglas!

BLOUNT. A wasp—where!—don't bwing it this way—some people don't mind them! I've a particlar dislike to wasps; they sting damnably!

EVE. I beg pardon—it's only a gadfly.

Enter PAGE, R.

PAGE. Sir John will be happy to see you in his study, Sir Frederick.
[*Exit* PAGE, C. L.

BLOUNT. Vewy well. (*rises and goes* R) Upon my word, there is something vewy nice about this girl. To be sure, I love Georgina—but if this one would take a fancy to me—(*thoughtfully*)—Well, I don't see what harm it could do me! *Au plaisir?* [*Exit*, R.

CLARA *takes her chair to* R. *of* L. *table.*

EVE. Clara!

CLARA. Cousin! (*coming forward*, L.)

EVE. And you, too, are a dependant?

CLARA. But on Lady Franklin, who seeks to make me forget it.

EVE. Ay, but can the world forget it? This insolent condescension—this coxcombry of admiration—more galling than the arrogance of contempt! Look you now—Robe Beauty in silk and cashmere—hand Virtue into her chariot—lackey their caprices—wrap them from the winds —fence them round with a golden circle—and Virtue and Beauty are as

goddesses both to peasant and to prince. Strip them of the adjuncts—
see Beauty and Virtue poor—dependant—solitary—walking the world
defenceless! oh, *then* the devotion changes its character—the same
crowd gather eagerly around—fools—fops—libertines—not to worship
at the shrine, but to sacrifice the victim!

CLARA. My cousin, you are cruel!—I can smile at the pointless insolence.

EVE. Smile—and he took your hand! Oh, Clara, you know not the
tortures that I suffer hourly! When others approach you—young—fair
—rich—the sleek darlings of the world—I accuse you of your very
beauty—I writhe beneath every smile that you bestow. (CLARA, *about to
speak*) No—speak not—my heart has broken its silence, and you shall
hear the rest. For you I have endured the weary bondage of this house
—the fools gibe—the hireling's sneer—the bread purchased by toils
that should have led me to loftier ends; yes, to see you—hear you—
breathe the same air—be ever at hand—that if others slighted, from one
at least you might receive the luxury of respect—for this—for this I
have lingered, suffered, and forborne. Oh, Clara! we are orphans both
—friendless both; you are all in the world to me; (*she turns away*) turn
not away—my very soul speaks in these words—I LOVE YOU! (*kneels.*)

CLARA. No—Evelyn—Alfred—no! Say it not; think it not! it were
madness.

EVE. Madness!—nay, hear me yet. I am poor, dependant—a beggar for bread to a dying servant. True! But I have a heart of iron. I
have knowledge—patience—health—and my love for you gives me at
last ambition! I have trifled with my own energies till now, for I despised all things till I loved you. With you to toil for—your step to
support—your path to smooth—and I—I, poor Alfred Evelyn—promise
at last to win for you even fame and fortune! Do not withdraw your
hand—*this* hand—shall it not be mine?

CLARA. Ah, Evelyn! Never—never! (*crosses to* R.)

EVE. Never? (*rises.*)

CLARA. Forget this folly; our union is impossible, and to talk of love
were to deceive both!

EVE. (*bitterly*). Because I am poor!

CLARA. And *I too!* A marriage of privation—of penury—of days that
dread the morrow! I have seen such a lot! Never return to this again.

EVE. Enough—you are obeyed. I deceived myself—ha—ha! I fancied that I too was loved. I, whose youth is already half gone with care
and toil—whose mind is soured—whom nobody *can* love—who ought to
have loved no one!

CLARA (*aside*). And if it were only ⸺ to suffer, or perhaps to starve!
Oh, what shall I say? (*aloud*) Evelyn—cousin!

EVE. Madam.

CLARA. Alfred! I I ⸺

EVE. Reject me?

CLARA. Yes. It is past!   [*Exit*, R.

EVE. Let me think. It was yesterday her hand trembled when mine
touched it. And the rose I gave her—yes, she pressed her lips to it
once when she seemed as if she saw me not. But it was a trap—a trick
—for I was as poor then as now. This will be a jest for them all!
Well, courage! it is but a poor heart that a coquette's contempt can
break. (*retires up to the table,* R.)

Enter LORD GLOSSMORE, *preceded by* PAGE, C. L.

PAGE. I will tell Sir John, my Lord. (*Exit,* R. EVELYN *takes up the
newspaper.*)

GLOSS. The secretary—hum! Fine day, sir; any news from the east?

EVE. Yes—all the wise men have gone back there!

SERVANT, C. L., *announces* MR. STOUT, R.

GLOSS. Ha! ha!—not all, for here comes Mr. Stout, the great political economist.

Enter STOUT, C. L.

STOUT (R. C). Good morning, Glossmore.

GLOSS. (L.). *Glossmore!*—the parvenu!

STOUT. Afraid I might be late—been detained at the vestry—astonishing how ignorant the English poor are! Took me an hour and a half to beat it into the head of a stupid old widow, with nine children, that to allow her three shillings a week was against all rules of public morality. (EVELYN *rises and comes down*, R.)

EVE. Excellent—admirable—your hand, sir!

GLOSS. What! you approve such doctrines, Mr. Evelyn? Are old women only fit to be starved?

EVE. Starved! popular delusion! Observe, my lord, (*crosses*, C.) to squander money upon those who starve is only to afford encouragement to starvation!

STOUT. A very superior person that!

GLOSS. Atrocious principles! Give me the good old times, when it was the duty of the rich to succor the distressed.

EVE. On second thoughts, *you* are right, my lord I, too, know a poor woman—ill—dying—in want. Shall *she*, too, perish?

GLOSS. Perish! horrible—in a Christian country! Perish! Heaven forbid!

EVE. (*holding out his hand*). What, then, will you give her?

GLOSS. Ahem! Sir, the parish ought to give.

STOUT. By no means!

GLOSS. By all means!

STOUT. No!—no!—no! Certainly not! (*with great vehemence.*)

GLOSS. No! no! But I say, yes! yes! And if the parish refuse to maintain the poor, the only way left to a man of firmness and resolution, holding the principles that I do, and adhering to the constitution of our fathers, is to force the poor *on* the parish by never giving them a farthing one's self.

STOUT. No!—no!—no!

GLOSS. Yes!—yes!—yes!

EVE. Gentlemen!—gentlemen!—perhaps Sir John will decide. (*pointing to* SIR JOHN *as he enters, and retires to table, takes up a book, reads.*)

Enter SIR JOHN, LADY FRANKLIN, GEORGINA, BLOUNT, PAGE, R. PAGE *goes off*, C. L. LADY FRANKLIN *goes to table*, L., *and sits.*

SIR J. How d'ye do? Ah! how d'ye do, gentlemen? This is a most melancholy meeting! The poor deceased! what a man he was!

BLOUNT (R.). I was chwistened Fwederick after him! He was my first cousin.

SIR J. (C.). And Georgina his own niece—next of kin! an excellent man, though odd—a kind heart, but no liver! I sent him twice a year thirty dozen of the Cheltenham waters. It's a comfort to reflect on these little attentions at such a time.

STOUT. And I, too, sent him the parliamentary debates regularly, bound in calf. He was my second cousin—sensible man—and a follower of Malthus; never married to increase the surplus population, and fritter away his money on his own children. And now——

EVE. He reaps the benefit of celibacy in the prospective gratitude of every cousin he had in the world!

LADY F. Ha! ha! ha!

SIR J. Hush! hush! decency, Lady Franklin; decency!

Enter PAGE, C. L.

PAGE. Mr. Graves—Mr. Sharp.

SIR J. Oh, here's Mr. Graves; that's Sharp the lawyer, who brought the will from Calcutta.

Enter MR. GRAVES. *and* MR. SHARP, *who goes immediately to* L. *table, and prepares his papers.*

Chorus of SIR JOHN, GLOSSMORE, BLOUNT, STOUT. Ah, sir—ah, Mr. Graves! (GEORGINA *holds her handkerchief to her eyes.*)

SIR J. A sad occasion!

GRAVES. But everything in life is sad. Be comforted, Miss Vesey! True, you have lost an uncle; but I—I have lost a wife—such a wife!— the first of her sex—and the second cousin of the defunct!

Enter SERVANTS, C.

Excuse me, Sir John; at the sight of your mourning my wounds bleed afresh. (SERVANTS *hand round wine and cake.*)

SIR J. Take some refreshment—a glass of wine.

GRAVES. Thank you!—(Very fine sherry!) Ah! my poor sainted Maria! Sherry was *her* wine! everything reminds me of Maria! Ah, Lady Franklin! *you* knew her. Nothing in life can charm me now. (*aside*) A monstrous fine woman that!

SIR J. And now to business. (*they each take a chair*) Evelyn, you may retire. (*All sit.* SERVANTS *retire,* C. EVELYN *rises.*)

SHARP (*looking at his notes*). Evelyn—any relation to Alfred Evelyn? (*to* EVELYN, *who is going,* C.)

EVE. The same.

SHARP. Cousin to the deceased, seven times removed. Be seated, sir; there may be some legacy, though trifling; all the relations, however distant, should be present. (EVELYN *reluctantly resumes his seat.*)

LADY F. Then Clara is related—I will go for her.   [*Exit.* R.

GEOR. Ah, Mr. Evelyn! I hope you will come in for something—a few hundreds, or even more.

SIR J. Silence! Hush! Wugh! Ugh! Attention!

While the Lawyer opens the will, re-enter LADY FRANKLIN *and* CLARA. *They cross behind the characters to* L., *up the stage, and sit.*

Disposition of Characters.

EVELYN.   LADY FRANKLIN, CLARA.
               SIR JOHN.   STOUT.   GLOSSMORE.
BLOUNT.   GEORGINA.   GRAVES.   SHARP.
     R.   L.

SHARP. The will is very short—being all personal property. He was a man that always came to the point.

SIR J. I wish there were more like him! (*groans and shakes his head.*)

SHARP (*reading*). "I, Frederick James Mordaunt, of Calcutta, being, at the present date, of sound mind, though infirm body, do hereby give, will, and bequeath—Imprimis, To my second cousin, Benjamin Stout, Esq., of Pall Mall, London—(STOUT *puts a large silk handkerchief to his eyes.* Chorus *exhibit lively emotion*) Being the value of the Parliamentary Debates with which he has been pleased to trouble me for some time past—deducting the carriage thereof, which he always forgot to pay—the sum of £14 2s. 4d." (STOUT *removes the handkerchief ; Chorus breathe more freely.*)

STOUT. Eh, what?—£14? Oh, hang the old miser!

SIR J. Decency—decency! Proceed, sir. Go on, sir, go on.

SHARP. "Item.—To Sir Frederick Blount, Baronet, my nearest male relative—" (*Chorus exhibit lively emotion.*)

BLOUNT. Poor old boy! (GEORGINA *puts her arm over* BLOUNT'S *chair.*)

SHARP. "Being, as I am informed, the best-dressed young gentleman in London, and in testimony to the only merit I ever heard he possessed, the sum of £500 to buy a dressing-case." (*Chorus breathe more freely ;* GEORGINA *catches her father's eye, and removes her arm.*)

BLOUNT (*laughing confusedly*). Ha! ha! ha! Vewy poor wit—low!—vewy—vewy low!

SIR J. Silence, now, will you? Go on, sir, go on.

SHARP. "Item.—To Charles Lord Glossmore—who asserts that he is my relation—my collection of dried butterflies, and the pedigree of the Mordaunts from the reign of King John. (*Chorus as before.*)

GLOSS. Butterflies!—Pedigree!—I disown the Plebeian!

SIR J. (*angrily*). Upon my word, this is too revolting! Decency! Go on, sir, go on.

SHARP. "Item.—To Sir John Vesey, Baronet, Knight of the Guelph, F.R.S., F.S.A., etc." (*Chorus as before.*)

SIR J. Hush! *Now* it is really interesting!

SHARP. "Who married my sister, and who senus me every year the Cheltenham waters, which nearly gave me my death, I bequeath—the empty bottles."

SIR J. Why, the ungrateful, rascally old——

LADY F. Decency, Sir John—decency!

CHORUS. Decency, Sir John—decency!

SHARP. "Item.—To Henry Graves, Esq., of the Albany—" (*Chorus as before.*)

GRAVES. Pooh! gentlemen—my usual luck—not even a ring, I dare swear.

SHARP. "The sum of £5,000 in the Three per Cents."

LADY F. I wish you joy!

GRAVES. Joy—pooh! Three per Cents.! Funds sure to go! Had it been *land*, now—though only an acre!—just like my luck.

SHARP. "Item.—To my niece, Georgina Vesey——(*chorus as before.*)

SIR J. Ah, now it comes!

SHARP. "The sum of £10,000 India Stock, being, with her father's reputed savings, as much as a single woman ought to possess."

SIR J. And what the devil, then, does the old fool do with all his money?

CHORUS. Really, Sir John, this is too revolting. Decency! Hush!

SHARP. "And, with the aforesaid legacies and exceptions, I do will and bequeath the whole of my fortune, in India Stock, Bonds, Exchequer Bills, Three per Cent. Consols, and in the Bank of Calcutta (constituting him hereby sole residuary legatee and joint executor with the aforesaid Henry Graves, Esq.), to—Alfred Evelyn, now, or formerly, of Trinity College, Cambridge—(*all turn to* EVELYN; *universal excitement.* EVELYN *starts up, closes his book, and casts it upon the table*) Being, I am told, an oddity, like myself—the only one of my relations who never fawned on me ; and who, having known privation, may the better employ wealth." (*all rise.* EVELYN *advances,* c., *as if in a dream*) And now, sir, I have only to wish you joy, and give you this letter from the deceased —I believe it is important. (*gives letter to* EVELYN.)

EVE. (*aside*). Ah, Clara, if you had but loved me !

CLARA (*turning away*). And his wealth, even more than poverty, separates us for ever ! (OMNES *crowd round to congratulate* EVELYN.)

SIR J. (*aside to* GEORGINA). Go, child, put a good face on it—he's an immense match ! (*aloud*) My dear fellow, I wish you joy; you are a great man now—a very great man ! I wish you joy. (*shakes his hand very warmly.*)

EVE. (*aside*). And *her* voice alone is silent !

GLOSS If I can be of any use to you——

STOUT. Or I, sir——.

BLOUNT. Or I ! Shall I put you up at the clubs ?

SHARP. You will want a man of business. I transacted all Mr. Mordaunt's affairs.

SIR J. Tush, tush ! Mr. Evelyn is at home *here*—always looked upon him as a son ! Nothing in the world we would not do for him ! Nothing !

EVE. Nothing ! then lend me £10 for my old nurse. (*Chorus put their hands in their pockets.*)

CURTAIN.

ACT II.

SCENE I.—*An anteroom in* EVELYN'S *new house ;* MR. SHARP *writing at a desk,* L., *books and parchments before him*—MR. CRIMSON. *the portrait painter ;* MR. GRABB, *the publisher ;* MR. MACSTUCCO, *the architect ;* MR. TABOURET, *the upholsterer ;* MR. MACFINCH, *the silversmith ;* MR. PATENT, *the coachmaker ;* MR. KITE, *the horse-dealer ; and* MR. FRANTZ, *the tailor.*

PATENT (*to* FRANTZ, *showing him a drawing).* Yes, sir ; this is the Evelyn vis-à-vis ! No one more the fashion than Mr. Evelyn. Money makes the man, sir.

FRANTZ. But de tailor, de schneider make de gentleman ! It is Mr. Frantz, of St. James',who take his measure and his cloth, and who make de fine handsome noblemen and gentry, where de faders and de mutters make only de ugly little naked boys !

MACSTUC (L. c.). He's an hon o' teeste, Mr. Evelyn. He taulks o' buying a veela (villa), just to pool down and build oop again. Ah, Mr. MacFinch ! a design for a piece of pleete, eh ?

MACFINCH (L., *showing the drawing*). Yees, sir ; the shield o' Alexander the Great to hold ices and lemonade ! It will coost two thousand poon' !

MACSTUC. And it's dirt cheap—ye're Scotch, arn't ye?

MACFINCH. Aberdounshire'—scraitch me, and I'll scraitch you !

Enter EVELYN, C. D. L.

EVE. A levee, as usual. Good day. Ah, Tabouret, (TABOURET *presents a drawing*) your designs for the draperies; very well. (*Exit* TABOURET, R.) And what do you want, Mr. Crimson?

CRIM. (R.). Sir, if you'd let me take your portrait, it would make my fortune. Every one says you're the finest judge of paintings.

EVE. Of paintings! paintings! Are you sure I'm a judge of paintings?

CRIM. Oh, sir, didn't you buy the great Corregio for £4,000?

EVE. True—I see. So £4,000 makes me an excellent judge of paintings. I'll call on you, Mr. Crimson—good day. (*Exit* CRIMSON, R. EVELYN *turns to the rest who surround him.*)

KITE. Thirty young horses from Yorkshire, sir!

PATENT (*showing drawing*). The Evelyn vis-à-vis!

MACFINCH (*showing drawing*). The Evelyn salver!

FRANTZ (*opening his bundle, and with dignity*). Sare, I have brought de coat—de great Evelyn coat.

EVE. Oh, go to—that is, go home. Make me as celebrated for a vis-à-vis, salvers, furniture, and coats, as I already am for painting, and shortly shall be for poetry. I resign myself to you—go! (*crosses*. L.)

[*Exeunt* MACFINCH, PATENT, *etc.*, R.*

Enter STOUT, R., *he places his hat on* R. *table.*

EVE. Stout, you look heated!

STOUT. I hear that you have just bought the great Groginhole property.

EVE. It is true. Sharp says it's a bargain.

STOUT. Well, my dear friend Hopkins, member for Groginhole, can't live another month—but the interests of mankind forbid regret for individuals! The patriot Popkins intends to start for the borough the instant Hopkins is dead—your interests will secure his election. Now is your time! put yourself forward in the march of enlightenment. (*turns and sees* GLOSSMORE) By all that is bigoted, here comes Glossmore! (*goes up the stage and listens.*)

Enter GLOSSMORE, R. EVELYN *crosses to meet him.*

GLOSS. So lucky to find you at home! Hopkins, of Groginhole, is not long for this world. Popkins, the brewer, is already canvassing underhand (so very ungentlemanlike!). Keep your interest for young Lord Cipher—a most valuable candidate. This is an awful moment—the CONSTITUTION depends on his return! Vote for Cipher.

STOUT (L.). Popkins is your man!

EVE. (*musingly*). Cipher and Popkins—Popkins and Cipher! Enlightenment and Popkins—Cipher and the Constitution! I AM puzzled! Stout, I am not known at Groginhole.

STOUT. Your *property's* known there!

EVE. But purity of election—independence of votes——

---

* The dialogue of this scene, up to this point, is sometimes omitted, and when that is the case, begin thus:—

Enter STOUT, *preceded by a* SERVANT, R.

SERV. I'll tell my master you wish to see him. Oh! Mr. Evelyn is here, sir!

Enter EVELYN, L.

STOUT. To be sure ; Cipher bribes *abominably.* Frustrate his schemes
—preserve the liberties of the borough—turn every man out of his house
who votes against enlightenment and Popkins !   `

EVE. Right !—down with those who take the liberty to admire any
liberty except *our* liberty ! That *is* liberty !

GLOSS. Cipher has a stake in the country—will have £50,000 a year
—Cipher will never give a vote without considering beforehand how people of £50,000 a year will be affected by the motion.

EVE. Right ! for as without law there would be no property, so to be
the law for property is the only proper property of law ! That *is*
law !

STOUT. Popkins is all for economy—there's a sad waste of the public
money—they give the Speaker £5,000 a year, when I've a brother-in-
law, who takes the chair at the vestry, and who assures me confidentially he'd consent to be Speaker for half the money !

GLOSS. Enough, Mr. Stout.   Mr. Evelyn has too much at stake for a
leveller.

STOUT. And too much sense for a bigot.

GLOSS. Bigot, sir ?

STOUT. Yes, sir, bigot!

EVE. Mr. Evelyn has no politics at all ! Did you ever play at *battledore ?*

BOTH. Battledore !

EVE. Battledore !—that is a contest between two parties ; both parties knock about something with singular skill—something is kept up—
high—low—here—there—everywhere—nowhere ! How grave are the
players ! how anxious the bystanders ! how noisy the battledores ! But
when this something falls to the ground, only fancy—it's nothing but
cork and feather ! Go, and play by yourselves—I'm no hand at it !
(*crosses,* L)

STOUT (*aside*). Sad ignorance !—Aristocrat ! (*crosses to* R. C.)

GLOSS. (*aside*). Heartless principles !—Parvenu ! (*goes up the stage.*)

STOUT. Then you don't go *against* us ? I'll bring Popkins to-morrow.
(*goes to* R. *table, gets his hat.*)

GLOSS. Keep yourself free till I present Cipher to you !

STOUT. I must go to inquire after Hopkins. The return of Popkins
will be an era in history !   [*Exit,* R.

GLOSS. I must be off to the club—the eyes of the country are upon
Groginhole. If Cipher fail, the constitution is gone !   [*Exit,* R

EVE. (R. C.). Both sides alike ! Money *versus* Man !—poor man !—
Sharp, come here—(SHARP *advances*) let me look at you ! You are my
agent, my lawyer, my man of business. I believe you honest ;—but
what *is* honesty ? where does it exist ?—in what part of us ?

SHARP. In the heart, I suppose, sir ?

EVE. Mr. Sharp, it exists in the breeches-pocket ! (*goes to table,* R.)
Observe : I lay this piece of yellow earth on the table—I contemplate
you both ; the man there—the gold here. Now, there is many a man
in those streets honest as you are, who moves, thinks, feels, and reasons
as well as we do ; excellent in form—imperishable in soul ! ; who, if his
pockets were three days empty, would sell thought, reason, body, and
soul, too, for that little coin ! Is that the fault of the man ?—no ! it is
the fault of mankind ! God made man ; behold what mankind have
made a god ! When I was poor, I hated the world ; now I am rich, I
despise it ! Fools—knaves—hypocrites !—By the bye, Sharp, send
£100 to the poor bricklayer whose house was burned down yesterday.
(SHARP *goes to his desk.*)

Enter GRAVES, R.

Ah, Graves, my dear friend, what a world this is!

GRAVES. It is an atrocious world! But astronomers say that there is a travelling comet which must set it on fire one day—and that's some comfort!

EVE Every hour brings its gloomy lesson—the temper sours—the affections wither—the heart hardens into stone!—Zounds, Sharp! what do you stand gaping there for?—have you no bowels?—why don't you go and see to the bricklayer! (*to* SHARP, *who is standing* R. *Exit* SHARP, L.) Graves, of all my new friends—and their name is Legion—you are the only one I esteem; there is sympathy between us—we take the same views of life. I am cordially glad to see you!

GRAVES (*groaning*). Ah! why should you be glad to see a man so miserable?

EVE (*sighs*). Because I am miserable myself.

GRAVES. You! Pshaw! *you* have not been condemned to lose a wife. (GRAVES *places his hat on table,* L.)

EVE. But, plague on it, man, I may be condemned to take one! Sit down, and listen. (*they seat themselves*—GRAVES L) I want a confidant! —Left fatherless when yet a boy, my poor mother grudged herself food to give me education. Some one had told her that learning was better than house and land—that's a lie, Graves!

GRAVES. A scandalous lie, Evelyn!

EVE. On the strength of that lie I was put to school—sent to college, a sizar. Do you know what a sizar is? In pride he is a gentleman—in knowledge he is a scholar—and he crawls about, amidst gentlemen and scholars, with the livery of a pauper on his back! I carried off the great prizes—I became distinguished—I looked to a high degree, leading to a fellowship; that is, an independence for myself—a home for my mother. One day a young lord insulted me—I retorted—he struck me —refused apology—refused redress. I was a sizar!—a Pariah! a thing —to *be* struck! Sir, I was at least a man, and I horsewhipped him in the hall before the eyes of the whole College! A few days, and the lord's chastisement was forgotten. The next day the sizar was expelled —the career of a life blasted! That is the difference between Rich and Poor; it takes a whirlwind to move the one—a breath may uproot the other! I came to London. As long as my mother lived, I had one to toil for; and I did toil—did hope—did struggle to be something yet. She died, and then, somehow, my spirit broke—I resigned myself to my fate; the Alps above me seemed too high to ascend—I ceased to care what became of me. At last I submitted to be the poor relation—the hanger-on and gentleman-lackey of Sir John Vesey. But I had an object in that—there was one in that house whom I had loved at the first sight.

GRAVES And were you loved again?

EVE. I fancied it, and was deceived. Not an hour before I inherited this mighty wealth I confessed my love, and was rejected because I was poor. Now, mark: you remember the letter which Sharp gave me when the will was read?

GRAVES. Perfectly! what were the contents?

EVE. After hints, cautions, and admonitions—half in irony, half in earnest (Ah, poor Mordaunt had known the world!) it proceeded—but I'll read it to you: "Having selected you as my heir, because I think money a trust to be placed where it seems likely to be best employed, I now—not impose a condition, but ask a favor. If you have formed no other and insuperable attachment, I could wish to suggest your choice;

my two nearest female relations are my niece Georgina, and my third cousin, Clara Douglas, the daughter of a once dear friend If you could see in either of these one whom you could make your wife, such would be a marriage that, if I live long enough to return to England, I would seek to bring about before I die." My friend, this is not a legal condition—the fortune does not *rest* on it ; yet, need I say that my gratitude considers it a moral obligation ? Several months have elapsed since thus called upon—I ought now to decide ; you hear the names—Clara Douglas is the woman who rejected me.

GRAVES. But now she would accept you !

EVE. And do you think I am so base a slave to passion, that I would owe to my gold what was denied to my affection ? (*rises and puts chair by* R. *table.*)

GRAVES. But you must choose one, in common gratitude ; you *ought* to do so. (GRAVES *replaces his chair.*)

EVE. Of the two, then, I would rather marry where I should exact the least. A marriage, to which each can bring sober esteem and calm regard, may not be happiness, but it may be content. But to marry one whom you could adore, and whose heart is closed to you—to yearn for the treasure, and only to claim the casket—to worship the statue that you never may warm to life. Oh ! such a marriage would be a hell, the more terrible because Paradise was in sight. (*crosses to* R.)

GRAVES. Ah, it is a comfort to think, my dear friend, as you are sure to be miserable, when you are married, that we can mingle our groans together. Georgina is pretty, but vain and frivolous.

EVE. You may misjudge Georgina ; she may have a nobler nature than appears on the surface. On the day, but before the hour, in which the will was read, a letter, in a strange or disguised hand, signed, " *From an unknown friend to Alfred Evelyn,*" and enclosing what to a girl would have been a considerable sum, was sent to a poor woman for whom I had implored charity, and whose address I had only given to Georgina.

GRAVES. Why not assure yourself ?

EVE. Because I have not dared. For sometimes, against my reason, I have hoped that it might be Clara. (*taking a letter from his bosom and looking at it*) No, I can't recognize the hand. Graves, I detest that girl. (*crosses to* R. *corner and back to* L.)

GRAVES. Who ? Georgina?

EVE. No ; Clara ! But I've already, thank Heaven, taken some revenge upon her. Come nearer. (*whispers*) I've bribed Sharp to say that Mordaunt's letter to me contained a codicil leaving Clara Douglas £20,000.

GRAVES. And didn't it *!*

EVE. Not a farthing. But I'm glad of it—I've paid the money—she's no more a dependant. No one can insult her now—she owes it all to me, and does not guess it, man—does not guess it—owes it to me—me, whom she rejected—me, the poor scholar ! Ha ! ha !—there's some spite in that, eh ?

GRAVES. You're a fine fellow, Evelyn, and we understand each other. Perhaps Clara may have seen the address, and dictated this letter after all ?

EVE. Do you think so—I'll go to the house this instant ! (*crosses to* R. *table for his hat and gloves.*)

GRAVES. Eh ! Humph ! Then I'll go with you. That Lady Franklin is a fine woman. If she were not so gay, I think—I could——

EVE. No, no ; don't think any such thing ; women are even worse than men

GRAVES. True ; to love is a boy's madness !

EVE. To feel is to suffer.

GRAVES. To hope is to be deceived.

EVE. I have done with romance !

GRAVES. Mine is buried with Maria !

EVE. If Clara did but write this——

GRAVES. Make haste, or Lady Franklin will be out! (EVELYN *catches his eye ; he changes his tone*) A vale of tears—a vale of tears !

EVE. A vale of tears, indeed !   [*Exeunt*, R.

Re-enter GRAVES *for his hat.*

GRAVES. And I left my hat behind me ! Just like my luck. If I had been bred a hatter, little boys would have come into the world without heads.   [*Exit*, R.

SCENE II.—*Drawing-rooms at* SIR JOHN VESEY'S, *as in Act I., Scene I.*

LADY FRANKLIN *and* CLARA, R.

LADY F. (R.). Ha! ha ! ha ! talking of marriage, I've certainly made a conquest of Mr. Graves.

CLARA (L.). Mr. Graves ! I thought he was inconsolable.

LADY F. For his sainted Maria ! Poor man ! not contented with plaguing him while she lived, she must needs haunt him now she is dead.

CLARA. But why does he regret her ?

LADY F. Why ? Because he has everything to make him happy— easy fortune, good health, respectable character. And since it is his delight to be miserable, he takes the only excuse the world will allow him. For the rest—it's the way with widowers; that is, whenever they mean to marry again. But, my dear Clara, you seem absent—pale— unhappy—tears, too ?

CLARA. No—no—not tears. No !

LADY F. Ever since Mr. Mordaunt left you £20,000 every one admires you. Sir Frederick is desperately smitten.

CLARA (*with disdain*). Sir Frederick !

LADY F. Ah, Clara, be comforted ! I am certain that Evelyn loves you.

CLARA. If he did, it is past now. You alone know the true reason why I rejected him. You know that if ever he should learn that reason, he will acquit me of the selfish motive he now imputes to me.

Enter SIR JOHN, R.C., *and turns over the books, etc., on the table, as if to look for the newspaper.*

LADY F. Let me only tell him that you dictated that letter—that you sent that money to his old nurse. Poor Clara ! it was your little all. He will then know, at least, if avarice be your sin.

CLARA He would have guessed it had *his* love been like *mine.*

LADY F. Guessed it—nonsense ! The hand-writing unknown to him —every reason to think it came from Georgina.

SIR J. (*aside*, R., *at table*). Hum ! Came from Georgina.

LADY F. Come, *let* me tell him *this.* I know the effect it will have upon his choice.

CLARA. Choice ! oh, that humiliating word. No, Lady Franklin, no ! Promise me !

LADY F. But——

CLARA. No ! Promise—faithfully—sacredly.

LADY F. Well, I promise.

CLARA. I—I—forgive me—I am not well.   [*Exit*, R.
LADY F. What fools these girls are!—they take as much pains to lose
a husband as a poor widow does to get one!
SIR J. Have you seen "The Times" newspaper? Where the deuce is
the newspaper? I can't find "The Times" newspaper.
LADY F. I think it is in my room. Shall I fetch it?
SIR J. My dear sister—you're the best creature. Do!
                                    [*Exit* LADY FRANKLIN, R.
Ugh! you unnatural conspirator against your own family! What can
this *letter* be? Ah! I recollect something.

Enter GEORGINA, R. C.

GEOR. (L.). Papa, I want—
SIR J. Yes, I know what you want well enough! Tell me!—were
you aware that Clara had sent money to that old nurse Evelyn bored us ·
about the day of the will?
GEOR. No! He gave me the address, and I promised, if——
SIR J. Gave you *the address*?—that's lucky! Hush!

Enter PAGE, C. L.

PAGE (*announces*). Mr. Graves—Mr. Evelyn.   [*Exit*, C. L.

Enter GRAVES *and* EVELYN, C. L.   EVELYN, *when he enters, goes to* SIR
   JOHN, *then converses with* GEORGINA, *who is seated* R. *of* L. *table.*

LADY F. (*returning*). Here is the newspaper.
GRAVES. Ay—read the newspapers!—they'll tell you what this world
is made of. Daily calendars of roguery and woe! Here, advertise-
ments from quacks, money-lenders, cheap warehouses, and spotted boys
with two heads. So much for dupes and impostors! Turn to the other
column—police reports, bankruptcies, swindling, forgery, and a bio-
graphical sketch of the snub-nosed man who murdered his own three
little cherubs at Pentonville. Do you fancy these but exceptions to the
general virtue and health of the nation?—Turn to the leading articles;
and your hair will stand on end at the horrible wickedness or melancholy idiotism of that half of the population who think differently from
yourself. In my day I have seen already eighteen crises, six annihi-
lations of Agriculture and Commerce, four overthrows of the Church,
and three last, final, awful, and irremediable destructions of the entire
Constitution. And that's a newspaper!
LADY F. (R. C.). Ha! ha! your usual vein; always so amusing and
good-humored!
GRAVES (L. C., *frowning and very angry*). Ma'am—good-humored!
LADY F. Ah, you should always wear that agreeable smile; you look
so much younger—so much handsomer—when you smile!
GRAVES (*softened*). Ma'am—(*aside*) A charming creature, upon my
word!
LADY F. You have not seen the last *Punch?* It is excellent. I think
it might make you *laugh*. But, by the bye, I don't think you can laugh.
GRAVES. Ma'am—I have not laughed since the death of my sainted
Ma——
LADY F. Ah! and that spiteful Sir Frederick says you never laugh,
because—But you'll be angry?
GRAVES. Angry!—pooh! I despise Sir Frederick too much to let

anything he says have the smallest influence over me! He says I don't laugh, because——

LADY F. You have lost your front teeth.

GRAVES. Lost my front teeth! Upon my word! Ha! ha! ha! That's too good—capital! Ha! ha! ha! (*laughing from ear to ear.*)

LADY F. Ha! ha! ha!   [*Exeunt* LADY FRANKLIN *and* GRAVES, C.

EVE. (*aside, at* R. *table*). Of course Clara will not appear! avoids me as usual! But what do I care?—what is she to me? Nothing!

SIR J. (*to* GEORGINA). Yes—yes—leave me to manage; you took his portrait, as I told you?

GEOR. Yes—but I could not catch the expression. I got Clara to touch it up.

SIR J. That girl's always in the way. (PAGE *from* C. L. *announces* CAPTAIN DUDLEY SMOOTH.)

Enter CAPTAIN DUDLEY SMOOTH, C. L.

SMOOTH. Good morning, dear John. Ah, Miss Vesey, you have no idea of the conquests you made at Almack's last night.

EVE. (*examining him curiously while* SMOOTH *is talking to* GEORGINA *at* L. *table*). And that's the celebrated Dudley Smooth!

SIR J. (R. C.). More commonly called Deadly Smooth!—the finest player at whist, écarté, billiards, chess, and picquet, between this and the Pyramids—the sweetest manners!—always calls you by your Christian name. But take care how you play at cards with him!

EVE. He does not cheat, I suppose?

SIR J. Hist! *No!*—but he always *wins!* He's an uncommonly clever fellow!

EVE. Clever? yes! When a man steals a loaf we cry down the knavery—when a man diverts his neighbor's mill-stream to grind his own corn, we cry up the cleverness! And every one courts Captain Dudley Smooth?

SIR J. Why, who could offend him?—the best-bred, civilest creature —and a dead shot! There is not a cleverer man in the three kingdoms.

EVE. A study—a study!—let me examine him! Such men are living satires on the world. (*rises.*)

SMOOTH (*passing his arm caressingly over* SIR JOHN'S *shoulder*). My dear John, how well you are looking! A new lease of life! Introduce me to Mr. Evelyn.

EVE. Sir, it's an honor I've long ardently desired. (*crosses to him— they bow and shake hands.* PAGE *announces* SIR FREDERICK BLOUNT.)

Enter SIR FREDERICK BLOUNT, C. L.

BLOUNT. How d'ye do, Sir John? Ah, Evelyn—I wished so much to see you. (*takes* EVELYN'S *arm and draws him towards* L. C.)

EVE. 'Tis my misfortune to be visible!

BLOUNT. A little this way. You know, perhaps, that I once paid my addwesses to Miss Vesey; but since that vowy eccentwic will Sir John has shuffled me off, and hints at a pwior attachment—(*aside*) which I know to be false.

EVE. (*seeing* CLARA). A prior attachment!—Ha! Clara! Well, another time, my dear Blount.

Enter CLARA, R.   *She seats herself* L. *of* R. *table.*

BLOUNT. Stay a moment. Why are you in such a howwid huwwy?
I want you to do me a favor with regard to Miss Douglas.

EVE. Miss Douglas!

BLOUNT. It is whispered about that you mean to pwopose to Georgina. Nay, Sir John more than hinted that was her pwior attachment!

EVE. Indeed!

BLOUNT. Yes. Now, as you are all in all with the family, if you could say a word for me to Miss Douglas, I don't see what harm it could do me!

EVE. 'Sdeath, man! speak for yourself! you are just the sort of man for young ladies to like—they understand you—you're of their own level. Pshaw! you're too modest—you want no mediator!

BLOUNT. My dear fellow, you flatter me. I'm well enough in my way. But you, you know, would cawwy evewything before you—you're so confoundedly wich!

EVE. You really think so, and you wish me to say a word for you to Miss Douglas? (*he takes* BLOUNT's *arm and walks him to* CLARA) Miss Douglas, what do you think of Sir Frederick Blount? Observe him. He is well dressed—young—tolerably handsome—(BLOUNT *bowing*) bows with an air—has plenty of small talk—everything to captivate. Yet he thinks that, if he and I were suitors to the same lady, I should be more successful because I am richer. What say you? Is love an auction?—and *do* women's hearts go to the highest bidder?

CLARA. Their hearts—no!

EVE. But their hands—yes! (*she turns away*) You turn away. Ah, you dare not answer that question! (BLOUNT *crosses to* CLARA, SMOOTH *and* SIR JOHN *go up the stage ;* EVELYN *goes to* GEORGINA, *at* L. *table.*)

BLOUNT I wish you would take my opewa-box next Saturday—'tis the best in the house. I'm not wich, but I spend what I have on myself. I make it a wule to have everything of the best in a quiet way. Best opewa-box—best dogs—best horses—best house in town of its kind. I want nothing to complete my establishment but the best wife.

CLARA. Oh, that will come in time.

GEOR. (*aside*). Sir Frederick flirting with Clara? I'll punish him for his perfidy. (*aloud*) You are the last person to talk so, Mr. Evelyn—you, whose wealth is your smallest attraction—you, whom every one admires —so witty, such taste, such talent! Ah, I'm very foolish.

SIR J. (*clapping* EVELYN *on the shoulder*). You must not turn my little girl's head. Oh, you're a sad fellow! Apropos, I must show you Georgina's last drawings. She's wonderfully improved since you gave her lessons in perspective.

GEOR. No, papa! No, pray, no! Nay, don't!

SIR J. Nonsense, child—it's very odd, but she's more afraid of you than of any one! (*goes to the folio stand.*)

SMOOTH (*aside*). He's an excellent father, our dear John! and supplies the place of a mother to her. (*lounges off,* C.)

CLARA (*aside*). So, so—he loves her! Misery—misery! But he shall not perceive it. No, no! (*aloud*) Ha, ha! Sir Frederick—excellent! excellent! You are so entertaining. (SIR JOHN *brings a portfolio and places it on the table ;* EVELYN *and* GEORGINA *look over the drawings ;* SIR JOHN *leans over them ;* SIR FREDERICK *converses with* CLARA ; EVELYN *watching them.*)

EVE Beautiful!—a view from Tivoli. (Death—she looks down while he speaks to her!) Is there a little fault in that coloring? (she positively blushes) But this Jupiter is superb. (What a d—d cocoxcomb it is?) (*rising*) Oh, she certainly loves him—I too, can be loved elsewhere—I, too, can see smiles and blushes on the face of another.

GEOR. Are you not well? (*going to him*, L. C.)

EVE. I beg pardon. Yes you are indeed improved. Ah, who so accomplished as Miss Vesey? (*re—rs with her to the table; taking up a portrait*) Why, what is this?—my own——

GEOR. You must not look at that—you must not, indeed. I did not know it was there.

SIR J. Your own portrait, Evelyn! Why, child, I was not aware you took likenesses—that's something new. Upon my word it's a strong resemblance.

GEOR. Oh, no—it does not do him justice. Give it to me. I will tear it. (*aside*) That odious Sir Frederick!

EVE. Nay you shall not. (CLARA *looks at him reproachfully, then talks with* SIR FREDERICK) But where is the new guitar you meant to buy, Miss Vesey—the one inlaid with tortoise shell? It it nearly a year since you set your heart on it, and I don't see it yet.

SIR J. (R. C., *taking him aside, confidentially*). The guitar—oh, to tell you a secret—she applied the money I gave her for it to a case of charity several months ago—the very day the will was read. I saw the letter lying on the table, with the money in it. Mind, not a word to her—she'd never forgive me.

EVE. Letter—money! What was the name of the person she relieved —not Stanton?

SIR J. I don't remember, indeed.

EVE. (*taking out letter*). This is not her hand!

SIR J. No! I observed at the time it was not her hand, but I got out from her that she did not wish the thing to *be known*, and had employed some one else to copy it. May I see the letter? Yes, I think this is the wording. Still, how did she know Mrs. Stanton's address?

EVE. I gave it to her, Sir John.

CLARA (*at the distance*). Yes, I'll go to the opera, if Lady Franklin will—on Saturday, then, Sir Frederick. (BLOUNT *bows to* CLARA *and goes off*, C. L.)

EVE. Sir John, to a man like me, this simple act of unostentatious generosity is worth all the accomplishments in the world. A good heart —a tender disposition—a charity that shuns the day—a modesty that blushes at its own excellence—an impulse towards something more divine than Mammon; such are the true accomplishments which preserve beauty for ever young. Such I have sought in the partner I would take for life—such have I found—alas! not where I had dreamed! Miss Vesey, I will be honest. (MISS VESEY *advances.* L. H.) I say then, frankly —(*raising his voice, as* CLARA *approaches, and looking fixedly at her*)—I have loved another—deeply—truly—bitterly—*vainly!* I cannot offer to you, as I did to her, the fair first love of the human heart—rich with all its blossoms and its verdure. But if esteem—if gratitude—if an earnest resolve to conquer every recollection that would wander from your image; if these can tempt you to accept my hand and fortune, my life shall be a study to deserve your confidence. (*during this speech* GEORGINA *has advanced*, L., CLARA *to a chair* H. *of* L. *table;* CLARA *sits motionless, clasping her hands.*)

SIR J. The happiest day of my life. (CLARA *falls back in her chair.*)

EVE. (*darting forward, aside*). She is pale; she faints. What have I done? Oh, Heaven! (*aloud*) Clara!

CLARA (*rising with a smile*). Be happy, my cousin—be happy! Yes, with my whole heart I say it—be happy, Alfred Evelyn! (*she sinks again into the chair, overcome by emotion; the rest form a picture of consternation and selfish joy.*)

CURTAIN. .

ACT III.

SCENE I.—*The drawing-rooms in* SIR JOHN VESEY'S *house, as before. The furniture arranged for the change to the next scene.*

SIR JOHN *and* GEORGINA *discovered, c.*

SIR J. And he has not pressed you to fix the wedding-day?

GEOR. No; and since he proposed he comes here so seldom, and seems so gloomy. Heigho! Poor Sir Frederick was twenty times more amusing.

SIR J. But Evelyn is fifty times as rich.

GEOR. But do you not fear lest he discover that Clara wrote the letter?

SIR J. No; and I shall get Clara out of the house. But there is something else that makes me very uneasy. You know that no sooner did Evelyn come into possession of his fortune than he launched out in the style of a prince. His house in London is a palace, and he has bought a great estate in the country. Look how he lives. Balls—banquets—fine arts—fiddlers—charities—and the devil to pay!

GEOR. But if he can afford it——

SIR J. Oh! so long as he stopped *there* I had no apprehension; but since he proposed for you he is more extravagant than ever. They say he has taken to gambling; and he is always with Captain Smooth. No fortune can stand Deadly Smooth! If he gets into a scrape he may fall off from the settlements. We must press the marriage at once.

GEOR. Heigho! Poor Frederick! You don't think he is *really* attached to Clara?

SIR J. Upon my word I can't say. Put on your bonnet, and come to Storr and Mortimer's to choose the jewels.

GEOR. The jewels—yes—the drive will do me good.

SIR J. Tell Clara to come to me. (*exit* GEORGINA, R.) Yes. I must press on this marriage. Georgina has not wit enough to manage him—at least till he's her husband, and then all women find it smooth sailing. This match will make me a man of prodigious importance! I suspect he'll give me up her ten thousand pounds. I can't think of his taking to gambling, for I love him as a son—and I look on his money as my own.

Enter CLARA, R.

SIR J. Clara, my love!

CLARA. Sir——

SIR J. My dear, what I am going to say may appear a little rude and unkind, but you know my character is frankness. To the point then; my poor child, I am aware of your attachment to Mr. Evelyn——

CLARA. Sir! *my attachment?*

SIR J. It is generally remarked. Lady Kind says you are falling away. My poor girl, I pity you—I do, indeed. (CLARA *weeps*) My dear Clara, don't take on so; I would not have said this for the world, if I was not a little anxious about my own girl. Georgina is so unhappy at what every one says of your attachment——

CLARA. Every one! Oh, torture!

SIR J. That it preys on her spirits—it even irritates her temper! In a word, I fear these little jealousies and suspicions will tend to embitter their future union. I'm a father—forgive me.

CLARA. What would you have me do, sir?

SIR J. Why, you're now independent. Lady Franklin seems resolved

to stay in town.   You are your own mistress.   Mrs. Carlton, aunt to my
late wife, is going abroad for a short time, and would be delighted if you
would accompany her.

CLARA. It is the very favor I would have asked of you. (*aside*) I shall
escape at least the struggle and the shame. (*aloud*) When does she go ?

SIR J. In five days—next Monday.—You forgive me ?

CLARA. Sir, I thank you.

SIR J. Suppose, then, you write a line to her yourself, and settle it at
once ?

Takes CLARA *to table,* L., *as the* PAGE *enters* C. L.

PAGE. The carriage, Sir John ; Miss Vesey is quite ready.

SIR J. Very well, James. If Mr. Serious, the clergyman, calls, say
I'm gone to the great meeting at Exeter Hall; if Lord Spruce calls, say
you believe I'm gone to the rehearsal of Cinderella. Oh ! and if Mac-
Finch should come (MacFinch who duns me three times a week), say
I've hurried off to Garraway's to bid for the great Bulstrode estate.
Just put the Duke of Lofty's card carelessly on the hall table. (*exit* SER-
VANT, R. C.) One must have a little management in this world. All hum-
bug !—all humbug, upon my soul !   [*Exit*, C. L.

CLARA (*folding the letter*). There, it is decided ! A few days, and we
are parted for ever !—a few weeks, and another will bear his name—his
wife ! Oh, happy fate ! She will have the right to say to him—though
the whole world should hear her—" I am thine !" And I embitter their
lot ! And yet, O Alfred ! if she loves thee—if she knows thee—if she
values thee—and, when thou wrong'st her, if she can forgive, as I do—I
can bless her when far away, and join her name in my prayer for thee !

EVE. (*without*). Miss Vesey just gone ! Well, I will write a line.

Enter EVELYN, C. L., *preceded by* PAGE, *who exits immediately*, C. L.

EVE. (*aside*). So—Clara ! (*she rises, crosses to* R.) Do not let me disturb
you, Miss Douglas.

CLARA (*going*, R.). Nay, I have done.

EVE. I see that my presence is always odious to you ; it is a reason
why I come so seldom. But be cheered, madam ; I am here but to fix
the day of my marriage, and I shall then go into the country—till—till
—In short, this is the last time my visit will banish you from the room
I enter. (*he places his hat on table*, L.)

CLARA (*aside*). The last time !—and we shall then meet no more !
And to thus part forever—In scorn—in anger—I cannot bear it ! (*approaches him*) Alfred, my cousin, it is true, this may be the last time we
shall meet—I have made my arrangements to quit England.

EVE. To quit England ? (*comes forward*, L)

CLARA. But let me thank you for many a past kindness,
which it is not for an orphan easily to forget.

EVE (*mechanically*). To quit England ?

CLARA. Yes, and now that you are betrothed to another—now, without recurring to the past—something of our old friendship may at least
return to us   And if, too, I dared, I have that on my mind which only
a friend—a sister—might presume to say to you.

EVE. (*moved*). Miss Douglas—Clara—if there is aught that I could do
—if, while hundreds—strangers—beggars tell me that I have the power,
by opening or shutting this worthless hand, to bid sorrow rejoice, or
poverty despair—if—if my life—my heart's blood—could render to *you*
one such service as my gold can give to others—why, speak !—and the
past you allude to—yes, even that bitter past—I will cancel and forget.

CLARA (*holding out her hand*). We are friends, then! [EVELYN *takes her hand*) You are again my cousin!—my brother!

EVE. (*dropping her hand*). Brother! Ah! say on!

CLARA. I speak, then, as a sister—herself weak, inexperienced—*might* speak to a brother, in whose career she felt the ambition of a man. Oh! Evelyn, when you inherited this vast wealth I pleased myself with imagining how you would wield the power delegated to your hands. I knew your benevolence—your intellect—your genius! I saw before me the noble and bright career open to you at last—and I often thought that, in after years, when far away—as I soon shall be—I should hear your name identified, not with what fortune can give the base, but with deeds an l ends to which, for the *great*, fortune is but the instrument ;—I often thought that I should say to my own heart—weeping proud and delicious tears—" And once this man loved me !"

EVE No more, Clara '—Oh, heavens !—no more!

CLARA. But *has* it been so !—have you been true to your own self ?—Pomp—parade—luxuries—pleasures—follies !—all these might distinguish others—they do but belie the ambition and the soul of Alfred Evelyn. Oh ! pardon me—I am too bold—I pain—I offend you.—Ah ! I should not have dared thus much had I not thought at times, that—that——

EVE. That these follies—these vanities—this dalliance with a loftier fate were your own work ! You thought that, and you were right ! Perhaps, indeed, after a youth, steeped to the lips in the hyssop and gall of penury—perhaps I might have wished royally to know the full value of that dazzling and starry life which, from the last step in the ladder, I had seen indignantly and from afar. But a month—a week, would have sufficed for that experience. Experience !—Oh, how soon we learn that hearts are as cold and souls as vile—no matter whether the sun shine on the noble in his palace, or the rain drench the rags of the beggar cowering at the porch. But you—did not you reject me because I was poor ? Despise me, if you please !—my revenge might be unworthy—I wished to show you the luxuries, the gaud, the splendor I thought you prized—to surround with the attributes your sex seems most to value—the station that, had you loved me, it would have been yours to command. But vain—vain alike my poverty and my wealth ! You loved me not in either, and my fate is sealed !

CLARA. A happy fate, Evelyn!—you love !

EVE. And at last I am beloved. (*after a pause, and turning to her abruptly*) Do you doubt it ?

CLARA. No, I believe it firmly !—And, now that there is nothing unkind between us—not even regret—and surely (*with a smile*) not revenge, my cousin, you will rise to your nobler self !—and so, farewell ! (*going*, R)

EVE. No ; stay, one moment ;—you still feel interest in my fate ? Have I been deceived ? Oh, why—why did you spurn the heart whose offerings were lavished at your feet ? Could you still—still—— ? Distraction—I know not what I say ;—my honor pledged to another—my vows accepted and returned ! Go, Clara, it is best so ! Yet you will miss some one, perhaps, more than me—some one to whose follies you have been more indulgent—some one to whom you would permit a yet tenderer name than that of brother ! (*goes to table*, L.)

CLARA (*aside*). It will make him, perhaps, happier to think it ! (*aloud*) Think so, if you will !—but part friends.

EVE. Friends—and that is all ! Look you—this is life ! The eyes that charmed away every sorrow—the hand whose lightest touch thrilled to the very core—the voice that, heard afar, filled space as with an

angel's music—a year—a month, a day, and we smile that we could
dream so idly. All—all—the sweetest enchantment, known but once,
never to return again, vanished from the world! And the one who forgets the soonest—the one who robs your earth for ever of its sunshine—
comes to you with a careless lip, and says—"Let us part friends!"—
Go, Clara—go—and be happy if you can! (*falls into a chair at* L. *table.*)
    CLARA (*weeping*). Cruel—cruel—to the last!   [*Exit*, R.
    EVE. (*rises*). Soft! let me recall her words, her tones, her looks.—
Does she love me ? There is a voice at my heart which tells me I have
been the rash slave of a jealous anger. But I have made my choice—I
must abide the issue. (*retires and sits at* R. *table.*)

Enter GRAVES, *preceded by* PAGE, L. C.

    PAGE. Lady Franklin is dressing, sir.
    GRAVES. Well, I'll wait. (*exit* PAGE, R.) She was worthy to have
known the lost Maria! So considerate to ask me hither—not to console
me, *that* is impossible—but to indulge the luxury of woe. It will be a
mournful scene. (*seeing* EVELYN) Is that you, Evelyn? I have just
heard that the borough of Broginhole is vacant at last. Why not stand
yourself—with your property you might come in without even a personal canvass.
    EVE. I, who despise these contests for the color of a straw. (*aside*) And
yet. Clara spoke of ambition. She would regret me if I could be distinguished. (*rises, aloud*) You are right, Graves, to be sure, after all. An
Englishman owes something to his country.
    GRAVES (L.). He does, indeed. (*counting on his fingers*) East winds,
Fogs, Rheumatism. Pulmonary Complaints, and Taxes. (EVELYN *walks
about in disorder*) Oh! you are a pretty fellow. One morning you tell
me you love Clara, or at least detest her, which is the same thing (poor
Maria often said she detested *me*), and that very afternoon you propose
to Georgina.
    EVE. Clara will easily console herself—thanks to Sir Frederick!
    GRAVES. Nevertheless, Clara has had the bad taste to refuse an offer
from Sir Frederick. I have it from Lady Franklin, to whom he con-
fided his despair in re-arranging his neck-cloth.
    EVE. My dear friend—is it possible ?
    GRAVES. But what then ? You *must* marry Georgina, who, to believe
Lady Franklin, is sincerely attached to—your fortune. Go and hang
yourself, Evelyn; you have been duped by them.
    EVE. By them—bah ! If deceived, I have been my own dupe. Is it
not a strange thing that in matters of reason—of the arithmetic and
logic of life—we are sensible, shrewd, prudent men; but touch our
hearts—move our passions—take us for an instant from the hard safety
of worldly calculation—and the philosopher is duler than the fool ?
(*crosses*, L.) *Duped*—if I thought it—but Georgina ?
    GRAVES. Plays affection to you in the afternoon, after practising with
Sir Frederick in the morning.
    EVE. On your life, sir, be serious; what do you mean ?
    GRAVES. That in passing this way I see her very often walking in the
square with Sir Frederick.
    EVE. Ha! say you so ?
    GRAVES. What then ? Man is born to be deceived. You look ner-
vous—your hand trembles; that comes of gaming. They say at the
clubs that you play deeply.
    EVE. Ha! ha! Do they say that? a few hundreds lost or won—a
cheap opiate—anything that can lay the memory to sleep. The poor

man drinks, and the rich man gambles—the same motive to both. But you are right—it is a base resource—I will play no more.

GRAVES. I am delighted to hear it, for your friend Captain Smooth has ruined half the young heirs in London. Even Sir John is alarmed. I met him just now in Pall Mall. By-the-bye, I forgot—do you bank with Flash, Brisk, Credit and Co. ?

EVE. So, Sir John is alarmed. (*aside*) Gulle 1 by this cozzing charlatan ? Aha! I may beat him yet at his own weapons. (*aloud*) Humph ! Bank with Flash ! Why do you ask me ?

GRAVES. Because Sir John has just heard that they are in a very bad way, and begs you to withdraw anything you have in their hands.

EVE. I'll see to it. So Sir John is *alarmed* at my gambling ?

GRAVES. Terribly ! He even told me he should go himself to the club this evening, to watch you.

EVE. To watch me—good—I will be there !

GRAVES. But you will promise not to play ?

EVE. Yes—to play. I feel it is impossible to give it up.

GRAVES. No—no ! 'Sdeath, man ! be as wretched as you please ; break your heart, that's nothing ! but damme, take care of your pockets.

EVE. Hark ye, Graves—if you are right, I will extricate myself yet. The duper shall be duped, in the next twenty-four hours. I may win back the happiness of a life. Oh ! if this scheme do but succeed !

GRAVES. Scheme ! What scheme ? (EVELYN *takes his hat from* L. *table*.) .

EVE. Yes, I will be there—I will play with Captain Smooth—I will lose as much as I please—thousands—millions—billions ; and if he presume to spy on my losses, hang me, if I don't lose Sir John himself into the bargain ! (*going out and returning*) I am so absent. What was the bank you mentioned ? Flash, Brisk and Credit ! B'ess me, how unlucky ! and it's too late to draw out to-day. Tell Sir John I'm very much obliged to him, and he'll find me at the club any time before daybreak, hard at work with my friend Smooth.   [*Exit*, C. L.

GRAVES. He's certainly crazy ! but I don't wonder at it. What the approach of the dog-days is to the canine species, the approach of the honeymoon is to the human race.

•

· *Enter* SERVANT, R.

SER. Lady Franklin's compliments—she will see you in the *boudoir*, sir.

GRAVES. In the *boudoir* !—go—go—I'll come directly. (*exit* SERVANT, R.) My heart beats—it must be for grief. Poor Maria ! (*searching his pockets for his handkerchief*) Not a white one—just like my luck ; I call on a lady to talk of the dear departed, and I've nothing about me but a cursed gaudy, flaunting, red, yellow and blue abomination from India, which it's even indecent for a disconsolate widower to exhibit. Ah ! Fortune never ceases to torment the susceptible. The *boudoir*—ha—ha ! the *boudoir* !   [*Exit*, R.

SCENE II.—*A boudoir in the same house. Two chairs brought on by a* PAGE, *who goes off*, L.

Enter LADY FRANKLIN, L.

LADY F. What if my little plot does not succeed ? The man insists on being wretched, and I pity him so much that I am determined to make him happy! Ha! ha! ha! He shall laugh, he shall sing, he shall dance, he shal!—(*composes herself*) Here he comes!

Enter GRAVES, R.

GRAVES (*sighing*). Ah, Lady Franklin!

LADY F. (*sighing*). Ah, Mr. Graves! (*they seat themselves*) Pray excuse me for having kept you so long. Is it not a charming day?

GRAVES. An east wind, ma'am! but nothing comes amiss to you—'t's a happy disposition! Poor Maria! *she*, too, was naturally gay.

LADY F. Yes, she was gay. So much life, and a great deal of spirit.

GRAVES. Spirit? Yes—nothing could master it! She *would* have her own way. Ah! there was nobody like her!

LADY F. And then, when her spirit was up, she looked so handsome! Her eyes grew so brilliant!

GRAVES. Did not they?—Ah! ah! ha! ha! ha! And do you remember her pretty trick of stamping her foot?—the tiniest little foot—I think I see her now. Ah! this conversation is very soothing!

LADY F. How well she acted in your private theatricals!

GRAVES. You remember her Mrs. Oakley, in "The Jealous Wife?" Ha! ha! how good it was!—ha! ha!

LADY F. Ha! ha! Yes, in the very first scene, when she came out with (*mimicking*) "Your unkindness and barbarity will be the death of me!"

GRAVES. No—no! that's not it! more energy. (*mimicking*) "Your unkindness and barbarity will be the DEATH of me!" Ha! ha! I ought to know how she said it, for she used to practice it on me twice a day. Ah! poor dear lamb! (*wipes his eyes.*)

LADY F. And then she sang so well! was such a composer! What was that little air she was so fond of?

GRAVES. Ha! ha! sprightly, was it not? Let me see—let me see.

LADY F. (*humming*). Tum ti—ti tum—ti—ti—ti. No, that's not it!

GRAVES (*humming*). Tum ti—ti—tum ti—ti—tum—tum—tum.

BOTH. Tum ti—ti—tum ti—ti—tum—tum—tum. Ha! ha!

GRAVES (*throwing himself back*). Ah! what recollection it revives! It is too affecting.

LADY F. It *is* affecting; but we are all mortal. (*sighs*) And at your Christmas party at Cyprus Lodge, do you remember her dancing the Scotch reel with Captain MacNaughten?

GRAVES. Ha! ha! ha! To be sure—to be sure.

LADY F. Can you think of the step?—somehow thus, was it not? (*dancing.*)

GRAVES. No—no—quite wrong!—just stand there. Now then—(*humming the tune*) La—la-la-la—La-la, etc. (*they dance*) That's it—excellent—admirable!

LADY F. (*aside*). Now 'tis coming.

Enter SIR JOHN, BLOUNT, GEORGINA, R. *They stand amazed.* LADY FRANKLIN *continues dancing.*

GRAVES. Bewitching—irresistible! 'Tis Maria herself that I see before me! Thus—thus—let me clasp——Oh, the devil! Just like my luck! (*stopping opposite* SIR JOHN. LADY FRANKLIN *runs off*, L.)

SIR J. Upon my word, Mr. Graves!

GEOR. *and* BLOUNT. Encore—encore! Bravo—bravo!

GRAVES. It's all a mistake! I—I—Sir John. Lady Franklin, you see—that is to say—I——Sainted Maria! you are spared, at least, this affliction!   [*Runs off*, R.

SIR JOHN, GEORGINA, *and* BLOUNT *follow.* PAGE *takes off the chairs*, L.

SCENE III.—*The interior of* * * * *'s Club; night; lights, etc., etc.*

Noise of conversation before the act-drop rises—murmurs as it ascends.

GLOSS. You don't often come to the Club, Stout?
STOUT. No; time is money.   An hour spent at a club is unproductive capital.
OLD MEMBER (*reading the newspaper*). Waiter! the snuff-box. (WAITER *brings a large round box on a salver.*)
GLOSS. So, Evelyn has taken to play?   I see Deadly Smooth, "hushed in grim repose, awaits his evening prey." Deep work to-night, I suspect, for Smooth is drinking lemonade—keeps his head clear—monstrous clever dog! (*murmurs as before;* STOUT *takes the snuff-box from* OLD MEMBER'S *table;* OLD MEMBER *looks at him savagely.*)

Enter EVELYN; *salutes and shakes hands with different* MEMBERS *in passing up the stage; places his hat on table*, C.

EVE. Ha, Flat, how well you are looking!—Green, how do you do? How d'ye do, Glossmore?   How are you, Stout? *you* don't play, I think?   Political Economy never plays at cards, eh?—never has time for anything more frivolous than Rents and Profits, Wages and Labor, High Prices, and Low—Corn-Laws, Poor-Laws, Tithes, Currency,—Dot-and-go-one—Rates, Puzzles, Taxes, Riddles, and Botheration!   Smooth is the man.   Aha! Smooth.   Piquet, eh?   You owe me my revenge! (*sits to play*, L. *of* R. *table;* MEMBERS *touch each other significantly.*)
SMOOTH. My dear Alfred, anything to oblige. (*murmurs.*)
OLD MEM. Waiter! the snuff-box. (WAITER *takes it from* STOUT *and brings it back to* OLD MEMBER. *Two* MEMBERS *from the top*, L., *come down and cross behind to* MEMBER R. *of centre table, whisper to him and go off*, C. WAITER *brings coffee to* MEMBER *behind the* OLD MEMBER, *and then takes away two coffee cups from* LORD GLOSSMORE *and* MEMBER, R. C. *Another* WAITER *brings a glass of brandy and water to* OLD MEMBER. *Having made the cards*, SMOOTH *deals.*)

Enter BLOUNT, C.; *he goes to* EVELYN'S *table, and stands in front of it for a moment.*

BLOUNT. So!   Evelyn at it again—eh, Glossmore?
GLOSS. Yes; Smooth sticks to him like a leech.   Clever fellow, that Smooth. (*murmurs.* SMOOTH *and* EVELYN *play.*)
SMOOTH. Your point?
EVE. Five!
SMOOTH. Not good.   Six—sequence—five!
EVE. Good!
SMOOTH. Three aces.
EVE. Good! (*they continue playing;* EVELYN *deals.*)
BLOUNT. Will you make up a wubber?
GLOSS. Have you got two others?
BLOUNT. Yes; Flat and Green.

_____

* For full disposition of this scene and characters as discovered, see the Synopsis of Scenery, page 3.

GLOSS. Bad players.

BLOUNT. I make it a wule to play with bad players; it is fire per cent. in one's favor I hate gambling. But a quiet wubber, if one is the best player out of four, can't do any harm

GLOSS. Clever fellow, that Blount. (*murmurs.* BLOUNT *takes up the snuff-box and walks off with it;* OLD MEMBER *looks at him savagely.* WAITER *fetches coffee-cup from* MEMBER, L.)

Enter a MEMBER *reading a long le ter ; sits,* C. *table.* BLOUNT, GLOSSMORE, FLAT, *and* GREEN, *make up a table at the bottom of the stage,* R.

SMOOTH. A thousand pardons, my dear Alfred—ninety repique—ten cards—game !

EVE. (*passing a note to him*). Game ! Before we go on, one question. This is Thursday—how much do you calculate to win of me before Tuesday next?

SMOOTH. *Ce cher Alfred !* He is so droll !

EVE. (*writing in his pocket-book*). Forty games a night—four nights, minus Sunday—our usual stakes—that would be right, I think.

SMOOTH (*glancing over the account*). Quite —if I win all—which is next to impossible.

EVE. It shall be possible to win twice as much, on one condition. Can you keep a secret ?

SMOOTH. My dear Alfred, I have kept myself ! I never inherited a farthing—I never spent less than £4,000 a year—and I never told a soul how I managed it.

EVE. Hark ye, then—it is a matter to me of vast importance—a word with you. (*they whisper.*)

OLD MEM. Waiter! the snuff-box. (WAITER *takes it from* BLOUNT, *etc. Murmurs.*)

Enter SIR JOHN, C.

EVE. You understand ?

SMOOTH. Perfectly ; anything to oblige.

EVE (*cutting*). It is for you to deal. (*murmurs. They go on playing.*)

WAITER *comes on with a note, on salver, and offers it to one of the* MEMBERS. *who is looking on at the whist-table : he scribbles an answer, at* C. *table, and sends the* WAITER *off with it.*

SIR J. There is my precious son-in-law, that is to be, spending *my* consequence, and making a fool of himself. (*takes up snuff-box ;* OLD MEMBER *looks at him.*)

EVE (*playing*). Six to the point.

SMOOTH. Good !

EVE. Three queens.

SMOOTH Not good—I have three kings and three knaves ! (*they deal out the cards until* SIR JOHN *speaks.*)

BLOUNT (*rising from the table ; another* MEMBER *takes his place*). I'm out. Flat, a pony on the odd twick. (*takes the money*) That's wight. (*comes down,* R. C., *counting money*) Well, Sir John, you don't play ?

SIR J. Play ? no ! (*looking over* EVELYN'S *hand*) Confound him—lost again !

EVE. Hang the cards!—double the stakes !

SMOOTH. Anything to oblige—done !

SIR J. Done, indeed !

OLD MEM. Waiter! the snuff-box. (WAITER *takes it from* SIR JOHN)

BLOUNT. I've won eight points and the bets—I never lose—I never play in the Deadly Smooth set! (*takes up the snuff-box;* OLD MEMBER *as before.*)

SIR J. (*looking over* SMOOTH's *hand, and fidgeting backwards and forwards*). Lord, have mercy on us! Smooth has seven for his point! What's the stakes?

EVE Don't disturb us—I only throw out four. Stakes, Sir John?—immense! Was ever such luck?—not a card for my point. Do stand back, Sir John—I'm getting irritable. (*all rise and gather round* EVELYN's *table; several in front, so as to hide the playing from the audience.*)

BLOUNT. One hundred pounds on the next game, Evelyn? (*going to the table.*)

SIR J. Nonsense—nonsense—don't disturb him! All the fishes come to the bait! Sharks and minnows all nibbling away at my son-in-law. (*goes and takes the snuff-box.*)

EVE. One hundred pounds, Blount? Oh, yes! the finest gentleman is never too fine a gentleman to pick up a guinea. Done! Treble the stakes, Smooth!

SIR J. I'm on the rack! Be cool, Evelyn! take care, my dear boy! Be cool—be cool! (SMOOTH *shows his cards.*)

EVE. What—what? You have four queens!—five to the king. Confound the cards! a fresh pack. (*throws the cards behind him over* SIR JOHN. WAITER *brings a new pack of cards to* EVELYN.)

OLD MEM. Waiter! the snuff-box. (*murmurs.* Different MEMBERS *gather round.*)

Two MEMBERS *re-enter, and advance to* EVELYN's *table. All the* WAITERS *on.*

FLAT (*with back to audience*). I never before saw Evelyn out of temper. He must be losing immensely!

GREEN (R.). Yes—this is interesting!

SIR J. Interesting! There's a wretch!

FLAT (*next to* GREEN). Poor fellow! he'll be ruined in a month

SIR J. I'm in a cold sweat!

GREEN. Smooth is the very devil.

SIR J. The devil's a joke to him!

GLOSS. (*slapping* SIR JOHN *on the back*). A clever fellow that Smooth, Sir John, eh? (*takes up the snuff-box;* OLD MEMBER *as before*) £100 on this game, Evelyn? (*going to the table.*)

EVE. (*half turning round*). You! well done the Constitution! yes, £100!

OLD MEM. Waiter! the snuff-box.

STOUT. I *think* I'll venture £200 on this game, Evelyn? (*goes in front of table,* R.)

EVE. (*quite turning round*). Ha! ha! ha!—Enlightenment and the Constitution on the same side of the question at last! Oh, Stout, Stout! —greatest happiness of the greatest number—greatest number, number one! Done, Stout!—£200! ha! ha! deal, Smooth. Well done, Political Economy—ha! ha! ha!

SIR J. Quite hysterical—drivelling! Aren't you ashamed of yourselves? His own cousins—all in a conspiracy—a perfect gang of them. (*takes snuff-box as before.* MEMBERS *indignant.*)

STOUT (*to* MEMBERS). Hush! he's to marry Sir John's daughter!

FLAT. What! Stingy Jack's? oh!

CHORUS OF MEMS. Oh! oh!

EVE. By Heaven, there never was such luck! It's enough to drive a man wild! This is mere child's play, Smooth—double or quits on the whole amount!

SMOOTH. Anything to oblige! (*murmurs ; they play quickly.*)

SIR J. Oh, dear—oh, dear! (*great excitement.*)

EVE. (*throwing down his cards, and rising in great agitation*). No more, no more—I've done!—quite enough! Glossmore, Stout, Blount—I'll pay you to-morrow. I—I—Death!—this is ruinous! (*crosses* L., *seizes the snuff-box, and goes up,* L. C., *to chair,* L. U. E. ; *sits.*)

SIR J. *Ruinous?* What has he lost? what *has* he lost, Smooth? Not much? eh? eh? (MEMBERS *look at* EVELYN; *others gather round* SMOOTH, C.)

SMOOTH. Oh, a trifle, dear John!—excuse me! We never tell our winnings. (*to* BLOUNT, L.) How d'ye do, Fred?—(*to* GLOSSMORE, R.) By the bye, Charles, don't you want to sell your house in Grosvenor square? —£12,000, eh?

GLOSS. Yes, and the furniture at valuation. About £3,000 more.

SMOOTH (*looking over his pocket-book*). Um! Well, we'll talk of it.

SIR J. (L. C.). 12 and 3—£15,000. What a cold-blooded rascal it is! —£15,000, Smooth?

SMOOTH. Oh, the house itself is a trifle ; but the establishment—I'm considering whether I have enough to keep it up, my dear John. (*goes* L.)

OLD MEM. Waiter! the snuff-box! (*scraping it round and with a wry face*) And it's all gone! (*gives it to the* WAITER *to fill.*)

SIR J. (*turning round*). And it's all gone!

EVE. (*starting up and laughing hysterically*). Ha! ha! all gone? not a bit of it. (*goes to* SMOOTH, C.) Smooth, this club is so noisy. Sir John, you are always in the way. Come to my house! come! Champagne and a broiled bone. Nothing venture, nothing have! The luck must turn, and by Jupiter we'll make a night of it! (*going ;* SIR JOHN *stops him.*)

SIR J. A night of it! For Heaven's sake, Evelyn! EVELYN!—think what you are about!—think of Georgina's feelings!—think of your poor lost mother!—think of the babes unborn!—think of—— ·

EVE. I'll think of nothing! Zounds!—you don't know what I have lost, man ; it's all your fault, distracting my attention. Pshaw—pshaw! Out of the way, do! (*throws* SIR JOHN *off,* L.) Come, Smooth. Ha! ha! a night of it, my boy—a night of it! [*Exeunt* SMOOTH *and* EVELYN, C.

SIR J. (*following*). You must not—you shall not! Evelyn, my dear Evelyn! he's drunk—he's mad! Will no one send for the police!
[*Exit,* C.

MEMS. Ha! ha! ha! Poor old Stingy Jack!

OLD MEM. (*rising for the first time, and in a great rage*). Waiter! the snuff-box!

MEMS. Ha! ha! ha! Stingy Jack! (*murmurs and laughter as the act-drop descends.*)

CURTAIN.

———

ACT IV.

SCENE I.—*An ante-room in* EVELYN'S *house.*

Enter TOKE, GLOSSMORE, *and* BLOUNT, R. *Chairs and tables with writing materials,* R. *and* L.

TOKE. My master is not very well, my lord ; but I'll let him know.
[*Exit* TOKE, C. D.

GLOSS. I am very curious to learn the result of his gambling tete-à-tete. There are strange reports abroad, and the tradesmen have taken the alarm.

BLOUNT. Oh, he's so howwidly wich, he can afford even a tete-à-tete with Deadly Smooth!

GLOSS. Poor old Stingy Jack! why, Georgina was *your* intended.

BLOUNT. Yes; and I weally liked the girl, though out of pique I pwoposed to her cousin. But what can a man do against money?

Enter EVELYN, c., *in a morning wrapper.*

If we could start fair, you'd see whom Georgina would pwefer; but she's sacwificed by her father! She as much as told me so! (*crosses*, R.)

EVE. (*aside*). Now to work still further upon Sir John, through these excellent friends of mine. (*aloud*) So, so—good morning, gentlemen! we've a little account to settle—one hundred each.

BOTH. Don't talk of it.

EVE. (*putting up his pocket-book*). Well, I'll not talk of it. (*taking* BLOUNT *aside*) Ha! ha! you'd hardly believe it—but I'd rather not pay you just at present; my money is locked up, and I must wait, you know, for the Groginhole rents. So, instead of owing you £100, suppose I owe you *five?* You can give me a check for the other four. And, harkye! not a word to Glossmore.

BLOUNT. Glossmore! the gweatest gossip in London! I shall be delighted! (*aside*) It never does harm to lend to a wich man; one gets it back somehow. (*aloud*) By the way, Evelyn, if you want my gwey cab-horse, you may have him for £200, and that will make seven.

EVE. (*aside*). That's the fashionable usury; your friend does not take interest—he sells you a horse. (*aloud*) Blount, it's a bargain. (BLOUNT *goes to* R. *table.*)

' BLOUNT (*writing a check, and musingly*). No; I don't see what harm it can do me; that off-leg must end in a spavin.

EVE. Now for my other friend. (*to* GLOSSMORE) That £100 I owe you is rather inconvenient at present; I've a large sum to make up for the Groginhole property—perhaps you would lend me five or six hundred more—just to go on with?

GLOSS. (L.). Certainly! Hopkins is dead; your interest for Cipher would——

EVE. Why, I can't promise *that* at this moment. But as a slight mark of friendship and gratitude, I shall be very much flattered if you'll accept a splendid gray cab-horse I bought to-day—cost £200!

GLOSS. (*aside*). Bought *to-day*—then I'm safe. (*aloud*) My dear fellow, you're always so princely!

EVE. Nonsense! just write the check; and, harkye, not a syllable to Blount!

GLOSS. Blount! He's the town-crier! (*goes to write at* L. *table.*)

BLOUNT (*rises, giving* EVELYN *the check*). Wansom's, Pall-mall East.

EVE. Thank you. So you *proposed* to Miss Douglas!

BLOUNT (R.). Hang it! yes; I could have sworn that she fancied me; her manner, for instance, the vewy day you pwoposed for Miss Vesey, otherwise Georgina——

EVE. Has only half what Miss Douglas has.

BLOUNT. You forget how much Stingy Jack must have saved! But I beg your pardon.

EVE. Never mind; but not a word to Sir John, or he'll fancy I'm ruined. (GLOSSMORE *comes down*, L)

GLOSS. (*giving the check*). Ransom's, Pall-mall East. Tell me, did you win or lose last night ?

EVE. Win ! lose ! oh ! No more of that, if you love me. I must send off at once to the banker's. (*looking at the two checks.*)

GLOSS. (*aside*). Why, he's borrowed from Blount, too !

BLOUNT (*aside*). That's a cheque from Lord Glossmore,

EVE. Excuse me ; I must dress ; I have not a moment to lose. You remember you dine with me to-day—seven o'clock. You'll meet Smooth. (*mournfully*) It may be the last time I shall ever welcome you here. My—what am I saying ? Oh, merely a joke—good bye—good bye. (*shaking them heartily by the hand. Exit, C. D. GLOSSMORE and BLOUNT look at each other for a moment, and then speak.*)

BLOUNT. Glossmore !

GLOSS. Blount !

BLOUNT. I am afwaid all's not wight !

GLOSS. I incline to your opinion.

BLOUNT. But I've sold my gway cab-horse.

GLOSS. Gray cab-horse ! you !—What is he really worth now ?

BLOUNT. Since he is sold, I will tell you—Not a sixpence.

GLOSS. Not a sixpence ? he gave it to me.

BLOUNT. That was devilish unhandsome ! Do you know, I feel nervous !

GLOSS. Nervous ! Let us run and stop payment of our checks.

Enter TOKE, C. D. ; *he runs across the stage towards* R.

BLOUNT. Hollo, John ! where so fast ?

TOKE (*in great haste*). Beg pardon, Sir Frederick, to Pall-mall East— Messrs. Ransom.   [*Exit*, R.

BLOUNT (*solemnly*) Glossmore, we are floored ?

GLOSS. Sir, the whole town shall know of it.   [*Exeunt*, R.

SCENE II.—*A splendid saloon in* EVELYN'S *house. Doors* C., *leading to the dining-room.*

EVELYN *and* GRAVES *discovered seated.*

GRAVES. You don't mean to say you've borrowed money of Sir John ?

EVE. Yes, five hundred pounds. Observe how I'll thank him for it ; observe how delighted he will be to find that five hundred was really of service to me.

GRAVES. I don't understand you. You've grown so mysterious of late. You've withdrawn your money from Flash and Brisk ?

EVE. (R. *of* L. *table*). No.

GRAVES. No—then——

Enter SIR JOHN, LADY FRANKLIN, *and* GEORGINA, R. GEORGINA *goes to table* L., *and listens to* EVELYN. LADY FRANKLIN *and* GRAVES *up* C.

SIR J. You got the check for £500 safely—too happy to—(*grasping* EVELYN'S *hand.*)

EVE. (*interrupting him*). My best thanks—my warmest gratitude ! So kind in you ! so seasonable—that £500—you don't know the value of that £500. I shall never forget your nobleness of conduct.

SIR J. Gratitude ! Nobleness ! (*aside*) I can't have been taken in ?

EVE. And in a moment of such distress !

SIR J. (*aside*). Such distress! He picks out the ugliest words in the whole dictionary.

EVE. You must know, my dear Sir John, I've done with Smooth. But I'm still a little crippled, and you must do me *another* favor. I've only as yet paid the deposit of ten per cent. for the great Groginhole property. I am to pay the rest this week—nay, I fear to-morrow. I've already sold out of the Funds for the purchase; the money lies at the bankers', and of course I can't touch it; for if I don't pay by a certain day, I forfeit the estate and the deposit.

SIR J. What's coming now, I wonder?

Enter SERVANT, R. *Announces* MR. STOUT *and exits. Enter* STOUT, *in evening dress.*

EVE. Georgina's fortune is £10,000. I always meant, my dear Sir John, to present you with that little sum.

SIR J. Oh, Evelyn! (*wipes his eyes;* STOUT *goes to* L. *table.*)

EVE. But the news of my losses has frightened my tradesmen! I have so many heavy debts at this moment that—that—that.—But I see Georgina is listening, and I'll say what I have to say to her. (*crosses to her,* R. C.)

SIR J. No, no—no, no. Girls don't understand business.

EVE. The very reason I speak to her. This is an affair not of business, but of *feeling*. Stout, show Sir John my Correggio.

SIR J. (*aside*). Devil take his Correggio! The man is born to torment me! (STOUT *takes him by the arm, and points off,* L. S. E)

EVE. My dear Georgina, whatever you may hear said of me, I flatter myself that you feel confidence in my honor.

GEOR. Can you doubt it?

EVE. I confess that I am embarrassed at this moment; I have been weak enough to lose money at play. I promise you never to gamble again as long as I live. My affairs can be retrieved; but for the first few years of our marriage it may be necessary to retrench,

GEOR. Retrench!

EVE. To live, perhaps, altogether in the country.

GEOR. Altogether in the country!

EVE. To confine ourselves to a modest competence.

GEOR. Modest competence! I knew something horrid was coming.

Enter SIR F. BLOUNT, R. ; *he salutes* EVELYN *and* LADY FRANKLIN.

EVE. And now, Georgina, you may have it in your power at this moment to save me from much anxiety and humiliation. My money is locked up—my debts of honor must be settled—you are of age—your £10,000 is in your own hands——

SIR J. (STOUT *listening as well as* SIR JOHN). I'm standing on hot iron.

EVE. If you could lend it to me for a few weeks. You hesitate. Can you give me this proof of your confidence? Remember, without confidence, what is wedlock?

SIR J. (*aside to her*). No! (EVELYN *turns sharply*) Yes, (*pointing his glass at the Correggio*) the painting may be fine.

STOUT. But you don't like the subject?

GEOR. (*aside*). He may be only trying me! Best leave it to papa.

EVE. Well——

GEOR. You—you shall hear from me to-morrow. (*aside*) Ah, there's that dear Sir Frederick! (*goes to* BLOUNT, *at the back.*)

Enter GLOSSMORE *and* SMOOTH, R. EVELYN *salutes them, paying* SMOOTH *servile respect ; takes his arm and crosses to* L., *and up the stage.*

LADY F. (R. C., *to* GRAVES). Ha! ha! To be so disturbed yesterday—was it not droll?

GRAVES. Never recur to that humiliating topic.

GLOSS. (C., *to* STOUT). See how Evelyn fawns upon Smooth.

STOUT. How mean in him!—*Smooth*—a professional gambler—a fellow who lives by his wits. I would not know such a man on any account. (SMOOTH *comes down,* C.)

SMOOTH (*to* GLOSSMORE). So Hopkins is dead—you want Cipher to come in for Groginhole, eh?

GLOSS. (L. C.). What—could *you* manage it? (*aside*) Why, he must have won his whole fortune.

SMOOTH. *Ce cher, Charles!*—anything to oblige.

GLOSS. It is not possible he can have lost Groginhole!

STOUT. Groginhole! What can he have done with Groginhole! Glossmore, present me to Smooth.

GLOSS. What! the gambler—the fellow who lives by his wits?

STOUT. Why, his wits seem to be an uncommonly productive capital? I'll introduce myself. (*crosses to* SMOOTH) How d'ye do, Captain Smooth? We have met at the club, I think—I am charmed to make your acquaintance in private. I say, sir, what do you think of the affairs of the nation? Bad! very bad—no enlightenment—great fall off in the revenue—no knowledge of finance! There's only one man who can save the country—and that's Popkins!

SMOOTH. Is he in Parliament, Mr. Stout? What's your Christian name, by-the-bye?

STOUT. Benjamin—No;—constituencies are so ignorant they don't understand his value. He's no orator; in fact, he stammers a little—that is, a great deal—but devilish profound. Could not we ensure him for Groginhole?

SMOOTH. My dear Benjamin, it is a thing to be thought on. (*they retire.*)

EVE. (*advancing*). My friends, pray be seated. (*they sit**) I wish to consult you. This day twelve months I succeeded to an immense income, and as, by a happy coincidence, on the same day I secured your esteem, so now I wish to ask you if you think I could have spent that income in a way more worthy your good opinion.

GLOSS. Impossible! excellent taste—beautiful house!

BLOUNT. Vewy good horses—(*aside, to* GLOSSMORE)—especially the gway cab.

LADY F. Splendid pictures!

GRAVES. And a magnificent cook, ma'am!

SMOOTH (*thrusting his hands into his pockets*). It is my opinion, Alfred —and I'm a judge—that you could not have spent your money better.

OMNES (*except* SIR JOHN). Very true!

GEOR. Certainly. (*coaxingly*) Don't retrench, my dear Alfred!

GLOSS. Retrench! nothing so plebeian!

STOUT. Plebeian, sir—worse than plebeian—it is against all rules of public morality. Every one knows, now-a-days, that extravagance is a

---

* All sit thus.

SIR FREDERICK.	GLOSSMORE.	STOUT.	SMOOTH.	GEORGINA.
LADY FRANKLIN.				EVELYN.
GRAVES.				SIR JOHN.
R.				L.

benefit to the population—encourages art—employs labor—and multi-
plies spinning jennies.

Eve. You reassure me! I own I did think that a man worthy of
friends so sincere might have done something better than feast—dress—
drink—play——

Gloss. Nonsense—we like you the better for it: (*aside*) I wish I had
my £600 back, though.

Eve. And you are as much my friends now as when you offered me
£10 for my old nurse?

Sir J. A thousand times more so, my dear boy. (Omnes *approve*.)

Enter Sharp, R.

Smooth. But who's our new friend?

Eve. Who? the very man who first announced to me the wealth
which you allow I have spent so well. But what's the matter, Sharp?
(*crosses to* Sharp, *who whispers to him.*)

Eve. (*aloud*). The bank's *broke!* (*all start up.*)

Sir J. Bank broke—what bank? (*coming down*, c.)

Eve. Flash, Brisk and Co.

Sir J. But I warned you—you withdrew?

Eve. Alas! no!

Sir J. Oh! Not much in their hands?

Eve. Why, I told you the purchase-money for Groginhole was at my
bankers'—but no, no; don't look so frightened! It was not placed with
Flash—it is at Hoare's—it is, indeed. Nay, I assure you it is. A mere
trifle at Flash's, upon my word, now! Don't groan in that way. You'll
frighten everybody! To-morrow, Sharp, we'll talk of this! One day
more—one day, at least for enjoyment. (*walks to and fro.*)

Sir J. Oh! a pretty enjoyment!

Blount. And he borrowed £700 of me!

Gloss. And £600 of me!　　　　　　　　　 } *All up the stage,* L. *and*

Sir J. And £500 of me!　　　　　　　　　　　　　　L. C.

Stout. Oh! a regular Jeremy Diddler! }

Stout (*to* Sir John). I say, you have placed your daughter in a very
unsafe investment. Transfer the stock.

Sir J. (*going to* Georgina). Ha! I'm afraid we've been very rude to
Sir Frederick. A monstrous fine young man!

Enter Toke, *with a letter,* R.

Toke (*to* Evelyn). Sir, I beg your pardon, but Mr. MacFinch insists
on my giving you this letter instantly.

Eve. (*reading*). How! Sir John, this fellow, MacFinch, has heard of
my misfortunes, and insists on being paid—a lawyer's letter—quite insolent. Here, read this letter—you'll be quite amused with it.

Toke. And, sir, Mr. Tabouret is below, and declares he will not stir
till he's paid.　　　　　　　　　　　　　　　　　　　　　　[*Exit,* R.

Eve. Not stir till he's paid! What's to be done, Sir John? Smooth,
what *is* to be done?

Smooth (*seated,* c.). If he'll not stir till he's paid, make him put up a
bed, and I'll take him in the inventory, as one of the fixtures, Alfred.

Eve. It is very well for you to joke, Mr. Smooth. But——

Enter Sheriff's Officer, *giving a paper to* Evelyn *and whispering.*

Eve. What's this? Frantz, the tailor. Why, the impudent scoundrel! Faith, this is more than I bargained for—Sir John, I'm arrested.

STOUT. He's arrested, (*slapping* SIR JOHN *on the back with glee*) old gentleman! But I didn't lend him a farthing.

EVE. And for a mere song—£150! Sir John, pay this fellow, will you? or see that my people kick out the bailiffs, or do it yourself, or something—while we go to dinner.

SIR J. Pay—kick—I'll be d—d if I do! Oh, my £500! my £500! Mr. Alfred Evelyn, I want my £500! (GRAVES *and* LADY FRANKLIN *come forward* R. C.)

GRAVES. I'm going to do a very silly thing—I shall lose both my friend and my money—just like my luck—Evelyn, go to dinner—I'll settle this for you.

LADY F. I love you for that!

GRAVES. Do you? then I am the nappiest—Ah! ma'am, I don't know what I am saying! (LADY FRANKLIN *retires*, R.   *Exeunt* GRAVES *and* OFFICER, R.)

EVE. (*to* GEORGINA, *who is* L. C.). Don't go by these appearances! I repeat, £10,000 will more than cover all my embarrassments. I shall hear from you to-morrow?

GEOR. Yes—yes! (*going*, R.)

EVE. But you're not going? You, too, Glossmore? you, Blount?—you, Stout!—you, Smooth!

SMOOTH. No. I'll stick by you as long as you've a guinea to stake!

GLOSS. Oh, this might have been expected from a man of such ambiguous political opinions! (*crosses*, R.)

STOUT. Don't stop me, sir. No man of common enlightenment would have squandered his substance in this way. Pictures and statues—baugh! (*crosses*, R.)

EVE. Why, you all said I could not spend my money better! Ha! ha! ha!—the absurdest mistake—you don't fancy I'm going to prison—Ha! ha! Why don't you laugh, Sir John?—ha! ha! ha! (*goes up the stage.* SIR JOHN *crosses to* R. C.)

SIR J. Sir, this horrible levity! Take Sir Frederick's arm, my poor, injured, innocent child.

SMOOTH. But, my dear John, they have no right to arrest the dinner.

The c. doors are thrown open by two SERVANTS, *a handsome dining-room is discovered, and a table elegantly set for ten persons. Enter* TOKE, C.

TOKE. Dinner is served.

GLOSS. (*pausing*). Dinner!

STOUT. Dinner! a very good smell!

EVE. (*to* SIR JOHN). Turtle and venison, too. (*they stop irresolute*) That's right—come along—come along—but one word first, Blount —Stout—Glossmore—Sir John—one word first; will you lend me £10 for my old nurse! (*they all fall back*) Ah, you fall back! Behold a lesson for all who build friendship upon their fortune, and not their virtues. You lent me hundreds this morning to squander upon pleasure—you would refuse me £10 now to bestow upon benevolence. Go—we have done with each other—go.

[*Exeunt, indignantly,* R., *all but* EVELYN *and* SMOOTH.

Re-enter GRAVES, R.

GRAVES. Heyday! what's all this?

EVE. Ha! ha!—the scheme prospers—the duper is duped! Come, my friends—come; when the standard of money goes down, in the great

battle between man and fate—why, a bumper to the brave hearts that
refuse to desert us. [*Exeunt,* c. *door.*
SMOOTH *and* GRAVES. Ha! ha! ha! (*ring down when* EVELYN *is seated.*)

CURTAIN.

ACT V.

SCENE I.—* * * *'*s Club;* SMOOTH, GLOSSMORE—*four other* MEMBERS
*discovered.**

GLOSS. Will his horses be sold, think you?
SMOOTH. Very possibly, Charles—a fine stud—hum—ha! Waiter, a
glass of sherry! (SMOOTH *is at breakfast at the* L. *table, where the* OLD MEM-
BER *sat.*)
Enter WAITER, c., *with sherry.*

GLOSS. They say he must go abroad.
SMOOTH. Well; 'tis the best time of year for travelling, Charles.
GLOSS. We are all to be paid to-day; and that looks suspicious!
SMOOTH. Very suspicious, Charles! Hum!—ah!
GLOSS. (*rises and crosses to* SMOOTH). My dear fellow, you must know
the rights of the matter; I wish you'd speak out. What have you really
won? Is the house itself gone?
SMOOTH. The house itself is certainly not gone, Charles, for I saw it
exactly in the same place this morning at half-past ten—it has not
moved an inch. (WAITER *gives a letter to* GLOSSMORE.)
GLOSS. (*reading*). From Groginhole—an express! What's this? I'm
amazed! (*reading*) "They've actually, at the eleventh hour, started Mr.
Evelyn; and nobody knows what his politics are! We shall be beat!—
the Constitution is gone—CIPHER!" Oh! this is infamous in Evelyn!
Gets into Parliament just to keep himself out of the Bench!
SMOOTH He's capable of it.
GLOSS. Not a doubt of it, sir! Not a doubt of it! The man saves
himself at the expense of his country—Groginhole is lost. There's an
end of the Constitution! [*Exit,* c.

Enter SIR JOHN *and* BLOUNT, c., *talking.*

SIR J. My dear boy, I'm not flint! I am but a man! If Georgina
really loves you—and I am sure that she *does*—I will never think of sac-
rificing her happiness to ambition—she is yours; I told her so this very
morning.
BLOUNT (*aside*). The old humbug!
SIR J. She's the best of daughters! Dine with me at seven, and we'll
talk of the settlements. (WAITER *brings a bill on a salver to* SMOOTH; *he
pays it*)
BLOUNT. Yes; I don't care for fortune—but——
SIR J. Her £10,000 will be settled on herself—that of course.
BLOUNT. *All* of it, sir? Weally, I——
SIR J. What *then,* my dear boy? I shall leave you both all I've laid
by. Ah, you know I'm a close fellow! "Stingy Jack,"—eh? After

---

* This Scene is frequently omitted.

all, worth makes the man! (WAITER *removes breakfast things and cloth from* SMOOTH's *table.*)

SMOOTH. (*rises*). And the more a man's worth, John, the worthier man he must be. (*Exeunt,* MEMBERS *and* SMOOTH, C. SIR JOHN *takes up a newspaper and reads.*)

BLOUNT (*aside*). Yes; he has no other child! She *must* have all his savings; I don't see what harm it could do me. Still, that £10,000—I want that £10,000; if she would but wun off one could get wid of the settlements.

Enter STOUT, C. (*wiping his forehead*), *and takes* SIR JOHN *aside,* L.

STOUT. Sir John, we've been played upon! My secretary is brother to Flash's head clerk; Evelyn had not £300 in the bank!

SIR J. (C.). Bless us and save us! you take away my breath! But then—Deadly Smooth—the execution—the—Oh, he must be done up!

STOUT. As to Smooth, he'd "do anything to oblige." All a trick, depend upon it. Smooth has already deceived me, for before the day's over, Evelyn will be member for Groginhole. I've had an express from Popkins; he's in despair! not for *himself*—but for the *country*, Sir John, —what's to become of the country?

SIR J. But what could be Evelyn's *object?*

STOUT. *Object?* Do you look for an object in a whimsical creature like that?—a man who has not even any political opinions! Object! Perhaps to break off his match with your daughter! Take care, Sir John, or the borough will be lost to your family.

SIR J. Aha! I begin to smell a rat.

STOUT. Do you!

SIR J. But it is not too late yet.

STOUT. My interest in Popkins made me run to Lord Spendquick, the late proprietor of Groginhole. I told him that Evelyn could not pay the rest of the money! and *he* told me that——

SIR J. What?

STOUT. Mr. Sharp had just paid it him; there's no hope for Popkins! England will rue this day. (*goes to table and looks at papers.*)

SIR J. *Georgina* shall lend him the money! *I'll* lend him—every man in my house shall lend him—I feel again what it is to be a father-in-law— Sir Frederick, excuse me—you can't dine with me to-day. And, on second thoughts, I see that it would be very unhandsome to desert poor Evelyn, now he's down in the world. Can't think of it, my dear boy— can't think of it! Very much honored, and happy to see you as a friend. Waiter, my carriage! Um! What, humbug *Stingy Jack*, will they? Ah! a good joke, indeed.   [*Exit,* C.

BLOUNT. Mr. Stout, what have you been saying to Sir John? Something about my chawacter; I know you have; don't deny it. Sir, I shall expect satisfaction!

STOUT. Satisfaction, Sir Frederick? Pooh, as if a man of enlightenment had any satisfaction in fighting! Did not mention your name; we were talking of Evelyn. Only think—he's no more ruined than you are.

BLOUNT. Not wuined! Aha, now I understand! So, so! Stay, let me see—she's to meet me in the square. (*pulls out his watch; a very small one.*)

STOUT (*pulling out his own; a very large one*). I must be off to the vestry.   [*Exit,* C.

BLOUNT. Just in time—ten thousand pounds! 'Gad, my blood's up, and I won't be tweated in *this* way if he were fifty times Stingy Jack!
                          [*Exit,* C.

SCENE II.—*The drawing-rooms in* SIR JOHN VESEY'S *house.*

Enter LADY FRANKLIN *and* GRAVES, L.

GRAVES. Well, well, I am certain that poor Evelyn loves Clara still, but you can't persuade me that she cares for him.

LADY F. She has been breaking her heart ever since she heard of his distress. Nay, I am sure she would give all she has, could it save him from the consequences of his own folly.

GRAVES. I should just like to sound her.

LADY F. (*ringing the bell*). And you shall. I take so much interest in her, that I forgive your friend everything but his offer to Georgina.

Enter PAGE, R.

Where are the young ladies ?

PAGE. Miss Vesey is, I believe, still in the square; Miss Douglas is just come in, my lady.

LADY F. What! did she go out with Miss Vesey ?

PAGE. No, my lady ; I attended her to Drummond's, the banker.
[*Exit*, R.

LADY F. Drummond's !

Enter CLARA. R.

Why, child, (*crosses to her*) what on earth could take you to Drummond's at this hour of the day ?

CLARA (*confused*). Oh, I—that is—I—Ah, Mr. Graves! (*crosses to* GRAVES) How is Mr. Evelyn ? How does he bear up against so sudden a reverse ?

GRAVES. With an awful calm. I fear all is not right here! (*touching his head*) The report in the town is, that he must go abroad instantly—perhaps to-day. (*crosses to* C.)

CLARA (c.). Abroad !—to-day !

GRAVES (L.). But all his creditors will be paid ; and he only seems anxious to know if Miss Vesey remains true in his misfortunes.

CLARA. Ah! he loves her so *much*, then ?

GRAVES. Um! That's more than I can say.

CLARA. She told me last night, that he said £10,000 would free him from all his liabilities—that was the sum, was it not ?

GRAVES. Yes ; he persists in the same assertion. Will Miss Vesey lend it ?

LADY F. (*aside*, R.). If she does, I shall not think so well of her poor dear mother ; for I am sure she'd be no child of Sir John's!

GRAVES. I should like to convince myself that my poor friend has nothing to hope from a woman's generosity.

LADY F. Civil! And are men, then, less covetous ?

GRAVES. I know one man at least, who, rejected in his poverty by one as poor as himself, no sooner came into a sudden fortune than he made his lawyer invent a codicil which the testator never dreamt of, bequeathing independence to the woman who had scorned him.

LADY F. And never told her ?

GRAVES. Never ! There's no such document at Doctors' Commons, depend on it. You seem incredulous, Miss Clara ! Good day ! (*crosses*, R.)

CLARA (*following him*). One word, for mercy's sake ! Do I understand you right ? Ah, how could I be so blind ? Generous Evelyn !

GRAVES. *You* appreciate, and *Georgina* will desert him. Miss Douglas,

he loves you still. If that's not just like me! Meddling with other
people's affairs, as if they were worth it—hang them!　　　　[*Exit*, R.

CLARA Georgina will desert him. Do you think so?

LADY F. She told me last night that she would never see him
again. To do her justice, she's less interested than her father—and as
much attached as she can be to another. Even while engaged to Evelyn, she has met Sir Frederick every day in the square.

CLARA. And he is alone—sad—forsaken—ruined. And I, whom he
enriched—I, the creature of his bounty—I, once the woman of his love
—I stand idly here to content myself with tears and prayers! Oh, Lady
Franklin, have pity on me—on him! We are both of kin to him—as relations we have both a right to comfort! Let us go to him—come!

LADY F. No! it would scarcely be right—remember the world—I
cannot!,

CLARA. All abandon him—then I will go alone! (*crosses*, R.)

LADY F. Alone—what will he think? What but——

CLARA. What but—that, if he love me still, I may have enough for
both, and I am by his side! But that is too bright a dream. He told
me I might call him brother! Where, now, should a sister be? But—
but—I—I—I—tremble! If, after all—if—if—In one word, am I too
bold? The world—my conscience can answer *that*—but do you think
that *he* could despise me?

LADY F. No, Clara, no! Your fair soul is too transparent for even
libertines to misconstrue. Something tells me that this meeting may
make the happiness of both. You cannot go alone. My presence jus-
tifies all. Give me your hand—we will go together.　　　　[*Exeunt*, R.

SCENE III.—*A room in* EVELYN'S *house, same as last of Act IV.* EVE-
LYN *discovered at table*, R.

EVE. Yes; as yet, all surpasses my expectations. I am sure of
Smooth—I have managed even Sharp; my election will seem but an
escape from a prison. Ha! ha! True, it cannot last long; but a few
hours more are all I require, and for that time at least I shall hope to
be thoroughly ruined. (*rises and goes* L.)

Enter GRAVES, R.

Well, Graves, and what do people say of me?

GRAVES. Everything that's bad!

EVE. Three days ago I was universally respected. I awake this
morning to find myself singularly infamous. Yet, I'm the same man.

GRAVES. Humph! why, gambling——

EVE. Cant! it was not criminal to gamble—it was criminal to lose.
Tut!—will you deny that if I had ruined Smooth instead of myself,
every hand would have grasped mine yet more cordially, and every
lip would have smiled congratulation on my success? Man—Man—I've
not been rich and poor for nothing. The Vices and the Virtues are
written in a language the world cannot construe; it reads them in a vile
translation, and the translators are—*failure* and *success!* You alone are
unchanged.

GRAVES. There's no merit in that I am always ready to mingle my
tears with any man. (*aside*) I know I'm a fool, but I can't help it. (*aloud*)
Hark ye, Evelyn, I like you—I'm rich; and anything I can do to get
you out of your hobble will give me an excuse to grumble for the rest
of my life. There, now 'tis out

EVE. (*touched*). There's something good in human nature, after all!

My dear friend, I will now confide in you ; I am not the spendthrift you think me—my losses have been trifling—not a month's income of my fortune. (GRAVES *shakes him heartily by the hand*) No! it has been but a stratagem to prove if the love, on which was to rest the happiness of a whole life, were given to the Money or the Man. Now you guess why I have asked from Georgina this one proof of confidence and affection.— Think you she will give it ?

GRAVES. Would you break your heart if she did not?

EVE It is vain to deny that I still love Clara ; our last conversation renewed feelings which would task all the energies of my soul to conquer. No! the heart was given to the soul as its ally, not as its traitor.

GRAVES What do you intend to do ?

EVE. This:—If Georgina prove, by her confidence and generosity, that she loves me for myself, I will shut Clara for ever from my thoughts. I am pledged to Georgina, and I will carry to the altar a soul resolute to deserve her affection and fulfill its vows.

GRAVES And if she reject you ?

EVE. (*joyfully*). If she do, I am free once more ! And then—then I will dare to ask, for I can ask without dishonor, if Clara can explain the past and bless the future ! (*crosses, R.*)

Enter SERVANT, R., *with a letter on a salver ;* EVELYN *takes it. Exit* SER-
VANT, R.

EVE. (*after reading it*). The die is cast—the dream is over. Generous girl ! Oh, Georgine ! I will deserve you yet.

GRAVES. Georgina ! is it possible ?

EVE. And the delicacy, the womanhood, the exquisite grace of this ! How we misjudge the depth of the human heart ! How, seeing the straws on the surface, we forget that the pearls may lie hid below ! I imagine her incapable of this devotion.

GRAVES. And I, too.

EVE. It were base in me to continue this trial a moment longer; I will write at once to undeceive that generous heart. (*goes to R. table and writes.*)

GRAVES. I would have given £1,000 if that little jade Clara had been beforehand. But just like my luck ; if I want a man to marry one woman, he s sure to marry another on purpose to vex me.

EVE. Graves, will you ring the bell ? (GRAVES *rings bell, L.*)

Enter SERVANT, R.

Take this instantly to Miss Vesey ; say I will call in an hour. (*exit* SER-
VANT) And now Clara is resigned forever. Why does my heart sink within me? Why, why, looking to the fate to come, do I see only the memory of what has been ? (*goes towards L.*)

GRAVES. You are re-engaged then to Georgina ?

EVE. Irrevocably.

Enter SERVANT, R., *announcing* LADY FRANKLIN *and* MISS DOUGLAS.

LADY F. My dear Evelyn, you may think it strange to receive such visitors at this moment; but, indeed, it is no time for ceremony. We are your relations—it is reported you are about to leave the country— we come to ask frankly what we can do to serve you !

EVE Madam—I——

LADY F. Come, come—do not hesitate to confide in us ; Clara is less a stranger to you than I am; your friend here will perhaps let me consult with him. (*crosses and speaks aside to* GRAVES) Let us leave them to themselves.

GRAVES. You're an angel of a widow; but you come too late, as whatever is good for anything generally does. (*they retire into the inner-room, out of sight, the doors of which should be partially open.*)

EVE. (L). Miss Douglas, I may well want words to thank you! this goodness—this sympathy——

CLARA (R., *abandoning herself to her emotion*). Evelyn! Evelyn! Do not talk thus! Goodness! sympathy—I have learned *all*—*all!* It is for ME to speak of *gratitude!* What! even when I had so wounded you —when you believed me mercenary and cold—when you thought that I was blind and base enough not to know you for what you are; even *at that time* you thought but of my happiness—my fortunes—my fate!— And to you—you—I owe all that has raised the poor orphan from servitude and dependence! While your words were so bitter, your deeds so gentle! Oh, noble Evelyn, this then was your revenge.

EVE. You owe me no thanks—that revenge was sweet! Think you it was nothing to feel that my presence haunted you, though you knew it not?—that in things the pettiest as the greatest, which that gold could buy—the very jewels you wore—the very robe in which, to other eyes, you might seem more fair—in all in which you took the woman's young and innocent delight—*I* had a part—a share! that, even if separated for ever—even if another's—even in distant years—perhaps in a happy home, listening to sweet voices that might call you "mother!"—even then should the uses of that dross bring to your lips one smile—that smile was mine—due to me—due as a sacred debt, to the hand that you rejected—to the love that you despised!

CLARA. Despised! See the proof that I despise you—see; in this hour, when they say you are again as poor as before, I forget the world —my pride—perhaps too much my sex; I remember but your sorrows —I am here!

EVE. And is this the same voice that, when I knelt at your feet—when I asked but *one day* the hope to call you mine—spoke only of poverty, and answered, "*Never?*"

CLARA. Because I had been unworthy of your love if I had insured your misery! Evelyn, hear me! My father, like you, was poor—generous; gifted, like you, with genius—ambition; sensitive, like you, to the least breath of insult. He married, as you would have done—married one whose only dower was penury and care! Alfred, I saw that genius the curse to itself—I saw that ambition wither to despair—I saw the struggle—the humiliation—the proud man's agony—the bitter life— the early death—and heard over his breathless clay my mother's groan of self-reproach! Alfred Evelyn, now speak! Was the woman you loved so nobly to repay you with such a doom?

EVE. Clara, we should have shared it.

CLARA. Shared? Never let the woman who really loves comfort her selfishness with such delusion! In marriages like this, the wife cannot share the burden; it is he—the husband—to provide, to scheme, to work, to endure—to grind out his strong heart at the miserable wheel! The wife, alas! cannot share the struggle—she can but witness the despair! And therefore, Alfred, I rejected you.

EVE. Yet you believe me as poor now as I was then?

CLARA. But *I* am not poor; *we* are not so poor. Of this fortune, which is all your own—if, as I hear, one-half would free you from your debts, why, we have the other half still left. Evelyn, it is humble—but it is not penury. You know me now.

EVE. Know you! Bright angel, too excellent for man's harder nature to understand—at least it is permitted me to revere. Why were such blessed words not vouchsafed to me before?—why, why come they now —too late? Oh, Heaven—too late!

CLARA. Too late! What, then, have I said?

EVE. Wealth! what is it without you? *With* you, I recognize its power; to forestall your every wish—to smooth your every path—to make all that life borrows from Grace and Beauty your ministrant and handmaid;—why, *that* were to make gold indeed a god! But vain—vain—vain! Bound by every tie of faith, gratitude, loyalty, and honor, to another!

CLARA. Another! Is she, then, true to your reverses? I did not know this—indeed I did not! And I have thus betrayed myself! (*aside*) O, shame! he must despise me now! (CLARA *goes up and sits at table,* R.)

Enter SIR JOHN, R.; *at the same time* GRAVES *and* LADY FRANKLIN *advance from the inner room.*

SIR J. (*with dignity and frankness*). Evelyn, I was hasty yesterday. You must own it natural that I should be so. But Georgina has been so urgent in your defence—(*as* LADY FRANKLIN *comes down,* R.) Sister, just shut the door, will you?—that I cannot resist her. What's money without happiness? So give me your security; for she insists on lending you the £10,000.

EVE. I know, and have already received it.

SIR J. (C.—*aside*). Already received it! Is he joking? Faith, for the last two days I believe I have been living amongst the Mysteries of Udolpho! (*aloud*) Sister, have you seen Georgina?

LADY F. (R.). Not since she went out to walk in the square.

SIR J. (*aside*). She's not in the square, nor the house—where the deuce can the girl be?

EVE. I have written to Miss Vesey—I have asked her to fix the day for our wedding.

SIR J. (*joyfully*). Have you? Go, Lady Franklin, find her instantly —she must be back by this time; take my carriage—it is but a step— you will not be two minutes gone. (*aside*) I'd go myself, but I'm afraid of leaving him a moment while he's in such excellent dispositions.

LADY F. (*repulsing* CLARA, *who rises to follow*). No, no; stay till I return. [*Exit,* R.

SIR J. And don't be down-hearted, my dear fellow; if the worst come to the worst, you will have everything I can leave you. Meantime, if I can in any way help you——

EVE. Ha!—you!—*you*, too? Sir John, you have seen my letter to Miss Vesey?—(*aside*) or could she have learned the truth before she ventured to be generous?

SIR J. No! on my honor. I only just called at the door on my way from Lord Spend—that is, from the City. Georgina was out;—was ever anything so unlucky? (*Voices without*—"Hurrah—hurrah! Blue for ever!") What's that?

Enter SHARP, R.

SHARP. Sir, a deputation from Groginhole—poll closed in an hour— you are returned! Holloa, sir—holloa!

EVE. (*aside*). And it was to please Clara!

SIR J. Mr. Sharp—Mr. Sharp—I say, how much has Mr. Evelyn lost by Messrs. Flash and Co.?

SHARP. Oh, a great deal, sir—a great deal!

SIR J. (*alarmed*). How?—a great deal!

EVE. Speak the truth, Sharp—concealment is all over. (*goes up the stage.*)

SHARP. £223 6s. 3l.—a great sum to throw away!

SIR J. Eh! what, my dear boy?—what? Ha! ha! all humbug, was it?—all humbug! So, Mr. Sharp, isn't he ruined, after all?—not the least wee, rascally little bit in the whole world ruined?

SHARP. Sir, he has never even lived up to his income.

SIR J. Worthy man! I could jump up to the ceiling! I am the happiest father-in-law in the three kingdoms. (*knock'ng*, R.) And that's my sister's knock, too!

CLARA (*rises*, R.). Since I was mistaken, cousin—since now you do not need me—forget what has passed; my business here is over. Farewell!

EVE. Could you but see my heart at this moment, with what love, what veneration, what anguish it is filled, you would know how little, in the great calamities of life, fortune is really worth. And must we part now, —now when—when—I——

Enter LADY FRANKLIN *and* GEORGINA, R., *followed by* BLOUNT, *who looks shy and embarrassed;* CLARA *retires and goes to* L. *table.*

GRAVES. Georgina herself—then there's no hope.

SIR J. (L.—*aside*). What the deuce brings that fellow Blount here? (*aloud*) Georgy, my dear Georgy, I want to——

EVE. (C.). Stand back, Sir John!

SIR J. But I must speak a word to her—I want to——

EVE. Stand back, I say—not a whisper—not a sign. If your daughter is to be my wife, to *her* heart only will I look for a reply to *mine*.—Georgina, it is true, then, that you trust me with your confidence—your fortune? It is also true, that when you did so you believed me ruined? Oh, pardon the doubt! Answer as if your father stood not there—answer me from that truth the world cannot yet have plucked from your soul—answer me as woman's heart, yet virgin and unpolluted, *should* answer to one who has trusted to it his all!

GEOR. (R. C.—*aside*). What can he mean?

SIR J. (L. C.—*making signs*). She'll not look this way—she will not—hang her—HEM!

EVE. You falter. I implore—I adjure you—answer!

LADY F. Speak! (SIR JOHN *makes an effort to speak;* EVELYN *observes it.*)

EVE. Silence, Sir John!

GEOR. Mr. Evelyn, your fortune might well dazzle me, as it dazzled others. Believe me, I sincerely pity your reverses.

SIR J. Good girl!—you hear her, Evelyn.

GEOR. What's money without happiness?

SIR J. Clever creature!—my own sentiments!

GEOR. And so, as our engagement is now annulled——

EVE. Annulled!

GEOR. Papa told me so this very morning—I have promised my hand where I have given my heart—to Sir Frederick Blount. (CLARA *goes down*, L.)

SIR J. I told you—I—No such thing—no such thing; you frighten her out of her wits—she don't know what she's saying! (*goes up and over to* R)

EVE. Am I awake? But this letter—this letter, received to-day——

LADY F. (*looking over the letter*). Drummond's—from a banker!

EVE. Rea'—read!

LADY F. " £10 000 just placed to your account—from the same un-known friend to Evelyn." Oh, Clara, I know now why you went to Drummond's this morning.

EVE. Clara! What!—and the former note with the same signature, on the faith of which I pledged my hand and sacrificed my heart——

LADY F. Was written under my eyes, and the secret kept that——

EVE. I see it all—how could I be so blind? I am free!—I am re-leased!—Clara, you forgive me?—you love me?—you are mine! We are rich—rich! I can give you fortune, power—I can devote to you my whole life, thought, heart, soul—I am all yours, Clara—my own—my wife! (*kneels ; she gives him her hand ; they embrace.*)

SIR J. (*to* GEORGINA). A pretty mess you've made, to humbug your own father! And you too, Lady Franklin—I am to thank you for this! (EVELYN *places* CLARA *in a chair up* L.)

LADY F. You've to thank me that she's not now on the road to Scotland with Sir Frederick. I chanced on them by the Park just in time to dis-suade and save her. But, to do her justice, a hint of your displeasure was sufficient.

GEOR. (*half-sobbing*). And you know, papa, you said this very morn-ing that poor Frederick had been very ill-used, and you would settle it all at the club.

BLOUNT. Come, Sir John, you can only blame yourself and Evelyn's cunning device. After all, I'm no such vewy bad match ; and as for the £10,000——

EVE I'll double it. Ah, Sir John, what's money without happiness? (*slaps* SIR JOHN *on the shoulder and retires.*)

SIR J. Pshaw—nonsense—stuff! Don't humbug me!

LADY F. But if you don't consent, she'll have no husband at all.

SIR J. Hum! there's something in that. (*aside to* EVELYN) Double it, will you? Then, settle it all *tightly* on her. Well—well—my foible is not avarice. Blount, make her happy. Child, I forgive you. (*pinching her arm*) Ugh, you fool! (BLOUNT *and* GEORGINA *go up*, L.)

GRAVES (*comes forward with* LADY FRANKLIN). I'm afraid it's catch-ing. What say you? I feel the symptoms of matrimony creeping all over me. Shall we, eh? Frankly, now, frankly——

LADY F. Frankly, now, there's my hand.

GRAVES. Accepted. Is it possible? Sainted Maria! thank Heaven you are spared this affliction! (*goes up* c.)

Enter SMOOTH, R.

SMOOTH. How d'ye do, Alfred? I intrude, I fear! Quite a family party.

BLOUNT. Wish us joy, Smooth—Georgina's mine, and——

SMOOTH. And our four friends there apparently have made up another rubber. John, my dear boy, you look as if you had something a. stake on the odd trick. (*crosses to* L.)

SIR J. Sir, your very—Confound the fellow—and he's a dead shot, too!

Enter STOUT *and* GLOSSMORE *hastily, talking with each other*, R.

GLOSS. My dear Evelyn, you were out of humor yesterday—but I for-give you. (EVELYN *takes his hand.*)

STOUT. Certainly! (EVELYN *crosses,* c.) what would become of public life if a man were obliged to be two days running in the same mind?—I rise to explain. Just heard of your return, Evelyn. Congratulate you.

The great motion of the session is fixed for Friday. We count on your vote. Progress with the times.

GLOSS. Preserve the Constitution!

STOUT. Your money will do wonders for the party! Advance!

GLOSS. The party respects men of your property. Stick fast!

EVE. I have the greatest respect, I assure you, for the worthy and intelligent flies upon both sides of the wheel; but whether we go too fast or too slow does not, I fancy, depend so much on the flies as on the Stout Gentleman who sits inside and pays the post-boys. Now, all my politics as yet is to consider what's best for the Stout Gentleman!

SMOOTH. Meaning John Bull. *Ce cher*, old John! (EVELYN *crosses to* SMOOTH *and takes his hand.*)

EVE. Smooth, we have yet to settle our first piquet account and our last. And I sincerely thank you for the service you have rendered to me, and the lesson you have given these gentlemen. (*returns to* C.; *all the characters take their positions for the end. Turning to* CLARA) Ah, Clara, you—you have succeeded where wealth had failed! You have reconciled me to the world and to mankind. My friends—we must confess it—amidst the humors and the follies, the vanities, deceits, and vices that play their parts in the great Comedy of Life—it is our own fault if we do not find such natures, though rare and few, as redeem the rest, brightening the shadows that are flung from the form and body of the *time* with glimpses of the everlasting holiness of truth and love.

GRAVES. But for the truth and the love, when found, to make us tolerably happy, we should not be without——

LADY F. Good health;

GRAVES. Good spirits;

CLARA. A good heart;

SMOOTH. An innocent rubber;

GEOR. Congenial tempers;

BLOUNT. A pwoper degwee of pwudence;

STOUT. Enlightened opinions;

GLOSS. Constitutional principles;

SIR J. Knowledge of the world;

EVE. And—plenty of money!

Disposition of the Characters at the fall of the Curtain.

	CLARA.	EVELYN.	
BLOUNT.			LADY FRANKLIN.
GEORGINA.			GRAVES.
GLOSSMORE.			SMOOTH.
STOUT.			SIR JOHN.
R.			L.

CURTAIN.

RICHELIEU.

ORIGINAL CAST OF CHARACTERS.

	Theatre Royal, Covent Garden, London, 1839.	Wallack's Old National Theatre, New York, Sept 4, 1839.
Louis XIII., King of France.........Mr. ELTON.		Mr. WALTON.
Gaston, Duke of Orleans (Brother to the King).......................Mr. DIDDEAR.		Mr. POWELL
Baradas (the King's Favorite)..... ....Mr. WARDE.		Mr. G. JAMESON.
Cardinal Richelieu.............. ....Mr. MACREADY.		Mr. EDWIN FOUREST.
The Chevalier de Mauprat............Mr. ANDERSON.		Mr.J.W.WALLACE,Jr.
The Sieur de Beringhen (in attendance on the King—one of the Conspirators)........ ....Mr. F. VINING.		Mr. HORNCASTLE.
Clermont (a Courtier).............		
Joseph, a Capuchin Monk (Richelieu's Confidant)........................Mr. PHELPS.		Mr. A. J. NEAFIE.
François (First Page to Richelieu).....Mr. HOWE.		Mrs. W. SEFTON.
Huguet (an Officer of Richelieu's Household Guard—a Spy)..............Mr. G. BENNETT.		
First Courtier........................ Mr. ROBERTS.		
First, Second, and Third Secretaries of State.	Mr. MATTHEWS. Mr. TILBURY. Mr. YARNOLD.	
Governor of the Bastile.................Mr. WALDRON.		
Jailer................................Mr. AYLIFFE.		
Julie de Mortemar (an Orphan, Ward to Richelieu)....................Miss HELEN FAUCIT.		Miss V. MONIER.
Marion de Lorme (Mistress to the Duke of Orleans, but in Richelieu's pay). Miss CHARLES.		Mrs. ROGERS.

Courtiers, Pages, Conspirators, Officers, Soldiers, etc.

TIME IN REPRESENTATION—THREE HOURS AND A QUARTER.

SCENE.—*Paris and the vicinity.*   PERIOD.—1642.

SCENERY.

ACT I., Scene 1.—Handsomely furnished room in the house of MARION DE LORME.

Entrance

3d Grooves.——— —— | | ——3d Grooves.

with curtains.

Table and		Table and	
R. 2 E.	* ◯ * Chairs.	* ◯ * Chairs.	L. 2 E.

R. 1 E.   L. 1 E.

At R. C. a handsome gilded table and four chairs; L. C. another table and two chairs ; wine, fruit, goblets, etc , on table R. C. The flats (in 3d grooves) represent a handsome chamber, D. L. F., concealed by curtains.

Scene II.—Room in the Cardinal's Palace.

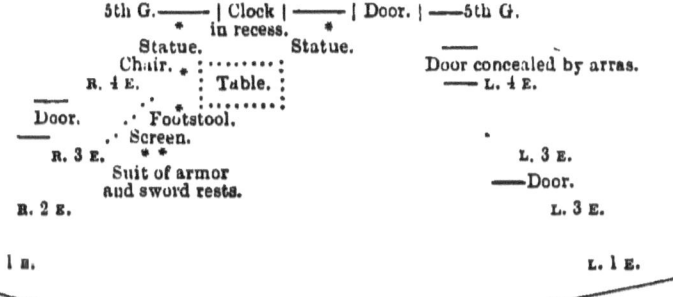

The walls are hung with tapestry in the 5th grooves. A large screen placed in a slanting direction, R. C. E. A door behind the arras, L. C. E. ; door L. H. F.; a rude clock in recess, C., over it a bust; weapons and banners hung about; statues at back, R. C., L. C., and L. H. ; a suit of armor R. C., and leaning on a rack or support near it a short sword and a large two-handed sword of the period; a large antique table with cover, C., upon which are books, papers, etc.; hand bell; R. H. of table a high antique arm-chair, with crimson seat and back ; by the side of it a footstool.

ACT II., Scene I.—Apartment in DE MAUPRAT'S new house. The flats in 3d grooves, and the wings represent the interior of a richly decorated apartment, large casements R. C. and L. C., hung with tapestry, and painted so as to represent being seen through the glass the gardens and domes of the Luxembourg Palace.

Scene II.—Same as Act I., Scene II.

ACT III., Scene I.—RICHELIEU'S Castle at Ruelle. The scene represents a large chamber in the Gothic style; large doors C. of F, which are in the 4th grooves; doors L. H. and R. H. between 2 and 3 E.; window L. C. F., through which the moonlight shines now and then ; the next scene closes in on 3d grooves. Table C., and chairs.

Scene II.—Room in the house of COUNT DE BARADAS, in the 3d grooves ; merely a representation of a richly-furnished apartment.

ACT IV., Scene I.—The Gardens of the Louvre. The flats in 4th grooves and the wings represent beautiful gardens : vases, fountains, etc., extending in perspective.

ACT V, Scene I.—A corridor in the Bastile. The flats in the 2d grooves represent massive, dismal-looking stone walls; door L. F., with bolts and lock ; door R. F.

Scene II—The King's closet in the Louvre. The wings represent the sides of a gorgeously fitted-up apartment. Folding-doors R. F., and the left half of flats represent in perspective a succession of rich rooms or gallery, so that on entering the King and suite appear to have traversed these apartments. Two richly gilded chairs at 3 E., both sides ; afterwards moved to R. C. and L. C.

COSTUMES.

Compiled Expressly for this Edition from the best French works.

LOUIS.—A complete suit of black velvet ; shoes, roses, and a black plume ; the Cross of St. Louis on his cloak and suspended round his neck.

GASTON.—Claret-colored doublet, cloak, and breeches ending with lace ; loose boots of buff leather; hat and plume ; Cross of St. Louis upon the cloak, and the order round the neck.

DE BERINGHEN, ⎫
CLERMONT, and ⎬ Similar styles, but of various colors.
    COURT.   ⎭

BARADAS.—Green velvet doublet, cloak, and breeches, slashed with yellow satin, trimmed with gold; shoes and roses; cloak with Star of St. Louis on it, order round the neck

CARDINAL RICHELIEU.—Scarlet cassock; tippet of white fur lined with scarlet; red stockings, shoes, and skull cap; a rich robe for the first dress.

DE MAUPRAT.—*1st Dress:* Plain dark velvet doublet, cloak, and breeches, terminating with lace; lace ruffles and collar; flap boots; hat and plume. *2d Dress:* Rich blue velvet doublet, cloak, and breeches, slashed with white satin and trimmed with gold and lace; lace collar, ruffles, and lace at end of breeches; shoes and roses; hat and feathers. *3d Dress:* Complete suit of steel armor. *4th Dress:* Same as 2d Dress.

JOSEPH.—A monk's brown frock, girdle, flesh-colored stockings, and plain sandals

HUGUET.—Buff jerkin, large red breeches, heavy boots and gauntlets; a gorget and morion; a bandoleer across the shoulder.

FRANCOIS.—*1st Dress:* White and red doublet, cloak, and breeches, slightly trimmed with gold; shoes. *2d Dress:* Buff-colored jerkin and breeches, steel back and breast plates; cross belt and waist belt, sword and boots and spurs. *3d Dress:* Plain jerkin and breeches, with shoes and rosettes; cap with rosette.

CAPT. OF ARCHERS —Green jerkin and breeches; waist belt, buff gloves, and boots; hat and feather.

SECRETARIES OF STATE.—Black velvet doublets, cloaks, and breeches; lace collars and cuffs; shoes and roses.

GOVERNOR OF BASTILE.—Dark-colored doublet and breeches; belt, shoes, and roses.

JAILER.—Dark-colored plain jerkin and breeches, with waist-belt and boots.

GUARDS.—Doublets with loose sleeves; breeches, stockings, and high shoes with rosettes; the letter " L " and a crown embroidered on the breast; hat and feathers.

PAGES.—Scarlet and purple doublets, cloaks, and breeches, slightly trimmed with gold; shoes and rosettes.

JULIE.—White satin, trimmed with blue and silver; a handsome travelling wrapper for 3d Act.

MARION DE LORME.—Amber and gold; very rich in jewels and ornaments; a veil for the 2d Act.

PROPERTIES.

ACT I., Scene 1.—Two richly-gilded tables and six chairs; wine, fruits, and goblets; dice and box; pieces of gold; swords for all; four arquebuses; parchment for BARADAS. *Scene* 2.—A large screen; large table and cover; books, papers, writing materials; quill pens; a rude sort of clock; massive antique chair with crimson seat and back; footstool; busts; statues; weapons and banners scattered about and against the wall; suit of armor; a long sword and a two-handled sword; small bell on table; carbine for HUGUET.

ACT II., Scene 1.—Large sheet of paper with seal attached for BARADAS; parchment scroll for him; table napkin for DE BERINGHEN. *Scene* 2.—As in Act I., Scene 2, but with purse and gold on table.

ACT III., Scene 1.—Antique table with chairs; books; purse with gold pieces for FRANCOIS; lamp on table; suit of armor and sword for DE MAUPRAT; antique couch and fittings. *Scene* 2.—Parchment for BARADAS; cross-bows for ARCHERS.

ACT IV., Scene 1.—Arquebuses for GUARDS; parchment for warrant.

ACT V., Scene 1.—Keys for JAILER; folded paper as a passport; sealed packet for DE BERINGHEN. *Scene* 2.—Watch for BARADAS; papers and large portfolios for the three SECRETARIES; two gilded chairs; parchment as before, and also sealed packet.

THE STORY OF THE PLAY.

THE opening of the play occurs during the reign of Louis XIII., King of France, at a period when the Cardinal Richelieu had risen high into power, having gradually but firmly worked his way up in a progressive journey of many years. But the weakness of the monarch, and the grand intellect, coupled with firmness, indeed, severity, of the minister operated to produce a spirit of discontent in the court, which had culminated in a powerful conspiracy, not for the love of nation, but for personal aggrandizement. Upon this state of things starts the play. Some idea of the character of the Cardinal, and the position of affairs, both before and at this time, are shown in the elegant "preface" of the distinguished author, and by the "Remarks" which accompany the present edition.

At the commement of the play, Gaston, Duke of Orleans, brother to the King, has formed a conspiracy for his dethronement, and possessing power, rank, and influence, has enlisted on his side, not only Baradas, the King's favorite, and one of his chief officers, but many other courtiers and presumed supporters of the crown ; not the least amongst them being the Duc de Bouillon, one of the great leaders of the French Army, then operating against the Spaniards ; for it is upon his support and that of his soldiers, that the hopes of the conspirators rest—hence, the importance attached to the "dispatch" introduced in the play.

The meetings are held at the house of Marion de Lorme, a fascinating beauty, mistress of the Duke of Orleans, but honestly in the service and pay of the Cardinal. It is at one of these meetings the play opens.

Baradas reveals to Orleans the proposed scheme for the Duc de Bouillon forsaking his allegiance to the King of France—joining his troops with those of his enemy, the King of Spain ; then marching on to Paris—dethroning the King, appointing Orleans Regent—and Baradas and the other lords members of the Council, when they would carry out more fully a preliminary treaty with Spain for an increase of wealth and power—and he produces the parchment to be signed by all who join in the compact.

The Duke of Orleans suggests, however, that Richelieu, with his well-known argus eyes and secret powers and appliances, might gain information of their schemes, and then—"good bye to life !"

Such a suggestion, however, Baradas meets boldly, and suggests, that whilst the dispatch, when duly signed, is sent to the Duc de Bouillon, the Cardinal, must, by some trusty hand, be sent to Heaven. To consider further, a meeting for the morrow is appointed.

Amongst the company present is a young courtier—the Chevalier de Mauprat—gay, dashing, brave, and of good birth, in fact, a Don Cæsar de Bazan of that period. He has been induced to play—lost all—and there is nothing left but his honor and his sword. The courtiers, therefore, having no more money to gain, leave him to himself ; but Baradas, keen-sighted and foreseeing, detects the presence of some grievance on his mind which will make him a ready tool for the purposes of the conspiracy, and remains to question him. He soon learns that hating the Cardinal, and under the influence and control of the Duke of Orleans, De Mauprat, some time previously had joined in a revolt against the King, in the Provinces, and aided by a number of daring, reckless spirits like himself, had gone so far as to seize upon a small town and hoist the flag of rebellion. Orleans, when he found affairs getting bad, and that he would be compelled to retreat, insisted that this had been done without his order or authority, and consequently, when he and his companions, being compelled to yield, received a general amnesty, the name of De Mauprat was erased from the pardon, Richelieu telling him to go and join the army then fighting against the Spaniards, and meet a soldier's fate rather than end his life upon a traitor's scaffold, beneath the headsman's axe. He proceeds to the seat of war, fights valiantly, and returns ; not to meet praise from the Cardinal, but the severest censure, with an intimation that though he has escaped the sword the axe may one day fall.

Upon this information, Baradas endeavors to induce him to side against the Cardinal, but De Mauprat knows his immense power and is proof against the temptation ; whereupon, Baradas hints artfully, that he loves the beautiful Julie de Mortemar, an orphan, under the Cardinal's protection, of whom he is himself deeply enamored. The shot is well aimed ; De Mauprat confesses to possess an antipathy to Richelieu, and at the same time admits his love for Julie—at this moment the order for his arrest arrives, and before further treaty can be made, he is conducted away.

Baradas rejoices ; in youth, strength valor, and now in love he had always been De Mauprat's inferior—but with his rival removed, success lay before him. Although the King, it was rumored, also loved Julie, he was determined to wed her—to become Minister of France—and by the aid of the parchment, when signed, and the assistance of the Duc de Bouillon and the Spanish Army he would accomplish ; dethrone the King, and " all in despite of my Lord Cardinal."

The scene then shifts to Richelieu's palace, where Joseph, a Capuchin monk, and his confidant, is acquainting him of the traitorous plot that is in progress—the parties concerned in it, and further, that the King has been charmed by Julie. Richelieu is grieved to hear this, but with a firm conceit and consciousness of his extraordinary power, he declares emphatically that the King must have no goddess but the State—and that State must be—himself ! Nothing daunted, Joseph asserts that the King, to conceal his love, and to bring Julie near him, intends to cause her to be married to Baradas. Richelieu determines to thwart this sacrifice, and vows that the only clasp round the neck of Baradas shall be the axe, and not the arms of his ward.

Julie arrives, and dispatching Joseph to his prayers, Richelieu feelingly tells her of her father's friendship, who, dying bequeathed her to his care, and that she shall find in him a second father, who will confer upon her a dowry of wealth, rank, and love worthy of the highest station. He closely and skillfully questions her of the attentions paid her by the King, Baradas and other courtiers, but without producing any effect, when Huguet, one of his officers, but also a spy against him, announces that the Chevalier de Mauprat waits an audience. Julie, thrown off her guard, starts at the name, and the Cardinal quickly detects the implied confession of love. He commands her to look higher for a match, and warns her that if she hates *his* foes, she *must* hate De Mauprat ; but she makes such an earnest appeal that his sternness is disarmed, and he consents to blot out his name from his list of foes.

Dismissing her into an adjoining chamber, he summons De Mauprat to his presence ; earnestly he reminds him of all the past events, and rebukes him bitterly for having since his return passed his time in wild and reckless living, and in a keen and smartly-telling speech, shows him that to live upon the means and labors of others, without the prospect of repaying them, is simply trickery and theft. His debts must be paid ; but when De Mauprat, answering boldly, says that he is ready to do so, but he should be glad to know where he can borrow the money, the humor of the Cardinal is touched, his severity relaxed, and he perceives at once that the Chevalier is exactly the man to serve the schemes he has in view, and prove a friend.

In one of the finest speeches in the play he tells him, though men say he is cruel, he is not so ; he is just, and portrays how he has reconstructed France, and from sloth and crime, raised her to wealth and power ; that France needs his aid—and though he came to meet him as a foe, he shall depart as a friend, with honor and wealth in store. De Mauprat is, very naturally, completely astounded at this sudden change ; under arrest, he came to the interview with the belief that after it, he should proceed to the Bastile and thence to the scaffold ; instead of which, there comes an offer of friendship and favor, nay, more, the Cardinal tells him he is aware of his love for Julie, and offers her in marriage. De Mauprat, feeling that the sentence of death still hangs over him, and that honor forbids the wedding, refuses. In apparent anger, the Cardinal directs his removal to the adjoining chamber (whither he has already sent Julie), and with mock solemnity bids him prepare to behold his execution—that his doom will be private—and to seek speedily for Heaven's mercy.

Summoning Joseph, the Cardinal gives orders for the preparation of the necessary deeds, and the arrangement of his house near the Luxembourg Palace, as a bridal present for his ward. Returning, overwhelmed with surprise and joy, De Mauprat and Julie receive his congratulations, and upon their departure, another brief but eloquent and thrilling speech, tells of the great man's power and his soul-binding, ardent love for his country.

> "France! I love thee!
> All earth sha'l never pluck thee from my hand!
> My mistress, France—my wedded wife—sweet France,
> Who shall proclaim divorce for thee and me?"

But the course of true love never did run smooth, and De Mauprat's case is no exception. Baradas has learned of the marriage—told the King, thus making him a foe to the husband, and exercising his influence, procures a royal warrant, forbidding De Mauprat communicating with Julie by word or letter, and so to continue until the formal annulment of the marriage is obtained, it being illegal. The sentence of death was still in force; Julie was a lady of the Court, and as such, according to the laws of France, could not lawfully be married without the King's permission. Armed with this order, Baradas repairs to De Mauprat's house immediately after the wedding, and meeting him, artfully and skillfully points out, that all which has taken place is only part of a wily, ambitious scheme of Richelieu's—the King loves Julie—to encourage this will increase the Cardinal's position and power—to avoid scandal she must first be married to some one, and in selecting De Mauprat, he had gratified two passions—ambition, by the grandeur of his ward, and vengeance by the dishonor of his foe. So skillfully, and with such subtlety is the story told that De Mauprat believes it; his anger is unbounded—again the tempter strikes, calling upon him to join the conspiracy; with Richelieu dead, and Baradas Prime Minister, all will be forgotten. Maddened with the thoughts of how basely he has been deceived, De Mauprat refuses to listen, and quits the spot; but not to escape. Another meeting is to take place to-night, when the compact is to be signed by all the League and forwarded to the Duc de Bouillon. Baradas determines that of this dispatch De Mauprat is to know nothing—he shall merely be posted as a sentry at the door—but he *shall* be the murderer of the Cardinal. At this moment, De Mauprat returns in a perfect state of frenzy. He has seen the King's carriage pass, and in the blindness of his passion, imagines he saw within it—Julie! Baradas promptly seizes the golden opportunity, and assures him that it was so. Mad with vengeance, De Mauprat believes him, consents to join the conspiracy, and swears that only the blood of Richelieu can obliterate the stain cast upon his honor.

In the meanwhile, Joseph has learned more of the proceedings, the plot for the assassination, and the intended meeting. The story rouses up all the latent energy of the great Minister; he speaks in glowing terms of the exploits of his youth, and bids his page bring to him the double-handed sword he once wielded with such force and skill. Alas! the strength of youth has fled. Sinking into his chair, he grasps his pen—that is now his weapon—and ruled by a master hand—

> "The pen is mightier than the sword!"

Marion arrives with further news of the meeting, and with the intimation that the Duke of Orleans had requested her to find a messenger upon whose fidelity she could rely, to convey dispatches that night to the Duc de Bouillon; and she had promised to send her brother. This is but a subterfuge to assist the Cardinal, to whom she leaves the selection; he chooses his favorite page, François, as being young, unnoted, faithful, brave, ambitious. He instructs him to arm himself, follow Marion, obtain the packet, and upon the fleetest steed he can procure, bring it to the Castle of Ruelle, whither the Cardinal intends to go for safety. He then questions Joseph as to the faithfulness of Huguet, who, unnoticed, enters, and overhears their conversation, by which he learns that certain honors he is expecting are to be promised to him but not granted. Breathing vengeance he retires unobserved; but returns shortly to receive instructions from the Cardinal to take steps for guarding every outlet and passage of the Castle. With triple walls, draw-bridge and portcullis, Huguet assures him that he can with twenty men hold out for a month against all comers, and he promises they shall be *well* chosen—from the conspirator's ranks.

It is midnight, and the Cardinal is at his castle, buried in deep meditation and waiting with great anxiety the coming of François. He does not wait long—François arrives, and falling at his feet, with bitter anguish tells him of the loss of the dispatch. Baradas had objected to his receiving it, but Orleans overcame his scruples, and giving it to him with a purse of gold, bade him hasten forward, promising him thousands more, when Bouillon's trumpets should sound through the streets of Paris.

As he mounted his horse, Marion came to him in the dark, and told him to speed well, for Orleans had sworn that before the morning dawned, Richelieu should cease to live. She fled, and at the same moment, a hand of iron fell upon him, and ere he could draw his sword, the packet was wrested from his keeping, whilst some one exclaimed, in a hoarse voice: "The spy is spared—the steel is for his lord!"

Although almost overwhelmed, Richelieu, in the greatness of his powerful intellect, is not subdued. The dispatch may yet be recovered; and telling François he has lost that which would have saved his country and made him great, he bids him away, and strive to regain it ; never to see him again until, by recovering it, he has acquired the right to do so—always bearing in mind there is no such word as "fail."

After his departure, Julie reaches the castle. In bitter anguish, she informs Richelieu that scarcely was she married when the King summoned her to the palace —told her the ceremony was unlawful—compelled her to remain—had even sought her chamber, making overtures she had indignantly repulsed. Not content with this, Baradas had approached her, and declared his love, but finding himself repulsed and defeated, he told her that De Mauprat was aware of the King's passion, and had only married her to further his own ends, by placing her in the King's power. In the moment of agony, she applied to the Queen, revealing everything, and by her aid, she was enabled to quit the palace. Hastening home—she found no home—all was desolate—no husband was there to meet her—and not being aware of his arrest, she believed him guilty, and had fled to the Cardinal for protection. Richelieu can hardly bring his mind to suspect De Mauprat ; he endeavors to soothe Julie, and conducts her to rest. The conspirators have entered the castle, and upon returning to the chamber, he meets De Mauprat, disguised in a suit of armor with his vizor down, who seizes him. In vain he calls for his guards! With a vigorous effort he releases himself, and in a fine burst of passionate eloquence, he tells him that Richelieu dies not by the hand of man—that there is no fiend created who would be a parricide of his native land by daring, in killing Richelieu, to murder France.

In bitter terms, De Mauprat taunts him with having spared a young soldier, then given him a mock pardon—and afterwards an angel for a bride, only to heap upon him dishonor and disgrace. No mercy could now be expected—retribution for the young soldier must follow, and the avenger was himself—De Mauprat. But the grand old Minister is cool and undaunted ; with stern dignity he orders his assailant to kneel and crawl for pardon ; he tells him that what he had done was to save Julie from the King, by giving her a brave and noble husband ; that she had been sheltered by him when her husband should have done it, and that she was now in the adjoining chamber ; from whence she enters to the amazement of the Chevalier.

In a few words the fearful deception is explained, and the treachery of Baradas revealed. De Mauprat informs the Cardinal of his danger—that his guards are not his trusty soldiers, but disguised conspirators of whom Huguet is captain. Loud shouts of "Death to the Cardinal!" are heard ; quick as lightning, De Mauprat and Julie hurry him away, and when Huguet and the other conspirators rush into the chamber, De Mauprat reappears from an adjoining room, and guarding the doorway, so that none may pass, he points to a couch at the other side of the room, upon which the Cardinal is laying apparently dead. He tells them that he strangled him so softly in his sleep, that all the world will say he died a natural death from exhausted nature, and he bids them hasten to Paris with the news, whilst he remains to lull suspicion and prepare for the interment.

The intelligence is swiftly borne to Baradas—now is the time for him to turn—Julie must be recovered—he has obtained another warrant for the arrest of De Mauprat—Marion de Lorme is in prison—and when Huguet, full of haste, rushes in to tell him of the murder, he calls the guard, and in spite of his struggles, and in spite of his attempts to inform him that he has something of importance to communicate—in fact, the missing packet—he is borne away to the Bastile. François returns to tell of the loss, and from the circumstance of the man who took the dispatch, from him being in armor, suspicion at once falls upon De Mauprat, whom Baradas tells François to find without the least delay. Fortune throws them together in a remote part of the palace gardens—and François making known who he is, De Mauprat tells him that whilst watching at the house, thinking he was a spy, he had seized the packet—and that since then he he had given it to—Huguet, he would have said—but at that moment he catches sight of Baradas approaching—drawing his sword, he rushes to attack him, but is seized by the guards, and prevented completing his story. But the dead come to life—astonished and amazed, they behold Richelieu appear upon the scene. Taking the writ, he appeals to the King for clemency, but without success, and De Mauprat is led off, not, however, before he tells François that he gave the packet to Huguet.

In a speech of magnificent force and eloquence, Richelieu calls upon the King to bear in mind all he has done for him, and for France—to do him justice—and to grant him protection. In vain the appeal; only when he sees him throw off his haughty bearing and kneels at the throne, will the King listen to his entreaties.

Now is the moment that Richelieu feels the bitterness of the struggle—yesterday he was the Cardinal King, the lord of life and death—to-day, a very weak old man. Only the possession of the dispatch can save him.

Returning to the palace, the King sends Clermont with an order for Julie to present herself before him, but she refuses to go, and in this Richelieu upholds her. Baradas arrives with a stern and positive command, when in one of the finest and most telling speeches in the play, Richelieu hurls defiance at the King, and dares him to take her from his protection under the penalty of the curse of Rome.

The excitement is too much, and the Cardinal sinks exhausted beneath it.

Baradas believes that De Mauprat has the dispatch, but he does not like to have him searched, fearing that if it should be found upon him open, as it undoubtedly would be, the contents would be read and made use of against his party. He cannot yet visit him personally, being obliged to keep close to the King night and day, to prevent any of the Cardinal's friends approaching him and whispering in his ear words which might disturb his influence and thwart his schemes. He looks upon Huguet's story as a mere trick to secure a respite, but to make sure, he sends De Beringhen to look into the matter. François, too, determined to redeem his honor, tries his utmost to obtain admission to Huguet, and for that purpose hovers about the prison gates, pretending to be his son. Joseph also makes every effort, but not even the threats of punishment from the church can move the Governor to depart from the rules. " Fortune favors the brave," and so it does in this case—De Beringhen arrives with an order to visit the prisoner, and being won over by the pathetic appeal of the presumed son, agrees to let him accompany him. Thrown off his guard by the order, and De Beringhen's entreaties that the boy may have a last word with his parent, the Governor tacitly consents, hinting that if when his lordship comes out the boy should slip in without his noticing him it is not his fault—it he does not see it, he cannot help it, and he will therefore go his rounds.

De Beringhen enters the prisoner's cell, and with beating heart, does François look through the key-hole. He hears high words between De Beringhen and Huguet—the cell is dimly lighted—they struggle in spite of Huguet's chains—but De Beringhen secures the packet. François hides behind the door, and lets him pass into the dark corridor when, dagger in hand, he springs upon him, tears the packet from his grasp and makes his escape.

In the last scene, we find the Court and all the leading conspirators assembled, laying plans for future operations.

The King, thinking she has changed her views, grants an audience to Julie, but she comes to appeal for her husband's pardon, which she does in exquisitely written, eloquent, and fervent language.

The King is moved, and directs Baradas to speak with her. He does so, and offers that if she will annul the marriage and become his wife, the same day shall D: Mauprat be free. With scorn and indignation, the chance is rejected, upon which he summons the guards and their prisoner, who assures Julie that life is short but love is immortal. As he is being led off, the Cardinal arrives, supported by Joseph, and apparently sinking fast. He appeals to Baradas in his present high position, to grant him one favor—De Mauprat's life. But the stakes are too heavy—" My head," replies the Minister, " I cannot lose one trick."

Seizing the opportunity of the King's return, the Cardinal, to the amazement of all assembled, announces his resignation, and calls upon his under secretaries to read their reports. They show such a state of trouble, revolt, and ruin in all the surrounding countries, whilst France alone is firm, made so, by Richelieu's skillful hand, that the King shudders to think there is no master mind like his to succeed him.

At this moment, François enters, and as he hands the dispatch to Richelieu observes lowly, " I have not failed." In an instant it is placed in the King's hands. With horror and dismay the conspirators hear it read, and their names repeated. The hour of triumph is too much for the Cardinal, who sinks exhausted, as a I think, dying. The King passionately implores him to live, if not for his sake, for his country—for France! Like a magician's charm does the word fall upon his ears, and with a superhuman power, all his latent energies revive. Orders are sent forth for the arrest of the Duc de Bouillon at the head of his army—one by one, the conspirators are dispatched to their doom—the death writ of De Mauprat thrown to the winds—happiness restored—and the Cardinal Minister, greater than ever, exclaims ;

> " My own dear France—I have thee yet—I have saved thee !
> I clasp thee still—it was thy voice that call'd me
> Back from the tomb ! What mistress like our country ?"

REMARKS.

THE few observations addressed to the reader of the Lady of Lyons (the first of the present new series of Bulwer's plays) are sufficient notes of the merits and high intellectual attainments and ability of the distinguished author of the two plays.

So enthusiastically was the Lady of Lyons received, so decided was its success in London and the Provinces, as well as in the United States, that he was encouraged speedily to attempt another play. Choosing for his theme a broader and a grander basis, he selected the History of France at a great and momentous period, to furnish the requisite materials.

Within twelve months after the successful launch of the Lady of Lyons, viz: in March, 1839, the literary and dramatic world were gratified by the production of one of the finest written and most skillfully constructed historical plays at any time offered to the public.

It was produced at the same establishment—the Theatre Royal, Covent Garden, London—and by a comparison of the cast of characters, it will be seen that many of the leading actors in that play appeared in this—in parts, equally, if not more, effective ; at any rate of a different and more powerful nature, calling forth all their energy and ability, and judging from the criticisms of the time, they were not found wanting.

In the United States, where it made its appearance very soon afterwards, only *one* of the actors in the Lady of Lyons appeared in Richelieu—but he was a host in himself—Edwin Forrest.

The author's preface to this play is more lengthy than to the former one, and is so beautifully and so clearly worded, that it would be the height of presumption to attempt to interfere with it. But a succinct account of the events previous to the commencement of the play, and the exact position of the chief persons, may prove interesting and afford the reader additional means for obtaining a clearer and more thorough knowledge of the story, and a keener and higher appreciation of the author's powers of dealing with his subject.

On the 13th of May, 1610, whilst Henry IV., King of France, was proceeding in his carriage through the Rue de la Ferroniere, a man named François Ravaillac, mounted upon the wheel and aimed a deadly blow at his side, a second followed, which reached his heart, and he immediately expired.

Louis XIII., who succeeded, was then nine years of age, and measures were instantly taken for placing the Regency in the hands of his mother, Mary De Medicis. It was not long, however, before matters assumed a very different aspect to that which had previously existed..

The government of a woman, and that woman a foreigner, could not maintain the lofty tone and vigor which had marked the reign of Henry. The Queen was a person of weak character and narrow understanding, ruled entirely by favorites and confidants. The usual consequences ensured—rival factions and internal disorder. In 1614, Louis attained his majority, when the body of Deputies and others known as the States General were assembled, and as one of the representatives of the clergy, then appeared Armand Duplessis de Richelieu, at that time Bishop of Luçon. To strengthen the government, it was determined to marry the young king to the Infanta Anne of Austria, a measure violently opposed by the Prince of Condé, then in great power, but warmly supported by the Queen Mother and Richelieu, who was silently, but surely, working his way to power, and by his advice, the Court took the bold step of arresting the Prince of Condé, and others of the nobility saved themselves by flight; riots took place in the City, but were soon suppressed, and Richelieu, for his good services, was made Secretary of State. He was a firm ally of the Queen Mother, supporting her strongly against all opposing factions. The military successes were great, but notwithstanding this, the Government fell into a lamentable state of weakness.

The King's chief advisers all stood in awe of Richelieu, whose commanding genius was apparent; but in spite of all opposition, the Queen Mother compelled Louis, in 1622, to make Richelieu a cardinal. Affairs grew worse and more unsteady, the King disliked the Cardinal, but under the importunities of the Queen Mother, he summoned him to his Council. He had not been in office six months before his supremacy was universally recognized ; the irresistible energy of his character, and extraordinary capacity for government, won their way. Attaining this high position, he started principles which he pursued vigorously through life, the annihilation of the Huguenots as a political party, the complete subjugation of the nobility to the royal authority, and the restoration of France to her predominant influence throughout Europe.

The first plot against him was in 1626, by Gaston, the King's only brother, and then Duke of Anjou ; but being detected, and being a mixture of weakness, cowardice and baseness, he betrayed his accomplices, for which the King was weak enough to make him Duke of Orleans and give him large revenues. Richelieu had his revenge by the execution or banishment of the other conspirators, and the triumph over this plot established his supremacy. From step to step he rose to greater fame, and notwithstanding his exalted rank and ecclesiastical character, he personally undertook the military operations at the siege of La Rochelle, and proved he possessed all the qualities of a great commander. In 1629, he was invested with the most extraordinary powers under the title of "Lieutenant General, representing the King's person." He assumed the supreme command of the army, and during 1630 fortress after fortress, in Italy and Savoy, fell before the French forces.

In 1637 another conspiracy was formed against him by the Duke of Orleans, which only failed through indecision. Richelieu was ill, a council was held at his residence ; unsuspectingly he descended the staircase surrounded by the conspirators, and at this moment his fate hung upon a thread. Gastou's nerve failed him, he hesitated to give the appointed signal, the others would not strike without orders, so the Cardinal escaped. Well might the noble author of the play put into the mouth of his hero the words :

> " Armand de Richelieu dies not by the hand
> Of man—the stars have said it—and the voice
> Of my own prophetic and oracular soul
> Confirms the shining Sibyls !"

In the year 1638, Richelieu received a severe blow by the death of his confidant, the Capuchin Joseph du Tremblay, who was a personage scarcely less remarkable in his own line, than Richelieu himself. He had been employed in all the most difficult and political negotiations of the time, performing his duties with unswerving fidelity to his master and the interests of France.

The King's health, always feeble, was now much impaired, and Richelieu began to reckon with certainty upon obtaining the Regency. But another attempt against him was to come. He had placed near the King, in the quality of Equerry, a gay and brilliant young nobleman, the Marquis of Cinq Mars, who quickly ingratiated himself with Louis, so much so, as to force his way into the Council Chamber, from which Richelieu at last sternly excluded him. From that moment, Cinq Mars exerted all his influence to ruin the Cardinal—enlisting all the Minister's ancient enemies, more or less, in the plot. Louis was attacked with a fit of illness, and to strengthen their position, in case of his death, they entered into a treaty with the Court of Spain, to assist them with troops and money, in return for which the King of Spain was to receive back all the places conquered by France.

In 1642, Louis and Richelieu, both in feeble health, journeyed towards the army of the south, but Richelieu became so unwell that he was compelled to remain at Narbonne, while the King went on. But Louis soon tired of command ; he found, that in the absence of Richelieu, he could depend upon no one for the conduct of affairs, and a messenger was dispatched to the Cardinal, assuring him that he stood higher than ever in the King's favor. At this moment, by a singular stroke of good fortune, Richelieu received from some unknown hand, a copy of the treaty—it was laid before the King—arrests ordered—additional powers given to Richelieu, and while Louis returned to Paris, the Cardinal embarked in a magnificent barge upon the Rhone, dragging in a boat behind him, Cinq Mars, and François du Thou, son of a celebrated historian of the time, and proceeded to Lyons, where they were tried and executed, Sept. 12th, 1642—the contemptible Duke of Orleans betraying his associates as usual, by acknowledging the treaty. He was, however, deprived of his dignity and domains, and banished, as was the case also with the Duc de Bouillon.

Everywhere now was Richelieu triumphant, but the end came. On returning to Paris, the ravages of a mortal disease, from which he had long suffered, reached a climax. On his death-bed he called God to witness that he had pursued no other object than the welfare of the church and of the kingdom ; and being asked whether he forgave his enemies, he replied he never had any except those who were enemies of the State.

He died Dec. 4th, 1642, at 58 years of age, and in May, 1643, Louis XIII. followed him.

Upon these facts (but as the author frankly observes, taking a little liberty with dates, etc.), is the play founded—a play, which is replete with action, interest and poetry. It is interesting to compare these historical facts with the story of the play, and see with what skill and ingenuity the author has constructed it.

Resuming the remarks, all the actors mentioned in the " Remarks " to the Lady of Lyons as appearing as Claude Melnotte, followed Macready's steps in this play, and it is therefore unnecessary to repeat here the observations regarding them which appear in those remarks, as they are equally applicable to their delineation of the character of Richelieu.

It was the same, also, in the United States. The play was produced at Wallack's Old National Theatre, New York, on Sept. 4th, 1839, with the great Edwin Forrest as the hero, and his keen appreciation and masterly execution of the telling beauties of the character, secured for him a success and fame unprecedented. He was followed by many others, well known to fame, and lastly by Mr. E. L. Davenport, who must be admitted to be as good a Richelieu as any on the stage, and probably the best in the United States.

The character of Richelieu, it will be observed upon close scrutiny, requires very great ability and power on the part of the actor to portray it with effect. There are so many sides of the wily but fearless old Cardinal—craftiness, courage, humor, infirmities, vanity, and potency of will, even to the very last all these passions require clean and delicate handling. There is little doubt that Macready on the English and Edwin Forrest on the American boards were two of the finest representatives of Richelieu on the stage, and that the present ones are Mr. Phelps (who was the original Joseph in the first representation in London) and Mr. E. L. Davenport.

The part of De Mauprat was originally filled in London by Mr. James Anderson, who afterwards rose to be himself a fine delineator of the leading character of the play, as well as of a large range of other characters. Indeed, that was the case with many others of the actors in the original cast. Then again the elegant and accomplished Miss Helen Faucit, who had made such a hit the preceding year as Pauline, in the Lady of Lyons, once more established herself as a great favorite in the part of Julie de Mortemar. There were probably also never a finer Joseph on the stage than Mr. Phelps, now the English father of Tragedians. So it will be seen that, as in the Lady of Lyons, not only was the leading character sustained by the greatest actor of the day, but he was well and effectively supported in every part by persons who must have rendered the characters well, as they afterwards advanced to the first rank of the profession.

At the Old National Theatre, Mr. J. W. Wallack, Jr., in the character of De Mauprat made a great hit. He was handsome in face and person, like all of the family, and capable, like most of his name, of appearing to the best possible advantage where action, fine and correct attitude and spirited declamation are needed. De Mauprat is brave, gay, and spirited—he is prompt to anger, easily aroused when he feels his honor at stake, and as easily subdued when convinced that he is in error. It is very probable that the stage has never had a finer De Mauprat than Mr. J. W. Wallack, Jr. He married a Miss Waring in 1842, visited London in 1851, succeeding Mr. Macready at the Haymarket Theatre, and he was afterwards manager of the Marylebone Theatre there.

Miss Monier, the original Julie here, was one of the most beautiful and accomplished girls of the period, and the daughter of parents who had been attached to the American stage for years. In 1836, after an absence of eight years, she reappeared in New York (where she had previously played as a child), and a more lovely face and form seldom graced the stage. For a short time she was the proprietor of a little theatre on Broadway, opposite St. Paul's Church, called "Miss Monier's Dramatic Saloon." In 1838 she succeeded Miss E. Wheatley at Wallack's, where she remained until its destruction in 1839. She afterwards married Captain Wynne of the British Army, appeared at Drury Lane Theatre, London, in July, 1846, as Mrs. Haller in "The Stranger," and then retired. So much for the original Julie, De Mauprat, and Richelieu.   J. M. K.

BILL FOR PROGRAMMES.

The events take place in the city of Paris, and the environs, and at the Castle of Ruelle, two leagues from Paris. Period, 1642.

ACT I.—The First Day.

Scene I.—ROOM IN THE HOUSE OF MARION DE LORME.

The Meeting of the Conspirators—The Female Spy—The Chevalier de Mauprat's Last Stake—The History of a Court Gallant——A Cardinal's Trick—Arrest of the Chevalier—A Rival's Triumph.

Scene II —A ROOM IN THE CARDINAL'S PALACE.

Richelieu and his Priestly Confidant—The Cardinal's Ward—A Story of Love—A Lesson to Youth—From an Enemy to a Friend—From a Lover to a Husband.

ACT II.—The Second Day.

Scene I.—APARTMENT IN THE CHEVALIER DE MAUPRAT'S NEW HOUSE.

A Bride but no Wife—The Royal Warrant—The King Loves Julie—The Trap Baited for a new Victim—The King Against the Cardinal—A Husband's Jealousy—The Compact of Death!

Scene II.—A ROOM IN THE CARDINAL'S PALACE.

The First Story of the Conspiracy—Which is to Win?—The Prowess of a Youthful Knight, but now an aged Minister—" The pen is mightier than the sword"—The Story of Marion de Lorme—The Tale of Treachery Divulged—The Trusty Messenger shall be the Page Francois—An Officer and a Traitor—The Prey upon the Alert.

ACT III.—The Second Day. Midnight.

Scene I.—RICHELIEU'S CASTLE AT RUELLE.

The Story of the Lost Dispatch—Away on the Search—There's no such word as " Fail"—The Story of an Insulted Wife—A Libertine King and a False Friend—The Mysterious Visitor—The Story of Vengeance and of Death—Discovery of the Snare—Approach of the Conspirators—The Flight and Supposed Death of Richelieu.

Scene II.—*Triumph of Baradas—Again the Lost Dispatch—The Chevalier de Mauprat Suspected—To-morrow France is Ours!*

ACT IV.—The Third Day.

Scene I.—THE GARDENS OF THE LOUVRE.

The King and the Conspirator—The Page and the Chevalier—Again the Lost Dispatch—The Mystery—The false Friend—Arrest of the Chevalier de Mauprat again—The Dead come to Life—The Appeal for Mercy— Again the Dispatch—An Appeal for Justice—The Star of Richelieu on the Wane—" Yesterday the Cardinal King ; to-day a very weak old man." —The King's commands to Julie—The Cardinal's Holy Shelter—" Power is my Stake, thy head is thine "—Who will Win the Trick ?

ACT V.—The Fourth Day.

SCENE I.—A CORRIDOR IN THE BASTILE.

Again the lost Dispatch—Father Joseph's attempt Foiled—A Page's Cunning—Filial Affection—A Courtier Snared—The Seizure—The Struggle and the Dispatch Secured.

SCENE II.—THE KING'S CLOSET AT THE PALACE OF THE LOUVRE.

Conspiracy in the Ascendant—A Wife's Appeal for Pardon—A Royal Favorite's Offer—The Hand or the Grave—"I or thy Husband?"—Virtue and Firmness—Richelieu to the Rescue—The Resignation—The Sinking Minister—"All is Safe!"—The Conspirators Gain—The Last Moment—Arrival of the Page with the lost Dispatch—"I have not failed"—Denouncement of the Traitors—Pardon of the Chevalier de Mauprat—Arrest of the Conspirators and Triumph of the Cardinal
RICHELIEU.

EXPLANATION OF THE STAGE DIRECTIONS.

The Actor is supposed to face the Audience.

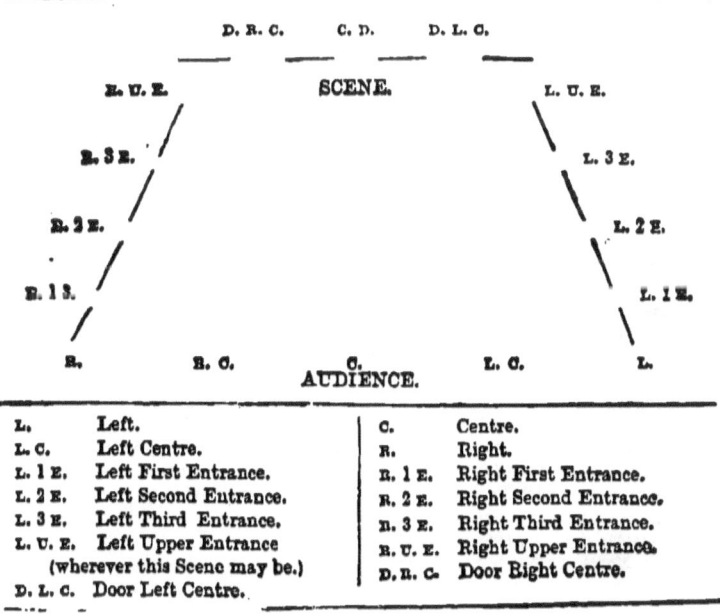

L.	Left.	C.	Centre.
L. C.	Left Centre.	R.	Right.
L. 1 E.	Left First Entrance.	R. 1 E.	Right First Entrance.
L. 2 E.	Left Second Entrance.	R. 2 E.	Right Second Entrance.
L. 3 E.	Left Third Entrance.	R. 3 E.	Right Third Entrance.
L. U. E.	Left Upper Entrance	R. U. E.	Right Upper Entrance.
	(wherever this Scene may be.)	D. R. C.	Door Right Centre.
D. L. C.	Door Left Centre.		

AUTHOR'S PREFACE.

THE administration of Cardinal Richelieu, whom (despite all his darker qualities) Voltaire and History justly consider the true architect of the French monarchy, and the great parent of French civilization, is characterized by features alike tragic and comic. A weak king—an ambitious favorite ; a despicable conspiracy against the minister, nearly always associated with a dangerous treason against the State—these, with little variety of names and dates, constitute the eventful cycle through which, with a dazzling case, and an arrogant confidence, the great luminary fulfilled its destinies. Blent together, in startling contrast, we see the grandest achievements and the pettiest agents—the spy—the mistress—the capuchin—the destruction of feudalism—the humiliation of Austria—the dismemberment of Spain.

Richelieu himself is still what he was in his own day—a man of two characters. If, on the one hand, he is justly represented as inflexible and vindictive, crafty and unscrupulous ; so, on the other, it cannot be denied that he was placed in times in which the long impunity of every license required stern examples—that he was beset by perils and intrigues, which gave a certain excuse to the subtlest inventions of self-defence—that his ambition was inseparably connected with a passionate love for the glory of his country—and that, if he was her dictator, he was not less her benefac'or. It has been fairly remarked, by the most impartial historians, that he was no less generous to merit than severe to crime—that in the various departments of the State, the Army, and the Church, he selected and distinguished the ablest aspirants—that the wars which he conducted were, for the most part, essential to the preservation of France, and Europe itself, from the formidable encroachments of the Austrain House—that, in spite of those wars, the people were not oppressed with exorbitant imposts—and that he left the kingdom he had governed in a more flourishing and vigorous state than at any former period of the French history, or at the decease of Louis XIV.

The cabals formed against this great statesman were not carried on by the patriotism of public virtue, or the emulation of equal talent ; they were but court struggles, in which the most worthless agents had recourse to the most desperate means. In each, as I have before observed, we see combined the twofold attempt to murder the minister and to betray the country. Such, then, are the agents, and such the designs, with which truth, in the Drama as in history, requires us to contrast the celebrated Cardinal—not disguising his foibles or his vices, but not unjust to the grander qualities (especially the love of country), by which they were often dignified, and, at times redeemed.

The historical drama is the concentration of historical events. In the attempt to place upon the stage the picture of an era, that license with dates and details which Poetry permits, and which the highest authorities in the Drama of France herself have sanctioned, has been, though not unsparingly, indulged. The conspiracy of the Duc de Bouillon is, for instance, amalgamated with the *dénouement* of *The Day of Dupes;* and circumstances connected with the treason of Cinq Mars (whose brilliant youth and gloomy catastrophe tend to subvert poetic and historic justice, by seducing us to forget his base ingratitude and his perfidious apostasy) are identified with the fate of the earlier favorite Baradas, whose sudden rise and as sudden fall passed into a proverb. I ought to add, that the noble romance of " Cinq Mars " suggested one of the scenes in the fifth act ; and that for the conception of some portion of the intrigue connected with De Mauprat and Julie, I am, with great alterations of incident, and considerable if not entire reconstruction of character, indebted to an early and admirable novel by the author of " Picciola."

London, March, 1839.

RICHELIEU;

OR, THE CONSPIRACY.

ACT I.

FIRST DAY.

SCENE I.—*A handsomely furnished room in the house of* MARION DE LORME ; *entrance* L. C., *hung with tapestry ; a table* R. (*with wine, fruits, etc.*). *at which are seated* BARADAS, L *of table, four* COURTIERS, *splendidly dressed in the costume of* 1641-2 ; *the* DUKE OF ORLEANS *seated* R. ; MARION DE LORME *standing at the back of his chair, offers him a goblet, and then retires. At another table,* L., DE BERINGHEN, DE MAUPRAT, *playing at dice ;* CLERMONT *and other* COURTIERS *looking on.*

ORLEANS (R. *of table, drinking*). Here's to our enterprise !
BARADAS (L. *of table, glancing at* MARION).   Hush. sir !
ORLEANS (*aside*).   Nay, Count,
     You may trust her ; she doats on me ; no house
     So safe as Marion's.
BAR.   Still, we have a secret.
     And oil and water—woman and a secret—
     Are hostile properties. (*noise of playing at* L. *table.*)
ORLEANS.   Well—Marion, see
     How the play prospers yonder.
     [MARION *goes to the* L. *table, looks on for a few moments, then exits,* L. C.
BAR. (*producing a parchment*).   I have now
     All the conditions drawn ; it only needs
     Our signatures ; upon receipt of this
     (Whereto is joined the schedule of our treaty
     With the Count-Duke, the Richelieu of the Escurial)
     Bouillon will join his army with the Spaniard,
     March on to Paris—there dethrone the King ;
     You will be Regent ; I, and ye, my Lords,
     Form the new Council. So much for the core
     Of our great scheme. (*noise at* L. *table.*)
ORLEANS.   But Richelieu is an Argus ;
     One of his hundred eyes will light upon us,
     And then—good-bye to life
BAR.   To gain the prize
     We must destroy the Argus. Ay, my Lords,
     The scroll the core, but blood must fill the veins,
     Of our design ;—while this dispatch'd to Bouillon,
     Richelieu dispatch'd to heaven ! The last *my* charge.
     Meet here to-morrow night. *You*, sir, as first

In honor and in hope, meanwhile select
Some trusty knave to bear the scroll to Bouillon;
Midst Richelieu's foes *I'll* find some desperate hand
To strike for vengeance, while we stride to power.
ORLEANS. So be it; to-morrow, midnight.—Come, my Lords.

Exeunt ORLEANS *and the* COURTIERS *in h s train,* L. C.   *Those at 'he* L. *table rise, salute* ORLEANS, *and re-seat themselves.* .

DE BER. Double the stakes.   .
DE MAU.   Done. (*throws.*)
DE BER.   Bravo! faith, it shames me
To bleed a purse already at its last gasp.
DE MAU. Nay, as you've had the patient to yourself
So long, no other doctor shall dispatch it. (DE MAUPRAT *throws.*)
OMNES. Lost! Ha, ha!—poor De Mauprat!
DE BER.   One throw more?
DE MAU. No; I am bankrupt. (*pushing gold*) There goes all—except
My honor and my sword. (*they rise ; he crosses* R.)
CLER.   Ay, take the sword
To Cardinal Richelieu; he gives gold for steel,
When worn by brave men.
DE MAU.   Richelieu!
DE BER. (*to* BARADAS).   At that name
He changes color, bites his nether lip.
Even in his brightest moments whisper "Richelieu,'
And you cloud all his sunshine.
BAR.   I have mark'd it,
And will learn the wherefore.
DE MAU. (*going to table,* R.).   The Egyptian
Dissolved her richest jewel in a draught;
Would I could so melt time and all its treasures,
And drain it thus. (*drinking.*)
DE BER.   Come, gentlemen, what say ye,
A walk on the parade?
CLER.   Ay; come, De Mauprat.
DE MAU. Pardon me; we shall meet again ere night-fall.
DE BER. Come, Baradas.
BAR.   I'll stay and comfort Mauprat.
DE BER.   '   Comfort!—when
We gallant fellows have run out a friend,
There's nothing left—except to run him through!
There's the last act of friendship.
DE MAU.   Let me keep
That favor in reserve ; in all besides
Your most obedient servant. [*Exeunt* DE BERINGHEN, *etc.,* L. C.
BAR. (L. C.).   You have lost—   '
Yet are not sad.
DE MAU.   Sad! Life and gold hath wings,
And must fly one day ; open, then, their cages
And wish them merry.
BAR.   You're a strange enigma—
Fiery in war—and yet to glory lukewarm ;
All mirth in action—in repose all gloom—
Fortune of late has sever'd us—and led
Me to the rank of Courtier, Count, and Favorite,
You to the titles of the wildest gallant

And bravest knight in France ; are you content ?
    (MAUPRAT *goes up and sits* L. *of* R. *table*)
No ;—trust in me—some gloomy secret——

DE MAU.   Ay—
A secret that doth haunt me, as, of old,
Men were possess'd of fiends ! (*rises*) Where'er I turn,
The grave yawns dark before me ! (*crosses* L.) I *will* trust you ;—
Hating the Cardinal, and beguiled by Orleans,
You know I joined the Languedoc revolt—
Was captured—sent to the Bastile——

BAR.   But shared
The general pardon, which the Duke of Orleans
Won for himself and all in the revolt,
Who but obey'd his orders.

DE MAU.   Note the phrase ;—
" *Obey'd his orders.*" Well, when on my way
To join the Duke in Languedoc, I (then
The down upon my lip—less man than boy)
Leading young valors—reckless as myself,
Seized on the town of Faviaux, and displaced
The Royal banners for the Rebel. Orleans
(Never too daring), when I reach'd the camp,
Blamed me for acting—mark—*without his orders ;*
Upon this quibble Richelieu razed my name
Out of the general pardon.

BAR.   Yet released you
From the Bastile——

DE MAU.   To call me to his presence,
And thus address me—" You have seized a town
Of France, without the orders of your leader,
And for this treason, but one sentence—DEATH."

BAR. Death !

DE MAU.   " I have pity on your youth and birth,
Nor wish to glut the headsman—join your troop,
Now on the march against the Spaniards—change
The traitor's scaffold for the soldier's grave—
Your memory stainless—they who shared your crime
Exiled or dead—your king shall never learn it."

BAR.   Well ?

DE MAU. You heard if I fought bravely. When the Cardinal
Review'd the troops—his eye met mine—he frown'd,
Summon'd me forth—" How's this ?" quoth he ; " you have
    shunn'd
The sword—beware the axe—'twill fall one day !"
He left me thus—we were recall'd to Paris,
And—you know all !

BAR.   And knowing this, why halt you,
Spell'd by the rattle-snake—while in the breasts
Of your firm friends beat hearts, that vow the death
Of your grim tyrant ? Wake ! Be one of us ;
The time invites—the King detests the Cardinal,
Dares not disgrace—but groans to be deliver'd
Of that too great a subject—join your friends,
Free France, and save yourself.

DE MAU.   Hush ! Richelieu bears
A charm'd life—to all, who have braved his power,
One common end—the block.

BAR.   Nay, if he live,
    The block your doom !
DE MAU.   Better the victim, Count,
    Than the assassin.   France requires a Richelieu,
    But does not need a Mauprat.   Truce to this—
    All time one midnight, where my thoughts are spectres.
    What to me fame ?   What love ? (*crosses gloomily to* R.)
BAR.   Yet dost thou love *not* ?
DE MAU. Love ? I am young——
BAR. And Julie fair ! (DE MAUPRAT *sinks into a chair*, R. *Aside*) It is so,
    Upon the margin of the grave—his hand
    Would pluck the rose that I would win and wear.
DE MAU. (*starting up gayly*). Since you have one secret, take the other;
        Never
    Unbury either !   Come (*crosses* L., *and takes his hat from table*)
    while yet we may,
    We'll bask us in the noon of rosy life—
    Lounge through the gardens—flaunt it in the taverns—
    Laugh—game—drink—feast—if so confined my days,
    Faith, I'll enclose the nights! (*goes to* BARADAS, *who is* R.) Pshaw !
            not so grave ;
    I'm a true Frenchman !   *Vive la bagatelle !*

As they are going out, enter HUGUET *and four* ARQUEBUSIERS, L. C.; *they*
    range at the back of the entrance. HUGUET *enters the chamber.*

HUGUET. Messire de Mauprat—I arrest you !   Follow
    To the Lord Cardinal.
DE MAU. (R. C).   You see, my friend,
    I'm out of my suspense—the tiger's play'd
    Long enough with his prey. (*gives his sword to* HUGUET) Farewell !
        Hereafter
    Say, when men name me, " Adrien de Mauprat.
    Lived without hope, and perished without fear."
                        [*Exeunt* DE MAUPRAT, HUGUET, *etc.*, L. C.
BAR. Farewell—I trust forever !   I design'd thee
    For Richelieu's murderer—but, as well his martyr!
    In childhood you the stronger—and I cursed you !
    In youth the fairer—and I cursed you still ;
    And now my rival !   While the name of Julie
    Hung on thy lips—I smiled—for then I saw,
    In my mind's eye, the cold and grinning Death
    Hang o'er thy head the pall !   By the King's aid
    I will be Julie's husband '—in despite
    Of my Lord Cardinal !—by the King's aid
    I will be Minister of France !—in spite
    Of my Lord Cardinal !   And then—what then ?
    The King loves Julie—feeble Prince—false master—(*producing*
    the parchment)
    Then, by the aid of Bouillon, and the Spaniard,
    I will dethrone the King ; and all—ha—ha—
    All, in despite of my Lord Cardinal.   [*Exit*, L.

SCENE II.—*A room in the Palais Cardinal, the walls hung with arras.   A*
    large screen, R. U. E., *a door behind the arras,* L U. E.—*doors* L. H *and*
    R. H.   *A table covered with books, papers, etc.,* C   *A rude clock in a*
    recess.   Busts, statues, book-cases, weapons of different periods, and ban-

ners suspended over RICHELIEU'S *chair. A panoply, a small and a two-handed sword,* R.

RICHELIEU *and* JOSEPH, R. D.

RICH. And so you think this new conspiracy
The craftiest trap yet laid for the old fox?—
Fox! Well, I like the nickname! What did Plutarch
Say of the Greek Lysander?

JOSEPH.   I forget.

RICH. That where the Lion's skin fell short, he eked it
Out with the fox's! A great statesman, Joseph,
That same Lysander!

JOS.   Orleans heads the traitors.

RICH. A very wooden head then! Well?

JOS.   The favorite,
Count Baradas——

RICH.   A weed of hasty growth;
First gentleman of the chamber—titles, lands,
And the King's ear! It cost me six long winters
To mount as high as in six little moons
This painted lizard——But I hold the ladder,
And when I shake—he falls! What more?

JOS. Your ward has charmed the King——

RICH.   Out on you.
Have I not, one by one, from such fair shoots
Pluck'd the insidious ivy of his love?
And shall it creep around my blossoming tree
Where innocent thoughts, like happy birds, make music
That spirits in heaven might hear? The King must have
No goddess but the State—the State—that's Richelieu! (*crosses
and sits* R. *of table.*)

JOS. (L.). This is not the worst—Louis, in all decorous,
And deeming you her least compliant guardian,
Would veil his suit by marriage with his minion,
Your prosperous foe, Count Baradas!

RICH.   Ha, ha!
I have another bride for Baradas.

JOS. You, my Lord?

RICH.   Ay—more faithful than the love
Of fickle woman—when the head lies lowliest,
Clasping him fondest. Sorrow never knew
So sure a soother—and her bed is stainless!

Enter FRANÇOIS, L. D.

FRAN. Mademoiselle de Mortemar.

RICH. Most opportune—admit her. (*Exit*, FRANÇOIS, L D.) In my closet
You'll find a rosary, Joseph; ere you tell
Three hundred beads, I'll summon you. (JOSEPH *going* C.) Stay,
Joseph;—
I did omit an Ave in my matins—
A grievous fault;—atone it for me, Joseph;
There is a scourge within; I am weak, you strong.
It were but charity to take my sin
On such broad shoulders.

JOS. (*aside*).   Troth a pleasant invitation!
[*Exit* JOSEPH, D. L. H.

Enter JULIE DE MORTEMAR, L. D. *She goes to* RICHELIEU *and sits at his*
feet, R.

RICH. That's my sweet Julie !
JULIE.   Are you gracious ?
     May I say " Father ? "
RICH.   Now and ever !
JULIE.   Father !
     A sweet word to an orphan.
RICH.   No ; not orphan
     While Richelieu lives ; thy father loved me well ;
     My friend, ere I had flatterers (now, I'm great,
     In other phrase, I'm friendless)—he died young
     In years, not service, and bequeath'd thee to me ;
     And thou shalt have a dowry, girl, to buy
     Thy mate amidst the mightiest. Drooping ?—sighs ?
     Art thou not happy at the court ?
JULIE.   Not often.
RICH. (*aside*). Can she love Baradas ?
     (*aloud*) Thou art admired—art young ;
     Does not his Majesty commend thy beauty—
     Ask thee to sing to him ?—and swear such sounds
     Had smooth'd the brows of Saul ?
JULIE.   He's very tiresome,
     Our worthy King. (RICHELIEU, *during this dialogue, is writing.*)
RICH.   Fie ! kings are never tiresome,
     Save to their ministers. What courtly gallants
     Charm ladies most ?—De Sourdiac, Cinq Mars, or
     The favorite, Baradas ?
JULIE.   A smileless man—
     I fear and shun him.
RICH.   Yet he courts thee ?
JULIE.   Then
     He is more tiresome than his Majesty.
RICH. Right, girl, shun Baradas. Yet of these flowers
     Of France, not one, in whose more honeyed breath
     Thy heart hears Summer whisper ?

                         Enter HUGUET, L. D.

HUGUET.   The Chevalier
     De Mauprat waits below.
JULIE (*starting up*).   De Mauprat !
RICH.   Hem !
     He has been tiresome too. Anon.   [*Exit* HUGUET, L. D.
JUDIE.   What doth he !—
     I mean—I—Does your Eminence—that is—
     Know you Messire de Mauprat ?
RICH. (*writing*).   Well !—and you-
     Has he address'd you often ?
JULIE.   Often !—no—
     Nine times—nay, ten ; the last time by the lattice
     Of the great staircase. (*in a melancholy tone*) The Court sees him
          rarely.
RICH (*writing*). A bold and forward royster ?
JULIE.   *He ?*—nay, modest,
     Gentle, and sad, methinks.

Rich. (*writing*). Wears gold and azure?
Julie. No; sable.
Rich. So you note his colors, Julie?
Shame on you, child ; look loftier. By the mass,
I have business with this modest gentleman.
Julie. You're angry with poor Julie. There's no cause.
Rich. No cause—you hate my foes?
Julie. I do !
Rich Hate Mauprat?
Julie. Not Mauprat. No, not Adrien, father.
Rich. Adrien !
Familiar ! Go, child ; (Julie *crosses to* L.) no—not *that* way; wait
In the tapestry chamber ; I will join you—go.
Julie (*crosses to* R., *then pauses*). His brows are knit; I dare not call him
father !
But I *must* speak—Your Eminence—(*approaches him timidly.*)
Rich. (*sternly*). Well, girl !
Julie (*kneels*). Nay,
Smile on me—one smile more ; there, now I'm happy.
Do not rank Mauprat with your foes ; he is not,
I know he *is* not; he loves France too well.
Rich. Not rank De Mauprat with my foes? So be it.
I'll blot him from that list.
Julie. That's my own father. [*Exit,* R. D.
Rich. (*ringing a small bell on the table*). Huguet !

Enter Huguet, L. D.

De Mauprat struggled not, nor murmured?
Huguet. No; proud and passive.
Rich. Bid him enter. Hold ;
Look that he hide no weapon. Humph ! despair
Makes victims sometimes victors. When he has enter'd
Glide round unseen—place thyself yonder. (*pointing to the screen*)
Watch him ;
If he shows violence—let me see thy carbine. (Huguet *gives it to
him*)
So, a good weapon—if he play the lion,
Why—the dog's death. (*returning the carbine.*)
Huguet. I never miss my mark.

Exit Huguet, L. D. ; Richelieu *resumes his pen, and slowly arranges the
papers before him. Enter* De Mauprat, *preceded by* Huguet, *who then
retires behind the screen,* R. U. E.

Rich. Approach, sir. (De Mauprat *advances*) Can you call to mind the
hour,
Now three years since, when in this room, methinks,
Your presence honor'd me ?
De Mau. (L. C.). It is, my Lord,
One of my most——
Rich. (*dryly*). Delightful recollections.
De Mau. (*aside*). St. Denis ! doth he make a jest of axe
And headsman ?
Rich. (*sternly*). I did then accord you
A mercy ill requited—you still live ?

DE MAU. To meet death face to face at last.
RICH.   Messire de Mauprat,
     Doom'd to sure death, how hast thou since consumed
     The time allotted thee for serious thought
     And solemn penitence?
DE MAU. (*embarrassed*).   The time, my lord?
RICH. Is not the question plain? I'll answer for thee.
     Thou hast sought nor priest nor shrine; no sackcloth chafed
     Thy delicate flesh. The rosary and the death's head
     Have not, with pious meditation, purged
     Earth from the carnal gaze. What thou hast *not* done
     Brief told; what done, a volume! Wild debauch,
     Turbulent riot—for the morn the dice-box—
     Noon claim'd the duel—and the night the wassail;
     These, your most holy, pure preparatives,
     For death and judgment. Do I wrong you, sir?
DE MAU. I was not always thus—if changed my nature,
     Blame that which changed my fate.
     Were you accursed with that which you inflicted—
     By bed and board, dogg'd by one ghastly spectre—
     The while within you youth beat high, and life
     Grew lovelier from the neighboring frown of death—
     Were this your fate, perchance,
     You would have err'd like me!
RICH.   I might, like you,
     Have been a brawler and a reveller; not,
     Like you, a trickster and a thief.
DE MAU. (*advancing threateningly*).   Lord Cardinal!
     Unsay those words! (HUGUET *deliberately raises the carbine.*)
RICH. (*waving his hand, aside*). Not so quick, friend Huguet;
     Messire de Mauprat is a patient man,
     And he can wait. (HUGUET *recovers, and withdraws behind the screen.*)
     (*aloud*) You have outrun your fortune—
     I blame you not, that you would be a beggar—
     Each to his taste. But I do charge you, sir,
     That being beggar'd, you would coin false moneys
     Out of that crucible, called DEBT. To live
     On means not yours—be brave in silks and laces,
     Gallant in steeds—splendid in banquets—all
     Not *yours*—given—uninherited—unpaid for;
     This is to be a trickster; and to filch
     Men's art and labor, which to them is wealth,
     Life, daily bread—quitting all scores with—" Friend,
     You're troublesome!" Why this, forgive me
     Is what—when done with a less dainty grace—
     Plain folks call " *theft!*" You owe eight thousand pistoles
     Minus one crown, two liards!
DE MAU. (*aside*).   The old conjurer!
RICH. This is scandalous, shaming your birth and blood.
     I tell you, sir, that you must pay your debts.
DE MAU. (*advancing boldly to the table*). With all my heart.
     My lord. Where shall I borrow, then, the money?
RICH. (*aside, and laughing*). A humorous dare-devil—the very man
     To suit my purpose—ready, frank, and bold.
     (*aloud*) Adrien de Mauprat, men have called me cruel—
     I am not—I am *just!* I found France rent asunder—
     The rich men despots, and the poor banditti—

Sloth in the mart, and schism within the temple ;
Brawls festering to a rebellion ; and weak laws
Rotting away with rust in antique sheaths.
I have re-created France ; and, from the ashes
Of the old feudal and decrepit carcase,
Civilization, on her luminous wings,
Soars, Phœnix-like, to Jove ! What was my art ?
Genius, some say—some, Fortune, Witchcraft some.
Not so—my art was JUSTICE ! (*rises*) Force and fraud
Misname it cruelty—you shall confute them !
My champion you ! You met me as your foe ;
Depart, my friend—you shall not die. France needs you.
You shall wipe off all stains—be rich, be honor'd,
Be great——(DE MAUPRAT *falls on his knee.* RICHELIEU *takes
his hand.*)
　　　　　I ask, sir, in return, this hand,
To gift it with a bride, whose dower shall match,
Yet not exceed her beauty. (RICHELIEU *raises him.*)

DE MAU.　　　　　　　　I, my lord ! (*hesitating*)
　　I have no wish to marry.

RICH.　　　　　　　　　Surely, sir,
　　To die were worse.

DE MAU.　　　　　　　　Scarcely ; the poorest coward
　　Must die—but knowingly to march to marriage—
　　My Lord, it asks the courage of a lion !

RICH. Traitor, thou triflest with me ! I know *all !*
　　Thou hast dared to love my ward—my charge.

DE MAU.　　　　　　　　　　　　　　　As rivers
　　May love the sunlight !—basking in the beams,
　　And hurrying on—

RICH.　　　　　　　　Thou hast told her of thy love ?

DE MAU. My Lord, if I had dared to love a maid,
　　Lowliest in France, I would not so have wronged her,
　　As bid her link rich life and virgin hope
　　With one, the deathman's gripe might, from her side,
　　Pluck at the nuptial altar.

RICH.　　　　　　　　I believe thee. (*sits*)
　　Yet since she knows not of thy love, renounce her—
　　Take life and fortune with another !—Silent ?

DE MAU. Your fate has been one triumph—you know not
　　How bless'd a thing it was in my dark hour
　　To nurse the one sweet thought you bid me banish.
　　Love hath no need of words ; nor less within
　　That holiest temple—the Heaven-builded soul—
　　Breathes the recorded vow. Base knight—false lover
　　Were he, who barter'd all that soothe in grief,
　　Or sanctified despair, for life and gold.
　　Revoke your mercy ; I prefer the fate
　　I look'd for !

RICH.　　　　　　　Huguet ! (HUGUET *comes forward,* R.) to the tapestry
　　　　chamber
　　Conduct your prisoner. (*to* MAUPRAT) You will there behold
　　The executioner ;—your doom be private—
　　And Heaven have mercy on you !

(DE MAUPRAT *crosses slowly to* R. ; *pauses ; then goes to* RICHELIEU.)

DE MAU.　　　　　　　　When I am dead,
　　Tell her I loved her.

Rich.   Keep such follies, sir,
        For fitter ears ;—go——
De Mau.   Does he mock me ?
                    [*Exeunt* De Mauprat *and* Huguet, R. D.
Rich.   Joseph,
        Come forth.
                    Enter Joseph, R. C., *down* L.

                        Methinks your cheek hath lost its rubies ;
        I fear you have been too lavish of the flesh ;
        The scourge is heavy.
Jos.   Pray you, change the subject.
Rich.   You good men are so modest !—Well, to business !
        Go instantly—deeds—notaries !—bid my stewards
        Arrange my house by the Luxembourg—*my* house
        No more !—a bridal present to my ward,
        Who weds to-morrow.
Jos.   Weds, with whom ?
Rich.   De Mauprat.
Jos.   Penniless husband !
Rich.   Bah ! the mate for beauty
        Should be a man, and not a money-chest! (*rises*) Who else,
        Look you, in all the court—who else so well,
        Brave, or supplant the favorite ;—balk the King—
        Baffle their schemes ;—I have tried him.   He has honor
        And courage ;—qualities that eagle-plume
        Men's souls—and fit them for the fiercest sun,
        Which ever melted the weak waxen minds
        That flutter in the beams of gaudy Power !
        Besides, he has taste, this Mauprat.   When my play
        Was acted to dull tiers of lifeless gapers,
        Who had no soul for poetry, I saw him
        Applaud in the proper places ;—(*crosses* L.) trust me, Joseph,
        He is a man of an uncommon promise !
Jos.   And yet your foe.
Rich.   Have I not foes enow ?
        Great men gain doubly when they make foes friends.
        Remember my grand maxims :—First employ
        All methods to conciliate.
Jos.   Failing these ?
Rich.   (*fiercely*). All means to crush ; as with the opening, and
        The clenching of this little hand, I will
        Crush the small venom of these stinging courtiers.
        So, so, we've baffled Baradas.
Jos.   And when
        Check the conspiracy ?
Rich.   Check, check ? Full way to it.
        Let it bud, ripen, flaunt i' the day, and burst
        To fruit—the Dead Sea's fruit of ashes ; ashes
        Which I will scatter to the winds. (*crosses and sits* R. *of table*, G),
                Joseph.   [*Exit* Joseph, L. D.

            Enter De Mauprat *and* Julie, R. D ; *they kneel.*

De Mau. Oh, speak, my Lord—I dare not think you mock me.
        And yet——
Rich.   How now ! Oh ! sir—you live !

De Mau.   Why, no, methinks,
    Elysium is not life !
Julie.   He smiles !—you smile,
    My father ! From my heart for ever, now,
    I'll blot the name of orphan !
Rich.   Rise, my children,
    For ye are mine—mine both ;—and in your sweet
    And young delight—your love—(life's first-born glory)
    My own lost youth breathes musical ! (*they rise.*)
De Mau.   I'll seek
    Temple and priest henceforward ;—were it but
    To learn Heaven's choicest blessings.
Rich.   Thou shalt seek
    Temple and priest right soon ; the morrow's sun
    Shall see across these barren thresholds pass
    The fairest bride in Paris. Go, my children ;
    Even *I* loved once ! (*they cross* L.) Be lovers while ye may !

As they are going, Richelieu *touches* Mauprat *on the right shoulder, and
    beckons him forward.*

    How is it with you, sir ? You bear it bravely,
    You know, it asks the courage of a lion.
                    [*Exeunt* Julie *and* De Mauprat, L. D.
    Oh, godlike Power ! Woe, Rapture, Penury, Wealth—
    Marriage and Death, for one infirm old man
    Through a great empire to dispense—withhold—
    As the will whispers ! And shall things—like motes
    That live in my daylight—lackeys of court wages,
    Dwarf'd starvelings—manikins, upon whose shoulders
    The burthen of a province were a load
    More heavy than the globe on Atlas—cast
    Lots for my robes and sceptre? France ! I love thee !
    All Earth shall never pluck thee from my heart !
    My mistress France—my wedded wife—sweet France,
    Who shall proclaim divorce for thee and me !
                    [*Exit* Richelieu, R. D.
                    CURTAIN.

                    ———

                    ACT II.

                    SECOND DAY.

SCENE I.—*A splendid apartment in* De Mauprat's *new house. Casements
    opening to the gardens, beyond which are seen the domes of the Luxem-
    bourg Palace.*
                    Enter Baradas, L. II.

Bar. Mauprat's new home—too splendid for a soldier !
    But o'er his floors—the while I stalk—methinks
    My shadow spreads gigantic to the gloom
    The old rude towers of the Bastile cast far
    Along the smoothness of the jocund day.
    Well, thou hast 'scaped the fierce caprice of Richelieu ;
    But art thou farther from the headsman, fool ?

Thy secret I have whisper'd to the King—
Thy marriage makes the King thy foe! Thou stand'st
On the abyss—and in the pool below
I saw a ghastly, headless phantom mirror'd—
Thy likeness ere the marriage moon hath waned.
Meanwhile—meanwhile—ha—ha, if thou art wedded,
Thou art not wived. (*retires, L.*)

Enter DE MAUPRAT, *splendidly dressed,* R.; *crosses to* L., *and back to* R.

DE MAU.   Was ever fate like mine ?
So blest, and yet so wretched !
BAR. (*comes forward,* L).   Joy, De Mauprat—
Why, what a brow, man, for your wedding day !
DE MAU. You know what chanced between
The Cardinal and myself ?
BAR.   This morning brought
Your letter—faith, a strange account ! I laugh'd
And wept at once for gladness.
DE MAU.   We were wed
At noon ; the rite perform'd, came hither—scarce
Arrived, when——
BAR.   Well ?
DE MAU.   Wide flew the doors, and lo,
Messire de Beringhen, and this epistle !
BAR. 'Tis the King's hand—-the royal seal !
DE MAU.   Read—read—
BAR. (*reading*). " Whereas Adrien de Mauprat, Colonel and Chevalier in
our armies, being already guilty of High Treason, by the seizure of our
town of Faviaux, has presumed, without our knowledge, consent, or sanc-
tion, to connect himself by marriage with Julie de Mortemar, a wealthy
orphan attached to the person of her Majesty—We do hereby proclaim
and declare the said marriage contrary to law. On penalty of death,
Adrien de Mauprat will not communicate with the said Julie de Mortemar, by word or letter, save in the presence of our faithful servant, the
Sieur de Beringhen, and then with such respect and decorum as are due
to a Demoiselle attached to the Court of France, until such time as it
may suit our royal pleasure to confer with the Holy Church on the formal annulment of the marriage, and with our Council on the punishment
to be awarded to Messire de Mauprat, who is cautioned for his own sake
to preserve silence as to our injunction, more especially to Mademoiselle
de Mortemar.

" Given under our hand and seal at the Louvre.
                        " LOUIS "
(*returning the letter*). Amazement ! Did not Richelieu say the King
Knew not your crime ?
DE MAU.   He said so.
BAR.   Poor De Mauprat !
See you the snare, the vengeance worse than death,
Of which you are the victim ?
DE MAU.   Ha !
BAR. (*aside*).   It works ! (*aloud*) What so clear ?
Richelieu has but two passions——
DE MAU.   Richelieu !
BAR.   Yes !
Ambition and revenge—in you both blended.

First for ambition—Julie is his ward,
Innocent—docile—pliant to his will—
He placed her at the court—foresaw the rest—
The King loves Julie !

DE MAU.   Merciful Heaven ! The King !

BAR. Such Cupids lend new plumes to Richelieu's wings ;
But the Court etiquette must give such Cupids
The veil of Hymen—(Hymen but in name).
He looked abroad—found you his foe—*thus* served
Ambition—by the grandeur of his ward,
And vengeance—by dishonor to his foe !

DE MAU. Prove this.

BAR   You have the proof—the royal letter—
Your strange exemption from the general pardon,
Known but to me and Richelieu ; can you doubt
Your friend to acquit your foe ?

DE MAU. I see it all ! Mock pardon—hurried nuptials—
False bounty—all—the serpent of that smile !
Oh ! it stings home ! (*crosses*, L.)

BAR.   You yet shall crush his malice ;
Our plans are sure—Orleans is at our head ;
We meet to-night ; join us, and with us triumph.

DE MAU. *To-night ?* But the King ?—but Julie ?

BAR. The King, infirm in health, in mind more feeble,
Is but the plaything of a minister's will.
Were Richelieu dead—his power were mine ; and Louis
Soon should forget his passion and your crime. (DE MAUPRAT
  goes to L.)
But whither now ?

DE MAU.   I know not ; I scarce hear thee ;
A little while for thought ; anon I'll join thee ;
But now, all air seems tainted, and I loathe
The face of man.   [*Exit* DE MAUPRAT, L.

BAR.   Start from the chase, my prey,
But as thou speed'st the hell-hounds of revenge
Pant in thy track and dog thee down.

Enter DE BERINGHEN, R., *his mouth full, a napkin in his hand.*

DE BER.   Chevalier,
Your cook's a miracle—what, my host gone ?
Faith, Count, my office is a post of danger—
A fiery fellow, Mauprat ! touch and go—
Match and saltpetre—pr-r-r-r— !

BAR.   You
Will be released ere long. The King resolves
To call the bride to Court this day.

DE BER.   Poor Mauprat !
Yet since *you* love the lady, why so careless
Of the King's suit ?
Is Louis still so chafed against the Fox
For snatching you fair dainty from the Lion ?

BAR. So chafed, that Richelieu totters. Yes, the King
Is half conspirator against the Cardinal.
Enough of this. I've found the man we wanted—
The man to head the hands that murder Richelieu—
The man whose name the synonym for daring.

DE BER. (*aside*). He must mean me. (*aloud*) No, Count, I am—I own,
   A valiant dog—but still——
BAR   Whom can I mean
   But Mauprat? Mark, to-night we meet at Marion's,
   There shall we sign ; thence send this scroll. (*showing it*) to
   Bouillon.
   You're in that secret—(*affectionately*) one of our new Council.
DE BER. But to admit the Spaniard—France's foe—
   Into the heart of France—dethrone the King—
   It looks like treason, and I smell the headsman.
BAR. Oh, sir, too late to falter ; when we meet
   We must arrange the separate—coarser scheme,
   For Richelieu's death. Of this dispatch, De Mauprat
   Must nothing learn. He only bites at vengeance,
   And he would start from treason. We must post him
   Without the door at Marion's—as a sentry.
   (*aside*) So, when his head is on the block—his tongue
   Cannot betray our most august designs.
DE BER. I'll meet you if the King can spare me. (*aside*) No !
   I am too old a goose to play with foxes,
   I'll roost at home. (*aloud*) Meanwhile in the next room
   There's a delicious pâté, let's discuss it.
BAR. Pshaw ! a man filled with a sublime ambition
   Has no time to discuss your pâtés.
DE BER.   Pshaw !
   And a man filled with as sublime a pâté
   Has no time to discuss ambition. Gad,
   I have the best of it !   [*Exit*, R.
BAR. Now will this fire his fever into madness !
   All is made clear ; Mauprat *must* murder Richelieu—
   Die for that crime—I shall console his Julie—
   This will reach Bouillon—from the wrecks of France
   I shall carve out—who knows—perchance a throne !
   All in despite of my Lord Cardinal.

                     Enter DE MAUPRAT, L.

DE MAU. Speak ! can it be ? Methought, that from the terrace
   I saw the carriage of the King—and Julie !
   No !—no ! my frenzy peoples the void air
   With its own phantoms !
BAR.   Nay, too true. Alas !
   Was ever lightning swifter, or more blasting,
   Than Richelieu's forked guile ?
DE MAU.   I'll to the Louvre——
BAR. And lose all hope ! The Louvre !—the sure gate
   To the Bastile !
DE MAU.   The King——
BAR.   Is but the wax,
   Which Richelieu stamps ! Break the malignant *seal*,
   And I will raze the print.
DE MAU.   Ghastly Vengeance !
   To thee, and thine august and solemn sister,
   The unrelenting Death, I dedicate
   The blood of Armand Richelieu ! When Dishonor
   Reaches our hearths Law dies, and Murther takes
   The angel shape of Justice ! (*crosses* R.)

BAR.   Bravely said!
At midnight—Marion's!—Nay, I cannot leave thee
To thoughts that——
DE MAU.   Speak not to me!—I am yours!—
But speak not! There's a voice within my soul,
Whose cry could drown the thunder. Oh! if men
Will play dark sorcery with the heart of man,
Let they, who raise the spell, beware the Fiend! [*Exeunt*, R.

SCENE II —*A room in the Palais Cardinal (as in the First Act.* RICHE-
LIEU *and* JOSEPH, L. D. FRANÇOIS *discovered arranging the footstool.*

JOS. (L.). Yes!—Huguet, taking his accustom'd round—
Disguised as some plain burger—heard these rufflers
Quoting your name;—he listen'd—" Pshaw!" said one,
" We are to seize the Cardinal in his palace
To-morrow!"—" How?" the other ask'd.—" You'll hear
The whole design to-night; the Duke of Orleans
And Baradas have got the map of action
At their fingers' end."—" So be it," quoth the other;
" I will be there—Marion de Lorme's—at midnight!"
RICH. I have them, man,—I have them!
JOS.   So they say
Of you, my Lord;—believe me, that their plans
Are mightier than you deem. You must employ
Means no less vast to meet them!
RICH.   Bah! in policy
We foil gigantic danger, not by giants,
But dwarfs. The statues of our stately fortune
Are sculptured by the chisel—not the axe!
Ah! were I younger—by the knightly heart
That beats beneath these priestly robes, I would
Have pastime with these cut-throats! Yea—as when,
Lured to the ambush of the expecting foe—
I clove my pathway through the plumed sea!
Reach me yon falchion, François—not that bauble
For carpet-warriors,—yonder—such a blade
As old Charles Martel might have wielded when
He drove the Saracen from France. (FRANÇOIS *brings him one of
        the long two-handed swords worn in the middle ages*) With this
I, at Rochelle, did hand to hand engage
The stalwart Englisher—no mongrels, boy,
Those island mastiffs—mark the notch—a deep one—
His casque made here,—I shore him to the waist!
A toy—a feather—then! (*tries to wield, and lets it fall*) You see, a
        child could
Slay Richelieu now. (*retires to the table and sits* R.)
FRAN. (*his hand on his hilt*). But now, at your command,
Are other weapons, my good Lord.
RICH. (*who has seated himself as to write, lifts the pen*). True—THIS!
Beneath the rule of men entirely great
The pen is mightier than the sword. Behold
The arch-enchanter's wand!—itself a nothing!—
But taking sorcery from the master-hand
To paralyze the Cæsars—and to strike
The loud earth breathless!—Take away the sword—

States can be saved without it ! (*looking at the clock.* FRANÇOIS *replaces the sword*) 'Tis the hour—
R*:*tire, sir.

FRANÇOIS *crosses behind and exits*, R. D.   *Three knocks are heard*, L. U. E.
RICHELIEU *repeats them. A door concealed in the arras is opened cautiously. Enter* MARION DE LORME, L. U. E.

JOS. (*amazed*). Marion de Lorme ! (*she passes behind to the* R. *of* RICHELIEU.)
RICH.   Hist ! Joseph,
    Keep guard. (JOSEPH *retires*, D. R.) My faithful Marion !
MARION (*kneeling*).   Good, my Lord,
    They meet to-night in my poor house. The Duke
    Of Orleans heads them.
RICH.   Yes—go on.
MAR.   His Highness
    Much question'd if I knew some brave, discreet,
    And vigilant man, whose tongue could keep a secret,
    And who had those twin qualities for service,
    The love of gold, the hate of Richelieu.
RICH.   You ?—
MAR Made answer, " Yes—my brother ; bold and trusty ;
    Whose faith my faith could pledge ;"—the Duke then bade me
    Have him equipp'd and arm'd—well-mounted—ready
    This night 'part for Italy.
RICH.   Aha !—
    His Bouillon too turn'd traitor ? So, methought !—
    What part of Italy ?
MAR   The Piedmont frontier,
    Where Bouillon lies encamp'd.
RICH.   Now there is danger
    Great danger ! If he tamper with the Spaniard,
    And Louis list not to my counsel, as,
    Without sure proof, he will not—France is lost.
    What more ?
MAR.   Dark hints of some design to seize
    Your person in your palace. Nothing clear—
    His Highness trembled while he spoke—the words
    Did choke each other.
RICH.   So !—who is the brother
    You recommended to the Duke ?
MAR.   Whoever
    Your Eminence may father !
RICH.   Darling Marion !
    (*rises and goes to the table, and returns with a large purse of gold*)
    There—pshaw—a trifle ! (*gives the purse to* MARION)
    You are sure they meet ?—the hour ?
MAR.   At midnight.
RICH.   And
    You will engage to give the Duke's dispatch
    To whom I send ?
MAR.   Ay, marry !
RICH. (*aside*).   Huguet ? No ;
    He will be wanted elsewhere—Joseph ?—zealous,
    But too well known—too much the *elder* brother !
    Mauprat—alas—it is his wedding day—
    François ?—the man of men !—unnoted—young—

Ambitious. (*goes to the door*) François !

Enter FRANÇOIS, R. D.

　　　　　　　Follow this fair lady ;
(Find him the suiting garments, Marion), take
My fleetest steed ; arm thyself to the teeth ;
A packet will be given you—with orders,
No matter what ! The instant that your hand
Closes upon it—clutch *it*, like your honor,
Which Death alone can steal, or ravish—set
Spurs to your steed—be breathless, till you stand
Again before me. (FRANÇOIS *is going*) Stay, sir ! You will find
　　me
Two short leagues hence—at Ruelle, in my castle.
Young man, be blithe—for—note me—from the hour
I grasp that packet—think your guiding star
Rains fortune on you.
FRAN.　　　　　　If I fail——
RICH.　　　　　　　　Fail—fail ?
In the lexicon of youth, which Fate reserves
For a bright manhood, there is no such word
As—*fail !* (You will instruct him further, Marion.
　　　　　　(MARION *crosses behind to* L. U. E.)
Follow her—but at a distance—speak not to her,
Till you are housed. Farewell, boy ! Never say
" *Fail* " again.
FRAN.　　　　　　I will not !
RICH. (*patting his locks*).　　There's my young hero !
　　　　　　[*Exeunt* FRANÇOIS *and* MARION, L. U. E.
So they would seize my person in this palace ?
I cannot guess their scheme—but my retinue
Is here too large ! a single traitor could
Strike impotent the fate of thousands. Joseph,

Enter JOSEPH, R. D.

Art sure of Huguet ? Think—we hanged his father !
JOS. But you have bought the son—heaped favors on him !
RICH. Trash !—favors past—that's nothing. (*crosses*, L.) In his hours
Of confidence with you, has he named the favors
To *come*—he counts on ?
JOS.　　　　　　Yes—a Colonel's rank,
And letters of nobility.

Here HUGUET *enters*, L. D., *as to address the* CARDINAL, *who does not perceive
him*.

RICH.　　　　　What, Huguet !—
HUGUET (*aside*). My own name, soft ! (*retires and listens.*)
RICH.　　　　　Colonel and nobleman !
My bashful Huguet—that can never be !
We have him not the less—we'll *promise it !*
And see the King withholds ! Ah, Kings are oft
A great convenience to a minister !
No wrong to Huguet either. Moralists

Say, Hope is sweeter than possession!   Yes!
We'll count on Huguet!
HUGUET. Ay, to thy cost, thou tyrant!   [*Exit*, L. D.
RICH.   You are right; this treason
Assumes a fearful aspect—but, once crushed,
Its very ashes shall manure the soil
Of power; and ripen such full sheaves of greatness,
That all the summer of my fate shall seem
Fruitless beside the autumn.
JOS.   The saints grant it!
RICH. (*solemnly*). Yes—for sweet France, Heaven grant it!   O my
      country,
For thee—thee only—though men deem it not—
Are toil and terror my familiars!   I
Have made thee great and fair—upon thy brows
Wreath'd the old Roman laurel; at thy feet
Bow'd nations down.   No pulse in my ambition
Whose beatings were not measured for thy heart!
And while I live—Richelieu and France are one. (*crosses to* R.)

              Enter HUGUET, L. D.

HUGUET.   My Lord Cardinal,
Your Eminence bade me seek you at this hour.
RICH. (*crossing*, C.). Did I?   True, Huguet.   So you overheard
Strange talk amongst these gallants?   Snares and traps
For Richelieu?   Well—we'll balk them; let me think—
The men-at-arms you head—how many?
HUGUET.   Twenty
My Lord.
RICH.   All trusty?
HUGUET.   Ay, my Lord.
RICH.   Ere the dawn be gray.
All could be arm'd, assembled, and at Ruelle
In my own hall?
HUGUET.   By one hour after midnight.
RICH. The castle's strong.   You know its outlets, Huguet?
Would twenty men, well posted, keep such guard
That not one step—(and Murther's step is stealthy)—
Could glide within—unseen?
HUGUET.   A triple wall—
A drawbridge and portcullis—twenty men
Under my lead, a month might hold that castle
Against a host.
RICH.   They do not strike till morning,
Yet I will shift the quarter.   Bid the grooms
Prepare the litter—I will hence to Ruelle
While daylight lasts—and one hour after midnight
You and your twenty saints shall seek me thither!
You're made to rise!   You are, sir; eyes of lynx,
Ears of the stag, a footfall like the snow;
You are a valiant fellow—yea, a trusty,
Religious, exemplary, incorrupt,
And precious jewel of a fellow, Huguet!
If I live long enough—ay, mark my words—
If I live long enough, you'll be a Colonel—
Noble, perhaps!   One hour, sir, after midnight.

HUGUET. You leave me dumb with gratitude, my Lord ;
  I'll pick the trustiest—(*aside*)—Marion's house can furnish.
                                                [*Exit* HUGUET, L D.
RICH.   Good—all favors,
  . If François be but bold, and Huguet honest.
  Huguet—I half suspect—he bow'd too low—
  . 'Tis not his way.
JOS.   This is the curse, my Lord,
  Of your high state—suspicion of all men.
RICH. (*sadly*). True—true—my leeches bribed to poisoners—pages
  To strangle me in sleep. My very King
  (This brain the unresting loom, from which was woven
  The purple of his greatness) leagued against me.
  Old—childless—friendless—broken—all forsake—
  All—all—but——
JOS.   What ?
RICH.   The indomitable heart
  Of Armand Richelieu ! (*crosses* R.)
J s   And Joseph——
RICH. (*after a pause*).   You——
  Yes, I believe you—yes—for all men fear you—
  And the world loves you not. And I, friend Joseph,
  I am the only man who could, my Joseph,
  Make you a Bishop. Come, we'll go to dinner,
  And talk the while of methods to advance
  Our Mother Church. Ah, Joseph—*Bishop Joseph* ! [*Exeunt*, R.

CURTAIN.

ACT III.

SECOND DAY (MIDNIGHT).

SCENE I.—RICHELIEU's *Castle at Ruelle. A Gothic Chamber. Moonlight at
the window, occasionally obscured. Large doors* C. ; *small doors* R. *and* L.

RICH. (*reading*). " In silence, and at night, the Conscience feels
  That life should soar to nobler ends than Power."
  So sayest thou, sage and sober moralist !
  O ! ye, whose hour-glass shifts its tranquil sands
  In the unvex'd silence of a student's cell ;
  Ye, whose untempted hearts have never toss'd
  Upon the dark and stormy tides where life
  Gives battle to the elements—
                          Ye safe and formal men,
  Who write the deeds, and with unfeverish hand
  Weigh in nice scales the motives of the Great,
  Ye cannot know what ye have never tried !
  Speak to me, moralist !—I'll heed thy counsel.
  Were it not best——

  Enter FRANÇOIS *hastily, and in part disguised*, D. L. S. E.

RICH. (*flinging away the book*). Philosophy, thou liest !
  Quick—the dispatch ! Power—Empire ! Boy—the packet !

FRAN. (*kneeling*). Kill me, my Lord !
RICH.   They knew thee—they suspected—
They gave it not——
FRAN.   He gave it—*he*—the Count
De Baradas—with his own hand he gave it !
RICH. Baradas ! Joy ! out with it !
FRAN.   Listen,
And then dismiss me to the headsman.
RICH.   Ha !
Go on.
FRAN.   They led me to a chamber—There
Orleans and Baradas—and some half-score,
Whom I know not—were met——
RICH.   Not more !
FRAN.   But from
The adjoining chamber broke the din of voices,
The clattering tread of armed men ; at times
A shriller cry, that yell'd out, " Death to Richelieu !"
RICH. Speak not of *me ;* thy *country* is in danger !
FRAN.   Baradas
Question'd me close—demurr'd—until, at last,
O'erruled by Orleans—gave the packet—told me
That life and death were in the scroll—this gold—(*showing purse.*)
RICH. Gold is no proof——
FRAN.   And Orleans promised thousands,
When Bouillon's trumpets in the streets of Paris
Rang out shrill answer. Hastening from the house,
My footstep in the stirrup, Marion stole
Across the threshold, whispering, " Lose no moment
Ere Richelieu have the packet ; tell him too—
Murder is in the winds of Night, and Orleans
Swears, ere the dawn the Cardinal shall be clay."
She said, and trembling fled within ; when, lo !
A hand of iron griped me ; thro' the dark
Gleam'd the dim shadow of an armed man :
Ere I could draw—the prize was wrested from me,
And a hoarse voice gasp'd—" Spy, I spare thee, for
This steel is virgin to thy Lord !" with that
He vanish'd   Scared and trembling for thy safety,
I mounted, fled, and kneeling at thy feet
Implore thee to acquit my faith—but not,
Like him, to spare my life.
RICH.   Who spake of *life ?*
I bade thee grasp that treasure as thine *honor*—
A jewel worth whole hecatombs of lives ! (*rises*)
Begone '—redeem thine honor—back to Marion—
Or Baradas—or Orleans—track the robber—
Regain the packet—or crawl on to Age—
Age and gray hairs like mine—and know, thou hast lost
That which had made thee great and saved thy country. (*crosses,*
R. FRANÇOIS *rises*)
See me not till thou'st bought the right to seek me.
Away !—Nay, cheer thee, thou hast not fail'd yet—
There's no such word as fail !"
FRAN.   Bless you, my Lord,
For that one smile !   [*Exit*, L. D.
RICH.   He will win it yet.

François!—He's gone. My murder! Marion's warning!
This bravo's threat! O for the morrow's dawn!
I'll set my spies to work—I'll make all space
(As does the sun) a Universal Eye—
Huguet shall track—Joseph confess—ha! ha!
Strange, while I laugh'd I shudder'd—and e'en now ＿
Thro' the chill air the beating of my heart
Sounds like a death-watch by a sick man's pillow;
If Huguet *could* deceive me—hoofs without—
The gates unclose—steps nearer and nearer!

Enter JULIE, L. D. S. E.

JULIE.   Cardinal!
My father! (*falls at his feet.*)
RICH.   Julie at this hour!—and tears!
What ails thee?
JULIE.   I am safe; I am with thee!—
RICH. Safe!   ·
JULIE.   That man—
Why did I love him?—clinging to a breast
That knows no shelter?
                       Listen—late at noon—
The marriage-day—e'en then no more a lover—
He left me coldly—well—I sought my chamber
To weep and wonder—but to hope and dream.
Sudden a mandate from the King—to attend
Forthwith his pleasure at the Louvre.
RICH.   Ha!
You did obey the summons; and the King
Reproach'd your hasty nuptials?
JULIE.   Were that all!
He frown'd and chid; proclaim'd the bond unlawful;
Bade me not quit my chamber in the palace,
And there at night—alone—this night—all still—
He sought my presence—dared—thou read'st the heart,
Read mine! I cannot speak it!
RICH.   He a king—
You—woman; well—you yielded!
JULIE.   Cardinal—
Dare you say " yielded?"—Humbled and abash'd,
He from the chamber crept—th mighty Louis;
Crept like a baffled felon!—yielded? Ah!
More royalty in woman's honest heart
Than dwells within the crowned majesty
And sceptred anger of a hundred kings!
Yielded!—Heavens!—yielded! (*goes L.*)
RICH.   To my breast.—close—close! (*they embrace*)
The world would never need a Richelieu, if
Men—bearded, mailed men—the Lords of Earth—
Resisted flattery, falsehood, avarice, pride
As this poor child with the dove's innocent scorn
Her sex's tempters, Vanity and Power!
He left you—well?
JULIE.   Then came a sharper trial!
At the King's suit the Count de Baradas
Sought me to soothe, to fawn, to flatter, while
On his smooth lip insult appear'd more hateful.

                                      Stung at last
By my disdain, the dim and glimmering sense
Of his cloak'd words broke into bolder light,
And THEN—ah! then, my haughty spirit fail'd me!
Then I was weak—wept—oh! such bitter tears!
For (turn thy face aside, and let me whisper
The horror to thine ear) then did I learn
That he—that Adrien—my husband—knew
The King's polluting suit, and deemed it *honor!*
Then all the terrible and loathesome truth
Glared on me;—coldness, waywardness, reserve—
Mystery of looks—words—all unravell'd—and
I saw the impostor, where I had loved the god!
RICH. I think thou wrong'st thy husband—but proceed.
JULIE. Did you say " wrong'd " him ?—Cardinal, my father,
Did you say " wrong'd ?"   Prove it, and life shall grow
One prayer for thy reward and his forgiveness.
RICH. Let me know all.
JULIE.   To the despair he caused
The courtier left me; but amid the chaos
Darted one guiding ray—to 'scape—to fly—
Reach Adrien, learn the worst—'twas then near midnight;
Trembling I left my chamber—sought the Queen—
Fell a' her feet—reveal'd the unholy peril—
Implored her aid to flee our joint disgrace.
Moved, she embraced and soothed me—nay, preserved ;
Her word sufficed to unlock the palace gates ;
I hasten'd home—but home was desolate—
No Adrien there! Fearing the worst, I fled
To thee, directed hither. As my wheels
Paused at thy gates—the clang of arms behind—
The ring of hoofs——
RICH.   'Twas but my guards, fair trembler.
(So Hugnet keeps his word, my omens wrong'd him.)
JULIE. Oh, in one hour what years of anguish crowd!
RICH. Nay, there's no danger now. Thou needst rest. (*takes a lamp
      from the table,* C.)
Come, thou shalt lodge beside me. Tush! be cheer'd,
My rosiest Amazon—thou wrong'st thy Theseus.
All will be well—yes, yet all well.
                                      [*Exeunt through a side door.* R. S. E.

Enter HUGUET—DE MAUPRAT, L. D., *in complete armor, his vizor down.
      The moonlight obscured at the casement.*

HUGUET.   Not here !
DE MAU. Oh, I will find him, fear not. Hence and guard (*crosses,* R.)
The galleries where the menials sleep—plant sentries
At every outlet—Chance should throw no shadow
Between the vengeance and the victim ! Go—
HUGUET.   Will you not want
      A second arm ?
DE MAU.   . To slay one weak old man ?
Away ! No lesser wrongs than mine can make
This murder lawful. Hence !
HUGUET.   A short farewell !
            [*Exit* HUGUET, L. D. DE MAUPRAT *conceals himself,* R.

Re-enter RICHELIEU, *not perceiving* DE MAUPRAT, R. D.

RICH. How heavy is the air! (*goes to the table and puts down the lamp.*)
The very darkness lends itself to fear—
To treason——

DE MAU.   And to death!

RICH.   My omens lied not!
What art thou, wretch?

DE MAU.   Thy doomsman!

RICH. (DE MAUPRAT *seizes him*).   Ho, my guards!
Huguet! Montbrassil! Vermont!

DE MAU.   Ay, thy spirits
Forsake thee, wizard; thy bold men of mail
Are *my confederates*. Stir not! but one step,
And know the next—thy grave!

RICH.   Thou liest, knave!
I am old, infirm—most feeble—but thou liest! (RICHELIEU *throws him off*)
Armand de Richelieu dies not by the hand
Of man—the stars have said it—and the voice
Of my own prophetic and oracular soul
Confirms the shining sibyls! Call them all—
Thy brother butchers! Earth has no such fiend—
No! as one parricide of his fatherland,
Who dares in Richelieu murder France! (*goes* L.)

DE MAU.   Thy stars
Deceive thee, Cardinal;
In his hot youth, a soldier, urged to crime
Against the State, placed in your hands his life—
You did not strike the blow—but o'er his head,
Upon the gossamer thread of your caprice,
Hover'd the axe.
One day you summon'd—mock'd him with smooth pardon—
Bade an angel's face
Turn Earth to Paradise——

RICH.   Well!

DE MAU.   Was this mercy?
A Cæsar's generous vengeance? Cardinal, no!
Judas, not Cæsar was the model! You
Saved him from death for shame; reserved to grow
The scorn of living men—
A kind convenience—a Sir Pandarus
To his own bride, and the august adulterer!
Then did the first great law of human hearts,
To which the patriot's, not the rebel's name,
Crown'd the first Brutus, when the Tarquin fell,
Make Misery royal—raise this desperate wretch
Into thy destiny! Expect no mercy!
Behold De Mauprat! (*lifts his vizor.*)

RICH.   To thy knees, and crawl
For pardon, or, I tell thee, thou shalt live
For such remorse, that, did I hate thee, I
Would bid thee strike, that I might be avenged!
It was to save my Julie from the King,
That in thy valor I forgave thy crime;
It was, when thou—the rash and ready tool—
Yea of that shame thou loath'st—didst leave thy hearth

To the polluter—in these arms thy bride
Found the protecting shelter thine withheld. (*goes to side door*, R.)
Julie De Mauprat—Julie! (MAUPRAT *crosses to* L.)

Enter JULIE.

                                        Lo, my witness!
DE MAU. (L.). What marvel's this ? I dream! my Julie—*thou!*
JULIE (L.). Henceforth all bond
Between us twain is broken. Were it not
For this old man, I might, in truth, have lost
The right—now mine—to scorn thee !
RICH. (C.).   So, you hear her ?
DE MAU. Thou with some slander hast her sense infected !
JULIE.   No, sir ; he did excuse thee. Thy *friend*—
Thy *confidant*—familiar—*Baradas*—
Himself reveal'd thy baseness !
DE MAU.   Baseness !
RICH.   Ay ;
That *thou* didst *court* dishonor.
DE MAU.   Baradas !
Where is thy thunder, Heaven ? Duped—snared—undone—
    (*sheaths his sword*)
Thou—thou couldst not believe him ! Thou dost love me !
JULIE (*aside*).   Love him ! Ah !
Be still, my heart ! (*aloud*) Love you I did !—how fondly
Woman—if women were my listeners now—
Alone could tell ! For ever fled my dream ;
Farewell—all's over !
RICH.   Nay, my daughter, these
Are but the blinding mists of daybreak love
Sprung from its very light, and heralding
A noon of happy summer. Take her hand
And speak the truth, with which your heart runs over—
That this Count Judas--this Incarnate Falsehood--
Never lied more, than when he told thy Julie
That Adrien loved her not—except, indeed,
When he told Adrien, Julie could betray him. (MAUPRAT *crosses to*
    JULIE.)
JULIE (*embracing* DE MAUPRAT). You love me, then !—you love me —
    and they wrong'd you !
DE MAU. Ah ! couldst thou doubt it ?
RICH.   Why, the very mole
Less blind than thou ! Baradas loves thy wife !—
Had hoped her hand—aspired to be that cloak
To the King's will, which to thy bluntness seems
The Centaur's poisonous robe—hopes even now
To make thy corpse his footstool to thy bed !
Where was thy wit, man ?—Ho ! these schemes are glass !
The very sun shines through them.
DE MAU.   O, my Lord,
Can you forgive me ?
RICH.   Ay, and save you !
DE MAU.   Save !—
Terrible word !—O, save *thyself ;*—these halls
Swarm with thy foes ; already for thy blood
Pants thirsty Murder ! (*draws his sword.*)

JULIE.   Murder !
RICH.   Hush ! put by
    The woman.   Hush ! a shriek—a cry—a breath
    Too loud, would startle from its horrent pause
    The swooping Death !   Go to the door, and listen !
    Now for escape !   (*crosses* R.   JULIE *kneels at the door listening*.)
DE MAU.   None—none !   Their blades shall pass
    This heart to thine !
RICH. (*dryly*).   An honorable outwork,
    But much too near the citadel.   I think
    That I can trust you now ;   (*slowly, and gazing on him*) yes, I can
        trust you.
    How many of my troop league with you ?
DE MAU.   All !—
    We *are* your troop !
RICH.   And Huguet ?
DE MAU.   Is our captain.
        (*watches the door and stands prepared for defence*.)
RICH. A retributive Power !   This comes of spies !
    All ?   then the lion's skin's too short to-night—
    Now for the fox's !—(*murmurs without*.)
JULIE.   A hoarse, gathering murmur !—
    Hurrrying and heavy footsteps !
RICH.   Ha !—the posterns !
DE MAU. No egress where no sentry !
RICH.   Follow me—
    I have it !—to my chamber—quick !   Come, Julie !
    Hush !   Mauprat, come !
        [*Exit* JULIE, DE MAUPRAT, *and* RICHELIEU, C. D.
murmurs at a distance).   Death to the Cardinal !
RICH. (*without*).   Bloodhounds, I laugh at ye !—ha ! ha !—we will
    Baffle them yet.   Ha ! ha !
HUGUET (*without*).   This way—this way !

        Enter HUGUET *and the* CONSPIRATORS, L. U. E.

HUGUET. De Mauprat's hand is never slow in battle ;
    Strange, if it falter now !   Ha ! gone !
FIRST CON.   Perchance
    The fox had crept to rest ; and to his lair
    Death, the dark hunter, tracks him.

Enter DE MAUPRAT, *throwing open the doors of the recess*, C., *in which there
    is a bed, whereon* RICHELIEU *lies extended*.

DE MAU.   Live the King ;
    Richelieu is dead !
HUGUET.   You have been long.
DE MAU.   I watch'd him till he slept.
    Heed me.   No trace of blood reveals the deed ;—
    Strangled in sleep.   His health hath long been broken—
    Found breathless in his bed.   So runs our tale,
    Remember !   Back to Paris—Orleans gives
    Ten thousand crowns, and Baradas a lordship,
    To him who first gluts vengeance with the news
    That Richelieu is in heaven !   Quick, that all France
    May share your joy !

HUGUET.   And you ?
DE MAU.   Will stay, to crush
  Eager suspicion—to forbid sharp eyes
  To dwell too closely on the clay ; prepare
  The rites, and place him on his bier—this *my* task.
  I leave to you, sirs, the more grateful lot
  Of wealth and honors. Hence !
HUGUET.   I shall be noble !
DE MAU. Away !
FIRST CON.   Ten thousand crowns !
OMNES.   To horse !—to horse !
  [*Exeunt* CONSPIRATORS, L. S. E.   DE MAUPRAT *stands on guard.*

SCENE II.—*A room in the house of* COUNT DE BARADAS.   ORLEANS *and*
                    DE BERINGHEN, R.

DE BER. I understand.   Mauprat kept guard without ;
  Knows naught of the dispatch—but heads the troop
  Whom the poor Cardinal fancies his protectors.
  Save us from such protection !

                    Enter BARADAS, R.

BAR.   Julie is fled ;—the King, whom I now left
  To a most thorny pillow, vows revenge
  On her—on Mauprat—and on Richelieu !   Well ;
  We loyal men anticipate his wish
  Upon the last—and as for Mauprat—(*showing a writ.*)
DE BER.   Hum !
  They say the devil invented printing !   Faith !
  He has some hand in writing parchment—eh, Count ?
  What mischief now ?
BAR.   The King, at Julie's flight
  Enraged, will brook no rival in a subject—
  So on this old offence—the affair of Faviaux—
  Ere Mauprat can tell tales of *us*, we build
  His bridge between the dungeon and the grave.
  Oh ! by the way—I had forgot your highness,
  Friend Huguet whispered me, " Beware of Marion ;
  I've seen her lurking near the Cardinal's palace."
  Upon that hint, I've found her lodgings elsewhere.
ORLEANS. You wrong her, Count.   Poor Marion ! she adores me.
BAR. (*apologetically*). Forgive me, but——

                    Enter PAGE, R.

PAGE.   My Lord, a rude, strange soldier,
  Breathless with haste, demands an audience.
BAR.   So !
  The archers ?
PAGE.   In the ante-room, my Lord,
  As you desired.
BAR.   'Tis well—admit the soldier.   [*Exit* PAGE, R.
  Huguet—I bade him seek me here.

                    Enter HUGUET, R.

HUGUET.   My Lords,
    The deed is done. Now, Count, fulfill your word,
    And make me noble!
BAR.   Richelieu dead ?—art sure ?
    . How died he ?
HUGUET.   Strangled in his sleep—no blood,
    No tell-tale violence.
BAR.   Strangled ?—monstrous villain !
    Reward for murder ! Ho, there ! (*stamping*.)

            Enter CAPTAIN *with five* ARCHERS, R.

HUGUET.   No, thou durst not !
BAR. Seize on the ruffian—bind him—gag him—(*they seize him*) Off
    To the Bastile !
HUGUET.   Your word—your plighted faith !
BAR. Insolent liar !—ho, away !
HUGUET.   Nay, Count ;
    I have that about me which——
BAR.   Away with him !
                    [*Exeunt* HUGUET *and* ARCHERS, R.
    Now, then, all's safe ; Huguet must die in prison,
    So Mauprat—coax or force the meaner crew
    To fly the country. Ha, ha ! thus, your highness,
    Great men make use of little men.
DE BER.   My Lords,
    Since our suspense is ended—you'll excuse me ;
    'Tis late—and *entre nous*, I have not supp'd yet !
    I'm one of the new Council now, remember ;
    I feel the public stirring here already ;
    A very craving monster. *Au revoir !* [*Exit* DE BERINGHEN, R.
ORLEANS. No fear now, Richelieu's dead.
BAR.   And could he come
    To life again, he could not keep life's life—
    His power—nor save De Mauprat from the scaffold—
    Nor Julie from these arms—nor Paris from
    The Spaniard—nor your highness from the throne !
    All ours ! all ours ! in spite of my Lord Cardinal !

                    Enter PAGE, R.

PAGE. A gentleman, my Lord, of better mien
    Than he who last——
BAR.   Well, he may enter.   [*Exit* PAGE, R.
ORLEANS.   Who
    Can this be ?
BAR.   One of the conspirators ;
    Mauprat himself, perhaps.

                    Enter FRANÇOIS, R.

FRAN.   My Lord——
BAR.   Ha, traitor ;
    In Paris still ?
FRAN.   .   The packet—the dispatch—
    Some knave play'd spy without and reft it from me,
    Ere I could draw my sword.

BAR. Played spy *without!*
Did he wear armor?
FRAN. Ay, from head to heel.
ORLEANS. One of our band. Oh, Heavens!
BAR. Could it be Mauprat?
Kept guard at the *door*—knew *naught of the dispatch*—
How he?—and yet, who other?
FRAN. Ha, De Mauprat!
The night was dark—his vizor closed.
BAR. 'Twas he!
How could he guess?—'sdeath! if he should betray us.
His hate to Richelieu dies with Richelieu—and
He was not great enough for treason. Hence!
Find Mauprat—beg, steal, filch, or force it back,
Or, as I live, the halter——
FRAN. By the morrow
I will regain it, (*aside*) and redeem my honor! [*Exit* FRANÇOIS, R.
ORLEANS. Oh, we are lost——
BAR. Not so! But cause on cause
For Mauprat's seizure—silence—death! Take courage.
ORLEANS. Should it once reach the King, the Cardinal's arm
Could smite us from the grave.
BAR. Sir, think it not!
I hold De Mauprat in my grasp. To-morrow,
And France is ours! [*Exeunt,* L.

CURTAIN.

ACT IV.

THIRD DAY.

SCENE I.—*The Gardens of the Louvre.* ORLEANS, BARADAS, DE BER-
INGHEN, COURTIERS, *etc.*, R. S. E.

ORLEANS (L. C.). How does my brother bear the Cardinal's death?
BAR. (R. C.). With grief, when thinking of the toils of state;
With joy, when thinking on the eyes of Julie;—
At times he sighs, "Who now shall govern France?"
Anon exclaims, "Who shall baffle Louis?"

Enter LOUIS *and other* COURTIERS, R. S. E. (*They uncover.*)

ORLEANS. Now, my liege, now, I can embrace a brother.
LOUIS. Dear Gaston, yes. I do believe you *love* me;—
Richelieu denied it—sever'd us too long.
A great man, Gaston! Who shall govern France? (*crosses* L. *and
back to* C.)
BAR. Yourself, my liege. That swart and potent star
Eclipsed your royal orb. He served the country,
But did he *serve*, or seek to *sway* the *King?*
LOUIS. You're right—he was an able politician—
Dear Count, this silliest Julie,
I know not why, she takes my fancy. Many

    As fair, and certainly more kind ; but yet
    It is so.
BAR.   Richelieu was most disloyal in that marriage.
LOUIS. (*querulously*). He knew that Julie pleased me ; a clear proof
    He never loved me !
BAR.   Oh, most clear !—But now
    No bar between your lady and your will !
    This writ makes all secure ; a week or two
    In the Bastile will sober Mauprat's love,
    And leave him eager to dissolve a hymen
    That brings him such a home.
LOUIS.   See to it, Count.
                   [*Exit* BARADAS, R.
    I'll summon Julie back. A word with you.
  [*Takes aside* FIRST COURTIER *and* DE BERINGHEN, *and exeunt,* L S. E.

Enter FRANÇOIS, R. U. E.

FRAN. All search, as yet, in vain for Mauprat ! Not
    At home since yesternoon—a soldier told me
    He saw him pass this way with hasty strides ;
    Should he meet Baradas—they'd rend it from him—
    And then—Oh, sweet fortune, smile upon me—
    I am thy son !—if thou desert'st me now,
    Come, Death, and snatch me from disgrace.   [*Exit,* L.

Enter DE MAUPRAT, R. U. E.

DE MAU.   Oh, let me—
    Let me but meet him foot to foot—I'll dig
    The Judas from his heart ;—albeit the King
    Should o'er him cast the purple !

Re-enter FRANÇOIS, L. U. E.

FRAN.   Mauprat ! hold !—
    Where is the——
DE MAU.   Well ! What would'st thou ?
FRAN.   The dispatch !
    The packet. LOOK ON ME—I serve the Cardinal—
    You know me. Did you not keep guard last night
    By Marion's house ?
DE MAU.   I did ;—no matter now !—
    They told me *he* was *here !* (*crosses to* L. *and up the stage.*)
FRAN.   O joy ! quick—quick—
    The packet thou didst wrest from me ?
DE MAU.   The packet !—
    What, art thou he I deemed the Cardinal's spy ?—
    (Dupe that I was) and overhearing Marion——
FRAN. The same—restore it !—haste !
DE MAU.   I have it not ;—
    Methought it but reveal'd our scheme to Richelieu,
    And, as we mounted, gave it to——

Enter BARADAS, R.

               Stand back !

Now, villain! now—I have thee! (*to* FRANÇOIS) Hence, sir!—
          Draw!
FRAN. Art mad?—the King's at hand! leave *him* to Richelieu!
          Speak—the dispatch—to whom——
DE MAU. (*dashing him aside, and rushing to* BARADAS). Thou triple slan-
          derer!
          I'll set my heel upon thy crest! (*a few passes.*)
FRAN.   Fly—fly!
          The King!—

Enter, L. S. E., LOUIS, ORLEANS, DE BERINGHEN, COURTIERS, *etc.* ; CAP-
          TAIN *and* GUARDS *hastily,* L. U. E.   *The* CAPTAIN *and* GUARDS *range*
          R., COURTIERS L , KING L. C., BARADAS L. C., DE MAUPRAT R.

LOUIS.   Swords drawn—before our very palace!—
          Have our laws died with Richelieu?
BAR. (R. *of the* KING).   Pardon, Sire,—
          My crime but self-defence. (*aside to* KING) It is De Mauprat.
LOUIS. Dare he thus brave us?
          (BARADAS *goes to the* CAPTAIN, *and gives the writ.*)
DE MAU.   Sire, in the Cardinal's name——
BAR. Seize him—disarm—to the Bastile!

DE MAUPRAT *resigns his sword. Enter* RICHELIEU *and* JOSEPH, *followed*
          by ARQUEBUSIERS, L. U. E.

BAR.   The dead
          Returned to life!
LOUIS (L. C.).   What! a *mock* death! this tops
          The Infinite of Insult.
DE MAU. (R.).   Priest and Hero!—
          For you are both—protect the truth!
RICH. (*taking the writ from the* CAPTAIN).   What's this?
DE BER. (L.). Fact in Philosophy. Foxes have got
          Nine lives, as well as cats!
BAR.   Be firm, my liege.
LOUIS. I have assumed the sceptre—I will wield it!
JOS. (*down* R). The tide runs counter—there'll be shipwreck somewhere.

BARADAS *and* ORLEANS *keep close to the* KING, *whispering and prompting*
          him when RICHELIEU *speaks.*

RICH. High treason!—Faviaux! still that stale pretence!
          My liege, bad men (ay, Count, most *knavish* men!)
          Abuse your royal goodness. For this soldier,
          France hath none braver—and his youth's folly,
          Misled (*to* ORLEANS)—(by whom *your Highness* may conjecture!)
          Is long since cancell'd by a loyal manhood.
          I, Sire, have pardon'd him.
LOUIS.   And we do give
          Your pardon to the winds. Sir, do your duty!
RICH. What, Sire?—you do not know—Oh, pardon me—
          You know not yet, that this brave, honest heart
          Stood between mine and murder! Sire, for my sake—
          For your old servant's sake—undo this wrong.
          See, let me rend the sentence.
LOUIS (*taking the paper from him*).   At your peril!

This is too much. Again, sir, do your duty! (MAUPRAT *is about*
   to expostulate.)
RICH. Speak not, but go—I would not see young valor
   So humbled as gray service.
DE MAU.   Fare you well! (*kisses* RICHELIEU'S *hand*)
   Save Julie, and console her.
FRAN. (*aside to* MAUPRAT, *as he is being led off*). The dispatch!
   Your fate, foes, life, hang upon a word—to whom?
DE MAU. To Huguet.   [*Exeunt* DE MAUPRAT *and* GUARD, L. U. E.
BAR. (*aside to* FRANÇOIS). Has he the packet?
FRAN.   He will not reveal—
   (*aside*) Work, brain—beat heart!—"*There's no such word as fail!*"
                      [*Exit* FRANÇOIS, R. U. E.
  (*All the* COURTIERS *have closed round the* KING, *shutting* RICHELIEU *out.*)
RICH. (*fiercely*). Room, my Lords, room! The Minister of France
   Can need no intercession with the King. (*they fall back.*)
LOUIS. What means this false report of death, Lord Cardinal?
RICH   Are you then anger'd, Sire, that I live still?
LOUIS. No; but such artifice——
RICH.   Not mine—look elsewhere!
   Louis—my castle swarm'd with the assassins.
BAR. (*advancing*, R.). We have punished them already. Huguet now
   In the Bastile. Oh, my Lord, *we* were prompt
   To avenge you—*we* were——
RICH.   WE? Ha! ha! you hear,
   My liege! What page, man, in the last Court grammar
   Made you a plural? Count, you have seized the *hireling;—*
   Sire, shall I name the *master?*
LOUIS.   Tush! my Lord,
   The old contrivance—ever does your wit
   Invent assassins—that ambition may
   Slay rivals—(BARADAS *crosses behind to the* KING.)
RICH.   Rivals, Sire, in what?
   Service to France! *I have none!* Lives the man
   Whom Europe, paled before your glory, deems
   Rival to Armand Richelieu?
LOUIS.   What, so haughty!
   Remember he who made can unmake.
RICH.   Never!
   Never! Your anger can recall your trust,
/   Annul my office, spoil me of my lands,
   Rifle my coffers—but my name—my deeds,
   Are royal in a land beyond your sceptre!
   Pass sentence on me, if you will; from Kings,
   Lo! I appeal to Time!
LOUIS (*turns haughtily to the* CARDINAL). Enough!
   Your Eminence must excuse a longer audience.
   To your own palace. For our conference, this
   Nor place—nor season.
RICH.   Good, my liege, for *Justice*
   All place a temple, and all season, summer!
   Do you deny me justice? Saints of Heaven!
   He turns from me! *Do you deny me justice?*
   For fifteen years, while in these hands dwelt Empire,
   The humblest craftsman—the obscurest vassal—
   The very leper shrinking from the sun,
   Tho' loathed by charity, might ask for justice!

Not with the fawning tone and crawling mien
Of some I see around you—Counts and Princes—
Kneeling for *favors ;*—but, erect and loud,
As men who ask man's rights ! my liege, my Louis,
Do you refuse me justice—audience even—
In the pale presence of the baffled Murther?

LOUIS. Lord Cardinal—one by one you have sever'd from me
The bonds of human love. All near and dear
Mark'd out for vengeance—exile or the scaffold.
You find me now amidst my trustiest friends,
My closest kindred—you would tear them from me ;
They murder *you,* forsooth, since *me* they love !
Eno' of plots and treasons for one reign !
Home!—Home! and sleep away these phantoms ! (*the* KING *and*
    all the COURT *cross to* R.)

RICH.   Sire !
I—patience, Heaven !—sweet Heaven !—from the foot
Of that Great Throne, these hands have raised aloft
On an Olympus, looking down on mortals
And worshipp'd by their awe—before the foot
Of that high throne—spurn you the gray-hair'd man,
Who gave you empire—and now sues for safety ?

LOUIS. No ; when we see your Eminence in truth
At the *foot* of the throne—we'll listen to you.
                    [*Exit* LOUIS, R., *followed by* COURTIERS.

ORLEANS.   Saved !

BAR. For this, deep thanks to Julie and to Mauprat !
                    [*Exeunt* BARADAS *and* ORLEANS, R.

RICH. Joseph—did you hear the King ?

JOS. (*down* L). I did—there's danger ! Had you been less haughty——

RICH. And suffer'd slaves to chuckle—" See the Cardinal—
How meek his Eminence is to-day "—I tell thee
This is a strife in which the loftiest look
Is the most subtle armor——

JOS.   But——

RICH.   No time
For ifs and buts. I will accuse these traitors !
François shall witness that De Baradas
Gave him the secret missive for De Bouillon,
And told him life and death were in the scroll.
I will—I will ! (*crosses,* R)

JOS.   Tush ! François is your creature ;
So they will say, and laugh at you !—*your witness*
Must be that same dispatch !

RICH.   Away to Marion !

JOS. I have been there—she is seized—removed—imprison'd—
By the Count's orders.

RICH.   Goddess of bright dreams,
My country—shalt thou lose me now, when most
Thou need'st thy worshipper ? My native land !
Let me but ward this dagger from thy heart,
And die—but on thy bosom !

Enter JULIE, L. S. E.

JULIE.   Heaven ! I thank thee !
It cannot be, or this all-powerful man

Would not stand idly thus.

RICH.   What dost *thou* here ?
Home!

JULIE. Home!—is *Adrien there ?*—you're dumb—yet strive
For words; I see them trembling on your lip,
But choked by pity. It *was* truth—all truth!
Seized—the Bastile—and in your presence, too !
Cardinal, where is Adrien ? Think—he saved
Your life—your name is infamy, if wrong
Should come to his !

RICH.   Be sooth'd, child.

JULIE.   Child no more.
I love, and I am woman !
Where is Adrien ?
Let thine eyes meet mine ;
Answer me but one word—I am a wife—
I ask thee for my *home*—my fate—my all !
Where is my *husband ?*

RICH.   You are Richelieu's ward,
A soldier's bride ; they who insist on truth
Must out-face fear—you ask me for your husband ?
There—where the clouds of heaven look darkest, o'er
The domes of the Bastile !

JULIE.   O, mercy, mercy !
Save him, restore him, father ! Art thou not
The Cardinal King ?—the Lord of life and death—
Art thou not Richelieu ?

RICH.   Yesterday I was !
To-day, a very weak old man ! To-morrow,
I know not what. (*crosses,* L.)

JULIE (*to* JOSEPH).   Do you conceive his meaning ?
Alas I cannot.

JOS. (R).   The King is chafed
Against his servant. Lady, while we speak,
The lackey of the ante-room is not
More powerless than the Minister of France.

Enter CLERMONT, R.

CLER.   Madame de Mauprat !
Pardon, your Eminence—even now I seek
This lady's home—commanded by the King
To pray her presence.

JULIE (*clinging to* RICHELIEU). Think of my dead father—
And take me to your breast.

RICH.   To those who sent you—
And say you found the virtue they would slay
Here—couch'd upon this heart, as at an altar,
And shelter'd by the wings of sacred Rome !
Begone !

CLER.   My Lord, I am your friend and servant—
Misjudge me not ; but never yet was Louis
So roused against you—shall I take this answer ?
It were to be your foe.

RICH.   All time my foe,
If I, a Priest, could cast this holy sorrow
Forth from her last asylum !

CLER.   He is lost!   [*Exit* CLERMONT, R.
RICH. God help thee, child!—she hears not! Look upon her!
The storm, that rends the oak, uproots the flower.
Her father loved me so! and in that age
When friends are brothers! She has been to me
Soother, nurse, plaything, daughter. Are these tears?
Oh! shame, shame!—dotage! (*places her in the arms of* JOSEPH.)
JOS.   Tears are not for eyes
That rather need the lightning! which can pierce
Through barred gates and triple walls, to smite
Crime, where it cowers in secret! The dispatch!
Set every spy to work—the morrow's sun
Must see that written treason in your hands,
Or rise upon your ruin.
RICH.   Ay—and close
Upon my corpse—I am not made to live—
Friends, glory, France, all reft from me—my star
Like some vain holiday mimicry of fire,
Piercing imperial heaven, and falling down
Rayless and blacken'd, to the dust—a thing
For all men's feet to trample! Yea!—to-morrow
Triumph or death! Look up; child! Lead us, Joseph!

   As they are going up C., *enter* BARADAS *and* DE BERINGHEN, R.

BAR. (R. C.). My Lord, the King cannot believe your Eminence
So far forgets your duty, and his greatness,
As to resist his mandate! Pray you, madam,
Obey the King—no cause for fear!
JULIE (L.).   My father!
RICH. (C.). She shall not stir!
BAR.   ·   You are not of her kindred—
An orphan——
RICH.   And her country is her mother.
BAR. The country is the King.
RICH.   Ay, is it so?
Then wakes the power which in the age of iron
Bursts forth to curb the great, and raise the low.
Mark, where she stands—around her form I draw
The awful circle of our solemn church!
Set but a foot within that holy ground
And on thy head—yea, though it wore a crown—
I launch the curse of Rome!
BAR.   I dare not brave you.
I do but speak the orders of my King,
The church, your rank, power, very word, my Lord,
Suffice you for resistance—blame yourself,
If it should cost your power.
RICH.   That *my* stake. Ah!
Dark gamester! *what is thine?* Look to it well—
Lose not a trick—By this same hour to-morrow
Thou shalt have France, or I thy head!
BAR. (*aside to* DE BERINGHEN).   He cannot
Have the dispatch?
JOS. (*aside, on* RICHELIEU'S R.). Patience is your game;
Reflect, you have not the dispatch!
RICH.   · O, monk!

Leave patience to the saints—for *I* am human!
(*to* JULIE) Did not thy father die for France, poor orphan?
And now they say thou hast *no* father!   Fie!
Art thou not pure and good?—if so, thou art
A part of that—the Beautiful, the sacred—
Which, in all climes, men that have hearts adore,
By the great title of their mother country!

BAR. (*aside*). He wanders!

RICH.   So cling close unto my breast,
Here where thou droop'st lies France! I am very feeble—
Of little use it seems to either now.
Well, well—we will go home. (*they go up the stage.*)

BAR.   In sooth, my Lord,
You do need rest—the burthens of the State
O'ertask your health!

RICH. (*to* JOSEPH, *pauses*).   I'm patient, see!

BAR. (*aside*).   His mind
And life are breaking fast.

RICH. (*overhearing him*). Irreverent ribald!
If so, beware the falling ruins!   Hark!
I tell thee, scorner of these whitening hairs,
When this snow melteth there shall come a flood!
Avaunt! my name is Richelieu—I defy thee!
Walk blindfold on; behind thee stalks the headsman.
Ha! ha!—how pale he is.   Heaven save my country! (*falls back
in* JOSEPH'S *arms.* JULIE *kneels at his side,* BARADAS *and* DE BER-
INGHEN *stand* R.

                      CURTAIN.

ACT V.

FOURTH DAY.

SCENE I.—*The Bastile—a corridor; in the background the door of one of
the condemned cells.*

Enter JOSEPH, *and* JAILER, *with a lamp,* R. D. F.

JAILER. Stay, father, I will call the governor.   [*Exit* JAILER, L.

JOS.   He has it then—this Huguet—so we learn
From François—Humph!   Now if I can but gain
One moment's access, all is ours!   The Cardinal
Trembles 'tween life and death.   His life is power;
Smite one—slay both!   No Æsculapian drugs,
By learned quacks baptized with Latin jargon,
E'er bore the healing which that scrap of parchment
Will medicine to ambition's flagging heart.
France shall be saved—and Joseph be a bishop.

Enter GOVERNOR *and* JAILER, L.

GOV.   Father, you wish to see the prisoners Huguet
And the young knight De Mauprat?

JOS.   So my office,
And the Lord Cardinal's order, warrant, son!

Gov. Father, it cannot be; Count Baradas
    Has summon'd to the Louvre Sieur de Mauprat.
Jos. Well, well! But Huguet——
Gov.   Dies at noon.
Jos.   At noon!
    No moment to delay the pious rites,
    Which fit the soul for death. Quick—quick—admit me!
Gov. You cannot enter, monk! Such are my orders.
Jos. Orders, vain man—the Cardinal still is Minister.
    His orders crush all others.
Gov. (*lifting his hat*).   Save his King's!
    See, monk, the royal sign and seal affix'd
    To the Count's mandate. None may have access
    To either prisoner, Huguet or De Mauprat.
    Not even a priest, without the special passport
    Of Count de Baradas. I'll hear no more!
Jos. (*aside*) Just Heaven! and are we baffled thus? Despair!
    (*aloud*) Think on the Cardinal's power—beware his anger.
Gov. I'll not be menaced, priest. Besides the Cardinal
    Is dying and disgraced—all Paris knows it:
    You hear the prisoner's knell! (*bell tolls*, L.)
Jos.   ·   I do beseech you—
    The Cardinal is *not* dying. But one moment,
    And hist—five thousand pistoles!
Gov.   How! a bribe—
    And to a soldier, gray with years of honor!
    Begone!
Jos.   Ten thousand—twenty!
Gov.   Jailer—put
    This monk without our walls.
Jos.   By those gray hairs—
    Yea, by this badge, (*touching the cross of St. Louis, worn by the*
    Governor)
            The guerdon of your valor—
    By all your toils—hard days and sleepless nights—
    Borne in your country's service, noble son—
    Let me but see the prisoner!
Gov.   No!
Jos.   He hath
    Secrets of State—papers in which——
Gov. (*interrupting*).   I know—
    Such was his message to Count Baradas;
    Doubtless the Count will see to it.
Jos (*aside*).   The Count!
    Then not a hope! (*aloud*) You shall——
Gov.   Betray my trust!
    Never—not one word more. You heard me, jailer!
Jos. What can be done? Distraction!
    Dare you refuse the Church her holiest rights?
Gov. I refuse nothing—I obey my orders.
Jos. And sell your country to her parricides!
    Oh, tremble yet—Richelieu——
Gov.   Begone!
Jos   Undone!   [*Exit* Joseph, R. D. F.
Gov. A most audacious shaveling—interdicted
    Above all others by the Count.
Jailer. Oh, by the way, that troublesome young fellow,

Who calls himself the prisoner Huguet's son,
Is here again—implores, weeps, raves to see him.
Gov. Poor youth, I pity him!

Enter DE BERINGHEN, *followed by* FRANÇOIS, R. D. F.

DE BER. (*to* FRANÇOIS). Now, prithee, friend,
Let go my cloak ; you really discompose me.
FRAN. (R.). No! they will drive me hence ; my father ! Oh!
Let me but see him once—but once—one moment !
DE BER. (*to* GOVERNOR). Your servant, Messire ; this poor rascal, Huguet,
Has sent to see the Count de Baradas,
Upon State secrets, that afflict his conscience.
The Count can't leave his Majesty an instant ;
I am his proxy.
Gov. (L. C.). The Count's word is law. (*beckons* JAILER *to un-*
lock L. D. F.
Again, young scapegrace ! How com'st thou admitted ?
DE BER. (R. C.). Oh! a most filial fellow ; Huguet's son !
I found him whimpering in the court below.
I pray his leave to say good bye to father,
Before that very long, unpleasant journey,
Father's about to take.
Gov. The Count's
Commands are strict. No one must visit Huguet
Without his passport.
DE BER. Here it is ! (*shows a paper*) Pshaw ! nonsense !
I'll be your surety. See, my Cerberus,
He is no Hercules !
Gov. Well, you're responsible.
Stand there, friend. If, when you come out, my Lord,
The youth slip in, 'tis *your* fault.
DE BER. So it is !
[*Exit,* L. D. F., *followed by the* JAILER.
Gov. Be calm, my lad. Don't fret so. I had once
A father, too ! I'll not be hard upon you,
And so stand close. I must not *see* you enter.
You understand ? •

Re-enter JAILER, L. D. F.

Come, we'll go our rounds ;
I'll give you just one quarter of an hour ;
And if my lord leave first, make my excuse.
Yet stay, the gallery's long and dark ; no sentry
Until we reach the gate below. He'd best
Wait till I come. If he should lose the way,
We may not be in call.
FRAN. I'll tell him, sir.
[*Exeunt* GOVERNOR *and* JAILER, R.
He's a wise son that knoweth his own father.
I've forged a precious one ! So far, so well !
Alas ! what then ? this wretch hath sent to Baradas—
Will sell the scroll to ransom life. Oh, Heaven !
On what a thread hangs hope ! (*listens at door*, L.)
Loud words—a cry ! (*looks through*
the key-hole.)

They struggle!   Ho—the packet! (*tries to open the door.*)
                                        Lost!   He has it—
The Courtier has it—Huguet, spite his chains.
Grapples!—well done!   Now—now! (*draws back.*)
                                      The gallery's long—
And this is left us! (*drawing dagger, and standing behind* R. *door.*)

Re-enter DE BERINGHEN, *with the packet.*

Victory! (*passes off at* R. D. F.) Yield it, robber! (*following him*)
Yield it—or die! (*a short struggle, without.*)
DE BER. (*without.*) Off! ho!—there!

SCENE II.—*The* KING'S *closet at the Louvre.   A suite of rooms in perspec-
                  tive at one side.*

Enter BARADAS *and* ORLEANS, R. C.

BAR. (R.). All smiles! the Cardinal's swoon of yesterday
     Heralds his death to-day.
     And yet, should this accurs'd De Mauprat
     Have given our packet to another—'Sdeath!
     I dare not think of it!
ORLEANS (L.).   You've sent to search him.
BAR. Sent, sir, to search ?—that hireling hands may find
     Upon him, naked, with its broken seal,
     That scroll, whose every word is death!   No—no—
     These hands alone must clutch that awful secret.
     I dare not leave the palace, night or day,
     While Richelieu lives—his minions—creatures—spies—
     Not one must reach the King!
ORLEANS.   What hast thou done?
BAR. Summon'd De Mauprat hither.
ORLEANS.   Could this Huguet,
     Who pray'd thy presence with so fierce a fervor,
     Have thieved the scroll?
BAR.   Huguet was housed with us,
     The very moment we dismiss'd the courier.
     It cannot be! a stale trick for reprieve.
     But, to make sure, I've sent our trustiest friend
     To see and sift him.   Hist—here comes the King.
     How fare you, Sire ?

Enter LOUIS, *followed by* PAGES, *and* COURT, L. C.

LOUIS.   In the same mind.   I have
     Decided!   Yes, he would forbid your presence,
     My brother—yours, my friend—then Julie, too!
     Thwarts—braves—defies—(*suddenly turning to* BARADAS We make
          you Minister.
     Gaston, for you—the baton of our armies,
     You love me, do you not?
ORLEANS.   Oh, love you, Sire ?
     (*aside*) Never so much as now. (*retires,* L. U. E., COURTIERS *sur-
          round him.*)
BAR.   May I deserve
     Your trust (*aside*) until you sign your abdication.

(*aloud*) My liege, but one way left to daunt de Mauprat,
And Julie to divorce.   We must prepare
The death-warrant; what, tho' sign'd and seal'd ? we can
Withhold the enforcement.
LOUIS.   Ah, you may prepare it ;
  We need not urge it to effect.
BAR.   Exactly !
  No haste, my liege. (*looking at his watch, and aside*) He may live
  one hour longer.

Enter PAGE, L. U. E.

PAGE. The Lady Julie, Sire, implores an audience.
LOUIS. Aha! repentant of her folly!   Well,
  Admit her.   [*Exit*, PAGE, L. U. E.
BAR.   Sire, she comes for Mauprat's pardon,
  And the conditions——
LOUIS.   You are Minister—
  We leave to you our answer,

As JULIE *enters* L. U. E., *the* CAPTAIN *of the* ARCHERS *enters* R. *door, and
    whispers* BARADAS.

CAPT.   The Chevalier
  De Mauprat waits below.
BAR. (*aside*).   Now the dispatch.
                            [*Exit with* OFFICER, R.
JULIE (L. C.). My liege, you sent for me. I come where grief
  Should come when guiltless, while the name of King
  Is holy on the earth! Here, at the feet
  Of Power, I kneel for mercy.
LOUIS (R. C.).   Mercy, Julie,
  Is an affair of state.   The Cardinal should
  In this be your interpreter.
JULIE.   Alas !
  I know not if that mighty spirit now
  Stoop to the things of earth.   Nay, while I speak,
  Perchance he hears the orphan by the throne
  Where Kings themselves need pardon! O, my liege,
  Be father to the fatherless ; in you
  Dwells my last hope.

Enter BARADAS, R.

BAR (*aside*).   He has not the dispatch ;
  Smil'd, while we search'd, and braves me—Oh !
LOUIS (*gently*).   What would'st thou ?
JULIE. A single life. You reign o'er millions. What
  Is *one man's* life to you?—and yet to *me*
  'Tis France—'tis earth—'tis everything—a life—
  A human life—my husband's !
LOUIS (*aside*).   Speak to her,
  I am not marble   Give her hope—or—(*retires ; speaks to* ORLEANS
      and COURTIERS.)
BAR.   ·   Madam,
  Vex not your King, whose heart, too soft for justice,
  Leaves to his ministers the solemn charge.

JULIE. You *were* his friend.
BAR. I *was* before I loved thee.
JULIE. Loved me!
BAR. Hush, Julie; could'st thou misinterpret
My acts, thoughts, motives, nay, my very words,
Here—in this palace?
JULIE. Now I know I'm mad;
Even that memory fail'd me.
BAR. I am young,
Well-born and brave as Mauprat—for thy sake
I peril what he has not—fortune—power;
All to great souls most dazzling. I alone
Can save thee from yon tyrant, now my puppet!
Be mine; annul the mockery of this marriage,
And on the day I clasp thee to my breast
De Mauprat shall be free.
JULIE. Thou durst not speak
Thus in *his* ear. (*pointing to* LOUIS) Thou double traitor! tremble.
I will unmask thee.
BAR. I will say thou ravest.
And see this scroll! its letters shall be blood!
Go to the King, count with me word for word;
And while you pray the life—I write the sentence!
JULIE. Stay, stay! (*rushing to the* KING) You have a kind and princely
heart,
Tho' sometimes it is silent; you were born
To *power*—it has not flush'd you into madness,
As it doth meaner men. Banish my husband—
Dissolve our marriage—cast me to that grave
Of human ties, where hearts congeal to ice,
In the dark convent's everlasting winter—
(Surely eno' for justice—hate—revenge)—
But spare this life, thus lonely, scathed, and bloomless;
And when thou stand'st for judgment on thine own,
The deed shall shine beside thee as an angel.
LOUIS (*much affected*). Go, go, to Baradas; annul thy marriage,
And——
JULIE (*anxiously, and watching his countenance*). Be his bride!
LOUIS. Yes!
JULIE. Oh thou sea of shame,
And not one star!

The KING *goes up the stage, and passes through the suite of rooms at the side,
in evident emotion. Exeunt* KING *and* COURT, R. U. E.

BAR. Well, thy election, Julie;
This hand—his grave?
JULIE. His grave! and I——
BAR. Can save him.
Swear to be mine.
JULIE. That were a bitterer death!
Avaunt, thou tempter. I did ask his life
A boon, and not the barter of dishonor.
The heart can break, and scorn you; wreck your malice;
Adrien and I will leave you this sad earth,
And pass together hand in hand to Heaven!
BAR. You have decided.

Beckons in CAPTAIN, *who enters* R.; BARADAS *whispers to him and he goes off quickly,* R.

Listen to me, Lady ;
I am no base intriguer.   I adored thee
From the first glance of those inspiring eyes ;
With thee entwined ambition, hope, the future.
I will not lose thee!   I can place thee nearest—
Ay, to the throne—nay, on the throne, perchance ;
My star is at its zenith.   Look upon me ;
Hast thou decided ?
JULIE.   No, no ; you can see
How weak I am ; be human, sir—one moment.

BARADAS *stamps his foot,* DE MAUPRAT *is brought on guarded,* R.; GUARDS *range* R.

BAR. Behold thy husband !   Shall he pass to death,
And know thou could'st have saved him ?
JULIE. (L.).   Adrien, speak,
But say you wish to *live !* if not, your wife,
Your slave—do with me as you will. (*crosses to him.*)
DE MAU. (R.).   Oh, think, my Julie,
Life, at the best, is short—but love immortal !
BAR. (*taking* JULIE'S *hand*). Ah, loveliest——
JULIE.   Go, that touch has made me iron.
We have decided (*embracing* MAUPRAT)—death !
BAR. (*to* DE MAUPRAT).   Now say to whom
Thou gavest the packet, and thou yet shalt live.
DE MAU. I'll tell thee nothing.
BAR.   Hark—the rack !
DE MAU.   Thy penance
For ever, wretch !   What rack is like the conscience ?
BAR. (*giving the writ to the* OFFICER, *who is* R.C.). Hence, to the heads-
man ! (*the doors are thrown open,* C.   *The* HUISSIER *announces*
" His Eminence the Cardinal Duke de Richelieu.")

Enter RICHELIEU, R. C., *attended by* PAGES, *etc., pale, feeble, and leaning on*
JOSEPH, *followed by three* SECRETARIES OF STATE, *attended by* SUB-
SECRETARIES *with papers, etc.*

JULIE (*rushing to* RICHELIEU). You live—you live—and Adrien shall
not die !
RICH. Not if an old man's prayers, himself near death,
Can aught avail thee, daughter !   Count, you now
Hold what I held on earth—one boon, my Lord,
This soldier's life.
BAR.   The stake—my head—you said it.
I cannot lose one trick.   Remove your prisoner.
JULIE (R. *of* RICHELIEU). No ! no !

Enter LOUIS *from* R. U. E., *attended by* COURT.

RICH. (*to* OFFICER).   Stay, sir, one moment.   My good liege,
Your worn out servant, willing, Sire, to spare you
Some pain of conscience, would forestall your wishes.

I do resign my office.

OMNES.   You!

JULIE.   All's over!

RICH. My end draws near. These sad ones, Sire, I love them.
I do not ask his life ; but suffer justice
To halt, until I can dismiss his soul,
Charged with an old man's blessing.

LOUIS (R. C.).   Surely!

(DE MAUPRAT goes behind, to the L. of RICHELIEU.,

BAR. (on the R. of the KING).   Sire——

LOUIS. Silence—small favor to a dying servant.

RICH. You would consign your armies to the baton
Of your most honored brother. Sire, so be it!
Your Minister, the Count de Baradas ;
A most sagacious choice! Your Secretaries
Of State attend me, Sire, to render up
The ledgers of a realm. I do beseech you,
Suffer these noble gentlemen to learn
The nature of the glorious task that waits them,
Here, in thy presence.

LOUIS.   You say well, my Lord.
Approach, sirs. (to SECRETARIES, as he seats himself. PAGES place
a chair for the KING, R. C.)

RICH.   I—I—faint—air—air ! (JOSEPH and a GENTLE-
MAN assist him to a chair, placed by PAGES, L. C.)
I thank you—
Draw near, my children.

BAR. (aside).   He's too weak to question,
Nay, scarce to speak ; all's safe.

JULIE kneeling beside the CARDINAL ; the OFFICER OF THE GUARD behind
MAUPRAT. JOSEPH near RICHELIEU, watching the KING. LOUIS
seated R. C. BARADAS at the back of the KING'S chair, anxious and
disturbed. ORLEANS at a greater distance, careless and triumphant. As
each SECRETARY advances in his turn, he takes the portfolios from the
SUB-SECRETARIES.

FIRST SEC. (kneeling).   The affairs of Portugal.
Most urgent, Sire. (gives a paper) One short month since the Duke
Braganza was a rebel,

LOUIS.   And is still !

FIRST SEC. No, Sire, he has succeeded ! He is now
Crown'd King of Portugal—craves instant succor
Against the arms of Spain.

LOUIS.   We will not grant it
Against his lawful King. Eh, Count ?

BAR.   No, Sire.

FIRST SEC. But Spain's your deadliest foe ; whatever
Can weaken Spain must strengthen France. The Cardinal
Would send the succors—(solemnly)·—balance, Sire, of Europe !
(gives another paper.)

LOUIS. The Cardinal—balance ! We'll consider—Eh, Count ?

BAR. Yes, Sire—fall back.

FIRST SEC. (rises).   But——

BAR.   Oh! fall back sir. (SECRETARY bows
and retires.)

JOS.   Humph !

SECOND SEC. (*advances and kneels*). The affairs of England, Sire, most
     urgent. (*gives paper*) Charles
     The First has lost a battle that decides
     One half his realm—craves moneys, Sire, and succor.
LOUIS. He shall have both. Eh, Baradas?
BAR.   Yes, Sire.
     (*aside*) Oh that dispatch!—my veins are fire!
RICH. (*feebly, but with great distinctness*). My liege—
     Forgive me—Charles's cause is lost. A man,
     Named Cromwell, risen—a great man—your succor
     Would fail—your loans be squander'd! Pause—reflect.
LOUIS. Reflect. Eh, Baradas?
BAR.   Reflect, Sire.
JOS.   Humph!
LOUIS (*aside*). I half repent! No successor to Richelieu!
     Round me thrones totter—dynasties dissolve—
     The soil he guards alone escapes the earthquake!
JOS. (*to* RICHELIEU). Our star not yet eclipsed—you mark the King?
     Oh! had we the dispatch!

                     Enter a PAGE, L. U. E.

RICH.   Ah!—Joseph!—Child—
     Would I could help thee!
             [PAGE *whispers* JOSEPH, *who exits hastily*, L. U. E.
BAR. (*to* SECRETARY).   Sir, fall back!
SECOND SEC. (*rises*).   But——
BAR.   Pshaw, sir!
             [SECOND SECRETARY *bows and retires*, L. C.
THIRD SEC. (*mysteriously, kneels*). The secret correspondence, Sire, most
     urgent—
     Accounts of spies—deserters—heretics—
     Assassins—poisoners—schemes against yourself! (*gives paper.*
     SECRETARY *rises.*)
LOUIS. *Myself!*—most urgent! (*the* KING *seizes that paper and drops the
     others.*)

Re-enter JOSEPH *with* FRANÇOIS, *whose pourpoint is streaked with blood.*
     FRANÇOIS *passes behind the* CARDINAL'S ATTENDANTS, *and, sheltered
     by them from the sight of* BARADAS, *etc., falls at* RICHELIEU'S *feet.*

FRAN. (L. *of* RICHELIEU).   My Lord!
     I have not fail'd. (*gives the packet.*)
RICH.   Hush! (*looking at the contents.*)
THIRD SEC. (*to* KING).   Sire, the Spaniards
     Have reinforced their army on the frontiers.
     The Duc de Bouillon——
RICH.   Hold! In this department—
     A paper—here, Sire—read yourself—then take
     The Count's advice on't. (*the* KING *takes the paper and goes* L.)

Enter DE BERINGHEN, L. U. E., *hastily, and draws aside* BARADAS, *and
     whispers.*

BAR. (*bursting from* DE BERINGHEN). What! and reft it from thee!
     Ha!—hold! (*going towards the* KING).
JOS. (L. C.).   Fall back, son, it is your turn now!

LOUIS (*reading, pacing the stage from* L. *to* R.). To Bouillon—and signd'd
    Orleans—
        Baradas, too!—league with our foes of Spain—
        Lead our Italian armies—what! to Paris!
        Capture the King—my health requires repose—
        Make me subscribe my proper abdication—
        Orleans, my brother, Regent! Saints of Heaven!
        These are the men I loved! (RICHELIEU *falls back.*)
JOS.   See to the Cardinal!
BAR. (R C.). He's dying—and I shall yet dupe the King!
LOUIS (*rushing to* RICHELIEU), Richelieu!—Lord Cardinal!—'tis *I* resign.
    Reign thou!
JOS. (*behind the chair*). Alas! too late—he faints!
LOUIS (R. *of* RICHELIEU).   Reign, Richelieu!
RICH (*feebly*). With absolute power?——
LOUIS.   Most absolute! Oh! live!
    If not for me—for France!
RICH   FRANCE!
LOUIS   Oh! this treason!
        The army—Orleans—Bouillon—Heavens!—the Spaniard!
        Where will they be next week?
RICH. (*starting up, seizing the paper and throwing it on the ground*). There,
        —at my feet! (*to* FIRST *and* SECOND SECRETARY)
        Ere the clock strike—the Envoys have their answer!
                                    [*Exit* SECRETARIES, L. U. E.
        (*to* THIRD SECRETARY, *with a ring*) This to De Chavigny—he knows
        the rest—
        No need of parchment here—he must not halt
        For sleep—for food—In *my* name—MINE!—he will
        Arrest the Duc de Bouillon at the head
        Of his army! (*Exit* THIRD SECRETARY, L. U. E.) Ho, there, Count
        de Baradas,
        Thou hast lost the stake! Away with him! (*as the* GUARDS *open,*
            BARADAS *passes through the line. Exeunt,* L) Ha! ha!—
    (*snatching* DE MAUPRAT'S *death-warrant from the* OFFICER *as he passes*)
        See here, De Mauprat's death-writ, Julie!
        Parchment for battledores! Embrace your husband—
        At last the old man blesses you!
JULIE (L. C.).   O, joy!
        You are saved; you live—I hold you in these arms.
DE MAU. Never to part——
JULIE.   No—never, Adrien—never!
LOUIS. (*peevishly*, R. C.). One moment makes a startling cure, Lord Car-
            dinal.
RICH. Ay, Sire, for in one moment there did pass
        Into this wither'd frame the might of France!—
        My own dear France—I have thee yet—I have saved thee!
        I clasp thee still!—it was thy voice that call'd me
        Back from the tomb!—What mistress like our country?
LOUIS. For Mauprat's pardon—well! But Julie—Richelieu,
        Leave me one thing to love!
RICH.   A subject's luxury!
        Yet if you must love something, Sire—*love me!*
LOUIS (*smiling in spite of himself*). Fair proxy for a young fresh Demoi-
            selle!
RICH. Your heart speaks for my clients. Kneel, my children;
        Thank your King. (RICHELIEU *passes up the stage; the* COURT *bow.*)

JULIE.   Ah, tears like these, my liege,
    Are dews that mount to Heaven.
LOUIS.   Rise—rise—be happy. (*retires.*)
        (RICHELIEU *comes forward and beckons to* DE BERINGHEN.)
DE BER. (*falteringly*, R.). My Lord—you are—most happily—recover'd
RICH. But you are pale, dear Beringhen;—this air
    Suits not your delicate frame—I long have thought so;—
    Sleep not another night in Paris. Go—
    Or else your precious life may be in danger.
    Leave France, dear Beringhen!
DE BER. St. Denis travelled without his head.
    I'm luckier than St. Denis.   [*Exit* DE BERINGHEN, R.
RICH. (*to* ORLEANS). For you repentance—absence—and confession!
                                         [*Exit* ORLEANS, R.
    (*to* FRANÇOIS, *who is* R. C.) Never say *fail* again. Brave boy! (*to* JOSEPH,
        crosses to C.) He'll be—
    A Bishop first.
JOS.   (R. C.).   Ah, Cardinal——
RICH. (C.).   Ah, Joseph! (*the* KING *advances*, R. C.)
        (*to* LOUIS, *as* DE MAUPRAT *and* JULIE *converse apart*)
    See, my liege—see thro' plots and counterplots—
    Thro' gain and loss—thro' glory and disgrace—
    Along the plains, where passionate Discord rears
    Eternal Babel—still the holy stream
    Of human happiness glides on!
LOUIS.   And must we
    Thank for *that* also—our Prime Minister?
RICH. No—let us own it :—there is ONE above
    Sways the harmonious mystery of the world,
    Even better than prime ministers :—
    Thus ends it.

    Position of the Characters at the fall of the Curtain.

                        PAGES.
        COURTIERS.   COURTIERS.
            LOUIS.   RICHELIEU.
                        C.
    FRANÇOIS.   JULIE.
        R. C.   L. C.
JOSEPH.   MAUPRAT.
    R.   L.

    The Characters are supposed to face the Audience.

                    CURTAIN.

THE RIGHTFUL HEIR.

CAST OF CHARACTERS.

Lyceum Theatre,
London, Oct. 3, 1868.

Vyvyan (Captain of the Privateer Dreadnaught)...........Mr. BANDMANN.
Sir Grey de Malpas (the Poor Cousin)..................... Mr. HERMANN VEZIN.
Wrecklyffe (a Gentleman turned Pirate)...................Mr. LAWLOR.
Lord Beaufort (Lady Montreville's Son)...................Mr. NEVILLE.
Sir Godfrey Seymour (a Magistrate).......................
Falkner, } (Vyvyan's Lieutenants)..................... { Mr. LIN RAYNE.
Harding, }   { Mr. ANDERSON.
Marsden (Seneschal of the Castle)........................Mr. DAVID EVANS.
Alton (a Village Priest).................................Mr. BASIL POTTER.
Sub-Officer of the Dreadnaught ....Mr. EVERARD.
Servant to Lady Montreville......... ....Mr. W. TEMPLETON.
Lady Montreville (a Widowed Countess)..... ....Mrs. HERMANN VEZIN.
Eveline (her Ward).......................................Miss MILLY PALMER.

Halberdiers, Retainers, Sailors, Peasantry, Servants, etc., etc.

TO ALL FRIENDS AND KINSFOLK

IN

THE AMERICAN COMMONWEALTH,

THIS DRAMA IS DEDICATED,

WITH AFFECTION AND RESPECT.

London. Sept. 28, 1868.

PREFACE.

MANY years ago this Drama was re-written from an earlier play by the same Author, called "The Sea Captain," the first idea of which was suggested by a striking situation in a novel by M. A. Dumas *Le Capitaine Paul*. The Author withdrew "The Sea Captain" from the stage (and even from printed publication), while it had not lost such degree of favor as the admirable acting of Mr. Macready chiefly contributed to obtain for it · intending to replace it before the public with some important changes in the histrionic cast, and certain slight alterations in the conduct of the story. But the alterations once commenced, became so extensive in character, diction and even in revision of plot, that a new play gradually rose from the foundations of the old one. The task thus undertaken, being delayed by other demands upon time and thought, was scarcely completed when Mr. Macready's retirement from his profession suspended the Author's literary connection with the stage, and "The Rightful Heir" has remained in tranquil seclusion till this year, when he submits his appeal to the proper tribunal; sure, that if he fail of a favorable hearing, it will not be the fault of the friends who take part in his cause and act in his behalf.

SCENERY.

ACT I.—SCENE I.—Castle Ruins in 4th grooves.

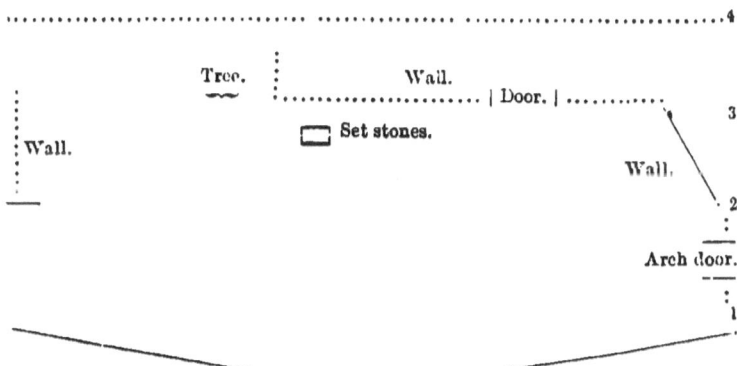

On flat, view of the sea; L. side, cliffs and castle; set wall, ruined, 10 to 12 feet high, along 3d grooves and L. 1 and 2 E.; open archway L. 1 E. set; low set wall R. 2 E.; a heap of set stones up C., to aid effect of picture; a set tree up R. C.; sky sinks and borders; curtain for covering the change of scene: dark velvet, heavily fringed and bordered deeply with gold, in two parts, to draw up and to each side; with coat of arms, royal English white lion and red griffin guarding shield and crown, in tapestry; over date in old English, 1588.

SCENE II.—Castle gardens in 5th grooves.

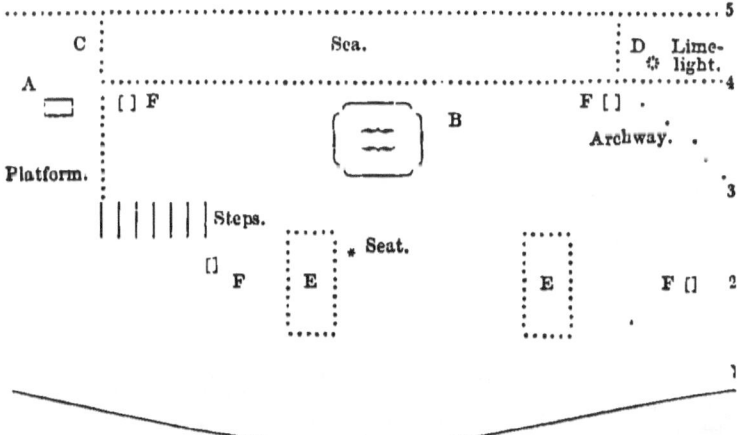

On flat foreground, dark blue sea, blending with the canvas down in U. E.; upper two-thirds light; bright sky; L. side, D., set wall of castle in U. E.; 3 E., set wall with open archway; 1st and 2d grooves wings, walls; all this side is dark; R. side c., set wall continuing the castle, supposed to be off R. 1 and 2 E.'s; the set cut with a cliff, running down into the sea; R. 2 and 3 E., set platform, reached by broad steps, six feet above stage level; A, a box, with large box-wood tree, trimmed into fantastic shape in the fashion of the Elizabethan age; R. 2 groove wing, tree, run in to mask end of platform; B., a fountain, playing in an oval basin; in front of the basin, a half-ring of canvas down, covered with flowers and moss; E E, two canvases, covered with flowers, for flower-beds; a garden seat to R. 1; F, F, F, F, statues, three-quarter life size; the upper pair kneeling satyrs, the front pair nymphs erect; limelight L. U. E., lighting up R. side.

ACT II.—SCENE I.—Interior, in 2d grooves; Gothic architecture; R. on F., wide hearth, with earl's coronet and shield on the keystone; R. on F., portrait of man, half length, to resemble the personator of VYVYAN in face; the painting on flat makes the stage seem to be part of the chamber thereon represented; open R. and L.; table and three chairs on at c., table has blue cloth, corded with gold and trimmed with red fringe; chairs have an old English M, surmounted by a coronet, in dead gold, on the back, inside.

SCENE II.—Court-yard and Castle. Exterior, in 5th grooves.

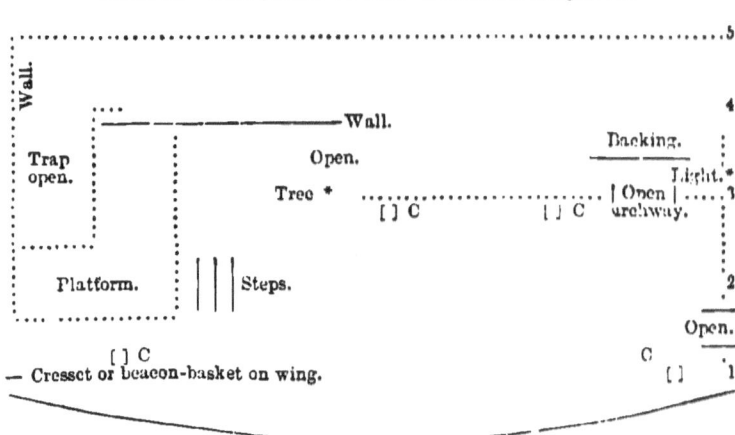

Sky on flat; the lower two-thirds is hidden by the set walls R. in 4th grooves, and in 3d grooves, c. to L.; L. side, 3 E., backing of wall, to large open archway in 3 g. set 1 and 2 E. closed in; small open archway in L. 1 E. set; dark, except L. 3 E., where there is a light; R. side 3 and 4 E., castle wall, ending in cliff over the sea; open trap, for the ditch, between platform (ten feet above stage level) and set wall; steps to platform 2 E.; wings are walls; sky sinks and borders; C, C, C, C, cannon on block carriages, the front pair pointed at each other, the upper pair pointed front; tree up R. of O., reaches to top of walls.

ACT III.—SCENE I.—Rocky landscape, sea and cliff, in 2d grooves; flat to roll up; view of sea, L. side; cliff running out over the water; all of 2 E. to sink and carry down the set rocks built up on it; along 1st grooves, low flat of rocks, to sink; sky sink and borders; trees and rocks for wings; sunset effect by limelight, L. U. E.

SCENE II.—Same as Act II., Scene II.; sunset effect L. U. E.; stage dark.

ACT IV.—SCENE I.—Same as Act II., Scene I.; table and chairs not on; a chair and a settee L.

SCENE II.—Cliff and Sea, in 4th grooves.

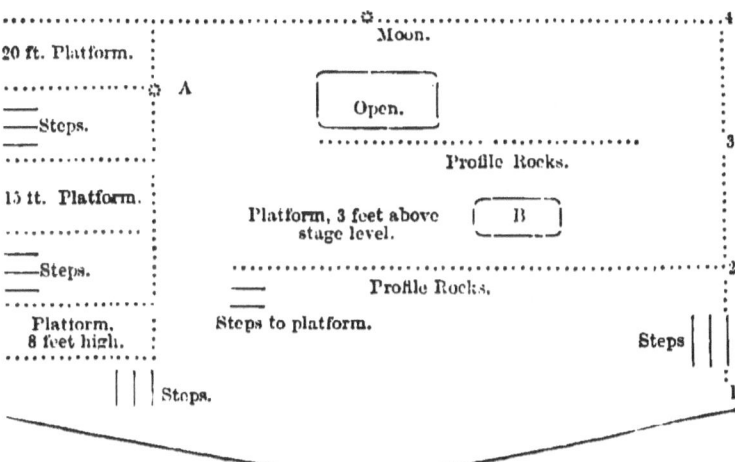

Limelight for moonlight, L. U. E.; sea on flat, with full moon at C.; the wing run in on 4th groove, R., is a profile edge of cliff; by having a piece stand out half way up its height, the piece will seem to be the base of another cliff, still further out in the sea; L. side, rocky cliff, covering in all; 1 E., set steps, leading from off down upon stage; sky wings, except L. 1 g., which is rocks; R. side, a series of rocks, forming steps and platforms; all practicable; A, a tree on the platform edge, joined to a piece facing the platform, so that, on VYVYAN seizing it, his weight brings it down, forces it to draw the piece joining it to L., and deposits him in open trap C., in 3 E.; B, a trap-net used in this scene.

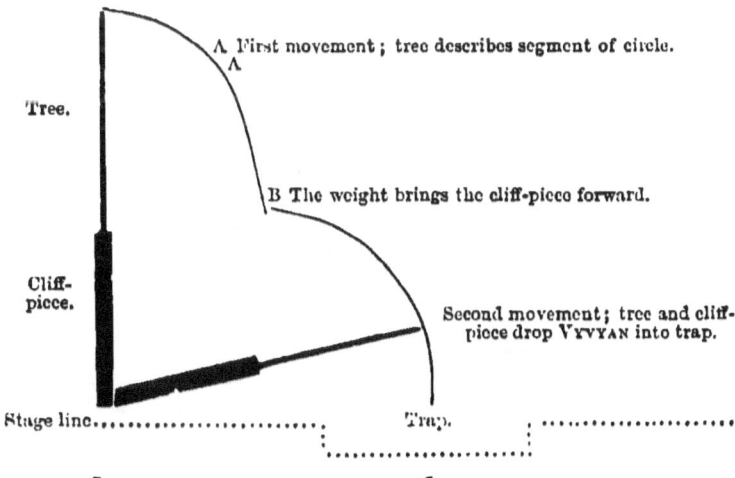

ACT V.—Scene I.—Same as Act IV., Scene II.; Trap B (see Act IV., Scene II.) is open; dark.

Scene II.—Interior, in 1st grooves; deep sink, rafters and ceiling; window R. C. in F. open; two chairs.

Scene III.—Hall in 5th grooves; closed in R. and L.; upper E. gallery to bear weight of spectators; large archway in its front, 4th grooves; L. 2 E., dais, with canopy over; royal arms behind chair; table L. C.; arch R. 3 E.; bannerets hung from wall; stained glass window in flat.

COSTUMES.

VYVYAN.—*Act I.:* Black hard felt hat, four or five inches high in the crown, with a white ostrich feather; steel gorget, polished; three yards long scarlet sash, six inches wide, fringed with gold at the end, from left shoulder to right hip, tied behind, with loose ends; buff leather jerkin, sleeveless : belt around waist; rapier, black and steel sheath, cut steel hilt; doublet and loose breeches of slate blue, striped up and down with black cord on the doublet, striped in *chevron* on the breeches; buff boots pulled up to above the knee; small satchel of buff leather, hung on right side, with dagger under it; short curl black wig, rather short; moustache and imperial; make-up after pictures of Essex, Raleigh or Drake. *Act II.—Scene I.:* Gorget and jerkin removed. *Scene II..* Red scarf; sword like the other, in similar sheath, for throwing aside. *Act III. and IV.:* Same as last; hat, no sword. *Act V.:* Half armor: helmet, with vizor to close; white plume; blue sash; steel-plated gauntlets, right hand one to be thrown on stage; high russet boots; thigh armor in plates.

GREY DE MALPAS.—Face made up for pale, cold, passionless expression, prematurely aged; moustache and imperial. *Act I.:* Brown doublet, striped with yellow cord; slate-colored tights; shoes. *Scene II.:* Same; fur cloak, with hanging sleeves; flat cap; cane. *Act V.:* Same as first dress; cane.

WRECKLYFFE.—Black wig, long loose hair; moustache, with flowing ends; chin beard; scar across right eyebrow and cheekbone; steel cap; long, narrow mantle of dark glazed sea-green water-proof, worn carelessly over one arm and about the body; short cutlass; brace of brass-mounted pistols stuck in belt; arms bare to the elbow; seaman's sleeveless jacket worn loosely over a breast-plate, tarnished.

GODFREY SEYMOUR.—Old man; white wig and moustache · black velvet skull-cap; red velvet doublet, with hanging sleeves, trimmed with gold lace; slate-colored tights; velvet shoes.

BEAUFORT.—*Act I.:* Handsome suit, blue and gold; sword : blue velvet round cap, with white plume russet boots drawn up to above the knee. *Act V.:* Red and black doublet; red tights; black velvet shoes; long dark mantle, with sleeves, trimmed deeply with ermine; face pale.

FALKNER.—Plumed hat; back and breast-plates · sword; high boots.

HARDING.—Like FALKNER, with variation in color of his doublet sleeves, of feather of his hat, etc.

ALTON.—Long white beard; white wig; dark cowl and long gown. *Act V.:* Skull-cap; staff.

MARSDEN.—Long white hair, white moustache and chin beard; handsome laced suit; doublet; trunk hose; velvet shoes, slashed and puffed; long white staff, with gilt coronet on top.

SERVANT.--Gray livery, turned up with orange.

SAILORS. - In Guernsey shirts, with belts supporting cutlasses and pistols; high boots; jackets gathered in at the waist by sashes; tights and shoes.

SERVANTS.—Like first servant.

CLERK TO SEYMOUR.—In black.

HALBERDIERS.—Steel caps; back, breast and thigh plates; boots; halberds for them.

VILLAGERS.—As usual.

LADY MONTREVILLE.—Fair-haired; make up after portraias of Queen Elizabeth; if the ruff does not look becomingly, have a deep ruffled lace collar open in front; jewelled stomacher; bodice cut square at the bosom; with lace let in; velvet boly and skirt, with deep border jewelled cross to long necklace; ear-rings; wedding-ring; velvet band, with jewelled beading, on the head, just behind the front puffs of the hair. *Act V.:* Dark velvet skirt and body; the bodice faced in the front with white lace, crossed with violet braid.

EVELINE.—Hair puffed in front, and in loose ringlets in a bunch at back of head; string of pearls three times around the neck, ending in locket and cross; blue body and skirt; skirt opens in front and shows white under-skirt; trimmed with gold cord. *Act V.:* White satin dress; face pale, with the white on the cheeks to come off and show color under, at a touch of hand dampened by a breath.

VILLAGE GIRLS.—As usual.

WAITING WOMEN FOR LADY MONTREVILLE.—As usual.

PROPERTIES, (See Scenery).

Act I.—Scene I.: Spade; coin for VYVYAN; weapons for sailors. *Scene II.:* A hand-ful of flowers for EVELINE to enter with, ready R. 1 E.; cane for MALPAS. *Act II.—Scene I.:* Table and three chairs; on table a two-handled silver goblet; cups and plates of fruit for three. *Scene II.:* Four cannon in block carriages, not to be touched; a cresset or beacon basket, at end of a rod, hung out from R. 1 E.; sheet of printed paper, foolscap size. *Act III.—Scene I.:* Staff; roll of MSS. tied up, for ALTON. *Scene II.:* Sword hilt in sheath, for VYVYAN to throw aside. *Act IV.—Scene I.:* MSS. roll, as in Act III., Scene I., for VYV-YAN to enter with, ready R. *Scene II.:* Profile miniature ship, to work from R. to L. U. E. line. *Act V.—Scene I.:* Canes, as before, for MALPAS and ALTON. *Scene II.·* Salver; gold cup, jewelled; letter, with sealed silk band, to be opened on stage; handful of flowers for EVELINE to enter with, ready R. *Scene III.* Table; chairs; quills, inkdishes, paper, books, on table; halberds for Halberdiers.

TIME OF PLAYING—TWO HOURS AND FORTY-FIVE MINUTES.

NOTE.

The few " cuts " are marked by enclosure between quotations, as " ———."

STORY OF THE PLAY.

Several years previous to the opening of the drama, very few of England's proud and wealthy nobles could boast of a fairer name, broader lands, or a more ancient pedigree than the Earl of Dartford. Left early in years a widower, his entire affection was centered upon an only daughter, the Lady Geraldine, for whom he destined a brilliant and powerful alliance. It so happened, however, that attached to the Earl's household was a young page, who, though his origin was somewhat lowly as compared with that of those by whom he was surrounded, could fairly boast of a comely form combined with intellect, gentleness, and courage. Despite the difference in rank, constant association brought about a unity of sentiment between the handsome page and the fair Geraldine, which speedily ripened into love, and was hallowed by a secret marriage. Their meetings remained undetected for some time, until one unfortunate evening, when a kinsman of the Earl's tracked the bridegroom to the lady's chamber. As ill news speeds apace so sped the kinsman to his noble relative with the fearful intelligence of his child's presumed dishonor.

With all the direful anger of a ruined house maddening his actions, the Earl, seizing his sword, hastened to his daughter's apartment, and forcing the door which was barred against his entrance, was prepared to inflict instant death upon the cause of his disgrace. But no culprit was there to meet his angry gaze; no one upon whom he could wreak his deadly vengeance—the only occupant of the chamber was his daughter, and she lay senseless upon the floor. But the wide opened casement told a tale that could deceive no one. Whoever had been there previously had by that means made his escape, hoping to save the lady's honor; only, however, to meet a certain death. The chamber was situated in the highest part of the castle, overlooking a long and steep descent of rocks, down which it was highly dangerous to pass with the best possible assistance—without it, fatal. The morning told the tale; the page's body was discovered at the foot of the rocks, fearfully mangled; a hasty midnight burial soon concealed his shattered remains and hid the bride's secret from the outer world.

After a few days of continued insensibility, a child was born, which was speedily removed to the shelter of Alton, the Earl's priest, and who being entirely dependent upon his noble patron, was easily bound to inviolable secrecy. The only wonder is that the infant was not destroyed, and thus all traces of the presumed crime obliterated. Fate, however, willed otherwise. The Lady Geraldine recovered, and often visited the priest's abode to bless and caress her offspring, and she placed in the holy man's keeping every proof that might at some future period be requisite to substantiate the infant's claims. But as the progress of time wears off the keen edge of sorrow, so fared it with the Lady Geraldine.

A lordly suitor came—ambition was grafted in her mind and soon brought forth its fruits; and forced by the surrounding circumstances of a haughty and threatening father, and the entreaties of a wily kinsman, she stifled a mother's feelings, forsook her child, and became the wife of the Earl of Montreville. New ties produced new affections, and the second nuptials brought another son, for whom the mother's love became warmer and more enduring than for her first-born. The poor priest, alarmed at the change, and fearing the direst results if his secret was divulged, observed the strictest silence, and continued for years to rear as one of his own, the infant entrusted to his care, until at a youthful age, the boy was enticed on board a vessel which happened to touch upon the coast, and borne away. This, however, was not the work of chance, but was really accomplished by the designs of a poor cousin of the family, Sir Grey de Malpas, who hoped some future day to obtain possession of the title and estates. At his instigation, Wrecklyffe, who had lost the fortune and position of a gentleman, and mixed himself up in piratical pursuits, sought the hamlet where the priest resided, and by his rough yet gallant bearing, so well adapted for winning the admiration of a youth of spirit, and his stories of danger, enterprise, and wealth soon secured a strong hold over his intended prize, and induced him to board his vessel and join in a cruise to the regions of affluence he had depicted.

Days afterwards, when far at sea, the true character of the ship was revealed. The pirate's flag was hoisted, and the captain in brief words told his captive that there was a choice of life or death before him—to join the pirate crew, or seek a last resting place in the ocean ; confessing that he had been well paid to get him out of the way. But the noble spirit of the youth was aroused by the desperate nature of the position in which he found himself; it was but the work of an instant to snatch a cutlass from the hands of a sailor near him, and in a moment more the pirate lay upon the deck weltering in blood. The scowling crew at first cried out for vengeance, but Wrecklyffe, who was second in command, was deeply imbued with a superstitious belief that it was unlucky to shed blood on board a ship unless in actual fighting, and he therefore managed to restrain their fierce anger, and directed them to seize the youth and bind him to a single plank. So soon as this was done he was cast over the vessel's side, and thus left to the m rcy of the elements and God; all sail was set, and very soon the little craft, which had promised to be the means of conveying him to a haven of happiness and prosperity, was lost to sight. For two days and nights was he tossed upon the waves until he lost all consciousness ; when he came to, he found that he had been discovered and rescued by one of the Queen's ships on her voyage to meet the Spanish cruisers.

With health restored, he was installed amongst the crew, and by his gallant and courageous bearing soon won a foremost position. During the vessel's cruise, he was instrumental in saving the lives of the Lady Eveline and her father from a band of Algerine pirates, and during the time she remained on the ship a mutual attachment sprung up between them, promising, if fate so willed it, a happy union at some future day. Vows of constancy and truth were exchanged when she was transferred to a homeward-bound ship. Time worked many changes ; the Earl of Dartford died; the Earl of Montreville also passed away, and the son of the second marriage succeeded to the estates, and became Lord Beaufort of Montreville. Eveline's father also was summoned to join his ancestors, and being related to the Montreville family, she became the ward and companion of the widowed Countess, in which position she inspired the young lord with strong feelings of love, though her heart remained true to, and silently yearned after, her sailor lover, who, under the name of Vyvyan, had risen to the rank of captain in command of the Dreadnaught, one of the smartest of the royal privateers.

Such then is the previous history of the characters who figure at the opening of the play. Sir Grey de Malpas has been installed as steward; still, the chains of poverty gall him, but he consoles himself by believing that he shall one day realize the ambition of his life, the title and revenues of the earldom, to which he is next in the succession upon the failure of the direct issue. But sore troubles are in store for him. Whilst working in the castle grounds his reveries are wofully disturbed by the sudden appearance of Wrecklyffe, whom he at first fails to recognize, and from whom he learns, to his dismay, not only that the boy still lives, but that Wrecklyffe, whilst secreting himself amongst the rocks that morning, has actually seen him approaching the castle. Whilst speaking he perceives Vyvyan approaching, and, pointing him out to Sir Grey, they withdraw to talk over the past, and lay down plans for the future.

Vyvyan is waiting orders to sail forth to meet the armament which Spain is fitting out for an intended attack upon England, and he takes the opportunity of his ship being at anchor in an adjacent bay to visit Montreville, and also to seek an interview with the priest, and endeavor to obtain from him the secret of his birth and such proofs as he may possess. With this object he bids Falkner, one of his lieutenants, seek out Alton, and inform him of his safe arrival and of his intended visit. These instructions are overheard by Sir Grey, who determines to prevent the interview.

It so happens that this day is the anniversary of the first son's birth, and a dream which the Countess has had calls the circumstance most forcibly to her mind ; but the thought that the ocean, in proving to be, as she imagines, his winding sheet, has wiped out shame and slander, tends to soothe and soften thoughts that might otherwise be distressing. She derives further support and joy, however, from the pride with which she sees Lord Beaufort increasing day by day in comely looks and gallant, princely bearing, entertaining for him an almost idolatrous love ; but she is vexed at his avowal of his love for Eveline, having determined he should make a far more exalted match. Whilst pondering over this obstacle to the fulfillment of her designs, Sir Grey seeks an interview, and in bitter and vindictive language conveys to her the startling intelligence that her first-born lives. With gloating revenge he points out to her how he has suffered the stings of poverty, and pictures how, if the elder son should prove his rights, Lord Beaufort must descend from his haughty state, and feel some of the pangs and sufferings he has himself endured. In agonizing terror she offers to give him gold in abundance to aid her in preventing this ; but scornfully rejecting it, he tells her how that when young he pined for gold, and sought her father's help to wed the ward he loved ; but the only answer he received was,

       " Poor cousins should not marry."

And again, in later years, when seeking to join the company of knights and gentlemen, her father's reply was,

       " He had need of his poor cousin
       At home, to be his huntsman and his falconer."

Even now, he reminds her, he is compelled to sit at the second table, bear the jokes of the menials, and submit tamely to the whims and caprices of the young lord. He consents, however, ultimately, to assist, promising he will only ask for payment when the work is done.

The meeting which now takes place between Vyvyan and Eveline is, as may well be imagined, a joyous one, but slightly clouded by the picture Eveline draws of the haughty bearing of the Countess. Vyvyan, however, bids her cheer up, and describes to her in glowing terms a fanciful home of happiness and bliss that will repay all their cares and suffering, leading her away to dream of every joy, and forget for the time that they are orphans.

Returning from their consultation, Sir Grey arranges to send a trusty messenger to the priest, and force from him whatever chance he may possess, and he abjures Lady Montreville to nerve herself to meet Vyvyan as a perfect stranger, detaining him as long as possible. Sir Grey has scarcely departed, when Eveline and Vyvyan return, and it requires very powerful efforts on the part of the Countess to meet his gaze, and request him to accept the hospitality of the castle.

During the interview which follows Vyvyan, at the earnest suggestion of Eveline, who thinks that the mournful tale of his early years will secure him a friend, describes the story of his past life, in language and incident well chosen and vigorously rendered. His ardor and enthusiasm enchant Eveline, and Lady Montreville, perceiving how devotedly they are attached to each other, determines to turn it to advantage by bringing about a speedy secret marriage, and an immediate departure, so as to prevent, or, at least, to delay considerably, Vyvyan's interview with the priest. But ere she can thoroughly mould her plans into shape, the pent-up feelings of a mother struggle to be free, and she hurriedly leaves to shed in solitude bitter, scalding tears for the child she dare not acknowledge.

In the course of wandering through the grounds Vyvyan and Eveline are observed by Lord Beaufort, to whom no introduction has yet been made. In the angry flashing of his haughty eye at perceiving a stranger walking with his cousin, Sir Grey quickly detects the rousing of jealousy, and determines to take advantage of it, and therefore tells him that during his absence the Countess had received the stranger as a guest and as a wooer of his cousin, and pretending not to know his name, suggests that Beaufort should inquire of Eveline herself. Angrily striding up to Vyvyan, he accosts him in haughty, overbearing terms, and when met with a reply as to the gallant calling he follows, he commands him not to presume too much, but to seek the steward of the castle, and by him be lodged with those who are more his equals. The insult thus offered calls forth a bitter reply from Vyvyan, and an encounter is only prevented by the arrival of Lady Montreville, and even then, when leaving, Beaufort whispers threateningly to Vyvyan, "Again, and soon, sir!"

Drawing her guest into conversation, Lady Montreville gleans from him that the object of his visit was twofold—to claim Eveline as his bride, and to discover, if Heaven so willed, a parent's heart; but if his country should be in danger, that call must be the first obeyed. In the promotion of these intentions the Countess warmly acquiesces. She points out the fiery temper of Beaufort, and urges Vyvyan to consent to a marriage that very night, promising a handsome dowry, and then to sail away at once, thus putting miles of distance between himself and bride and his jealous rival; and she promises further to use all her power and wealth in tracing out his parents. It is a heavy trial, and she almost betrays herself, when Vyvyan passionately implores her to find him a mother with eyes like her own, and when she kisses him, he pictures to her an angel's hand lifting up the veil of time, and revealing to him a face like hers bending over his infant couch.

Falkner now returns with tidings from the English Admiral Drake that the Spanish fleet, known as the Armada, has set sail; and he also brings word that the priest has ample proofs of Vyvyan's birth, and will meet him with them at St. Kinian's Cliff—a lone spot in the neighborhood where they are not likely to be observed. Vyvyan determines to see Eveline and then the priest, whilst his trusty lieutenant, Falkner, calls the crews together, and gets the vessels ready for sea.

By the activity of Falkner in reaching Alton before Sir Grey's agent, his designs to obtain the papers are thwarted, and consequently, at the meeting which takes place between Alton and Vyvyan, the latter learns the particulars of his birth, and, with a throbbing heart, hastens to seek Lady Montreville, and claim a mother's fond embrace.

In the meantime she makes Sir Grey acquainted with her plans, and she also seeks Lord Beaufort to sound him as to his feelings should reverses overtake him. Proudly he upbraids her for such fancies, and in glowing terms portrays the high position that he holds—the ancient name he bears in trust for sons unborn—and so warmly and boldly is the picture drawn, that remorse is stilled within the mother's bosom, and she swears to know no other son, closing the gates of feeling against the stranger guest.

Vyvyan makes Eveline acquainted with his sudden departure, and whilst doing so is interrupted by the arrival of Lord Beaufort and Sir Grey de Malpas. The latter artfully draws Eveline aside, whilst Beaufort, writhing with anger and jealousy at the new proofs of love he has witnessed, demands of Vyvyan to name the spot and hour where they shall meet again. To this Vyvyan readily consents, and names St. Kinian's Cliff, determining to go there unarmed, and, after revealing the newly discovered secret, to embrace, and not to fight, a brother.

Sir Grey now sees that he has succeeded in raising a storm, but the ultimate result, skillful schemer as he is, is not quite clear to him; help, however, is at hand. Wrecklyffe has overheard the appointment, and he tells Sir Grey that he will be there to have revenge upon Vyvyan, who had caused him to be branded with the name of felon. Sir Grey at once perceives a way to work out his schemes; he beseeches Wrecklyff to hold back and let Vyvyan first meet Beaufort, to watch them, and if Beaufort should slay Vyvyan, who will be unarmed, not to prevent it nor assist. Wrecklyffe suggests that this is murder, which is precisely what Sir Grey intends it should be, for then the murderer would die beneath the headsman's axe, and, the two lives thus removed, Sir Grey de Malpas would be Lord of Montreville, in which case he promises to make Wrecklyffe the richest squire in all his train. The scheme savors well of success to the outcast pirate, but he suggests that Beaufort may fail or relent. For this emergency Sir Grey is prepared. Should such an event occur, Wrecklyffe could then gratify his revenge. Vyvyan's corpse would be found upon the spot where Beaufort, armed, had arranged to meet him, and suspicion would fall, with almost unerring certainty, upon Beaufort, when the secret of

his presumed victim's birth and rivalry in love were known. Wrecklyffe is satisfied, and departs with the firm determination that by the hand of himself or Beau-
tort, that night, the unsuspecting Vyvyan dies. Then, in a well-conceived and
finely-expressed soliloquy, Sir Grey pictures his rise from poverty to wealth, and as
he retires, chuckling with delight over his cunning scheme, he observes :

> "Back, conscience, back! Go scowl on boors and beggars!
> Room, smiling flatterers, room for the new Earl!"

Before setting out, Vyvyan determines to seek an audience of Lady Montreville,
and acquaint her with the information he has gained. She nerves herself to the
trial; vehemently accuses him of being an imposter, and calls upon her attendants
to cast him forth, but when they come to do her bidding she falters; the image of
her husband stands before her, and she cannot give the order. Left alone, she describes
in an agony of grief the sufferings she has endured ; her belief in his death, and the
growth of her strong affection for Beaufort. She pictures the desolation that will
now be wrought by this sudden rising from the grave, as it were, and proffering him
wealth in abundance, implores his acceptance, and, blessed with Eveline's love, his
renunciation of his mother forever. All this he rejects; he will never renounce her ;
but for the papers, the proofs of birth, he will treat them as worthless; no lands and
noble title did he seek, but the richest prize of all, a parent's love ; and he asks only
that he may be able to say in years to come that he received a mother's blessing.
The victory is gained, and with a passionate embrace, the weeping Countess invokes
the blessing of Heaven upon her first-born. Then shines forth the true nobility of
Vyvyan's nature ; he stifles his emotion ; a single kiss declares the seal of secrecy
upon his lips ; that henceforth he will be dead to her, and whilst he receives a fervent prayer for his welfare, he bids her farewell for ever.

Beaufort is punctual in his appointment at St. Kinian's Cliff, though he is very
nearly forestalled by Wrecklyffe, who conceals himself amongst the rocks as he hears
the shouts of the approaching Vyvyan. The pent-up anger of Beaufort bursts forth
upon his arrival, and as he seizes Vyvyan he reminds him that though he may presume upon his youthful years, his playmates have been veterans, his toy a sword,
and his first lesson valor.

But Vyvyan is immovable to anger, and bids him strike and then tell his mother
that he pardoned and pitied him. At this moment the signal guns are heard calling
all hands to the ships, and pushing him aside, Vyvyan endeavors to force his path
towards the bay. Exasperated almost to madness, Beaufort with drawn sword im-
pedes the attempt, presses him to the edge of the lofty overhanging cliff, and calls
upon him to stand or die. It is in vain that Vyvyan urges him to forbear ; every
vein runs fire; he is lost to all reason; he presses still closer, Vyvyan catches hold
of the bough of a tree for support, and as Beaufort raises his sword to strike, the
treacherous branch gives way beneath Vyvyan's weight, and he is cast over the edge
of the precipice. With a cry of horror at the sudden disappearance of his rival,
Beaufort falls senseless ; at the same moment, Wrecklyffe hurries from his hiding-
place and hastens down the sides of the cliff, determined to complete the deed should
any signs of life remain.

Twelve months elapse, and no tidings have been heard of either Vyvyan or the
pirate; people imagine they must have gone off in the ships; but to Sir Grey their
disappearance is easily accounted for. Wrecklyffe must have seen, and perhaps assisted, in the murder of Vyvyan, and then been well paid to depart. Of Beaufort's
guilt, Sir Grey has no doubt ; he has been seized with a fixed melancholy, lonely,
wandering habits, and a mind always ill at ease; and the grief and seclusion of
Lady Montreville confirm Sir Grey's views. But how to prove the fact ? Where
is the evidence to back up the charge?

> "How cry, 'Lo! murder!' yet produce no corpse?"

Whilst thus debating, the priest arrives with the intelligence that Falkner has
just returned from his voyage, and that Vyvyan did not accompany him. The old
man's heart is bowed with grief as he hints that murder must have been at work ;
an idea which Sir Grey repudiates with affected indignation, but suggests that a

careful search should be made and the assistance obtained of Sir Godfrey Seymour, a great magistrate of the neighborhood Falkner now arriving with some of his crew, learns the full particulars of the rivalry and challenge of Beaufort. The hour, night—the meeting place, the very spot on which he is now standing; crags, caves and chasms below, with gushing streams, and ledges jutting out, forming slender and half-hidden resting places ; might not in one of these the bones of Vy. vyan rest! With the brave and faithful sailor thought is action, and ere the others can surmise his intention, he disappears from amongst them and attempts the perilous descent of the cliff, watched, with straining eyeballs, by Sir Grey, who prays that some evidence may be found to support the charge he intends to make.

The grief and agony Lady Montreville endures from the change which has taken place in Beaufort is almost unbearable ; her heart bleeds as she sees him throw aside all the pursuits in which he once so spiritedly indulged ; moving about with hollow tread and listless gaze, as though life had ceased to possess for him a single charm. His reason seems impaired, for when she tells him that the Queen has been pleased to appoint him one of her chosen knights, and that the noblest gentleman in the land, the Earl of Essex, is on his way from his victory over the Spaniards, and intends to pay him a visit, it fails to arouse his wonted ardor and enthusiasm, and he coldly and sternly refuses to welcome Essex or to put on his knightly trappings. The spirit of madness seems to be working through the household, for poor Eveline appears stricken down, wandering about the place, singing dolefully :—

> " Blossoms, I weave ye
> To drift on the sea,
> Say when you find him
> Who sang ' Woe is me !' "

as she casts the garlands upon the waters without, and watches the waves toss them to and fro, with a sort of childish glee.

All this, not particularly pleasant domestic felicity, is interrupted by the arrival of Sir Godfrey Seymour, who, having been made acquainted with the particulars of Vyvyan's disappearance, has summoned a court of justice to be held in the great hall of the castle, and commanded the attendance of the persons interested.

It is pretty certain to all that in this inquiry the truth will be elicited, for Sir Godfrey Seymour bears a high repute as being not only a stern but a very shrewd judge ; and when the announcement is made that the plume and various gems and ornaments known to belong to Vyvyan have been found amongst a heap of human bones discovered at the bottom of the precipice, Sir Grey's heart beats with delight at the prospective certainty of success.

Falkner is a stern accuser, but at the same time is much moved by the deep remorse which Beaufort exhibits, and he makes an earnest appeal to him to confess that, in jealous phrenzy, swords were drawn, and they fought as man to man. But the young lord is silent, and his mother urges him to remember his birth and rank, to remain firm and unmoved, and to confess nothing. The trial proceeds, and it seems clear that jealousy was the cause of the quarrel, upon which grounds the judge appears inclined to deal leniently with the accused, when Sir Grey, seizing the opportunity, forces the priest to the witness stand, and the secret of Vyvyan's birth is revealed. The shock is too great for Beaufort, and, rejecting the accusation of assassin, proclaims himself a fratricide. But Eveline, firm in faith of the wondrous power which has hitherto preserved Vyvyan, still believes that he is living, whilst the distracted mother endeavors to shield her son by suggesting that the law will spare him if it can be shown that she had urged him to do the deed. It is in vain ; Sir Godfrey is inflexible, and, sternly chiding, commits her and her son to the custody of the future earl, Sir Grey de Malpas, to be held as prisoners for further trial.

The triumph of the arch-schemer, however, is very brief, for, before he can remove the accused, the attendants announce the approach of a knight belonging to the cavalcade of the Earl of Essex, then in the vicinity of the castle, and who, hearing of the proceedings going on, is hastening to the hall, and follows the messenger upon the scene. Fully equipped, and with his vizor down, none can recognize the new-comer, who, quickly understanding the position of affairs, throws down his gauntlet as a challenge to any one who dares assert that Beaufort and his mother are guilty. He then relates the circumstances of the meeting: the breaking of the bough ; that Vyvyan's fall was broken by a bush-grown ledge, upon which he lay for some minutes insensible, and that, when recovering, he saw upon a crag near him the pirate, Wrecklyffe, with uplifted steel, prepared to slay him ; but at that instant the crag gave way, and the would-be assassin fell to the bottom of the abyss. As soon as he could gather strength, Vyvyan crawled down the rocks, and reached the dying man in sufficient time to receive his confession of the murderous trap that had been prepared. Staggered and bewildered at this recital, Sir Grey summons up all his courage, and, drawing his sword, asserts vehemently that Vyvyan died by Beaufort's hand, as he is prepared to prove ; but the knight calmly bids him write the lie upon the face of truth, and, raising his vizor, gives convincing proof of the innocence of the accused by discovering himself as the missing Vyvyan. Sinking senseless and defeated into the arms of the attendants, Sir Grey de Malpas finishes his career of villainy. Vyvyan briefly explains by what means, finding his vessel gone, he had joined the army of the Earl of Essex, and won his way to fame, receiving the honour of knighthood. Then, embracing with joy his faithful Eveline and stricken mother, he proclaims his will that his erring brother shall share with him his fortune and his parent's love, although to the title and estates of Montre-ville he alone becomes THE RIGHTFUL HEIR.

REMARKS.

IN the year 1839, the noble author of the " Lady of Lyons " and " Richelieu " made another venture to obtain the favorable applause of the play-going public, by pro-ducing a piece called " The Sea Captain," the idea of which had been suggested by a striking situation in one of Alexandre Dumas' novels, " Le Capitaine Paul."

In October of that year, the eminent tragedian, Mr. Macready, resigned his labors at the Theatre Royal, Covent Garden, London, and transferred himself to the Thea-tre Royal, Haymarket, then under the management of Mr. Benjamin Webster, with whom he entered into an engagement at a salary of £100 per week (about 500 dol-lars). The manuscript of the new play was put into his hands for perusal, and meeting with his approval, was at once placed in rehearsal, in which the author assisted.

It received, as a matter of course, from an actor and manager of such skill and liberality as Mr. Webster, every attention possible as regards mounting it on the stage, and it was also well cast. Mr. Macready enacted the part of Norman, a character corresponding to that of Vyvyan in the present play, and all the other parts were filled by the best available talent of the profession.

It was produced October 30, 1839, and was received with a very fair degree of en-thusiasm, Mr. Macready being honored with a call upon the occasion. The general opinion, however, was not a very flattering one, and what favor it did receive was solely due to his admirable acting. It was played occasionally afterwards, but only for a brief period.

Following up the plan pursued with the author's previous plays, this one, as with them, was very soon transplanted in the United States. In the middle of the fol-lowing year, the Sea Captain's flag was hoisted on this side of the Atlantic—the play being produced at the Park Theatre, New York, on June 9, 1840, upon the oc-casion of Mr. Hield's benefit, when the leading characters were cast as follows:—

Norman	Mr. CRESWICK.
Lord Ashdale	Mr. WHEATLEY.
Sir Maurice Beevor	Mr. HIELD.
Giles Gaussen	Mr. RICHINGS.
Lady Arundel	Miss CUSHMAN.
Violet	Miss S. CUSHMAN.

The above characters corresponding to those in the present play of *Vyvyan*, *Lord Beaufort*, *Sir Grey de Malpas*, *Lady Montreville*, and *Eveline*. But although, as will be seen, it had the support of some of the best actors and actresses upon the stage, it was very tamely received, and, I believe, never acted again.

As before observed, the excellent acting of Mr. Macready secured for the piece a short run, but it was one of such doubtful favor that the author withdrew the play from the stage (and even from printed publication) intending to replace it before the public with some important changes in the histrionic cast, and certain slight alterations in the conduct of the story. But these alterations became so extensive in character, diction, and even in revision of plot, that a new play gradually rose from the foundations of the old one. The task thus undertaken was much delayed by other demands upon the author's time and thought, and it was scarcely completed when Mr. Macready's retirement from his profession suspended the author's literary connection with the stage, and "The Rightful Heir" remained in tranquil seclusion until 1868. In that year, the Lyceum Theatre, London, was under the management of Mr. E. T. Smith, who had for many years previously been one of the most enterprising and successful managers of the Theatre Royal, Drury Lane. Having secured the services of Mr. Bandmann, an actor of much excellence and fame, he opened negotiations with the author, which resulted in the production of the piece on October 3, 1868. Mr. Bandmann was supported by an excellent and good working company, including such well-known talented professionals as Mr. Herman Vezin and his wife (formerly a Mrs. Charles Young), Mr. Neville (a most painstaking actor, who has since risen to a very high position in London), and Mr. Basil Potter, than whom there were few more clever in high class melo-drama, especially of the French school.

I did not, however, have a very successful career, and I am not aware of its being played afterwards in England or on the American stage.

One little gratifying incident in connection with the piece may be mentioned. Upon its publication, the author took the opportunity to make known his good feeling towards the people of the United States, for the appreciation bestowed upon his previous productions, and at the commencement of a brief preface he stated that he dedicated the drama

" To all friends and kinsfolk in the American Commonwealth, with affection and respect."

As the noble author observes that he set to work to alter " The Sea Captain " and produced a new play, so might similar labor be bestowed upon the present piece with a corresponding result, and by judicious alterations and curtailment of some of the lengthy speeches and scenes, with the introduction of a few new incidents, there is little doubt an excellent drama could be produced.

The chief fault is that the plot is too commonplace and of the old melo-dramatic type to create any very great interest ; nevertheless it affords scope for some very beautiful speeches and sentiments ; as an artist would say, the dressy and showy verbiage is hung upon a very weak lay figure.

The character of Vyvyan is very ably drawn, but his departure after escaping so miraculously from death, and being cognizant of his rank and birth, as also passionately in love, is a very great stretch of dramatic license.

The character of Lady Montreville is also very admirably drawn. Believing her first-born dead, and gradually drifting out of a state of remorse and suffering into one of peace and affection for her second son, it is naturally a fearful struggle for her to proclaim to the world her shame, and to disinherit and cast forth as a beggar, as it were, the young noble who had been reared with all the care and luxury that pride and wealth could bestow. The scene in which this struggle is portrayed (Act 1, Scene 1) is a very lengthy one, but for vigorous and appropriate language of the finest class, will bear comparison with any of the author's compositions. So also will the first scene in the Second Act, where Vyvyan, at the request of Eveline, relates to Lady Montreville the story of his early life. The great fault, however, of both these scenes is the extreme length ; the idea and language are unexceptionable.

Another fine piece of descriptive poetry is the imaginary home for a sailor's bride, which Vyvyan pictures to Eveline in the Second Scene of the First Act, and which very much resembles, in idea and execution, a similar but grander flight of poetic fancy in the Second Act of the Lady of Lyons.

The character of Alton, the priest, is very neatly drawn, and his story of Vyvyan's birth (Act III, Scene 1), couched in easy and appropriate language.'

Sir Grey de Malpas, the leading villain of the drama, is skillfully depicted ; his sarcastic remarks upon the poverty he endures and the insults to which he is subjected, are pointedly given, and his interview with Lady Montreville and the soliloquy upon his anticipated succession to rank and wealth are finely described.

Lord Beaufort, proud and impetuous, is also well done, as is the blunt but faithful friend of Vyvyan, Falkner. Eveline is tame ; she is made, for what reason one fails to see, a sort of melo-dramatic Ophelia, with nothing of much importance to do or say.

Altogether, however, the play reads well, and though there is the drawback of a rather weak, improbable, and commonplace plot, there is much beauty of language and many telling points.   J. M. K.

BILL FOR PROGRAMMES, ETC.

The events of the Play take place at, and in the vicinity of, the Castle of Montreville, on the coast of England, in the years 1588-9, during the reign of Queen Elizabeth.

ACT I.

Scene I.—RUINS NEAR THE CASTLE OF MONTREVILLE.

The Poor Cousin—A Strange Wreck from the Sea—Arrival of Captain Vyvyan on a Love Cruise—The Secret of Birth—The Hour to Solve the Mystery.

Scene II.—GARDENS OF THE CASTLE.

A Mother's Love for the Living and the Dead—Eveline's Song of Woe—Insult to the Poor Cousin—Story of the Missing Heir of Montreville—The Proofs Exist—The Compact !—Poetry of Love, and the Bright Home for a Sailor's Bride—Dismay of Lady Montreville.

ACT II.

Scene I. A ROOM IN THE CASTLE.

The Mother and her First-born—Vyvyan's Vivid Story of His Life—The Plot to Destroy him.

Scene II.—THE CASTLE YARD.

Interview between Beaufort and Vyvyan—The Sailor and the Gallant—The Quarrel—A Rival in Fortune, Name, and Love—A Hasty Marriage and a Quiet Departure—The Snake in the Grass—Proclamation of Queen Elizabeth against the Invasion by Spain—The Call to Arms—Preparations for Battle.

ACT III.

Scene I.—ROCKY VIEW ON THE COAST.

*The Priest Reveals to Vyvyan the Secret of his Birth—" The Proofs ?"—
" Are Here ! "—" Now then to Find and Claim a Mother ! "*

Scene II.—EXTERIOR OF THE CASTLE.

*The Poor Cousin and the Pirate—The Schemers Outwitted—Preparing for
Defence—Pride and Poverty—The Challenge !—The Lord and the Sai-
lor—" We meet again, no Living Eye to see us ! "—A Pirate's Revenge
—Plotting for Murder.*

ACT IV.

Scene I.—A ROOM IN THE CASTLE.

*Postponement of the Wedding—The Lost Son—Heart-rending Appeal to a
Mother—A Parent's Agony—Struggle between Pride and Affection—
Priceless Value of a Mother's Blessing.*

Scene II.—CLIFFS AND ROCKY PASS ON THE COAST.

*The Rival in Love and Fortune—The Pirate on the Watch—The Trap for
the Unarmed Sailor—The Quarrel—The Pursuit—Life on the Edge of
a Rock—The Fatal Trap—The Broken Bough—Vyvyan is hurled from
the Cliff !*

Twelve months elapse between these Acts.

ACT V.

Scene I.—CLIFFS AND ROCKY PASS.

*The Schemer's Success—The Poor Cousin future Lord of Montreville—Vyv-
yan's Fate—Suspicion Points to Beaufort – The Search for the Corpse
—" Bring up but Bones, and Round the Skull I'll Wreath my Coronet ! "*

Scene II.—A ROOM IN THE CASTLE.

*Beaufort's Remorse—A Distressed Mind and a Mother's Grief—Dis-
covery of Proofs of Guilt—The Summons to the Hall of Justice.*

Scene III.—THE GREAT HALL IN THE CASTLE OF MONTRE-VILLE.

*The Court Assembled—The Charge of the Poor Cousin—The Accusation
—Proofs of Murder—The Secret of Birth Revealed—The Suspected
Fratricide—An Unlooked-for and Mysterious Visitor—The Tables
Turned—" The Bones are those of Wrecklyffe, the Intended Assas-
sin, and thou, Sir Grey, the Schemer ! "—Confusion of Villainy and
Triumph of Innocence—Unity of Mother and Brothers—True Love
Rewarded—Joyous Recognition of Vyvyan as*

THE RIGHTFUL HEIR.

THE RIGHTFUL HEIR.

ACT I.

SCENE I.—*Castle Ruins in 4th grooves.*   *Music.*

Discover SIR GREY, *digging, up* C., *throws down his spade and comes down* C

SIR GREY. I cannot dig. Fie, what a helpless thing
    Is the white hand of well-born poverty!
    And yet between this squalor and that pomp (*looks up* L.)
    Stand but two lives, a woman's and a boy's—
    But two frail lives. I may outlive them both. (R. C.)

Enter WRECKLYFFE, L. 1 E.

WRECK. Ay, that's the house—the same; the master changed,
    But less than I am. Winter creeps on him,
    Lightning hath stricken me. Good-day.
SIR G.   Pass on.
    No spendrift hospitable fool spreads here
    The board for strangers. Pass.
WRECK.   Have years so dimmed
    Eyes once so keen, De Malpas?
SIR. G. (*after a pause*).   Ha! Thy hand.
    What brings thee hither?
WRECK.   " Brings me? " say " hurled back."
    First, yellow pestilence, whose ghastly wings
    Guard, like the fabled griffin, India's gold;
    Unequal battle next; then wolfish famine;
    And lastly storm (rough welcome to England)
    Swept decks from stern to stem; to shore was flung
    A lonely pirate on a battered hulk!
    One wreck rots stranded;—you behold the other.
SIR G. Penury hath still it's crust and roof-tree—share them.
    Time has dealt hardly with us both, since first
    We two made friendship—thou straight-limbed, well-favored,
    Stern-hearted, disinherited dare-devil.
WRECK. And thou?——
SIR G. (*smiles*).   A stroke paints me. My lord's poor cousin.
    How strong thou wert, yet I could twist and wind thee
    Round these slight hands; that is the use of brains.

WRECK. Still jokes and stings ?
SIR. G.   Still a poor cousin's weapons.
WRECK. Boast brains, yet starve ?
SIR G.   Still a poor cousin s fate, sir.
Pardon my brains, since oft' thy boasts they pardoned ;
(Sad change since then). when rufflers aped thy swagger,
And village maidens sighed and, wondering, asked
Why heaven made men so wicked—and so comely.
WRECK. (*gruffly*) 'Sdeath ! Wilt thou cease ?
SIR G.   That scar upon thy
Front bespeaks grim service.
WRECK.   In thy cause, De Malpas ;
The boy, whom at thine instance I allured
On board my bark, left me this brand of Cain.
SIR G. That boy——
WRECK.   Is now a man, (SIR GREY *starts*) and on these shores.
This morn I peered from yonder rocks that hid me,
And saw his face. I whetted then this steel :
Need'st thou his death ? In me behold Revenge !
SIR G. He lives—he lives ! There is a third between
The beggar and the earldom.
WRECK. (*looks* R).   Steps and voices ;
When shall we meet alone ? Hush ! it is he.
SIR G. He with the plume ?
WRECK.   Ay.
SIR G.   Quick ; within.
WRECK.   And thou ?
SIR G. I dig the earth ; see the grave-digger's tool. (*goes up* R. C)
                    [*Exit* WRECKYLFFE, D *in* 3 G., *set flat.*

Enter HARDING *and* SAILORS, R. 1 E.

HARD. Surely 'twas here the captain bade us meet him
While he went forth for news ?
FIRST SAILOR.   He comes.

Enter VYVYAN, L. 1 E.

HARD.   Well, captain.
What tidings of the Spaniard's armament ?
VYV. Bad, for they say the fighting is put off,
And storm in Biscay driven back the Dons.
This is but rumor—we will learn the truth.
Harding, take horse and bear these lines to Drake—(*gives paper*
If yet our country needs stout hearts to guard her,
He'll not forget the men on board the Dreadnaught.
Thou canst be back ere sunset with his answer,
And find me in yon towers of Montreville.
                    [*Exit* HARDING, R. 1 E.
Meanwhile make merry in the hostel, lads,
And drink me out these ducats in this toast :—(*gives coin*)
" No foes be tall eno' to wade the moat
Which girds the fort whose only walls are men "
                    [SAILORS *cheer, and exeunt* R. 1 E.

VYV. (c.). I never hailed reprieve from war till now.
Heaven grant but time to see mine Eveline,
And learn my birth from Alton.

Enter FALKNER, L. 1 E.

FALK. Captain. (*meets* VYVYAN, C.)
VYV. Falkner!
So soon returned? Thy smile seems fresh from home.
All well there?
FALK. Just in time to make all well.
My poor old father!—bailiffs at his door;
He tills another's land, and crops had failed.
I poured mine Indian gold into his lap,
And cried, " O father wilt thou now forgive
The son who went to sea against thy will?"
VYV. And he forgave.—Now tell me of thy mother;
I never knew one, but I love to mark
The quiver of a strong man's bearded lip
When his voice lingers on the name of mother.
Thy mother bless'd thee——
FALK. Yes, I——(*falters and turns aside.*)
Pshaw! methought
Her joy was weeping on my breast again!
VYV. I envy thee those tears.
FALK. Enough of me!
Now for thyself What news? Thy fair betrothed—
The maid we rescued from the turband corsair
With her brave father in the Indian seas—
Found and still faithful?
VYV. Faithful I will swear it;
But not yet found. Her sire is dead—the stranger
Sits at his hearth—and with her next of kin,
Hard by this spot—yea, in yon sunlit towers (*points up* L.)
Mine Eveline dwells.
FALK. Thy foster father, Alton,
Hast thou seen him?
VYV. Not yet. My Falkner, serve me.
His house is scarce a two hours' journey hence,
The nearest hamlet will afford a guide;
Seek him and break the news of my return,
Say I shall see him ere the day be sped.
And, hearken, friend (good men at home are apt
To judge us sailors harshly), tell him this—
On the far seas his foster son recalled
Prayers taught by age to childhood, and implored
Blessings on that gray head. Farewell! (FALKNER *exits* R. 1 E.)
Now, Eveline. [*Exit*, VYVYAN L. 1 E.
SIR G. (*comes down* L. C.). Thou seekest those towers—go! I will meet
thee there.
He must not see the priest—the hour is come
Absolving Alton's vow to guard the secret;
Since the boy left, two 'scutcheons moulder o'er
The dust of tombs from which his rights ascend;
He must not see the priest—but how forestall him?—
Within! For there dwells Want, Wit's counsellor,
Harboring grim Force, which is Ambition's tool.
[*Exit* SIR GREY, D *in* 3 G. *flat.*

Drop Curtain for change. Music during wait.

Scene changes to

SCENE II.—*Castle Gardens in 5th grooves.*

Enter, R. U. E., LADY MONTREVILLE, *by steps to* C.

LADY M. This were his birthday, were he living still!
But the wide ocean is his winding sheet,
And his grave—here! (*hand to heart*) I dreamed of him last
night.
Peace! with the dead, died shame and glozing slander;
In the son left me still, I clasp a world
Of blossoming hopes which flower beneath my love,
And take frank beauty from the flattering day.
And——but my Clarence—in his princely smile
How the air brightens.

Enter LORD BEAUFORT *and* MARSDEN, L. 3 E.

LORD B. (*to* MARSDEN).   Yes, my gallant roan,
And stay—be sure the falcon, which my lord
Of Leicester sent me ; we will try its metal. (*goes up* R. C.)
MARS. Your eyes do bless him, madam, so do mine :
A gracious spring ; Heaven grant we see its summer !
Forgive, dear lady, your old servant's freedom.
LADY M. Who loves him best, with me ranks highest, Marsden.
                                        [*Exit* MARSDEN, L. 2 E.
Clarence, you see me not.
LORD B (*comes down*).   Dear mother, welcome. (R *of* LADY M.)
Why do I miss my soft-eyed cousin here ?
LADY M. It doth not please me, son, that thou should'st haunt
Her steps, and witch with dulcet words her ear.
Eveline is fair, but not the mate for Beaufort.
LORD B. Mate! Awful word! Can youth not gaze on beauty
Save by the torch of Hymen? To be gallant,
Melt speech in sighs, or murder sense in sonnets ;
Veer with each change in Fancy's April skies,
And o'er each sun-shower fling its fleeting rainbow.
All this——
LADY M. (*gloomily*). Alas, is love.
LORD B.   No! Love's light prologue,
The sportive opening to the serious drama ;
The pastime practice of Don Cupid's bow,
Against that solemn venture at the butts
At which fools make so many random shafts,
And rarely hit the white! Nay, smile, my mother ;
How does this plume become me ?
LADY M.   .   Foolish boy !
It sweeps too loosely.
LORD B.   Now-a-days, man's love
Is worn as loosely as I wear this plume—
A glancing feather stirred with every wind
Into new shadows o'er a giddy brain,
Such as your son's. Let the plume play, sweet mother.
LADY M. Would I could chide thee ! (*to* R. C.)
LORD B.   Hark, I hear my steed

Neighing impatience; and my falcon frets
Noon's lazy air with lively silver bells ;
Now, madam, look to it—no smile from me
When next we meet,—no kiss of filial duty,
Unless my fair-faced cousin stand beside you;
Blushing "Peccavi" for all former sins—
Shy looks, cold words, this last unnatural absence,
And taught how cousins should behave to cousins.

[Exit Lord Beaufort, L. 2 E.

Lady M. Trifler! And yet the faults that quicker fear
Make us more fond—we parents love to pardon. (goes up c.)

Enter Eveline, R. 1 E., weaving flowers—not seeing Lady Montreville.

Evel. (sings). Bud from the blossom,
    And leaf from the tree,
    Guess why in weaving
    I sing " Woe is me ! " (goes up c. to wall.)

    'Tis that I weave you
    To drift on the sea,
    And say, when ye find him,
    Who sang " Woe is me ! "
 (casts garland over wall, blows a kiss, and comes down c.)

Lady M. A quaint but mournful rhyme.
Evel.   You, madam !—pardon!
Lady M. What tells the song ?
Evel.   A simple village tale
Of a lost seaman, and a crazed girl,
His plighted bride—good Marsden knew her well,
And oft-times marked her singing on the beach,
Then launch her flowers, and smile upon the sea.
I know not why—both rhyme and tale do haunt me.
Lady M. Sad thoughts haunt not young hearts, thou senseless child.
Evel. Is not the child an orphan ? (both at c., she R. of Lady M.)
Lady M.   In those eyes
Is there no moisture softer than the tears
Which mourn a father? Roves thy glance for Beaufort ?
Vain girl, beware! The flattery of the great
Is but the eagle's swoop upon the dove,
And, in descent, destroys
Evel.   Can you speak thus,
Yet bid me grieve not that I am an orphan ?

[Exit, thoughtfully, L. 2 E.

Lady M. (aside). I have high dreams for Beaufort; bright desires!
Son of a race whose lives shine down on Time
From lofty tombs, like beacon-towers o'er ocean,
He stands amidst the darkness of my thought,
Radiant as Hope in some lone captive's cell.
Far from the gloom around, mine eyes, inspired,
Pierce to the future, when these bones are dust,
And see him loftiest of the lordly choirs
Whose swords and coronals blaze around the throne,
The guardian stars of the imperial isle—
Kings shall revere his mother.

(seats herself in garden seat thoughtfully)

Enter, R 1 E., SIR GREY, *speaking to* SERVANT.

SIR G. What say'st thou?
SER7ANT (*insolently*). Sir Grey—ha! ha!—Lord Beaufort craves your
 pardon,
 He shot your hound—its bark disturbed the deer.
SIR G. The only voice that welcomed me! A dog—
 Grudges he that? (R. C.)
SERVANT.   Oh, sir, 'twas done in kindness
 To you and him; the dog was wondrous lean, sir!
SIR G. I thank my lord!   [*Exit* SERVANT, R. 1 E., *laughing.*
 So my poor Tray is killed!
 And yet *that* dog but barked—can *this* not bite?
 (*approaches* LADY MONTREVILLE, *vindictively in a whisper.*)
 He lives!
LADY M.   He! who?
SIR G.   The heir of Montreville!
 Another, and an elder Beaufort, lives! (LADY M. *rises.*)
 (*Aside.*) So—the fang fixes fast—good—good! (L. C. *front.*)
LADY M.   Thou saidst
 Ten years ago—" Thy first-born is no more—
 Died in far seas."
SIR G.   So swore my false informant.
 But now, the deep that took the harmless boy
 Casts from its breast the bold-eyed daring man.
LADY M. Clarence! My poor proud Clarence! (C)
SIR G. (L. C. *front*).   Ay, *poor* Clarence!
 True; since his father, by his former nuptials,
 Had other sons, if you, too, own an elder,
 Clarence is poor, as his poor cousin.
 Ugh! but the air is keen, and Poverty
 Is thinly clad; subject to rheums and agues, (*shivers*)
 Asthma and phthisic, (*coughs*) pains in the loins and limbs,
 And leans upon a crutch, like your poor cousin.
 If Poverty begs. Law sets it in the stocks;
 If it is ill, the doctors mangle it;
 If it is dying, the priests scold at it;
 And, when 'tis dead, rich kinsmen cry, " Thank heaven! "
 Ah! If the elder prove his rights, dear lady,
 Your younger son will know what's poverty!
LADY M. Malignant, peace! why doest thou torture me?
 The priest who shares alone with us the secret
 Hath sworn to guard it.
SIR G.   Only while thy sire
 And second lord survived. Yet, what avails
 In law his tale, unbacked by thy confession?
LADY M. He hath proofs, clear proofs. Thrice woe to Clarence!
SIR G. Proofs—written proofs?
LADY M.   Of marriage, and the birth!
SIR G. Wherefore so long was this concealed from me?
LADY M. (*haughtily*). Thou wert my father's agent, Grey De Malpas,
 Not my familiar.
SIR G. (*proudly*).   Here, then, ends mine errand. (*going* L.)
LADY M. Stay, sir—forgive my rash and eager temper;
 Stay, stay, and counsel me. What! sullen still?
 Needest thou gold? befriend, and find me grateful.

Sir G. Lady of Montreville, I was once young,
    And pined for gold, to wed the maid I loved:
    Your father said, " Poor cousins should not marry,"
    And gave that sage advice in lieu of gold.
    A few years later, and I grew ambitious,
    And longed for wars and fame, and foolish honors:
    Then I lacked gold, to join the knights, mine equals,
    As might become a Malpas, and your kinsman:
    Your father said he had need of his poor cousin
    At home to be his huntsman, and his falconer!
Lady M. Forgetful! After my first fatal nuptials
    And their sad fruit, count you as naught——
Sir G.   My hire!
    For service and for silence ; not a gift.
Lady M. And spent in riot, waste, and wild debauch!
Sir G. True ; in the pauper's grand inebriate wish
    To know what wealth is,—tho' but for an hour.
Lady M. But blame you me or mine, if spendthrift wassail
    Run to the dregs ? Mine halls stand open to you ;
    My noble Beaufort hath not spurned your converse;
    You have been welcomed——
Sir G.   At your second table,
    And as the butt of unchastised lackeys ;
    While your kind son, in pity of my want,
    Hath this day killed the faithful dog that shared it.
    'Tis well ; you need my aid, as did your father,
    And tempt, like him, with gold. I take the service;
    And, when the task is done will talk of payment.
    Hist! the boughs rustle. Closer space were safer ;
    Vouchsafe your hand, let us confer within.
Lady M. Well might I dream last night! A fearful dream.
   [*Exeunt* Lady Montreville *and* Sir Grey, *by steps, and off* R. 2. E.
     conversing.
             Enter Eveline, L. 2 E.

Evel. Oh, for some fairy talisman to conjure
    Up to these longing eyes the form they pine for !
    And yet, in love, there's no such word as absence ;
    The loved one glides beside our steps forever ; (*seated in garden*
     seat.)
    Its presence gave such beauty to the world,
    That all things beautiful its tokens are,
    And aught in sound most sweet, to sight most fair,
    Breathes with its voice, and haunts us with its aspect.

             Enter Vyvyan, L. 3 E.

    There spoke my fancy, not my heart! Where art thou,
    My unforgotten Vyvyan ?
Vyv. (*kneels to her*).   At thy feet! (*pauses and rises*)
    Look up—look up !—these are the arms that sheltered
    When the storm howled around ; and these the lips
    Where, till this hour, the sad and holy kiss
    Of parting lingered, as the fragance left
    By angels, when they touch the earth and vanish.
    Look up ; night never hungered for the sun
    As for thine eyes my soul!

Evel. (*embraces* Vyvyan).   Oh! joy, joy, joy !
Vyv. Yet weeping still, tho' leaning on my breast!
My sailor's bride, hast thou no voice but blushes ?
Nay from those drooping roses let me steal
The coy reluctant sweetness !
Evel.   And, methought
I had treasured words, 'twould take a life to utter
When we should meet again !
Vyv.   Recall them later.
We shall have time eno', when life with life
Blends into one ;—(Eveline *looks* R.) why dost thou start and
    tremble ?
Evel. Methought I heard her slow and solemn footfall ! (*rises.*)
Vyv. *Her !* Why, thou speak'st of woman : the meek word
Which never chimes with terror.
Evel.   You know not
The dame of Montreville. (c.)
Vyv. (R. *of* Eveline).   Is she so stern ?
Evel. Not stern, but haughty ; as if high-born virtue
Swept o'er the earth to scorn the faults it pardoned.
Vyv. Haughty to thee ?
Evel.   To all, e'en when the kindest ;
Nay, I do wrong her; never to her son ;
And when those proud eyes moisten as they hail him,
Hearts lately stung, yearn to a heart so human !
Alas, that parent love ! how in its loss
All life seems shelterless !
Vyv.   Like thee, perchance,
Looking round earth for that same parent shelter,
I too may find but tombs. So, turn we both,
Orphans, to that lone parent of the lonely,
That doth like Sorrow ever upward gaze
On calm consoling stars ; the mother Sea..
Evel. Call not the cruel sea by that mild name.
Vyv. She is not cruel if her breast swell high
Against the winds that thwart her loving aim
To link, by every raft whose course she speeds,
Man's common brotherhood from pole to pole ;
Grant she hath danger—danger schools the brave,
And bravery leaves all cruel things to cowards.
Grant that she harden us to fear, the hearts
Most proof to fear are easiest moved to love,
As on the oak whose roots defy the storm,
All the leaves tremble when the south-wind stirs.
Yet If the sea dismay thee, (*right arm around* Eveline's *waist*)
    on the shores
Kissed by her waves, and far, as fairy isles
In poet dreams, from this gray care-worn world,
Blooms many a bower for the Sea Rover's bride.
I know a land where feathering palm-trees shade
To delicate twilight, suns benign as those
Whose dawning gilded Eden ; Nature, there,
Like a gay spendthrift in his flush of youth,
Flings her whole treasure on the lap of Time.
There, steeped in roseate hues, the lakelike sea
Heaves to an air whose breathing is ambrosia ;
And, all the while, bright-winged and warbling birds,

Like happy souls released, melodious float
Thro' blissful light, and teach the ravished earth
How joy finds voice in Heaven.　Come, rest we yonder,
And, side by side, forget that we are orphans!
　　　　　[VYVYAN *and* EVELINE *exeunt*, L. 1 L.

Enter LADY MONTREVILLE *and* SIR GREY, R. 2 E., *and down the steps.*

LADY M. Yet still, if Alton sees——
SIR G.　　　　　　　　　　Without the proofs,
Why, Alton's story were but idle wind ;
The man I send is swift and strong, and ere
This Vyvyan (who would have been here before me
But that I took the shorter path) depart
From your own threshold to the priest's abode,
Our agent gains the solitary dwelling,
And——
LADY M. But no violence !
SIR G.　　　　　　　　　Nay, none but fear—
Fear will suffice to force from trembling age
Your safety, and preserve your Beaufort's birthright.
LADY M. Let me not hear the ignominious means ;
Gain thou the end ;—quick—quick !
SIR G.　　　　　　　　　　And if, meanwhile.
This sailor come, be nerved to meet a stranger ;
And to detain a guest.
LADY M.　　　　　　My heart is wax,
But my will, iron.—Go. (R. C. *by seat.*)
SIR G. (*aside.*)　　　　To fear add force—
And this hand closes on the proofs, and welds
That iron to a tool.　　　　[*Exit* SIR GREY, R. I E.

Enter VYVYAN *and* EVELINE, L. 1 E., *up to* L. C.

EVEL.　　　　　　　Nay, Vyvyan—nay,
Your guess can fathom not how proud her temper.
VYV. Tut for her pride ! a king upon the deck
Is every subject's equal in the hall.
I will advance. (*he uncovers.*)
LADY M. (*aside*).　　　Avenging angels, spare me !
　　　　　(*great emotion, unable to look at* VYVYAN.]
VYV. Pardon the seeming boldness of my presence.
EVEL.* Our gallant countryman, of whom my father
So often spake—who from the Algerine
Rescued our lives and freedom.
LADY M.　　　　　　Ah ! Your name, sir ?
VYV. The name I bear is Vyvyan, noble lady.
LADY M. Sir, you are welcome.　Walk within, and hold
Our home your hostel, while it lists you.
VYV.　　　　　　　　　　Madam,
I shall be prouder in all after time
For having been your guest.
LADY M　　　　　　　How love and dread

| *LADY M. | VYVYAN. | EVELINE. |
| R. *of* C. | C. | L. C. |

Make tempest here!   I pray you follow me.
                         [*Exit* LADY MONTREVILLE, R. 2 E.
Vyv.   A most majestic lady—her fair face
Made my heart tremble, and called back old dreams:
Thou saidst she had a son?
EVEL.   Ah, yes.
Vyv.   In truth
A happy man.
EVEL.   Yet he might envy thee:
Vyv.   Most arch reprover, yes.   As kings themselves
⌠ Might envy one whose arm entwines his all.
⌡   [*arm around* EVELINE, *exeunt* R. 2 E.   *Music.*

CURTAIN.

ACT II.

SCENE I.—*Room in 2d grooves.*

Discover LADY MONTREVILLE *and* VYVYAN *seated at table, and* EVELINE
                    L. C. *front.**

Vyv.   Ha! ha!   In truth we made a scurvy figure
After our shipwreck.
LADY M.   You jest merrily
On your misfortunes.
Vyv.   'Tis the way with sailors:
Still in extremes.   Ah! I can be sad sometimes.
LADY M. That sigh, in truth, speaks sadness.   Sir, if I
In aught could serve you, trust me.
EVEL.   Trust her, Vyvyan.
Methinks the mournful tale of thy young years
Would raise thee up a friend, wherever pity
Lives in the heart of woman.
Vyv.   Gentle lady,
The key of some charmed music in your voice
Unlocks a haunted chamber in my soul;
And—would you listen to an outcast's tale,
'Tis briefly told.   Until my fifteenth year,
Beneath the roof of a poor village priest,
Not far from hence, my childhood wore away;
Then stirred within me restless thoughts and deep;
Throughout the liberal and harmonious nature
Something seemed absent,—what, I scarcely knew,
Till one calm night, when over slumbering seas
Watched the still heaven, and down on every wave
Looked some soft lulling star—the instinctive want
Learned what it pined for; and I asked the priest
With a quick sigh—" Why I was motherless?"

LADY M.*: table.   :*VYVYAN.
                              *EVELINE.

LADY M. And he ?—

VYV.   Replied that—I was nobly born,
And that the cloud which dimmed a dawning sun,
Oft but foretold its splendor at the noon.
As thus he spoke, faint memories struggling came—
Faint as the things some former life hath known.

LADY M. Of what?

VYV. (*rises, keeps his eyes on* LADY M). A face sweet with a stately
    sorrow,
And lips which breathed the words that mothers murmur.

LADY M. (*aside*). Back, tell-tale tears ! (*weeping.*)

VYV.   About that time, a stranger
Came to our hamlet ; rough, yet, some said, well-born ;
Roysterer, and comrade, such as youth delights in.
Sailor he called himself, and naught belied
The sailor's metal ringing in his talk
Of El Dorados, and Enchanted Isles,
Of hardy Raleigh, and of dauntless Drake,
And great Columbus with prophetic eyes
Fixed on a dawning world.   His legends fired me—
And, from the deep whose billows washed our walls,
The alluring wave called with a Siren's music.
And thus I left my home with that wild seaman.

LADY M. The priest, consenting, still divulged not more?

VYV. No; nor rebuked mine ardor.   " Go," he said,
" The noblest of all nobles are the men
In whom their country feels herself ennobled."

LADY M. (*aside*). I breathe again. (*aloud*) ·Well, thus you left these
    shores——

VYV. Scarce had the brisker sea-wind filled our sails,
When the false traitor who had lured my trust
Cast me to chains and darkness.   Days went by,
At length—one belt of desolate waters round,
And on the decks one scowl of swarthy brows,
(A hideous crew, the refuse of all shores)—
Under the flapping of his raven flag
The pirate stood revealed, and called his captive.
Grimly he heard my boyish loud upbraidings,
And grimly smiled in answering : " I, like thee,
Cast off, and disinherited, and desperate,
Had but one choice, death or the pirate's flag—
Choose *thou*—I am more gracious than thy kindred ;
I proffer life ; the gold *they* gave me paid
Thy grave in ocean !"

LADY M.   Hold !   The demon lied !

VYV. Swift, as I answered so, his blade flashed forth ;
But self-defence is swifter still than slaughter ;
I plucked a sword from one who stood beside me,
        (*gesture of parrying a thrust and replying by a down cut*)
And smote the slanderer to my feet.   Then all
That human hell broke loose ; oaths rang. steel lightened ;
When in the death-swoon of the caitiff chief,
The pirate next in rank forced back the swarm,
And,—in that superstition of the sea
Which makes the sole religion of its outlaws—
Forbade my doom by bloodshed—griped and bound me
To a slight plank ; spread to the winds the sail,

And left me on the waves alone with God.

EVEL. Pause, (*standing beside* VYVYAN) Let my hand take thine—feel
    its warm life,
    And, shuddering less, thank Him whose eye was o'er thee.

VYV. That day, and all that night, upon the seas
    Tossed the frail barrier between life and death;
    Heaven lulled the gales; and when the stars came forth,
    All looked so bland and gentle that I wept,
    Recalled that wretch's words, and murmured, "All,
    E'en wave and wind, are kinder than my kindred!"
    But—nay, sweet lady——

LADY M. (*sobbing*). Heed me not. (*with an effort*) Night passed——

VYV. Day dawned; and, glittering in the sun, behold
    A sail—a flag!

EVEL.   Well—well?

VYV.   Like Hope, it vanished!
    Noon glaring came—with noon came thirst and famine,
    And with parched lips I called on death, and sought
    To wrench my limbs from the stiff cords that gnawed
    Into the flesh, and drop into the deep:
    And then—the clear wave trembled, and below
    I saw a dark, swift-moving, shapeless thing,
    With watchful, glassy eyes ;—the ghastly shark
    Swam hungering round its prey—then life once more
    Grew sweet, and with a strained and horrent gaze
    And lifted hair I floated on, till sense
    Grew dim, and dimmer ; and a terrible sleep
    (In which still—still those livid eyes met mine)
    Fell on me—and——

EVEL.   Quick—quick!

VYV.   I woke, and heard
    My native tongue! Kind looks were bent upon me.
    I lay on deck—escaped the ravening death—
    For God had watched the sleeper.

EVEL.   Oh, such memories
    Make earth, forever after, nearer heaven ;
    And each new hour an altar for thanksgiving.

LADY M. Break not the tale my ear yet strains to listen.

VYV. True lion of the ocean was the chief
    Of that good ship. Beneath his fostering eyes,
    Nor all ungraced by Drake's illustrious praise,
    And the frank clasp of Raleigh's kingly hand,
    I fought my way to manhood. At his death
    The veteran left me a more absolute throne
    Than Cæsar filled—his war-ship; for my realm
    Add to the ocean, hope—and measure it!
    Nameless, I took his name. My tale is done—
    And each past sorrow, like a wave on shore,
    Dies on this golden hour. (*goes* L. *with* EVELINE, *tenderly.*)

LADY M. (*observing them*). He loves my ward,
    Whom Clarence, too—that thought piles fear on fear ;
    Yet, hold—that very rivalship gives safety—
    Affords pretext to urge the secret nuptials,
    And the prompt parting, ere he meet with Alton.
    I—but till Nature sobs itself to peace,
    Here's that which chokes all reason. Will ye not

Taste summer air, cooled through yon shadowy alleys?
Anon I'll join you.   [*Exit* LADY MONTREVILLE, R. 1 E.
VYV.   We will wait your leisure.
A most compassionate and courteous lady—
How could'st thou call her proud?
EVEL.   Nay, ever henceforth,
For the soft pity she has shown to thee,
I'll love her as a mother.
VYV.   Thus I thank thee. (*kissing her hand.*)
           [*Exeunt,* L. 1 E.

SCENE II.—*Castle yard, in 5th grooves.*

Enter SIR GREY DE MALPAS, L 2 E.

LORD B. (*speaking off* L. 2 E.). A noble falcon! Marsden, hood him
    gently.

Enter LORD BEAUFORT, D. *in* 3 G. *set.*

Good-day, old knight, thou hast a lowering look,
As if still ruffled by some dire affray
With lawless mice, at riot in thy larder.
SIR G. Mice in my house! magnificent dreamer, mice!
The last was found three years ago last Christmas,
Stretched out beside a bone; so lean and worn
With pious fast—'twas piteous to behold it;
I canonized its corpse in spirits of wine,
And set it in the porch—a solemn warning
To its poor cousins! (*aside*) Shall I be avenged?
He killed my dog too.

Enter VYVYAN *and* EVELINE, R. 2 E., *remaining up* R. *on platform.*

LORD B. (L. C.).   Knight, look here!—A stranger,
And whispering with my cousin.
SIR G. (L. C. *front, aside*).   Jealous? Ha!
Something should come of this: Hail, green-eyed fiend!
(*aloud*) Let us withdraw—tho' old, I have been young;
The whispered talk of lovers should be sacred.
LORD B. Lovers!
SIR G.   Ah! true! You know not, in your absence
Your mother hath received a welcome guest
In your fair cousin's wooer. Note him well,
A stalwart, comely gallant.
LORD B.   Art thou serious?
A wooer to my cousin—quick, his name!
SIR G. His name?—my memory doth begin to fail me—
Your mother will recall it. Seek—ask *her*——
       (VYVYAN *and* EVELINE *come down* R. C.)
LORD B. (*to* C.). Whom have we here? Familiar sir, excuse me,
I do not see the golden spurs of knighthood.
VYV.* Alack, we sailors have not so much gold
That we should waste it on our heels! The steeds
We ride to battle need no spurs, Sir Landsman;

---

     * EVELINE.   VYVYAN.   BEAUFORT.   SIR GREY.
      R. *of* C.   C.   L. C.

LORD B. And overleap all laws ; (*sneeringly*) methinks thou art
    One of those wild Sea Rovers, who——
VYV. (*quickly*).   Refuse
    To yield to Spain's proud tyranny, her claim
    To treat as thieves and pirates all who cross
    The line Spain's finger draws across God's ocean.
    We, the Sea Rovers, on our dauntless decks
    Carry our land, its language, laws, and freedom ;
    We wrest from Spain the sceptre of the seas,
    And in the New World build up a new England.
    For this high task, if we fulfill it duly,
    The Old and New World both shall bless the names
    Of Walter Raleigh and his bold Sea Rovers.
LORD B. Of those names thine is——
VYV.   Vyvyan.
LORD B.   Master Vyvyan,
    Our rank scarce fits us for a fair encounter
    With the loud talk of blustering mariners.
    We bar you not our hospitality ;
    Our converse, yes. Go ask the Seneschal
    To lodge you with your equals !
VYV.   Equals, stripling !
    Mine equals truly should be bearded men,
    Noble with titles carpet lords should bow to—
    Memories of dangers dared, and service done,
    And scars on bosoms that have bled for England !
SIR. G. Nay, coz, he has thee there. (*restraining* BEAUFORT *from draw-
    ing sword.*)
                 Thou shalt not, Clarence.
    Strike *me.* I'm weak and safe—but *he* is dangerous.

Enter LADY MONTREVILLE, R. 1 E., *as* LORD BEAUFORT *breaks from* SIR
    GREY *and draws his sword.*

EVEL. Protect your guest from your rash son.
LADY M.   Thy sword
    Drawn on thy——(c.) Back, boy ! I command thee, back!
    To you, sir guest, have I in aught so failed,
    That in the son you would rebuke the mother ?
VYV.* Madam, believe, my sole offence was this,
    That rated as a serf, I spoke as man.
LADY M. Wherefore, Lord Beaufort, such unseemly humors ?
LORD B. (*drawing her aside*). Wherefore ?—and while we speak his
    touch profanes her !
    Who is this man ? Dost thou approve his suit ?
    Beware !
LADY M.   You would not threaten——Oh, my Clarence,
    Hear me—you——
LORD B.   Learned in childhood from my mother
    To brook no rival—and to curb no passion.
    Aid'st thou yon scatterling against thy son,
    Where most his heart is set ?
LADY M.   Thy heart, perverse one ?
    Thou saidst it was not love.

---

* EVELINE.	VYVYAN.	LADY M.	BEAUFORT.	SIR GREY.
R.	R. C.	C.	L. C.	L.

LORD B.   That was before
A rival made it love—nay, fear not mother,
If you dismiss this insolent; but, mark me,
Dismiss him straight, or by mine honor, madam,
Blood will be shed.

LADY B.   Thrice miserable boy!
Let the heavens hear thee not!

LORD B. (*whispering to* VYVYAN *as he crosses* R.) Again, and soon, sir!
                                        [*Exit* R 1 E.

LADY M. (*seeing* SIR GREY). Villain!—but no, I dare not yet up-
braid——
(*aloud*) After him, quick! Appease, soothe, humor him.

SIR G. Ay, madam, trust to your poor cousin.   [*Exit* R. 1 E

LADY M. (*aside*).   Eveline,
Thou lov'st this Vyvyan?

EVEL. (*aside*).   Lady—I—be saved
My life and honor.

LADY M. (*aside*).   Leave us, gentle child,
I wou'd confer with him.   May both be happy!

EVEL. (*to* VYVYAN). Hush! she consents; well mayst then bid me
love her.   [*Exit* EVELINE, L. 1 E.

LADY M. Sir, if I gather rightly from your speech,
You do not mean long sojourn on these shores?

VYV. Lady, in sooth, mine errand here was two-fold.
First, to behold, and, if I dare assume
That you will ratify her father's promise,
To claim my long affianced; next to learn
If Heaven vouchsafe me yet a parent's heart.
I gained these shores to hear of war and danger—
The long-suspended thunderbolt of Spain
Threatened the air.   I have dispatched an envoy
To mine old leader, Drake, to crave sure tidings;
I wait reply: If England be in peril,
Hers my first service; if,·as rumor runs,
The cloud already melts without a storm,
Then, my bride gained, and my birth tracked, I sail
Back to the Indian seas, where wild adventure
Fulfills in life what boyhood dreamed in song.

LADY M. 'Tis frankly spoken—frankly I reply.
First—England's danger; now, for five slow years
Have Spain's dull trumpets blared their braggart war,
And Rome's gray monk-craft muttered new crusades;
Well, we live still—and all this deluge dies
In harmless spray on England's scornful cliffs.
And, trust me, sir, if war beleaguer England,
Small need of one man's valor: lacked she soldiers,
Methinks a Mars would strike in childhood's arm,
And woman be Bellona!

VYV.   Stately matron,
So would our mother country speak and look,
Could she take visible image!

LADY M.   Claim thy bride
With my assent, and joyous gratulation.
She shall not go undowried to your arms.
Nor deem me wanting to herself and you
If I adjure prompt nuptials and departure.
Beaufort—thou see'st how fiery is his mood—

In my ward's lover would avenge a rival :
Indulge the impatient terrors of a mother,
And quit these shores. Why not this night ?

Vyv.   This night ?
With her—my bride ?

Lady M.   So from the nuptial altar
Pledge thou thy faith to part—to spread the sail
And put wide seas between my son and thee.

Vyv. This night, with Eveline !—dream of rapture ! (*changes look from
     joy to pain*) yet—
My birth untracked—

Lady M.   Delay not for a doubt
Bliss when assured   And, heed me, I have wealth
To sharpen law. and power to strengthen justice ;
I will explore the mazes of this mystery ;
I—I will track your parents.

Vyv.   Blessed lady ;
My parents !—Find me one with eyes like thine,
                                        (Lady M. *starts*)
And were she lowliest of the hamlet born,
I would not change with monarchs.

Lady M. (*aside*).   Can I bear this ?
(*aloud*) Your Eveline well nigh is my daughter ; you
Her plighted spouse ; pray you this kiss—O sweet !
     (Vyvyan *sinks on one knee as* Lady M. *kisses his forehead.*)

Vyv. Ah. as I kneel, and as thou bendest o'er me,
Methinks an angel's hand lifts up the veil
Of Time, the great magician and I see
Above mine infant couch, a face like thine.

Lady M. Mine, stranger !

Vyv. (*rising*).   Pardon me ; a vain wild thought
I know it is ; but on my faith, I think
My mother was like thee.

Lady M.   Peace, peace ! We talk
And fool grave hours away. Inform thy bride ;
Then to thy bark, and bid thy crew prepare ;
Meanwhile, I give due orders to my chaplain.
Beside the altar we shall meet once more ,—
(*voice breaks*) And then—and then—Heaven's blessing and farewe'l !
                    [*Exit* Lady Montreville, l. 1 e., *wildly.*

Vyv. Most feeling heart ! its softness hath contagion,
And melts mine own ! Her aspect wears a charm
That half divides my soul with Eveline's love !
Strange ! while I muse, a chill and ominous awe
Creeps thro' my reins ! Away, ye vague forebodings !
Eveline ! At thy dear name the phantoms vanish,
And the glad future breaks like land on sea,
When rain-mists melt beneath the golden morn.

Enter, d. in 3 g. *set*, Falkner.

Falk. Ha ! Vyvyan !

Vyv.   Thou !

Falk.   Breathless with speed to reach thee,
I guessed thee lingering here. Thy foster sire
Hath proofs that clear the shadow from thy birth.
Go—he awaits thee where yon cloud-capt rock

Jags air with barbed peaks—St. Kinian's Cliff.

[*Shouts off* L., *faintly.*

Vyv. My birth! My parents live?

Falk.   I know no more.

Enter, D. *in* 3 G. *set,* Harding.

Hard. Captain, the rumor lied. I bring such news
As drums and clarions and resounding anvils
Fashioning the scythes of reapers into swords,
Shall ring from Thames to Tweed.

Vyv.   The foeman comes!

Hard. (*gives letter*). These lines will tell thee; Drake's own hand.

[*Goes up* L. C.

Vyv. (*reads*).   "The Armada
Has left the Groyne, and we are ranging battle.
Come! in the van I leave one gap for thee."
Poor Eveline! Shame on such unworthy weakness!

Falk. Time to see her and keep thy tryst with Alton
Leave me to call the crews and arm the decks.
Not till the moon rise, in the second hour
After the sunset, will the deepening tide
Float us from harbor—ere that hour be past
Our ship shall wait thee by St. Kinian's Cliff.
Small need to pray thee not to miss the moment
Whose loss would lose thee honor.

Vyv.   If I come not
Ere the waves reel to thy third signal gun.
Deem Death alone could so delay from duty,
And step into my post as o'er my corpse.

Falk. Justly, my captain. thou rebuk'st my warning.
And couldst thou fail us, I would hold the signal
As if thy funeral knell—crowd every sail,
And know thy soul——

Vyv.   Was with my country still. (*shouts off* L.)

Enter, D. *in* 3 G. *set,* Sub-officer, Sailors, Retainers, *and* Villagers
confusedly.

Sub-officer (*with broadsheet*). Captain, look here. Just come!

Vyv.   The Queen's Address
From her own lips to the armed lines at Tilbury.

Voices. Read it, sir, read it—

Vyv.   Hush then. (*reads*) "Loving people,
Let tyrants fear! I, under Heaven, have placed
In loyal hearts my chiefest strength and safeguard,
Being resolved in the midst and heat of the battle
To live and die amongst you all, content
To lay down, for my God and for my people
My life blood even in the dust: I know
I have the body of a feeble woman,
But a King's heart a King of England's too;
And think foul scorn that Parma, Spain, or Europe,
Dare to invade the borders of my realm!
Where England fights—with concord in the camp,
Trust in the chief, and valor in the field,

Swift be her victory over every foe
Threatening her crown, her altars, and her people."

The noble Woman King ! These words of fire
Will send warm blood through all the veins of Freedom
Till England is a dream ! Uncover, lads !
God and St. George ! Hurrah for England's Queen !
(*Cheers, all cheer.*)

VILLAGERS. *   *   *   *   *   * VILLAGERS.
FALKNER.*   * VYVYAN. * HARDING.

QUICK CURTAIN.

ACT III.

SCENE I.—*Rocky Landscape in 2d grooves.*

Discover ALTON *and* VYVYAN, *seated c., on low rocks.*

ALTON. And I believed them when they said " He died
    In the far seas." Ten years of desolate sorrow
    Passed as one night—Now thy warm hand awakes me.
VYV Dear friend, the sun sets fast.
ALTON.   Alas ! then listen.
    There was a page, fair, gentle, brave, but low-born—
    And in those years when, to young eyes the world,
    With all the rough disparities of fortune,
    Floats level thro' the morning haze of fancy,
    He loved the heiress of a lordly house :
    She scarce from childhood, listening, loved again,
    And secret nuptials hallowed stolen meetings—
    'Till one—I know not whom (perchance a kinsman,
    Heir to that house—if childless died its daughter)
    Spied—tracked the bridegroom to the bridal bower,
    Aroused the sire, and said, " Thy child's dishonored ! "
    Snatching his sword, the father sought the chamber ;
    Burst the closed portal—but his lifted hand
    Escaped the crime. Cold as a fallen statue,
    Cast from its blessed pedestal forever,
    The bride lay senseless on the lonely floor
    By the ope'd casement, from whose terrible height
    The generous boy, to save her life or honor,
    Had plunged into his own sure death below.
VYV. A happy death, if it saved her he loved !
ALTON. A midnight grave concealed the mangled clay,
    And buried the bride's secret. Few nights after,
    Darkly as life from him had passed away,
    Life dawned on thee—and, from the unconscious mother,
    Stern hands conveyed the pledge of fatal nuptials
    To the poor priest, who to thy loftier kindred
    Owed the mean roof that sheltered thee.

VYV.   Oh, say
  I have a mother still!
ALTON.   Yes!
VYV. (*with joy*).   Oh!
ALTON.   She survived—
  Her vows, thy birth, by the blind world unguessed;
  And, after years of woe and vain resistance,
  Forced to a lordlier husband's arms.
VYV.   "My soul
  Ofttimes recalls a shadowy mournfulness,
  With woman's patient brow, and saddest tears
  Dropped fast from woman's eyes;—they were my mother's.
ALTON. In stealth a wife—in stealth a mother! yes,
  Then did she love thee, *then* aspired to own
  In coming times, and bade me hoard these proofs
  For that blest day." Alas! new ties
  Brought new affections—to the second nuptials
  A second son was born; she loved him better,
  Better than thee—than her own soul!
VYV.   Poor mother!
ALTON. And haughtier thoughts on riper life arose,
  And worldly greatness feared the world's dread shame.
  And she forsook her visits to thy pillow,
  And the sire threatened, and the kinsman prayed,
  Till, over-urged by terror for thy safety,
  I took reluctant vows to mask the truth
  And hush thy rights while lived thy mother's sire
  And he, her second unsuspecting lord.
  Thus thy youth, nameless, left my lonely roof
  The sire and husband died while thou wert absent.
  Thou liv'st—thou hast returned; mine oath is freed;
  These scrolls attest my tale and prove thy birthright—
  Hail, Lord of Beaufort—Heir of Montreville!
VYV. 'Tis she—'tis she! At the first glance I loved her!
  And when I told my woes, she wept—she wept!
  This is her writing. Look—look where she calls me
  "Edmond and child." Old man, how thou hast wronged her!
  Joy—joy! I fly to claim and find a mother!
        [*Exit* VYVYAN, L. 1 E.
ALTON. Just power, propitiate Nature to that cry,
  "And from the hardened rock, let living streams
  Gush as in Horeb! Ah, how faintly flags,
  Strained by unwonted action, weary age!
  I'll seek the neighboring hamlet—rest and pray." .
        [*Exit* ALTON, R. 1 E.

SCENE II.—*Castle Exterior as in* SCENE II., *Act II. Sunset.*

Enter SIR GREY *and* WRECKLYFFE, D. *in* 3 G. flat.

SIR G. The priest has left his home?
WRECK.   The hour I reached it.
SIR G. With but one man? Did'st thou not hound the foot-track?
WRECK. I did.
SIR G.   Thou didst—and yet the prey escaped!
  I have done. I gave thee thy soul's wish, revenge,
  Revenge on Vyvyan—and thou leav'st his way

Clear to a height as high from thy revenge
As is yon watch-tower from a pirate's gibbet.

WRECK Silence! thou——

SIR. G (*haughtily*).   Sir!

WRECK. (*subdued and cowed*). Along the moors I track'd them.
But only came in sight and reach of spring
Just as they gained the broad and thronging road,
Aloud with eager strides, and clamorous voices—
A surge of tumult, wave to wave rebooming
How all the might of Parma and of Spain
Hurried its thunders on. (*gas gradually down during this scene.*)

SIR G.   Dolt, what to us
Parma and Spain ? The beggar has no country !

WRECK. But deeds like that which thou dost urge me to
Are not risked madly in the populous day.
I come to thy sharp wit for safer orders.

SIR G. My wit is dulled by time, and must be ground
Into an edge by thought.   Hist !—the door jars,
She comes. Skulk yonder—hide thee--but in call !
A moment sometimes makes or marreth fortune,
Just as the fiend Occasion springs to hand—
Be *thou* that fiend !   [WRECKLYFFE *exits up* R. C.

Enter LADY MONTREVILLE, L. 1 E.

LADY M.   Look on me ' What, nor tremble ?
Couldst thou have deemed my father's gold a bribe
For my son's murder ? Sold to pirates ! Cast
On the wild seas !

SIR G.   How ! I knew naught of this.
If such the truth, peace to thy father's sins,
For of those sins is this. Let the past sleep,
Meet present ills—the priest hath left his home
With Vyvyan's comrade, and our scheme is foiled.

LADY M I will, myself, see Alton on the morrow—
Edmond can scarce forestall me ; for this night
Fear sails with him to the far Indian main.

SIR G. Let me do homage to thy genius. Sorceress,
What was thy magic ?

LADY M.   Terror for my Cla·ence,
And Edmond's love for Eveline.

SIR G. (*aside*).   I see !
Bribed by the prize of which she robs his rival !
This night—so soon ?—this night—

LADY M.   I save my Clarence !
Till then, keep close, close to his side. Thou hast soothed him ?

SIR G. Fear not—these sudden tidings of the foe
With larger fires have paled receding love—
But where is Vyvyan ?

LADY M.   Doubtless with his crew,
Preparing for departure.

LORD B. (*without*).   This way, Marsden.

Enter, L. 2 E., LORD BEAUFORT *with* MARSDEN *and armed* ATTENDANTS.

LORD B. '*To* R ' Repair yon broken parapets at dawn ;
Yonder the culverins ,—delve down more sharply

That bank ;—clear out the moat. Those trees—eh—Marsden,
Should fall ? They'd serve to screen the foe ! (*comes to* c.) Ah,
  mother,
Make me a scarf to wear above the armor
In which thy father, 'mid the shouts of kings,
Shivered French lances at the Cloth of Gold.
MARS. Nay, my young lord, too vast for you that armor.
LORD B. No ; you forget that the breast swells in danger,
And honor adds a cubit to the stature.
LADY M. Embrace me, Clarence, I myself will arm thee.
Look at him, Marsden—yet they say I spoil him !
SIR G. (*draws* LADY M. *to* L. c., *and whispers*). I mark i' the distance
  swift disordered strides,
And the light bound of an impatient spirit ;
Vyvyan speeds hither, and the speed seems joy.
He sought his crew—Alton might there await him.
LADY M. His speed is to a bride.
SIR G.   Ay, true—old age
Forgets that Love's as eager as Ambition ;
Yet hold thyself prepared.
LADY M. (*to herself.*)   And if it were so !
Come, I will sound the depths of Beaufort's heart !
And, as that answers, hush or yield to conscience.
Lead off these men.
    [*Exeunt* SIR GREY *and* ATTENDANTS, D. *in* 3 G. *fl.it.*
(*to* MARSDEN)   Go, meet my this day's guest,
And see he enter through the garden postern.
              [*Exit* MARSDEN, L. 1 E.
Clarence, come back.
LORD B. (*peevishly.*) What now ? (R.)
LADY M.   Speak kindly, Clarence.
Alas, thou'lt know not till the grave close o'er me,
How I did need thy kindness !
LORD B.   Pardon, mother,
My blunt speech now, and froward heat this morning.
LADY M. Be all such follies of the past, as leaves
Shed from the petals of the bursting flower.
Think thy soul slept, till honor's sudden dawn
Flashed, and the soil bloomed with one hero more !
Ah, Clarence, had I, too, an elder-born,
As had thy father by his former nuptials !—
Could thy sword carve out fortune ?
LORD B.   Ay, my mother !
LADY M. "Well tho bold answer rushes from thy lips ! "
Yet, tell me frankly, dost thou not, in truth,
Prize over much the outward show of things ;
And couldst thou—rich with valor, health and beauty,
And hope—the priceless treasure of the young—
Couldst thou endure descent from that vain height
Where pride builds towers the heart inhabits not ;
To live less gorgeously, and curb thy wants
Within the state, not of the heir to earls,
But of a simple gentleman ?
LORD B.   If reared to it,
Perchance contented so ; but *now*—no, never !
Such as I am, thy lofty self hath made me ;
Ambitious, haughty, prodigal ; and pomp

A part of my very life. If I could fall
From my high state, it were as Romans fell,
On their swords' point!
LADY M. (*in horror*).   Oh!
LORD B.   Why is your cheek so hueless?
Why daunt yourself with airiest fantasies?
Who can deprive me of mine heritage—
"The titles borne at Palestine and Crecy?
The seignory, ancient as the throne it guards,"
That will be mine in trust for sons unborn,
When time—from this day may the date be far!—
Transfers the circlet on thy stately brows
(Forgive the boast!) to no unworthy heir.
LADY M. (*aside*). My proud soul speaks in his, and stills remorse;
I'll know no other son! (*aloud*) Now go, Lord Beaufort.
LORD B. So formal—fie!—has Clarence then offended?
LADY M. Offended?—thou! Resume thy noble duties,
Sole heir of Montreville!   [*Exit* LORD BEAUFORT, L. 2 E.
My choice is made.
As one who holds a fortress for his king,
I guard this heart for Clarence, and I close
Its gates against the stranger. Let him come.
[*Exit*, L. 1. E.

Enter, D. *in* 3 G. *flat*, VYVYAN *and* EVELINE.

EVEL. I would not bid thee stay, thy country calls thee—
But thou hast stunned my heart i' the midst of joy
With this dread sudden word—part—part!
VYV.   Live not
In the brief present. Go forth to the fu ure!
Wouldst thou not see me worthier of thy love?
EVEL. Thou canst not be so.
VYV.   Sweet one, I am now
Obscure and nameless. What if at thy feet
I could lay rank and fortune?
EVEL.   These could give
To me no bliss save as they bless thyself.
Into the life of him she loves, the life
Of woman flows, and nevermore reflects
Sunshine or shadow on a separate wave.
Be his lot great, for his sake she loves greatness;
Humble—a cot with *him* is Arcady!
Thou art ambitious; thou wouldst arm for fame,
Fame then fires me too, and without a tear
I bid thee go where fame is won—as now:
Win it and I rejoice; but fail to win,
Were it not joy to think I could console?
VYV. Oh, that I could give vent to this full heart!
Time rushes on, each glimmering star rebukes me—
Is that the Countess yonder? This way—come. (*up* C.)
[*Moonlight falls on* L. *side now*.

Enter LORD BEAUFORT *and* SIR GREY, L. 1 E.

LORD B. Leave England, say'st thou—and with her?
SIR G.   Thou hast wrung

The secret from me. Mark—I have thy promise
Not to betray me to thy mother.

LORD B.   Ah !
Thought she to dupe me with that pomp of words,
And blind ambition while she beggar'd life ?
No, by yon heavens, she shall not so befool me !

SIR G.—Be patient. Had I guessed how this had galled,
I had been dumb.

LORD B.   Stand from the light ! Distraction !
She hangs upon his breast ! (*hurries to* VYVYAN, *and then un-
covering with an attempt at courtesy, draws him to front*)

LORD B.   Sir, one word with you.
This day such looks and converse passed between us
As men who wear these vouchers for esteem,
Cancel with deeds.

VYV. (*aside*).   The brave boy ! How I love him !

LORD B. What saidst thou, sir ?

EVEL. (*approaching*).   Oh, Clarence.

LORD B.   Fear not, cousin.
I do but make excuses for my rudeness
At noon, to this fair cavalier.

SIR G.   If so,
Let us not mar such courteous purpose, lady.

EVEL. But—

SIR G.   Nay, you are too timid ! (*draws* EVELINE *up* L)

LORD B.   Be we brief, sir.
You quit these parts to-night. This place beseems not
The only conference we should hold. I pray you
Name spot and hour in which to meet again,
Unwitnessed save by the broad early moon.

VYV. Meet thee again—oh, yes !

LORD B.   There speaks a soldier,
And now I own an equal. Hour and place ?

VYV. Wait here till I have——

LORD B.   No, sir, on thy road.
Here we are spied.

VYV.   So be it, on my road.
(*aside*) [There where I learned that heaven had given a brother,
There the embrace.] Within the hour I pass
St. Kinian's Cliff.

LORD B.   Alone ?

VYV.   Alone.

LORD B. Farewell !

SIR. G. (*catching at* LORD BEAUFORT *as he goes out.*) I heard St
Kinian's Cliff. I'll warn the Countess.*

LORD B. Do it, and famish !

SIR G.   Well, thy fence is skillful.

LORD B. And my hand firm.

SIR G.   But when ?

LORD B.   Within the hour !
                              [*Exit* LORD BEAUFORT, L. 1 E.

EVEL. I do conjure thee on thine honor, Vyvyan,
Hath he not—

VYV.   What ? (R. C.)

EVEL.   Forced quarrel on thee ? (C.)

VYV.   Quarrel
That were beyond his power. Upon mine honor,
No, and thrice no !

EVEL   I scarce dare yet believe thee.
VYV. Why then, I thus defy thee still to tremble.
    Away this weapon. (*throwing sword off* R. 1 E.) If I meet thy
        cousin,
    Both must be safe, for one will be unarmed.
EVEL. Mine own frank hero-lover, pardon me ;
    Yet need'st thou not——
VYV.   Oh, as against the Spaniard,
    There will be swords enow in Vyvyan's war-ship—
    But art thou sure his heart is touched so lightly ?
EVEL. Jealous, and now !
VYV.   No, the fair boy, 'tis pity !

                Enter MARSDEN, L. 2 E.,

MARS.* My lady, sir, invites you to her presence;
    Pray you this way.
EVEL.   Remember—O, remember,
    One word again, before we part; but one !
VYV. One word.   Heaven make it joyous.
EVEL.   Joyous !
VYV. Soft, let me take that echo from thy lips
    As a good omen.   How my loud heart beats ! (*aside.*)
    Friend, to your lady   [*Exeunt* VYVYAN *and* MARSDEN, L. 1 E.
EVEL.   Gone !   The twilight world
    Hath its stars still—but mine ! Ah, woe is me !
                         [*Exit* EVELINE, L. 1 E.
SIR G. Why take the challenge, yet cast off the weapon ?
    Perchance, if, gentle, he forbears the boy ;
    " Perchance, if worldly wise, he fears the noble ;
    Or hath he, in his absence, chanced with Alton ?
    It matters not.   Like some dark necromancer,
    I raise the storm, then rule it thro' the fiend !
    Where waits this man without a hope ?
WRECK. (*coming down* C.).   Save vengeance !
SIR G. Wert thou as near when Beaufort spoke with Vyvyan ?
WRECK. Shall I repeat what Vyvyan said to Beaufort ?
SIR G. Thou know'st——
WRECK.   I know, that to St. Kinian's Cliff
    Will come the man whose hand wrote " felon " here.
                                    (*touches face.*)
SIR G. Mark, what I ask is harder than to strike ;
    'Tis to forbear—but 'tis revenge with safety.
    Let Vyvyan first meet Beaufort ; watch what pass,
    And if the boy, whose hand obeys all passion,
    Should slay thy foeman, and forestall thy vengeance,
    Upon thy life (thou know'st, of old, Grey Malpas)
    Prevent not, nor assist.
WRECK.   That boy slay Vyvyan !
SIR G. For Vyvyan is unarmed.
WRECK.   Law calls that—murder !
SIR G. Which by thy witness, not unbacked by proof,
    Would give the murderer to the headsman's axe,
    And leave Grey Malpas heir of Montreville,
    And thee the richest squire in all his train.

_____

        *VYVYAN.   EVEL.   MARSDEN.   SIR GREY.
                         C.   L., *up.*

WRECK. I do conceive the scheme. But if the youth
Fail or relent——
SIR G. I balk not thy revenge.
And, if the corpse of Beaufort's rival be
Found on the spot where armed Beaufort met him,
To whom would justice track the death blow?—Beaufort!
WRECK. No further words. Or his, or mine the hand,
Count one life less on earth; and weave thy scheme—
As doth the worm its coils—around the dead.
[*Exit* WRECKLYFFE, D. *in* 3 G. *flat.*
SIR G. " One death avails as three, since for the mother
Conscience and shame were sharper than the steel."
So, I o'erleap the gulf, nor gaze below.
On this side, desolate ruin; bread begrudged;
And ribald scorn on impotent gray hairs;
The base poor cousin Boyhood threats with famine—
Whose very dog is butchered if it bark :—
On that side bended knees and fawning smiles,
Ho! ho! there—Room for my lord's knights and pages!
Room at the Court—room there, beside the throne!
Ah, the new Earl of Montreville! His lands
Cover two shires. Such man should rule the state—
A gracious lord—the envious call him old;
Not so—the coronet conceals gray hairs.
He limp'd, they say, when he wore hose of serge.
Tut, the slow march becomes the robes of ermine.
Back, conscience, back! Go scowl on boors and beggars—
Room, smiling flatterers, room for the new Earl!
(*comes down fron', proudly, as falls the*)

CURTAIN.

ACT IV.

SCENE I.—*Same as Scene I., Act II.*

Discover LADY MONTREVILLE, R. *Enter* VYVYAN, L.

LADY M. Thou com'st already to demand thy bride?
VYV. Alas! such nuptials are deferred. This night
The invader summons me—my sole bride, Honor,
And my sole altar—England ' (*aside*) How to break it?
LADY M. My Clarence on the land, and thou on sea,
Both for their country armed! Heaven shield ye both!
VYV. Say you that? *Both?*—You who so love your son?
LADY M. Better than life, I love him!
VYV. (*aside*). I must rush
Into the thick. Time goads me! (*aloud*) Had you not
Another son? A first born?
LADY M. Sir!
VYV. A son,
On whom those eyes dwelt first—whose infant cry
Broke first on that divine and holiest chord

In the deep heart of woman, which awakes
All Nature's tenderest music ? Turn not from me
I know the mystery of thy mournful life.
Will it displease thee—will it—to believe
That son is living still ?

LADY M.   Sir—sir—such license
Expels your listener. (*turns* R.)

VYV.   No, thou wilt not leave me ?
I say, thou wilt not leave me—on my knees (*kneeling*)
I say, thou *shalt* not leave me!

LADY M.   Loose thine hold!

VYV. *I* am thy son—thine Edmond—thine own child !
Saved from the steel, the deep, the storm, the battle;
Rising from death to thee—the source of life!
Flung by kind Heaven once more upon thy breast,
Kissing thy robe, and clinging to thy knees.
Dost thou reject thy son ?

LADY M.   I have no son,
Save Clarence Beaufort.

VYV.   Do not—do not hear her,
Thou who, enthroned amid the pomp of stars,
Dost take no holier name than that of Father !
Thou hast no other son ?   O, cruel one !
Look—look—these letters to the priest who reared him—
See where thou call'st him " Edmond "—" child " —" life's all ! '
Can the words be so fresh on this frail record,
Yet fade, obliterate from the undying soul ?
By these—by these—by all the solemn past,
By thy youth's lover—by his secret grave,
By every kiss upon thine infant's cheek—
By every tear that wept his fancied death—
Grieve not that still a first-born calls thee " mother !

LADY M. Rise. If these prove that such a son once lived,
Where are your proofs that still he lives in you ?

VYV. There ! in thine heart !—thine eyes that dare not face me !
Thy trembling limbs, each power, each pulse of being,
That vibrates at my voice ! Let pride encase thee
With nine-fold adamant, it rends asunder
At the great spell of Nature—Nature calls
Parent, come forth !

LADY M. (*aside*) Resolve gives way ! Lost Clarence ! (*he rises*)
What! " Fall as Romans fell, on their swords' point ? '
No, Clarence, no ! (*turning fiercely*) Imposter ! If thy craft
Hath, by suborning most unworthy spies,
Sought in the ruins of a mourner's life
Some base whereon to pile this labored falsehood,
Let law laugh down the fable—Quit my presence.

VYV. No. I will not.

LADY M.   Will not ! Ho !

VYV.   Call your hirelings,
And let them hear me. (*to* R. C) Lo, beneath thy roof,
And on the sacred hearth of sires to both,
Under their 'scutcheon, and before their forms
Which from the ghostly canvas I invoke
To hail their son—I take my dauntless stand,
Armed with my rights ; now bid your menials thrust
From his own hearth the heir of Montreville !

Enter SERVANTS I.

LADY M. Seize on—— (*clasping her hands before her face*)
      Out—out! (*aside*) His father stands before me
  In the son's image No I dare not!
FIRST SERVANT   Madam,
  Did you not summon us?
Vvv.   They wait your mandate,
  Lady of Montreville.
LADY M.   I called not. Go!
                [*Exeunt* SERVANTS. L.
  Art thou my son? If so, have mercy, Edmond!
  Let Heaven attest with what remorseful soul
  I yielded to my ruthless father's will,
  And with cold lips profaned a second vow.
  I *had* a child—I was a parent true;
  But exiled from the parent's paradise.
  Not mine the frank joy in the face of day.
  The pride, the boast, the triumph, and the rapture;
  Thy couch was sought as with a felon's step,
  And whispering nature shuddered at detection.
  Ah, could'st thou guess what hell to loftier minds
  It is to live in one eternal lie
  Yet, spite of all, how dear thou wert!
Vvv   I was?
  Is the time past forever? What my sin?
LADY M. I loved thee till another son was born,
  A blossom 'mid the snows. Thou wert afar,
  Seen rarely—alien—on a stranger's breast
  Leaning for life. (*with great feeling*) But *this* thrice-blessed one
  Smiled in mine eyes took being from my breast,
  Slept in mine arms; *here* love asked no concealment—
  Here the tear shamed not—*here* the kiss was glory—
  Here I put on my royalty of woman—
  The guardian, the protector; food, health, life—
  It clung to me for all. Mother and child,
  Each was the all to each.
Vvv.   O, prodigal,
  Such wealth to him, yet naught to spare to me!
LADY M. My boy grew up, my Clarence. Looking on him
  Men prized his mother more—so fair and stately,
  And the world deemed to such high state the heir!
  Years went; they told me that by Nature's death
  Thou hadst in boyhood passed away to heaven.
  I wept thy fate; and long ere tears were dried,
  The thought that danger, too, expired for Clarence,
  Did make thy memory gentle.
Vvv.   Do you wish
  That I were still what once you wept to deem me?
LADY M. I did rejoice when my lip kissed thy brow;
  I did rejoice to give thy heart its bride;
  I would have drained my coffers for her dowry;
  But wouldst thou ask me if I can rejoice
  That a life rises from the grave abrupt
  To doom the life I cradled, reared, and wrapt
  From every breeze, to desolation?—No!

Vyv   What would you have me do ?

Lady M.   Accept the dowry,
And blest with Eveline's love, renounce thy mother

Vyv   Renounce thee! No—*these* lips belie not Nature!
Never!

Lady M.   Enough—I can be mean no more,
E'en in the prayer that asked his life. Go, slay it.

Vyv.   Why must my life slay his ?

Lady M.   Since his was shaped
To soar to power—not grovel to dependence—
And I do seal his death-writ when I say,
" Down to the dust, Usurper ; bow the knee
And sue for alms to the true Lord of Beaufort."
Those words shall not be said—I ll find some nobler.
Thy rights are clear.   The law might long defer them—
I do forestall the law.   These lands be thine.
Wait not my death to lord it in my hall :
Thus I say not to Clarence, " Be dependent "—
But I *can* say, " Share poverty with me."
I go to seek him; at his side depart;
He spurns thine alms; I wronged thee—take thy vengeance!

Vyv.   Merciless—hold, and hear me—I—alms!—vengeance!—
True—true, this heart a mother never cradled,
Or she had known it better.

Lady M.   Edmond !

Vyv.   Hush !
Call me that name no more—it dies forever!
Nay, I renounce thee not, for that were treason
On the child s lip.   Parent, renounce—thy—child !
As for these nothings, (*giving papers*) take them : if you dread
To find words, once too fond, they're blurr'd already—
You'll see but tears : tears of such sweetness, madam.
I did not think of lands and halls, pale Countess,
I did but think—these arms shall clasp a mother.
" Now they are worthless—take them.   Never guess
How covetous I was—how hearts, cast off,
Pine for their rights—rights not of parchment, lady."
Part we, then, thus ? No, put thine arms around me ;
Let me remember in the years to come,
That I have lived to say, a mother blessed me ! (*kneels.*)

Lady M. Oh, Edmond, Edmond, thou hast conquered !
Thy father's voice !—his eyes ! Look down from heaven,
Bridegroom, and pardon me ; I bless thy child !

Vyv. Hark ! she has blessed her son ! It mounts to heaven,
The blessing of the mother on her child !
Mother, and mother ;—how the word thrills thro' me !
Mother again, dear mother ! Place thy hand
Here—on my heart Now thou hast felt it beat,
Wilt thou misjudge it more ?

Lady M.   Oh !

Vyv.   Recoil'st thou still ?

Lady M (*breaking from him*). What have I done ?—betrayed, condemned my Clarence ! (*to* R., *frantically.*)

Vyv. (c.). Condemned thy Clarence ! By thy blessing, No !
That blessing was my birthright.   I have won
That which I claimed.   Give Clarence all the rest.
Silent, as sacred, be the memory

Of this atoning hour. Look, evermore (*kissing her*)
Thus—thus I seal the secret of thy first-born '
Now, only Clarence lives ' Heaven guard thy Clarence'
Now deem me dead to thee. Farewell, farewell !
                                        [*Exit* Vyvyan, L.
Lady M. (*rushing after him*). Hold, hold—too generous, hold ! Come
     back, my son !   [*Exit* Lady Montreville, L.

Scene changes to

SCENE II.—*Sea and Rocks in 4th grooves.*

Enter Lord Beaufort, L. 1 E.

Lord B. And still not here ! The hour has long since passed.
    I'll climb yon tallest peak, and strain mine eyes
    Down the sole path between the cliff and ocean.
                            (*goes up steps R., and off* R. 2 E.)

Enter Wrecklyffe, L. 1 E.

Wreck. The boors first grinned, then paled, and crept away ;
    The tavern-keeper slunk, and muttered " Hangdog ! "
    And the she-drudge whose rough hand served the drink,
    Stifled her shriek, and let the tankard fall !
    It was not so in the old merry days :
    Then the scarred hangdog was " fair gentleman."
    And—but the reckoning waits. Why tarries he ? (*beat on bass
        drum, with diminuendo beats, for signal gun, and its echoes.*)
    A signal ! Ha !
Vyv. (*off L.*)   I come, I come !
Wreck. (*grasping his cutlass, but receding as he sees* Beaufort *enter*
    R. 1 E.)   Hot lordling !
    I had well nigh forestalled thee. Patience !
                            [*Exit around set rock,* L. C.
Lord B. (*R. 2 E., on platform.*)   Good !
    From crag to crag he bounds—my doubts belied him ;
    His haste is eager as my own.

Enter Vyvyan, L. 1 E., *crossing and going up* R. *steps.*

                    *Sir, welcome.
                    (*both on first platform,* R. U. E.)
Vyv. Stay me not, stay me not ! Thou hast all else
    But honor—rob me not of that ! Unhand me !
Lord B. Unhand thee ? yes—to take thy ground and draw.
Vyv. Thou know'st not what thou sayest. Let me go !
Lord B. Thyself didst name the place and hour :
Vyv.   For here
    I thought to clasp—(*aside*) I have no brother now !
Lord B. He thought to clasp his Eveline. Death and madness !
Vyv. Eveline ! Thou lov'st not Eveline. " Be consoled.
    Thou hast not known affliction—hast not stood
    Without the porch of the sweet home of men ;
    Thou hast leaned upon no reed that pierced the heart;
    Thou hast not known what it is, when in the desert

The hopeless find the fountain." Happy boy,
Thou hast not loved   Leave love to man and sorrow!
Lord B. Dost thou presume upon my years? Dull scoffer!
The brave is man betimes—the coward never.
Boy if I be, my playmates have been veterans;
My toy a sword, and my first lesson valor.
And, had I taken challenge as thou hast,
And on the ground replied to bold defiance
With random words implying dastard taunts,
"With folded arms, pale lip, and haggard brow,"
I'd never live to call myself a man.
Thus says the boy, since manhood is so sluggard,
Soldier and captain. Do not let me strike thee!
Vyv. Do it,—and tell thy mother, when thy hand
Outraged my cheek, I pardoned thee, and pitied.
Lord B. Measureless insult! Pitied! (*drum for gun as before.*)
Vyv.   There again!
And still so far! Out of my path, insane one!
Were there naught else, thy youth, thy mother's love
Should make thee sacred to a warrior's arm—
Out of my path. Thus, then. (*suddenly lifts, and puts him aside.*)
                        Oh, England—England!
Do not reject me too!—I come! I come!
                        (*up the steps to upper platform.*)
Lord B. Thrust from his pathway—every vein runs fire!
Thou shalt not thus escape me—Stand or die!
    (*sword in hand, drives* Vyvyan *to the edge of the cliff, and he
    grasps, for support, the bough of tree.*)
Vyv. Forbear, forbear!
Lord B.   Thy blood on thine own head! (*drum for gun
    as before.   As* Beaufort *lifts his sword and strikes,* Vyvyan
    retreats—the bough breaks, and* Vyvyan *swings* L., *and down
    into centre trap.*)
Wreck. (*rises* R. C. *by trap*). Is the deed done? If not, this steel
    completes it. (*waves cutlass and exit down trap.* Lord
    Beaufort *sinks on his knee in horror. Work ship on* R. *to
    L., across.*)

                    SLOW CURTAIN.

                    ACT V.

        SCENE I.—*Same as Act IV., Scene II.*

    Enter Sir Grey de Malpas, L., *leaning on cane.*

Sir G. A year—and Wrecklyffe still is mute and absent,
Even as Vyvyan is! Most clear! He saw,
And haply shared, the murderous deed of Beaufort;
And Beaufort's wealth hath bribed him to desert
Penury and me. That Clarence slew his brother
I cannot doubt. He shuts me from his presence;
But I have watched him, wandering, lone, yet haunted—

Marked the white lip and glassy eyes of one
For whom the grave has ghosts, and silence, horror.
His mother, on vague pretext of mistrust
That I did sell her first-born to the pirate,
Excludes me from her sight, but sends me alms
Lest the world cry, " See, her poor cousin starves ! "
Can she guess Beaufort's guilt ? Nay ! For she lives !
I know that deed, which, told unto the world,
Would make me heir of Montreville. O, mockery !
For how proceed ?—no proof ! How charge ?—no witness !
How cry, " Lo ! murder ! " yet produce no corpse !

Enter ALTON, R.

ALTON. Sir Grey de Malpas ! I was on my way
        To your own house.
SIR G.   Good Alton—can I serve you ?
ALTON. The boy I took from thee, returned a man
        Twelve months ago : mine oath absolved.
SIR G.   'Tis true.
ALTON. Here did I hail the rightful lord of Montreville,
        And from these arms he rushed to claim his birthright.
SIR G. (*aside*). She never told me this
ALTON.   That night his war-ship
        Sailed to our fleet. I deemed him with the battle.
        Time went ; Heaven's breath had scattered the Armada.
        I sate at my porch to welcome him—he came not
        I said, " His mother has abjured her offspring,
        And law detains him while he arms for justice."
        Hope sustained patience till to-day.
SIR G.   To-day ?
ALTON. The very friend who had led me to his breast
        Returns and——
SIR G. (*soothingly.*) Well ?
ALTON.   He fought not with his country.
SIR G. And this cold friend lets question sleep a year ?
ALTON. His bark too rashly chased the flying foe ;
        Was wrecked on hostile shores ; and he a prisoner.
SIR G. Lean on my arm, thou'rt faint.
ALTON.   Oh, Grey de Malpas,
        Can men so vanish—save in murderous graves ?
        You turn away.
SIR G.   What murder without motive ?
        And who had motive here ?
ALTON.   Unnatural kindred.
SIR G. Kindred ! Ensnare me not ! Mine, too, that kindred.
        Old man, beware how thou asperse (*pause*) Lord Beaufort !
ALTON. Beaufort ! Oh, horror ! How the instinctive truth
        Starts from thy lips !
SIR G.   From mine ?
ALTON.   Yes. Not of man
        Ask pardon, if accomplice——
SIR G.   I, accomplice !
        Nay, since 'tis my good name thou sulliest now—
        This is mine answer : Probe ; examine ; search ;
        And call on justice to belie thy slander.
        Go, seek the aid of stout Sir Godfrey Seymour ;

A dauntless magistrate ; strict, upright, honest ;
(*aside*). At heart a Puritan, and hates a Lord,
With other slides that fit into my grooves.

ALTON. He bears with all the righteous name thou giv'st him,
Thy zeal acquits thyself.

SIR G.   And charges none.

ALTON. Heaven reads the heart.   Man can but track the deed.
My task is stern.   [*Exit* ALTON, L.

SIR G   Scent lies—suspicion dogs,
And with hot breath pants on the flight of conscience.
Ah ! who comes here ?   Sharp wit, round all occasion !

Enter FALKNER *with* SAILORS, L.

FALK. Learn all you can—when latest seen, and where—
Meanwhile I seek you towers.   [*Exeunt* SAILORS, L.

SIR G.   Doubtless, fair sir,
I speak to Vyvyan's friend.   My name is Malpas—
Can it be true, as Alton doth inform me,
That you suspect your comrade died by murder ?

FALK. Murder !

SIR G.   And by a rival's hand ?   Amazed !
Yet surely so I did conceive the priest.

FALK. Murder !—a rival !—true, he loved a maiden !

SIR G. In yonder halls !

FALK.   Despair !   Am I too late
For all but vengeance !   Speak, sir—who this rival ?

SIR G. Vengeance !—fie—seek those towers, and learn compassion.
Sad change indeed, since here, at silent night,
Your Vyvyan met the challenge of Lord Beaufort.

FALK. A challenge ?—here ?—at night ?

SIR G.   Yes, this the place.
How sheer the edge ! crag, cave, and chasm below !
If the foot slipped,—nay, let us think slipped heedless,—
Or some weak wounded man were headlong plunged,
What burial place more secret ?

FALK.   Hither, look !
Look where, far down the horrible descent,
Through some fresh cleft rush subterranean waves,
How wheel and circle ghastly swooping wings !

SIR G. The sea-gulls ere a storm,

FALK.   No !   Heaven is clear !
The storm *they* tell, speeds lightning towards the guilty.
So have I seen the foul birds in lone creeks
Sporting around the shipwrecked seaman's bones.
Guide me, ye spectral harbingers ! (*down* c *trap.   Music.*)

SIR G.   From bough
To bough he swings—from peak to slippery peak
I see him dwindl ng down ;—the loose stones rattle ;
He falls—he falls—but 'lights on yonder ledge,
And from the glaring sun turns steadfast eyes
Where still the sea-gulls wheel ; now crawls, now leaps ;
Crags close around him—not a glimpse nor sound !
O, diver for the dead ! (*sinks down as if watching* FALKNER ;
then *rises*) Bring up but bones,
And round the sku'l I'll wreathe my coronet.   [*Exit*, R.

Scene changes to

SCENE II.—*Interior in 1st grooves.*

Enter LADY MONTREVILLE *and* MARSDEN, L.

LADY M. Will he nor hunt nor hawk ? This constant gloom!
Canst thou not guess the cause ? He *was* so joyous !
MARS. Young plants need air and sun ; man's youth the world.
Young men should pine for action. Comfort, madam,
The cause is clear, if you recall the date.
LADY M. Thou hast marked the date ?
MARS. Since that bold seaman's visit.
LADY M. Thy tongue runs riot, man. How should that stranger—
I say a stranger, strike dismay in Beaufort ?
MARS. Dismay ! Not that, but emulation !
LADY M. Ay !
You speak my thoughts, and I have prayed our Queen
To rank your young lord with her chivalry ;
This day mine envoy should return.
MARS. This day ?
Let me ride forth and meet him !
LADY M. Go ! [*Exit* MARSDEN, L.
'Tis true !
Such was the date. Hath Clarence guessed the secret—
Guessed that a first-born lives ? I dread to question !
Yet sure the wronged was faithful, and the wrong
Is my heart's canker-worm and gnaws unseen.
Where wanderest thou, sad Edmond ? Not one **word**
To say thou liv'st—thy very bride forsaken,
As if love, frozen at the parent well-spring,
Left every channel dry ! What hollow tread,
Heavy and weary falls ? Is that the step
Which touched the mean earth with a lightsome scorn,
As if the air its element ?

Enter, BEAUFORT, R., *in mantle.*

LORD B. Cold ! cold !
And yet I saw the beggar doff his frieze,
Warm in his rags. I shiver under ermine.
For me 'tis never summer—never—never !
LADY M. How fares my precious one ?
LORD B. Well ;—but so cold.
Ho ! there ! without !

Enter SERVANT, L.

Wine ! wine ! [*Exit* SERVANT, L.
LADY M. Alas ! alas !
Why, this is fever—thy hand burns.
LORD B. That hand !
Ay, *that* hand always burns.

Re-enter SERVANT, L., *with wine in goblet, on salver.*

Look you—the cup

The wondrous Tuscan jeweller, Cellini,
Made for a king! A king's gift to thy father!
What? Serve such gauds to me!

LADY M. Thyself so ordered
In the proud whims thy light heart made so graceful.

LORD B. Was I proud once? Ha! ha! what's this?—not wine?

SERVANT. The Malvoisie your lordship's friends, last year,
Esteemed your rarest.

LORD B. How one little year
Hath soured it into nausea! Faugh—'tis rank.

LADY M. (to SERVANT). Send for the leech—quick—go.
[Exit SERVANT, L.
Oh, Clarence! Clarence!
Is this the body's sickness, or the soul's?
Is it life's youngest sorrow, love misplaced?
Thou dost not still love Eveline?

LORD B. Did I love her?

LADY M. Or one whose birth might more offend my pride?
Well, I am proud. But I would hail as daughter
The meanest maiden from whose smile thy lip
Caught smiles again. Thy smile is day to me.

LORD B. Poor mother, fear not. Never hermit-monk,
Gazing on skulls in lone sepulchral cells,
Had heart as proof to woman's smile as mine.

LADY M. The court—the camp—ambition——

Enter MARSDEN, *with a letter*, R.

MARS. From the Queen!
(*while the* COUNTESS *reads,* MARSDEN, *turning to* LORD BEAUFORT)
My dear young lord, be gay! The noblest knight,
In all the land, Lord Essex, on his road
From conquered Cadiz, "with the armed suite
That won his laurels," sends before to greet you,
And prays you will receive him in your halls.

LORD B. The flower of England's gentry, spotless Essex!
Sully him not, old man, bid him pass on.

LADY M. Joy, Beaufort, joy! August Elizabeth
Owns thee her knight, and bids thee wear her colors,
And break thy maiden lance for England's lady.

LORD B. I will not go. Barbed steeds and knightly banners—
Baubles and gewgaws!

MARS. Glorious to the young.

LORD B. Ay—to the young! Oh, when did poet dreams
Ever shape forth such a fairy land as youth!
Gossamer hopes, pearled with the dews of morn,
Gay valor, bounding light on welcome peril,—
Errors themselves, the sparkling overflow,
Of life as headlong, but as pure as streams
That rush from sunniest hill-tops kissing heaven,—
Lo! *that* is youth. Look on my soul, old man,
Well—is it not more gray than those blanched hairs? (*falls in
seat, c.*)

LADY M. He raves. Heed not his words. Go speed the leech!
[*Exit* MARSDEN, R., *quickly.*
(*aside*). I know these signs—by mine own soul I know them;
This is nor love, nor honor's sigh for action,

Nor Nature's milder suffering. This is guilt! (*sits*, L. c.)
Clarence—now, side by side, I sit with thee!
Put thine arms round me, lean upon my breast—
It is a mother's breast. So, that is well;
Now—whisper low—what is thy crime?

LORD B. (*bursting into tears*).   Oh, mother!
Would thou hadst never borne me!

LADY M.   Ah, ungrateful!

LORD B. No—for thy sake I speak. Thou—justly proud,
For thou art pure; thou, on whose whitest name
Detraction spies no soil—dost thou say "crime"
Unto thy son; and is his answer tears?

Enter EVELINE, R., *weaving flowers as in Act I.*

EVEL.   Blossoms, I weave ye
                     To drift on the sea,
                     Say when ye find him
                     Who sang "Woe is me!"
(*approaching* BEAUFORT) Have you no news?

LORD B.   Of whom?

EVEL.   Of Vyvyan?

LORD B. That name! Her reason wanders; and oh, mother,
When that name's uttered—so doth mine—hush, hush it.
          (EVELINE *goes to window, and throws garland through*)

LADY M. Kill me at once—or when I ask again,
What is thy crime?—reply, "No harm to Vyvyan!"

LORD B. (*breaking away*). Unhand me! Let me go!
                         [*Exit* LORD BEAUFORT, L., *wildly.*

LADY M.   This pulse beats still!
Nature rejects me!

EVEL.   Come, come—see the garland,
It dances on the waves so merrily.

Enter MARSDEN, R.

MARS. (*drawing aside* LADY M.). Forgive this haste. Amid St. Kini-
      an's Cliffs
Where, once an age, on glassy peaks may glide
The shadow of a man, a stranger venturing
Hath found bleached human bones, and to your hall,
Nearest at hand, and ever famed for justice,
Leads on the crowd, and saith the dead was Vyvyan.

EVEL. Ha! who named Vyvyan? Has he then come back?

MARS. Fair mistress, no.

LADY M.   If on this terrible earth
Pity lives still—lead her away. Be tender.

EVEL. (*approaching* LADY M.), I promised him to love you as a mo-
      ther.
Kiss me, and trust in Heaven! He will return!
                         [*Exeunt* EVELINE *and* MARSDEN, R.

LADY M. These horrors are unreal.

Enter SERVANT, R.

SERVANT.   Noble mistress.

Sir Godfrey Seymour, summoned here in haste,
Craves your high presence in the Justice Hall.
LADY M. Mine—mine? Where goest thou?
SERVANT.   Sir Godfrey bade me
    Seek my young lord.
LADY M.   Stir not. My son is ill.
Thyself canst witness how the fever—(*hurrying* R.) Marsden!

Enter MARSDEN, R.

My stricken Clarence!—In his state, a rumor
Of—of what passes here, might blast life—reason:
Go, lure him hence—if he resist, use force
As to a maniac. Ah! good old man, thou lov'st him;
His innocent childhood played around thy knees—
I know I can trust *thee*—Quick—speak not:—Save!
                              [*Exit* MARSDEN, L.
(*to* SERVANT) Announce my coming.   [*Exit* SERVANT, R.
                              This day, life to shield
The living son:—Death, with the dead, to-morrow!
                              [*Exit* LADY MONTREVILLE, R.

SCENE III.—*Castle Hall, in 5th grooves.*

Discover SIR GODFREY SEYMOUR *seated,* L. CLERK, *at table, employed in
    writing.* SIR GREY DE MALPAS *standing up* L., *near* SIR GODFREY.
    FALKNER, L. C. HALBERDIERS, SERVANTS.

SIR GODF. (*to* FALKNER). Be patient, sir, and give us ampler proof
    To deem yon undistinguishable bones
    The relics of your friend.
FALK.   That gentleman
    Can back my oath, that these, the plume, the gem
    Which Vyvyan wore—I found them on the cliff.
SIR GODF. Verily, is it so?
SIR G. (*with assumed reluctance*). Sith law compel me—
    Yes, I must vouch it.

Enter SERVANT, R. 2 E.

SERVANT (*placing a chair of state*). Sir, my lady comes.
SIR G.   And her son.

Enter, R. 2 E., LADY MONTREVILLE, *and seats herself,* R. C.

SIR GODF. You pardon, madam, mine imperious duties,
    And know my dismal task——
LADY M.   Pray you be brief, sir.
SIR GODF. Was, this time year, the captain of a war-ship,
    Vyvyan his name, your guest?
LADY M.   But one short day—
    To see my ward, whom he had saved from pirates.
SIR GODF. I pray you, madam, in his converse with you
    Spoke he of any foe, concealed or open,
    Whom he had cause to fear?
LADY M.   Of none!
SIR GODF.   Nor know you
    Of any such?

LADY M. (*after a pause*). I do not.
SIR GODF. (*aside to* FALKNER). Would you farther
Question this lady, sir?
FALK. No, she is a woman,
And mother; let her go. I wait Lord Beaufort.
SIR GODF. Madam, no longer will we task your p esence.

Enter LORD BEAUFORT, C. D. R., *breaking from* MARSDEN, *and other* AT-
TENDANTS.

LORD B. Off, dotard, off! Guests in our hall!
LADY M. He is ill.
Sore ill—fierce fever—I will lead him forth.
Come, Clarence; darling come!
LORD B. Who is this man?
FALK. The friend of Vyvyan, whose pale bones plead yonder.
LORD B. I—I will go. L t's steal away, my mother.
FALK. Lost friend, in war, how oft thy word was "Spare."—
Methinks I hear thee now. (*draws* LORD BEAUFORT *to* R. C.)
Young lord, I came
Into these halls, demanding blood for blood—
But thy remorse (this *is* remorse) disarms me.
Speak; do but say—(look, I am young myself,
And know how hot is youth;) speak—do but say,
After warm wo ls. struck out from jealous frenzy,
Quick swords were drawn: Man's open strife with man—
Passion, not murder: Say this, and may law
Pardon thee, as a soldier does!
SIR GREY (*to* MARSDEN). Call Eveline,
She can attest our young lord's innocence. [*Exit* MARSDEN,
FALK. He will not speak, sir, let my charge proceed.
LADY M. (*aside*). Whа e'er the truth—of that—of that hereafter,
Now but remember, child, thy birth, thy name;—
Thy mother's heart, it beats beside thee—take
Strength from its pulses.
LORD B. Keep close, and for thy sake
I will not cry—" 'Twas passion, yet still, murder!"
SIR GODF. (*who has been conversing aside with* SIR GREY). Then jealous
love the motive? Likelier that
Than Alton's wilder story.

Enter EVELINE *and* MARSDEN, C. D. R.

Sweet young madam,
If I be blunt, forgive me; we are met
On solemn matters which relate to one
Who, it is said, was your betrothed:
EVEL. To Vyvyan!
SIR GODF. 'Tis also said, Lord Beaufort crossed his suit,
And your betrother resented.
EVEL. No! forgave.
SIR G. Yes, when you feared some challenge from Lord Beaufort,
Did Vyvyan not cast down his sword and say,
"Both will be safe, for one will be unarmed? (*great sensation
through the hall.*)
FALKNER *and* SIR GODFREY. Unarmed!
EVEL. His very words!

FALK.   Oh, vile assassin!
SIR GODF. Accuser, peace! This is most grave. Lord Beaufort,
    Upon such tokens, with your own strange bearing,
    As ask appeal to more august tribunal,
    You stand accused of purposed felon murder
    On one named Vyvyan, Captain of the *Dreadnaught*—
    " Wouldst thou say aught against this solemn charge?"
EVEL. Murdered!—he—Vyvyan! Thou his murderer, Clarence,
    In whose rash heat my hero loved frank valor?
    Lo! I, to whom his life is as the sun
    Is to the world—with my calm trust in Heaven
    Mantle thee thus. Now, speak!
LADY M. (*aside*). Be firm—deny, and live.
LORD B. (*attempting to be haughty*). You call my bearing " strange ?"
    —what marvel, sir?
    Stunned by such charges, of a crime so dread.
    What proof against me? (SIR GREY *meets* ALTON *up* R. *and
        keeps him in talk*)
LADY M.   Words deposed by whom?
    A man unknown ;—a girl's vague fear of quarrel—
    His motive what? A jealous anger! Phantoms!
    Is not my son mine all? And yet this maid
    I plighted to another. Had I done so
    If loved by him, and at the risk of life?
    Again, I ask all present what the motive?
ALTON. (*comes down with* SIR GREY).* Rank, fortune, birthright.
        Miserable woman!
LADY M. Whence com'st thou, pale accuser?
ALTON.   From the dead!
    Which of ye two will take the post I leave?
    Which of ye two will draw aside that veil,
    Look on the bones behind, and cry, " I'm guiltless?"
    Hast thou conspired with him to slay thy first-born,
    Or knows he not that Vyvyan was his brother? (LADY MONTRE-
        VILLE *swoons*. EVELINE *rushes to* LADY MONTREVILLE.)
LORD B. My brother! No, no, no! (*clutching hold of* SIR GREY.) Kins-
    man, he lies!
SIR G. Alas! (R. *front*.)
LORD B.   Wake, mother wake. I ask not speech.
    Lift but thy brow—one flash of thy proud eye
    Would strike these liars dumb!
ALTON.   Read but those looks
    To learn that thou art——
LORD B. Cain! (*grasping* FALKNER) Out with thy sword—(L.)
    Hew off this hand. Thou calledst me " assassin!"
    Too mild—say "fratricide!" Cain, Cain, thy brother! (*falls
        sobbing,* C. *front*)
EVEL. It cannot be so! No. Thou wondrous Mercy,
    That, from the pirate's knife, the funeral seas
    And all their shapes of death, didst save the lone one,
    To prove to earth how vainly man despairs
    While God is in the heavens—I cling to thee,
    As Faith unto its anchor! (*to* SIR GREY) Back, false kinsman!
    I tell thee Vyvyan lives—the boy is guiltless!

---

*EVEL.   LADY M. .   BEAUF.   ALTON.   SIR GREY.   SIR GODFREY.
 R.   R. C.   C.   L. C.   L.

" FALK. Poor, noble maid ! How my heart bleeds for her ! "
LADY M. (*starting up*). Sentence us both ! or stay,—would law con-
demn
   A child so young, if I had urged him to it ?
SIR GODF. Unnatural mother, hush ! Sir Grey, to you,
   Perchance ere long, by lives too justly forfeit,
   Raised to this earldom, I entrust these—prisoners. (*motions to*
   HALBERDIERS, *who advance to arrest* BEAUFORT, *who rises,*
   and LADY MONTREVILLE.)
MARS. Oh, day of woe !
SIR G.   Woe—yes ! Make way for us. (*trumpet.*)

Enter SERVANT, C. D. R.

SERVANT. My lord of Essex just hath passed the gates ;
   But an armed knight who rode beside the Earl,
   After brief question to the crowd without,
   Sprang from his steed, and forces here his way ! (*trumpet*
   flourish.)

Enter VYVYAN, C. D. R., *in armor, his vizor three parts down.*

VYV. Forgiveness of all present !
SIR GODF.   Who art thou ?
VYV. A soldier, knighted by the hand of Essex
   Upon the breach of Cadiz.
SIR GODF.   What thy business ?
VYV. To speak the truth. Who is the man accused
   Of Vyvyan's murder ?
SIR G.   You behold him yonder.
VYV. 'Tis false.
SIR G. (R. *front*). His own lips have confessed his crime.
VYV. (*throwing down his gauntlet, to* R.). This to the man whose crush-
ing lie bows down
   Upon the mother's bosom that young head !
   Say you " confess'd ! " Oh, tender, tender conscience !
   Vyvyan, rough sailor, galled him and provoked ;
   He raised his hand. To the sharp verge of the cliff
   Vyvyan recoiled, backed by an outstretched bough,
   The bough gave way—he fell, but not to perish ;
   Saved by a bush-grown ledge that broke his fall ;
   Long stunned he lay ; when opening dizzy eyes,
   On a gray crag between him and the abyss
   He saw the face of an old pirate foe ;
   Saw the steel lifted, saw it flash and vanish,
   As a dark mass rushed thro' the moonlit air
   Dumb into deeps below—the indignant soil
   Had slid like glass beneath the murderer's feet,
   And his own death-spring whirled him to his doom.
   Then Vyvyan rose, and, crawling down the rock,
   Stood by the foe, who, stung to late remorse
   By hastening death, gasped forth a dread confession.
   The bones ye find are those of Murder's agent—
   Murder's arch-schemer—Who ? Ho ! Grey De Malpas,
   Stand forth ! Thou art the man !
SIR GREY. (*aside, vehemently*).   Hemm'd round with toils,

Soul, crouch no more! (*aloud*) Base hireling, doff thy mask,
And my sword writes the lie upon thy front.
By Beaufort's hand died Vyvyan—(*draws sword.*)

VYV.   As the spell
Shatters the sorcerer when his fiends desert him,
Let thine own words bring doom upon thyself!
Now face the front on which to write the lie. (*removes hemlet,
taken away by* PAGES. SIR GREY *drops his sword and staggers
back into the arms of* MARSDEN *and* ALTON, R. *front.*)

EVEL. Thou liv'st, thou liv'st—(*removes white from her checks and shows
the color.*)

VYV. (*kneeling to her,* C.). Is life worth something still?

SIR GREY. Air, air—my staff—some chord seems broken here. (*pressing his heart.*)
Marsden, your lord shot his poor cousin's dog;
In the dog's grave—mark!—bury the poor cousin. (*sinks exhausted, and is borne out,* R. 2 E.)

VYV. Mine all on earth, if I may call thee mine.

EVEL. Thine, thine, thro' life, thro' death—one heart, one grave!
 "I knew thou wouldst return, for I have lived
 In thee so utterly, thou couldst not die
 And I live still.—The dial needs the sun;
 But love reflects the image of the loved,
 Tho' every beam be absent!—Thine, all thine!"

LADY M. My place is forfeit on thy breast, not his. (*pointing
to* BEAUFORT.)
Clarence, embrace thy brother, and my first-born.
His rights are clear—my love for thee suppressed them—
He may forgive me yet—wilt *thou*?

BEAU.   Forgive thee!
Oh mother, what is rank to him who hath stood
Banished from out the social pale of men,
Bowed like a slave, and trembling as a felon?
Heaven gives me back mine ermine, innocence;
And my lost dignity of manhood, honor.
I miss naught else.—Room there for me, my brother!

VYV. Mother, come first!—love is as large as heaven!
"FALK. But why so long——

VYV.   What! could I face thee, friend,
Or claim my bride, till I had won back honor?
The fleet had sailed—the foeman was defeated—
And on the earth I laid me down to die.
The prince of England's youth, frank-hearted Essex,
Passed by—— But later I will tell you how
Pity woke question; soldier felt for soldier.
Essex then, nobly envying Drake's renown,
Conceived a scheme, kept secret till our clarions,
Startling the towers of Spain, told earth and time
How England answers the invader. Clarence,"
Look brother—I have won the golden spurs of knighthood!
For worldly gifts, we'll share them—hush, my brother;
Love me, and thy gift is as large as mine.
Fortune stints gold to some; impartial Nature
Shames her in proffering more than gold to all—
Joy in the sunshine, beauty on the earth,
And love reflected in the glass of conscience;
Are these so mean? Place grief and guilt beside them,

Decked in a sultan's splendor, and compare!
The world's most royal heritage is his
Who most enjoys, most loves, and most forgives.

All form picture. Music.

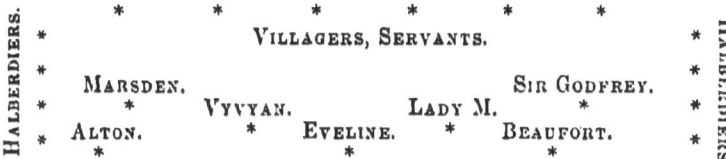

HALBERDIERS.

*   *   *   *   *   *

VILLAGERS, SERVANTS.

MARSDEN.   SIR GODFREY.
*   VYVYAN.   LADY M.   *
ALTON.   *   EVELINE.   *   BEAUFORT.
*

HALBERDIERS.

CURTAIN (slow).

EXPLANATION OF THE STAGE DIRECTIONS.

The Actor is supposed to face the Audience.

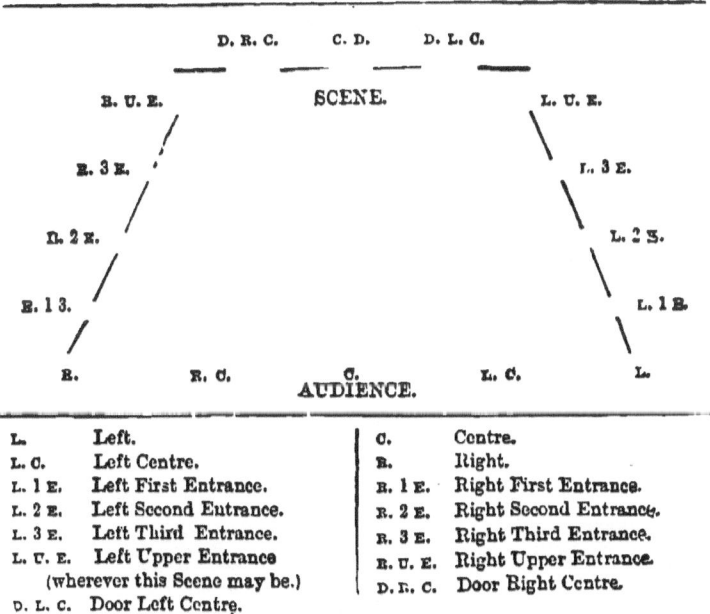

L.	Left.	O.	Centre.
L. O.	Left Centre.	R.	Right.
L. 1 E.	Left First Entrance.	R. 1 E.	Right First Entrance.
L. 2 E.	Left Second Entrance.	R. 2 E.	Right Second Entrance.
L. 3 E.	Left Third Entrance.	R. 3 E.	Right Third Entrance.
L. U. E.	Left Upper Entrance	R. U. E.	Right Upper Entrance.
	(wherever this Scene may be.)	D. R. C.	Door Right Centre.
D. L. C.	Door Left Centre.		

WALPOLE.

CAST OF CHARACTERS.

THE RIGHT HON. SIR ROBERT WALPOLE (Member of the English Parliament, Chancellor of the Exchequer, and Prime Minister to King George the First).

JOHN VEASEY (also a Member of Parliament, and his Confidant).

SELDEN BLOUNT (another Member of Parliament, and a very active and powerful Leader of a Party in strong opposition to Walpole).

SIR SIDNEY BELLAIR (another Member of Parliament—a fashionable and wealthy young Baronet, and also an opponent to Walpole).

LORD NITHSDALE (a young Scotch Nobleman—a firm Jacobite Supporter of the Pretender).

FIRST JACOBITE LORD } (Supporters of the Pretender).
SECOND JACOBITE LORD }

LUCY WILMOT (an Orphan, and the Protegé of Selden Blount).

MRS. VIZARD (a widowed matronly Lady, having charge of Lucy, and in the pay of Selden Blount, at the same time not objecting to assist the Jacobite Party).

Coffee-House Loungers, Waiters, Footmen, Servants, Newsmen, etc.

PERIOD—1717—the commencement of the reign of George I., King of England.

SCENERY (English.)

ACT I.—TOM'S Coffee-House, in, London in 4th grooves.

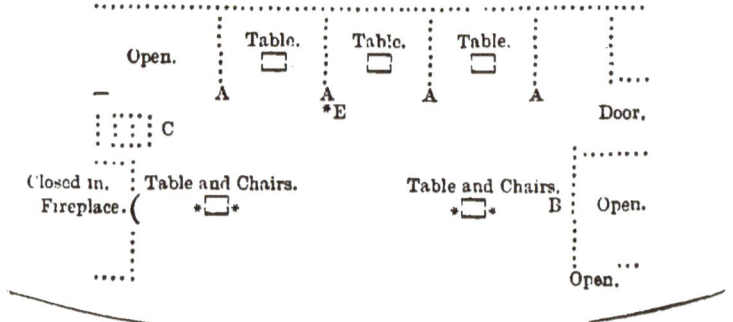

The walls in panelling, dark red oak a few framed oil paintings, portraits of Queen Anne, Marlborough, Charles I., after Vandyke, the Battle of Blenheim, etc. ; statuette of Bacchus, print of Sir Walter Raleigh smoking; a framed set of curious tobacco-pipes arranged as a trophy; East Indian curiosities; a stuffed raccoon, a handbill on a nail: "Distressed Mother....His Majesty's Servants....Prices of the Places," a handbill "£25 Reward. Whereas certain........known for their excesses....MOHOCKS did set upon........maltreat....rolled the said Sarah Frost, in a hogshead, down Holborn Hill....on the night of...." Old muskets and swords crossed, over fireplace, under a map. A, A, A, A, partitions of panelled oak, five feet high, making small rooms or "boxes," of the space between them, in which is a table with a seat running around three sides of each box. C, stairs leading off up from stage. R. U. E., open for WAITERS to exit as to kitchen, for coffee, etc. L. 2 E., double door. B, a bar, with oyster patties, meat pies, newspapers, books, tobacco jars, red, with gilt Arms of Great Britain on them, and "TOM'S" in black letters · a public snuff-box, large. E, a cheval glass, on a stand, in which the LOUNGERS look before going off L. D. Curtains to the boxes, red.

ACT II.—Sc ne 1.—Room in 21 grooves. Portraits on wall; rich tables; chair; writing materials, etc.

Scene II.—Room in 2d grooves.

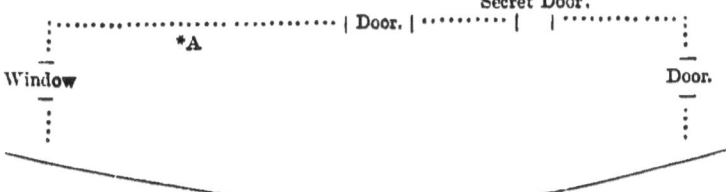

A, a clock. Balcony outside of window.

Scene III.—Outside of a House, court and garden wall in 5th grooves.

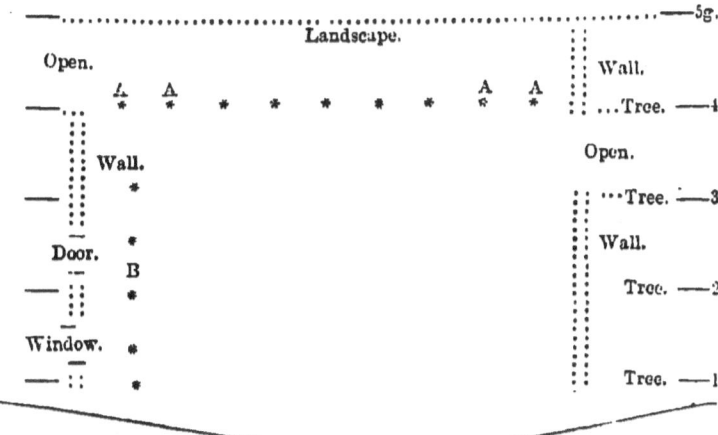

On flat, view of housetops, with a park or trees between. 4th groove line, a row of blue posts, set near enough to prevent a cart passing between them, four feet high. L. U. E., closed in by a garden wall or hedge. L. 1 and 2 E., a garden wall, six feet high, with spikes on top, and a creeping plant. R. 3 E., a low wall. R. 1 and 2 E., a set house front, on the ground floor a window, 1 E., and D. 2 E. above it, a practicable window with balcony. B, iron railing, with posts to the door, with lamps, and iron sockets, such as were used as extinguishers for torches.

ACT III.—Scene I.—St. James's Park in 1st grooves (or can be painted on canvas to roll up); two benches to be pushed on R. and L. Sunset effect. Tree wings. Sky sink and borders.

Scene II.—Same as *Scene I.*, Act *II.*, in 2d grooves.

Scene III.—Same as *Scene II.*, Act *II.*, but set in 3d grooves instead of 2d.

PROPERTIES.

ACT I.: Trays; plates; blue china cups and saucers; chocolate dishes; eatable; a joint of meat, a ham, some preserves, on bar; pipes, tobacco, etc. *Act II.—Scene 1st* Writing materials, books and papers on table; three chairs. *Scene 2d:* A purse, filled; poker; hand-bell. *Scene 3d:* Pebbles. *Act III.—Scene 1st:* Note. *Scene 2d:* Note as before candles in candle-sticks; book on table; hand-bell pocket-book. *Scene 3d:* Lamp; miniature for LUCY; note-book; key.

COSTUMES.

WALPOLE.—*Act I:* Square-cut coat and long-flapped waistcoat of dark-colored cloth, the cuffs of the coat broad and trimmed with lace; silk hose drawn up high over the knees so as to join the breeches, of a similar material to the coat, underneath the waistcoat flaps; white lace neckcloth with long ends; three-cornered hat, black, with the sides turned up; long curled wig; high-heeled shoes, and buckles; fob watch, seals, snuff-box, and court sword. *Act II.:* A rich suit of similar style to the above of dark-blue velvet, embroidered with gold; lace ruffles, etc.; white silk stockings. *Act III.:* Same as Act 1, with a dark-colored roquelaure to throw over him.

SELDEN BLOUNT.—A similar style of dress to that worn by WALPOLE, of a claret-colored velvet; black silk stockings; lace ruffles; court sword; high-heeled shoes, etc., rich snuff-box.

BELLAIR.—A rich showy dress of the same style, but of light-blue velvet, with rich lace ruffles and lace neckcloth; richly-embroidered waistcoat; light-colored wig; laced hat; white silk stockings, with breeches of the same material as the coat; high-heeled shoes, and buckles; handsome court sword, and jewelled snuff-box.

LORD NITHSDALE.—Scarlet velvet coat, waistcoat, and breeches; black silk stockings; shoes and buckles; wig of long black hair like a woman's; lace ruffles and neckcloth; a gray gown with red flowers upon it, and a black cloth mantle, trimmed with ermine, for the disguise in Scene 2, Act 2, to be followed by a dark gown, and a mantle with a hood to it.

VEASEY.—A similar style of dress to WALPOLE'S dress in Act 1, but of black cloth or quiet-colored material, with black silk hose, shoes, buckles, hat, sword, etc.

JACOBITE LORDS.—Similar dresses to LORD NITHSDALE; short wig; swords; hats, and short cloaks of dark velvet to throw over their dresses.

LOUNGERS IN THE COFFEE HOUSE.—Dresses of various materials, but all of a similar style, some more showy than others; wigs, some long and some short; swords, gold-headed canes, etc., so as to give variety to the scene.

FOOTMEN AND SERVANTS.—Silk stockings, shoes, and buckles; black, and blue breeches; claret-colored coats, with silver buttons; white neckcloths; short wigs.

WAITERS.—Black sleeveless waistcoats and knee-breeches, of dark material; white stockings; shoes and buckles; long white aprons, white neckcloths, and long skirts to coats.

LUCY WILMOT.—Plain embroidered silk dress of amber color, with looped skirt; white petticoat; shoes and buckles; loose sleeves, with lace undersleeves; hair in curls.

MRS. VIZARD.—A full old-fashioned style of dress, of dark flowered silk; shoes and buckles; cap trimmed with lace; small shawl to throw over shoulders; small lace trimming to the sleeves; a small patch of black court-plaister near the mouth and on one cheek; hair bound up in close curls. In the 3d Act, cloak, with hood.

TIME OF PLAYING—ONE HOUR AND THREE QUARTERS.

STORY OF THE PLAY AND REMARKS.

In the present instance, dealing with an unacted play, it has been thought desirable and advisable to deviate from the plan previously followed of giving the Story and Remarks separately, and in this case to amalgamate them as being a course more likely to supply a better understanding of the plot of the piece, the characters introduced, and the position of affairs at the period selected for the story of the comedy.

The scene is laid in London in the year 1717, in the third year of the reign of George the First. For years the whole country had been put to much trouble by attempts made both in Scotland and England, as also in France, to place upon the throne, one Charles Stuart, who claimed to be a lineal descendant of James the Second, King of England (who abdicated the throne in 1688), and who, as such descendant, considered himself entitled to wear the crown. He was known throughout the country by the cognomen of " The Pretender," and his adherents were denominated " Jacobites," from *Jacobus*, the Latin for James. His claims were supported by numerous powerful factions both in France and other countries, and by many noblemen and gentlemen of wealth and distinction ; but although his cause was honestly and bravely advocated, it was compelled to succumb to the sovereign power, and was finally extinguished. So far then as is necessary to explain the terms used in the play in connection with the character of Lord Nithsdale and his confederates ; the next point to be touched upon is the political position.

The legislature of England is divided into two parts: the House of Lords, composed of members of the peerage, who are entitled to that position by right of birth, royal decree, or from occupying the position of a Bishop or Archbishop of the Protestant church ; and the House of Commons, which is composed of gentlemen elected by the people of the various towns and cities. They amount (at the present time) to over 600 in number, and so long as they hold the appointment (to which, it may be mentioned, there is no pay attached, the honor of the position and the patronage it affords being considered an ample equivalent for the expenses of election and the labor attending the performance of the duties belonging to it) they are entitled to put the letters M.P. after their name, signifying their position as Members of Parliament. The House of Commons has absolute control over the expenditure of the funds of the country, the levying of taxes, and the collection of the National Revenues from all sources; hence it is, no matter which political party is in power, the leader of that party is generally appointed to the post of Chancellor of the Exchequer, or First Lord of the Treasury, and holds the position of Prime Minister, or chief adviser to the reigning sovereign.

After all the elections have been made, the members assemble, and continue sitting in Parliament for a certain number of years (at the time of the play it was three, it is now seven), at the end of which period it is dissolved, and a new election takes place all over the country, which is termed a " General Election." This, however, only applies to the House of Commons, the members of the House of Lords holding their positions for life. But instead of waiting for the natural expiration of the term for sitting, the Prime Minister, if he should be defeated upon any important question, has the power of causing the House of Commons to be dissolved, and a general election to be had before the specified time, in the hopes of turning out some of his opponents and bringing in persons who are favorable to him, so that when the new Parliament meets, he can be certain of a sufficient number of votes to carry any measures he may propose. These explanations are necessary to show the immense power wielded by Walpole and the meaning of his allusion to a general election in the first scene of the Second Act.

Again, the members of both Houses of Parliament are divided into different parties, bearing names identifying the particular principles they advocate. At the period in question, there were only two classes, known as *Whigs* and *Tories* : terms which originated in England during the reign of Charles the First or Second. Those who supported the king in his high, exacting, and oppressive claims were called *Tories*, and those who sided with the people and were advocates of liberal measures, upholding popular rights, were denominated *Whigs.* Frequent allusion to both will be found in the play.

Of all the ministers who had succeeded in wielding unlimited power, and offering strong opposition to the adversaries of kingly rule, few surpassed Robert Walpole.

For many years his family had been staunch whigs, but the change of succession to the crown from the Stuart family, of which Queen Anne was the last representative in power, to that of the family of the Elector of Hanover, wrought a wonderful difference. During her reign the Tories held high office, but upon her decease the tables were turned, and their strong Jacobite likings and prejudices rendered them unpopular and unsuited for power. The consequence was, the Whigs came into full authority, and Walpole soon worked himself into the foremost position. Out of the large family, of which he was the greatest member, one only had deserted their principles, a sister, of whom he was passionately fond, who married a Tory and a Jacobite, and of whom no tidings had been heard for years. Could he have traced her husband he vows he would have made him turn Whig, by giving him something worth having, which he had unlimited power to do—for, according to the records of the times, he was made Plenipotentiary in regard to the disposal of all offices and posts of State. He had absolute sway ; and was perfectly unscrupulous; no minister ever before or since exceeded him in bribery and corruption, and it was by such means he constantly managed the Parliaments under his direction. *Each man had his price,** or his weakness seemed to be so well studied by Walpole, that there was always some alluring bait thrown out to catch or gratify him; buying and selling of elections, iniquitous jobs and contracts, inordinate extravagance, but a great passion for the fine arts, were the essence of his administration ; his views being to make the king absolute, and preserve the power in his own hands. Such is a picture of Sir Robert Walpole, who figures in the play. With this necessary introduction, we will now proceed with the action of the drama.

It is Walpole's great aim to retain for a longer term his high position, and to prevent anything arising that may occasion risk to the crown by a rebellious outbreak amongst the partisians of the Pretender—and the only way by which he can possibly succeed in doing this is to get the sitting of Parliament extended from three to seven years, so that those in office may continue to work harmoniously together, and by so doing perfect the plans they have formed for laying down a sound foundation for the new dynasty. This is, however, a very difficult task, for Walpole cannot reckon with any certainty upon a majority of votes to support his measures, and the ranks of the opposing party are strong, more especially, two portions, one led by Sir Sidney Bellair, a young baronet of good family, gay disposition, great wealth and brilliant expectations, the other by Selden Blount, a man of more mature years and experience, and in every respect a gentleman of birth, education, influence, and position, bearing the reputation of a staunch, patriotic member. Walpole calculates that these two members control some sixty or seventy votes; if, therefore, by bribery, or getting them into some dangerous dilemma, he can manage to win them over to his side of the house, the votes they would bring would give him a swimming majority, and enable him to carry out his plans with a certainty of success. Now Walpole applies his principle—that each man has his price—and circumstances occur which not only promote his designs and enable him to achieve success, but, most unquestionably verify the truth of his axiom.

It so happens that some time previous to the commencement of the play, Selden Blount, in the course of his travels, stopped at an obscure village inn. Amongst the inmates were two females, who, although then in most reduced circumstances, had evidently seen better days. Interest and curiosity were excited in him, but although he failed to gratify the latter, he succeeded with the former, and his well-

* These words which the author makes use of for his second title are the exact words descriptive of Walpole, printed in an old work I have inspected, entitled " Prime Ministers in England," published at London, in 1763.

filled purse supplied ample means for lightening the sufferings of the ladies until death removed the elder of the two, leaving the younger one alone in the world. It was then only that he gathered from her the information that her father had been a staunch adherent of the Pretender, and had died in his cause; and that her mother's death had been occasioned by the suffering and trouble she had undergone. Smitten deeply by her amiability and attractiveness, and his generous sympathy excited by her piteous story, Selden Blount, under the assumed name of John Jones, persuaded her to accept his offer of protection, as a father, and journey with him to London, where he promised to place her under the care of a matronly friend with whom she could improve her education and live in ease and comfort until such time as an opportunity presented itself for settling down in life. With gratitude and full faith in the integrity of her new-found friend's proposition, Lucy Wilmot was only too glad to accept the offer, and accompanied him accordingly to London, where she was committed to the motherly charge of his particular friend and agent, Mrs. Vizard.

Constant visits to Lucy gradually brought about a feeling rather different to that of charity and disinterested affection, and when Blount began one day to scrutinize himself rather more closely than he had hitherto done, he was compelled to acknowledge that there was a slight undercurrent of love for his protegé running through his mind. At first, he was somewhat in doubt, but a circumstance occurred which convinced him of the fact, and led to an avowal of his passion.

About two weeks before the commencement of the play, Mrs. Vizard had relaxed somewhat the strict care with which she had guarded Lucy, and taken her to church one evening. On their return, they were interrupted and annoyed by a set of young profligates, who made it a practice to roam through the streets after nightfall, insulting every female who might chance to cross their path unprotected. Lucy's cries for assistance when she found herself and guardian thus surrounded, brought to their aid Sir Sidney Bellair, who happened to be upon his way home from the Parliament house, and drawing his sword he soon put the offenders to flight, and escorted the ladies in safety to their dwelling. Struck with the beauty and simple grace of Lucy, he made an excuse to call the following day; but although grateful for his timely assistance, Mrs. Vizard respectfully declined the favor of any further visits; she saw he was young, fascinating and handsome, and she feared that serious results might ensue from the meeting of her young charge and the youthful baronet, injurious to her own interests and detrimental to those of her patron and employer. So thus the matter stood.

Now, Walpole has a firm confidant in Sir John Veasey, a tried member of Parliament, and to him he reveals frankly the dilemma in which he finds himself, and discusses the chances that appear to offer of getting safely out of it. Amongst the arrests he has caused to be made, is that of Lord Nithsdale, a young Scotch nobleman just married, and a staunch adherent of the Pretender. Rumor says that Walpole has rejected all appeals made to him to spare the young man's life; but in truth he is determined to do so if possible, and only the evening previous to the opening of the play, has given his wife an order of admission to the Tower of London, where her husband is confined, in the hopes that he may manage to effect his escape: this he accomplishes, and the clemency thus shown by Walpole turns out afterwards to be of the greatest benefit to his designs.

Veasey, however, has great doubts of Walpole being able to win over Blount or Bellair; they are staunch and firm to their party and principles; nevertheless, Walpole asserts his unbounded faith in his favorite theory, that every man has his price, and either by money, place, rank, or danger, he is determined to secure his men. Bellair arriving, Walpole, with a complimentary remark upon a most effective speech he has recently delivered, leaves him to the care of Veasey to sound him upon the subject at issue. He does so, and suggests that there is the daughter of a Duke who would be a most excellent match, and if he agrees, Walpole, who wishes to increase the strength of the House of Lords, will raise him to the peerage; but Bellair declines, remarking, sarcastically, that he prefers remaining in the House of

Commons, where the members have the pleasure occasionally of badgering and baiting the Prime Minister. Veasey perceives very plainly there is no chance of winning
him over in that way, and retires to consider what other scheme is likely to suit his
leader's purpose.

At an interview which follows, between Bellair and Blount, the former jokes the
latter upon having seen him the previous evening, muffled up in his cloak, hurrying
up the court leading to Mrs. Vizard's house. Blount is astounded at Bellair having
any knowledge of this person, but the more so when he mentions the name of the
young lady in her charge, and relates the circumstances under which he became
acquainted with her, confessing frankly that he is deeply in love with her, and that
although forbidden the house, he visits the neighborhood every day and exchanges
salutations from the window. He begs Blount—who admits that he knows the parties—to make him acquainted with her history; but Blount excuses himself, assuring Bellair that she is of very humble origin, and vastly beneath him in position.
But the young baronet is not to be put off so easily ; he assures Blount that his love
is genuine and honorable, and he makes him promise to mention the matter to Lucy
and to plead his cause.

Walpole's plan for the escape of Nithsdale turns out as he expecteded, and he is
just in receipt of the information when Blount calls upon him, and he takes the
opportunity of sounding him.

This interview is most admirably described ; in witty, sharp, and well chosen language, Walpole boldly opens up his plan for saving the nation, offering place and
patronage in return for the support of Blount and his party, and pushing pen and
paper towards him to write his own terms. Blount does so, and with a low bow
hands his reply to Walpole, striding haughtily away. To his chagrin, the minister
finds written down :

> " 'Mongst the men who are bought to save England inscribe me,
> And my bribe is the head of the man who would bribe me !"

But Walpole is not to be beaten so easily ; certainly to threaten impeachment
and desire the forfeit of his head is rather high, and, at the same time, rather objec-
tionable ambition, and he observes, facetiously :

> " So he calls himself honest ! What highwayman's worse
> Thus to threaten my life when I offer my purse ?
> Hem ! he can't be in debt, as the common talk runs,
> For the man who scorns money has never known duns ;
> And yet have him I must ! Shall I force or entice ?
> Let me think—let me think ; every man has his price."

It so happens that Mrs. Vizard's house is not only an asylum for Lucy, but is also
a meeting place for some of the Jacobite leaders. Accordingly, upon making his
escape, disguised in his wife's garments,* Nithsdale is conducted there by his confederates, who represent him as the wife of one of their party now in exile, and
that they are seeking to hide her until sunset, when she will be able to make her
way down to the river and get on board a vessel bound for France. Mrs. Vizard
agrees to this, and they arrange to send a carriage at sunset, when a stone thrown
up at the window shall be the signal that a trusty messenger is in waiting.

They are interrupted by a knocking at the door, and effect a hasty retreat by
a secret passage, as Mrs. Vizard conceals Nithsdale, and calmly receives the unlooked for visit of Selden Blount. In a very few words he tells her he has heard of
the occurrence which took place on the return from church, and directs that Lucy
shall be sent to him and that they shall be left alone. In a very pretty speech, he
points out to his protégé the danger of an intimacy with such a gay gallant as Sir Sid-

---

* The visit of Lord Nithsdale's wife, as mentioned in the play, is not historically
correct. He and six other lords were arrested for treason as supporting the rebellion, all but one pleaded guilty. Nithsdale and two others were ordered for immediate execution ; but the night before he had the good fortune to escape in clothes
which his *mother* brought him. The others were beheaded the next morning.

ney Bellair, and pictures to her the joy and happiness of a beautiful cottage and gardens where, as soon as he is daily freed from the toil of business, he can share with her love, name and fortune. Completely overcome by this sudden avowal, Lucy withdraws to her chamber, whilst Blount considering the matter settled, bids Mrs. Vizard prepare for departure, as he is going at once in search of a parson. At this moment a newsman passing through the street, calls out the intelligence of the escape of Nithsdale, and the offer of one thousand guineas for his apprehension. As she listens to the description of the dress, it strikes Mrs. Vizard that her guest is the escaped lord, and she determines to lock up both him and Lucy whilst she hastens to give the information and secure the reward. But Lucy, overhearing Blount tell Mrs. Vizard to lock the door safely, slips out and conceals herself behind the window curtains as her guardian carefully fastens the door of the empty chamber. As soon as she is gone, Lucy is alarmed by a violent rapping at the outer door of the apartment, and before she can recover from her fright, it is burst open and Nithsdale appears. In a few hurried words he excuses his disguise to Lucy, as his companions did to Mrs. Vizard, and urges her to furnish him with other clothes; she tells him that her chamber door is fastened, when, with an abruptness which startles her, he produces a very effective key in the shape of a poker which has already opened one door and now does duty a second time. He obtains a hood, gown, and mantle, for which he warmly thanks and kisses Lucy, who, astonished and bewildered at his Amazonian conduct, innocently remarks,

" What a wonderful girl !"

Bellair, anxious to know the result of Blount's labors in his behalf, hastens in his carriage towards Mrs. Vizard's house, and leaving it close by, meets with Blount, who is vainly endeavoring to find a parson. Blount assures him that Lucy has rejected his offer and promised her hand to another, and leaving him to reflect upon the intelligence, goes upon his search. But Bellair determines to know the truth from Lucy's own lips, and accordingly, as he perceives some one at the window, throws up a pebble. This is the agreed Jacobite signal, so Nithsdale jumps down into the arms of Bellair, who, believing it to be Lucy, attempts a kiss, only to receive a smart box on the ears. Although somewhat staggered at such a reception, he vows that he will not be baffled, and raises the hood ; a struggle follows, and he declares unless an explanation is given that he will call for the watch. Nithsdale speaks out boldly, and avows that he owes his life to Lucy, imploring him to save or sell him quickly. Bellair determines to do the former, and though he thus risks his own life by aiding the escape of a rebel, the mention of Lucy's name overcomes all scruples ; he escorts Nithsdale to the carriage and starts him off to the river side. Returning he meets Lucy at the window, and earnestly pleading his love, vowing eternal constancy and truth, he gains her promise to elope with him that night.

Blount succeeds at last in finding a parson, and he determines that after a brief honeymoon he will return to his seat in Parliament, and there taunt Walpole with the bribes he offered. Whilst thus laying down plans for future action, Bellair, full of gayety and delight, happens to meet him and tells him of his plans for running off with Lucy, and begs him to attend at his house and give her away, having arranged for two of his aunts to be present at the ceremony. At this moment one of the Jacobite lords enters, and requesting a few minutes private conversation with Bellair, hands to him a letter of thanks from Nithsdale. Veasey arriving, observes the two in conversation, and knowing the Jacobite, watches them closely. Bellair tells Blount, never suspecting him, to beware of Mrs. Vizard, as she has attempted to surrender Nithsdale, whom he confesses to having assisted in his escape, in proof of which he shows the letter just received. Blount reads it carefully, advises him to be cautious in concealing it, and pretending to place the important document in Bellair's pocket, but letting it drop, as the young baronet hurries away, picks it up.

Now then is the time to turn the tables upon his rival ; he informs Veasey of the discovery he has made, and it is determined that a warrant shall be at once issued for the arrest of Bellair, which will enable Blount to secure Lucy.

Walpole is much pleased at the success of his scheme for the escape of Nithsdale, any very much more so at the news he receives of Bellair's share in the transaction. He at once issues a warrant for his detention, and requests Veasey to keep company with the prisoner until sent for, as he is going to Mrs. Vizard's to make inquiries with respect to a young female whom his agent had found confined there upon searching for Nithsdale. Dismissing Veasey, Walpole summons Mrs. Vizard to his presence, and learns from her the particulars respecting Selden Blount and Lucy; and his curiosity and interest are strongly excited when she relates certain things which go far to show that Lucy is most probably the child of his wayward sister.

Arrived at Mrs. Vizard's house, an interview, most sweetly and effectively described, coupled with the production of a portrait of the deceased mother, convince Walpole that Lucy is his niece. He questions her as to her love for Bellair, and when she confesses her intended flight, his anger is aroused, believing that the baronet intended to play false. He dispatches his servant for him and Veasey, determining to test the truth of his intentions. At this moment a pebble strikes the window; looking out, Walpole perceives a rope ladder and the figure of a man. Bidding Lucy confide in him and her happiness shall yet be secured, he tells her to open the window and call out that she needs help as she is chained to the floor, and then withdraws to watch the result. In a few moments Blount appears, to Lucy's unfeigned surprise, her manner showing she expected some one else. Angry and indignant at such a reception, he declares that his affections have been trifled with and outraged, and she shall either remain as his victim or depart as his bride. But the hand of Walpole falls heavy upon his shoulder; discomfited at this unexpected appearance of the minister, Blount endeavors to escape by the window, but Walpole is too quick for him, and pushes away the ladder. Sir Sidney Bellair now arrives, and not noticing Walpole, bitterly upbraids Blount for betraying his friendship, and for insulting him by bringing him there; but the minister steps between them, and sternly demands to know if his intentions towards Lucy, apparently penniless and so far beneath him, are honorable. Bellair frankly declares that they are, and whatever his fate may be, his sentiments are fixed and unchangeable; upon which, Walpole makes known that she is his niece, and that he sanctions the union, at the same time remarking artfully, that it will never do for the nephew to outvote his uncle. Bellair acknowledges that he is vanquished, and promises his cordial support. Following up his success, Walpole appeals to Blount, suggesting that all that has happened had better be hushed up, with which proposition his recent opponent warmly coincides, and promises his support. So the minister thus gains over his two adversaries and their votes, practically demonstrating the truth of his assertion —that every man has his price.

I am not aware that this piece has ever been placed upon the stage; why, I must confess, I am at a loss to conceive. It is a very neatly constructed comedy, admirably written; the rhyme very perfect, and the language flowing, easy, and polished. The plot is very well put together; it does not exceed the bounds of dramatic probability, and is interesting and entertaining, when the history of the country where the scene is laid, the period chosen for the action, and the position of society at the time, are understood. This has been attempted in the early part of these remarks and, it is to be hoped, with success. I have no hesitation in saying that with an audience possessing such knowledge, and with the piece well mounted in the very excellent style for which the managers of this city are so justly celebrated, and acted with the judgment, ability, and care exhibited by many members of the profession, possessing talents admirably suited to the characters of this piece, there are many modern comedies that would not afford one-half the entertainment and amusement for a couple of hours, as that which might be derived from a finished representation of WALPOLE.   J. M. K.

BILL FOR PROGRAMMES, ETC.

ACT I.

SCENE I.—INTERIOR OF TOM'S COFFEE-HOUSE IN LONDON.

The Prime Minister and his Confidant—Jacobite Plots and Troublesome Times—A Scheme of Bribery to support the Crown—Bellair's Story of the Rescued Angel—Blount's Astonishment—Rivals in Love—News of the Escape from the Tower of London of the Jacobite Rebel, Lord Nithsdale—Consternation!

ACT II.

SCENE I.—HANDSOME APARTMENT IN THE MANSION OF SIR ROBERT WALPOLE.

The Minister's Interview with Selden Blount—Attempted Bribery—The Offer Rejected—Political Diplomacy in a Fix—A Great Minister never Fails for Resources—Walpole's Resolution to Win—Every Man has his Price.

SCENE II.—ROOM IN THE HOUSE OF MRS. VIZARD.

The Meeting Place of the Conspirators—Lord Nithsdale in Disguise—The Caged Beauty—Interview of Selden Blount with his Protegé, Lucy Wilmot—Declaration of Love, and Proposed Marriage—News of the Reward for Lord Nithsdale's Apprehension—A Woman's Deceit—Money Wins—Mrs. Vizard Locks up her Prisoners, and goes for the Reward—A Poker for a Key—One Angel aids Another (in belief)—Lord Nithsdale's Second Escape.

SCENE III.—THE EXTERIOR OF MRS. VIZARD'S HOUSE.

Rivals in Love—Another Version of Romeo and Juliet—Amazonian and Unladylike Descent of Lord Nithsdale from the Balcony—A Lover's Embraces Repulsed—Perplexing Situation—Discovery and Surprise—A True Friend in the Hour of Need—Lord Nithsdale's Third Escape—Bellair Declares his Love, and Lucy Consents to Elope with him.

ACT III.

SCENE I.—A VIEW IN ST. JAMES'S PARK, LONDON.

Very Awkward Position of the Rivals in Love—The Expecting Husband asked to be the Bride's Father—The Story of Nithsdale's Escape—The Treasonous Letter—Plot and Counterplot—Falsity of a Friend—The Scheme for Arrest.

SCENE II.—APARTMENT IN WALPOLE'S HOUSE.

The Proofs of Bellair's Treason—State Warrant for his Arrest—Walpole's Story of his Lost Sister—Proposed Journey to Mrs. Vizard's House to Solve the Mystery.

SCENE III.—APARTMENT IN THE HOUSE OF MRS. VIZARD.

Lucy Preparing to Elope—An Unexpected Visitor—The Story of Trial and

Suffering—The Portrait—Joyful Recognition of Lucy as the Minister's Niece—The Test of Affection and the Trial of Honor—Blount's Offer of Love Refused—Arrival of Bellair—Explanations and Promises—The Reward of Virtue and Faith—Union of Bellair and Lucy—Opposition Votes Secured—The Struggle for Power Won—And Triumphant Success of

W A L P O L E.

EXPLANATION OF THE STAGE DIRECTIONS.

The Actor is supposed to face the Audience.

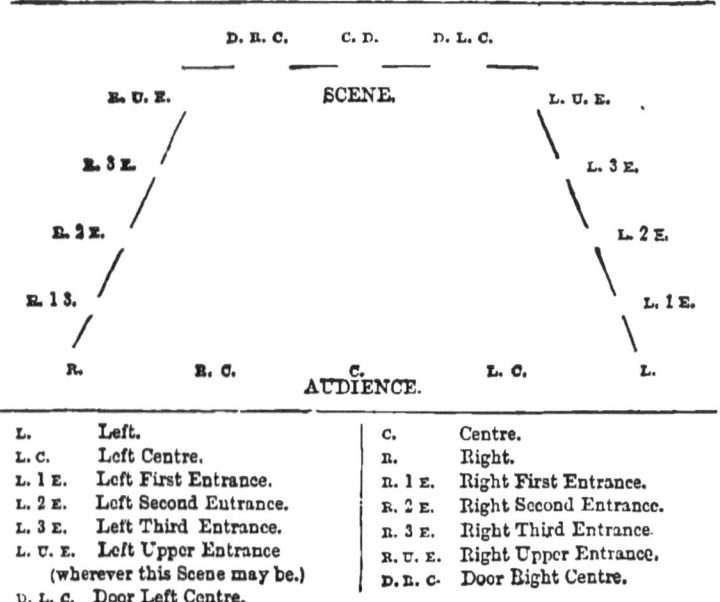

L.	Left.	c.	Centre.
L. C.	Left Centre.	R.	Right.
L. 1 E.	Left First Entrance.	R. 1 E.	Right First Entrance.
L. 2 E.	Left Second Entrance.	R. 2 E.	Right Second Entrance.
L. 3 E.	Left Third Entrance.	R. 3 E.	Right Third Entrance.
L. U. E.	Left Upper Entrance	R. U. E.	Right Upper Entrance.
	(wherever this Scene may be.)	D. R. C.	Door Right Centre.
D. L. C.	Door Left Centre.		

WALPOLE

ACT I.

SCENE.—Tom's *Coffee-house, in 4th grooves—At back,* Gentlemen *seated in the different " boxes."*

Enter Walpole, l. d., *and* Veasey, r. 2 e., *down steps, both to* c. *front.*

Veasey. Ha! good day, my dear patron.

Walpole.   Good day, my dear friend ;
You can spare me five minutes ?

Veasey.   Five thousand.

Walpole.   Attend ;
I am just from the king, and I failed not to press him
To secure to his service John Veasey.

Veasey.   God bless him !

Walpole. George's reign, just begun, your tried worth will distinguish.

Veasey. Oh, a true English king !

Walpole.   Tho' he cannot *speak* English.

Veasey. You must find that defect a misfortune, I fear ?

Walpole. The reverse ; (*smiles*) for no rivals can get at his ear.
It is something to be the one public man put in
The new language that now governs England, dog Latin.

Veasey. Happy thing for these kingdoms that *you* have that gift,
Or, alas ! on what shoals all our counsels would drift.

Walpole. (*jauntily*). Yes, the change from Queen Anne to King
George, we must own,
Renders me and the Whigs the sole props of the throne.
For the Tories their Jacobite leanings disgrace,
And a Whig is the only safe man for a place.

Veasey. And the Walpoles of Houghton, in all their relations,
Have been Whigs to the backbone for three generations.

Walpole. Ay, my father and mother contrived to produce
Their eighteen sucking Whigs for the family use,
Of which number one only, without due reflection,
Braved the wrath of her house by a Tory connection.
But, by Jove, if her Jacobite husband be living,
I will make him a Whig.

Veasey.   How ?

Walpole.   By something worth giving ;
For I loved her in boyhood, that pale pretty sister ;

And in counting the Walpoles still left, I have miss'd her.
(*pauses in emotion, but quickly recovers himself*)
What *was* it I said? Oh—the State and the Guelph,
For their safety, must henceforth depend on myself.
The revolt, scarcely quenched, has live sparks in its ashes;
Nay, fresh seeds for combustion were sown by its flashes.
Each example we make dangerous pity bequeathes;
For no Briton likes blood in the air that he breathes.

VEASEY.   Yes; at least there's one rebel whose doom to the block
Tho' deserved, gives this soft-hearted people a shock.

WALPOLE.   Lord Nithsdale, you mean; handsome, young, and just
wedded—
A poor body—'twould do us much harm if beheaded.

VEASEY.   Yet, they say, *you* rejected all prayers for his life.

WALPOLE.   It is true; but *in private* I've talked to his wife;
She had orders to see him last night in the Tower,
And——

VEASEY.   Well?—

WALPOLE (*looking at his watch*). Wait for the news—'tis not yet quite
the hour.
Ah! poor England, I fear, at the General Election,
Will vote strong in a mad anti-Whiggish direction.
From a Jacobite Parliament we must defend her,
Or the King will be Stuart, and Guelph the Pretender.
And I know but one measure to rescue our land
From the worst of all ills—Civil War.

VEASEY (*solemnly*).   True; we stand
At that dread turning-point in the life of a State
When its free choice would favor what freedom should
hate;
When the popular cause, could we poll population——

WALPOLE.   Would be found the least popular thing in the nation.

VEASEY.   Scarce a fourth of this people are sound in their reason——

WALPOLE.   But we can't hang the other three-fourths for high treason!

VEASEY.   Tell me, what is the measure your wisdom proposes?

WALPOLE.   In its third year. by law, this Whig Parliament closes.
But the law! What's the law in a moment so critical?
Church.and State must be saved from a House Jacobitical.
Let this Parliament then, under favor of Heaven,
Lengthen out its existence from three years to seven.

VEASEY.   Brilliant thought! could the State keep its present directors
Undisturbed for a time by those rowdy electors,
While this new German tree, just transplanted, takes root,
Dropping down on the lap of each friend golden fruit,
Britain then would be saved from all chance of reaction
To the craft and corruption of Jacobite faction.
But ah! think you the Commons would swallow the question?

WALPOLE.   That depends on what pills may assist their digestion.
I could make—see this list—our majority sure,
If by buying two men I could sixty secure;
For as each of these two is the chief of a section
That will vote black or white at its leader's direction,
Let the pipe of the shepherd but lure the bell-wether,
And he folds the whole flock, wool and cry. altogether.
Well, the first of these two worthy members you guess.

VEASEY.   Sure, you cannot mean Blount, virtuous Selden Blount?

WALPOLE.   Yes.

VEASEY. What! your sternest opponent, half Cato, half Brutus,
He, whose vote incorruptible——
WALPOLE. Just now would suit us ;
For a patriot so staunch could with dauntless effrontery—
VEASEY. Sell himself ?
WALPOLE. Why, of course, for the good of his country.
True, his price will be high—he is worth forty votes,
And his salary must pay for the change in their coats.
Prithee, has not his zeal for his fatherland—rather
Overburthened the lands he received from his father ?
VEASEY. Well, 'tis whispered in clubs that his debts somewhat tease him.
WALPOLE. I must see him in private, and study to ease him.
Will you kindly arrange that he call upon me
At my *home, not* my office, to-day—just at three ?
Not a word that can hint of the object in view——
Say some (*slight pause*) bill in the House that concerns him
and you ;
And on which, as distinct from all party disputes,
Members meet without tearing each other like brutes.
VEASEY. Lucky thought !—Blount and I both agree in Committee
On a bill for amending the dues of the City——
WALPOLE. And the Government wants to enlighten its soul
On the price which the public should pay for its coal.
We shall have him, this Puritan chief of my foes.
Now the next one to catch is the chief of the Beaux ;
All our young members mimic his nod or his laugh ;
And if Blount be worth forty votes, he is worth half.
VEASEY. Eh ! Bellair, whose defence of the Jacobite peers——
WALPOLE. Thrilled the House ; Mr. Speaker himself was in tears.
Faith, I thought he'd have beat us. (*taking snuff.*)
VEASEY. That fierce peroration——
WALPOLE. Which compared me to Nero—superb (*brushing the snuff
from his lace lappet*) declamation !
VEASEY. Yes ; a very fine speaker.
WALPOLE. Of that there's no doubt
For he speaks about things he knows nothing about.
But I still to our party intend to unite him——
Secret Service Department—Bellair—a small item.
VEASEY. Nay, you just—for this gay maiden knight in debate,
To a promise so brilliant adds fortune so great——
WALPOLE. That he is not a man to be bought by hard cash ;
But he's vain and conceited, light-hearted and rash.
Every favorite of fortune hopes still to be greater,
And a beau must want something to turn a debater.
Hem ! I know a Duke's daughter, young, sprightly and fair ;
She will wed as I wish her ; hint that to Bellair ;
Ay, and if he will put himself under my steerage,
Say that with the Duke's daughter I throw in the peerage.
VEASEY. (*thoughtfully*). Those are baits that a vain man of wit *may*
seduce.
WALPOLE. Or, if not, his political creed must be loose ;
To some Jacobite plot he will not be a stranger,
And to win him securely——
VEASEY. We'll get him in danger
Hist !

Enter BELLAIR, *humming a tune,* L. D.

WALPOLE. Good-morning, Sir Sidney; your speech did you credit;
    And whatever your party, in time you will head it.
    Your attack on myself was exceedingly striking,
    Though the subject you cho se was not quite to my liking.
    Tut! I never bear malice.   You hunt?

BELLAIR.   Yes, of la e

WALPOLE. And you ride as you speak?

BELLIAR.   Well, in both a light weight.

WALPOLE. But light weights have the odds in their favor, I fear.
    Come and hunt with my harriers at Houghton this year;
    I can show you some sport.

BELLAIR.   Sir, there's no doubt of that.

WALPOLE. We will turn out a fox.

BELLAIR. (aside).   As a bait for a rat!

WALPOLE. I expect you next autumn! Agreed then; good-day.
            [They salute; exit WALPOLE, L. D.

BELLAIR. Well, I don't know a pleasanter man in his way;
    'Tis no wonder his friends are so fond of their chief.

VEASEY. That you are not among them is matter for grief.
    Ah, a man of such stake in the land as yourself,
    Could command any post in the court of the Guelph.

BELLAIR. No, no; I'm appalled.

VEASEY.   By the king? Can you doubt him?

BELLAIR. I'm appalled by those Gorgons, the ladies about him.

VEASEY. Good! ha, ha! yes, in beauty his taste may be wrong,
    But he has what we want, sir, a government strong.

BELLAIR. Meaning petticoat government? Mine too is such,
    But my rulers don't frighten their subjects so much.

VEASEY. Nay, your rulers? Why plural? Legitimate sway
    Can admit but one ruler to love——

BELLAIR.   And obey.
    What a wife! Constitutional monarchy? Well,
    If I choose my own sovereign I might not rebel.

VEASEY. You may choose at your will! With your parts, wealth, con-
        dition,
    You in marriage could link all the ends of ambition
    There is a young beauty—the highest in birth
    And her father, the Duke——

BELLAIR.   Oh, a Duke!

VEASEY.   Knows your worth
    Listen; Walpole, desiring to strengthen the Lords
    With the very best men whom the country affords,
    Has implied to his Grace, that his choice should be clear.
(carelessly) If you wed the Dukes's daughter, of course you're a peer.

BELLAIR. With the Lords and the lady would Walpole ally me?

VEASEY. Yes; and if I were you——

BELLAIR   He would certainly buy me;
    But I,—being a man——(draws himself up haughtily)

VEASEY.   No offence. Why that frown?

BELLAIR (relapsing into his habitual ease). Nay, forgive me. Tho' man,
    I'm a man about town;
    And so graceful a compliment could not offend
    Any man about town, from a Minister's friend.
    Still, if not from the frailty of mortals exempt,
    Can a mortal be tempted where sins do not tempt?
    Of my rank and my fortune I am so conce ted,
    That I don't, with a wife, want those blessings repeated.

And tho' flattered to learn I should strengthen the Peers—
Give me still our rough House with its laughter and
cheers.
Let the Lords have their chamber—I grudge not its powers;
But for badgering a Minister nothing like ours !
Whisper that to the Minister ;—sir, your obedient. (*turns
away,.*R. *to* GENTLEMEN *at table.*)

VEASEY (*aside*). Humph ! I see we must hazard the ruder expedient.
If some Jacobite pit for his feet we can d'g,
He shall hang as a Tory, or vote as a Whig. (VEASEY *re-
tires up stage*)

BELLAIR (*seating himself*, R. c. *front*). Oh, how little these formalist
middle-aged schemers
Know of *us* the bold youngsters, half sages, half dreamers !
Sages half ? Yes, because of the time rushing on,
Part and parcel are *we ; they* belong to time gone.
Dreamers half ? Yes, because in a woman's fair face
We imagine the heaven they find in a place.
At this moment I, courted by Whig and by Tory,
For the spangles and tinsel which clothe me with glory,
Am a monster so callous, I should not feel sorrow
If an earthquake engulfed Whig and Tory to-morrow
" What a heartless assertion ! " the aged would say ;
True, the young have no heart, for they give it away.
Ah, I love ! and here—joy ! comes the man who may aid me.

Enter BLOUNT, L. D.

BLOUNT (*to Coffee-house loungers, who gather round him as he comes down
the stage*).
Yes, sir, just from Guildhall, where the City has paid me
The great honor I never can merit enough,
Of this box, dedicated to Virtue——(*Coffee-house loungers
gather around*)

VEASEY.   And snuff.

BLOUNT. Yes, sir, Higgins the Patriot, who deals in rappee,
Stored that box with pulvillio, superfluous to me ;
For a public man gives his whole life to the nation,
And his nose has no time for a vain titillation.

VEASEY. On the dues upon coal—apropos of the City—
We agreed——

BLOUNT.   And were beat ; Walpole bribed the Committee.

VEASEY. You mistake ; he leans tow'rds us, and begs you to call
At his house—three o'clock.

BLOUNT (*declaiming as if in Parliament*). But I say, once for all,
That the dues——

VEASEY.   Put the case as you only can do,
And we carry the question.

BLOUNT.   I'll call, sir, at two.

VEASEY.   He said three.

BLOUNT. I say *two*, sir ; my honor's at stake,
To amend every motion that Ministers make. (VEASEY *retires
into the background.*)

BLOUNT. (*advancing to* BELLAIR). Young debater, your hand. One
might tear into shreds
All your plea for not cutting off Jacobite heads ;
But that burst against Walpole redeemed your whole speech.

Be but honest, and high is the fame you will reach.
BELLAIR. (R. C.). Blount, your praise would delight, but your caution
      offends.
BLOUNT (C.). 'Tis my way—I'm plain spoken to foes and to friends.
     What are talents but snares to mislead and pervert you,
     Unless they converge in one end—Public Virtue!
     Fine debaters abound ; we applaud and despise them ;
     For when the House cheers them the Minister buys them.
     Come, be honest, I say, sir—away with all doubt ;
     Public Virtue commands !   Vote the Minister out !
BELLAIR. Public virtue when construed means private ambition.
BLOUNT. This to me—to a Patriot——
BELLAIR   In fierce opposition ;
     But you ask for my vote.
BLOUNT.   England wants every man.
BELLAIR. Well, tho' Walpole can't buy me, I think that you can.
     Blount, I saw you last evening cloaked up to your chin,
     But I had not a guess who lay, *perdu*, within
     All those bales of broadcloth—when a gust of wind rose,
     And uplifting your beaver it let out your nose.
BLOUNT. (*somewhat confusedly*). Yes, I always am cloaked—half disguised
       when I go
     Certain rounds—real charity hides itself so ;
     For one good deed concealed is worth fifty paraded.
BELLAIR. Finely said   Quitting, doubtless, the poor you had aided,
     You shot by me before I had time to accost you,
     Down a court which contains but one house ;—there I lost
      you.
BLOUNT. One house !
BELLAIR.   Where a widow named Vizard——
BLOUNT. (*aside*).   I tremble.
     Yes——
BELLAIR. Resides with an angel——
BLOUNT. (*aside*).   'Twere best to dissemble.
     With an angel ! bah ! say with a girl—what's her name?
BELLAIR. On this earth Lucy Wilmot.
BLOUNT.   Eh !—Wilmot ?
BELLAIR.   The same.
BLOUNT. (*after a short pause*). And how knew you these ladies ?
BELLAIR.   Will you be my friend ?.
BLOUNT. I ? of course. Tell me all from beginning to end.
BELLAIR. Oh, my story is short. Just a fortnight ago,
     Coming home tow'rds the night from my club——
BLOUNT.   Drunk ?
BELLAIR.   So, so.
     " Help me, help !" cries a voice—'tis a woman's—I run—
     Which may prove I'd drunk less than I often have done.
     And I find—but, dear Blount, you have heard the renown
     Of a set called the Mohawks ?
BLOUNT.   The scourge of the town.
     A lewd band of night savages, scouring the street,
     Sword in hand,—and the terror of all whom they meet
     Not as bad as themselves ;—*you* were safe, sir ; proceed.
BELLAIR In the midst of the Mohawks I saw her and freed——
BLOUNT. You saw *her*—Lucy Wilmot—at night, and alone ?
BELLAIR. No, she had a protector—the face of that crone.
BLOUNT. Mistress Vizard ?

BELLAIR.   —   The same, yet, tho' strange it appear,
When the rogues saw her face they did *not* fly in fear.
Brief—I came, saw and conquered—but own, on the whole,
That my conquest was helped by the City Patrol.
I escorted them home—at their threshold we part ——
And I mourn since that night for the loss of my heart.

BLOUNT.   Did you call the next day to demand back that treasure ?

BELLAIR.   Yes.

BLOUNT.   And saw the young lady ?

BELLAIR.   I had not that pleasure ;
I saw the old widow, who to'd me politely
That her house was too quiet for visits so sprightly ;
That young females brought up in the school of propriety
Must regard all young males as the pests of society.
I will spare you her lectures, she showed me the door,
And closed it.

BLOUNT.   You've seen Lucy Wilmot no more ?

BELLAIR.   Pardon, yes—very often ; that is once a day.
Every hou-e has its windows——

BLOUNT.   Ah ! what did you say ?

BELLAIR.   Well, by words very little, but much by the eyes.
Now instruct me in turn,—from what part of the skies
Did my angel descend ? What her parents and race ?
She is well-born, no doubt—one sees *that* in her face.
What to her is Dame Vizard—that awful duenna,
With the look of a griffiness fed upon senna ?
Tell me all. Ho there !—drawer, a bottle of clary !
                    [*Exit,* WAITER, R. U. E.

BLOUNT.   Leave in peace the poor girl whom you never could marry.

BELLAIR.   Why ?

BLOUNT.   Her station's too mean. In a small country town
Her poor mother taught music.

BELLAIR.   Her father ?

Enter WAITER, R. U. E., *and places wine and glasses on the table.* R. C.

BLOUNT.   Unknown.
From the mother's deathbed, from the evil and danger
That might threaten her youth, she was brought by a stran-
    ger.
To the house of the lady who——

BELLAIR.   Showed me the door ?

BLOUNT.   Till instructed to live like her mother before,
As a teacher of music. My noble young friend,
To a match so unmeet you could never descend.
You assure me, I trust, that all thought is dismist
Of a love so misplaced.

BELLAIR.   No—(*filling* BLOUNT's *glass*)—her health !

BLOUNT.   You persist ?
Dare you, sir, to a man of my tenets austere,
Even to hint your design if your suit persevere ?
What !—you still would besiege her ?

BELLAIR.   Of course, if I love.

BLOUNT.   I am virtue's defender, sir—there is my glove. (*flings down
his glove, and rises in angry excitement.*)

BELLAIR.   Noble heart ! I esteem you still more for this heat,
In the list of my sins there's no room for deceit ;

And to plot against innocence helpless and weak—
I'd as soon pick a pocket!

BLOUNT.   What mean you then ?   Speak.

BELLAIR. Blount, I mean you to grant me the favor I ask,

BLOUNT.   What is that ?

BELLAIR.   To yourself an agreeable task.
Since you know this Dame Vizard, you call there to-day,
And to her and to Lucy say all I would say.
You attest what I am—fortune, quality, birth,
Adding all that your friendship allows me of worth.
Blount, I have not a father; I claim you as one;
You will plead for my bride as you'd speak for a son.
All arranged—to the altar we go in your carriage,
And I'll vote as you wish the month after my marriage.

BLOUNT (*aside*). Can I stifle my fury ?

Enter NEWSMAN, *with papers*, L. D.

NEWSMAN. Great news! (*music, animated, piano.*)

BELLAIR.   Silence ape ! (*coffee-house loungers rise and crowd
round the* NEWSMAN, L. C.—VEASEY *snatching the paper.*)

OMNES.   Read.

VEASEY   (*reading through the music*). "Lord Nithsdale, the rebel, has
made his escape.
His wife, by permission of Walpole, last night,
Saw her lord in the tower——"(*great sensation.*)

BELLAIR (*to* BLOUNT).   You will make it all right.

VEASEY (*continuing*). "And the traitor escaped in her mantle and
dress."

BELLAIR (*to* BLOUNT). Now my fate's in your hands—I may count on
you.

BLOUNT (*loudly*). Yes. (*music forte.*)

QUICK CURTAIN.

———

ACT II.

SCENE I.—*A room in* WAPOLE'S *house.*

Discover WALPOLE *and* VEASEY *seated at table.*

WALPOLE. And so Nithsdale's escaped !   His wife's mantle and gown ;
Well—ha, ha ! let us hope he's now out of this town,
And in safer disguise than my lady's attire,
Gliding fast down the Thames —which he'll not set on fire.

VEASEY.   All your colleagues are furious.

WALPOLE.   Ah, yes ; if they catch him,
Not a hand from the crown of the martyr could snatch him !
Of a martyr so pitied the troublesome ghost
Would do more for his cause than the arms of a host.
These reports from our agents, in boro' and shire,
Show how slowly the sparks of red embers expire.
Ah ! what thousands will hail in a general election
The wild turbulent signal for——

VEASEY.   Fresh insurrection.

WALOPLE. (*gravely*). Worse than that ; Civil War!—at all risk, at all cost,
    We must carry this bill, or the nation is lost.
VEASEY. Will not Tory and Roundhead against it unite ?
WALPOLE. Every man has his price ; I must bribe left and right.
    So you've failed with Bellair—a fresh bait we must try.
    As for Blount——

Enter SERVANT, L.

SERVANT. Mr. Blount.
WALPOLE. Pray admit him. Good-bye.   [*Exit* VEASEY R.

SERVANT *bows in* BLOUNT, L.

BLOUNT. Mr. Walpole, you ask my advice on the dues
    Which the City imposes on coal.
WALPOLE. (*motions* BLOUNT *to take seat*, L, C.). Sir, excuse
    That pretence for some talk on more weighty a theme,
    With a man who commands——
BLOUNT. (*aside*).   Forty votes.
WALPOLE.   My esteem.
    You're a patriot, and therefore I counted this visit,
    Hark! your country's in danger—great danger, sir.
BLOUNT (*drily*).   Is it ?
WALPOLE. And I ask you to save it from certain perdition.
BLOUNT. Me !—I am——
WALPOLE. Yes, at present in hot opposition.
    But what's party ? Mere cricket—some out and some in;
    I have been out myself. At that time I was thin.
    Atrabilious, sir,—jaundiced ; now rosy and stout,
    Nothing pulls down a statesman like long fagging out.
    And to come to the point, now there's nobody by,
    Be as stout and as rosy, dear Selden, as I.
    What! when bad men conspire, shall not good men combine ?
    There's a place—the Paymastership—just in your line ;
    I may say that the fees a e ten thousand a year,
    Besides extras—not mentioned. (*aside*) The rogue will cost
      dear.
BLOUNT. What has that, sir, to do with the national danger
    To which——
WALPOLE.   You're too wise to be wholly a stranger,
    Need I name to a man of your Protestant true heart
    All the risks we yet run from the Pope and the Stuart ?
    And the indolent public is so unenlightened
    That 'tis not to be trusted, and scarce to be frightened.
    When the term of this Parliament draws to its close,
    Should King George call another, 'tis filled with his foes.
BLOUNT. You pay soldiers eno' if the Jacobites rise——
WALPOLE. But a Jacobite house would soon stop their supplies.
    There's a General on whom you must own on reflection,
    The Pretender relies.
BLOUNT.   Who ?
WALPOLE.   The General Election.
BLOUNT. That election must come ; you have no other choice.
    Would you juggle the People and stifle its voice ?
WALPOLE. That is just what young men fresh from college would say
    And the People's a very good thing in its way.
    But what is the People ?—the mere population ?

No, the sound-thinking part of this practical nation,
Who support peace and order, and steadily all poll
For the weal of the land !
BLOUNT (*aside*).   In plain words, for Bob Walpole.
WALPOLE. Of a people like this I've no doubt, or mistrustings,
But I have of the fools who vote wrong at the hustings.
Sir, in short, I am always frank-spoken and hearty,
England needs all the patriots that go with your party.
We must make the three years of this Parliament seven,
And stave off Civil War. You agree ?
BLOUNT (*rises*).   Gracious heaven !
Thus to silence the nation, to baffle its laws,
And expect Selden Blount to defend such a cause !
What could ever atone for so foul a disgrace ?
WALPOLE. Everlasting renown—(*aside*) and the Paymaster's place,
BLOUNT.   Sir, your servant—good day; I am not what you thought;
I am honest——(*going* L.)
WALPOLE.   Who doubts it ? (*rises*.)
BLOUNT.   And not to be bought.
WALPOLE (*stays* BLOUNT *at* L. C.). You are not to be bought, sir--as-
tonishing man !
Let us argue that point. (*to* C.) If creation you scan,
You will find that the children of Adam prevail
O'er the beasts of the field but by barter and sale.
Talk of coals—if it were not for buying and selling,
Could you coax from Newcastle a coal to your dwelling ?
You would be to your own fellow-men good for naught,
Were it true, as you say, that you're not to be bought.
If you find men worth nothing—say, don't you despise them ?
And what proves them worth nothing ?—why nobody buys
them.
But a man of such worth as yourself! nonsense—come,
Sir, to business ; I want you—I buy you ; the sum ?
BLOUNT.   Is corruption so brazen ? are manners so base ?
WALPOLE   (*aside*). That means he don't much like the Paymaster's place.
(*with earnestness and dignity*)
Pardon. Blount, I spoke lightly ; but do not mistake,—
On mine honor the peace of the land is at stake.
Yes, the peace and the freedom ! Were Hampden himself
Living still, would he side with the Stuart or Guelph ?
When the Cæsars the freedom of Rome overthrew,
All its forms they maintained—'twas its spirit they slew !
Shall the freedom of England go down to the grave ?
No ! the forms let us scorn, so the spirit we save.
BLOUNT.   England's peace and her freedom depend on your bill ?
WALPOLE (*seriously*). Thou know'st it—and therefore——
BLOUNT.   My aid you ask still !
WALPOLE. Nay, no longer *I* ask, 'tis thy country petitions.
BLOUNT. But you talked about terms.
WALPOLE (*pushing pen and paper to him*). There, then, write your condi-
ditions. (BLOUNT *writes, folds the paper, gives it to* WAL-
POLE, *bows and exit*, L. D.)
WALPOLE. (*reading*). "'Mongst the men who are bought to save Eng-
land inscribe me,
And my bribe is the head of the man who would bribe me."
Eh ! my head ! That's amb'tion much too high-reaching ;
I suspect that the crocodile hints at impeaching.

And he calls himself honest! What highwayman's worse?
Thus to threaten my life when I offer my purse.
Hem! he can't be in debt, as the common talk runs,
For the man who scorns money has never known duns.
And yet have him I must! Shall I force or entice?
Let me think—let me think; every man has his price.

[*Exit* WALPOLE, *slowly*, R.

Scene changes to

SCENE II.—*A room in* MRS. VIZARD'S *house.*

Enter MRS. VIZARD, R.

MRS. VIZARD. 'Tis the day when the Jacobite nobles bespeak
This safe room for a chat on affairs once a-week. (*knock without,* L.)
Ah, they come.

Enter, D. F., *two* JACOBITE LORDS, *and* NITHSDALE, *disguised as a woman.*

FIRST LORD. Ma'am, well knowing your zeal for our king,
To your house we have ventured this lady to bring.
She will quit you at sunset—nay, haply, much sooner—
For a voyage to France in some t usty Du ch schooner.
Hist!—her husband in exile she goes to rejoin,
And our homes are so watched——
MRS. VIZ.   That she's safer in mine.
Come with me, my dear lady, I have in my care
A young ward——
FIRST L.   Who must see her not! Till we prepare
Her departure, conceal her from all prying eyes;
She is timid, and looks on new faces as spies.
Send your servant on business that keeps her away
Until nightfall;—her trouble permit me to pay. (*giving a purse.*)
MRS. VIZ. Nay, my lord, I don't need——
FIRST L.   Quick—your servant release.
MRS. VIZ. I will send her to Kent with a note to my niece.

[*Exit,* MRS. VIZARD, R.

FIRST L. (*to* NITHSDALE). Here you are safe; still I tremble until you
are freed;
Keep sharp watch at the window—the signal's agreed,
When a pebble's thrown up at the pane, you will know
'Tis my envoy;—a carriage will wait you below.
NITHSDALE. And, if, ere you can send him, some peril befall?
FIRST L. Risk your flight to the inn near the steps at Blackwall.

Re-enter MRS. VIZARD, R.

MRS. VIZ. She is gone.
FIRST L.   Lead the lady at once to her room.
MRS. VIZ. (*opening* L. D.). No man dares enter here.
NITHSDALE (*aside*).   Where she sleeps, I presume.

[*Exeunt* MRS. VIZARD *and* NITHSDALE, L. D.

SECOND L. You still firmly believe, tho' revolt is put down,
That King James is as sure to recover his crown.

FIRST LORD. Yes; but wait till this Parliament's close is decreed,
    And then up with our banner from Thames to the Tweed.
        (*knock at back*, R. *side*)
    Who knocks? Some new friend?

                Enter MRS. VIZARD, L., *crosses to* R.

MRS. V. (*looking out of the window*, R). Oh! quick—quick - do not stay!
        It is Blount.
BOTH LORDS.   What, the Roundhead?
MRS. V. (*opening concealed door*, L. *in* F.). Here—here—the back way.
                            [*Exit* MRS. VIZARD, D. F.
FIRST L. (*as they get to* L. D. *in* F.). Hush! and wait till he's safe within
        doors.
SECOND L.   But our foes
        She admits?
FIRST L.   By my sanction—their plans to disclose.

Exeunt JACOBITE LORDS, L. D. *in* F., *just as enter* BLOUNT *and* MRS. VIZ-
                ARD, D. F.

MRS. VIZ. I had sent out my servant; this is not your hour.
BLOUNT. Mistress Vizard.
MRS VIZ.   Sweet sir! (*aside*) He looks horridly sour.
BLOUNT. I enjoined you when trusting my ward to your care——
MRS. VIZ. To conceal from herself the true name that you bear.
BLOUNT. And she still has no guess——
MRS. VIZ.   That in Jones, christened John,
    'Tis the great Selden Blount whom she gazes upon.
BLOUNT. And my second injunction——
MRS. VIZ.   Was duly to teach her
    To respect all you say, as if said by a preacher.
BLOUNT. A preacher!—not so ; as a man she should rather
    Confide in, look up to, and love as——
MRS. VIZ.   A father.
BLOUNT. Hold! I did not say " Father." You might, for you can,
    Call me——
MRS. VIZ.   What?
BLOUNT.   Hang it, madam, a fine-looking man.
    But at once to the truth which your cunning secretes,
    How came Lucy and you, ma'am, at night in the streets?
MRS. VIZ. I remember. Poor Lucy so begged and so cried——
    On that day, a year since——
BLOUNT.   Well !
MRS. VIZ.   Her poor mother died ;
    And all her wounds opened, recalling that day ;
    She insisted—I had not the heart to say nay—
    On the solace religion alone can bestow ;
    So I led her to church,—does that anger you?
BLOUNT.   No !
    But at nightfall——
MRS. VIZ.   I knew that the church would be dark ;
    And thus nobody saw us, not even the clerk.*
BLOUNT. And returning——

_____

*Clerk, like " Derby," is often pronounced broadly, as if " Clark " and " Darby,"
throughout England.

MRS. VIZ.   We fell into terrible danger.
                  Sir, the Mohawks——
BLOUNT.   I know; you were saved by a stranger.
                  He escorted you home; called the next day, I hear.
MRS. VIZ.   But I soon sent him off with a flea in his ear.
BLOUNT.   Since that day the young villain has seen her.
MRS. VIZ   Oh, no!
BLOUNT   Yes.
MRS. VIZ.   And where?
BLOUNT.   At the window.
MRS. VIZ.   You do not say so!
                  What deceivers girls are! how all watch they befool!
                  One should marry them off, ere one sends them to school!
BLOUNT.   Ay, I think you are right.   All our plans have miscarried.
                  Go; send Lucy to me—it is time she were married.
                                    [Exit MRS. VIZARD, R. D.
BLOUNT (alone at c.). When I first took this orphan, forlorn and alone,
                  From the poor village inn where I sojourned unknown,
                  My compassion no feeling more sensitive masked.
                  She was grateful—that pleased me; was more than I asked.
                  'Twas in kindness I screened myself under false names,
                  For she told me her father had fought for King James;
                  And, imbued in the Jacobite's pestilent error,
                  In a Roundhead she sees but a bugbear of terror.
                  And from me, Selden Blount, who invoked our free laws
                  To behead or to hang all who side with that cause,
                  She would start with a shudder! O fool! how above
                  Human weakness I thought myself? This, then, is love!
                  Heavens! to lose her—resign to another those charms!
                  No, no! never! Why yield to such idle alarms?
                  What's that fop she has seen scarcely once in a way
                  To a man like myself, whom she sees every day?
                  Mine she must be! but how!—the world's laughter I dread.
                  Tut! the world will not know, if in secret we wed.

                        Enter LUCY, by R. D.

LUCY.   Dear sir, you look pale.   Are you ill?
BLOUNT.   Ay, what then?
                  What am I in your thoughts?
LUCY.   The most generous of men.
                  Can you doubt of the orphan's respectful affection,
                  When she owes even a home to your sainted protection?
BLOUNT.   In that home I had hoped for your youth to secure
                  Safe escape from the perils that threaten the pure;
                  But, alas! where a daughter of Eve is, I fear
                  That the serpent will still be found close at her ear.
LUCY.   You alarm me!
BLOUNT.   I ought. Ah, what danger you ran!
                  You have seen—have conversed with——
LUCY.   Well, well.
BLOUNT (c).   A young man.
LUCY (R. c.) Nay, he is not so frightful, dear, sir, as you deem;
                  If you only but knew him, I'm sure you'd esteem.
                  He's so civil—so pleasant—the sole thing I fear
                  I—heigh-ho! are fine gentlemen always sincere?
BLOUNT.   You are lost if you heed not the words that I say.

Ah! young men are not now what they were in my day.
Then their fashion was manhood, their language was truth,
And their love was as fresh as a world in its youth;
Now they fawn like a courtier, and fib like his flunkeys,
And their hearts are as old as the faces of monkeys.

LUCY.   Ah! you know not Sir Sidney——
BLOUNT.   His nature I do,
For he owned to my friend his designs upon you.
LUCY.   What designs? (comes nearer to BLOUNT.)
BLOUNT.   Of a nature too dreadful to name.
LUCY.   How! His words full of honor——
BLOUNT.   Veiled thoughts full of shame.
Heard you never of sheep in wolf's clothing? Why weep?
LUCY.   Indeed, sir, he don't look the least like a sheep.
BLOUNT.   No, the sheepskin for clothing much fitter he trucks;
Wolves are nowaday clad not as sheep—but as bucks.
'Tis a false heart you find where a fine dress you see,
And a lover sincere is a plain man like me.
Dismiss, then, dear child, this young beau from your mind—
A young beau should be loathed by good young womankind.
At the best he's a creature accustomed to roam ;
'Tis at sixty man learns how to value a home.
Idle fancies throng quick at your credulous age,
And their cure is companionship, cheerful, but sage.
So, in fu'ure, I'll give you much more of my own.
Weeping still!—I've a heart, and it is not of stone.
LUCY.   Pardon, sir, these vain tears ; nor believe that I mourn
For a false-hearted——
BLOUNT.   Coxcomb, who merits but scorn.
We must give you some change—purer air, livelier scene—
And your mind will soon win back its temper serene.
You must quit this dull court with its shocking look-out.
Yes, a cot is the home of contentment, no doubt.
A sweet cot with a garden—walled round—shall be ours,
Where our hearts shall unite in the passion—for flowers.
Ah! I know a retreat, from all turmoil remote,
In the suburb of Lambeth—soon reached by a boat.
So that every spare moment to business not due
I can give, my sweet Lucy, to rapture and you.
LUCY (aside). What means he? His words and his looks are alarming ;
(aloud) Mr. Jones, you're too good!
BLOUNT.   What, to find you so charming?
Yes; tho' Fortune has placed my condition above you,
Yet Love levels all ranks. Be not startled—I love you.
From all dreams less exalted your fancies arouse ;
The poor orphan I raise to the rank of my spouse.
LUCY (aside). What! His spouse! Do I dream?
BLOUNT.   Till that moment arrives,
Train your mind to reflect on the duty of wives.
I must see Mistress Vizard, and all things prepare ;
To secure our retreat shall this day be my care.
And—despising the wretch who has caused us such sorrow—
Our two lives shall unite in the cottage to-morrow.
LUCY.   Pray excuse me—this talk is so strangely——
BLOUNT.   Delightful!
LUCY (aside). I am faint ; I am all of a tremble ; how frightful!
                                        [Exit, R. D.

BLOUNT.   Good ; my mind overawes her! From fear love will grow,
And by this time to-morrow a fig for the beau. (*calling off*, R.)
Mistress Vizard !

Enter MRS. VIZARD, R. D.

BLOUNT.   Guard well my dear Lucy to-day,
For to-morrow I free you, and bear her away.
I agree with yourself—it is time she were married,
And I only regret that so long I have tarried.
Eno'! I've proposed.
MRS. VIZ.   She consented ?
BLOUNT.   Of course ;
Must a man like myself get a wife, ma'am, by force ? (*voice
of* NEWSMAN, *at back, and the ringing of hand-bell*)
Great news. (*crosses* L. *to* R., *while crying out*)
MRS. VIZ. (*running to the window, listening and repeating*). What! " Lord
Nithsdale escaped from the Tower." (NITHSDALE *peeps
through* L. D.
" In his wife's clothes disguised! the gown gray, with red
flower,
Mantle black, trimmed with ermine " My hearing is hard.
Mr. Blount, Mr. Blount! Do you hear the reward ?
BLOUNT.   Yes ; a thousand——
MRS. VIZ.   What ! guineas ?
BLOUNT.   Of course ; come away.
I go now for the parson—do heed what I say. (NITHSDALE
shakes his fist at MRS. VIZARD, *and retreats*)
We shall marry to-morrow—no witness but you ;
For the marriage is private. I'm Jones still. Adieu .
[*Exit* BLOUNT, D. F. LUCY *peeps out* R. D.
MRS. VIZ. Ha! a thousand good guineas ! (*looks* L. D.)

Re-enter BLOUNT, D. F.

BLOUNT.   Guard closely my treasure.
That's her door ; for precaution just lock it.
MRS. VIZ.   With pleasure. (*as she shows
out* BLOUNT, D. F., LUCY *slips out* R. D. *and goes up* L.)
LUCY (*tries* L. D.). Eh! locked up! No, I yet may escape if I hide. (*gets
behind the window-curtains, up* R.)

Re-enter MRS. VIZARD, D. F.

MRS. VIZ. Shall I act on this news ? I must quickly decide.
Surely Nithsdale it is! Gray gown, sprigged with red ;
Did not walk like a woman—a stride, not a tread (*locks* R. D)
Both my lambs are in fold ; I'll steal out and inquire.
Robert Walpole might make the reward somewhat higher.
[*Exit* MRS. VIZARD, D. F.
LUCY (*looking out of window*). She has locked the street door. She has
gone with the key, ·
And the servant is out. No escape ; woe is me !
How I love him, and yet I must see him with loathing.
Why should wolves be disguised in such beautiful clothing ?
NITHSDALE (*knocking violently at* L. D). Let me out. I'll not perish en-
trapped. From your snare

Thus I break——(*bursts open* L. D., *and comes down brandishing*
   a poker.) Treacherous hag!
LUCY.   'Tis the wolf. Spare me ; spare! (*kneeling* C.,
   and hiding her face.)
NITHSDALE. She's a witch, and has changed herself?
LUCY.   Do not come near me.
NITHSDALE. Nay, young lady, look up!
LUCY.   'Tis a woman!
NITHSDALE.   Why fear me?
   Perchance, like myself, you're a prisoner?
LUCY.   Ah, yes!
NITHSDALE. And your kinsfolk are true to the Stuart, I guess?
LUCY.   My poor father took arms for King James.
NITHSDALE.   So did I.
‑LUCY. You!—a woman! How brave.
NITHSDALE.   For that crime I must die
   If you will not assist me.
LUCY.   Assist you—how? Say.
NITHSDALE. That she-Judas will sell me, and goes to betray.
LUCY. Fly! Alas! she has locked the street-door!
NITHSDALE.   Lady fair,
Does not Love laugh at locksmiths? Well so does Despair!
   (*glancing at the window*)
Flight is here. But this dress my detection ensures.
If I could but exchange hood and mantle for yours!
Dare I ask you to save me?
LUCY.   Nay, doubt not my will;
   But my own door is locked.
NITHSDALE (*raising the poker*). And the key is *here* still. (*bursts* R. D. *open*
   and exits, R. D.)
LUCY. I have read of the Amazons; this must be one!
NITHSDALE (*entering by* R. D., *with hood, gown, and mantle on his arm*). I
   have found all I need for the risk I must run.
LUCY. Can I help you?
NITHSDALE.   Heaven bless thee, sweet Innocence, no.
Haste, and look if no backway is open below.
Stay ; your father has served the king over the water ;
And this locket may please your brave father's true daughter.
The gray hair of poor Charles, interwined with the pearl.
Go ; vouchsafe me this kiss. (*kisses her hand, and exits,* L. D.)
LUCY.   What a wonderful girl! [*Exit,* R. D.

Scene changes to

SCENE III.—*Exterior of* MRS. VIZARD's *house.*

Enter BLOUNT, L. 3 E, *to* L. C. *front.*

BLOUNT. For the curse of celebrity nothing atones.
The sharp parson I call on as simple John Jones,
Has no sooner set eyes on my popular front,
Than he cries, " Ha ! the Patriot, the great Selden Blount!"
Mistress Vizard must hunt up some priest just from Cam,
Who may gaze on these features, nor guess who I am. (*knocks*
   at D. F. *in* L 2 R. *set.*)
Not at home. Servant out too! Ah ! gone forth, I guess,

To enchant the young bride with a new wedding-dress.
I must search for a parson myself.

Enter BELLAIR R U. E., *and through posts.*

BELLAIR. (*slapping* BLOUNT *on the shoulder*). Blount, your news ?
BLOUNT. You! and here, sir ! What means——
BELLAIR. My impatience excuse.
You have seen her ?
BLOUNT. I have.
BELLAIR. And have pleaded my cause :
And of course she consents, for she loves me. You pause.
BLOUNT. Nay, alas ! my dear friend——
BELLAIR. Speak, and tell me my fate.
BLOUNT. Quick and rash though your wooing be, it is too late ;
She has promised her hand to another. Bear up.
BELLAIR. There is many a slip 'twixt the lip and the cup.
Ah ! my rival I'll fight. Say his name if you can.
BLOUNT. Mr. Jones. I am told he's a fine-looking man.
BELLAIR. His address?
BLOUNT. Wherefore ask ? You kill *her* in this duel—
Slay the choice of her heart ;
BELLAIR Of her heart ; you are cruel.
But if so, why, Heaven bless her !
BLOUNT. My arm—come away !
BELLAIR No, my carriage waits yonder. I thank you. Good-day.
[*Exit*, L. 3 E.
BLOUNT. He is gone ; I am safe—(*shaking his left hand with his right*)
wish you joy, my dear Jones ! [*Exit*, R. U. E.

NITHSDALE, *disguised in* LUCY'S *dress and mantle, opens the upper window.*

NITHSDALE. All is still. How to jump without breaking my bones ? (*trying to flatten his petticoats, and with one leg over the balcony*)
Curse these petticoats ! Heaven ! out of all my lost riches,
Why couldst thou not save me one thin pair of breeches !
Steps ! (*gets back—shuts the window.*)

Re-enter BELLAIR, L D. 3 E.

BELLAIR. But Blount may be wrong. From her own lips alone
Will I learn. (*looking up at the window*) I see some one ; I'll
venture this stone. (*picks up, and throws a pebble at upper window.*)
NITHSDALE (*opening the window*). Joy ! —the signal !
BELLAIR. Tis you ; say my friend was deceived. (NITHSDALE *nods*)
You were snared into——
NITHSDALE. Hush !
BELLAIR. Could you guess how I grieved !
But oh ! fly from this jail ; I'm still full of alarms.
I've a carriage at hand ; trust yourself to these arms.

NITHSDALE *tucks up his petticoats, gets down the balcony backwards, setting
his foot on the area rail.*

BELLAIR. Powers above !—what a leg !

Lord Nithsdale *turns round on the rail, rejects* Bellair's *hand and jumps down.*

Bellair.   O my charmer! one kiss,
Nithsdale. Are you out of your senses ?
Bellair (*trying to pull up her hood*). With rapture !
Nithsdale (*striking him*).   Take this.
Bellair. What a fist !   If it hits one so hard before marriage,
    What *would* it do after ?
Nithsdale.   Quick—where is the carriage ?
    Now, sir, give me your hand.
Bellair.   I'll be hanged if I do
    Till I snatch my first kiss ! (*lifts the hood and recoils astounded*)
            Who the devil are you ? (Nitusdale
        tries to get from him.   A struggle. Bellair *prevails.*)
Bellair (c.). I will give you in charge, or this moment confess
        How you pass as my Lucy, and wear her own dress ?
Nitasdale (*aside*). What ! His Lucy ? I'm saved.
                         .   To her pity I owe
    This last chance for my life ; would you sell it, sir ?
Bellair.   ·   No.
    But your life ! What's your name ? Mine is Sidney Bellair.
Nithsdale. Who in Parliament pleaded so nobly to spare
        From the axe——
Bellair.   The chiefs doomed in the Jacobite rise ?
Nithsdale (*with dignity*). I am Nithsdale.—Quick—sell me or free me
        —time flies.
Bellair. Come this way.   There's my coach. (*points* l.) I will take
        you myself
        Where you will ;—ship you off.
Nithsdale.   Do you side with the Guelph ?
Bellair. Yes.   What then ?
Nithsdale.   You would risk your own life by his laws
    Did you ship me to France.   They who fight in a cause
    Should alone share its perils.   Farewell, generous stranger !
        (*goes up.*)
Bellair. Pooh ! no gentleman leaves a young lady in danger ;
    You'd be mobbed ere you got half a yard through the town ;
    Why that stride and that calf—let me settle your gown.
        (*clinging to him and leading him* l *, and speaking as they
        exeunt* l. 3 e.
    No, no ; I will see you at least to my carriage. (*off* l.)
    To what place shall it drive ?
Nithsdale (*off* l).   To Blackwall.

Lucy *appears at the window.*

Lucy.   Hateful marriage !
    But where's that poor lady ? What !—gone ? She is free !
    Could she leap from the window ? I wish I were she. (*retreats.*)

Re-enter Bellair, l. 3 e.

Bellair. Now she's safe in my coach, on condition I own,
        Not flattering, sweet creature, to leave her alone.
Lucy (*peeping*). It is he.

BELLAIR.   Ah! If Lucy would only appear! (*stoops to pick up*
a stone, and in the act to fling it LUCY *reappears*)
O my Lucy!—mine angel!

LUCY.   Why is he so dear?

BELLAIR. Is it true? From that face am I evermore banished?
In your love was the dream of my life! Is it vanished?
Have you pledged to another your hand and your heart?

LUCY. Not my heart. Oh, not that.

BELLAIR.   But your hand? By what art,
By what force, are you won heart and hand to dissever,
And consent to loathed nuptials that part us forever?

LUCY. Would that pain you so much?

BELLAIR.   Can you ask? Oh, believe me,
You're my all in the world!

LUCY.   I am told you deceive me;
That you harbor designs which my lips dare not name,
And your words full of honor veil thoughts full of shame
Ah, sir! I'm so young and so friendless—so weak!
Do not ask for my heart if you take it to break.

BELLAIR. Who can slander me thus! Not my friend, I am sure,

LUCY. His friend!

BELLAIR.   Can my love know one feeling impure
When I lay at your feet all I have in this life——
Wealth and rank name and honor—and woo you as wife?

LUCY. As your wife! All about you seems so much above
My mean lot——

BELLAIR.   And so worthless compared to your love.
You reject, then, this suitor?—my hand you accept?

LUCY. Ah! but do you not see in what prison I'm kept?
And this suitor——

BELLAIR.   You hate him!

LUCY.   Till this day, say rather——

BELLAIR. What?

LUCY. I loved him.

BELLAIR.   You loved!

LUCY.   ·As I might a grandfather.
He has shielded the orphan;—I had not a notion
That he claimed from me more than a grandchild's devotion.
And my heart ceased to beat between terror and sorrow
When he said he would make me his wife and to-morrow.

BELLAIR. Fly with me, and at once!

LUCY.   She has locked the street-door.

BELLAIR. And my angel's not made to jump down from that floor.
Listen—quick; I hear voices;—I save you; this night
I'll arrange all we need both for wedlock and flight.
At what time after dark does your she dragon close
Her sweet eyes, and her household consign to repose?

LUCY. About nine in this season of winter. What then?

BELLAIR. By the window keep watch. When the clock has struck ten
A slight stone smites the casement; below I attend.
You will see a safe ladder; at once you descend.
We then reach your new home, priest and friends shall be
      there.
Proud to bless the young bride of Sir Sidney Bellair.
Hush! the step come this way; do not fail! She is won.
                  [*Exit* BELLAIR, L. D.

LUCY Stay;—I tremble as guilty. Heavens! what have I done?

            CURTAIN.

ACT III.

SCENE I.—*St. James's Park.*

Enter BLOUNT.

BOUNT.   So the parson is found and the cottage is hired—
Every fear was dispelled when my rival retired.
Even my stern mother country must spare from my life,
A brief moon of that honey one tastes with a wife!
And then strong as a giant, recruited by sleep,
On corruption and Walpole my fury shall sweep,
'Mid the cheers of the House I will state in my place
How the bribes that he proffered were flung in his f.ce.
Men shall class me amid those examples of worth
Which, alas! become daily more rare on this earth; (*takes
seat on bench,* L.)
And Posterity, setting its brand on the front
Of a Walpole, select for its homage a Blount.

Enter BELLAIR, R., *gayly singing.*

BELLAIR.   " The dove builds where the leaves are still green on the
tree——"
BLOUNT (*rising*).   Ha !
BELLAIR.   " For May and December can never agree."
BLOUNT.   I am glad you've so quickly got over that blow.
BELLAIR.   Fallala !
BLOUNT (*aside*).   What this levity means I must know.
(*aloud*) The friend I best loved was your father, Bellair—
Let me hope your strange mirth is no laugh of despair.
BELLAIR.   On the wit of the wisest man it is no stigma
If the heart of a girl is to him an enigma ;
That my Lucy was lost to my arms you believed—
Wish me joy, my dear Bount, you were grossly deceived.
She is mine !—What on earth are you thinking about ?
Do you hear ?
BLOUNT.   I am racked !
BELLAIR.   What ?
BLOUNT.   A twinge of the gout   (*reseating himself.*)
Pray excuse me.
BELLAIR.   Nay, rather myself I reproach
For not heeding your pain.   Let me call you a coach.
BLOUNT.   Nay, nay, it is gone.   I am eager to hear
How I've been thus deceived—make my blunder more clear.
You have seen her ?
BELLAIR.   Of course.   From her own lips I gather
That your good Mr. Jones might be Lucy's grandfather.
Childish fear, or of Vizard—who seems a virago—
Or the old man himself——
BLOUNT.   Oh !
BELLAIR.   You groan ?
BLOUNT.   The lumbago !
BELLAIR.   Ah ! they say gout is shifty—now here and now there.
BLOUNT.   Pooh !—continue.   The girl then——

BELLAIR.   I found in despair.
But no matter—all's happily settled at last.
BLOUNT.   Ah! eloped from the house?
BELLAIR.   No, the door was made fast.
But to-night I would ask you a favor.
BLOUNT.   What? Say.
BELLAIR.   If your pain should have left you, to give her away.
For myself it is meet that I take every care
That my kinsfolk shall hail the new Lady Bellair.
I've induced my two aunts (who are prudish) to grace
With their presence my house. where the nuptials take place.
And to act as her father there's no man so fit
As yourself, dear old Blount, if the gout will permit.
BLOUNT.   'Tis an honor——
BELLAIR.   Say pleasure.
BLOUNT.   Great pleasure! Proceed.
How is *she*, if the door is still fast, to be freed?
Is the house to be stormed?
BELLAIR.   Nay; I told you before
That a house has its windows as well as its door.
And a stone at the pane for a signal suffices,
While a ladder——
BLOUNT.   I see. (*aside*) What infernal devices!
Has she no maiden fear——
BELLAIR.   From the ladder to fall?
Ask her that—when we meet at my house in Whitehall.

Enter FIRST JACOBITE LORD, L.

LORD (*giving note to* BELLAIR). If I err not I speak to Sir Sidney Bellair?
Pray vouchsafe me one moment in private. (*draws him aside*, L.)
BLOUNT.   Despair!
How prevent?—how forestall? Could I win but delay,
I might yet brush this stinging fly out of my way.

While he speaks, enter VEASEY, R.

VEASEY.   Ah! Bellair whispering close with that Jacobite lord——
Are they hatching some plot? (*hides between wing and scene*, R.,
listening.)
BELLAIR (*reading*).   So he's safely on board——
LORD.   And should Fortune shake out other lots from her urn,
We poor friends of the Stuart, might serve you in turn.
You were talking with Blount—Selden Blount—is he one
Of your friends?
BELLAIR.   Ay, the truest.
LORD.   Then warn him to shun
That vile Jezabel's man trap—I know he goes there.
Whom she welcomes she sells.
BELLAIR.   I will bid him beware. (*shakes hands.*)
[*Exit* JACOBITE LORD, L.
BELLAIR (*to* BLOUNT). I have just learned a secret, 'tis fit I should tell
you.
Go no more to old Vizard's, or know she will sell you.
Nithsdale hid in her house when the scaffold he fled.
She received him, and went for the price on his head;

But—the droilest mistake—of that tale by-and-bye—
He was freed ; is safe now !

BLOUNT. ·   Who delivered him?
BELLAIR.   I.
BLOUNT.   Ha ! you—did !
BELLAIR.   See, he sends me this letter of thanks.
BLOUNT (*reading*). Which invites you to join with the Jacobite ranks.
And when James has his kingdom——
BELLAIR.   That chance is remote ;
BLOUNT.   Hints an earldom for you.
BELLAIR.   Bah !
BLOUNT.   Take care of this note. (*appears
to thrust it into* BELLAIR'S *coat-pocket—lets it fall and puts
his foot on it.*)
BELLAIR.   Had I guessed that the hag was so greedy of gold,
Long ago I had bought Lucy out of her hold ;
But to-night the dear child will be free from her power.
Adieu ! I expect, then——
BLOUNT.   Hold ! at what hour ?
BELLAIR.   By the window at ten, self and ladder await her ;
The wedding—eleven ; you will not be later.   [*Exit*, R.
BLOUNT (*picking up the letter*). Nithsdale's letter. Bright thought!—and
what luck ! I see Veasey.

Re-enter BELLAIR, R.

BELLAIR.   Blount, I say, will o'd Jones be to-morrow uneasy ?
Can't you fancy his face ?
BLOUNT.   Yes ; ha ! ha !
BELLAIR.   I am off.   [*Exit*, R.
BLOUNT.   What ! shall I Selden Blount, be a popp'njay's scoff ?
Mr. Veasey, your servant.
VEASEY.   I trust, on the whole,
That you've settled with Walpole the prices of coal.
BLOUNT.   Coals be—lighted below !   Sir, the country's in danger.
VEASEY.   To that fact Walpole says that no patriot's a stranger.
BLOUNT.   With the safety of England myself I will task,
If you hold yourself licensed to grant what I ask.
VEASEY.   Whatsoever the terms of a patriot so staunch,
Walpole gives you—I speak as his proxy—*carte blanche.*
BLOUNT.   If I break private ties where the Public's at stake,
Still my friend is my friend ; the condition I make
Is to keep him shut up from all share in rash strife,
And secure him from danger, to fortune and life.
VEASEY.   Blount—agreed.   And this friend ?   Scarce a moment ago
I marked Sidney Bellair in close talk with——
BLOUNT.   I know.
There's a plot to be checked ere it start into shape.
Hark ! Bellair had a hand in Lord Nithsdale's escape !
VEASEY.   That's abetment of treason.
BLOUNT.   Read this, and attend. (*gives* NITHS-
DALE'S *note to* BELLAIR, *which* VEASEY *reads*)
Snares atrocious are set to entrap my poor friend
In an outbreak to follow that Jacobite's flight——
VEASEY.   In an outbreak ?   Where ?—when ?
BLOUNT.   Hush ! in London to-night

He is thoughtless and young.   Act on this information.
Quick, arrest him at once; and watch over the nation.
VEASEY.   No precaution too great against men disaffected.
BLOUNT.   And the law gives you leave to confine the suspected.
VEASEY.   Ay, this note will suffice for a warrant.   Be sure,
Ere the clock strike the quarter, your friend is secure.
                                          [*Exit* VEASEY, R.
BLOUNT.   Good ; my rival to-night will be swept from my way,
And John Jones shall wake easy eno' the next day.
Do I still love this girl ?   No, my hate is so strong,
That to me, whom she mocks, she alone shall belong.
I need trust to that saleable Vizard no more.
Ha ! I stand as Bellair the bride's window before.
Oh, when love comes so late how it maddens the brain,
Between shame for our folly, and rage at our pain ! [*Exit*, L.

Scene changes to

SCENE II.—*Room in* WALPOLE'S *house.*

Enter WALPOLE, R.

WALPOLE. So Lord Nithsdale's shipped off.   There's an end of one
     trouble
When his head's at Boulogne the reward shall be double
     (*seating himself*, R. C, *takes up a book—glances at it, and
     throws it down*)
Stuff! I wonder what lies the Historians will tell
When they babble of one Robert Walpole !   Well, well,
Let them sneer at his blunders, declaim on his vices,
Cite the rogues whom he purchased, and rail at the prices,
They shall own that all lust for revenge he withstood ;
And, if lavish of gold, he was sparing of blood ;
That when E gland was threatened by France and by Rome,
He forced peace from abroad and encamped at her home
And th' Freedom he left rooted firm in mild laws,
May o'ershadow the faults of deeds done in her cause !

Enter VEASEY, L.

VEASEY (*giving note*). Famous news ! see, Bellair has delivered himself
     To your hands.   He must go heart and soul with the Guelph,
     And vote straight, or he's ruined.
WALPOLE (*reading*).   This note makes it clear
     That he's guilty of Nithsdale's escape.
VEASEY.   And I hear
     That to-night he will head some tumultuous revolt,
     Unless chained to his stall like a mischievous colt.
WALPOLE. Your informant ?
VEASEY.   Guess !   Blount ; but on promise to save
     His young friend's life and fortune !
WALPOLE.   What Blount says is grave.
     He would never thus speak if not sure of this fact. (*signing
     warrant*)
     Here, then, take my State warrant ; but cautiously act.
     Bid Bellair keep his house—forbid exits and entries ;—
     To make sure, at his door place a couple of sentries.

Say I mean him no ill; but these times will excuse
Much less gentle precautions than those which I use.
Stay, Dame Vizard is waiting without; to her den
Nithsdale fled. She came here to betray him.

VEASEY.   What then?

WALPOLE. Why, I kept her, perforce, till I sent on the sly,
To prevent her from hearing Lord Nithsdale's good-bye.
When my agent arrived, I'm delighted to say
That the cage-wires were broken,—the bird flown away;
But he found one poor captive imprisoned and weeping;
I must learn how that captive came into such keeping.
Now, then, off—nay, a moment; you would not be loth
Just to stay with Bellair?—I may send for you both.

VEASEY. With a host more delightful no mortal could sup,
But a guest so unlooked for——

WALPOLE   Will cheer the boy up!
[Exit VEASEY, L.

WALPOLE (ringing hand-bell).

                           Enter SERVANT, L.

Usher in Mistress Vizard.
[Exit SERVANT, who ushers in MRS. VIZARD.—Then exit SERVANT.

WALPOLE.   Quite shocked to detain you,
But I knew a mistake, if there were one, would pain you.

MRS. VIZ. Sir, mistake there is not; that vile creature is no man.

WALPOLE. But you locked the door?

MRS. VIZ.   Fast.

WALPOLE.   Then, no doubt, 'tis a woman,
For she slipped thro' the window.

MRS. VIZ.   No woman durst!

WALPOLE.   Nay.
When did woman want courage to go her own way?

MRS. VIZ. You jest, sir. To me 'tis no subject for laughter.

WALPOLE. Do not weep. The reward? We'll discuss that hereafter.

MRS. VIZ. You'd not wrong a poor widow who brought you such news?

WALPOLE. Wrong a widow!—there's oil to put in her cruse. (giving a
pocket-book)
Meanwhile, the tried agent dispatched to your house,
In that trap found a poor little terrified mouse,
Which did call itself "Wilmot"—a name known to me,
Pray, you, how in your trap did that mouse come to be?

MRS. VIZ (hesitatingly). Sir, believe me——

WALPOLE   Speak truth—for your own sake you ought.

MRS. VIZ. By a gentleman, sir, to my house she was brought.

WALPOLE. Oh! some Jacobite kinsman perhaps?

MRS. VIZ.   Bless you, no;
A respectable Roundhead. You frighten me so.

WALPOLE. A respectable Roundhead entrust to your care
A young girl whom you guard as in prison!—Beware!
'Gainst decoy for vile purpose the law is severe.

MRS. VIZ. Fie! you libel a saint, sir, of morals austere.

WALPOLE Do you mean Judith Vizard?

MRS. VIZ.   I mean Selden Blount.

WALPOLE. I'm bewildered! But why does this saint (no affront)
To your pious retreat a fair damsel confide!

MRS. VIZ. To protect her as ward till he claims her as bride.
WALPOLE Faith, his saintship does well until that day arrive
To imprison the maid he proposes to wive.
But these Roundheads are wont but with Roundheads to
wed,
And the name of this lady is Wilmot, she said.
Every Wilmot I know of is to the backbone
A rank Jacobite; say can that name be her own ?
MRS. VIZ. Not a doubt; more than once I have heard the girl say
That her father had fought for King James on the day
When the ranks of the Stuart were crushed at the Boyne.
He escaped from the slaughter, and fled to rejoin
At the Court of St. Germain's his new-wedded bride.
Long their hearth without prattlers; a year ere he died,
Lucy came to console her who mourned him, bereft
Of all else in this world.
WALPOLE (*eagerly*).   But the widow he left ;
She lives still ?
MRS. VIZ.   No ; her child is now motherless.
WALPOLE (*aside*).   Fled !
Fled again from us, sister ! How stern are the dead !
Their dumb lips have no pardon ' Tut ! shall I build grief
On a guess that perchance only fools my belief?
This may *not* be her child. (*rings.*)

Enter SERVANT, L.

My coach waits ?
SERVANT.   At the door.
WALPOLE. Come ; your house teems with secrets I long to explore.
[*Exeunt* WALPOLE *and* MRS. VIZARD, L.—*Exit* SERVANT. L.

Scene changes to

SCENE III.—MRS. VIZARD'S *house, as before. A lamp on a table*, R. C.

Enter LUCY, R. D.

LUCY.   Mistress Vizard still out ! (*looking at the clock*) What ! so late ?
O my heart !—
How it beats ! Have I promised in stealth to depart ?
Trust him—yes ! But will *he*, ah ! long after this night,
Trust the wife wooed so briefly, and won but by flight?
My lost mother ! (*takes a miniature from her breast*) Oh couldst
thou yet counsel thy child !
No, this lip does not smile as it yesterday smiled.
From thine heaven can no warning voice come to mine ear;
Save thy child from herself ;—'tis myself that I fear.

Enter WALPOLE *and* MRS. VIZARD, *through the secret door*

MRS VIZ. Lucy, love, in this gentleman (curtsey, my dear)
See a friend.
WALPOLE.   Peace, and leave us.   [*Exit* MRS. VIZARD. R.
WALPOLE (C.).   Fair girl, I would hear
From yourself, if your parents——

LUCY (R. C.).   My parents; Oh say
Did you know them ?—my mother?
WALPOLE.   The years roll away.
I behold a gray hall backed by woodlands of pine;
I behold a fair face—eyes and tresses like thine—
By her side a rude boy full of turbulent life,
All impatient of rest, and all burning for strife—
They are brother and sister. Unconscious they stand—
On the spot where their paths shall divide—hand in hand.
Hush! a moment, and lo! as if lost amid night,
She is gone from his side, she is snatched from his sight.
Time has flowed on its course—that wild boy lives in me;
But the sister I lost! Does she bloom back in thee?
Speak—the name of thy mother, ere changing her own
For her lord's—who her parents?
LUCY.   I never have known.
When she married my father, they spurned her, she said,
Bade her hold herself henceforth to them as the dead;
Slandered him in whose honor she gloried as wife,
Urged attaint on his name, plotted snares for his life;
And one day when I asked what her lineage, she sighed
" From the heart they so tortured their memory has died."
WALPOLE Civil war slays all kindred—all mercy, all ruth.
LUCY.   Did you know her ?—if so, was this like her in youth? (giv-
          ing miniature.)
WALPOLE. It is she; the lips speak! Oh, I knew it!—thou art
My lost sister restored!—to mine arms, to mine heart,
That wild brother the wrongs of his race shall atone;
He has stormed his way up to the foot of the throne.
Yes! thy mate thou shalt choose 'mid the chiefs of the land.
Dost thou shrink ?—heard I right ?—is it promised this hand?
And to one, too, of years so unsuited to thine?
LUCY.   Dare I tell you?
WALPOLE.   Speak, sure that thy choice shall be mine.
LUCY.   When my mother lay stricken in mind and in frame,
All our scant savings gone, to our succor there came
A rich stranger, who lodged at the inn whence they sought
To expel us as vagrants. Their mercy he bought;
Ever since I was left in the wide world alone,
I have owed to his pity this roof——
WALPOLE.   Will you own
What you gave in return?
LUCY.   Grateful reverence.
WALPOLE.   And so
He asked more!
LUCY.   Ah! that more was not mine to bestow.
WALPOLE. What! your heart some one younger already had won.
Is he handsome?
LUCY   Oh, yes!
WALPOLE.   And a gentleman's son?
LUCY.   Sir, he looks it.
WALPOLE.   His name is——
LUCY.   Sir Sidney Bellair.
WALPOLE. Eh! that brilliant Lothario? Dear Lucy, beware;
Men of temper so light may make love in mere sport.
Where on earth did you meet ?— in what terms did he court?

Why so troubled ? Why turn on the timepiece your eye ?
Orphan, trust me.

LUCY.   I will. I half promised to fly——

WALPOLE. With Bellair. (*aside*) He shall answer for this with his life.
Fly to-night as his—what !

LUCY.   Turn your face—as his wife. (LUCY
sinks down, burying her face in her hands.)

WALPOLE. (*going to* D. F.) Jasper—ho !

Enter SERVANT, D. F., *as he writes on his tablets.*

Take my coach to Sir Sidney's, Whitehall.
Mr. Veasey is there ; give him this—that is all. (*tearing out
the leaf from the tablet and folding it up*)
Go out the back way ; it is nearest my carriage.* (*opens the
secret door* L. *in* F , *through which exit* SERVANT)
I shall very soon know if the puppy means marriage.

LUCY.   Listen ; ah ! that's his signal ! (*tap at window.*)

WALPOLE.   A stone at the pane !
But it can't be Bellair—*he* is safe.

LUCY.   There, again !

WALPOLE (*peeps out of window*). Ho!—a ladder ! Niece, do as I bid you ;
confide
In my word, and I promise Sir Sidney his bride !
Ope the window and whisper, " I'm chained to the floor ;
Pray come up and release me."

LUCY (*calls out of window*).   " I'm chained to the floor,
Pray, come up and release me."

WALPOLE.   I watch by this door.
                    [*Exit,* R. D., *and peeps out.*

BLOUNT *enters through window.*

LUCY.   Saints in Heaven, Mr. Jones ! (L. C.)

WALPOLE (*aside*)   Selden Blount, by old Nick !

BLOUNT.   What ! you are not then chained ! Must each word be a
trick ?
Ah ! you looked for a gallant more dainty and trim ;
He deputes me to say he abandons his whim ;
By his special request I am here in his place,
Saving him from a crime and yourself from disgrace.
Still ungrateful, excuse for your folly I make—
Still the prize he disd ins to my heart I can take.
Fly with me, as with him you would rashly have fled ;—
He but sought to degrade you, I seek but to wed.
Take revenge on the false heart, give bliss to the true !

LUCY.   If he's false to myself, I were falser to you,
Could I say I forget him ?

BLOUNT.   You will, when my wife.

LUCY.   That can never be——

BLOUNT.   Never !

LUCY.   One love lasts thro' life !

BLOUNT.   Traitress ! think not this insult can tamely be borne——

---

*In obeying this instruction, the servant would not see the ladder, which (as the reader will learn by what immediately follows) is placed against the balcony in the front of the house.

Hearts like mine are too proud for submission to scorn.
You are here at my mercy—that mercy has died ;
You remain as my victim or part as my bride. (*locks* L. D.)
See, escape is in vain, and all others desert you ;
Let these arms be your refuge.
WALPOLE (*tapping him on the shoulder*). Well said, Public Virtue !

BLOUNT, *stupified, drops the key, which* WALPOLE *takes up, stepping out into
the balcony, to return as* BLOUNT, *recovering himself, makes a rush at
the window.*

WALPOLE (*stopping him*). As you justly observed, '' See, escape is in
                                vain "—
          I have pushed down the ladder.
BLOUNT (*laying his hand on his sword*). 'Sdeath ! draw, sa !——
WALPOLE.   Austain
          From that worst of all blunders, a profitless crime.
          Cut my innocent throat ? Fie ! one sin at a time.
BLOUNT.   Sir, mock on, I deserve it ; expose me to shame,
          I've o'erthrown my life's labor,—an honest man's name.
LUCY (*stealing up to* BLOUNT). No ; a moment of madness can not sweep
                                away
          All I owed, and—forgive me—have failed to repay. (*to* WAL-
                                POLE)
          Be that moment a secret,
WALPOLE.   If woman can keep one,
          Then a secret's a secret. Gad, Blount, you're a deep one !
          (*knock at* D. F.—WALPOLE *opens it.*)

Enter, D. F., BELLAIR *and* VEASEY, *followed by* MRS. VIZARD.

BELLAIR. (*not seeing* WALPOLE, *who is concealed behind the door which he
          opens, and hurrying to* BLOUNT).
          Faithless man, canst thou look on my face undismayed ?
          Nithsdale's letter disclosed, and my friendship betrayed !
          What ! and *here* too ! Why *here ?*
BLOUNT (*aside*).   I shall be the town's scoff.
WALPOLE (*to* BELLAIR *and* VEASEY). Sirs, methinks that you see not
                                that lady—hats off.
          I requested your presence, Sir Sidney Bellair,
          To make known what you owe to the friend who stands there.
          For that letter disclosed, your harsh language recant—
          Its condition your pardon ;—full pardon I grant.
          He is here—you ask why ; 'tis to save you to-night
          From degrading your bride by the scandal of flight. (*drawing
                                him aside*)
          Or—hist !—*did* you intend (whisper close in my ear)
          Honest wedlock with one so beneath you I fear ?
          You of lineage so ancient——
BELLAIR.   Must mean what I say,
          Do their ancestors teach the well-born to betray ?
WALPOLE. Wed her friendless and penniless ?
BELLAIR.   Ay.
WALPOLE.   Strange caprice !
          Deign to ask, then, from Walpole the hand of his niece.
          Should he give his consent, thank the friend you abuse.

BELLAIR (*embracing* BLOUNT). Best and noblest of men my blind fury
      excus'.
WALPOLE. H rk! her father's lost lands may yet serve for her dower.
BELLAIR. All the earth has no lands worth the bloom of this flower.
LUCY. Ah! too soon fades the flower.
BELLAIR.   True, I alter the name.
      Be my perfect pure chrysolite—ever the same.
WALPOLE. Hold! I know not a chrysolite from a carbuncle, (*with in-
      sinuating blandishment of voice and look*)
      But my nephew-in-law should not vote out his uncle.
BELLAIR. Robert Walpole, at last you have bought me, I fear.
WALPOLE. Every man has his price. My majority's clear.
      If,—— (*crossing quickly to* BLOUNT)
      Dear Blount, did your goodness not rank with the best,
      What you feel as reproach, you would treat as a jest.
      Raise your head—and with me keep a laugh for the ass
      Who has never gone out of his wits for a lass;
      Live again for your country—reflect on my bill.
BLOUNT (*with emotion, grasping* WALPOLE'S *hand*). You are generous; I
      thank you. Vote *with* you?—I will!
VEASEY. How dispersed are the clouds seeming lately so sinister!
WALPOLE. Yes, I think that the glass stands at Fair—for the Minister.
VEASEY. Ah! what more could you do for the People and Throne?
WALPOLE. Now I'm safe in my office, I'd leave well alone.

SERVANTS AT BACK.

MRS. VIZARD.

BELLAIR.   LUCY.   BLOUNT.   VEASEY.
              WALPOLE.

CURTAIN.

NOT SO BAD AS WE SEEM.

CAST OF CHARACTERS.

	Burton's Theatre, New, York, Aug. 29, 1851.	Theatre Royal, Haymarket, London, Feb. 12, 1853.
The Duke of Middlesex (a peer attached to the son of James II., commonly called the First Pretender..	Mr. MOORHOUSE.	Mr. STUART.
The Earl of Loftus (also a peer attached to the son of James II.........		
Lord Wilmot (a young man at the head of the Mode more than a century ago, son to Lord Loftus)......Mr. DYOTT.		Mr. LEIGH MURRAY.
Mr. Shadowly Softhead (a young gentleman from the city friend and double to Lord Wilmot)............Mr. BURTON.		Mr. KEELEY.
Hardman (a rising Member of Parliament, and adherent of Sir Robert Walpole).......................Mr. BLAND.		Mr. BARRY SULLIVAN.
Sir Geoffrey Thornside (a gentleman of good family and estate)............		Mr. B. WEBSTER
Mr. Goodenough Easy (in business, highly respectable, and a friend of Sir Geoffrey)........... ....Mr. J. DUNN.		Mr. BUCKSTONE.
Colonel Flint (a Fire-eater)............		
Mr. Jacob Tonson (a Bookseller).... ..		
Smart (Valet to Lord Wilmot).... ....*		
Hodge (Servant to Sir Geoffrey Thornside)......................		
Paddy O'Sullivan (Mr. Fallen's Landlord)........		
Mr. David Fallen (Grubb Street Author and Phamphleteer)..........Mr. PARDAY.		Mr. HOWE.
First Watchman.....		
Lucy (Daughter to Sir Geoffrey Thornside)............... ....Miss WESTON.		Miss ROSE BENNETT.
Barbara (Daughter to Mr. Easy).... ..Miss M. BARTON.		Miss AMELIA VINING.
Lady Ellinor (the Lady of Deadman's Lane)............................		

Coffee House Loungers, Drawers, Newsmen, Watchmen, etc.

PERIOD—1720.—REIGN OF GEORGE I.

SCENE—LONDON.

TIME IN REPRESENTATION—THREE HOURS AND A QUARTER.

The events of the Play are supposed to take place between the morning of one day and the afternoon of the second day following.

SCENERY.

ACT I., Scene I.—LORD WILMOT's apartment in St. James's. A handsomely furnished apartment richly carpeted, closed in, set scene. In 4th grooves the flats represent one side with folding doors, c. Gilded panels and large paintings. Doors

R. 3 E. and L. 3 E. in a slanting direction; near each of them two rich gilt tables upon which are books and papers; on either side of the tables similar kind of chairs and also between the doors; the panels on either side are hung with pictures. Handbell on table, R. 2 E. Everything betokens a rich and elegantly furnished apartment.

ACT II., Scene I.—Library in the house of SIR GEOFFREY THORNSIDE. Flats in 4th grooves represent one side of the apartment with dark and heavy looking oak panels, partly gilded; the sides represent the same. At the back, c., a large window opening nearly to the ground. Doors L. 3 E. and R. 3 E.; the scene beyond the window represents a garden wall, with vines, etc., trained up it. Antique tables, with books and papers, R. 2 E. and L. 2 E.; antique high-backed chairs with velvet seats on either side of the tables.

ACT III., Scene 1—Will's Coffee House.

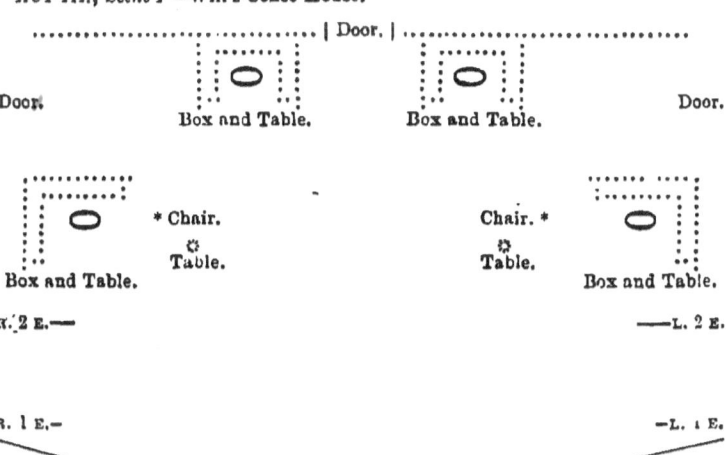

.....................| Door. |.....................

Door.   Door.
Box and Table.   Box and Table.

* Chair.   Chair. *
Table.   Table.
Box and Table.   Box and Table.

R. 2 E.—   —L. 2 E.

R. 1 E.—   —L. 1 E.

The flats set in the back grooves represent dark oak panelling, decorated with paintings. In the centre a doorway, panelling of passage beyond; on either side of the doorway two partitions four or five feet high, forming a sort of open box, and between them a table, with a seat running round three sides of the box, leaving one side open to the audience. Doors R. U. E. and L. U. E. Nearer the audience R. and L., a similar sort of box, with the seat running round two sides only, the sides next the centre of the stage and facing the audience being open. Over the door in the centre are the gilded arms of England, and on the panels of the room are various placards—"Army Increase," "More Treason," "Defeat of the Ministry," "More Jacobite Plots," "One Thousand Guineas Reward," etc. Writing materials in the open box, R. Two small round tables and chairs near the open boxes, R. and L., with newspapers, etc.

Scene II.—Library in SIR GEOFFREY'S house. Flats as in Act 2, Scene 1, but set in 2d grooves. Chair pushed on R. 2 E.

Scene III.—An old fashioned street scene set in 4th grooves. The corner of a gloomy-looking house, R. 3 E., apparently the beginning of an alley, upon the corner of it is inscribed "Deadman's Lane." Belonging to it in a slanting direction is a heavy-looking doorway, over which is fixed a massive crown and portcullis.

ACT IV., Scene I.—Library in SIR GEOFFREY'S house, as in Act 3, Scene 2.

Scene II.—David Fallen's garret. The flats set in the back grooves represent the side of a dilapidated garret; a low small casement with broken and patched panes, c. A cupboard, R. C. A low bedstead with blanket and scanty bedding, L. U. E. Two or three old pictures on the wall. Door R. 3 E. Common table and two chairs near the window; writing materials.

Scene III.—The Mall. The flats in the 3d grooves represent rows of trees and gravelled walk; the wings to correspond.

ACT V., Scene I.—Old Mill near the Thames. The flats in the 2d grooves represent river banks, with an old mill and outbuildings.

Scene II.—Apartment in the house in Deadman's Lane. The flats set full back represent a very old fashioned and sombre-looking room, with heavy tapestry on the wall, very much faded. Old style of fire-place, with high heavy carved mantelpiece in the centre, over which is a dingy crown and portcullis. The tapestry, R., is partially drawn back, and shows a door; a window, L; a roughly carved antique table, C., with writing materials upon it; three chairs near it of a similar style, and chairs R. and L.

NOTE.—If the Epilogue of "David Fallen is Dead" is given, the scene is set the same as Scene 1 in Act 1, with the addition of wine, fruit, etc.

COSTUMES.

Compiled from the works of Planche, Fairholt, and Martin.

LORD WILMOT.—Square-cut coat and long-flapped waistcoat, of scarlet cloth or velvet, with pockets in them. Broad lappels to the pockets of the coat just below the hips, trimmed with gold lace, buttons, and embroidered button holes; white neckcloth, lace, with long ends. Three-cornered hat with the sides turned up. Silk hose drawn up over the knee so high that they join the breeches under the long waistcoat flaps—the breeches may therefore be of the same or any other color, and of silk or velvet. High-heeled shoes and buckles. Large hanging cuffs to the coat, with lace ruffles. Very long curled wig. Court sword. *2d Dress :* Plain black coat, waistcoat, and trunks of a similar style, without ornament; shoes and buckles; short wig; linen neckcloth, and plain three-cornered hat. This is only used when disguised as Curll.

HARDMAN.—A similar dress, of blue velvet or cloth, but more quietly ornamented; hat, wig, shoes, buckles, and sword.

SHADOWLY SOFTHEAD.—Square-cut coat, fancifully embroidered, blue satin waistcoat, flowered with silk designs; lace neckcloth and ruffles; shoes, buckles, three-cornered hat and small feather, blue hose and short breeches, as above mentioned; gold-headed cane; full wig.

DUKE OF MIDDLESEX, } Precisely similar style of dress and equipments—one being
LORD LOTFUS. } of a cinnamon or pale brown color, and the other plum colored.

SIR GEOFFREY THORNSIDE.—Square cut coat of a claret color and waistcoat to match, without ornaments; neckcloth, ruffles, black silk hose, breeches, plain three-cornered hat, shoes, buckles, short wig, and sword.

MR. GOODENOUGH EASY.—Plain black suit of a similar shape and make; black silk hose, shoes, buckles, hat, short wig, plain neckcloth; neither ruffles nor sword.

JACOB TONSON.—Plain black suit of similar kind.

COLONEL FLINT.—Similar style of dress, varied in the colors.

DAVID FALLEN.—*1st Dress :* Well worn black coat and waistcoat; breeches and hose; hat, shoes, buckles, linen neckcloth, and long wig. *2d Dress :* The coat thrown aside, and waistcoat, shoes, hose, and everything in dishabille.

SMART.—Silk stockings, shoes, and buckles; black breeches; coat of claret-colored cloth, with plated buttons; plain neckcloth; short wig.

HODGE.—Similar dress of a cherry color, and a highly figured waistcoat underneath; knee breeches; cotton hose; shoes and buckles; short wig.

PADDY O'SULLIVAN.—Plain short coat of rough material; plain neckcloth; knee breeches, worsted hose, shoes, buckles, and short wig.

WATCHMEN.—Long coats of dark frieze, buttoned up; worsted hose, breeches, shoes, buckles; rather short wigs; three-cornered hats.

Lucy.—Full skirt and bodice of silk (any color), with wide open sleeves to the elbow trimmed with lace, and lace undersleeves ; a light lace cap over the head fastened with ribbons; the hair dressed high and thrown back. High-heeled shoes and buckles; fan ; a light muslin handkerchief thrown over the shoulders and the ends thrust into the bosom ; round low-crowned hat

Barbara.—A similar kind of dress, but varied in the colors.

Lady Ellinor.—A similar kind of dress, but concealed during the early scenes of the play by the use of a dark mantle, hood, and mask.

General Dresses.—The loungers about Will's Coffee House are dressed in similar style, but of varied quality. The drawers with long white aprons, black stockings and breeches ; sleeveless waistcoats and long coats; short wigs ; shoes, buckles, and plain neckcloths.

PROPERTIES.

ACT I., Scene 1.—Four gilt tables ; eight or ten gilt chairs; paintings ; books ; papers ; handbell ; card with address on it ; gold-headed cane.

ACT II., Scene 1 —Two heavy antique tables, with books and papers; four antique high-backed chairs with velvet seats ; bunch of flowers ; sword for Sir Geoffrey ; gold snuff-box for Wilmot.

ACT III., Scene 1.—Two round mahogany tables with newspapers ; newspapers for newsman ; decanters and wine glasses; trays, etc. ; letter; card with address. *Scene* 2.—Antique chairs. *Scene* 3 —Pipe for Easy ; rattles, staves, and lanterns for Watchmen.

ACT IV., Scene 2.—Old pictures on wall ; common table and two chairs; writing materials ; handsomely ornamented portfolio with papers and letter ; common bedstead with blanket and a few old bed clothes ; canvas bag with coin. *Scene* 3. —Phial for Softhead.

ACT V., Scene 1.—Folded paper ; address card ; pocket tablets for Hardman. *Scene* 2.—Roughly carved table and five chairs ; written paper for Hardman ; writing materials ; letter ; portfolio as before, papers and letter ; spectacles for the Duke.

Note.—If the Epilogue is given, the properties are the same as in Scene 1, Act 1, with the addition of wine, decanters, glasses, silver fruit dishes, fruit, etc.

STORY OF THE PLAY.

The period chosen for the action of the story is during the reign of the first George, king of England, when efforts were still being made to place upon the throne the Jacobite son of James the Second, commonly called the First Pretender. The constant reverses which had hitherto attended his efforts had slightly damped the ardor and decreased the number of his adherents ; nevertheless, many of the embers of the fire still existed, and his cause found favor and support among several of the leading nobility of the period, including therein two, represented in the play as the Duke of Middlesex and Lord Loftus, names which, it is hardly necessary to say, are created for the occasion. Their connection with the rebel cause is made use of to work out the story and bring about a successful and happy conclusion.

The Duke of Middlesex is represented as being the head of a noble house whose fame is so ancient and so great as to form a part of the history of the country—the very fountain of truth and honor. But, as then was and even now is the case with many other great families, there was a dark spot on the escutcheon—there was one member who satiated himself with dissipation, whose vanity and pride were of the most extensive kind, and who, casting aside the proverbial truth and honor of his race, whose word was always considered sacred, did not hesitate to boast openly of the female conquests he made, and, if he had been unsuccessful, felt no compunction in bringing a lie to his assistance, and asserting, utterly regardless of the consequences, that he had been honored with the lady's favors. Such was the character of the Duke's brother, Lord Henry de Mowbray.

Amongst the numerous ladies with whom this dangerous nobleman came in contact few surpassed in personal or mental charms and graces Lady Ellinor, the young and idolized wife of a wealthy gentleman, Sir Geoffrey Morland, one of England's sterling men, bearing an ancient and spotless name, and master of large domains. For a long time did the unscrupulous seducer exercise his most skillful arts to trap his new victim, but in vain ; purity and firmness formed an invulnerable shield. Finding himself continuously baffled, and his vanity and pride of conquest thus mortified, Lord Henry resorted to lying to uphold his prestige as a successful libertine, and by wily artifices and ready tools he soon had it gradually noised abroad that the Lady Morland had not been quite so circumspect and guarded in her conduct as to preserve her husband's honor untarnished. And in this diabolical scheme he was much aided by a letter which she had incautiously written to him, and the language of which he artfully perverted to suit his purposes. The sparks thus thrown about soon produced a flame. An inquiry was instituted by the distracted husband to trace out the origin of the slander, and relying unsuspectingly upon the presumed sacred truthfulness of the word of a Mowbray, he banished from his house the idolized wife of his bosom shortly after she had given birth to a daughter. He then sought the supposed seducer, forced him to a duel, and wounded him so severely that, thinking he had killed him, he fled from men's tongues and the story and scene of his dishonor to a distant land, which he did not quit until many years afterwards, when, broken down in mind and body, he returned to his native land, changing for another the name which De Mowbray had blighted. His only comfort was his daughter, but even with her there was a dark side in his thoughts, for doubts would sometimes cross his mind as to her true parentage.

Previous to the duel Lady Morland sought refuge in the house of her father; but sorrows come not singly. The very day she reached there he was compelled to fly the country to save his life, having been concerned in a Jacobite plot which had just been discovered. Deprived of all other ties, husband, home, and child, she accompanied her father into exile—proving herself his stay, his hope, his all. His lands were confiscated ; but although so highly born and so tenderly reared, she worked nobly for his support until his troubles and wants were silenced in the grave. She then entered a convent, and prepared to take the noviciate, when she learned most unexpectedly that inquiries had been instituted about her in Paris and elsewhere by a person who stated that Lord de Mowbray had died recently, and upon his death had retracted to the fullest extent possible the foul slander of which he was the instigator, and that he had left behind him written memoirs, papers, and letters acquitting her beyond the shadow of a doubt. The documents were stated also to explain clearly the circumstances under which he received the letter from Lady Morland, and how he made use of it, so that her entire innocence could be fully established. The image of her darling child, from whom she had been separated so many years—the hope of once again embracing the husband of her youth, urged her to active and energetic exertions, and returning to England, she obtained information which enabled her to trace out her husband's dwelling and assumed name. A few days before the opening of the play she had taken up her residence in an old, gloomy, and hitherto deserted house immediately adjacent to her husband's mansion, and was at once known as the mysterious masked lady of Deadman's Lane ; he as Sir Geoffrey Thornside, and their child as Lucy Thornside, now passing from girlhood into womanhood. Here in disguise and masked would the mother wander round the premises, stealing cautiously, like a thief, to the window to obtain one glance of all that remained in the world to love and live for, waiting patiently, full of hope and faith, for time to place within her power the proofs of her innocence. So far then as these parties are concerned this is the position of affairs at the opening of the play.

She has frequently observed from the window of her lonely house overlooking Sir Geoffrey's garden a gay young spark of the period, Lord Wilmot, walking there with Lucy, and she contrives to obtain an interview with him, when she learns that Lucy very often mourns with tears in her eyes the want of a mother's love, believing that she had died in her infancy. Lady Morland entreats him at the next meeting to say that he had seen a friend of this mother who had something to impart which might probably be to the happiness of both. This he consents to do, and a visitor approaching, she gives him her address and appoints a meeting for the evening.

Now Lord Wilmot was one of the youthful leaders of the fashionable world, for which position a handsome person, a refined intellect, and polished manners rendered him well qualified. As is frequently the case, every young man in the possession of wealth, but very little else, eagerly sought his society and struggled desperately to win the honor of his acquaintance, making him a sort of idolatrous model, proud beyond description of his patronage and playful familiarities, and endeavoring, though with very little success, to imitate him in every possible way. Such a one is Mr. Shadowly Softhead, the son of an opulent clothier possessing great weight and influence among the city companies, but not much known beyond. Whatever Wilmot did, said, or thought, Softhead would try to do, say, and think the same; in fact, he was Wilmot's double, though not one of the most approved description. Another friend of Wilmot's, but of a very different sort, is Mr. Hardman. Unknown to himself he is the son of the foster brother of Sir Geoffrey, who promised his father, in compliance with his dying wish, that the boy should never know the favors he intended to bestow upon him, so that he should not feel the yoke of dependence; and Sir Geoffrey kept his word. He managed matters so skillfully and secretly that the youth received a good education, wrote works which brought his name into high notice and favor (Sir Geoffrey paying the publisher to produce them), obtained an annuity for some trifling service, and a seat in Parliament without a shilling of expense, never for one moment doubting that all this he had himself accomplished by energy, perseverance, talent, and application, instead of owing it to the watchful care and long purse of Sir Geoffrey Thornside, otherwise Morland. At the opening of the play Hardman is in the proud position of a rising member of the English Parliament and a strong adherent of the Prime Minister, Sir Robert Walpole.*

At an interview which takes place between Wilmot and the Duke the former alludes to a report which is going through fashionable circles that Lord Mowbray has left behind him certain confessions or memoirs which, from the well known gay and dissolute life he pursued, are likely to prove highly rich and interesting in their details. This is particularly unpleasant news for the Duke, who views with horror the odium and ridicule that are likely to be cast upon the family by the discovery and publication of these papers; and if it be possible by any means whatever he entreats Wilmot to obtain possession of them and not let them fall into the hands of some greedy publisher. Wilmot promises to do all he possibly can, as he considers it the duty of all noble gentlemen to suppress scandal so injurious to their class. Pleased with his ready acquiescence, the Duke reveals to him his connection with the Jacobite cause, urging him to join, observing in a magniloquent way, " If we succeed, you restore the son of a Stuart ; if we fail, you will go to the scaffold by the side of John, Duke of Middlesex !"

Strange as it may seem, however, Wilmot cannot see the particular advantage or honor in thus running the risk of putting an end to his youthful and, at present, pleasurable career ; consequently he very respectfully declines the offer ; but he learns enough to lead him to suspect that his father, Lord Loftus, is mixed up in the treasonable plot. Unable, however, to obtain further information of the Duke, and not being upon friendly terms with his parent, he determines to put Hardman

---

* A full description of this eminent statesman will be found in the introductory portion of a comedy in rhyme, by the same author, entitled, " Walpole; or, Every Man has his Price."

on the inquiry, and to apply to the poor author, David Fallen, who, it is well known, is more or less concerned in all the schemes of the Pretender's party. Hardman is in love with Lucy, and half suspects that Wilmot is also, and so before he departs on the mission he throws out a hint—" One is always safe from a rival, both in love and ambition, if one will watch to detect and then scheme to destroy." Wilmot is really in love with Lucy, and determines to put Sir Geoffrey on a wrong scent with regard to his passion, and therefore he induces Shadowly Softhead, though not without some difficulty, to make pretended love to her, whilst he will do the same towards Barbara Easy, of whom Softhead is deeply enamored, and then when opportunity occurs matters can be reversed ; as Wilmot wittily observes, they can " change partners, hands across, down the middle, and up again."

Sir Geoffrey in his retirement has grown suspicious, petu ant, and irritable, and this disposition is not improved by the rustic bluntness of his eccentric attendant, Hodge, whom he has brought to London from his country house. For some few days he has been much annoyed by nosegays being thrown in at the window, in which he is convinced there is some attempt upon his life; then again, when he walks in the garden, he feels sure that some one, or something, is watching from the window of the lone house in Deadman's Lane. Another great source of annoyance is the frequent calling of Wilmot, who, as he says, pretending to have saved Lucy from footpads, persists in repeating the calls daily, only an excuse, he is confident, for making love to her, which angers him much, as he has not the slightest liking or respect for a lord ; all of which he reveals to Goodenough Easy.

The arrival of the young ladies, accompanied by Wilmot and Softhead, affords an opportunity for some amusing by-play, by means of which Wi.mot skillfully plays upon Sir Geoffrey and then upon Easy, so that he induces the latter to take the former into an adjoining room to talk over his views with regard to Lucy, thus leaving Softhead and Barbara to a battle of love, and giving Wilmot an opportunity to make Lucy acquainted with the visit from a friend of her mother's.

The arrival of Hardman breaks up the meeting, and although partners are changed as arranged, Hardman is very suspicious, but having ascertained from David Fallen that Wilmot's father really is mixed up in treasonous plots, he determines to use that knowledge as a hold upon the son, should occasion need. Barbara confides to Wilmot her love for Softhead and her father's dislike to him for having quitted the sober business city life in which he was reared, to ape and imitate the man of fashion and the ways of those far above him in rank and position, for which reason their union has been forbidden. But Wilmot cheers her up and promises to work a great change in the steady young city merchant, and although Barbara declares that her father is one of the soberest men living, and exceedingly severe against a cheerful glass, Wilmot determines to lead him into a tipsy bout and turn the incident to advantage.

At a meeting the same evening, at Will's Coffee House, a noted resort for all the gay young lords, politicians, authors, and noted men of the day, Easy is induced to be a visitor. Hardman is there also, to have have a further interview with David Fallen ; so also are Lord Loftus and the Duke, who choose the place for meeting as from its publicity they are less likely to excite suspicion than in using a more pri. vate one.

Loftus expects a messenger from the Pretender, and leaves it to Fallen to name the meeting place and time, which he fixes for the ensuing day at an old secluded mill on the banks of the river Thames. As soon as they are gone, he tells Hardman what has taken place, and urges him to save the infatuated noblemen from danger and not to destroy them, observing, that though he is resigned to the name of starving poet and hireling, he is not, and cannot be, to that of butcher. In warm language he tells how he commenced life in devotion to two causes—the throne of the Stuarts and the glory of Letters. Politicians of both sides served him alike ; no matter which was in power, he starved ; and he is now in that position ; he is paid for information and scurrilous pamphlets, from which source he ekes out a scanty subsistence.

Hardman at this moment is very much disposed to throw up his post, for, believing he has a claim upon the prime minister for past services, he has applied to him for a vacant official appointment, only, however, to meet with a refusal from Walpole, which so angers him that he is almost inclined to forsake his allegiance; but a little reflection bids him wait.

Wilmot now appears upon the scene to put his scheme into operation. Accompanied by his idolizing double, Softhead, he invites the leading members of the company to a grand dinner, and artfully contrives that there shall be just *one* wanting to complete the party. Of course his eye drops upon Easy, and in spite of his protestations that he is unused and objects to such scenes, he is compelled to agree to make up the number, which brings forth another side to his character; with the excitement of the scene, he forgets his previous steady going merchant principles and speaks boastingly to acquaintances around him of the honor, ability, and pleasantry of his *friend*, Lord Wilmot.

Now is the time for looking after the memoirs, so Wilmot broaches the subject to Tonson (a celebrated publisher and an employer of distressed and suffering, but talented, authors at starvation prices), and from him he finds that they are in the possession of David Fallen, who refuses to part with them, although Tonson has offered the magnificent sum of two hundred guineas. This is good news for Wilmot, who obtains the poet's address and determines to visit him at his house, alone.

Tonson also speaks of the subject to Hardman, expatiating warmly upon the extreme attractiveness of the papers if they could only be secured for publication; a full account of the love adventures of Lord Mowbray; *such* a confession about the beautiful Lady Morland; satires upon the Duke; Jacobite family secrets; ever so much scandal; would sell like wildfire; such glorious nuts for the public to crack! But to all this Hardman turns a deaf ear.

Now Tonson's great fear is that one Curll, a most unscrupulous publisher, author and trafficker in literary matter, should forestall him in the possession of these memoirs and force them upon the market in spite of all the trouble he has taken, and he therefore mentions the subject to Wilmot, begging him to be upon his guard and not let the secret of the ownership get wind. This gives a new idea to Wilmot; he once dressed like and imitated this Curll so well that the great poet Pope was himself deceived, and ordered him out of the room, so he determines again to adopt this disguise to assist him in dealing with Fallen, and not to appear in his proper person.

Observing Hardman somewhat moody, he learns from him the minister's refusal of the sought for place, which if he had secured would have given him courage to ask for and obtain the hand of the lady he loves; and his spirits are by no means cheered up when Wilmot avows to him his own love for Lucy. Hardman, however, is not to be so easily baffled, the knowledge of the treason of Lord Loftus and the Duke is in his keeping, for which he can demand from Wilmot any price he pleases, and he determines that such price shall be his resignation of the hand of Lucy. With dissembling friendship he bids him adieu:—

"To-day I'm your envoy; to-morrow your master."

Now Wilmot is half jesting; he sees that every man's character has different sides to it, and he thinks it too cruel a joke that for want of the official appointment Hardman should lose the chance of winning the woman. Wilmot has a very scarce and valuable painting by the celebrated artist Murillo; the weak side of Walpole's character was a strong infatuation for paintings. The game is quite clear: Wilmot will make him a present of the painting in exchange for the appointment—in fact, he will bribe the Prime Minister—Walpole shall have the Murillo, and Hardman shall have the place, and the wife, if he can win her.

In an interview which takes place in Sir Geoffrey's library, Lucy alludes to the visits of Wilmot under pretence of loving Barbara, and affectionately urges him to forbid them, confessing that they make her too happy, and yet may grieve him. The old baronet is struck with this token of affection; she must be his child; how to console her? "By speaking of my mother," timidly suggests Lucy. The father's brow darkens as he forbids her ever to mention the name of one who had dishonored him. "It is false!" speaks a low voice, and the masked female disappears from the window of the apartment where she had been a spectator of the scene. At this moment Hardman arrives with the news that Wilmot is not in love with Barbara, but with Lucy, and whilst the baronet informs him that he already knows it, and they agree that the nosegays and the watch kept on the house are evidently part of a plan to entrap her, the masked female glides past the window. With a startled cry Hardman, who observes the movement, leaps out in pursuit; carefully tracks her to the house in Deadman's Lane, and determines that the morrow shall solve the mystery.

Wilmot's dinner takes place as arranged, and so skillfully does he carry out his plans that he works Easy into a glorious state of jovial exhilaration, in which he declares his undying antipathy for lords, and binds himself irrevocably to accept Softhead as his son-in-law; thus Wilmot achieves success for his plot number one. Scenes of rough play in the streets between young sparks and the night watchmen were common occurrences at the period of the play; indeed, it was not considered the proper thing to wind up an evening's carousal without something of the kind. As a matter of course Wilmot takes care that his party shall be no exception to the custom, and he therefore leads his friends into such a scene, as it happens, in the vicinity of Deadman's Lane. Goodenough Easy, under the influence of his frequent draughts, forgets his civic dignity, and bestriding a fallen watchman, affords much amusement by fancying himself the chairman of a jovial meeting and the watchman's body the table. The arrival of the other members of the watch however interrupt his delusion, and he is borne away to the watch-house, still shouting, however, the glorious principles of the constitution and the pride he feels at the exalted position to which he has been raised—the shoulders of the watchmen. Wilmot, having taken Softhead aside, now points out to him the lone house, and so works upon his fears by the picture he draws of things within, that when the masked lady suddenly appears, he darts away frightened out of his wits. She beckons, and Wilmot follows her into the house.

Hardman now takes an opportunity of an interview with Sir Geoffrey to ask for Lucy's hand. He relates in glowing terms his career from boyhood; his struggles for fortune and fame; with all of which the baronet is of course acquainted; but when he tells him that not an hour previously he had received the appointment which had been refused, the baronet is sorely puzzled to know who could have done that. However, charmed by his frankness, Sir Geoffrey gives his consent, if Lucy so inclines, and then tells him that upon examining the nosegays thrown in at the window he finds they are made up in the very form in which he used to make up those he sent to his wife in the days of their courtship. He tells him also of his supposed dishonor, and reveals his true name—Morland—and that of the presumed seducer. Tonson's words about the memoirs flash to Hardman's recollection, and he determines to seek an interview with David Fallon.

Wilmot is not slow on the same track. Disguising himself as Mr. Curll, he visits Fallon in his wretched garret, when the forlorn poet is about to pawn the last blanket he possesses to obtain food for his children. He offers three hundred guineas for the memoirs, but, poor as he is, Fallen refuses; honor and poverty are still left to him. He relates how they were given to him by Lord Mowbray on his death-bed; that they contain a confession as to the lady he once foully injured, which would serve to clear the name he himself had aspersed, and that they had been received with a promise to seek her and place them in her hands to enable her to establish her innocence. She was of a Jacobite family, and as a Jacobite agent Fallen was supposed to have the best chance of tracing her; he exerted himself to the utmost, but only to hear that she had died in France. Having thus failed, he was determined that no money should induce him to open up the secrets of homes to public scoff and ridicule. For a moment baffled, the prize seems lost, when Wilmot informs him he comes from Lord Mowbray's brother, the Duke of Middlesex. This only makes matters worse. Fallen relates in bitter words the circumstances under which he met the Duke some years previously, when a kind word, a nod of recognition would have made his fortune. He had inscribed to the Duke a new poem, took it to his house and waited in the hall, when the great man appeared and said: "Oh, you are the poet? take this," extending his alms as if to a beggar. "You look very thin, sir; stay and dine with my people." He meant his servants! Fallen points out that these memoirs made public, would make the Duke the jeer of his own lackeys; but he will be no tool for working out a dead brother's revenge, and his pride prevents him receiving money.

Charmed by the nobility of Fallen's conduct, Wilmot tells him who he is, that the Duke is his father's friend, and ought to possess the papers as a family secret, and expresses warmly his admiration for one who, in the midst of poverty, could spurn a bribe to his honor, but who might now humble by such a valuable gift, the great and haughty noble, who had insulted him by alms. Fallen surrenders the memoirs, and Wilmot departs, promising him for life a yearly sum equal to that which he had refused as a bribe.

Hardman arrives only to find the true nature of the documents; that Lady Morland's letter was with them, and that they are now on their way to the Duke. Baffled in this, there is left yet the meeting with the Pretender's agent. If he can only obtain the treasonous dispatch, he will force the memoirs from the Duke; the masked female must be Lady Morland; establish her innocence and he wins Lucy.

Wilmot places the documents in the hands of the Duke, and then sends a letter to Lucy to meet and accompany him to the lone house.

Acting upon his knowledge of the meeting-place and the password, Hardman obtains the dispatch, and upon the Duke's arrival he reveals to him his knowledge of all that has passed respecting his brother and Lady Morland, and that he knows of the papers being in his possession, and the nature of them. He appeals to him, not as a proud peer of England, but as a man, to surrender the papers, and by so doing restore a wife to the husband she loves and forgives—to the girl for whom her heart yearns. Pride struggles with honor and justice in the breast of the haughty nobleman, but the latter triumphs, and he takes his leave, promising to meet Hardman forthwith and hand over to him the memoirs.

In a state of the greatest alarm, Softhead arrives with the information that he has seen Lucy and Wilmot enter the lone house at Deadman's Lane. Enraged at being thus forestalled, Hardman gives him a note to the justice to send and post officers at the door to await his orders, and also a message to Sir Geoffrey to meet him there; and hastening thither, he arrives shortly after Wilmot has united mother and daughter. In vehement language he reminds him of his love for Lucy; he tells him that instead of sounding his father, he has detected him in what history and party feeling call *zeal*, but the law *high treason!* producing the dispatch calling for arms and money to dethrone the king, signed by the Duke and Lord Loftus.

Astounded by the intelligence, Wilmot locks the door and attempts to secure the paper, but Hardman coolly informs him that officers are waiting below, and the effort is futile. He then pictures his love for Lucy, and that he had schemed to save his father, not to injure him; had the dispatch fallen into the hands of a spy the result would have been very different, and he now only asks that he may himself place it in the hands of Lord Loftus, with such words as will save him and others from similar perilous hazards in the future. Wilmot departs therefore to secure the presence of his father and the Duke.

As soon as he is gone, Hardman seeks an interview with Lucy, in which he declares his love, telling her of her father's wish, and that he will soon dispel all the clouds which have darkened his life, and make her mother the pride of their home. She blesses him for the promise, but warns him that her heart may not go with her hand. He is content; he will try and win it. Her father is coming full of suspicion; she must appear as his betrothed and accepted; he will restore her mother's name; secure her parents' reunion; her hand the pledge—she gives it.

Followed by Easy, Softhead, and Barbara, Sir Geoffrey bursts into the room in search of Wilmot, by whom he thinks his daughter has been taken off and finding Hardman there, believes that he has been the means of saving her from disgrace.

Then comes to light the whole secret of Hardman's past career, of the unknown hand that raised him, and, more astounding than all, the fact that he owes his official appointment to Wilmot. He is overwhelmed at such generosity, and informs Sir Geoffrey why Lucy was brought there. With indignation at the snare laid to bring him and his wife together, Sir Geoffrey is about to depart, when the Duke arrives with the memoirs, which he hands over to Hardman. The inspection of them and of the letter convinces Sir Geoffrey of his wife's innocence, and with a burst of joy he receives her in his arms. But Hardman's task is not yet done. He gives up the dispatch, with the information that the cause is hopeless, the Pretender having abjured his faith and fled to Rome. He feels that Lucy's heart yearns towards Wilmot, so taking her hand he places it in his, remarking to Sir Geoffrey, "You placed her happiness in my charge—here, she loves and is loved."

The fever is catching, and as Softhead always liked to imitate a lord, he suggests being married to Barbara. To this, however, Mr. Goodenough Easy strongly objects, but Wilmot slyly reminds him that when he was chairman of the impromptu meeting of the previous night he had promised, nay, insisted upon it, that Softhead should be his son-in-law, and offers to explain to the company the circumstances. This is too much for Goodenough Easy, so he consents.

All are made happy—treason is crushed—love is promoted—and the conclusion is arrived at by all the party assembled, that, with all their faults, they are not so bad as they seem.

REMARKS.

"NOT so bad as we seem" was written by the author more with a view to its production in private on a special occasion than to its representation upon the stage; hence it is that many of the ideas are elaborately worked out, and many of the incidents, slight in themselves, unduly and needlessly extended.

The late Duke of Devonshire was, and had been for many years of his life, a warm and earnest patron of Literature and the Drama. To all who were connected with those professions he ever extended a genial and noble sympathy, and was always ready to befriend every member, high or low, of what he was pleased to call his "brotherhood." He was also the founder of an institution for rendering assistance to any one of the class who should unfortunately, as was too often the case, be in need of it.

Having made arrangements to give a grand entertainment to Her Majesty, Queen Victoria, at his palatial house in London, Bulwer readily entered into his desire to make the occasion one worthy of note, and accordingly constructed the present play. It was produced in a theatre especially erected for the purpose, fitted up in the most complete and costly manner, and was performed before the Queen and one of the most noble and brilliant audiences ever assembled; all the parts being filled by amateur ladies and gentlemen of eminent position and ability. The result may well be imagined; the sparkling wit, refined language and polished manners of all the actors naturally met with approval from such a select audience, and it was duly announced as being a great and decided success. But when the composition was submitted to a public ordeal, and its merits judged by a severer tribunal, the weak nature of the plot, the undue extension of the details, and a faulty construction, caused it to fail in producing a confirmatory verdict.

The American stage bore off the palm of making the first attempt to test the merits of the new work by its production in public, bringing it out at Burton's Chambers Street Theatre on August 29th, 1851. It was well mounted, but to no good—lack of interest, want of incident, and the absence of effective situations were not to be atoned for by fine language and occasionally long speeches; the consequence was an unsatisfactory reception, and an early withdrawal. It should be noted, however, that while the cast of the characters embraced the names of several excellent players, scarcely any of them had a part suitable to their peculiar talents. Burton, Dyott, Dunn, Bland, and Parday were admirable actors in their respective lines ; but in this cast they were singularly out of their proper places.

Two years afterwards the London stage made the attempt, by producing it at the Theatre Royal Haymarket, where it had the advantage of actors in every respect admirably adapted to the characters personated, backed up by the best mounting possible. Like the attempt in New York, it met with very little favor, was withdrawn after a short run, and has not been produced since. That this was a true test of the merits of the play is beyond a doubt ; for all that professional ability could do to ensure success was unquestionably done. It is a curious fact that every one of the actors engaged, rose afterwards to the top of the profession in their several branches ; one more especially, Mr. Barry Sullivan, who has attained a most distinguished position amongst the many candidates for high histrionic honors. All of them too, curiously enough, became lessees and managers of the principal London theatres.

It seems to have been the author's aim to present each of the personages in a particular style, and to change him into quite an opposite one.

In Hardman he represents a young, energetic, and talented man, overcoming every obstacle in his path of ambition, and achieving all that he desires ; loving warmly, and yet so moved by the generosity of his rival, and a sense of honor, that when he becomes aware that the heart of the girl he adores is not his, though her hand may be, for services rendered to her father, he does not hesitate to sacrifice his own desires for her happiness, and surrenders her to Wilmot, knowing their affection to be warm and mutual. Again, he secures the treasonous secret of Lord Loftus and the Duke to further his designs in winning Lucy, but throws over his intentions and saves them from an untimely death.

The Duke of Middlesex is the type of a proud, haughty, and conceited class, of whom, at that period, there were many representatives ; but on the other side of his character there is a spirit of honor and chivalry in him highly to be commended. The production of the Confession and Memoirs of his brother, Lord Mowbray, is certain, by the exposure of their loose and scandalous contents, to bring ridicule and shame upon himself and the family name ; his vanity consequently recoils at the prospect, but when he learns that a woman's honor is at stake, and the salvation of a wife and mother is to be achieved, he hesitates no longer ; like a truehearted man and a gentleman he agrees to surrender the document quite regardless whether the result be unpleasant to him or not. Thus we see the different sides to his character.

Lord Wilmot is like many young men of that, and even of the present, day—wealthy, light-hearted, and gay. His passion for Lucy is of very rapid growth, and he is one of those persons who strike quickly. Smitten by her charms, he soon tells his love, although aware of the existence of a prior candidate. Yet, in spite of his affection, there is such a feeling of generosity in him that he grieves to see his rival disappointed in a chance of winning her, so he sets to work and procures for him the official appointment he had failed to obtain, although it is likely to raise him considerably in the eyes of his ladylove, and render him a more formidable opponent. Here again we have different sides of another character.

Mr. Goodenough Easy has but one idea of the proper course of life to pursue—trade. He was born and bred in business in the city, and there he must remain and die, believing that a man has no right to move out of the sphere in which he entered life. But even he has to change his character and ideas, and to give way to the influence of rank and position, and actually boasts of the pride he feels in the new-made friendship of a lord, yielding most amiably to his wishes.

As for Shadowly Softhead, he represents a class of which we constantly meet specimens ; but there is nothing particularly new or striking in his character, or in that of either of the ladies, to call for any special notice.

David Fallen, the poor poet, is a prettily conceived character. The description of his career in Act IV. is well drawn, and is a truthful illustration of the life of

many talented men in the last century. Might we not also say in this ? Notwithstanding all the vicissitudes, tria's, and sufferings through which he has passed,
honor remains intact. Finding the original purpose for which he was intrusted
with Lord Mowbray's Memoirs and Confession cannot be carried out, he does not
hesitate to give them up to the Duke, rather than allow the secrets of a high family
and a home to be scattered abroad, bringing scandal and disgrace upon all its members.

Sir Geoffrey Thornside, after all he has endured, is, as we might naturally expect,
a suspicious, discontented, and irritable old gentleman ; his mind fixed upon one
point—a firm conviction of his wife's guilt, which nothing can move. But this character also has to undergo a change and exhibit another side, so when the time comes
to make all things clear, the old love comes up as bright as ever, and every trouble
vanishes.

There are not many telling situations in the play, nor any particular display of
fine writing, until towards the end, in the Fourth and Fifth Acts. It bears evident
signs of hurried composition, and it would be difficult for any one to believe, by a
perusal of the work, supposing him, of course, to be ignorant of the fact that it had
emanated from the same source as Richelieu, Money, and the Lady of Lyons. There
is, however, groundwork for a neat drama by using some little excision and making
a few alterations in the arrangement of the incidents. The female parts are very
tame ; indeed, there are no very strongly marked and distinctive characters in it,
drawn in the brilliant colors which distinguish other productions of the noble author.
The imaginary chairmanship of Easy in the Third Scene of Act III. is ludicrous.
The interview between Lord Wilmot and David Fallen is very well done, and the
bitter feelings with which the latter relates the circumstance of the insult he received from the Duke are excellently rendered. So also is that portion of the Third
Scene in Act IV., where Wilmot describes to Softhead his interview with the Prime
Minister, Walpole, and how he managed to obtain from him the place for Hardman
in exchange for his Murillo painting. In the hands of an able actor this can certainly be made the gem of the play. The language is witty, sharp, and well chosen,
and if delivered clearly, rapidly, and judiciously, the speech cannot fail to ensure
applause. But perhaps the neatest portion of the composition is that entitled
"David Fallen is Dead !" intended as a sort of key to the play. It was to have been
spoken at the original amateur performance ; not being ready, however, it did not
appear until the work was published, when it was introduced as an after scene—as
an acted epilogue. The idea is a novel one, and the language well chosen, witty,
appropriate, and telling.

At any rate, the design of the play is a good one, and if not carried out so well and
effectively as it might be, the principle is established that there are " many sides to
a character," and that all of us are " Not so Bad as we Seem."   J. M. K.

BILL FOR PROGRAMMES, ETC.

The events of the Play take place in London. Period—1720.

ACT I.

Scene I.—LORD WILMOT'S APARTMENT IN ST. JAMES'S

The Mysterious Lady—The Invitation—An Ambitious Citizen—Haughty Nobility and an aspiring Youth—A Small Man and a Great Mind - Memoirs of a Gay Nobleman—The Jacobite Plot—Treason and its Adherents—The Compact.

ACT II.

Scene I.—LIBRARY IN THE HOUSE OF SIR GEOFFREY THORNSIDE

An Irritable Master and his Country Servant—Suspicions and Fears—The Mysterious Nosegay—Poison in Flowers—An exalted Trader—A Ruse of Love--A Declaration of Affection—The Rival Lovers—Hardman and Wilmot—The Conspiracy.

ACT III.

Scene I.—WILL'S COFFEE-HOUSE.

Nobility, Wit, and Learning—Poetry and Wine—Plot and Counterplot— The Noble Conspirators—A Jacobite Agent—The Secret Dispatch—The Meeting Betrayed—A Poet's Story of Politics and Starvation—Confessions of a Seducer—A Dinner for Six—The Trap Laid.

Scene II.—LIBRARY IN SIR GEOFFREY'S HOUSE.

Father and Daughter—A Masked Listener—The Mysterious Voice—The Baronet's Suspicions of a Wife's Honor—The Interruption--The Pursuit of the Unknown.

Scene III.—OLD STREET IN LONDON AND DEADMAN'S LANE.

Tracking the Masked Lady—The Result of the Dinner—Wine and its Effects—Mr. Goodenough Easy as Chairman—An Election for the City— A Living Table—A March to the Watch-house—A Softhead by Name and Nature—The Masked Lady again—Wilmot in Pursuit.

ACT IV.

Scene I.—LIBRARY IN SIR GEOFFREY'S HOUSE.

Hardman's Story of his Life and Career—Sir Geoffrey Reveals his True Name and the Secret of his Dishonor—Hardman on the Track for the Memoirs and Confession of the Culprit.

Scene II.—THE GARRET HOME OF DAVID FALLEN.

Poetry and Poverty—Milk Scores in Arrear—A Warm-hearted Irishman— The Hunt for the Memoirs—The Poet's Story of Indignity and Insult— Nobility of Nature—The Bribe Refused—Heroic Example of Generosity —Wilmot obtains the Memoirs—Hardman Defeated—"Now then for the Treasonous Dispatch!"

Scene III.—THE MALL.

The Duke and the Memoirs—How Wilmot bribed the Prime Minister— Value of Painting—Lucy on the way to her Mother.

ACT V.

Scene I.—OLD MILL ON THE BANKS OF THE THAMES.

Hardman secures the Dispatch—Proofs of Treason—The Story of Lady Morland's Wrongs—The Injured Wife and a Seducer's Confession—A Rival in Love—Officers ordered for Deadman's Lane.

Scene II.—APARTMENT IN THE LONE HOUSE IN DEADMAN'S LANE.

The Meeting of Mother and Daughter—Hardman in Pursuit—The Dispatch to the Pretender—A Father's Treason and a Son's Ruin—A Lover's Appeal—An Enraged Parent—The Story of the Unknown Benefactor—Proofs of Innocence—Reunion of Husband and Wife—A Noble Sacrifice—Lovers made Happy—Treason Destroyed—All Prove they are not so Bad as they Seem!

EXPLANATION OF THE STAGE DIRECTIONS.

The Actor is supposed to face the Audience.

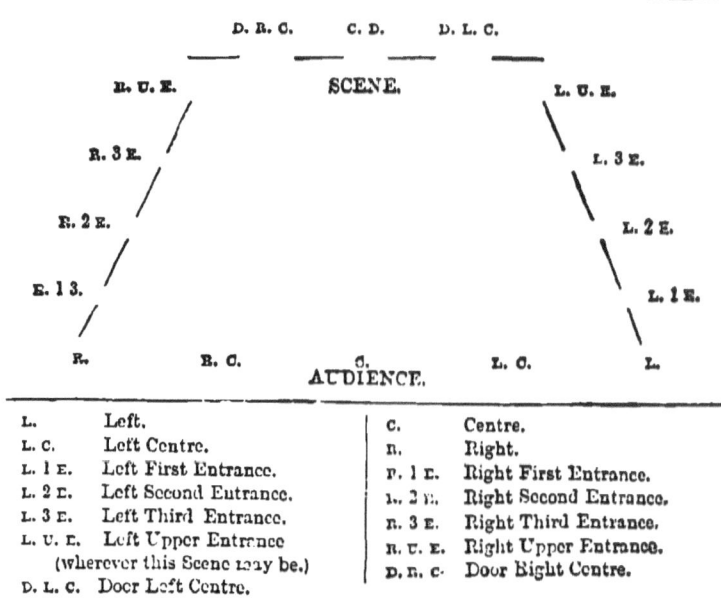

L.	Left.	C.	Centre.
L. C.	Left Centre.	R.	Right.
L. 1 E.	Left First Entrance.	R. 1 E.	Right First Entrance.
L. 2 E.	Left Second Entrance.	R. 2 E.	Right Second Entrance.
L. 3 E.	Left Third Entrance.	R. 3 E.	Right Third Entrance.
L. U. E.	Left Upper Entrance	R. U. E.	Right Upper Entrance.
	(wherever this Scene may be.)	D. R. C.	Door Right Centre.
D. L. C.	Door Left Centre.		

NOT SO BAD AS WE SEEM;

OR, MANY SIDES TO A CHARACTER.

ACT I

SCENE I.—Lord Wilmot's *apartment in St. James's.*

Enter Smart, c. d. l., *showing in* Lady Ellinor, *masked.*

Smart. My Lord is dressing. As you say, madam, it is late. But though he never wants sleep more than once a week, yet when he does sleep, I am proud to say he sleeps better than any man in the three kingdoms.

Lady E. I have heard much of Lord Wilmot's eccentricities—but also of his generosity and honor.

Smart. Yes, madam, nobody like him for speaking ill of himself and doing good to another.

Enter Wilmot, r. d.

Wilmot. "And sleepless lovers just at twelve awake." Any duels to-day, Smart? No—I see something more dangerous—a woman. (*to* Smart) Vanish. (*exit* Smart, c. d. *Places a chair,* l. c., *for* Lady E. *She sits and he also, near her*) Madam, have I the honor to know you? Condescend to remove your vizard. (Lady E. *lifts her mask. Aside*) Very fine woman, still—decidedly dangerous. (*aloud*) Madam, allow me one precautionary observation—My affections are engaged.

Lady. So I conjectured; for I have noticed you from the window of my house, walking in the garden of Sir Geoffrey Thornside with his fair daughter; and she seems worthy to fix the affections of the most fickle.

Wil. My dear madam, do you know Sir Geoffrey? Bind me to you for life, and say a kind word to him in my favor.

Lady E. Can you need it?—young, highborn, accomplished——

Wil. Sir Geoffrey's very objections against me. He says I am a fine gentleman, and has a vehement aversion to that section of mortals, because he implies that a fine gentleman once did him a mortal injury. But you seem moved—dear lady, what is your interest in Sir Geoffrey or myself?

Lady E. You shall know later. Tell me, did Lucy Thornside ever speak to you of her mother?

Wil. Only to regret, with tears in her eyes, that she had never known a mother—that lady died, I believe, while Lucy was but an infant.

Lady E. When you next have occasion to speak to her, say that you have seen a friend of her mother, who has something to impart that may contribute to her father's happiness and her own.

WIL. I will do your bidding this day, and——
SOFT. (*without*). Oh, never mind announcing me, Smart.
LADY E (*starting up*). I would not be seen here—I must be gone. Call on me at nine o'clock this evening ; this is my address.

SOFTHEAD, *enters* C. D. L., *as* LORD WILMOT *is protecting* LADY E.'s *retreat, and stares aghast.*

WIL. (*aside*). Do not fear him—best little fellow in the world, ambitious to be thought good for nothing, and frightened out of his wits at the sight of a petticoat. (*aloud, as he attends her out*) Allow me to escort your ladyship.   [*Exits.* C D. L., *with* LADY E.
SOFT. Ladyship ! lucky dog. But then he's such a villain !
WIL. (*returning, and looking at card*). Very mysterious visitor—sign of Crown and Portcullis, Deadman's Lane—a very funereal residence. (*observing his visitor apparently for the first time*) Ha, Softhead ! my Pylades—my second self ! *Animæ——*
SOFT. (*astonished, not understanding Latin*). Enemy !
WIL. *Dimidium meæ.*
SOFT. (*aside*). *Dimi !* that's the oath last in fashion, I warrant. (*aloud, with a swagger and a slap on* WILMOT's *back*) *Dimidum meæ !* how d'ye do ? But what is that lady ?—masked too ? Oh, Fred, Fred ; you are a monster !
WIL. Monster ! ay, horrible ! That lady may well wear a mask. She has poisoned three husbands.
SOFT. *Dimidam meæ.*
WIL. A mere ha mless gallantry has no longer a charm for me.
SOFT. Nor for me, either ! (*aside*) Never had.
WIL. Nothing should excite us true men of pleasure but some colossal atrocity, to bring our necks within an inch of the gallows.
SOFT. (*aside*). He's a perfect demon ! Alas, I shall never come up to *his* mark !
Re-enter SMART.

SMART. Mr. Hardman, my Lord.
WIL. Hush ! Must not shock Mr. Hardman, the most friendly, obliging man, and so clever—will be a minister some day. But not of our set.

Enter HARDMAN, C D. L.   *Exit* SMART.

HARD. And how fares my dear Lord ?
WIL. (C.). Bravely—and you ? Ah ! you men who live for others have a hard life of it. Let me present you to my friend, Mr. Shadowly Softhead. (*they salute each other.*)
HARD. (L. C) The son of the great clothier who has such weight in the Guild ? I have heard of you from Mr. Easy and others, though never so fortunate as to meet you before, Mr. Softhead.
SOFT (*bowing*, N. C.). *Shadowly* Softhead—my grandmother was one of the Shadowlys—a genteel family that move about court. She married a Softhead——
WIL. A race much esteemed in the city.
HARD. (*turning aside and glancing at painting*, L.). A new picture, my Lord ? I'm no very great judge—but it seems to me quite a masterpiece
WIL. I've a passion for art. Sold off my stud to buy that picture. (*aside*) And please my poor father. (*aloud*) 'Tis a Murillo.
HARD. A Murillo ! you know that Walpole, too, has a passion for

pictures. In despair at this moment that he can't find a Murillo to hang up in his gallery. If ever you want to corrupt the Prime Minister's virtue, you have only to say, " I have got a Murillo."

WIL. Well, if, instead of the pictures, he'll just hang up the *men* he has bought, you may tell him he shall have my Murillo for nothing !

HARD. Bought? now really, my Lord, this is so vulgar a scandal against Sir Robert. Let me assure your Lordship——

WIL. Lordship! Plague on these titles among friends. Why, if the Duke of Middlesex himself—commonly styled "the Proud Duke "—who said to his Duchess, when she astonished his dignity one day with a kiss, " Madam, my first wife was a Percy, and *she* never took such a liberty——" *

HARD. Ha! ha! well, if "the Proud Duke——"

WIL. Could deign to come here, we would say, " How d'ye do, my dear Middlesex!"

SOFT. So we would, Fred! Middlesex. Shouldn't you like to know a Duke, Mr. Hardman ?

HARD. I have known one or two—in opposition ; and had rather too much of 'em.

SOFT. Too much of a Duke! La! I could never have eno' of a Duke!

HARD. You may live to think otherwise.

Re-enter SMART.

SMART. His Grace the Duke of Middlesex.

Enter DUKE, C. D. L.   *Exit* SMART.

DUKE. My Lord Wilmot, your most obedient servant.

WIL. (*aside*). Now then, courage! (*aloud*) How d'ye do, my dear Middlesex?

DUKE. "How d'ye do?" "Middlesex!" Gracious Heaven; what will this age come to ? (*sits in chair*, C.)

HARD. (*aside, crossing over to* SOFTHEAD). Well, it *may* be the fashion, —yet I could *hardly* advise you to adopt it.

SOFT. But if Fred——

HARD. Oh! certainly Fred is an excellent model——

SOFT. Yet there's something very awful in a live Duke.

HARD. Tut, a mere mortal like ourselves, after all.

SOFT. D'ye really think so ?—upon your honor ?

HARD. Sir, I'm sure of it--upon my honor, a mortal !

DUKE (*turning stiffly round, and half rising from his chair in majestic condescension*). Your Lordship's friends ? A good day to you, gentlemen.

SOFT. And a good day to yourself. My Lord Du—I mean, my dear boy '—Middlesex; how d'ye do ?

DUKE. " Mid !"—" boy !"—" sex !"—" dear !" I must be in a dream.

WIL. (*to* SOFTHEAD). Apologize to the Duke. (*to* HARDMAN) Then

---

* This well-known anecdote of " the Proud Duke " of Somerset, and some other recorded traits of the same eminent personage, have been freely applied to the character, intended to illustrate the humor of pride, in the comedy. None of our English memoirs afford, however, instances of that infirmity so extravagant as are to be found in the French. Tallamant has an anecdote of the celebrated *Duchess de Longueville*, which enlivens the burlesque by a bull that no Irish imagination ever surpassed. A surgeon having probably saved her life by bleeding her too suddenly and without sufficient ceremonial—the *Duchess* said, on recovering herself, that " he was an insolent fellow to have bled her—*in her presence*."

hurry him off into the next room. (*to the* DUKE) Allow me to explain to your Grace.

SOFT. (*to* HARDMAN). But what shall I say?

HARD. Anything most civil and servile.

SOFT. (*aloud, and crossing over toward* L. C., *followed by* HARDMAN). I—I —my Lord Duke, I really most humbly entreat your Grace's pardon, I——

DUKE. Small man, your pardon is granted, for your existence is effaced. So far as my recognition is necessary to your sense of being, consider yourself henceforth—annihilated!

SOFT. (L. C.). I humbly thank your Grace! (*aside, to* HARDMAN) Annihilated! what's that?

HARD. Duke's English for excused. (SOFTHEAD *wants to get back to the* DUKE) What! have not you had enough of the Duke?

SOFT. No, now we've made up. I never bear malice. I should like to know more of him; one can't get at a Duke every day. If he did call me "small man," he is a Duke—and such a remarkably fine one!

HARD. (*drawing him away*). You deserve to be haunted by him! No —no! Come into the next room.

[*Exeunt through side-door,* L. SOFTHEAD *very reluctant to leave the* DUKE.

DUKE. There's something portentous in that small man's audacity. Quite an aberration of Nature! But we are alone now, we two gentlemen. (*motions to* WILMOT *to sit near him—he does so*) Your father is my friend, and his son must have courage and honor.

WIL. Faith, I had the courage to say I would call your Grace "Middlesex," and the honor to keep my word. So I've given good proof that I've honor and courage for anything!

DUKE (*affectionately*). You're a wild boy. You have levities and follies. But alas! even rank does not exempt its possessor from the faults of humanity. Very strange! My own dead brother—(*with a look of disgust.*)

WIL. Your brother, Lord Henry de Mowbray? My dear Duke, pray forgive me; but I hope there's no truth in what Tonson, the bookseller, told me at Will's—that your brother had left behind certain Confessions or Memoirs, which are all that might be apprehended from a man of a temper so cynical, and whose success in the gay world was so—terrible. (*aside*) Determined seducer and implacable cut-throat!

DUKE. Ha! then those Memoirs exist! My brother kept his profligate threat. I shall be ridiculed, lampooned. I, the head of the Mowbrays! Powers above, is nothing on earth then left sacred! Can you learn in whose hands is this scandalous record?

WIL. I will try. Leave it to me. I know Lord Henry bore you a grudge for renouncing his connection on account of his faults—of humanity! I remember an anecdote, how he fought with a husband, some poor devil named Morland, for a boast in a tavern, which—Oh, but we'll not speak of that. We must get the Memoir. We gentlemen have all common cause here.

DUKE (*taking his hand*). Worthy son of your father. You deserve indeed the trust that I come to confide to you. Listen. His Majesty, King James, having been deceived by vague promises in the Expedition of 'Fifteen, has very properly refused to imperil his rights again, unless upon the positive pledge of a sufficient number of persons of influence to risk life and all in his service. Myself and some others, not wholly unknown to you, propose to join in a pledge which our King with such reason exacts. Your assistance, my Lord, would be valuable, for you are the idol of the young. Doubts were entertained of your loyalty. I have come to dispel them—a word will suffice. If we succeed, you restore the son of a Stuart; if we fail—you will go to the scaffold by the side of John, Duke of Middlesex! Can you hesitate? or is silence assent?

WIL. My dear Duke, forgive me that I dismiss with a jest a subject so fatal, if gravely entertained. I have so many other engagements at present that, just to recollect them, I must keep my head on my shoulders. Accept my humblest excuses.

DUKE. Accept mine for mistaking the son of Lord Loftus. (*rises and goes up to* C. D.)

WIL. Lord Loftus again! (*rising*) Stay. Your Grace spoke of persons not wholly unknown to me. I entreat you to explain.

DUKE. My Lord, I have trusted you with my own life; but to compromise by a word the life of another!—permit me to remind your Lordship that I am John, Duke of Middlesex.　　　[*Exit*, C D. L

WIL. Can my father have entangled himself in some Jacobite plot? How shall I find out? Ha! Hardman, Hardman, I say! Here's a man who finds everything out.

Re-enter HARDMAN *and* SOFTHEAD.

Softhead, continue annihilated for the next five minutes or so. These books will help to the cessation of your existence, mental and bodily. Mr. Locke, on the Understanding, will show that you have not an innate idea; and the Essay of Bishop Berkeley will prove you have not an atom of matter.

SOFT. But——

WIL. No buts!—they're the fashion.

SOFT. Oh, if they're the fashion—(*seats himself at the table*, R. 3 E., *and commences to read vigorously, gradually subsiding into dozing*)

WIL. (C.—*to* HARDMAN, L. C.). My dear Hardman, you are the only one of my friends whom, in spite of your politics, my high Tory father condescends to approve of. Every one knows that his family were stout cavaliers attached to the Stuarts.

HARD. (*aside*). Ah! I guess why the Jacobite Duke has been here. I must look up David Fallen; he is in all the schemes for the Stuarts. Well—and——

WIL. And the Jacobites are daring and numerous; and—in short, I should just like to know that my father views things with the eyes of our more wise generation.

HARD. Why not ask him yourself?

WIL. Alas! I'm in disgrace; he even begs me not to come to his house. You see he wants me to marry.

HARD. But your father bade me tell you he would leave your choice to yourself;—would marriage then seem so dreadful a sacrifice?

WIL. Sacrifice! Leave my choice to myself? My dear father. (*rings the hand-bell*) Smart! (*re-enter* SMART) Order my coach.　　　[*Exit* SMART.

HARD. This impatience looks very like love.

WIL. Pooh! what do you know about love?—you—who love only ambition! Solemn old jilt, with whom one's never safe from a rival.

HARD. Yes;—always safe from a rival, both in love and ambition, if one will watch to detect, and then scheme to destroy him.

WIL. Destroy—ruthless exterminator! May we never be rivals! Pray keep to ambition.

HARD. But ambition lures me to love. (*aside*) This fair Lucy Thornside, as rich as she's fair! woe indeed to the man who shall be my rival with her. (*aloud*) I will call there to-day.

WIL. Then you'll see my father, and sound him?

HARD. I will do so.

WIL. You are the best friend I have. If ever I can serve you in return——

HARD. Tut! in serving my friends 'tis myself that I serve.
                                                    [*Exit*, C. D. L.

WIL (*after a moment's thought*). Now to Lucy. Ha! Softhead.

SOFT. (*waking up*). Heh!

WIL. (*aside*). I must put this suspicious Sir Geoffrey on a wrong scent. If Softhead were to make love to the girl—violently—desperately.

SOFT. (*yawning*). I would give the world to be tucked up in bed now.

WIL. I've a project—an intrigue—be all life and all fire! Why, you tremble——

SOFT. With excitement. (*rises and advances*) Proceed!

WIL. There's a certain snarling, suspicious Sir Geoffrey Thornside, with a beautiful daughter, to whom he is a sort of a one-sided bear of a father—all growl and no hug.

SOFT. I know him!

WIL You? How?

SOFT. Why, his most intimate friend is Mr. Goodenough Easy.

WIL Lucy presented me to a Mistress Barbara Easy. Pretty girl.

SOFT. You are not courting her?

WIL. Not at present. Are you?

SOFT. Why, my father wants me to marry her.

WIL. You refused?

SOFT. No. I did not.

WIL. Had *she* that impertinence?

SOFT. No; but her father had. He wished for it once; but since I've become *à la mode*, and made a sensation at St. James's, he says that his daughter shall be courted no more by a man of such fashion. Oh! he's low—Mr. Easy; very good-humored and hearty, but respectable, sober, and square-toed;—decidedly low!—City bred! So I can't go much to his house; but I see Barbara sometimes at Sir Geoffrey's.

WIL Excellent! Listen. I am bent upon adding Lucy Thornside to the list of my conquests. But her churl of a father has already given me to understand that he hates a lord——

SOFT. Hates a lord! Can such men be?

WIL. And despises a man *à la mode*.

SOFT. I knew he was eccentric, but this is downright insanity.

WIL. Brief. I see very well that he'll soon shut his doors in my face, unless I make him believe that it is not his daughter who attracts me to his house; so I tell you what we will do;—you shall make love to Lucy —violent love, you rogue.

SOFT. But Sir Geoffrey knows I'm in love with the other.

WIL. That's over. Father refused you—transfer of affection; natural pique and human inconstancy. And, in return, to oblige you, I'll make love just as violent to Mistress Barbara Easy.

SOFT. Stop, stop; I don't see the necessity of that.

WIL. Pooh! nothing more clear. Having thus duped the two lookers-on, we shall have ample opportunity to change partners, and hands across, then down the middle, and up again.

Re-enter SMART.

SMART.. Your coach waits, my Lord.

WIL. Come along. Fie! that's not the way to conduct a cane. (*acts as though he had a cane in his hand*) Has not Mr. Pope, our great poet of fashion, given you the nicest instructions in that art? (SOFTHEAD *imitates him with intense admiration*.)

> " Sir Plume, of amber snuff-box justly vain,
> And the nice conduct of a clouded cane."

The cane does not conduct you; you conduct the cane. Thus, with a *debonnair* swing. Now, t'other hand on your haunch ; easy, *dégagé*—impudently graceful; with the air of a gentleman, and the heart of a— monster! *Allons ! Vive la joie.*

SOFT. *Vive la jaw*, indeed. I feel as if I were going to be hanged. *Allons ! Vive la jaw !*   [*Exeunt*, C. D.

ACT II.

SCENE I.—*Library in the house of* SIR GEOFFREY THORNSIDE.

Enter SIR GEOFFREY *and* HODGE, L. D.

SIR GEOFFREY. But I say the dog did howl last night, and it is a most suspicious circumstance.

HODGE. Fegs. my dear measter, if you'se think that these Lunnon thieves have found out that your honor's rents were paid last wolk, mayhap I'd best sleep here in the loibery.

SIR GEOF. (*aside*). How does he know I keep my moneys here ?

HODGE. Zooks! I'se the old b.underbuss, and that will boite better than any dog, I'se warrant !

SIR GEOF. (*aside*). I begin to suspecthim. For ten years have I nursed that viper at my heart, and now he wants to sleep in my library, with a loaded blunderbuss, in case I should come in and detect him. I see murder in his very face. How blind I've been ! (*aloud*) Hodge, you are very good—very; come closer. (*aside*) What a felon step he has ! (*aloud*, But I don't keep my rents here, they're all gone to the banker's.

HODGE. Mayhap I'd best go and lock up the plate ; or will you send that to the banker's ?

SIR GEOF. (*aside*). I wonder if he has got an accomplice at the banker's ! It looks uncommonly like it. (*aloud*) No, I'll not send the plate to the banker's; I'll—consider. You've ot detected the miscreant who has been flinging flowers into the library the last four days ?—or observed any one watching your master when he walks in his garden, from the window of that ugly old house in Deadman's Lane ?

HODGE. With the sign of the Crown and Poor Cully ? Why, it maun be very leately. 'Tint a week ago 'sin it war empty.

SIR GEOF. (*aside*). How he evades the question—just as they do at the Old Bailey. (*aloud*) Get along with you and feed the house-dog—*he's honest !*

HODGE. Yes, your honor.   [*Exit*, L. D.

SIR GEOF. (C.). I'm a very unhappy man, very. Never did harm to any one—done good to many. And ever since I was a babe in the cradle, all the world have been conspiring and plotting against me. It certainly is an exceedingly wicked world ; and what its attraction can be to the other worlds, that they should have kept it spinning through space for six thousand years, I can't possibly conceive—unless they are as bad as itself; I should not wonder. That new theory of atrraction is a very suspicious circumstances against the planets—there's a gang of 'em! (*a bunch of flowers is thrown in at the window*) Heaven defend me! There it is again! This is the fifth bunch of flowers that's been thrown at me through the window—what can it possibly mean?—the most alarming circumstance. (*cautiously poking at the flowers with his sword.*)

MR. GOODENOUGH EASY (*without*, L.). Yes, Barbara, go and find Mistress Lucy. (*entering*, R. D.) How d'ye do, my hearty?

SIR GEOF. Ugh! hearty, indeed!

EASY. Why, what's the matter? what are you poking at those flowers for?—is there a snake in them?

SIR GEOF. Worse than that, I suspect! Hem! Goodenough Easy, I believe I may trust you——

EASY. You trusted me once with five thousands pounds.

SIR GEOF. Dear, dear, I forgot that. But you paid me back, Easy?

EASY. Of course; but the loan saved my credit, and made my fortune; so the favor's the same.

SIR GEOF. Ugh! Don't say that; favors and perfidy go together! a truth I learned early in life. What favors I heaped on my foster brother. And did not he conspire with my cousin to set my own father against me, and trick me out of my heritage?

EASY. But you've heaped favors as great on the son of that scamp of a foster brother; and he——

SIR GEOF. Ay! but he don't know of them. And then there was my—that girl's mother——

EASY. Ah! that was an affliction which might well turn a man, pre-inclined to suspicion, into a thorough self-tormentor for the rest of his life. But she loved you dearly once, old friend; and were she yet alive, an I could be proved guiltless after all——

SIR GEOF. Guiltless! Sir?

EASY. Well—well!, we agreed never to talk upon that subject. Come, come, what of the nosegay?

SIR GEOF. Yes, yes, the nosegay! Hark! I suspect some design on my life. The dog howled last night. When I walk in the garden some-body or something (can't see what it is) seems at the watch at a window in Deadman's Lane—pleasant name for a street at the back of one's premises! And what looks blacker than all, for five days running, has been thrown in at me, yonder, surreptitiously and anonymously, what you call—a nosegay!

EASY. Ha, ha! you lucky dog!—you are still not bad-looking. Depend on it the flowers come from a woman.

SIR GEOF. A woman!—my worst fears are confirmed! In the small city of Placentia, in one year, there were no less than seven hundred cases of slow poisoning, and all by woman. Flowers were among the instruments they employed, steeped in laurel water and other mephitic preparations. Those flowers are poisoned. Not a doubt of it!—how very awful!

EASY. But why should any one take the trouble to poison you, Geoffrey?

SIR GEOF. I don't know. But I don't know why seven hundred people in one year were poisoned in Placentia. Hodge! Hodge!

Re-enter HODGE.

Sweep away those flowers—lock 'em up with the rest in the coal-hole. I ll examine them all chemically, by and by, with precaution. (HODGE *picks up the bunch of flowers*) Don't smell at 'em; and, above all, don't let the house dog smell at 'em.   [*Exit* HODGE, L. D.

EASY. Ha! ha!

SIR GEOF. (*aside*). Ugh!—that brute's laughing—no more feeling than a brick-bat. (*aloud*) Goodenough Easy, you are a very happy man.

EASY. Happy, yes. I could be happy on bread and water.

SIR GEOF. And would toast your bread at a conflagration, and fill your jug from a deluge! Ugh! I've a trouble you are more likely to feel for, as you've a girl of your own to keep out of mischief. A man named Wilmot, and styled "my Lord," has called here a great many times; he pretends he saved my——ahem!—that is, Lucy, from foot-pads, when she was coming home from your house in a sedan chair. And I suspect that man means to make love to her!——

EASY. Egad! that's the only likely suspicion you've hit on this many a day. I've heard of Lord Wilmot. Softhead professes to copy him. Softhead, the son of a trader! he be a lounger at White's and Will's, and dine with wits and fine gentlemen! He live with lords!—he mimic fashion! No! I've respect for even the faults of a man; but I've none for the tricks of a monkey.

SIR GEOF. Ugh! you're so savage on Softhead, I suspect 'tis from envy. Man and monkey, indeed! If a ribbon is tied to the tail of a monkey, it is not the man it enrages; it is some other monkey whose tail has no ribbon!

EASY (*angrily*). I disdain your insinuations. Do you mean to imply that I am a monkey? I will not praise myself; but at least a more steady, respectable, sober——

SIR GEOF. Ugh! sober!—I suspect you'd get as drunk as a lord, if a lord passed the bottle.

EASY. Now, now, now. Take care;—you'll put me in a passion.

SIR GEOF. There—there—beg pardon. But I fear you've a sneaking respect for a lord.

EASY. Sir, I respect the British Constitution and the House of Peers as a part of it; but as for a lord in himself, with a mere handle to his name, a paltry title! That can have no effect on a Briton of independence and sense. And that's just the difference between Softhead and me. But as you don't like for a son-in-law the real fine gentleman, perhaps you've a mind to the copy. I am sure you are welcome to Softhead.

SIR GEOF. Ugh! I've other designs for the girl.

EASY. Have you? What? Perhaps your favorite, young Hardman?—by the way, I've not met him here lately.

Enter LUCY *and* BARBARA, R. D.

LUCY. O, my dear father, forgive me if I disturb you; but I did so long to see you!

SIR GEOF. Why?

LUCY. Ah, father, is it so strange that your child——

SIR GEOF. (*interrupting her*). Why?

LUCY. Because Hodge told me you'd been alarmed last night—the dog howled! But it was full moon last night, and he will howl at the moon!

SIR GEOF. (*aside*). How did she know it was full moon? I suspect she was looking out of the window——

Re-enter HODGE.

HODGE. Lord Wilmot and Mr. Shadowly Softhead.   [*Exit* HODGE.

SIR GEOF. (*aside*). Wilmot! my suspicions are confirmed; she *was* looking out of the window! This comes of Shakespeare having written that infernal incendiary trash about Romeo and Juliet!

Enter WILMOT *and* SOFTHEAD, L. D.

WIL. Your servant, ladies;—Sir Geoffrey, your servant. I could not refuse Mr. Softhead's request to inquire after your health.

SIR GEOF. I thank your Lordship; but when my health wants inquiring after I send for the doctor.

WIL. Is it possible you can do anything so dangerous and rash?

SIR GEOF. How?—how?

WIL. Send for the very man who has an interest in your being ill!

SIR GEOF. (*aside*). That's very true. I did not think he had so much sense in him! (SIR GEOFFREY *and* EASY *retire up the stage.*)

WIL. I need not inquire how you are, ladies. When Hebe retired from the world, she divided her bloom between you. Mistress Barbara, vouchsafe me the honor a queen accords to the meanest of her gentlemen. (*kisses* BARBARA'S *hand, and leads her aside, conversing in dumb show.*)

SOFT. Ah, Mistress Lucy, vouchsafe me the honor which—(*aside*) But she don't hold her hand in the same position.

EASY (*advancing and patting him on the shoulder*). Bravo!—bravo! Master Softhead!—*Encore!*

SOFT. Bravo!—*Encore!* I don't understand you, Mr. Easy.

EASY. That bow of yours! Perfect. Plain to see you have not forgotten the old dancing master in Crooked Lane.

SOFT. (*aside*). I'm not an inconstant man; but I'll show that city fellow there are other ladies in town besides his daughter. (*aloud*) *Dimidium meæ*, how pretty you are, Mistress Lucy! (*walks aside with her.*)

SIR GEOF. That popinjay of a lord is more attentive to Barbara than ever he was to the other.

EASY. Hey! hey! D'ye think so?

SIR GEOF. I suspect he has heard how rich you are. (WILMOT *and* BARBARA *approach.*)

BAR. Papa, Lord Wilmot begs to be presented to you. ·(*bows interchanged.* WILMOT *offers snuff-box.* EASY *at first declines then accepts—sneezes violently ; unused to snuff.*)

SIR GEOF. He! he! quite clear! titled fortune-hunter. Over head and ears in debt, I dare say. (*takes* WILMOT *aside*) Pretty girl, Mistress Barbara! Eh?

WIL. Pretty! Say beautiful!

SIR GEOF. He! he! Her father will give her fifty thousand pounds down on the wedding day.

WIL. I venerate the British merchant who can give his daughter fifty thousand pounds! What a smile she has! (*hooking his arm into* SIR GEOFFREY'S) I say, Sir Geoffrey, you see I'm very shy—bashful, indeed —and Mr. Easy is watching every word I say to his daughter; so embarrassing! Couldn't you get him out of the room?

SIR GEOF. Mighty bashful, indeed! Turn the oldest friend I have out of my room, in order that you may make love to his daughter! (*turns away.*)

WIL. (*to* EASY). I say, Mr. Easy. My double there, Softhead, is so shy—bashful, indeed—and that suspicious Sir Geoffrey is watching every word he says to Mistress Lucy; so embarrassing! Do get your friend out of the room, will you?

EASY. Ha! ha! Certainly, my Lord. (*aside*) I see he wants to be alone with my Barbara. What will they say in Lombard street when she's my lady? Shouldn't wonder if they returned me M.P. for the city. (*aloud*)

Come into the next room, Geoffrey, and tell me your designs for
Lucy.

Sir Geof. Oh, very well! You wish to encourage that pampered
young—satrap! (*aside*) How he does love a lord, and how a lord does
love fifty thousand pounds! He! he!

[*Exeunt* Sir Geoffrey *and* Easy, R. D.

Wil. (*running to* Lucy *and pushing aside* Softhead). Return to your
native allegiance. Truce with the enemy and exchange of prisoners.
(*leads* Lucy *aside—she rather grave and reluctant.*)

Bar. So you'll not speak to me, Mr. Softhead; words are too rare
with you fine gentlemen to throw away upon old friends.

Soft. Ahem!

Bar. You don't remember the winter evenings you used to pass at
our fireside? nor the mistletoe bough at Christmas? nor the pleasant
games at Blindman's Buff and Hunt the Slipper? nor the strong tea I
made you when you had the migraine? Nor how I prevented your
eating Banbury cake at supper, when you know it always disagrees with
you? But I suppose you are so hardened that you can eat Banbury
cake every night now! I'm sure 'tis nothing to me!

Soft. Those recollections of one's early innocence are very melting!
One renounces a great deal of happiness for renown and ambition. Barbara!

Bar. Shadowly!

Soft. However one may rise in life—however the fashion may compel
one to be a monster——

Bar. A monster!

Soft. Yes, Fred and I are both monsters! Still—still—still—'Ecod,
I do love you with all my heart, and that's the truth of it.

Wilmot *and* Lucy *advancing.*

Lucy. A friend of my lost mother's. Oh! yes, dear Lord Wilmot, do
see her again—learn what she has to say. There are times when I so
long to speak of that—my mother; but my father shuns even to mention her name. Ah, he must have loved her well!

Wil. What genuine susceptibility! I have found what I have sought all
my life, the union of womanly feeling and childlike innocence. (*attempts
to take her hand;* Lucy *withdraws it coyly*) Nay, nay, if the renunciation
of all youthful levities and follies, if the most steadfast adherence to
your side—despite all the chances of life, all temptations, all dangers—
(Hardman's *voice without,* L.)

Bar. Hist! some one coming.

Wil. Change partners; hands across. (Wilmot *joins* Barbara, Softhead *joins* Lucy) My angel Barbara!

Enter Hardman, L. D.

Hard. (*aside, astonished*). Lord Wilmot here!

Wil. (*aside to* Barbara). What! does *he* know Sir Geoffrey?

Bar. Oh, yes. Sir Geoffrey thinks there's nobody like him.

Wil. (*aloud*). Well met, my dear Hardman. So you are intimate
here?

Hard. Ay; and you?

Wil. An acquaintance in its cradle. Droll man, Sir Geoffrey; I delight in odd characters. Besides, here are other attractions. (*returning
to* Barbara.)

Hard. (*aside*). If he be my rival! Hum! I hear from David Fallen that his father's on the brink of high treason! That secret gives a hold on the son. (*joins* LUCY.)

WIL. (*to* BARBARA). You understand; 'tis a compact. You will favor my stratagem?

BAR. Yes; and you'll engage to cure Softhead of his taste for the fashion, and send him back to—the city.

WIL. Since you live in the city, and condescend to regard such a monster!

BAR. Why, we were brought up together. His health is so delicate; I should like to take care of him. Heigho! I am afraid 'tis too late, and papa will never forgive his past follies.

WIL. Yet papa seems very good-natured. Perhaps there's another side to his character?

BAR. Oh, yes! He is such a very independent man, my papa! and has *such* a contempt for people who go out of their own rank, and make fools of themselves for the sake of example.

WIL. Never fear; I'll ask him to dine, and open his heart with a cheerful glass.

BAR. Cheerful glass! You don't know papa—the soberest man! If there's anything on which he's severe, 'tis a cheerful glass.

WIL. So so! does not he *ever*—get a little excited?

BAR. Excited! Don't think of it! Besides, he is so in awe of Sir Geoffrey, who would tease him out of his life, if he could but hear that papa was so inconsistent as to—as to——

WIL. As to get—a little excited? (*aside*) These hints should suffice me! 'Gad, if I could make him tipsy for once in a way! I'll try. (*aloud*) Adieu, my sweet Barbara, and rely on the zeal of your faithful ally. Stay! tell Mr. Easy that he must lounge into Will's. I will look out for him there in about a couple of hours. He'll meet many friends from the city, and all the wits and fine gentlemen. *Allons! Vive la joie!* Softhead, we'll have a night of it!

SOFT. Ah! those were pleasant nights when one went to bed at half after ten. Heigho! (*as* HARDMAN *kisses* LUCY's *hand,* WILMOT *gayly kisses* BARBARA'S—HARDMAN *observes him with a little suspicion*—WILMOT *returns his look lightly and carelessly*—LUCY *and* BARBARA *conscious*

ACT III.

SCENE I.—*Will's Coffee House; occupying the depth of the stage.* JACOB TONSON *and various groups; some seated in boxes, some standing. In the half-open box at the side,* R., DAVID FALLEN, *seated writing.*

Enter EASY, C. D. L., *speaking to various acquaintances as he passes round.*

EASY. How d'ye do? Have you seen my Lord Wilmot? Good day. Yes; I seldom come here; but I've promised to meet an intimate friend of mine—Lord Wilmot. Servant, sir!—looking for my friend Wilmot. Oh! not come yet!—hum—ha!—charming young man, Wilmot; head of the mode; generous, but prudent. I know all his affairs. (*mixes with the group, conversing with* TONSON, *etc.*)

Enter NEWSMAN, C. D., *with papers.*

NEWSMAN. Great news! great news! Suspected Jacobite Plot! Fears of Ministers! Army to be increased! Great news! (*Coffee-house frequenters gather round* NEWSMAN—*take papers—form themselves into fresh groups about the stage.*)

Enter HARDMAN, L. 2 E.

HARD I have sent off my letter to Sir Robert Walpole. This place, he must give it; the first favor I have asked. Hope smiles; I am at peace with all men. Now to save Wilmot's father. (*approaches the box at which* DAVID FALLEN *is writing, and stoops down, as if arranging his buckle; to* FALLEN) Hist! Whatever the secret, remember, not a word save to me. (*passes up the stage, and is eagerly greeted by various frequenters of the Coffee house.*)

Enter LORD LOFTUS, C. D. L., *and advances to the half open box,* L.

LORD LOFTUS. Drawer, I engage this box; give me the newspaper. So—" Rumored Jacobite Plot."

The DUKE OF MIDDLESEX *enters,* C. D L., *and proceeds to join* LOFTUS.

DUKE. My dear Lord, I obey your appointment. But is not the place you select rather strange?

LOF. Be seated, I pray you. No place so fit for our purpose. First, because its very publicity prevents all suspicion. We come to a coffee-house, where all ranks and all parties assemble, to hear the news, like the rest. And, secondly, we could scarcely meet our agent anywhere else. He is a Tory pamphleteer; was imprisoned for our sake in the time of William and Mary. If we, so well known to be Tories, are seen to confer with him here, 'twill only be thought that we are suggesting some points in a pamphlet. May I beckon our agent?

DUKE. Certainly. He risks his life for us; he shall be duly rewarded. Let him sit by our side. (LORD LOFTUS *motions to* DAVID FALLEN, *who takes his pamphlet and approaches open'y*) I have certainly seen somewhere before that very thin man. Be seated, sir. Honorable danger makes all men equal.

FAL. No, my Lord Duke. I know you not. It is the Earl I confer with. (*aside*) I never stood in *his* hall, with lackeys and porters.

DUKE (*to* LOFTUS). Powers above! That scare-crow rejects my acquaintance! Portentous! (*stunned and astonished.*)

LOF. Observe Duke, we speak in a sort of jargon. Pamphlet means messenger. (*to* FALLEN *aloud*) Well, Mr. Fallen, when will the pamphlet be ready?

FAL. (*aloud*). To-morrow, my Lord, exactly at one o'clock.

DUKE (*still bewildered*). I don't understand——

LOF. (*aside*). Hush! Walpole laughs at pamphlets, but would hang messengers. (*aloud*) To-morrow, not to-day! Well, more time for——

FAL. Subscribers. Thank you, my Lord. (*whispering*) Where shall the messenger meet you?

LOF. At the back of the Duke's new house there is a quiet, lone place——

FAL. (*whispering*). By the old mill near the Thames? I know it. The messenger shall be there. The signal word " Marston Moor." No conversation should pass. But who brings the packet? That's the first step of danger.

DUKE (*suddenly rousing himself, and with dignity*). Then 'tis mine, sir, in right of my birth.

FAL. (*aloud*). I'll attend to all your Lordship's suggestions; they're excellent, and will startle this vile administration. Many thanks to your Lordship. (*returns to his table and resumes his writing. Groups point and murmur.* JACOB TONSON *and* EASY *advance.*)

EASY. That pestilence scribbler, David Fallen! Another libellous pamphlet as bitter as the last, I'll swear.

TON. Bitter as gall, sir, I am proud to say. Your servant, Jacob Tonson, the bookseller—at your service. I advanced a pound upon it. (*they continue talking and mingle with the others.*)

DUKE (*to* LOFTUS) I will meet you in the Mall to-morrow, a quarter after one precisely. We may go now? (*they rise and go towards* C. D., LOFTUS *in front*) Powers above—his mind's distracted—he walks out before me!

LOF. (*drawing back at the door*). I follow you, Duke.

DUKE. My dear friend—if you really insist on it.

[*Exeunt,* C. D. L., *bowing.*

DRAWER *enters,* R. D., *with wine, etc., which he places on the table,* R.

HARD. Let me offer you a glass of wine, Mr. Fallen. (*aside to him*) Well? (*sits near* FALLEN. FALLEN, *who has been writing, pushes the paper towards him.*)

HARD. (*reading*). "At one to-morrow—by the old mill near the Thames – Marston Moor—the Duke in person." So! We must save these men. I will call on you in the morning, and concert the means.

FAL. Yes; save, not destroy, these enthusiasts. I'm resigned to the name of hireling—not to that of a butcher!

HARD. You serve both Whig and Jacobite; do you care then for either?

FAL. Sneering politician! what has either cared for me? I entered the world, devoted heart and soul to two causes—the throne of the Stuart, the glory of Letters. I saw them both as a poet. My father left me no heritage but loyalty and learning. Charles the Second praised my verse, and I starved; James the Second praised my prose, and I starved; the reign of King William—I passed *that* in prison.

HARD. But the ministers of Anne were gracious to writers.

FAL. And offered me a pension to belie my past life, and write Odes on the Queen who had dethroned her own father. I was not then disenchanted—I refused. That's years ago. If I starved, I had fame. Now came my worst foes, my own fellow writers. What is fame but a fashion? A jest upon Grub Street, a rhyme from young Pope, could jeer a score of gray laborers like me out of their last consolation. Time and hunger tame all. I could still starve myself; I have six children at home—they must live.

HARD. (*aside*). This man has genius—he might have been a grace to his age. I'm perplexed. (*aloud*) Sir Robert——

FAL. Disdains letters—I've renounced them. He pays services like these. Well, I serve him. Leave me; go!

HARD. (*rising, aside*). Not so bad as he seems—another side to the character.

Enter DRAWER, L. D., *with a letter to* HARDMAN.

HARD. (*aside*). From Walpole! Now then! my fate—my love—my fortunes!

EASY. (*peeping over* HARDMAN'S *shoulder*). He has got a letter from the Prime Minister, marked " private and confidential." (*great agitation*) After all, he *is* a very clever fellow. (*Coffee-house frequenters evince the readiest assent, and the liveliest admiration.*)

HARD. (*advancing and reading the letter*). "My dear Hardman,—Extremely sorry. Place in question absolutely wanted to conciliate some noble family otherwise dangerous.* Another time, more fortunate. Fully sensible of your valuable service.—ROBERT WALPOLE."—Refused! Let him look to himself! I will—I will—alas! he is needed by my country; and I am powerless against him. (*seats himself.*)

Enter WILMOT *and* SOFTHEAD, C. D. L.

WIL. Drawer! a private room—covers for six—dinner in an hour!† And—drawer! Tell Mr. Tonson not to go yet. Softhead, we'll have an orgie to-night, worthy the days of King Charles the Second. Softhead, let me present you to our boon companions—my friend, Lord Strongbow (hardest in drinker England); Sir John Bruin, best boxer in England --threshed Figg; quarrelsome but pleasant; Colonel Flint—finest gentleman in England and, out and out, the best fencer; mild as a lamb, but can't bear contradiction, and on the point of honor, inexorable. Now for the sixth. Ha, Mr. Easy! (I ask him to serve you) Easy, your hand! So charmed that you've come. You'll dine with us—give up five invitations on purpose. Do—*sans cérémonie.*

EASY. Why, really, my Lord, a plain, sober man like me would be out of place——

WIL. If that's all, never fear. Live with us, and we'll make another man of you, Easy.

EASY. What captivating familiarity! Well, I cannot resist your Lordship. (*strutting down the room, and speaking to his acquaintances*) Yes, my friend Wilmot—Lord Wilmot—will make me dine with him   Pleasant man, my friend Wilmot. We dine together to-day. (SOFTHEAD *retires to the background with the other invited guests; but trying hard to escape* SIR JOHN BRUIN, *the boxer, and* COLONEL FLINT, *the fencer, fastens himself on* EASY *with an air of patronage.*)

WIL. (*aside*). Now to serve the dear Duke. (*aloud*) You have not yet bought the Memoir of a late Man of Quality.

TON. Not yet, my Lord; just been trying; hard work. (*wipes his forehead*) But the person who has it is luckily very poor! one of my own authors.

WIL. (*aside*). His eye turns to that forlorn-looking spectre I saw him tormenting. (*aloud*) That must be one of your authors; he look so lean, Mr. Tonson.

TON. Hush; that's the man! made a noise in his day; David Fallen.

WIL. David Fallen, whose books, when I was but a schoolboy, made me first take to reading—not as task-work, but pleasure. How much I do owe him! (*bows very low to* MR. FALLEN.)

TON. My Lord bows very low! Oh, if your Lordship knows Mr. Fallen, pray tell him not to stand in his own light. I would give him a vast sum for the memoir—two hundred guineas; on my honor I would! (*whispering*) Scandal, my Lord; sell like wild-fire.—I say, Mr Hardman, I observed you speak to poor David. Can't you help me here! (*whispering*) Lord Henry de Mowbray's Private Memoirs! Fallen has them, and refuses to sell. Love Adventures; nuts for the public. Only

---

* As Walpole was little inclined to make it a part of his policy to conciliate those whose opposition might be dangerous, while he was so fond of power as to be jealous of talent not wholly subservient to him, the reluctance to promote Mr. Hardman, implied in the insincerity of his excuse, may be supposed to arise from his knowledge of that gentleman's restless ambition and determined self-will.

† It was not the custom at Will's to serve dinners; and the exception in favor of my Lord Wilmot proves his influence as a man à la mode.

just got a peep myself. But *such* a confession about the beautiful Lady Morland.

HARD. Hang Lady Morland!

TON Besides—shows up his own brother! Jacobite family secrets. Such a card for the Whigs!

HARD. Confound the Whigs! What do I care?

WIL I'll see to it, Tonson. Give me Mr. Fallen's private address.

TON. But pray be discreet, my Lord If that knave Curll should get wind of the scent, he'd try to spoil my market with my own author. The villain!

WIL. (*aside*). Curll? Why, I have mimick'd Curll so exactly that Pope himself was deceived, and, stifling with rage, ordered me out of the room I have it! Mr. Curll shall call upon Fallen the first thing in the morning, and outbid Mr Tonson. (*aloud*) Thank you, sir. (*taking the address*) Moody, Hardman? some problem in political ethics? You turn away —you have a grief you'll not tell me—why, this morning I asked you a favor; from that moment I had a right to your confidence, for a favo degrades when it does not come from a friend.

HARD. You charm, you subdue me, and I feel for once how necessary to a man is the sympathy of another. Your hand, Wilmot. This is secret—I, too, then presume to love. One above me in fortune; it may be in birth. But a free state lifts those it employs to a par with its nobles. A post in the Treasury of such nature is vacant; I have served the minister men say, with some credit; and I asked for the gift without shame—'twas my due. Walpole needs the office, not for reward to the zealous, but for bribe to the doubtful. See, (*giving letter*) "Noble family to conciliate." Ah, the drones have the honey!

WIL. (*reading and returning the letter*). And had you this post, you think you could gain the lady you love?

HARD. At least it would have given me courage to ask. Well, well, well,—a truce with my egotism,—you at least, my fair Wilmot, fair in form, fair in fortune, you need fear no rebuff where you place your affections.

WIL Why, the lady's father sees only demerits in what you think my advantages.

HARD. You mistake, I know the man much better than you do; and look, even now he is gazing upon you as fondly as if on the coronet that shall blazon the coach of my lady, his daughter.

WIL. Gazing on me?—where?

HARD. Yonder—Ha! is it not Mr. Easy, whose——

WIL. Mr. Easy! you too taken in! Hark, secret for secret—'tis Lucy Thornside I love,

HARD. You—stun me!

WIL But what a despot love is, allows no thought not its slave! They told me below that my father had been here; have you seen him? HARD. Ay.

WIL. And sounded?

HARD. No—better than that—I have taken precautions. I must leave you now; you shall know the result to-morrow afternoon. (*aside*) Your father's life in these hands—his ransom what I please to demand.—Ah, joy! I am myself once again. Fool to think man could be my friend! Ah, joy! born but for the strife and the struggle, it is only 'mid foes that my invention is quickened! Half-way to my triumph, now that I know the rival to vanquish! (*to* FALLEN) Engage the messenger at one, forget not. Nothing else till I see you (*to* WILMOT) Your hand once again. To-day I'm your envoy; (*aside*) to-morrow your master.

[*Exit*, C. D. L. FALLEN *folds up papers and exits*, C. D. L.

WIL. The friendliest man that ever lived since the days of Damon and
Pythias: I'm a brute if I don't serve him in return. To lose the woman
he loves for want of this pitiful place. Saint Cupid forbid! Let me
consider! Many sides to a character—I think I could here hit the right
one better than Hardman. Ha! ha! Excellent! My Murillo! I'll
not sell myself, but I'll buy the Prime Minister! Excuse me, my
friends; urgent business; I shall be back ere the dinner hour; the
room is prepared. Drawer, show in these gentlemen; Hardman shall
have his place and his wife, and I'll bribe the arch-briber! Ho! my
lackeys, my coach, there! Ha, ha! bribe the Prime Minister! There
never was such a fellow as I am for crime and audacity.

[Exit WILMOT, C. D. L.

COL. FLINT. Your arm, Mr. Softhead.

SOFT. And Fred leaves me in the very paws of this tiger!

[*Exeunt*, C. D. L., *as the scene closes in, the loungers making way for them.*]

SCENE II.—*The Library in* SIR GEOFFREY'S *house.*

Enter SIR GEOFFREY, L. 1 E.

SIR GEOF. I'm followed! I'm dogged! I go out for a walk unsuspi-
ciously; and behind creeps a step, pit, pat; feline and stealthy; I turn,
not a soul to be seen—I walk on; pit, pat, stealthy and feline! turn
again; and lo! a dark form like a phantom, muffled and masked—just
seen and just gone. Ouf! The plot thickens around me—I can struggle
no more. (*sinks into seat*, R.)

Enter LUCY, L. 1 E.

Who is there?

LUCY. But your child, my dear father.

SIR GEOF. Child, ugh! what do you want?

LUCY. Ah, speak to me gently. It is your heart that I want:

SIR GEOF. Heart—I suspect I'm to be coaxed out of something!
Eh; eh! Why she's weeping. What ails thee, poor darling? (*rises.*)

LUCY. So kind. Now I have courage to tell you. I was sitting alone,
and I thought to myself—"my father often doubts of me—doubts of
all——"

SIR GEOF. Ugh!—what now?

LUCY. "Yet his true nature is generous—it could not always have
been so. Perhaps in old times he has been deceived where he loved.
Ah, his Lucy, at least, shall never deceive him." So I rose and listened for your footstep—I heard it—and I am here—here, on your
bosom, my own father!

SIR GEOF. You'll never deceive me—right, right—go on, pretty one,
go on. (*aside*) If she should be my child after all!

LUCY. There is one who has come here lately—one who appears to
displease you—one whom you've been led to believe comes not on my
account, but my friend's. It is not so, my father; it is for me that he
comes. Let him come no more—let me see him no more—for—for—I
feel that his presence might make me too happy—and that would grieve
you, O my father! (LADY ELLINOR *appears at the window watching.*)

SIR GEOF. (*aside*). She must be my child! Bless her! (*aloud*) I'll
never doubt you again. I'll bite out my tongue if it says a harsh word
to you. I'm not so bad as I seem. Grieve me?—yes, it would break
my heart. You don't know these gay courtiers—I do!—tut—tut—tut
—don't cry. How can I console her?

LUCY. Shall I say?—let me speak to you of my mother.

SIR GEOF. (*recoiling*). Ah!

LUCY. Would it not soothe you to hear that a friend of hers was in London, who——

SIR GEOF. (*changing in his whole deportment*). I forbid you to speak to me of your mother—she dishonored me——

LADY E. (*in a low voice of emotion*). It is false! (*she disappears, R.*)

SIR GEOF. (*starting*). D.d you say "false?"

LUCY (*sobbing*). No—no—but my heart said it!

SIR GEOF. Strange! or was it but my own fancy?

LUCY. Oh, father, father! How I shall pity you if you discover that your suspicions erred. And again I say—I feel—feel in my heart of woman—that the mother of the child who so loves and honors you was innocent.

HARDMAN (*without, L.*). Is Sir Geoffrey at home?

LUCY *starts up and exits, R.* 1 E. *Twilight; during the preceding dialogue the stage has gradually darkened. Enter* HARDMAN, L. 1 E.

HARD. Sir Geoffrey, you were deceived; Lord Wilmot has no thought of Mr. Easy's daughter.

SIR GEOF. I know that—Lucy has told me all, and begged me not to let him come here again.

HARD. (*joyfully*). She has! Then she does not love this Lord Wilmot? But still be on your guard against him. Remember the arts of corruption—the emissary—the letter—the go-between—the spy!

SIR GEOFF. Arts! Spy! Ha! if Easy was right after all. If those flowers thrown in at the window; the watch from that house in the lane; the masked figure that followed me; all bode designs but on Lucy——

HARD. Flowers have been thrown in at the window? You've been watched? A masked figure has followed you? One question more. All this since Lord Wilmot knew Lucy?

SIR GEOF. Yes, to be sure; how blind I have been! (LADY ELLINOR *appears again, R.*)

HARD. Ha! look yonder! Let me track this mystery; (*she disappears, L.*) and if it conceal a scheme of Lord Wilmot's against your daughter's honor, it shall need not your sword to protect her.

[*Pushes open the window, leaps out, and exits,* L.

SIR GEOF. What does he mean? Not *my* sword? Zounds! he don't think of his own! If he does, I'll discard him. I'm not a coward, to let other men risk their lives in my quarrel. Served as a volunteer under Marlbro', at Blenheim; and marched on a cannon! Whatever my faults, no one can say I'm not brave. (*starting*) Ha! bless my life! What is that? I thought I heard something—I'm all on a tremble! Who the deuce *can* be brave when he's surrounded by poisoners—followed by phantoms, with an ugly black face peering in at his window? Hodge, come and bar up the shutters—lock the door – let out the house-dog! Hodge! Hodge! Where on earth is that scoundrel?

[*Exit,* L. 1 E.

SCENE III.—*The Streets. In perspective an alley, inscribed Deadman's Lane. A large, old-fashioned, gloomy house in the corner, with the door on the stage, above which is impanelled a sign of the Crown and Portcullis.* LADY ELLINOR, *masked, enters,* L. 1 E.—*looks round, pauses, and enters the door, R. Dark; lights down.*

Enter HARDMAN, L. 1 E.

HARD. Ha! enters that house. I have my hand on the clue! some pretext to call on the morrow, and I shall quickly unravel the skein.

[*Exit*, R. 2 E.

GOODENOUGH EASY (*singing without*, L.)

> "Old King Cole
> Was a jolly old soul,
> And a jolly old soul was he——

Enters, L 3 E., *with* LORD WILMOT *and* SOFTHEAD ; EASY, *his dress disordered, a pipe in his mouth, in a state of intoxication, hilarious, musical, and oratorical;* SOFTHEAD *in a state of intoxication, abject, remorseful, and lachrymose ;* WILMOT *sober, but affecting inebriety.*

> "He called for his pipe, and he called for his bowl,
> And he called for his fiddlers three."

WIL. Ha, ha! I imagine myself like Bacchus between Silenus and his—ass!

EASY. Wilmot, you're a jolly old soul, and I'll give you my Barbara.

SOFT. (*blubbering*). Hegh! hegh! hegh! Betrayed in my tenderest affections.

WIL. My dear Mr. Easy, I've told you already that I'm pre-engaged.

EASY. Pre-engaged! that's devilish unhandsome! But now I look at you, you do seem double; and if you're double, you're not single; and if you're not single, why, you can't marry Barbara, for that would be bigamy! But I don't care; you're a jolly old soul!

WIL. Not a bit of it. Quite mistaken, Mr. Easy. But if you want, for a son-in-law, a jolly old soul—there he is!

SOFT. (*bursting out afresh*). Hegh! hegh! hegh!

EASY. Hang a lord! What's a lord? I'm a respectable, independent family Briton! Softhead, give us your fist ; you're a jolly old soul, and *you* shall have my Barbara.

SOFT Hegh! hegh! I'm not a jolly old soul. I'm a sinful, wicked, miserable monster. Hegh! hegh!

EASY. What's a monster? I like a monster! My girl shan't go a-begging any farther. You're a precious good fellow, and your father's an alderman, and has got a great many votes, and I'll stand for the city ; and you *shall* have my Barbara.

SOFT. I don't deserve her, Mr. Easy ; I don't deserve such an angel! I'm not precious good. Lords and tigers have corrupted my innocence. Hegh! hegh! I'm going to be hanged.

WATCH. (*without*, L.). Half-past eight o'clock!

WIL. Come along, gentlemen ; we shall have the watch on us.

EASY.—

> "And the bands that guard the city,
> Cried—'Rebels, yield or die!'"

Enter WATCHMAN, *with staff, rattle and lantern*, L. 3 E.

WATCH. Half-past eight o'clock—move on! move on!

EASY. Order, order! Mr. Vice and gentlemen, here's a stranger disturbing the harmony of the evening. I knock him down for a song. (*seizes the* WATCHMAN'S *rattle*) Half-past eight, Esq., on his legs! Sing, sir ; I knock you down for a song.

WATCH. Help! help! Watch! watch! (*cries within*, L , " Watch!")

SOFT. Hark! the officers of justice! My wicked career is approaching its close!

EASY. (*who has got astride on the* WATCHMAN'S *head, and persuades himself that the rest of the* WATCHMAN *is the table*). Mr. Vice and gentlemen, the toast of the evening—what's the matter with the table ? 'Tis bobbing up and down. The table's drunk ! Order for the chair—you table, you! (*thumps the* WATCHMAN *with the rattle*) Fill your glasses—a bumper toast. Prosperity to the city of London—nine times nine—Hip, hip, hurrah ! (*waves the rattle over his head ; the rattle springs, he is amazed*) Why, the Chairman's hammer is as drunk as the table !

Enter WATCHMEN, L. 3 E., *with staves, springing their rattles.*

WIL. (*drawing* SOFTHEAD *off into a corner*). Hold your tongue—they'll not see us here !
WATCH. (*escaping*). Murder !—murder !—this is the fellow—most desperate ruffian. (EASY *is upset by the escape of the* WATCHMAN, *and after some effort to remove him otherwise, the Guardians of the Night hoist him on their shoulders.*)
EASY. I'm being chaired member for the city ! Freemen and Electors ! For this elevation to the post of member for your metropolis, I return you my heartfelt thanks ! Steady, there, steady ! The proudest day of my life. 'Tis the boast of the British Constitution that a plain, sober man like me may rise to honors the most exalted ! Long live the British Constitution. Hip—hip—hurrah ! (*is carried off waving the rattle.* SOFTHEAD *continues to weep in speechless sorrow.*)
WIL. (*coming forth*). Ha ! ha ! ha ! My family Briton being chaired for the city ! "So severe on a cheerful glass." Well, he has chosen a son-in-law drunk ; and egad ! he shall keep to him sober ! Stand up ; how do you feel ?
SOFT. *Feel !* I'm a ruin !
WIL. Faith, I never saw a more mournful one ! It must be near Sir Geoffrey's ! Led them here—on my way to this sepulchral appointment, Deadman's Lane. Where the plague can it be ? Ha ! the very place. Looks like it ! How get rid of Softhead ? Ha, ha ! I have it. Softhead awake ! the night has begun—the time for monsters and their prey. Now will I lift the dark veil from the mysteries of London. Behold that house, Deadman's Lane !
SOFT. Deadman's Lane ! I'm in a cold prespiration !
WIL. In that house—under the antique sign of Crown and Portcullis —are such delightful horrors at work as would make the wigs of holy men stand on end ! The adventure is dangerous, but deliriously exciting. Into that abode will we plunge, and gaze, like Macbeth, "on deeds without a name."

LADY E., *masked, enters from the door in Deadman's Lane, and approaches* WILMOT, *who has, till now, hold of* SOFTHEAD.

SOFT. Hegh ! hegh ! hegh ! I won't gaze on deeds without a name ! I won't plunge into Deadmen's abodes ! (*perceiving the figure*) Ha ! Look there ! Dark veil, indeed ! Mysteries of London ! Horrible apparition, avaunt ! (*breaks from* WILMOT, *who releases him as he sees the figure*) Hegh ! hegh ! I'll go home to my mother !   [*Exit,* R. 1 E.

LADY E. *motions to* WILMOT *and exits into the house, followed by* WILMOT.

ACT IV.

SCENE I.—*The Library in* SIR GEOFFREY'S *house.*

Enter HARDMAN *and* SIR GEOFFREY, L. 1 E.

SIR GEOF. Yes! I've seen that you're not indifferent to Lucy. But before I approve or discourage, just tell me more of yourself—your birth, your fortune, past life. Of course, you are the son of a gentleman? (*aside*) Now as he speaks truly or falsely I will discard him as a liar, or reward him with Lucy's hand. He turns aside. H · will lie!

HARD. Sir, at the risk of my hopes, I will speak the hard truth. "The son of a gentleman?" I think not. My infancy passed in the house of a farmer; the children with whom I played told me I was an orphan. I was next dropped, how I know not, in the midst of that rough world called school. "You have talent," said the master; "but you're idle; you have no right to holidays; you must force your way through life; you are sent here by charity."

SIR GEOF. Charity! *There*, the old fool was wrong!

HARD. My idleness vanished—I became the head of the school. Then I resolved no longer to be the pupil of—charity. At the age of sixteen I escaped, and took for my motto—the words of the master:— "You must force your way through life." Hope and pride whispered— "You shall force it."

SIR GEOF. Poor fellow! What then?

HARD. Eight years of wandering, adventure, hardship, and trial I often wanted bread—never courage. At the end of those years I had risen—to what? A desk at a lawyer's office in Norfolk——

SIR GEOF. (*aside*). My own lawyer? where I first caught trace of him again.

HARD. Party spirit ran high in town. Politics began to bewitch me. There was a Speaking Club, and I spoke. My ambition rose higher —took the flight of an author. I came up to London with ten pounds in my pocket, and a work on the "State of the Nation." It sold well; the publisher brought me four hundred pounds. "Vast fortunes," said he, " are made in the South Sea Scheme. Venture your hundreds,—I'll send you a broker "——

SIR GEOF. He! he! I hope he was clever, that broker?

HARD. Clever indeed; in a fortnight he said to me, " Your hundreds have swelled into thousands. For this money I can get you an annuity on land, just enough for a parliamentary qualification." The last hint fired me—I bought the annuity. You now know my fortune, and how it was made.

SIR GEOF. (*aside*). He! he! I must tell this to Easy; how he'll enjoy it.

HARD. Not long after, at a political coffee-house, a man took me aside. "Sir," said he, "you are Mr. Hardman who wrote the famous work on 'The State of the Nation.' Will you come into Parliament? We want a man like you for our borough; we'll return you free of expense; not a shilling of bribery."

SIR GEOF. He! he! Wonderful! not a shilling of bribery.

HARD. The man kept his word, and I came into Parliament—inexperienced and friendless. I spoke, and was laughed at; spoke again, and was listened to; failed often; succeeded at last. Here, yesterday, in ending my tale I must have said, looking down, "Can you give your child to a man of birth more than doubtful, and of fortunes so humble?

Yet aspiring even then to the hand of your heiress, I wrote to Sir Robert for a place just vacated by a man of high rank, who is raised to the peerage. He refused.

SIR GEOF. Of course. (aside) I suspect he's very rash and presuming.

HARD. To-day the refusal is retracted—the office is mine.

SIR GEOF. (astonished and aside). Ha ! I had no hand in that !

HARD I am now one—if not of the highest—yet still o·e of that Government through which the Majesty of England administers her laws. And, with front erect, I say to you—as I would to the first peer of the realm—" I have no charts of broad lands, and no roll of proud fathers. But alone and unfriended I have fought my way against Fortune. Did your ancestors more ? My country has truste l the new man to her councils, and the man whom she honors is the equal of all."

SIR GEOF. Brave fellow, your hand. Win Lucy's consent, and you have mine. Hush! no thanks! Now listen ; I have told you my dark story—these flowers cannot come from Wilmot. I have examined them again—they are made up in the very form of the posies I had the folly to send, in the days of our courtship, to the wife who afterwards betrayed me——   .

HARD. Be not so sure that she betrayed. No proof but the boast of a profligate.

SIR GEOF. Who had been my intimate friend for years—so that, O torture ! I am haunted with the doubt whether my heiress be my own child !—and to whom (by the confession of a servant) she sent a letter in secret the very day on which I struck the mocking boast from the villain's lips in a public tavern. Ah, he was always a wit and a scoffer—perhaps it is from him that these flowers are sent, in token of gibe and insult. He has discovered the man he dishonored, in spite of the change of name——

HARD You changed your name for an inheritance. You have not told me that which you formerly bore.

SIR GEOF. Morland.

HARD. Morland ? Ha—and the seducer's——

SIR GEOF. Lord Henry de Mowbray——

HARD. The reprobate brother of the Duke of Middlesex. He died a few months since.

SIR GEOF (staggering) Died too ! Both dead !

HARD. (aside). Tonson spoke of Lord Henry's Memoir—Confession about Lady Morland in Fallen's hands I will go to Fallen at once. (aloud) You have given me a new clue. I will follow it up. When can I see you again ?

SIR GEOF. I'm going to Easy's—you'll find me there all the morning. But don't forget Lucy—we must save her from Wilmot.

HARD. Fear Wilmot no more. This day he shall abandon his suit.
                                                    [Exit HARDMAN, L. 1 E.

SIR GEOF. Hodge! Well—well——

Enter HODGE, R. 1 E.

Hodge, take your hat and your bludgeon—attend me to the city: (aside) She'll be happy with Hardman. Ah ! if she were my own child after all !   [Exeunt SIR GEOFFREY and HODGE, L. 1 E.

SCENE II.—DAVID FALLEN'S *Garret. The scene resembling that of Hogarth's " Distrest Poet "* FALLEN *discovered seated at table.*

FAL. (opening the casement). So, the morning air breathes fresh ! One moment's respite from drudgery. Another line to this poem, my grand bequest to my country! Ah! this description; unfinished; good, good.

> " Methinks we walk in dreams on fairy land,
> Where—golden ore—lies mix'd with——" *

Enter PADDY, R. D.

PADDY. Please, sir, the milkwoman's score!

FAL. Stay, stay ;—

> " Lies mixed with—common sand !"

Eh ? Milkwoman? She must be·paid, or the children—I—I—(*fumbling in his pocket, and looking about the table*) There's another blanket on the bed ; pawn it.

PADDY. Agh, now, don't be so ungrateful to your ould friend, the blanket. When Mr. Tonson, the great bookshiller, tould me, says he, " Paddy, I'd give two hunder gould guineas for the papursh Mr. Fallen has in his disk!"

FAL. Go, go! (*knock without*, R.)

PADDY. Agh, murther! Who can that be distarbin' the door at the top of the mornin' ?   [*Exit*, R. D.

FAL. Oh! that fatal Memoir! My own labors scarce keep me from starving, and this wretched scrawl of a profligate worth what to me were Golconda! Heaven sustain me! I'm tempted.

Re-enter PADDY, *with* WILMOT, *disguised as* EDMUND CURLL.

PADDY. Stoop your head, sir. 'Tis not a dun, sir; 'tis Mr. Curll ; says he's come to outbid Mr. Tonson, sir.

FAL. Go quick ; pawn the blanket. Let me think my children are fed. (*exit* PADDY, R. D.) Now, sir, what do you want ?

WIL. (*taking out his handkerchief and whimpering*). My dear, good Mr. Fallen—no offence—I do so feel for the distresses of genius. I am a bookseller, but I have a heart—and I'm come to buy——

FAL. Have you? this poem ? it is nearly finished—twelve books—twenty years' labor—twenty-four thousand lines!—ten pounds, Mr. Curll, ten pounds ?

WIL. Price of *Paradise Lost!* ˙Can't expect such prices for poetry now-a-days, my dear Mr. Fallen. Nothing takes that is not sharp and spicy. Hum! I hear you have come most interesting papers ; private Memoirs and Confessions of a Man of Quality recently deceased. Nay, nay, Mr. Fallen, don't shrink back ; I'm not like that shabby dog, Tonson. Three hundred guineas for the Memoir of Lord Henry de Mowbray.

FAL. Three hundred guineas for that·garbage !—not ten for the poem ! —and—the children ! Well ! (*goes to the cupboard and take out the Memoir in a portfolio, splendidly bound, with the arms and supporters of the Mowbrays blazoned on the sides*) Ah!—but the honor of a woman—the secrets of a family—the——

WIL. (*grasping at the portfolio, which* FALLEN *still detains*). Nothing sells better, my dear, dear Mr. Fallen! But how, how did you come by these treasures, my excellent friend ?

FAL. How? Lord Henry gave them to me himself, on his death-bed.

---

* As it would be obviously presumptuous to assign to an author so eminent as Mr. David Fallen any verses composed by a living writer, the two lines in the text are taken from Mr. Dryden's *Indian Emperor.*

Wil.. Nay; what could he give them for but to publish, my sweet Mr. Fallen? no doubt to immortalize all tho ladies who loved him.

Fal No, sir; profligate as he was, and vile as may be much in this Memoir, that was not his dying intention, though it might be his first. There was a lady he had once foully injured—the sole woman he had ever loved eno' for remorse. This Memoir contains a confession that might serve to clear the name he himself had aspersed; and in the sudden repentance of his last moments, he bade me seek the lady and place the whole in her hands, to use as best might serve to establish her innocence.

Wil. How could you know the lady, my benevolent friend?

Fal. I did not; but she was supposed to be abroad with her father— a Jacobite exile—and I, then a Jacobite agent, had the best chance to trace her.

Wil. And you did?

Fal. But to hear she had died somewhere in France.

Wil. Then, of course, you may *now* gratify our intelligent public, for your own personal profit. Clear as day, my magnanimous friend! Three hundred guineas! I have 'em here in a bag! (*shows it.*)

Fal. Begone! I will not sell a man's hearth to the public.

Wil. (*aside*). Noble fellow! (*aloud*) Gently, gently, my too warm, but high-spirited friend! To say the truth, I don't come on my own account. To whom, my dear sir, since the lady is dead, *should* be given these papers, if unfit for a virtuous, but inquisitive public? Why, surely to Lord Henry's nearest relation. I am employed by the rich Duke of Middlesex. Name your terms.

Fal. Ha! ha! Then at last he comes crawling to me, your proud Duke? Sir, years ago, when a kind word from his Grace, a nod of his head, a touch of his hand, would have turned my foes into flatterers, I had the meanness to name him my patron—inscribed to him a work, took it to his house, and waited in his hall among porters and lackeys—till, sweeping by his carriage, he said, "Oh, you are the poet? take this;" and extending his alms, as if to a beggar. "You look very thin, sir; stay and dine with my people" People—his servants!

Wil. Calm yourself, my good Mr. Fallen! 'Tis his Grace's innocent way with us all.

Fal. Go! let him know what these memoirs contain! They would make the Proud Duke the butt of the town—the jeer of the lackeys, who jeered at my rags; expose his frailties, his follies, his personal secrets. Tell him this; and then say that my poverty shall not be the tool of his brother's revenge; but my pride shall not stoop from its pedestal to take money from him. Now, sir, am I right? Reply, not as tempter to pauper; but if one spark of manhood be in you, as man speaks to man.

Wil. (*resuming his own manner*). I reply, sir, as man to man, and gentleman to gentleman. I am Frederick, Lord Wilmot. Pardon this imposture. The Duke is my father's friend. I am here to obtain, what it is clear that he alone should possess. Mr. Fallen, your works first raised me from the world of the senses, and taught me to believe in such nobleness as I now hope for in you. Give me this record to take to the Duke—no price, sir; for such things are priceless—and let me go hence with the sight of this poverty before my eyes, and on my soul the grand picture of the man who has spurned the bribe to his honor, and can humble by a gift the great prince who insulted him by alms.

Fal. Take it—take it! (*gives the portfolio*) I am save! from temptation. God bless you, young man!

Wil. Now you indeed make me twofold your debtor—in your books, the rich thought; in yourself the heroic example. Accept from my superfluities, in small part of such debt, a yearly sum equal to that which your poverty refused as a bribe from Mr. Tonson.

FAL. My Lord—my Lord! (*bursts into tears.*)

WIL. Oh, trust me the day shall come, when men will feel that it is not charity we owe to the ennoblers of life—it is tribute! When your Order shall rise with the civilization it called into being, and shall refer its claim to just rank among freemen, to some Queen whom even a Milton might have sung, and even a Hampden have died for.

FAL. O, dream of my youth! My heart swells and chokes me!

Enter HARDMAN, R. D.

HARD. (*aside*). What's this? Fallen weeping? Ah! is not that the tyrannical sneak, Edmund Curll?——

WIL. *changing his tone to* FALLEN *into one of imperiousness*). Can't hear of the poem, Mr. Fallen. Don't tell me. Ah, Mr. Hardman (*concealing the portfolio*), your most humble! Sir—sir—if you want to publish something smart and spicy—Secret Anecdotes of Cabinets—Sir Robert Walpole's Adventures with the Ladies—I'll come down as handsomely as any man in the Row—smart and spicy——

HARD. Offer to bribe *me*, you insolent rascal!

WIL. Oh, my dear, good Mr. Hardman, I've bribed the Premier himself. Ha! ha! Servant, sir; servant. [*Exit*, R. D.

HARD. Loathsome vagabond! My dear Mr. Fallen, you have the manuscript Memoir of Lord Henry de Mowbray. I know its great value. Name your own price to permit me just to inspect it.

FAL. It is gone; and to the hands of his brother, the Duke.

HARD. The Duke! This is a thunder-stroke! Say, sir; you have read this Memoir—does it contain aught respecting a certain Lady Morland?

FAL. It does. It confesses that Lord Henry slandered her reputation as a woman in order to sustain his own as a seducer. That part of the Memoir was writ on his death-bed.

HARD. His boast, then——

FAL. Was caused by the scorn of her letter rejecting his suit.

HARD. What joy for Sir Geoffrey! And that letter?

FAL. Is one of the documents that make up the Memoir.

HARD. And these documents are now in the hands of the Duke?

FAL. They are. For, since Lady Morland is dead——

HARD. Are you sure she is dead?

FAL. I only go by report.

HARD. Report often lies. (*aside*) Who but Lady Morland can this mask be? I will go at once to the house and clear up that doubt myself. But the Duke's appointment! Ah! that must not be forgotten; my rival must be removed ere Lucy can be won. And what hold on the Duke himself to produce the Memoir, if I get the dispatch. (*aloud*) Well, Mr. Fallen, there is no more to be said as to the Memoir. Your messenger will meet his Grace, as we settled. I shall be close at hand; and mark, the messenger must give me the dispatch which is meant for the Pretender. [*Exit* HARDMAN, R. D.

Re-enter PADDY.

PADDY. Plase, sur, an' I've paid the milk score——

FAL. (*interrupting him*). I'm to be rich—so rich! 'Tis my turn now. I've shared your pittance, you shall share my plenty. (*sinks down on chair, seizing* PADDY'S *hand and shaking it heartily as the scene closes in.*)

SCENE III.—*The Mall.*

Enter SOFTHEAD, L. 3 E., *his arms folded, and in deep thought, as though forming a virtuous resolution.*

SOFT. Little did I foresee, in the days of my innocence, when Mr. Lillo read to me his affecting tragedy of George Barnwell,* how I myself was to be led on, step by step, to the brink of deeds without a name. Dead-man's Lane—that funereal apparition in black—a warning to startle the most obdurate conscience.

Enter EASY, R. 3 E., *recently dismissed from the Watch-house ; slovenly, skulking, and crestfallen.*

EASY. Not a coach on the stand ! A pretty pickle I'm in if any one sees me ! A sober, respectable man like me, to awake in the watch-house, be kept there till noon among thieves and pickpockets, and at last to be fined five shillings for drunkenness and disorderly conduct ; all from dining with a lord who had no thoughts of making Barbara my Lady after all ! Deuce take him ! (*discovering* SOFTHEAD, *aside*) Softhead ! how shall I escape him ?

SOFT. (*aside, discovering* EASY). Easy ! What a fall ! I'll appear not to remember. Barbara's father should not feel degraded in the eyes of a wretch like myself! (*aloud*) How d'ye do, Mr. Easy ? You're out early, to-day.

EASY. (*aside*). Ha ! He was so drunk himself he has forgotten all about it. (*aloud*) Yes, a headache. You were so pleasant at dinner. I wanted the air of the park.

SOFT. Why, you look rather poorly, Mr. Easy !

EASY. Indeed, I feel so. A man in business can't afford to be laid up—so I thought, before I went home to the city, that I'd just look into —Ha, ha! a seasoned toper like you will laugh when I tell you—I thought I'd just look into the 'pothecary's !

SOFT. Just been there myself, Mr. Easy. (*showing a phial.*)

EASY (*regarding it with mournful disgust*). Not taken physic since I was a boy ! It looks very nasty !

SOFT. 'Tis worse than it looks ! And this is called *Pleasure !* Ah, Mr. Easy, don't give way to Fred's fascination ; you don't know how it ends !

EASY. Indeed I do, (*aside*) It ends in the watch-house. (*aloud*) And I'm shocked to think what will become of yourself, if you are thus every night led away by a lord, who——

SOFT. Hush ! talk of the devil—look ! he's coming up the Mall ! (SOFTHEAD *retires back.*)

EASY. He is ? then I'm off ; I see a sedan-chair. Chair ! chair ! stop —chair ! chair !   [*Exit*, R. 2 E.

Enter WILMOT *and* DUKE *with portfolio,* L. 3 E.

DUKE (*looking at portfolio*). Infamous, indeed ! His own base lie against that poor lady, whose husband he wounded. Her very letter attached to it. Ha!—what is this ? Such ribaldry on me ! Gracious

---

* We have only, I fear, Mr. Softhead's authority for supposing *George Barnwell* to be then written ; it was not acted till some years afterwards.

Heaven! My name thus dragged through the dirt, and by a son of my own house! Oh! my Lord, how shall I thank you?

WIL. Thank not me; but the poet, whom your Grace left in the hall.

DUKE. Name it not—I'll beg his pardon myself! Adieu; I must go home and lock up this scandal till I've leisure to read and destroy it; never again shall it come to the day! And then, sure that no blot shall be seen in my 'scutcheon, I can peril my life without fear in the cause of my king.   [*Exit* DUKE, R. 2 E.

WIL. (*chanting*).

"Gather your rosebuds while you may,
    For time is still a-flying."

Since my visit last night to Deadman's Lane, and my hope to give Lu y such happiness, I feel as if I trod upon air (*discovers* SOFTHEAD) Ah. Softhead! why, you stand there as languid and lifeless as if you were capable of—fishing!

SOFT. I've been thinking—(*advances.*)

WIL. Thinking! you *do* look fatigued! What a horrid exertion it must have been to you!

SOFT. Ah! Fred, Fred, don't be so hardened. What atrocity did you perpetrate last night?

WIL. Last night? Oh, at Deadman's Lane; monstrous, indeed. And this morning, too, another! Never had so many atrocities on my hands as within the last twenty-four hours. But they are all nothing to that which I perpetrated yesterday, just before dinner. Hark! I bribed the Prime Minister.

SOFT. Saints in heaven!

WIL. Ha! ha! Hit him plump on the jolly blunt side of his character! I must tell you about it. Drove home from Will's; put my Murillo in the carriage, and off to Sir Robert's—shown into his office,— "Ah! my Lord Wilmot," says he, with that merry roll of his eye; "this *is* an honor, what can I do for you?"—"Sir Robert," says I, "we men of the world soon come to the point; 'tis a maxim of yours that all have their price."—"Not quite that," says Sir Robert, "but let us suppose that it is." Another roll of his eye, as much as to say, "I shall get this rogue a bargain!"—"So, Sir Robert," quoth I, with a bow, "I've come to buy the Prime Minister."—"Buy me," cried Sir Robert, and he laughed till I thought he'd have choked; "my price is rather high, I'm afraid." Then I go to the door, bid my lackeys bring in the Murillo. "Look at that if you please; about the mark, is it not?" Sir Robert runs to the picture, his breast heaves, his eyes sparkle; "A Murillo!" cries he, "name your price!"—"I have named it." Then he looks at me *so*, and I look at him *so!*—turn out the lackeys, place pen, ink and paper before him; "That place in the Treasury just vacant, and the Murillo is yours."—"For yourself?—I am charmed," cried Sir Robert. "No, 'tis for a friend of your own, who's in want of it."— "Oh, that alters the case; I've so many friends troubled with the same sort of want."—"Yes, but the Murillo is *genuine,*—pray, what are the friends?" Out laughed Sir Robert, "There's no resisting you and the Murillo together! There's the appointment. And now, since your Lordship has bought me, I must insist upon buying your Lordship. Fair play is a jewel." Then I take my grand holiday air. "Sir Robert," said I, "you've bought me long ago. You've given us peace where we feared civil war; and a Constitutional King instead of a despot. And if that's not enough to buy the vote of an Englishman, believe me, Sir Robert, he's not worth the buying." Then he stretched out his bluff, hearty hand, and I gave it a bluff, hearty shake. He got the Murillo—Hardman the place. And here stand I, the only man in all England who can boast that he bought the Prime Minister! Faith, you may well call me hardened; I don't feel the least bit of remorse.

Soft. Hardman! you got Hardman the place?

Wil. I did not say Hardman——

Soft. You did say Hardman. But as 'tis a secret that might get you into trouble, I'll keep it. Yet, *Dimidum meæ*, that's not behaving much like a monster?

Wil. Why, it does seem betraying the Good Old Cause—but if there's honor among thieves, there is among monsters; and Hardman is in the same scrape as ourselves—in love—his place may secure him the hand of the lady. But mind—he's not to know I've been meddling with his affairs. Hang it! no one likes that. Not a word then.

Soft. Not a word. My dear Fred, I'm so glad you're not so bad as you seem. I'd half a mind to desert you; but I have not the heart; and I'll stick by you as long as I live!

Wil. (*aside*). Whew! This will never do! Poor dear little fellow! I'm sorry to lose him; but my word's passed to Barbara, and 'tis all for his good. (*aloud*) As long as you live! Alas! that reminds me of your little affair. I'm to be your second, you know.

Soft. Second!—affair!

Wil. With that fierce Colonel Flint. I warned you against him; but you have such a deuce of a spirit. Don't you remember?

Soft. No; why, what was it all about?

Wil. Let me see—oh, Flint said something insolent about Mistress Barbara.

Soft. He did? Ruffian!

Wil. So—you called him out! But if you'll empower me in your name to retract and apologize——

Soft. Not a bit of it. Insolent to Barbara! *Dimidum meæ*. I'd fight him if he were the first swordsman in England.

Wil. Why, that's just what he is!

Soft. Don't care; I'm his man—though a dead one.

Wil. (*aside*). Hang it—he's as brave as myself on that side of his character. I must turn to another. (*aloud*) No, Softhead, that was not the cause of the quarrel—said it to rouse you, as you seemed rather low. The fact is that it was a jest on yourself that you took up rather warmly.

Soft. Was that all—only myself?

Wil. No larger subject; and Flint is *such* a good fencer!

Soft. My dear Fred, I retract, I apologize; I despise duelling—absurd and unchristianlike.

Wil. Leave all to me. Dismiss the subject. I'll settle it; only, Softhead, you see our set has very stiff rules on such matters. And if you apologize to a brave like Flint; nay, if you don't actually, cheerfully, rapturously fight him—though sure to be killed—I fear you must resign all ideas of high life!

Soft. *Dimidum meæ*, but low life is better than no life at all!

Wil. There's no denying that proposition. It will console you to think that Mr. Easy's kind side is Cheapside. And you may get upon one if you return to the other.

Soft. I was thinking so when you found me—*thinking*—(*hesitatingly*) But to leave you——

Wil. Oh, not yet! Retire at least with *éclat*. Share with me one grand, crowning, last, daring, and desperate adventure.

Soft. Deadman's Lane again, I suppose? I thank you for nothing. Fred, I have long been your faithful follower. (*with emotion*) Now, my

Lord, I'm your humble servant.* (*aside*) Barbara will comfort me. She's perhaps at Sir Geoffrey's.   [*Exit*, R. 1 E.

WIL. Well! his love will repay him, and the City of London will present me with her freedom, in a gold box, for restoring her prodigal son to her Metropolitan bosom.   Deadman's Lane—that was an adventure, indeed.   Lucy's mother still living—implores me to get her the sight of her child.   Will Lucy believe me?   Will——

Enter SMART, L. 1 E.

Ha, Smart!   Well—well?   You—baffled Sir Geoffrey?

SMART. He was out.

WIL. And you gave the young lady my letter?

SMART. Hist! my Lord, it so affected her—that—here she comes.
                    [*Exit* SMART, R. 1 E.

Enter LUCY, L. 1 E.

LUCY. Oh, my Lord is this true?   Can it be?   A mother lives!   Do you wonder that I forget all else?—that I am here—and with but one prayer, lead me to that mother!   She says, too, she has been slandered —blesses me—that my heart defended her, but—but—this is no snare— you do not deceive me?

WIL. Deceive you!   Oh, Lucy—I have a sister myself at the hearth of my father.

LUCY. Forgive me—lead on—quick, quick—oh, mother, mother!
                    [*Exeunt* LUCY *and* WILMOT, R. 1 E.

ACT V.

SCENE I.—*Old Mill near the Thames.*

Enter HARDMAN, L. 1 E.

HARD. The dispatch to the Pretender. (*opening it*) Ho! Wilmot is in my power; here ends his rivalry.   The Duke's life, too, in exchange for the Memoir!   No!   Fear is not his weak point; but can this haughtiest of men ever yield such memorials?   Even admit the base lie of his brother?   Still her story has that which may touch him.   Since I have seen her, I feel sure of her innocence.   The Duke comes; now all depends on my chance to hit the right side of a character.

Enter DUKE OF MIDDLESEX, R. 1 E.

DUKE. Lord Loftus not here yet!   Strange!

HARD. My Lord Duke—forgive this intrusion!

DUKE (*aside*). T'other man I met at Lord Wilmot's. (*aloud*) Sir, your servant; I'm somewhat in haste.

HARD. Still I presume to delay your Grace, for it is on a question of honor.

DUKE. Honor! that goes before all!   Sir, my time is your own.

HARD Your Grace is the head of a house whose fame is a part of our

---

* A play upon words plagiarised from Farquhar.   The reader must regret that the author had not the courage to plagiarize more from Farquhar.

history; it is therefore that I speak to you boldly, since it may be that wrongs were inflicted by one of its members——

DUKE. How, sir!

HARD. Assured that if so (and should it be still in your power), your Grace will frankly repair them, as a duty you took with the ermine and coronet.

DUKE. You speak well, sir. (*aside*) Very much like a gentleman!

HARD. Your Grace had a brother, Lord Henry de Mowbray.

DUKE. Ah! Sir, to the point.

HARD. At once, my Lord Duke. Many years ago a duel took place between Lord Henry and Sir Geoffrey Morland—your Grace knows the cause.

DUKE. Hem! yes; a lady—who—who——

HARD. Was banished her husband's home and her infant's cradle on account of suspicions based, my Lord Duke, on—what your Grace cannot wonder that the husband believed—the word of a Mowbray!

DUKE (*aside*). Villain! (*aloud*) But what became of the husband, never since heard of? He——

HARD. Fled abroad from men's tongues and dishonor. He did not return to his native land till he had changed for another the name that a Mowbray had blighted. Unhappy man! he still lives.

DUKE. And the lady—the lady——

HARD. Before the duel had gone to the house of her father, who was forced that very day to fly the country. His life was in danger.

DUKE. How?

HARD. He was loyal to the Stuarts, and—a plot was discovered.

DUKE. Brave, noble gentleman! Go on, sir.

HARD. Her other ties wrenched from her, his daughter went with him into exile—his stay, his hope, his all. His lands were confiscated. She was high-born; she worked for a father's bread. Conceive yourself, my Lord Duke, in the place of that father—loyal and penniless; noble; proscribed; dependent on the toils of a daughter; and that daughter's name sullied by——

DUKE. A word?——

HARD. From the son of that house to which all the chivalry of England looked for example.

DUKE. (*aside*). Oh, Heaven! can my glory thus be turned to my shame? (*aloud*) But they said she had died, sir.

HARD. When her father had gone to the grave, she herself spread or sanctioned that rumor—for she resolved to die to the world. She entered a convent, prepared to take the noviciate—when she suddenly learned that a person had been inquiring for her at Paris, who stated that Lord Henry de Mowbray had left behind him a Memoir——

DUKE. Ah!

HARD. Which acquits her. She learned, too, the clue to her husband —resolved to come hither—arrived six days since. No proof of her innocence save those for which I now appeal to your Grace!

DUKE (*aside*). O pride, be my succor! (*aloud, haughtily*) Appeal to me, sir—and wherefore?

HARD. The sole evidence alleged against this lady are the fact of a letter sent from herself to Lord Henry, and the boast of a man now no more. She asserts that that letter would establish her innocence. She believes that, on his deathbed, your brother retracted his boast, and that the Memoir he left will attest to its falsehood.

DUKE. Asserts—believes!—go on—go on.

HARD. No, my Lord Duke, I have done. I know that that letter, that Memoir exists; that they are now in your hands. If her assertion

be .alse—if they prove not her innocence—a word, nay, a sign, from the
chief of a house so renowned for its honor, suffices. I take my leave,
and condemn her. But if her story be true, you have heard the last
chance of a wife and a mother to be restored to the husband she loves
and forgives, to the child who has grown into womanhood remote from
her care ; and these blessings I pledged her by my faith to obtain if
that letter, that Memoir, should prove that the boast was——

DUKE. A lie, sir, a lie, a black lie!—the coward's worst crime—a lie
on the fair name of a woman ! Sir, this heat, perhaps, is unseemly ;
thus to brand my own brother ! But if we, the peers of England, and
the representatives of her gentlemen, can hear, can think, of vile things
done, whoever the doer, with calm pulse and cold heart—perish our
titles ; where would be the use of a Duke ?

HARD. (aside). A very bright side of his character.

DUKE. Sir, you are right. T:.e Memoir you speak of is in my hands,
and with it, Lady Morland's own letter. Much in that Memoir relates
to myself; and so galls all the pride I am said to possess, that not ten
minutes since methought I had rather my duchy were forfeit than have
exposed its contents to the pity or laugh of a stranger. I think no more
of myself. A woman has appealed for her name to mine honor as a
man. Now, sir, your commands.

HARD. No passage is needed, save that which acquits Lady Morland.
Let the Memoir still rest in your hands. Condescend but to bring it
forthwith to my house ; and may I hope that my Lord Loftus may accompany you—there is an affair of moment on which I would speak to
you both.

DUKE. Your address, sir. (HARDMAN gives him card) I will but return
home for the documents and proceed at once to your house. Hurry
not; I will wait. Allow me to take your hand, sir. You know how to
speak to the heart of a gentleman.   [Exit, r. 1 E.

HARD. Yet how ignorant we are of men's hearts till we see them
lit up by a passion ! This noble has made what is honor so clear to my
eyes. Let me pause—let me think—let me choose ! I feel as if I stood
at the crisis of life.

Enter SOFTHEAD, L. 1 E.

SOFT. (aside). What have I seen ? Where go ? Whom consult ? (sees
HARDMAN) Oh, Mr. Hardman ! You're a friend of Lord Wilmot's, of
Sir Geoffrey's, of Lucy's ?

HARD. Speak—quick—to the purpose.

SOFT. On my way to Sir Geoffrey's, I passed by a house of the most
villainous character. (aside) I dare not say how Wilmot himself has described it. (aloud, earnestly) Oh, sir, you know Wilmot ! you know his
sentiments on marriage. I saw Wilmot and Lucy Thornside enter that
infamous house—Deadman's Lane !

HARD. (aside). Deadman's Lane ? He takes her to the arms of her
mother ! forestalls my own plan, will reap my reward. Have I schemed,
then, for him ?—No, by yon heavens !

SOFT. I ran on to Sir Geoffrey's—he was out.

HARD. (who has been writing in his tablets, tears out a page) Take this to
Justice Kite's, hard by ; he will send two special officers, placed at the
door, Deadman's Lane, to wait my instructions. They must go instantly
—arrive as soon as myself Then hasten to Mr. Easy's ; Sir Geoffrey is
there. Break your news with precaution, and bring him straight to
that house. Leave the rest to my care. Away with you, quick.

SOFT. I know he will kill me! But I'm right. And when I'm right
—*Dimidum meæ!*   [*Exit,* R. 1 E.
HARD. Ho! ho! It is war! My choice is made. I am armed at all
points, and strike for the victory.   [*Exit,* L. 1 R.

SCENE II.—*Apartment in the house, Deadman's Lane.*

LUCY *and* LADY ELLINOR *discovered seated* R. *of table,* WILMOT L.

LADY E. And you believe me? Dear child—this indeed is happiness.
Ah! If your cruel father——
LUCY. Hush—he will believe you, too.
LADY E. No; I could not venture into his presence without the proof
that he had wronged me.
WIL. (*rising*). Oh, that I had known before what interest you had in
this Memoir!—how can I recover it from the Duke?
LUCY (*rising and approaching him*). You will—you must—dear—dear
Lord Wilmot—you have restored me to my mother; restore my mother
to her home. (*clasps his hand.*)
WIL. Ah—and this hand—would you withdraw it then?
LUCY. Never from him who reunites my parents.
LADY E. (*rising*). Ha!—a voice without—steps!
WIL. If it should be Sir Geoffrey—in some rash violence he might—
Retire—quick—quick.
                    [*Exeunt* LADY ELLINOR *and* LUCY *in the inner room.*

Enter HARDMAN, L. 3 E.

HARD. Alone! Where is Lucy, my Lord?
WIL. In the next room with——
HARD. Her mother?
WIL. What! you know?
HARD. I know that between us two there is a strife, and I am come
to decide it; you love Lucy Thornside
WIL. Well! I told you so.
HARD. You told it my Lord, to a rival. Ay, smile. You have
wealth, rank, fashion, and wit; I have none of these, and I need them
not. But I say to you, (*taking out watch and looking at it*) that ere the
hand on this dial moves to that near point in time, your love will be
hopeless and your suit be withdrawn.
WIL. The man's mad. Unless, sir, you wish me to believe that my
life hangs on your sword, I cannot quite comprehend why my love
should go by your watch.
HARD. I command you, Lord Wilmot, to change this tone of levity;
I command it in the name of a life which, I think, you prize more than
your own—a life that is now in my hands. You told me to sound your
father. I have not done so—I have detected——
WIL. Detected! Hold, sir! that word implies crime
HARD. Ay, the crime of the great. History calls it ZEAL   Law styles
it HIGH TREASON.
WIL. What do I hear? Heavens!—my father! Sir, your word is no
proof?
HARD. But *this* is? (*producing the Requisition to the Pretender*) 'Tis
high treason, conspiring to levy arms against the King on the throne—
here called the Usurper. High treason to promise to greet with banner
and trump a pretender—here called James the Third. Such is the
purport of the paper I hold—and here is the name of your father.

WIL. (*aside*). Both are armed and alone. (*locks the outer door by which he is standing.*)

HARD. (*aside*). So, I guess his intention. (*crosses to R., and opens the window and looks out*) Good, the officers are come.

WIL. What the law calls high treason I know not; what the honest call treason I know. Traitor, thou who hast used the confidence of a son against the life of a father, thou shalt not quit these walls with that life in thy grasp—yield the proof thou hast plundered or forged. (*seizes him.*)

HARD. 'St! the officers of justice are below; loose thine hold, or the life thou demandest falls from these hands into theirs.

WIL. (*recoiling*) Foiled! Foiled! How act! what do? And thy son set you bloodhound on thy track, O my father! Sir, you are my rival; I guess the terms you now come to impose!

HARD. I impose no terms. What needs the demand? Have you an option? I think better of you. We both love the same woman; I have loved her a year, you a week; you have her father's dislike, I his consent. One must yield—why should I? Rule son of the people though I be, why must I be thrust from the sunshine because you cross my path as the fair and the high-born? What have I owed to your order or you?

WIL. To me, sir? Well, if to me you owed some slight favor, I should scorn at this moment to speak it.

HARD. I owe favor, the slightest, to no man; 'tis my boast. Listen still, I schemed to save your father, not to injure. Had you rather this scroll had fallen into the hands of a spy? And now, if I place it in yours—save your name from attainder, your fortunes from confiscation, your father from the axe of the headsman—why should I ask terms? Would it be possible for you to say, " Sir, I thank you; and in return I would do my best to rob your life of the woman you love, and whom I have just known a week?" Could you, peer's son, and gentleman, thus reply—when, if I know aught of this grand people of England, not a mechanic who walks thro' yon streets, from the loom to the hovel, but what would cry "Shame!" on such answer?

WIL. Sir, I cannot argue with, I cannot rival the man who has my father's life at his will, whether to offer it as a barter, or to yield it as a boon. Either way, rivalry between us is henceforth impossible. Fear mine no more! Give me the scroll—I depart.

HARD. (*aside*). His manliness moves me! (*aloud*) Nay, let me pray your permission to give it myself to your father, and with such words as will save him, and others whose names are hereto attached, from such perilous hazards in future.

WIL. In this, too, I fear that you leave me no choice; I must trust as I may to your honor! but heed well if——

HARD. Menace not; you doubt, then, my honor?

WIL. (*with suppressed passion*). Plainly, I do; our characters differ. I had held myself dishonored for ever if our positions had been reversed —if I had taken such confidence as was placed in you—concealed the rivalry—prepared the scheme—timed the moment—forced the condition in the guise of benefit. No, sir, no; that may be talent, it is not honor.

HARD. (*aside*). This stings! scornful fool that he is, not to see that I was half relenting. And now I feel but the foe! How sting again? I will summon him back to witness himself my triumph. (*aloud*) Stay, my Lord! (*writing at the table*) You doubt that I should yield up the document to your father? Bring him hither at once! He is now at my house with the Duke of Middlesex; pray them both to come here, and give this note to the Duke. (*with a smile*) You will do it, my Lord?

WIL. Ay, indeed—and when my father is safe, I will try to think that I wronged you. (*aside*) And not one parting word to—to—'Sdeath—I am unmanned. Show such emotion to him—No, no! And if I cannot watch over that gentle life, why, the angels will! (*aloud, as he unlocks the door*) I—I go, sir—fulfill the compact; I have paid the price.

[*Exit, L. D.*

HARD. He loves her more than I thought for. But she? Does she love him? (*goes to the door at back*) Mistress Lucy! (*leads forth* LUCY, D.F.)

LUCY. Lord Wilmot gone!

HARD. Nay, speak not of him. If ever he hoped that your father could have overcome a repugnance to his suit, he is now compelled to resign that hope, and for ever. (LUCY *turns aside, and weeps quietly*) Let us speak of your parents—your mother——

LUCY. O, yes—my dear mother—I so love her already.

HARD. You have heard her tale! Would you restore her, no blot on her name, to the hearth of your father?

LUCY. Speak!—speak!—can it be so?

HARD. If it cost you some sacrifice?

LUCY. Life has none for an object thus holy.

HARD. Hear, and decide. It is the wish of your father that I should ask for this hand——

LUCY. No!—no!

HARD. Is the sacrifice so hard? Wait and hear the atonement. You come from the stolen embrace of a mother; I will make that mother the pride of your home. You have yearned for the love of a father; I will break down the wall between yourself and his heart—I will dispel all the clouds that have darkened his life.

LUCY. You will?—you will? O blessings upon you.

HARD. Those blessings this hand can confer!

LUCY. But—but—the heart—the heart—*that* does *not* go with the hand.

HARD. Later it will. I only pray for a trial. I ask but to conquer that heart, not to break it. Your father will soon be here—every moment I expect him. He comes in the full force of suspicion—deeming you lured here by Wilmot—fearing (pardon the vile word) your dishonor. How explain? You cannot speak of your mother till I first prove her guiltless. Could they meet till I do, words would pass that would make even union hereafter too bitter to her pride as a woman. Give me the power at once to destroy suspicion, remove fear, delay other explanations. Let me speak—let me act as your betrothed, your accepted. Hark! voices below—your father comes! I have no time to plead; excuse what is harsh—seems ungenerous——

SIR GEOF. (*without, L.*). Out of my way!—loose my sword!

LUCY. Oh, save my mother! Let him not see my mother!

HARD. Grant me this trial—pledge this hand now—retract hereafter if you will. Your mother's name—your parents' reunion! Ay or no! —will you pledge it?

LUCY. Can you doubt their child's answer? I pledge it!

Enter SIR GEOFFREY, L. D., *struggling from* EASY, SOFTHEAD, *and* BARBARA.

SIR GEOF. Where is he? where is this villain? let me get at him! What, what! gone? (*falling on* HARDMAN's *breast*) Oh, Hardman! You came, you came! I dare not look at her yet. *Is* she saved?

HARD. Your daughter is innocent in thought as in deed—I speak in the name of the rights she has given me; you permitted me to ask for her hand, and here she has pledged it!

SIR GEOF. (*embracing her*). O my child! my child! I never called you
that name before. Did I? Hush! I know now that thou art my child
—know it by my anguish—know it by my joy. Who could wring from
me tears like these but a child?

EASY. But how is it all, Mr. Hardman? you know everything! That
fool Softhead, with his cock-and-bull story, frightened us out of our wits.

SOFT. That's the thanks I get! How is it all, Mr. Hardman?

SIR GEOF. Ugh, what so clear? He came here—he saved her! My
child was grateful. Approach, Hardman, near, near. Forgive me if
your childhood was lonely; forgive me if you seemed so unfriended.
Your father made me promise that you should not know the temptations
that he thought had corrupted himself—should not know of my favors,
to be galled by what he called my suspicions—should not feel the yoke
of dependence;—should believe that you forced your own way through
the world—till it was made. Now it is so. Ah, not in vain did I pardon him his wrongs against me; not in vain fulfill that sad promise
which gave a smile to his lips in dying; not in vain have I bestowed
benefits on you. You have saved—I know it—I feel it—saved from infamy—my child.

LUCY. Hush, sir, hush! (*throws herself into* BARBARA'S *arms.*)

HARD. My father? Benefits? You smile, Mr. Easy. What means
he? No man on this earth ever bestowed benefits on me!

EASY. Ha! ha! ha! Nay, excuse me; but when I think that that's
said by a clever fellow like you—ha! ha!—the jest is too good; as if
any one ever drove a coach through this world but what some other one
built the carriage, or harnessed the horses! Why, who gave you the
education that helped to make you what you are? Who slyly paid Tonson, the publisher, to bring out the work that first raised you into notice? Who sent you the broker with the tale of the South Sea Scheme?
From whose purse came the sum that bought your annuity? Whose
land does the annuity burthen? Who told Fleece'em, the borough-
monger, to offer you a seat in Parliament? Who paid for the election
that did not cost you a shilling?—who, but my suspicious, ill-tempered,
good-hearted friend there? And you are the son of his foster-brother,
the man who first wronged and betrayed him!

SOFT. And this is the gentleman who knows everybody and everything! Did not even know his own father! La! why, he's been quite
a take-in! Ha! ha!

EASY. Ha! ha! ha!

HARD. And all the while I thought I was standing apart from others
—needing none; served by none; mastering men; moulding them—
the man whom my father had wronged went before me with noiseless
beneficence, and opened my path through the mountain I fancied this
right hand had hewn!

SIR GEOF. Tut! I did but level the ground; till you were strong
eno' to rise of yourself; I did not give you the post that you named with
so manly a pride; I did not raise you to the councils of your country as
the "equal of all!"

SOFT. No! for that you'll thank Fred. He bribed the Prime Minister
with his favorite Murillo. He said you wanted the post to win the lady
you loved. *Dimidum mei* - I think you might have told him what lady it
was.

HARD. So! Wilmot! It needed but this!

EASY. Pooh, Mr. Softhead! Sir Geoffrey would never consent to a
lord. Quite right. Practical, steady fellow is Mr. Hardman; and as to
his father, a disreputable connection—quite right not to know him! All
you want, Geoffrey, is to secure Lucy's happiness.

SIR GEOF. All! That, now, is his charge.

HARD. I accept it. But first I secure yours, O my benefactor! This house, in which you feared to meet infamy, is the home of sorrow and virtue; the home of a woman unsullied, but slandered—of her who, loving you still, followed your footsteps; watched you night and day from you windows; sent you those flowers, the tokens of innocence and youth; in romance, it is true—the romance only known to a woman—the romance only known to the pure! Lord Wilmot is guiltless! He led your child to the arms of a mother,

SIR GEOF. Silence him!—silence him!—'tis a snare! I retract! He shall not have this girl! Her house? Do I breathe the same air as the woman so loved and so faithless?

LUCY. Pity, for my mother! No, no; justice for her! Pity for yourself and for me!

SIR GEOF. Come away, or you shall not be my child, I'll disown you. That man speaks——

Enter WILMOT, DUKE, *with portfolio and papers, and* LORD LOFTUS, L. D.

HARD. I speak, and I prove. (*to the* DUKE) The Memoirs. (*glancing over them*) Here is the very letter that the menial informed you your wife sent to Lord Henry. Read it, and judge if such scorn would not goad such a man to revenge. What revenge could he wield? Why, a boast!

SIR GEOF. (*reading*). The date of the very day that he boasted. Ha, brave words! proud heart! I suspect!—I suspect!

HARD. Lord Henry's confession. It was writ on his deathbed.

LOF. 'Tis his hand. I attest it.

DUKE. I, too, John, Duke of Middlesex.

SIR GEOF. (*who has been reading the confession*). Heaven forgive me! Can *she?* The flowers; the figures; the—How blind I've been! Where is she? where is she? You said she was here! (LADY ELLINOR *appears at* D. F.) Ellinor! Ellinor! to my arms—to my heart—O, my wife! Pardon! Pardon! (*embracing her rapturously.*)

LADY E. Nay, all was forgiven when I once more embraced our child.

HARD. (*to* LOFTUS *and* DUKE). My Lord, destroy this Requisition! When you signed it, you doubtless believed that the Prince you would serve was of the Church of your Protestant fathers? You are safe evermore; for your honor is freed. The Prince has retired to Rome, and abjured your faith. I will convince you of this later, (DUKE *and* SOFTHEAD *continue to shun each other with mutual apprehension.*)

EASY (*to* WILMOT). Glad to find you are not so bad as you seemed, my Lord; and now that Lucy is engaged to Mr. Hardman——

WIL. Engaged already! (*aside*) So! he asked me here to insult me with his triumph! (*aloud*) Well!

HARD. Lucy, your parents are united—my promise fulfilled; permit me—(*takes her hand*) Sir Geoffrey, the son of him who so wronged you, and whose wrongs you pardoned, now reminds you, that he is entrusted with the charge to ensure the happiness of your child! Behold the man of her choice, and take from his presence your own cure of distrust. With his faults on the surface, and with no fault that is worse than that of concealing his virtues;—Here she loves and is loved! And thus I discharge the trust, and ensure the happiness! (*takes* LUCY's *hand and places it in* WILMOT's.)

SIR GEOF. How?

LADY E. It is true—do you not read in her blush the secret of her heart?

WIL. How can I accept at the price of——

HARD. Hush! For the third time to-day, you have but one option. You cannot affect to be generous to me at the cost of a heart all your own. Take your right. Come, my Lord, lest I tell all the world how you bribed the Prime Minister.

SOFT. (who has taken EASY aside). But, indeed, Mr. Easy, I reform; I repent. Mr. Hardman will have a bride in the country—let me have a bride in the city. After all, I was not such a very bad monster.

EASY. Pooh! Won't hear of it! Want to marry only just to mimic my Lord.

BAR. Dear Lord Wilmot; do say a good word for us.

EASY. No, sir; no! Your head's been turned by a lord.

WIL. Not the first man whose head has been turned by a lord, with the help of the Duke of Burgundy—eh, Mr. Easy? I'll just appeal to Sir Geoffrey.

EASY. No—no—hold your tongue, my Lord.

WIL. And you insisted upon giving your daughter to Mr. Softhead; forced her upon him.

EASY. I—never! When?

WIL. Last night, when you were chaired member for the City of London. I'll just explain the case to Sir Geoffrey——

EASY. Confound it—hold—hold! You like this young reprobate, Barbara?

BAR. Dear papa, his health is so delicate. I should like to take care of him.

EASY. There go, and take care of each other. Ha! ha! I suppose it is all for the best.

DUKE *takes forth, and puts on, his spectacles; examines* SOFTHEAD *curiously —is convinced that he is human, approaches, and offers his hand, which* SOFTHEAD, *emboldened by* BARBARA, *though not without misgivings, accepts—the* DUKE *shakes his hand—does the same with* BARBARA, *and passes to the left where* LORD LOFTUS *joins him.*

A great deal of dry stuff, called philosophy, is written about life. But the grand thing is to take it coolly, and have a good-humored indulgence——

WIL. For the force of example, Mr. Easy. (*bowing to him.*)

SOFT. Ha! ha! ha!

WIL. For the follies of fashion, and the crimes of monsters like myself, and that terrible Softhead!

SIR GEOF. Ha! ha!

HARD. You see, my dear Wilmot, many sides to a character!

WIL. Plague on it, yes! But get at them all, and we're not so bad as we seem——

SOFT. No, Fred, not quite so bad.

WIL. Taking us as we stand—ALTOGETHER!

Position of Characters.

WILMOT *and* LUCY.   HARDMAN.   SOFTHEAD *and* BARBARA.

SIR GEOFFREY *and* LADY ELLINOR.   EASY.   DUKE *and* LORD LOFTUS.

CURTAIN.

"DAVID FALLEN IS DEAD!"

OR, A KEY TO THE PLAY.

(AN AFTER SCENE BY WAY OF AN EPILOGUE.)

(Intended to have been spoken by the Original Amateur Performers.)

SCENE.—WILMOT'S *Apartment.* WILMOT, SIR GEOFFREY, SOFTHEAD,
. EASY, *and* HARDMAN, *seated at a table. Wine, fruits,* etc.

WIL. Pass the wine—what's the news ?
EASY.   Funds have risen to-day.
SIR GEOF. I suspect it will rain.
EASY.   Well, I've got in my hay.
HARD. DAVID FALLEN IS DEAD !
OMNES.   DAVID FALLEN !
WIL.   Poor fellow !
SIR GEOF. I should like to have seen him !
SOFT.   *I* saw him ! *So* yellow !
HARD. Your annuity killed him !
WIL.   How ?—how ? to the point.
HARD. By the shock on his nerves—at the sight of a joint.
     A very great genius——
EASY.   I own—now he's dead,
     That a writer more charming——
WIL.   Was never worse fed !
HARD. His country was grateful——
SOFT. (*surprised*).   He looked very shabby !
HARD. His bones——
SOFT.   You might count them !——
HARD.   Repose in the Abbey !
SOFT. (*after a stare of astonishment*). So *that* is the way that a country is
         grateful !
     Ere his nerves grew so weak—if she'd sent him a plateful.
EASY (*hastily producing a long paper*).   *My Taxes !*
     Your notions are perfectly hateful ! (*pause. Evident feeling that*
         there's no getting over MR. EASY'S *paper.*)
WIL Pope's epigram stung him.
HARD.   Yes, Pope has a sting.
WIL But who writes the epitaph ?
HARD.   Pope ; a sweet thing !
WIL. 'Gad, if I were an author, I'd rather, instead,
     Have the epitaph living—the epigram dead.
     If Pope had but just reconsidered that matter,
     Poor David——
SOFT.   Had gone to the Abbey much fatter !
EASY. He was rather a scamp !
WIL.   Put yourself in his place.

EASY (*horror-struck*). Heaven forbid!

HARD.   Let us deem him the Last of a Race!

SIR GEOF. But the race that succeeds may have little more pelf.

HARD. Ay; and trials as sharp. I'm an author myself.

    But the remedy? Wherefore should authors not build——

EASY. An almshouse?

HARD.   No, merchant, their own noble guild!

    Some fortress for youth in the battle for fame;

    Some shelter that Age is not humbled to claim;

    Some roof from the storm for the Pilgrim of Knowledge.

WIL. Not unlike what our ancestors meant by—a College;

    Where teacher and student alike the subscriber,

    Untaxing the Patron——

EASY.   The State——

HARD.   Or the briber——

WIL. The son of proud Learning shall knock at the door

    And cry *This** is rich, and not whine *That†* is poor.

HARD. Oh right! For these men govern earth from their graves—

    Shall the dead be as kings, and the living as slaves?

EASY. It is all their own fault—they so slave one another;

    Not a son of proud Learning but knocks—down his brother!

WIL. Yes! other vocations, from Thames to the Border,

    Have some *esprit de corps*, and some pride in their order;

    Lawyers, soldiers, and doctors, if quarrels do pass,

    Still soften their spite from respect to their class;

    Why should authors be spitting and scratching like tabbies,

    To leave but dry bones——

SOFT.   For those grateful cold Abbeys?

HARD. Worst side of their character!

WIL.   True to the letter.

    Are their sides, then, so fat, we can't hit on a better?

HARD. Why—the sticks in the fable —our Guild be the tether.

WIL. Ay; then the thorns are rubbed off when the sticks cling together.

SOFT. (*musingly*). I could *be*—yes—I *could* be a Pilgrim of Knowledge,

    If you'd change Deadman's Lane to a snug little College.

SIR GEOF. Ugh! stuff—it takes money a College to found.

EASY. I will head the subscription myself—with a pound.

HARD. Quite enough from a friend; for we authors should feel

    We must put our own shoulders like men to the wheel.

    Be thrifty when thriving—take heed of the morrow——

EASY. And not get in debt——

SIR GEOF.   Where the deuce could they borrow?

HARD. Let us think of a scheme.

EASY.   He is always so knowing.

WIL. A scheme! I have got one; the wheel's set a-going!

    A play from one author.

HARD.   With authors for actors——

WIL. And some benefit nights——

BOTH.   For the world's benefactors.

SIR GEOF. Who'll give you the play? it will not be worth giving,

    Authors now are so bad; always are while they're living!

EASY. Ah! if David Fallen, great genius, were he——

OMNES. Great genius!

HARD.   A man whom all time shall revere;

SOFT. (*impatiently*). But he's dead.

---

     * The head.   † The pocket.

OMNES. (*lugubriously*).   He is dead!
EASY.   The true Classical School, sir!
Ah! could he come back!
WIL.   He'll not be such a fool, sir. (*taking*
HARDMAN *aside, whispers.*)
We know of an author.
HARD. (*doubtfully*).   Ye—s—s, David was brighter.
OMNES. But he's dead!
HARD.   This might do—as a live sort of writer.
EASY. Alive! that looks bad.
SOFT.   Must we take a live man?
WIL. To oblige us he'll be, sir—as dead as he can!
SOFT. Alive; and *will* write, sir?
HARD.   With pleasure, sir.
SOFT.   *Pleasure!*
HARD. With less than your wit, he has more than your leisure.
Coquettes with the Muse——
SIR GEOF.   Lucky dog to afford her!
WIL. Can we get his good side?
HARD.   Yes, he's proud of his order.
WIL. Then he'll do!
SIR GEOF.   As for wit—he has books on his shelves.
HARD. Now the actors?
WIL.   By Jove, we'll act it ourselves. (OMNES *at first*
surprised into enthusiasm, succeeded by great consternation)
SIR GEOF. Ugh, not I!
SOFT.   Lord ha' mercy!
EASY.   A plain, sober, steady——
WIL. I'll appeal to Sir Geoffrey. There's one caught already!
This suspicious old knight; to his blind side direct us.
HARD. Your part is to act——
WIL.   True; and his to suspect us.
I rely upon you.
HARD. (*looking at his watch*). Me! I have not a minute!
WIL. If the play has a plot, he is sure to be in it.
Come, Softhead!
SOFT.   I won't. I'll go home to my mother.
WIL. Pooh! monsters like us always help one another.
SIR GEOF. I suspect you will act.
SOFT.   Well, I've this consolation—
Still to imitate one——
HARD.   Who defies imitation.
WIL. Let the public but favor the plan we have hit on,
And we'll chair through all London—our Family Briton.
SIR GEOF. What? what? Look at Easy! He's drunk, or I dream——
EASY (*rising*). The toast of the evening—SUCCESS TO THE SCHEME.

CURTAIN.

THE
DUCHESS DE LA VALLIÈRE.

CAST OF CHARACTERS.

	Theatre Royal, Covent Garden, London, Jan. 4, 1837.	Park Theatre, New York, May 13, 1837.
Louis the Fourteenth, King of France ..Mr. VANDENHOFF.		Mr. MASON.
The Duke de Lauzun...............Mr. W. FARREN.		Mr. CHIPPENDALE.
The Count de Grammont........ ....Mr. PRITCHARD.		Mr. NIXSEN.
The Marquis Alphonso de Bragelone (Betrothed to Louise de la Vallière)Mr. MACREADY.		Mr. FREDERICKS.
Bertrand (Armorer to the Marquis)......Mr. TILBURY.		Mr. ISHERWOOD.
Gentleman in Attendance..............		Mr. RUSSELL.
First, Second, and Third Courtiers......		
Maria Theresa, Queeen of France........		Mrs. ARCHER.
Louise (afterwards Duchess) de la VallièreMiss HELEN FAUCIT.		Miss ELLEN TREE.
Madame de la Vallière (her mother).....Mrs. W. WEST.		Mrs. WHEATLEIGH.
Madame de Montespan (Rival of the Duchess, and one of the King's Mistresses.................. ....Miss PELHAM.		Mrs. DURIE.
First, Second, and Third Ladies of the Court and Maids of Honor to the Queen.........................		
The Lady Abbess (Superioress of the Convent of the Carmelites)		

Courtiers, Gentleman of the Chamber, Priests, Nuns, Ladies, Maids of Honor, etc.

TIME IN REPRESENTATION—THREE HOURS AND THIRTY MINUTES.

SCENE.—The Chateau de la Vallière some leagues from Paris; the Palaces of Fontainebleau and Versailles; and the Convent of the Carmelites in the vicinity of the Chateau.

PERIOD—1672-1674.

SCENERY.

ACT I., Scene I.—The Chateau de la Vallière and Convent of the Carmelites in the distance. In a slanting direction, L., the entrance and a part of the buildings of an old Chateau; the back scene represents woods and vineyards, and through the openings a river. The turrets of the Carmelite Convent are seen at the hack, R., in the distance.

Scene II.—Armory in the Castle of Bragelone. The flats in the second grooves represent heavy grained stone archways and pillars, upon which appear to be hanging various pieces of armor and different weapons.

Scene III.—Antechamber in the Palace of Fontainebleau. The flats in the second grooves represent the interior of a rich apartment.

Scene IV.—Gardens of the Palace of Fontainebleau. The stage is thrown open to the full extent; the wings represent branches of trees hung with colored lamps—vases of flowers on pedestals are placed, at pleasure, about the stage; the flats represent in perspective a continuation of the gardens, with fountains. In the centre, at the upper part of the stage, a large pavilion, with gilded pillars and dome with trellis-work. It is made to open out, and when open there is seen inside a figure representing the Goddess of Fortune with an illuminated wheel at her feet—at either side of her a gilt vase, over which preside two figures emblematical of Merit and Honor.

ACT II., Scene I.—Gardens of the Palace of Fontainebleau. The flats in the third grooves represent, in perspective, beautiful gardens, fountains, statuary, etc. The wings in the second grooves project some distance on the stage, and are cut representing slender trees entwining. A rustic bench in a slanting position, L. 2 E.

Scene II.—Cabinet of the King at Fontainebleau. The flats in the fourth grooves represent a richly decorated apartment. An antique table, c., far back so as to allow of the next scene closing in—papers and writing materials on the table—chairs R. and I. of table.

Scene III.—Cloisters of a Convent. The flats representing heavy stone walls close in on the third grooves. Long windows, through which flashes of lightning are seen.

ACT III, Scene I.—Antechamber in the Palace of the Duchess de la Vallière at Versailles. The flats in the second grooves represent the interior of a handsome apartment.

Scene II.—Saloon in the King's Palace. The flats in the fourth grooves represent a magnificently decorated room. An arched entrance, c., with rich heavy curtains. Doors R. 2 E. and L. 2 F. A richly-gilded table, R., with chess-board and pieces—chairs to match R. and L. of table. Another table, L., with writing materials upon it, and two chairs. A candelabra lighted upon each table.

Scene III.—The Gardens of Versailles. The flats as in Act II., Scene I., placed in the second grooves.

Scene IV.—Grand Saloon in the Palace of Versailles. The flats in the fourth grooves represent a magnificent apartment; a large archway, c., beyond which, represented in perspective, a suite of apartments of similar style.

ACT IV., Scene I.—The Gardens at Versailles. The flats, as in Act II., Scene I., placed in the second grooves.

Scene II.—Private apartment in the Palace of the Duchess de la Vallière. A richly-decorated saloon; the flats in the fourth grooves. Folding doors c. Doors L. 3 E. and R. 3 E. Small gilt tables and chairs R. and L., opposite the doors.

ACT V., Scene I.—The Gardens at Versailles. Same as Act IV., Scene I., but in the front grooves.

Scene II.—The old Chateau de la Vallière. The same as Act I., Scene I.

Scene III.—Exterior of the Convent of the Carmelites. The flats in the second grooves represent the Gothic entrance of the Convent. Massive doors, c., partially open. Windows illumined R. and L.

Scene IV.—Interior of the Chapel of the Carmelite Convent. The whole stage is thrown open, and represents the pillared and vaulted aisles of a Gothic chapel. In the centre at the back appears the altar, with raised steps approaching to it, fitted up in a gorgeous manner with figures, etc., lit up with tapers; from the arched roof hang down lights; priests and officials walk to and fro swinging censers.

PROPERTIES.

ACT I., Scene 1.—Bell to sound for vespers. *Scene* 2.—Long and heavy sword for BERTRAND; letter for servant; bugle. *Scene* 4.—Various jewels and rich ornaments, a heavy diamond bracelet; vases, flowers, and pedestals; colored lamps.
ACT II., Scene 1.—Rustic bench; miniature handsomely set with jewels. *Scene* 2.— An antique table and two chairs; papers and writing materials. Folded parchment for the King. *Scene* 3.—Tolling bell; trumpet; thunder; lightning.
ACT III., Scene 1.—Two richly-gilded tables and four chairs; chess-board and pieces; two candelabras, lighted; writing materials; letter. *Scene* 4.—Folded parchment for memorial.
ACT IV., Scene 1.—Two small gilt tables; four chairs; faded scarf for BRAGELONE; golden goblet and salver.
ACT V., Scene 2.—Bell for vespers; glove for Duchess. *Scene* 3.—Letter for LAUZUN. *Scene* 4.—Organ; swinging censers with incense; lights suspended along the aisle, and tapers placed on and about the altar.

COSTUMES.

Compiled expressly for this Edition from the best French authorities.

LOUIS.—A richly-embroidered purple velvet loose waistcoat, or jacket body without sleeves, fasteued at the throat and loose downwards; rich lace collar, full lawn shirt, sleeves puffed with purple ribbons and finished with lace ruffles; a short skirt of purple velvet, with embroidery and lace fringed at the bottom; full leggings of black silk; high-heeled shoes; bands of purple satin ribbon gartered round the knees, with rosettes or drooping ends, and bows or rosettes on shoes. Auburn colored hair in long ringlets. A richly-embroidered sash from the left shoulder to below the right hip, from which hangs a rich court sword in an almost horizontal position. Broad hat with feathers on either side. The Order of Saint Esprit on left breast. An embroidered overcloak trimmed with ermine in Act 2, Scene 3, and in Act 5.

LAUZUN.—Short velvet coat (any color), with embroidered cuffs, rich lace ruffles and collar, with silk bows. Long curl wig. Hat wide, and partially looped up on one side, with feathers. A gold embroidered silk sash from the right shoulder to low down on the left hip, from which hangs a court sword in an almost horizontal position. Silk stockings and high-heeled shoes, with large silk bows. An overcloak in Act 2, Scene 3, and in Act 5, Scene 3 and last Scene.

DE GRAMMONT.—A Similar dress.

BRAGELONE.—*Act* 1: Suit of plain armor, consisting of coat of mail, with half sleeves, thigh pieces, and buff leather arm pieces, and leggings and garters with buff leather shoes, and spurs; steel helmet, with vizor raised; sword and cross-belt. *Act* 2, *Scene* 1: Rich blue velvet coat embroidered with gold both back and front and round the cuffs, with large lace ruffles and collar. An under-skirt of silk. Full and loose half-breeches of silk, fastened at the knee with garters of colored silk and long ends or rosettes. Silk stockings and high-heeled shoes, with broad lappets or rosettes of silk. Long curl wig, and hat slightly looped up, with feathers. Richly embroidered sash, reaching across to left hip, and sword hanging almost horizontally. *Act* 4: A monk's long gown of dark serge, fastened round the waist with a band of same material; black stockings and sandals; cowl to gown, and bald wig.

BERTRAND.—Buff leather jerkin and breeches; gaiters and high-heeled shoes, lace collar, waist-belt, and short wig.

GENTLEMAN.—A loose coat of velvet, embroidered, and reaching to the knees, with sleeves embroidered and looped with ribbons; loose and full half-breeches, stockings, and high-heeled shoes, with lappets or bows; long curl wig.

COURTIERS.—Similar dresses to LAUZUN and BRAGELONE, but not of such rich description. The dresses should be varied, however, by some of them wearing silk tights and large deep lace ruffles round the knees. The hair in curls; shoes and rosettes; swords.

PRIESTS.—Long and full black gowns, with tight sleeves, over which are suspended lawn robes, fastened at the neck, with large sleeves; some of them wearing slightly embroidered or ornamental robes; silk stockings and sandals; full hair.

LOUISE.—*Act* 1, *Scene* 1: Plain velvet bodice with lace up the front, loose sleeves, with muslin under sleeves; long sweeping skirt. Sleeves and neck trimmed with lace; bracelets and necklace; hair in curls; low hat and feathers; rich silk scarf. *Scene* 4: A handsome velvet bodice with gold embroidery, trimmed at neck and sleeves with lace and ribbons; long skirt of blue silk richly ornamented with gold, embroidery and puffings of ribbons; high-heeled shoes and rosettes; hair in curls. *Act* 2, *Scene* 3: A full cloak thrown over dress and fastened at the neck and waist with silk cords. *Act* 3, *Scene* 2: Rich velvet bodice coming down in a peak in front and then sloping off on either side to form a train. The skirt portion edged round with puffs of amber silk; the bodice is laced together in front with gold and silver cords; short sleeves, half way between shoulder and elbow, bound round with puffs of ribbon, and continued in loose white under sleeves of lace, and rows of lace round the neck; rich satin under skirt and train; high-heeled shoes, and bows; bracelets and necklace; hair in long curls; hat with feather, when needed.* *Act* 5, *Scene* 2: Similar dress to Act 1, Scene 1, with cloak as in Act 2. *Scene* 3: Hat and feathers, and gloves. *Scene* 4: Rich bridal costume of white satin bodice, full sleeves, skirt and train, trimmed with wreaths of flowers and rosettes round the head; under skirt of white silk; high-heeled white leather shoes; followed, in the change, by a plain black loose robe, with white collar and cuffs, and the hair without any ornaments.

THE QUEEN.—A similar costume to the DUCHESS, but varied in the color and arrangement, and more highly ornamented with a greater display of jewelry; high-heeled shoes; hair in curls.

DE MONTESPAN.—A similar costume, but varied during the play in each Act. A breast knot of colors in Act 3, and in the last Act a light overcloak, hat and feathers; high-heeled shoes; hair in curls.

MADAME DE LA VALLIERE.—A full-bodied dark velvet dress, with short sleeves trimmed with lace, and lace round the neck; velvet train, trimmed with ribbons, and under skirt of dark silk; high-heeled shoes; fan; hat and feathers.

LADIES OF THE COURT AND MAIDS OF HONOR.—Similar dresses in construction and arrangement to those previously described, but not of such rich material or so highly ornamented. All the ladies wear long curls, high-heeled shoes, and rosettes, and in Act 3 breast-knots.

STORY OF THE PLAY.

SOME years previous to the commencement of the play, Madame de la Vallière had been left a widow by the untimely death of the Lord de Vallière in one of the battles which took place during the campaign between the French and the Dutch. One daughter was the only offspring of the marriage, and upon her was bestowed all that a mother's care and affection could provide. Beautiful, warm-hearted, and loving, it may easily be imagined how great was the treasure the widow possessed, and with what fear and trembling she received an intimation that the reigning sovereign, Louis the XIV., desired the presence of her daughter at court. Of the state of affairs at the period selected for the incidents of the play, and of the character of Louis, a very good idea may be gathered from the " Remarks " which will be found hereafter.

Occupying a time-honored chateau, Madame and Louise de la Vallière were happy and contented; and the latter had the additional happiness of a lover, Alphonse Marquis de Bragelone, one of the most noble and gallant knights of the period. When quite a stripling, he had bravely won his spurs, by saving De Vallière's standard from the grasp of the enemy, and upon another occasion, he threw himself in front of the king, and received in his breast a stab, in spite of his coat of mail, which would probably have terminated the monarch's life. Bragelone was one who never left debts unpaid, and he discharged this by cleaving in two the head of his assailant. His courage and skill gained him the friendship of his peers, and combined with his handsome and gallant bearing, the love and admiration of the softer sex; it was not long, therefore, before he found great favor in the eyes of the beautiful Louise de la Vallière.

True love, it is known, never runs smooth; the king's wish was law, and Louise was bound to go to the court.

The play opens on the evening previous to her departure, when, accompanied by her mother, she is taking a parting view, perhaps forever, of the abode of childhood, youth, and innocence—naturally, the scene is an affecting and trying one; the mother

* The design of this dress is taken from an old painting of the Queen, Maria Theresa, but it is thought proper to adapt it to the Duchess, she being the conspicuous character of the play.

has every faith and confidence in her child; a firm belief, that by instinct she will shrink from wrong; and that the thought of a parent's love, and the voice of a pure conscience, will guide her safely through all temptations, even through those at that time existing in the gayest and most profligate court in Europe. Louise bids her look well after the poor peasants, who will miss her in the winter, and her birds, and then comes the germs of danger—the story of the visions she has frequently had of royalty, love, and empire. The mother endeavors to convince her it is mere imagination, conjured up by her father's stories, who, in her early years, was always instilling into her mind the old knightly faith of France, "To honor God, and love the king." Louise admits it might be so, but thinks it strange to have had the dream so often. The arrival of her lover, Bragelone, prevents further discussion. He, too, has been summoned away; not to court, but to the wars, and he rejoices that when she is gone he will not be left behind, alone to haunt the spots they had so often sought together, and mourn her absence day after day. In warm language, he relates to her the story of his love and its growth—the idolatry of his passion, and points out to her the vast difference between his own honest heart, that never wronged a friend or shunned a foe, and that of the courtiers she will meet, mere minions of the king; proud to the humble, servile to the great. With a strangely mingled feeling, that she does, and yet she does not, love Bragelone, she binds her scarf across his coat of mail, and bids him farewell.

In due course, she reaches the court, where her grace and beauty attract the admiration of all, of the king more especially. A letter from her mother, to Bragelone, informs him of all this, and he is so proud of her triumph, that he vows the king, for the favor and praise he has bestowed upon the idol of his love, shall find in him henceforward, a tenfold better soldier. Telling his joys to the old family armorer, Bertrand the faithful retainer is proud, indeed, to learn the secret of his master's love, and is half wild with glee, at the prospect of a marriage, and nursing upon his knee an infant likeness of his young lord.

Gossip and scandal are not long, however, before they attack Louise. The subject of her early visions are formed into reality by the gorgeous scenes surrounding her. When first beholding the king's portrait, young, gallant, and handsome as he is, a vague feeling of a wild, romantic fancy for him, not yet ripened into actual love, steals over her, and the passion becomes stronger when they meet. The courtiers, but more especially, the wily Duke de Lauzun, are pleased with this. According to his views, the king must have a mistress, and by that mistress he must mount to fame and power. A brilliant fête which takes place in the gardens of the Fontainebleau palace, affords him an excellent opportunity of furthering his projects. In the confidence of the king, they converse freely, respecting Louise; and in honeyed words, the Duke tells him of the court gossip. Louise approaching, they draw aside, and overhear her describe to the ladies of the court, in the most glowing language, her admiration of the king. The ladies retire, to join in the dance, and she is about to follow, when he intercepts her, and the Duke judiciously slips away. Thus left alone, the king, in passionate language, declares his love. A strong struggle rends her heart; she implores him to unsay his words, and reminding him that she is but a poor, simple girl, who, though she loves her king, loves honor more, flies from his presence. Her coyness only increases the intensity of his passion, and another opportunity is soon afforded him to further show her the ardor of his love. Amongst the varied amusements is one, the Temple of Fortune, presided over by Merit and Honor. Each person draws a ticket from the vase of Merit, and presenting it to Honor, receives in return some article of jewelry which is presented to the presumed object of affection. The king draws a magnificent diamond bracelet, every eye is upon him, each lady hoping to be the happy recipient of the royal favor; quickly and gallantly he clasps it upon the arm of Louise, and the first step towards the path of sin is taken.

Strange rumors reach Bragelone, of the sudden advancement of Louise at court; insinuations are strongly uttered that she is the king's chosen favorite, and although the young knight cannot bring himself to believe that it is needed, he determines to seek her; to warn, advise, protect, and, if required, to save her. Arriving at Fontainebleau, in strolling through the gardens, he encounters Lauzun, who relates to him the gossip of the court, and throws out broad hints as to the chastity of Louise. The indignation of Bragelone is aroused; although a rough, stern soldier, taught from youth to maintain his words by his sword, he restrains himself, and implores Lauzun to unsay the story; meeting with a refusal and a repetition, they fight, and though Bragelone disarms him, he scorns to take his life. They separate, but Bragelone, returning to the spot, comes unexpectedly upon Louise, who is gazing with admiration upon a portrait of the king, and breathing his name in tender accents. Bragelone speaks to her with all his fervent love; he pictures to her in vivid terms, the image of what she was, and what he is now led to believe she is. With true indignation, she denies the charge; still he insinuates its truth, telling her how deeply and devotedly he loved her, but now that confidence and hope have fled, his heart is crushed, and life hath charms no more. She beseeches him not to be hasty in his judgment; she will fly back to the old chateau and quit the court forever. Still doubting, he reminds her that even there the king can reach, and that there is only one safe place of shelter left—the house of God. In great agony she half-consents, but urges that she should see the king once more, to take a last farewell; Bragelone reminds her, most touchingly, of the love of her mother, who is then blessing Heaven for her birth, but to-morrow may be wishing she were dead. The scruples of Louise are vanquished by this touching appeal, and she flies with Bragelone.

At an interview between the king and Lauzun, to whom he is giving the lands and lordship of one of the French provinces as a token of his gratitude for the zeal with which the wily courtier serves him, Louis again tells him of the depth of his love for Louise; during which, news is brought him of her flight. In a torrent of passion, he proclaims that she is, to him, more than his crown, from which not all the arms of Europe dare take a single jewel, and that all who stand between him and her are traitors to the throne.

Louise reaches in safety the Convent of the Carmelites; but she cannot command peace of mind or repose. She feels that she loves the king, though it is guilty so to do, and she would not, if she could, be happy and forget him. Sounds of alarm at this moment ring through the building, and the king, accompanied by Lauzun, arrives to claim, if needs be, to compel, the return of Louise. Surrounded by affrighted nuns, the Lady Abbess reminds him that the walls of the holy building are sacred against the power of the strongest monarch. But Louis is not to be thwarted, and notwithstanding the threatened curses of the church of Rome, he claims the right to converse with Louise alone; she has not yet taken the vows, she is a fatherless child over whom, as one of his court, he lawfully has control, and therefore he commands a private interview. Most reluctantly the Lady Abbess yields, and left alone, he appeals passionately to Louise to retrace her steps. At first she firmly resists his importunities, but his solemn declaration of true, undying, and enduring love, which he, the proudest and most powerful monarch in Europe, offers to her on his knee, are too flattering tributes to her vanity; she acknowledges her love for him and yields, returning to the court to—fall.

In a brief period, wealth, position, and splendor are bestowed upon Louise: but, as so frequently the case, they bring neither happiness nor friendship. She is raised to the rank of a Duchess and soon finds a powerful rival, in the person of Madame de Montespan, one of the maids of honor, a woman of almost equal beauty, but not of such genuine tenderness and devotion as Louise. Madame de Montespan is artful, intriguing, and ambitious; and she finds a ready helpmate in Lauzun, who has assisted her in her schemes on more than one occasion. He willingly joins his forces, as he has not found in the Duchess the friendship and support he had been expecting to receive from her so soon as she attained a high position. Madame de Montespan had once loved Lauzun, she might even love him now, but she loves ambition and power more. She needs a guide, but once successful in her schemes, she must have no partner; then, with all his haughty air, she will bind him in her charms—she will lead but not be led.

An opportunity too soon occurs to put their schemes in motion, and work the downfall of the Duchess. During one of their private hours of enjoyment, over a game of chess, the king tells Louise of sad news he has received, and that both himself and France mourn the loss of one of his bravest subjects, who should have died a marshal had not death struck so soon. With true and innocent sympathy she inquires his name, that she, too, may mourn his untimely end; and it is in vain she endeavors to conceal her emotion, when the answer comes, "Bragelone!"

The king questions her, and she does not attempt to conceal from him that they were betrothed in youth; then flashes across his mind with all the weight of truth, Lauzun's assertions, that Louise loved another, and that it was not the king who had won her virgin heart. Jealousy, disappointed pride, and anger, are alternately aroused : he reproaches her bitterly for sorrowing over lost virtue; forgetting that she is placed next in rank to the latest, but not the least, of the great Bourbon race of kings, and he sternly commands her to greet him for the future with smiles, and not with tears. Dissembling, however, they separate, she in the belief that the storm has blown over—he, to consult his wily favorite, Lauzun, and with the assistance of his wit and knavery, endeavor to find some new attraction in the place of her whom he had so ardently sought, but of whom he now grows weary.

At this unfortunate moment for the Duchess, Madame de Montespan arrives, and learning that the king has gone off in anger, quickly perceives the value of the opportunity fortune has thrown in her way. There is a great fête in preparation, and as she serves the queen, and will consequently meet the king before sunset, she suggests that Louise should write to him, and promises herself to place the letter in his hands. The gentle and unsuspecting Duchess falls into the snare; she tells Madame de Montespan of the discovery of her love for Bragelone, and gives her the letter to the king, with heart-felt joy, at having found in the hour of trouble so true a friend. The clue thus found, Madame de Montespan determines to follow up until it leads the Duchess to destruction—herself to favor, and, perhaps, the throne. During the progress of the fête, the king reveals to Lauzun his fancy for Madame de Montespan, and the wily courtier perceiving she is approaching, withdraws so as to leave them together. With well assumed diffidence, and deceptive modesty of demeanor, she presents the letter. The king is struck with her beauty, which had hitherto escaped his notice; she perceives the impression she has made, and so artfully constructs her speech, that she rouses an ardent passion within him, which he openly declares. Following up the advantage thus gained, she rejects his offers, and hurriedly retreats, thus making him still more anxious to secure a successor to the Duchess. A further opportunity occurs to contribute to her downfall. A courtier, believing in her influence and power with the king, presents a memorial for a vacant appointment as colonel in the royal guards. Louise, however, tells him that merit, rather than favor, should obtain the post, and declines to interfere; not so, however, with Madame de Montespan who observes the chance, takes the paper and promises the king shall see it and grant the request. In an interview that follows, this is achieved, even in the presence of Louise, who sees with grief and anguish, the mastery that her rival is assuming. And yet another blow falls. A knightly tournament is to be held, at which each combatant is to wear the colors of the lady he now chooses. Louise, in her confiding nature, believes that the king will, as hitherto, receive hers; but when she takes the breast-knot from her bosom, and offers it, he turns aside, and selects one from Madame de Montespan. The Duchess is crushed, but the wily Lauzun bids her conceal her emotion, and artfully suggests how differently he would have acted.

As quickly as the Duchess rose to wealth and power, so does Madame de Montespan rise. Now is the time for Lauzun to act; he is very poor, his creditors very pressing, the Duchess is rich and a valuable prize—though a blemish exists, it is obscured by her wealth ; why should he not marry her? Warily, and cautiously, he mentions the subject to the king, who at first receives the proposition with anger, love still lingering in his breast : but ultimately he gives his approval to the suit.

Madame De la Vallière is dead, and the sorrows and sufferings of the Duchess are increased by the knowledge that she is now alone in the world. A visit from Lauzun gives her a momentary hope of joy; believing he brings a message from the king, but this is soon dispelled 1 y the proffer of Lauzun's hand. Bowed down by grief and shame, there is still some honesty and virtue left, and learning that the king himself has encouraged, even wished for the union, she indignantly rejects the offer, and bids him, as the king's friend, depart; not wishing to see him so debased as to be refused by the cast-off mistress of his master.

Immediately after this interview, Bragelone, whose reported death is untrue, arrives in the garb of a Franciscan Friar, and craves an audience of the Duchess. In the course of this interview, he acquaints her with the particulars of her lover's supposed death—he depicts the fervency of his affection, and the crushing blow that fell upon him when he received the tidings of her fall from virtue. In agony, she listens to the story of his sufferings, and he hands her a faded scarf, the one she had twined around his coat of mail. An inward, undefined feeling prompts her to ask who he is, and he tells her, "Bragelone's brother," upon which she implores him to be a friend to the friendless. This he promises, and further informs her, that as a priest, he had engaged to wait until her guilty fame was tarnished, then to seek her, and lead her to repentance and atonement. In the deepest agony she listens to the story of her mother's death, which had been hastened by her shame; that on her death-bed, in the once joyous home of honor, peace and purity, the mother was about to curse, when Bragelone, who attended her whilst life held out, arrested her lips, and her dying breath yielded forth a blessing In frantic anguish, the Duchess can bear no more, and rushes madly from the room. Ere Bragelone can depart, the king arrives, and the friar boldly reproaches him with his perfidious conduct. He pictures his greatness, as viewed in the world, and then paints him as he appears before an humble minister of Heaven.

> "You are the king who has betray'd his trust—
> Beggar'd a nation, but to bloat a court,
> Seen in men's lives the pastime to ambition,
> Look'd but on virtue as the toy for vice;
> And, for the first time, from a subject's lips,
> Now learns the name he leaves to Time and God!"

Angered, as the king is, the friar is undaunted; more powerful, more eloquent and more impassioned in his language, he warns him to beware of the consequences of his cruelty, voluptuousness, and vice, and leaves him astounded at the truthful, but audacious speech. A good draught of wine soon nerves the king for his interview with the Duchess, in which he urges the marriage with Lauzun. She tells him of the refusal, and that she has made another choice, of which he shall be in due time informed; thus satisfied, he departs. Bragelone returns; her struggles have been great, but the desire for repentance has triumphed, and she agrees to accompany the friar to the Convent of the Carmelites.

The news of the second flight of the Duchess creates much sensation, but Madame de Montespan asserts that a month's fasting and penance will send her back again. Matters have not gone on well with the new mistress and Lauzun; he is chafed at her constant allusions to his love for the Duchess, and she, by his retort, that it is something to love the only woman whom the king had ever *honored*. She threatens to exert her influence, and procure his banishment; and thus forewarned, he determines to increase the coldness with which the king has already begun to look upon his new mistress, observing, with appropriate sarcasm:

> "The war's declared—'tis clear that one must fall,
> I'll be polite—the *lady* to the wall!"

Upon leaving the palace, Bragelone, still unknown, conducts the Duchess to the old chateau, to take a farewell look of the former abode of childhood, purity, and happiness. It is too severe a trial, and she swoons in his arms. As he bends over and imprints a kiss upon her lips—

> "A brother's kiss—it has no guilt;
> Kind Heaven, it has no guilt!"

he breathes aloud her name. Slowly reviving, she hears and recognizes him: he passionately tells her that his last task before death, is to lead her soul to peace, and on the day that she takes the veil, one more, one last meeting, and then—she to a convent, he to a hermit's cell without.

The king has undergone another change; the coarseness and artfulness of Madame de Montespan, as compared with the gentleness and innocence of the Duchess, have displeased him, and he sends a letter to Louise full of his old affection: but it is too late, she is firm in her resolution. He is not, however, to be thwarted thus, and he hurries forward to stop the ceremony, and secure, if possible, her return.

In the meantime, the tables are shifting between Lauzun and Madame de Montespan. He exerts his power and influence with success, and at the very moment that she is congratulating herself upon her agreeable progress so far, and again threatens Lauzun, her fall is consummated by his producing a letter from the king, excusing her further attendance at court, and banishing her from Paris. Thus far successful, Lauzun hastens to join the king in his efforts to secure the Duchess.

Reaching the convent, and forcing their way to the altar, through the crowd assembled to witness the imposing ceremony, Bragelone stops the king's advance, calling upon the priests of Heaven to complete their task, and invoking the curse of the Church upon him who would interfere. Before the ceremony is over, the king obtains an interview with the Duchess: in the most humble and imploring language, he confesses his errors, and beseeches her to return: renewed love, wealth, power, rank—all shall be lavished upon her. Too late! Her reply is:

> "For Louis Heaven was left—and now I leave
> Louis, when tenfold more beloved, for Heaven!"

The end is reached   The church claims as her own, the beautiful mistress of Louis the XIV., King of France: and the world, with all its glories, pomp, and vanities, are forever shut out from the gaze of—*The Duchess de la Vallière!*

REMARKS.

PURSUING the plan adopted in the historical play of Richelieu, a brief notice of the royal personage who figures so conspicuously in this play, and of the position of affairs at the period, will, it is hoped, prove interesting.

Louis XIII. (who figures in Richelieu), died in 1643, leaving one son, aged five years, over whom he appointed a Council of Regency, consisting of his queen, Anne of Austria, the Duke of Orleans, Cardinal Mazarin (a staunch disciple of, and successor to, Richelieu), the Prince of Conde, and others. But immediately after his death, the Queen took steps to do away with all her deceased husband's arrangements; she procured his will to be cancelled by the Parliament, and assumed the supreme authority of government, bestowing, to the surprise of all, upon Cardinal Mazarin, the faithful adherent and follower of Richelieu, her persevering enemy, the office of Prime Minister.

During this regency, which lasted for a period of nearly eighteen years, there was a constant succession of wars, intrigues, and civil dissensions, which were not put an end to, and indeed, then only temporarily, until 1660, when Louis XIV., then twenty-two years of age, was married to Maria Theresa, the Infanta of Spain; and immediately upon the death of Cardinal Mazarin, in the year following, personally assumed the supreme direction of affairs. From all accounts, he was well qualified for the task. He possessed a sound, though not a brilliant intellect; a firm and resolute will; considerable sagacity and penetration; much aptitude for business; industry, and perseverance. Mazarin said of him: "There is enough in him to make four kings and one honest man."

Louis imbibed the most extravagant ideas of the nature and extent of the royal prerogative. Regarding his authority as delegated immediately from Heaven, he strove to concentrate in himself individually, all the powers and functions of government. According to his view, the sovereign was not only the guardian and dispenser, but the fountain and author of all law, and of all justice. His fixed principle was, "The State is myself;" and the peculiar position in which he found the affairs of the kingdom, enabled him almost literally to verify this lofty maxim. Never, in the whole history of the world, was there a more complete, nor a more favorable or successful specimen of absolute irresponsible monarchy than that which he established.

During the early years of his reign, Louis lived in habits of unrestrained licentiousness. He formed an attachment for Maria di Mancini, a niece of Cardinal Mazarin; but the wily minister had no faith in the happiness of such a union, neither was it suited to his political intrigues and designs, so the young lady was removed from court, and the marriage with the Infanta of Spain brought about. This union, however, in no way checked the lax principles of morality in Louis; it is doubtful, indeed, if he entertained any real affection for his wife; if he did, he did not allow either that feeling, or one of respect even, to prevent his openly indulging in licentious pursuits. It is recorded, on the best authorities, that his first object of serious attachment was Louise de la Vallière, the heroine of this play, who, after having borne him two children, retired into a convent. This incident the author has selected for his subject, and it will be seen how well and truly he depicts the character of the king—strictly in keeping with that derived from the best authorities, as above described. He omits, however, all mention of the children; and the banishment of Madame de Montespan, as stated in the play, is merely a dramatic liberty with truth; the records refer to nothing of the kind; on the contrary, they show that immediately upon the retirement of the Duchess de la Vallière, Madame de Montespan continued to retain the royal affections and became the mother of eight children, who were all declared legitimate and intermarried with some of the noblest families in the realm.

In 1678, when forty years of age, Louis became enamored with Françoise D'Aubigne, grand-daughter of the great Protestant historian, and, who afterwards became so celebrated as Madame de Maintenon. She had been recommended to Madame de Montespan as governess to her children, in which capacity the King saw her constantly, and by degrees she acquired an influence and control over him which lasted until his death. Amidst all these licentious intrigues, the queen could not have led a very happy life; however, she does not appear to have taken it very much to heart; she lived for twenty-three years after her marriage, and died in 1683. The year following, the king was secretly married to Madame de Maintenon by his confessor, La Chaise, in the presence of the Archbishop of Paris; but the marriage was never acknowledged, in consequence of which, her position at court was rather anomalous and equivocal, but her influence over the royal mind in private was unbounded, extending to all subjects, domestic, political, and religious.

After a constant succession of intrigues and wars, during which occurred some of the greatest and most splendid battles upon record, Louis XIV. closed his career in 1715, having consequently reigned seventy-two years, the longest period of kingly rule upon record.

As a general rule, the first dramatic productions of an author, no matter what his position in the other varied paths of literature may be, is seldom, or ever, attended with success; and notwithstanding the high intellect, cultivation and ability of the eminent writer of the present play, it was no exception to this general rule. In all first productions, there is almost invariably found a weakness of plot, and a want of consistency in the arrangement and a crudeness of construction, which can only be overcome by practice and observation, and the opposite of which cannot be born with the genius of the author.

The story worked out in the Duchess de la Vallière is simple, and although it is sufficient for an excellent reading play, it is not sufficiently interesting, nor filled enough with good points and situations, to make it an interesting and attractive play in a theatrical sense. That this view is a true one, and that the talented author himself so felt, is verified by his observations in the preface to the succeeding production of his pen, the Lady of Lyons, in which, after admitting the comparative failure of the present piece upon the stage, he states that one of his reasons for making a second attempt, was to see whether certain critics had truly declared that it was not in his power to attain the art of dramatic construction and theatrical effect. He admits that he felt it was in this that a writer accustomed to the narrative class of composition, had much both to learn and unlearn, and accordingly, he had directed his chief attention to the development and a careful arrangement of the incidents, throwing whatever belonged to poetry less into the diction and the "felicity of words," than into the construction of the story, the creation of the characters, and the spirit of the prevailing sentiment.

But, although thus deficient as a dramatic work, there are unquestionably many beauties in the language of the present play, which, as before observed, render it an entertaining work for perusal. For instance, in the opening scene, the conversation between mother and daughter; the story of her dreams of ambition, and the interview between her and her lover, Bragelone, are prettily rendered ; the conversation between Bragelone and the armorer, Bertrand, in a subsequent scene, is characteristically and well drawn ; and though the part of the armorer is but a small one, it is capable of being made a very telling and effective one, and a neat little picture in any representation of the play. The meeting of Bragelone and Louise after her arrival at court, and his endeavors to get at the truth of the evil rumors he has heard, is also well drawn ; but more particularly good is his short speech upon the strength and purity of his love. Again, also, is this the case, in the third act, when the king discovers the love of Louise for Bragelone, and the meeting between her and the latter character.

But probably the finest written and most effectively drawn portion of the whole play, is the scene in the fourth act, between the king and Bragelone, in his character of the Franciscan friar, in which, in well-chosen, eloquent, and powerful language, he vehemently upbraids the king for his base conduct, in having raised a maiden to a Duchess, to gratify his desires ; trampled, without thought or regret, upon her gallant father's memory as a brave and loyal subject; tarnished her mother's stainless honor as a matron, and rendered her home and expiring life desolate; and crushed the hopes and anticipated happiness of her affianced husband, who had served him well, and saved his life. From this subject, Bragelone dashes fiercely and rapidly into a review of the king's principles, and pictures to him the scenes of gayety, flattery, and licentiousness then surrounding him, and which had so long existed, and those which may await him—a scaffold where the palace rises—the axe —the headsman—and the victim! It is hardly possible for any writer to equal, much less to surpass the beauty and sarcastic keenness of the language here used ; it is, most undoubtedly, the most brilliant portion of the play, and in the hands of a fine actor, must invariably make a hit. Other good portions could be selected, but it is the lack of interest and faulty dramatic construction, that mars and damages this otherwise fine play. However pleasingly the speeches read, they are too prosy for the stage ; and we do not meet with the noble and beautiful sentiments expressed in the perfectly eloquent and poetical language which mark the noble author's subsequent productions. Nothing in the play will bear comparison with the love scenes in the Lady of Lyons, or the jealousy and indignation of De Mauprat, in Richelieu. One great point, however, must not be overlooked. It is not often the case, that in selecting a great historical personage like Louis XIV, for one of the principal characters in a play, that the author adheres strictly to the authentic records of the habits, life, and disposition of that person. In the present instance, nothing has been omitted, or aught exaggerated, and the character of Louis " the Great" is as finely painted by the pen of the renowned scholar and poet, as it has been portrayed by that of the great historians, who were contemporaneous with the king.

If the play were reduced to about two-thirds of its present length and slightly rearranged, it would make a very fair acting drama ; but I am not aware of its ever having been played in such a way, or in any other shape than in its entirety, as first produced in London, when, although it had the grand support of the eminent tragedian, Mr. Macready, the beautiful and accomplished Helen Faucit (as to whom, see the remarks to the Lady of Lyons), Mr. Vandenhoff, and other excellent actors, it failed to prove a success. This was the case also in New York, upon its production at the Park Theatre, in 1837, although it was well mounted and well cast, having the great actress, Miss Ellen Tree (afterwards Mrs Charles Kean), in the part of the Duchess. It was this want of success, which induced the author to turn his attention directly to a close study of the principles of dramatic construction, and which he mastered with progressively, grand, and perfect results, as the undying reputation of his subsequent plays, the Lady of Lyons, Richelieu, and Money will prove.

J. M. K.

BILL FOR PROGRAMMES.

ACT I.

SCENE I.—THE CHATEAU DE LA VALLIÈRE AND CONVENT OF THE CARMELITES.

Mother and Daughter—The Evening of Departure for the Court—Story of a Lover—The Scarf of Beauty

SCENE II —ARMORY IN THE CASTLE OF BRAGELONE.

A Faithful Servant—Tales of Heroism and Daring—News of Louise de la Vallière's Arrival at Court—Anticipations of Marriage—An Armorer's Joy.

SCENE III.—APARTMENT IN THE PALACE OF FONTAINE-BLEAU.

Gossip of the Court—A Wily Courtier—Wit and Cunning beat Sword and Spear—The King must have a Mistress —It must be Louise.

SCENE IV.—GARDENS OF THE PALACE ILLUMINATED FOR A ROYAL FÉTE.

The King and his Courtiers—The Monarch caught by the Maid—Scandal amongst the Ladies of Honor—Rivalry and Jealousy—The King's Declaration of Love—The Wheel of Fortune—Royal Gift to Louise —Envy and Consternation.

ACT II.

SCENE I —GARDENS OF THE PALACE OF FONTAINEBLEAU.

A Lover's Search—The Tale of Scandal—Louise is the King's Favorite —The Quarrel and the Duel—The Portrait—Unexpected Interruption—A Lover's Appeal—" Fly before you fall ! Mother ! Honor ! Duty! all call upon thee ere too late "—She yields !—Flight of Louise and Bragelone.

SCENE II.—THE KING'S CABINET AT FONTAINEBLEAU.

A Noble Gift to the Wily Courtier, Lauzun—The King reveals his Love—Vews of Louise's Flight—Anger of the King, and Orders for Pursuit.

SCENE III —CLOISTERS OF A CONVENT.

Distress of Louise The Signal of Alarm—Arrival of the King and Lauzun—The Lady Abbess or the King—Convent or Court—Appeal of Love, and Departure for the Palace once more.

ACT III.

SCENE I.—ANTECHAMBER IN THE PALACE OF THE DUCHESS DE LA VALLIÈRE AT VERSAILLES.

A Rise in Rank but a Fall from Virtue—Louise now a Duchess—The Conspiracy—The Wily Courtier and Maid of Honor—Woman against Woman—The Compact to the Death !

SCENE II.—SALOON IN THE KING'S PALACE.

A Royal Game of Chess—Story of the Death of the Bravest Knight in France, Bragelone—Agitation of Louise—The King's Suspicions—The Quarrel —Disgrace Approaching—A Rival Mistress and a False Friend—The Trap laid—An Unsuspecting Victim—The Fatal Letter.

Scene III.—THE GARDENS OF VERSAILLES.

A Court Serpent - A False Messenger—The Star of Louise is Falling - The King finds a new Mistress.

Scene IV.—GRAND SALOON IN THE PALACE OF VERSAILLES.

A Royal Gathering—Jealousy begins the Game—Proposal for a Knightly Tournament—The Colors of Louise Refused—Triumph of Madame de Montespan, and Betrayal of Louise.

ACT IV.

Scene I.—THE GARDENS AT VERSAILLES.

Lauzun lays Plans for Marrying the Duchess—She still Loves the King— His Victim, not his Mistress.

Scene II.—PRIVATE APARTMENT IN THE PALACE OF THE DUCHESS DE LA VALLIÈRE.

Desolation of Louise—A Mother's Death—Lauzun pleads his Suit—Virtue not yet Dead—A Rejected Lover—Arrival of a Holy Friar—Interview with the Duchess—Story of Bragelone's Love and Forgiveness—A Mother's last words changed from Curses to Blessings—Agony of Louise—Arrival of the King—Anger at a Monk's Reproaches—The Warning Voice of the Church—" Beware, Proud King! Beware!"—Louise Consents to Wed.

ACT V.

Scene I.—THE GARDENS AT VERSAILLES.

Story of the Flight of the Duchess—Lauzun and the King's new Mistress— Reproaches and Revenge—" You've played the Knave and Thrown away the King."

Scene II.—THE OLD CHATEAU DE LA VALLIÈRE AND CONVENT OF THE CARMELITES

A Last Visit to the Home of Childhood and Virtue—The Disclosure—Bragelone still Lives!—The Priest's Vow—The World is Lost, but the Convent and the Monastery remain.

Scene III.—EXTERIOR OF THE CONVENT OF THE CARMELITES.

" Ere the Clock strikes Louise takes the Veil!"—Lauzun and Madame de Montespan—Plot against Plot—Banishment of the new Favorite—A Woman's Curse.

Scene IV.—INTERIOR OF THE CHAPEL OF THE CONVENT.

Preparation for Taking the Veil—Arrival of the King—A Last Appeal-- " Thy Rival Banished, no other Love but Thee!"—Too late! Repentance Triumphs! The Life of Sin is Ended! The Passage to the Outer World forever Closed—A Last Farewell, and Heaven claims the Sacrifice of

THE DUCHESS DE LA VALLIÈRE.

[For Stage Directions see page 68.]

PROLOGUE.

To paint the Past, yet in the Past portray
Such shapes as seem dim prophets of to-day ;—
To trace, through all the garish streams of art,
Nature's deep fountain—woman's silent heart ;—
On the stirr'd surface of the soften'd mind
To leave the print of holier truths behind ;—
And, while through joy or grief—through calm or strife,
Bound the wild Passions on the course of life,
To share the race—yet point the proper goal,
And make the Affections preachers to the soul ;—
Such is the aim with which a gaudier age
Now woos the brief revival of the stage ;—
Such is the moral, though unseen it flows,
In Lauzun's wiles and soft La Vallère's woes ;
Such the design our Author boldly drew,
And, losing boldness, now submits to you.
   Not new to climes where dreamy fable dwells—
That magic Prospero of the Isle of Spells—
Now first the wanderer treads, with anxious fear,
The fairy land whose flowers allured him here.
Dread is the court our alien pleads before ;
Your verdict makes his exile from the shore.
Yet, e'en if banish'd, let him think, in pride,
He trod the path with no unhallow'd guide ;
Chasing the light, whose face, though veil'd and dim,
Perchance a meteor, seem'd a star to him,
Hoping the ray might rest where TRUTH appears
Beneath her native well—your smiles and tears.
   When a wide waste, to Law itself unknown,
Lay that fair world the DRAMA calls its own ;
When all might riot on the mines of Thought,
And Genius starved amidst the wealth it wrought ;
He who now ventures on the haunted soil
For nobler laborers won the rights of toil,
And his the boast—that Fame now rests in ease

Beneath the shade of her own laurel-trees.
Yes, if with all the critic on their brow,
His clients once have grown his judges now,
And watch, like spirits on the Elysian side,
Their brother ferried o'er the Stygian tide,
To where, on souls untried, austerely sit
(The triple Minos)—Gallery—Boxes—Pit—
'Twill soothe to think, howe'er the verdict end,
In every rival he hath served a friend.
  But well we know, and, knowing, we rejoice,
The mightiest Critic is the PUBLIC VOICE.
Awed, yet resign'd, our novice trusts in you,
Hard to the practised, gentle to the new.
Whate'er the anxious strife of hope and fear,
He asks no favor—let the stage be clear.
If from the life his shapes the poet draws,
In man's deep breast lie all the critic's laws ;
If not, in vain the nicely-poised design,
Vain the cold music of the labor'd line,
Before our eyes, behold the living rules ;—
The soul has instincts wiser than the schools !
Yours is the great Tribunal of the Heart,
And touch'd Emotion makes the test of Art.
Judges august !—the same in every age,
While Passions weave the sorcery of the Stage—
While Nature's sympathies are Art's best laws—
To you a stranger has referr'd his cause ;—
If the soft tale he woos the soul to hear
Bequeaths the moral, while it claims the tear,
Each gentler thought to faults in others shown
He calls in court—a pleader for his own !

THE DUCHESS DE LA VALLIERE.

ACT I.

SCENE I.—*Time—sunset. On the foreground,* L., *an old chateau ; beyond vineyards and woods which present through their openings, views of a river, reflecting the sunset. At a distance,* R *, the turrets of the Convent of the Carmelites.*

MADAME *and* MADEMOISELLE DE LA VALLIÈRE *enter from chateau.*

MDLLE. DE LA V. 'Tis our last eve, my mother !
MME. DE LA V.   Thou regrett'st it,
  My own Louise ! albeit the court invites thee—
  A court beside whose glories, dull and dim
  The pomp of Eastern kings, by poets told ;
  A court——
MDLLE. DE LA V. In which I shall not see my mother!
  Nor those old walls, in which, from every stone,
  Childhood speaks eloquent of happy years ;
  Nor vines and woods, which bade me love the earth,
  Nor yonder spires, which raised that love to God. (*the vesper bell*
    tolls)
  The vesper bell !—my mother, when, once more,
  I hear from those gray towers that holy chime,
  May thy child's heart be still as full of heaven,
  And callous to all thoughts of earth, save those
  Which mirror Eden in the face of Home !
MME. DE LA V. Do I not know thy soul ?—through every snare
  My gentle dove shall 'scape with spotless plumes,
  Alone in courts, I have no fear for *thee* ;
  Some natures take from Innocence the lore
  Experience teaches; and their delicate leaves,
  Like the soft plant, shut out all wrong, and shrink
  From vice by instinct, as the wise by knowledge ;
  And such is thine ! *My* voice thou wilt not hear,
  But Thought shall whisper where my voice would warn,
  And Conscience be thy mother and thy guide !
MDLLE. DE LA V. Oh, may I merit all thy care, and most
  Thy present trust ! Thou'lt write to me, my mother,
  And tell me of thyself; amidst the court
  My childhood's images shall rise. Be kind
  To the poor cotters in the wood—alas !
  They'll miss me in the winter !—and my birds ?—
  Thy hand will feed them ?——

MME. DE LA V.   And that noble heart
That loves thee as my daughter should be loved—
The gallant Bragelone?*—should I hear
Some tidings Fame forgets—if in the din
Of camps I learn thy image makes his solace,
Shall I not write of *him ?*
MDLLE. DE LA V. (*with indifference*). His name will breathe
Of home and friendship—yes!
MME. DE LA V.   Of naught beside?
MDLLE DE LA V. Nay, why so pressing?—let me change the theme.
The king—you have seen him—is he, as they say,
So fair—so stately?
MME. DE LA V.   Ay, in truth, my daughter,
A king that wins the awe he might command.
Splendid in peace, and terrible in war ;
Wise in council—gentle in the bower.
MDLLE. DE LA V. Strange, that so often through mine early dreams
A royal vision flitted—a proud form,
Upon whose brow Nature had written "empire ;"
While, on the lip,—love, smiling, wrapp'd in sunshine
The charmed world that was its worshipper—
A form like that which clothed the gods of old,
Lured from Olympus by some mortal maid—
Youthful it seemed—but with ambrosial youth ;
And beautiful—but half as beauty were
A garb too earthly for a thing divine—
Was is not strange, my mother?
MME. DE LA V.   A child's fancy,
Breathed into life by thy brave father's soul.
He taught thee, in thy cradle yet, to lisp
Thy sovereign's name in prayer—and still together,
In thy first infant creed, were link'd the lessons
" *To honor God and love the king ;* " it was
A part of that old knightly faith of France
Which made it half religion to be loyal.
MDLLE. DE LA V. It might be so. I have preserved the lesson,
E'en with too weak a reverence—Yet, 'tis strange!
A dream so oft renew'd !
MME. DE LA. V.   Here comes thy lover !
Thou wilt not blame him if his lips repeat
The question mine have asked?

Enter BRAGELONE, R. 2 E.

                    Alphonso, welcome !
BRAGE. My own Louise!—ah ! dare I call thee so ?
War never seem'd so welcome ! since we part,
Since the soft sunshine of thy smiles must fade
From these dear scenes, it soothes, at least to think
I shall not linger on the haunted spot,
And feel, forlorn amidst the gloom of absence,
How dark is all once lighted by thine eyes. (MADAME DE LA
          VALLIÈRE *retires into the chateau.*)
MDLLE. DE LA V. Can friendship flatter thus—or wouldst thou train
My ear betimes to learn the courtier's speech ?

* The author has, throughout this play, availed himself of poetical license to
give to the name of Bragelone the Italian pronunciation, and to accent the final *e.*

BRAGE. Louise! Louise! this is our parting hour;
　　Me war demands—and thee the court allures.
　　In such an hour, the old romance allow'd
　　The maid to soften from her coy reserve,
　　And her true knight, from some kind words, to take
　　Hope's talisman to battle—Dear Louise!
　　Say, canst thou love me?
MDLLE. DE LA V.　　　　　　Sir—I—love—methinks
　　It is a word that——
BRAGE.　　　　　　　　Sounds upon thy lips
　　Like " land " upon the mariner's, and speaks
　　Of home and rest after a stormy sea.
　　Sweet girl, my youth has pass'd in camps ; and war
　　Hath somewhat scathed my manhood ere my time.
　　Our years are scarce well-mated ; the soft spring
　　Is thine, and o'er my summer's waning noon
　　Grave autumn creeps. Thou say'st " I flatter !"—well
　　Love taught me first the golden words in which
　　The honest heart still coins its massive ore.
　　But fairer words, from falser lips, will soon
　　Make *my* plain courtship rude. Louise! thy sire
　　Bethroth'd us in thy childhood ; I have watch'd thee
　　Bud into virgin May, and in thy youth
　　Have seem'd to hoard my own ! I think of *thee!*
　　And I am youthful still! The passionate prayer—
　　The wild idolatry—the purple light
　　Bathing the cold earth from a Hebe's urn ;
　　Yea, all the soul's divine excess which youth
　　Claims as its own, came back when first I loved thee !
　　And yet so well I love, that if thy heart
　　Recoil from mine—if but one single wish,
　　A shade more timid than the fear which ever
　　Blends trembling twilight with the starry hope
　　Of maiden dreams, would start thee from our union,—
　　Speak, and my suit is tongueless !
MDLLE. DE LA V.　　　　　Oh, my lord!
　　If to believe all France's chivalry
　　Boasts not a nobler champion—if to feel
　　Proud in your friendship, honor'd in your trust—
　　If this be love, and I have known no other,
　　Why then——
BRAGE.　　　　Why then, thou lov'st me ?
MDLLE. DE LA V. (*aside*).　　　　Shall I say it ?
　　I feel 'twere to deceive him. Is it love ?
　　Love, no, it is *not* love ! (*aloud*) My noble lord,
　　As yet I know not all mine own weak heart ;
　　I would not pain thee, yet would not betray.
　　Legend and song have often painted love,
　　And my heart whispers not the love which should be
　　The answer to thine own—thou hadst best forget me !
BRAGE. Forget!
MDLLE. DE LA V. I am not worthy of thee !
BRAGE.　　　　　　　　　Hold!
　　My soul is less heroic than I deem'd it.
　　Perchance my passion asks too much from thine
　　And would forestall the fruit ere yet the blossom
　　Blushes from out the coy and maiden leaves.

No! let *me* love ; and say, perchance the time
May come when *thou* wilt bid me not forget thee.
Absence may plead my cause ; it hath some magic ;
I fear not contrast with the courtier herd ;
And thou art not Louise if thou art won
By a smooth outside and a honey'd tongue.
No! when thou seest these hunters after power,
These shadows, minion'd to the royal sun—
Proud to the humble, servile to the great—
Perchance thou'lt learn how much one honest heart,
That never wrong'd a friend or shunn'd a foe—
How much the old hereditary knighthood,
Faithful to God, to glory, and to love,
Outweighs a universe of cringing courtiers !
Louise, I ask no more—I bide my time !

Re-enter MADAME DE LA VALLIÈRE *from the chateau.*

MME. DE LA V. The twilight darkens.   Art thou, now, Alphonso, .
Convinced her heart is such as thou wouldst have it?
BRAGE. It is a heavenly tablet—but my name
God angels have not writ there !
MME. DE LA V.   Nay, as yet,
Love wears the mask of friendship, she must love thee.
BRAGE. (*half incredulously*). Think'st thou so?
MME. DE LA V.   Ay, be sure !
BRAGE.   I'll think so too.
          (*turns to* MADEMOISELLE DE LA VALLIÈRE)
Bright lady of my heart ! (*aside*) By Heaven ! 'tis true !
The rose grows richer on her cheek, like hues
That in the silence of the virgin dawn,
Predict, in blushes, light that glads the earth.
Her mother spoke aright—ah, yes, she loves me !
(*aloud*) Bright lady of my heart, farewell ! and yet
Again farewell !
MDLLE. DE LA V.   Honor and health be with you !
MME. DE LA V. Nay, my Louise, when warriors wend to battle,
The maid they serve grows half a warrior, too ;
And does not blush to bind on mailed bosoms
The banner of her colors.
BRAGE.   Dare I ask it ?
MDLLE. DE LA V. A soldier's child could never blush, my lord,
     To belt so brave a breast ;—and yet—well, wear it. (*placing her
          scarf around* BRAGELONE'S *hauberk.*)
BRAGE. Ah ! add for thy sake.
MDLLE. DE LA V.   For the sake of one
Who honors worth, and ne'er since Bayard fell,
Have banners flaunted o'er a knight more true
     To France and Fame ;——
BRAGE.   And love ?
MDLLE. DE LA V.   Nay, hush, my lord ;
     I said not that.
BRAGE.   But France and Fame shall say it !
Yes, if thou hear'st men speak of Bragelone.
If proudest chiefs confess he bore him bravely,
Come life, come death, his glory shall be thine ;
And all the light it borrowed from thine eyes,

Shall gild thy name. Ah, scorn not *then* to say,
" He loved me well!"   How well! God shield and bless thee!
                                    [*Exit* BRAGELONE, R. 2 E.

MDLLE. DE LA V. (*aside*). Most worthy love! *why* can I love him not?

MME. DE LA V. Peace to his gallant heart! when next we meet,
May I have gained a son—and thou——

MDLLE. DE LA V. (*quickly*).   My mother,
This night let every thought be given to *thee!*
Beautiful scene, farewell—farewell, my home!
And thou, gray convent, whose inspiring chime
Measures the hours with prayer, that morn and eve
Life may ascend the ladder of the angels,
And climb to heaven! Serene retreats, farewell!
And now, my mother—no! some hours must yet
Pass ere our parting.

MME. DE LA V.   Cheer thee, my Louise!
And let us now within; the dews are falling—

MDLLE. DE LA V. And I forget how ill thy frame may bear them.
Pardon!—within, within! (*stopping short, and gazing fondly on*
MADAME DE LA VALLIÈRE) Your hand, dear mother!
                                    [*Exeunt into chateau.*

SCENE II.—*An old armory, of the heavy French Architecture preceding the
time of Francis the First, in the castle of* BRAGELONE. BERTRAND, *the
armorer, employed in polishing a sword, enters,* L. 1 E.

BER.   There now! I think this blade will scarcely shame
My gallant master's hand; it was the weapon,
So legends say, with which the old Lord Rodolph
Slew, by the postern gate, his lady's leman!
Oh, we're a haughty race—we old French lords;
Our honor is unrusted as our steel,
And, when provoked, as ruthless!

             Enter BRAGELONE, R. 1 E., *without sword.*

BRAGE.   Ah, old Bertrand!
Why, your brave spirit, 'mid these coats of mail,
Grows young again. So! this, then, is the sword
You'd have me wear. God wot! a tranchant blade!
Not of the modern fashion.

BER.   My good lord,
Yourself are scarcely of the modern fashion.
They tell me, that to serve one's king for nothing,
To deem one's country worthier than one's self,
To hold one's honor not a phrase to swear by—
They tell me now, all *this* is out of fashion.
Come, take the sword, my lord; (*offering it*) you have your father's
Stout arm and lordly heart; they're out of fashion,
And yet you keep the one—come, take the other.

BRAGE. Why, you turn satirist! (*takes the sword.*)

BER.   Satirist! what is that?

BRAGE. Satirists, my friend, are men who speak the truth
That courts may say, they do not know the fashion!
Satire on Vice is Wit's revenge on fools
That slander Virtue. (*examines sword*) How now! look ye, Bertrand!
Methinks there is a notch here.

BER.   Ah, my lord !
I would not grind it out ;—'twas here the blade
Clove through the helmet, e'en to the chin,
Of that irreverent and most scoundrel Dutchman,
Who stabb'd you through your hauberk-joints—what time
You placed your breast before the king.

BRAGE.   Hence, ever
Be it believed, that, in his hour of need,
A king's sole safeguard are his subjects' hearts !
Ha ! ha ! good sword ! that was a famous stroke !
Thou didst brave deeds that day, thou quaint old servant,
Though now—thou'rt not the fashion. (*hands back the sword.*)

BER.   Bless that look,
And that glad laugh ! they bring me back the day
When first old Bertrand arm'd you for the wars,—
A fair-faced stripling ; yet, beshrew my heart,
You spurr'd that field before the bearded chins,
And saved the gallant Lord La Vallière's standard,
And yet you were a stripling then .

BRAGE.   La Vallière !
The very name goes dancing through my veins.
Bertrand, look round the armory. Is there naught
I wore that first campaign ? Nay, nay ! no matter !
I wear the *name within* me. Hark ye, Bertrand !
We're not so young as then we were ; when next
We meet, old friend, we both will end our labors,
And find some nook, amidst yon antique tropies,
Wherein to hang this idle mail.

BER.   Huzza!
The village dames speak truth—my lord will marry !
And I shall nurse, in these old wither'd arms,
Another boy—for France another hero.
Ha ! ha ! I am so happy !

BRAGE.   Good old man !
Why this looks like my father's hall—since thus
My father's servants love me.

BER.   All must love you!

BRAGE. All—let me think so. (*bugle without,* L.) Hark, the impatient bugle !
I hear the neigh of my exultant charger,
Breathing from far the glorious air of war.
Give me the sword ! (*takes it, and girdles it on.*)

Enter SERVANT, L. 1 E., *with a letter, which he hands to* BRAGELONE, *and
exits.*

                              Her mother's hand—" Louise,
Arrived at court, writes sadly, and amidst
The splendor pines for home,"—I knew she would !
My own Louise !—" speaks much of the king's goodness ; "
Goodness to her !—that thought shall give the king
A tenfold better soldier !—" From thy friend,
Who trusts ere long to hail thee as her son."
Her son !—a blessed name. These lines shall be
My heart's true shield, and ward away each weapon.
He who shall wed Louise has conquer'd Fate,
And smiles at earthly foes. (*bugle without,* L.) Again the bugle !
Give me your hand, old man. My fiery youth

Went not to battle with so blithe a soul
As now burns in me. So! she pines for home—
I knew she would—I knew it! Farewell, Bertrand!
[*Exit* BRAGELONE, L. 1 E.

BER. Oh! there'll be merry doings in the hall
When my dear lord returns. A merry wedding!
And then—and then—oh, such a merry christening!
How well I fancy his grave, manly face
Brightening upon his first born.

As he is going, re-enter BRAGELONE.

BRAGE.   Ho, there! Bertrand!
One charge I had forgot—Be sure they train
The woodbine richly round the western wing—
My mother's old apartment. Well, man, well!
Do you not hear me?
BER.   *You*, my lord! the woodbine?
BRAGE. Yes; see it duly done. I know she loves it;
It clambers round her lattice. I would not
Have one thing absent she could miss. Remember.
[*Exit* BRAGELONE, L. 1 E.
BER. And this is he whom warriors call "the Stern!"
The dove's heart beats beneath that lion breast.
Pray Heaven his lady may deserve him! Oh,
What news for my good dame!—i' faith, I'm glad
I was the first to learn the secret. So,
This year a wife—next year a boy! I'll teach
The young rogue how his father clove the Dutchman
Down to the chin! (*chuckling merrily*) Ha, ha! old Bertrand now
Will be of use again on winter nights—
I know he'll be the picture of his father. [*Exit* BERTRAND, L. 1 E.

SCENE III.—*An antechamber in the Palace of Fontainebleau.*

Enter LAUZUN, L. 1 E, *and* GRAMMONT, R. 1 E.

LAU. Ah, Count, good day! Were you at court last night?
GRAM. Yes; and the court has grown the richer by
A young new beauty.
LAU.   So! her name?
GRAM.   La Vallière.
LAU. Ay, I have heard! a maid of honor?
GRAM.   Yes.
The women say she's plain.
LAU.   The women? oh,
The case it is that's plain—*she* must be lovely.
GRAM. The dear, kind gossips of the court declare
The pretty novice hath conceived a fancy—
A wild, romantic, innocent, strange fancy—
For our young king; a girlish love, like that
Told of in fairy tales; she saw his picture,
Sigh'd to the canvas, murmur'd to the colors,
And fell in love with carmine and gamboge.
LAU. The simple dreamer! Well, she saw the king?
GRAM. And while she saw him, like a rose, when May
Breathes o'er its bending bloom, she seem'd to shrink

Into her modest self, and a low sigh
Shook blushes (sweetest rose-leaves!) from her beauty.

LAU.   You paint it well.

GRAM.   And ever since that hour
She bears the smiling malice of her comrades
With an unconscious and an easy sweetness ;
As if alike *her* virtue and *his* greatness
Made love impossible ; so down the stream
Of purest thought, her heart glides on to danger.

LAU.   Did Louis note her ?—Has he heard the gossip ?

GRAM   Neither, methinks ; his Majesty is cold,
The art of pomp, and not the art of love,
Tutors his skill—Augustus more than Ovid.

LAU.   The time will come.   The king as yet is young,
Flush'd with the novelty of sway, and fired
With the great dream of cutting Dutchmen's throats ;
A tiresome dream—the poets call it " Glory."

GRAM.   So much the better—'tis one rival less ;
The handsome king would prove a dangerous suitor.

LAU.   Oh, hang the danger !   He must have a mistress ;
'Tis an essential to a court ; how many
Favors, one scarcely likes to ask a king,
One flatters from a king's inamorata !
We courtiers fatten on the royal vices ;
And, while the king lives chaste, he cheats, he robs me
Of ninety-nine per cent. !

GRAM.   Ha! ha!   Well, duke,
We meet to-night.   You join the revels ?
Till then, adieu.

LAU.   Adieu, dear count.   [*Exit* GRAMMONT, L. 1 E.
                                            The king
Must have a mistress ; I must lead that mistress.
The times are changed—'twas by the sword and spear,
Our fathers bought ambition—vulgar butchers !
But now our wit's our spear—intrigue our armor ;
The antechamber is our field of battle ;
And the best hero is—the cleverest rogue !

                                    [*Exit* LAUZUN, R. 1 E.

SCENE IV.—*Night—the garden of the Fontainebleau, brilliantly illuminated with colored lamps—Fountains, vases, and statues in perspective*—A pavilion in the background—to the right, the Palace of Fontainebleau, illuminated.   Enter* COURTIERS, LADIES, *etc.,* L. U. E., *and* LAUZUN, C. *A dance.*

        Enter LOUIS, R. U. E., *followed by* COURTIERS, *etc.*

LOUIS.   Fair eve and pleasant revels to you all !
Ah, duke—a word with you ! (COURTIERS *give way.*)
                          Thou hast seen, my Lauzun,
The new and fairest flowret of our court,
This youngest of the graces—sweet La Vallière,
Blushing beneath the world's admiring eyes ?

LAU.   (*aside*). So. so !—he's caught ! (*aloud*) Your Majesty speaks
            warmly ;
Your praise is just—and grateful——

The effect of the scene should be principally made by jets-d'eau, waterfalls, etc.

LOUIS.   Grateful ?
LAU.   Ay.
   Know you not, Sire, it is the jest, among
The pretty prattlers of the royal chamber,
That this young Dian of the woods has found
Endymion in a king—a summer dream,
Bright, but with vestal fancies ! Scarcely love,
But that wild interval of hopes and fears
Through which the child glides, trembling to the woman ?
LOUIS. Blest thought ! Oh, what a picture of delight
   Your words have painted.
LAU.   While we speak, behold,
Through yonder alleys, with her sister planets,
Your moonlight beauty gleams.
LOUIS.   'Tis she—this shade
   Shall hide us—quick ! (*enters one of the bosquets,** L. 2 E.)
LAU. (*following him*), I trust my creditors
   Will grow the merrier from this night's adventure.

Enter MADEMOISELLE DE LA VALLIÈRE, R. U. E., *and* MAIDS OF HONOR.
               They advance.

FIRST MAID. How handsome looks the Duke de Guiche, to-night !
SECOND MAID. Well, to my taste, the graceful Grammont bears
   The bell from all.
THIRD MAID.   But, then, that charming Lauzun
   Has so much wit.
FIRST MAID.   And which, of all these gallants,
   May please the fair Vallière most ?
MDLLE. DE LA V.   In truth,
   I scarcely mark'd them ; when the king is by,
Who can have eye, or ear, or thought for others ?
FIRST MAID. You raise your fancies high !
SECOND MAID.   And raise them vainly !
   The king disdains all love !
MDLLE. DE LA V.   Who spoke of love ?
   The sunflower, gazing on the Lord of Heaven,
Asks but its sun to shine ! Who spoke of love ?
And who would wish the bright and lofty Louis
To stoop from glory ? Love should not confound
So great a spirit with the herd of men.
Who spoke of love——
FIRST MAID.   My country friend, you talk
   Extremely well ; but some young lord will teach you
To think of Louis less, and more of love.
MDLLE DE LA V. Nay, e'en the very presence of his greatness
   Exalts the heart from each more low temptation.
He seems to walk the earth as if to raise
And purify our wandering thoughts, by fixing
Thought on himself—and she who thinks on Louis
Shuts out the world, and scorns the name of love !
FIRST MAID. Wait till you're tired. (*music*) But hark ! the music chides
     us
For waiting this most heavenly night so idly.
Come, let us join the dancers ! [*Exeunt* MAIDS, L. 2 *and* 3 E.

---

* *Bosquet* is a small arbor or shady retreat.

As LA VALLIÈRE *follows, the* KING *steals from the bosquet, and takes her hand, while* LAUZUN *retires in the opposite direction.*

LOUIS.   Sweet La Vallière!
MDLLE. DE LA V. Ah!
LOUIS.   Nay, fair lady, fly not, ere we welcome
   Her who gives night its beauty!
MDLLE. DE LA V.   Sire, permit me!
   My comrades wait me.
LOUIS.   What! my loveliest subject
   So soon a rebel? Silent! Well, *be* mute,
   And teach the world the eloquence of blushes.
MDLLE. DE LA V. I may not listen——
LOUIS.   What if *I* had set
   Thyself the example? What if *I* had listen'd,
   Veil'd by yon friendly boughs, and dared to dream
   That one blest word which spoke of Louis absent
   Might charm his presence, and make nature music?
MDLLE. DE LA V. You did not, Sire! you could not!
LOUIS.   Could not hear thee!
   Nor pine for these divine, unwitness'd moments,
   To pray thee, dearest lady, to divorce
   No more the thought of love from him who loves thee.
   And—faithful still to glory—swears thy heart
   Unfolds the fairest world a king can conquer!
   Hear me, Louise.
MDLLE. DE LA V.   No Sire; forget those words!
   I am not what their foolish meaning spoke me,
   But a poor simple girl, who loves her king,
   And honor *more*. Forget, and do not scorn me!
             [*Exit* MADEMOISELLE DE LA VALLIÈRE, L. 2 E.
LOUIS. Her modest coyness fires me more than all
   Her half unconscious and most virgin love!

Enter COURTIERS, MAIDS OF HONOR, LADIES, GUESTS, *etc.*, L. C. LAUZUN
   advances, GRAMMONT *and* MONTESPAN *enter*, R. C.

   Well, would the dancers pause awhile?
LAU.   E'en pleasure
   Wearies at last.
LOUIS.   We've but to change its aspect
   And it resumes its freshness. Ere the banquet
   Calls us, my friends, we have prepared a game
   To shame the lottery of this life, wherein
   Each prize is neighbor'd by a thousand blanks
   Methinks it is the duty of a monarch
   To set the balance right, and bid the wheel
   Shower naught but prizes on the hearts he loves.
   What ho, there! with a merry music, raise
   Fortune, to show how Merit conquers Honors! (*music.*)

The pavilion at the back of the stage opens, and discovers the Temple of Fortune superbly illuminated. Fortune ; at her feet, a wheel of light ; at either hand, a golden vase, over each of which presides a figure—the one representing Merit, the other Honor.

LOUIS. Approach, fair dames and gallants! Aye, as now,

May Fortune smile upon the friends of Louis! (*the* COURTIERS *and* LADIES *group around the vases. From the one over which Merit presides they draw lots, and receive in return from Honor, various gifts of jewels, etc.*)

Enter MADEMOISELLE DE LA VALLIÈRE, *at the back of the stage, and advances,* L.

LOUIS (*to* MADEMOISELLE DE LA VALLIERE). Nay, if you smile not on me, then the scene
    Hath lost its charm.
MDLLE. DE LA V. Oh, Sire, all eyes are on us!
LOUIS. All eyes *should* learn where homage should be render'd.
MDLLE. DE LA V. I pray you, Sire——
LAU.   Wilt please your Majesty
    To try your fortune?
LOUIS.   Fortune! Sweet La Vallière,
    I only seek my fortune in thine eyes. (*music.* LOUIS *draws, and receives a diamond bracelet.* LADIES *crowd round*)
FIRST LADY.   How beautiful!
SECOND LADY.   Each gem is worth a duchy!
THIRD LADY. Oh, happy she upon whose arm the king
    Will bind the priceless band!
LOUIS (*approaching* MADEMOISELLE DE LA VALLIÈRE). Permit me,
    lady! (*clasps the bracelet.*)
LAU. Well done—well play'd! In that droll game call'd Woman,
    Diamonds are always trumps for hearts.
FIRST LADY.   Her hair's
    Too light!
SECOND LADY.   Her walk is so provincial!
THIRD LADY. D'ye think she paints?
LAU.   Ha, ha! What envious eyes,
    What fawning smiles await the king's new mistress!

ACT II.

SCENE I.—*The gardens of the Fontainebleau.*

Enter BRAGELONE, L. U. E.

BRAGE. (*advancing*). Why did we suffer her to seek the court?
    It is a soil in which the reptile Slander
    Still coils in slime around the fairest flower.
    Can it be true?—Strange rumors pierced my tent
    Coupling her name with—pah—how foul the thought is!—
    The maid the king loves!—Fie! I'll not believe it!
    I left the camp—sped hither; if she's lost,
    Why then—down—down, base heart! wouldst *thou* suspect her?
    Thou—who shouldst be her shelter from suspicion?
    But I may warn, advise, protect, and save her—
    Save—'tis a fearful word!

Enter LAUZUN, R. U. E.

LAU.   Lord Bragelone!

Methought your warrior spirit never breathed
The air of palaces! No evil tidings,
I trust, from Dunkirk?
BRAGE.   No. The *fleur-de-lis*
Rears her white crest unstain'd. Mine own affairs
Call me to court.
LAU.   Affairs? I hate the word;
It sounds like debts.
BRAGE. (*aside*).   This courtier may instruct me.
(*aloud*) Our king—he bears him well?
LAU.   Oh, bravely, Marquis;
Engaged with this new palace of Versailles.
It costs some forty millions!
BRAGE.   Ay, the people
Groan at the burthen.
LAU.   People—what's the *people*?
I never heard that word at court! The *people*!
BRAGE. I doubt not, duke. The people like the air,
Is rarely heard, save when it speaks in thunder.
I pray you grace for that old fashion'd phrase.
What is the latest news?
LAU.   His Majesty
Dines half an hour before his usual time.
That's the last news at court!—it makes sensation!
BRAGE. Is there no weightier news? I heard at Dunkirk
How the king loved a—loved a certain maiden—
The brave La Vallière's daughter.
LAU.   How, my lord,
How can you vegetate in such a place?
I fancy the next tidings heard at Dunkirk
Will be that—Adam's dead!
BRAGE.   The news is old, then?
LAU. News! *news*, indeed! Why, by this time, our lackeys
Have worn the gossip threadbare. News!
BRAGE.   The lady
(She is a soldier's child) hath not yet bartered
Her birthright for ambition? She rejects him?
Speak!—She rejects him?
LAU.   Humph!
BRAGE.   Oh, duke, I know
This courtier air—this most significant silence—
With which your delicate race are wont to lie
Away all virtue! Shame upon your manhood!
Speak out, and say Louise La Vallière lives
To prove to courts—that woman *can* be honest!
LAU. Marquis, you're warm.
BRAGE. You dare not speak; I knew it!
LAU.   Dare not?
BRAGE. Oh, yes, you dare, with hints and smiles
To darken fame—to ruin the defenceless,
Blight with a gesture—wither with a sneer!
Did I say " dare not?"—No man dares it better!
LAU. My lord, these words must pass not!
BRAGE.   Duke, forgive me!
I am a rough, stern soldier—taught from youth
To brave offence, and by the sword alone
Maintain the license of my speech. Oh, say—

Say but one word—say this poor maid is sinless,
And, for her father's sake—(*her father* loved me!)
I'll kneel to thee for pardon!

LAU.   Good, my lord,
I know not your interest in this matter ;
'Tis said that Louis loves the fair La Vallière ;
But what of that—good taste is not a crime !
'Tis said La Vallière does not hate the king ;
But what of that—it does but prove her—loyal !
I know no more. I trust you're satisfied ;
If not——

BRAGE.   Thou liest!

LAU.   Nay, then, draw! (*they fight—after a few
passes* LAUZUN *is disarmed.*)

BRAGE. (*picking up* LAUZUN's *sword*).   There, take
Thy sword. Alas! each slanderer wears a weapon
No honest arm can baffle—*this* is edgeless. (LAUZUN *receives sword.*)
                        [*Exit* BRAGELONE, R. U. E.

LAU. Pleasant! This comes, now, of one's condescending
To talk with men who cannot understand
The tone of good society. Poor fellow! [*Exit* LAUZUN, R. U. E.

Enter MADEMOISELLE DE LA VALLIÈRE, L. U. E.

MDLLE. DE LA V. (*advancing to* C). He loves me, then!   He loves me !
Love! wild word !
Did I say love ? Dishonor, shame, and crime
Dwell on the thought! and yet—and yet—*he loves me !*

Re-enter BRAGELONE. *He pauses. She takes out the* KING's *picture.*

Mine early dreams were prophets! (BRAGELONE *advances*) Stops!
The king ?

BRAGE. No, lady ; pardon me—a joint mistake ;
You sought the king—and *I* Louise La Vallière !

MDLLE. DE LA V. 'You here, my lord !—you here!

BRAGE.   There was a maiden
Fairer than many fair ; but sweet and humble,
And good and spotless, through the vale of life
She walk'd, her modest path with blessings strew'd
(For all men bless'd her) ; from her crystal name,
Like the breath i' the mirror, even envy passed :
I sought that maiden at the court; none knew her.
May I ask you—where now Louise La Vallière ?

MDLLE. DE LA V. Cruel—unjust ! You were my father's friend,
Dare you speak thus to me ?

BRAGE.   Dare! dare! 'Tis well !
You have learnt your state betimes——

MDLLE. DE LA V.   My state, my lord ?
I know not by what right you thus assume
The privilege of insult !

BRAGE.   Ay, reproach !
The harlot's trick—for shame ! Oh, no, your pardon !
You are too high for shame ; and so—farewell !

MDLLE. DE LA V. My lord !—my lord, in pity—No—*in justice*,
Leave me not thus !

BRAGE.   Louise !

MDLLE. DE LA V.   Have they belied me ?
     Speak, my good lord !   What crime have I committed ?
BRAGE. No crime—at courts!   'Tis only Heaven and Honor
     That deem it aught but—most admired good fortune !
     Many, who sweep in careless pride before
     The shrinking, spotless, timorous La Vallière,
     Will now fawn round thee, and with bended knees
     Implore sweet favor of the king's kind mistress.
     Ha ! ha ! this is not crime !   Who calls it crime ?
     Do prudes say " Crime ?"   Go, bribe them, and they'll swear
     Its name is greatness.   Crime, indeed !—ha, ha !
MDLLE. DE LA V. My heart finds words at length !   'Tis false !
BRAGE.   'Tis false !
     Why, speak again !   Say once more it is false—
     'Tis *false*—again *'tis false !*
MDLLE. DE LA V.   Alas ! I'm wretched !
BRAGE. No, lady, no ! not wretched, if not guilty ! (MADEMOISELLE DE
     LA VALLIÈRE, *after walking to and fro in great agitation, seats
     herself on the bench, L., and covers her face with her hands.)*
     (aside) Are these the tokens of remorse ?   No matter !
     I loved her well !   And love is pride, not love,
     If it forsake e'en guilt amidst its sorrows !
     (aloud) Louise ! Louise !   Speak to thy friend, Louise !
     Thy father's friend—thine own !
MDLLE. DE LA V.   This hated court !
     Why came I hither ?   Wherefore have I closed
     My heart against its own most pleading dictates ?
     Why clung to virtue, if the brand of vice
     Sear my good name ?   .
BRAGE.   That, when thou pray'st to Heaven,
     Thy soul may ask for *comfort—not forgiveness !*
MDLLE. DE LA V. *(rising, eagerly).*   A blessed thought !
  .   I thank thee !
BRAGE. (C.).   Thou art innocent !
     Thou hast denied the king ?
MDLLE. DE LA V. (L. C)   I *have* denied him.
BRAGE. Curst be the lies that wrong'd thee !—doubly curst
     The hard, the icy selfishness of soul,
     That, but to pander to an hour's caprice,
     Blasted that flower of life—fair fame !   Accurst
     The king who casts his purple o'er his vices !
MDLLE. DE LA V. Hold !—thou malign'st thy king !
BRAGE.   He spared not thee !
MDLLE. DE LA V. The king—Heaven bless him !
BRAGE.   Wouldst thou madden me ?
     Thou !—No—thou lov'st him not !—thou hid'st not thy face !
     Woman, thou tremblest !   Lord of Hosts, who
     Hast thou preserved me from the foeman's sword,
     And through the incarnadined and raging seas
     Of war upheld me—made both life and soul
     The sleepless priests to that fair idol—Honor ?
     Was it for this ?   I loved thee not, Louise,
     As gallants love ?   Thou wert this life's ideal,
     Breathing through earth the lovely and the holy,
     And clothing Poetry in human beauty !
     When in this gloomy world they spoke of sin,
     I thought of thee, and smiled—for thou wert sinless !

And when they told me of some diviner act
That made our nature noble, my heart whisper'd—
" So would have done Louise !"—'Twas thus I loved thee !
To lose thee, I can bear it ; but to lose,
With thee, all hope, all confidence of virtue—
This—*this* is hard ! Oh ! I am sick of earth ! (*paces to and fro*)

MDLLE. DE LA V. Nay, speak not thus—be gentle with me. Come,
I am not what thou deem'st me, Bragelone ;
Woman I am, and weak. Support, advise me !
Forget the lover, but be still the friend.
Do not desert me—*thou !*

BRAGE. (*stopping suddenly*).   Thou lov'st the king !

MDLLE. DE LA V. But I can fly from love.

BRAGE.   Poor child ! And whither ?

MDLLE. DE LA V. (*appealingly, laying her hand upon his arm*). Take me to
the old castle, to my mother !

BRAGE. The king can reach thee there !

MDLLE. DE LA V.   He'll not attempt it !
Alas ! in courts, how quickly men forget !

BRAGE. Not till their victim hath surrender'd all !
Hadst thou but yielded, why thou might'st have lived
Beside his very threshold, safe, unheeded ;
But thus, with all thy bloom of heart unrified—
The fortress storm'd, not conquer'd—why man's pride,
If not man's lust, would shut thee from escape !
Art thou in earnest—wouldst thou truly fly
From gorgeous infamy to tranquil honor,
God's house alone may shelter thee !

MDLLE. DE LA V.   The convent !
Alas ! alas ! to meet those eyes no more !
Never to hear that voice !

BRAGE. (*departing*).   Enough !

MDLLE. DE LA V.   Yet, stay !
I'll see him once ! One last farewell—and then—
Yes, to the convent !

BRAGE.   I have done—and yet,
Ere I depart, (*takes off scarf and offers it*) take back the scarf thou
gav'st me.
Then didst " thou honor worth !" now, gift and giver
Alike are worthless.

MDLLE. DE LA V.   Worthless ! Didst thou hear me ?
Have I not said that——

BRAGE.   Thou wouldst see the king !
Vice first, and virtue after ! O'er the marge
Of the abyss thou tremblest. One step more,
And from all heaven the angels shall cry, "*Lost !*"
Thou ask'st that single step ! Wouldst thou be saved ?
Lose not a moment. Come !

MDLLE. DE LA V. (*in great agony*). Beside that tree,
When stars shone soft, he vowed for aye to love me !

BRAGE. Think of thy mother ! At this very hour
She blesses Heaven that thou wert born—the last
Fair scion of a proud and stainless race.
To-morrow, and thy shame may cast a shade
Over a hundred 'scutcheons, and thy mother
Feel thou wert born that *she* might long to die !
Come !

MDLLE. DE LA V. I am ready—take my hand. (*as she puts out her hand,*
    her eye falls on the bracelet) Away !
    This is his gift ! And shall I leave him thus ?
    Not one kind word to break the shock of parting—
BRAGE. And break a mother's heart !
MDLLE DE LA V.   Be still ! Thou'rt man !
    Thou canst not feel as woman feels !—her weakness
    Thou canst not sound. O Louis, Heaven protect thee !
    May fate look on thee with La Vallière's eyes !
    Now I am ready, sir. Thou'st seen how weak
    Woman is ever where she loves. *Now,* learn,
    Proportion'd to that weakness is the strength
    With which she conquers love ! O Louis ! Louis !
    Quick ! take me hence ! (*clasping his arm and bending down her*
    head.)
BRAGE. (*aside*). The heart she wrongs hath saved her !
    And is that all !—The shelter for mine age—
    The Hope that was the garner for affection—
    The fair and lovely tree, beneath whose shade
    The wearied soldier thought to rest at last,
    And watch life's sun go calm and cloudless down,
    Smiling the day to sleep—all, all lie shatter'd !
    No matter. (*aloud*) I have saved thy soul from sorrow,
    Whose hideous depth thy vision cannot fathom.
    Joy !—I have saved thee !
MDLLE. DE LA V.   ·   Ah ! when last we parted
    I told thee, of thy love I was not worthy.
    Another shall replace me !
BRAGE. (*smiling sadly*).   Hush ! Another ?
    No ! (*replacing scarf*) See, I wear thy colors still ! Though Hope
    Wanes from the plate, the dial still remains,
    And takes no light from stars ! I—*I* am nothing !
    But thou—Nay, weep not ! Yet these tears are honest ;
    Thou hast not lived to make the Past one blot,
    Which life in vain would weep away ! Poor maiden !
    I could not cheer thee *then.* Now, joy !—I've saved thee !
[*Exeunt* MADEMOISELLE DE LA VALLIÈRE *and* BRAGELONE, R. U. E.

SCENE II.—*The* KING's *cabinet at Fontainebleau ;** *Table* C., *covered with*
    papers, the KING *seated* R. *of table, writing.*

Enter LAUZUN, L. 2 E.

LOUIS. Lauzun, I sent for you. Your zeal has served me,
    And I am grateful. There, this order gives you
    The lands and lordship of De Vesci.
LAU. (*advances, kneels and receives the parchment*). Sire,
    How shall I thank your goodness ?
LOUIS.   Hush !—by silence !
LAU. (*rising, aside*). A king's forbidden fruit has pretty windfalls !
LOUIS. The beautiful Louise ! I never loved
    Till now.

---

    * To some it may be interesting to remember that this cabinet, in which the most
powerful of the Bourbon kings is represented as rewarding the minister of his pleasure, is the same as that in which is yet shown the table upon which Napoleon Bonaparte (son of a gentleman of Corsica), signed the abdication of the titles and domin-
ions of Charlemagne !

LAU.   She yields not yet ?
LOUIS.   But gives refusal
A voice that puts e'en passion to the blush
To own one wish so soft a heart denies it!
LAU.   A woman's No! is but a crooked path
Unto a woman's Yes! Your Majesty
Saw her to-day ?
LOUIS.   No!—Grammont undertakes
To bear, in secret, to her hand, some lines
That pray a meeting.—I await his news. (*continues writing.*)
LAU.   (*aside, advancing*, L. C.). I'll not relate my tilt with Bragelone.
First, I came off the worst. No man of sense
Ever confesses that! And, secondly,
This most officious, curious, hot-brained Quixote
Might make him jealous; jealous kings are peevish;
And, if he fall to questioning the lady,
She'll learn who told the tale, and spite the teller.
Oh! the great use of logic! (*crosses to* R.)
LOUIS.   'Tis in vain
I strive by business to beguile impatience!
How my heart beats!—Well, count ?

Enter GRAMMONT, L. 2 E.

GRAM.   Alas, my liege ?
LOUIS. Alas! Speak out!
GRAM.   The court has lost La Vallière!
LOUIS (*starting up*). Ha!—lost!
GRAM.   She has fled, and none guess whither.
LOUIS. (*advancing quickly to* C.).   Fled!
I ll not believe it!—Fled!
LAU. (R. C.).   What matters, Sire ?
No spot is sacred from the king!
LOUIS (*passionately, walking to and fro*). By Heaven,
I *am* a king!—Not all the arms of Europe
Could wrest one jewel from my crown. And she—
What is my crown to her ? I am a king!
Who stands between the king and her he loves
Becomes a traitor—and may find a tryrant!
Follow me!   [*Exit* LOUIS, L. 1 E.
GRAM.   Who e'er heard of Maids of Honor
Flying from kings ?
LAU.   Ah, had *you* been a maid,
How kind you would have been, you rogue!—Come on!
         [*Exeunt* LAUZUN *and* GRAMMONT, L. 1 E.

SCENE III.—*The cloisters of a Convent—Night—Thunder and lightning, the latter made visible through the long oriel windows.*

MADEMOISELLE DE LA VALLIÈRE *enters, wearily,* L. 2 E.

MDLLE. DE LA V. Darkly the night sweeps on. No thought of sleep
Steals to my heart. What sleep is to the world
Prayer is to me—life's balm, and grief's oblivion!
Yet, e'en before the altar of my God,
Unhallow'd fire is raging through my veins—
Heav'n on my lips, but earth within my heart—

And while I pray *his* memory prompts the prayer,
And all I ask of Heaven is, " Guard my Louis ! "
Forget him—*that* I dare not pray !   I would not,
E'en if I could, be happy, and forget him ! (*thunder*)
Roll on, roll on, dark chariot of the storm,
Whose wheels are thunder—the rack'd elements
Can furnish forth no tempest like the war
Of passion in one weak and erring heart ! (*the bell tolls one*)
Hark ! to-night's funeral knell !   How through the roar
Of winds and thunder thrills that single sound,
Solemnly audible !—the tongue of time,
In time's most desolate hour—it bids us muse
On worlds which love can reach not !   Life runs fast
To its last sands !   To bed, to bed !—to tears
And wishes for the grave !—to bed, to bed ! (*1 trumpet is heard
without*, L.)

Two or three NUNS *enter*, L. 2 E., *and hurry across the stage.*

FIRST NUN. Most strange !
SECOND NUN.   In such a night, too !   The great gates
That ne'er unclose save to a royal guest,
Unbarr'd ! (NUNS *draw aside towards* R. 1 E.)
MDLLE. DE LA V. What fear, what hope, by turns distracts me ! (*the
trumpet sounds again.*)
FIRST NUN. Hark ! in the court, the ring of hoofs !—the door
Creaks on the sullen hinge !
LAU. (*without*).   Make way—the king !

Enter LOUIS *and* LAUZUN, L. 1 E.

MDLLE. DE LA V. (*rushing forward*). Oh, Louis—oh, beloved ! (*then paus-
ing abruptly*) No, touch me not !
Leave me ! in pity leave me !   Heavenly Father,
I fly to thee !   Protect me from his arms—
Protect me from myself !
LOUIS.   Oh bliss !   Louise !

Enter ABBESS *and* NUNS, R. 1 E.

ABBESS. Peace, peace !   What clamor desecrates the shrine
And solitudes of God ?
LAU. (L. C.).   Madam, your knee—
The king !
ABBESS.   The king !—you mock me, sir !
LOUIS (*quitting* MADEMOISELLE DE LA VALLIÈRE). Behold
Your sovereign, reverend mother !—We have come
To thank you for your shelter of this lady,
And to reclaim our charge.
ABBESS.   My liege, these walls
Are sacred even from the purple robe
And sceptred hand.
LOUIS.   She hath not ta'en the vow !
She's free—we claim her !—she is of our court !
Woman,—go to !
ABBESS.   The maiden, Sire, is free !
Your royal lips have said it !—She is free !

And if this shrine her choice, whoe'er compels her
Forth from the refuge, doth incur the curse
The Roman Church awards to even kings !
Speak, lady—dost thou claim against the court
The asylum of the cloister ?

LOUIS.   Darest thou brave us ?
LAU. (aside to LOUIS). Pardon, my liege !—reflect ! Let not the world
Say that the king——
LOUIS (aside to LAUZUN).   Can break his bonds !—Away !
I was a man before I was a king ! (aloud, approaching MADEMOI-
        SELLE DE LA VALLIERE)
Lady, we do command your presence ! (lowering his voice) Swee !
Adored Louise !—if ever to your ear
My whispers spoke in music—if my life
Be worth the saving, do not now desert me !
MDLLE. DE LA V. Let me not hear him, Heaven !—Strike all my senses !
Make—make me dumb, deaf, blind—but keep me honest !
ABBESS. Sire, you have heard her answer !
LOUIS (advancing passionately, pauses, and then with great dignity). Abbess,
        no !
This lady was intrusted to our charge—
A fatherless child !—The king is now her father !
Madam, we would not wrong you ; but we know
That sometimes most unhallow'd motives wake
' Your zeal for converts !—This young maid is wealthy,
And nobly born !—Such proselytes may make
A convent's pride but oft a convent's victims !
No more !—we claim the right the law awards us,
Free and alone to commune with this maid.
If then her choice go with you—be it so ;
We are no tyrant !   Peace !—retire !
ABBESS.   My liege !
Forgive——
LOUIS.   We do !   Retire !
                [LAUZUN, the ABBESS, etc., withdraw, R. 1 E.
LOUIS (C.).   We are alone !
MDLLE. DE LA V. Alone !—No, God is present, and the conscience !
LOUIS. Ah ! fear'st thou, then, that heart that would resign
E'en love itself to guard one pang from thee ?
MDLLE. DE LA V. I must speak !—Sire, if every drop of blood
Were in itself a life, I'd shed them all
For one hour's joy to thee !   But fame and virtue—
My father's grave—my mother's lonely age—
These, these—(thunder) I hear their voice !—the fires of Heaven
Seem to me like the eyes of angels, and
Warn me against myself !—Farewell !
LOUIS.   Louise,
I will not hear thee !   What ! farewell ! that word
Sounds like a knell to all that's worth the living !
Farewell !   why, then, farewell all peace to Louis,
And the poor king is once more but a thing
Of state and forms.   The impulse and the passion—
The blessed air of happy human life—
The all that made him envy not his subjects,
Dies in that word !   Ah, canst thou—dar'st thou say it ?
MDLLE. DE LA V. Oh, speak not thus !—Speak harshly ! threat, com-
        mand !—

Be all the king !
Louis (*kneeling*).   The king ! he kneels to thee!
Mdlle. de la V. I'm weak!—be generous ! My own soul betrays me;
But *thou* betray me not !
Louis.   Nay, hear me, sweet one !
Desert me not this once, and I will swear
To know no guiltier wish—to curb my heart—
To banish hope from love—and nurse no dream
Thy spotless soul itself shall blush to cherish !
Hear me, Louise—thou lov'st me ?
Mdlle. de la V.   Love thee, Louis !
Louis. Thou lov'st me—then confide ! Who loves *trusts* ever !
Mdlle. de la V. Trust thee!—ah ! *dare* I ?
Louis (*rising and clasping her in his arms*). Ay, till death! What ho!
Lauzun ! I say !

Lauzun re-enters quickly, and advances.

Mdlle. de la V.   No, no !
Louis.   *Not trust me*, dearest ?

She falls on his shoulder. The Abbess re-enters followed by Nuns.

Abbess. Still firm !
Lau. (L.).   No, madam ! Way there for the king !

———

ACT III.

SCENE I.—*An antechamber in the palace of* Madame la Duchess de la
Vallière, *at Versailles.*

Enter Lauzun, l. 1 e., *and* Madame de Montespan, r. 1 e.

Lau. Ha ! my fair friend, well met—how fairs Athenè ?
Mme de Mon. Weary with too much gayety ! Now, tell me !
Do *you* ne'er tire of splendor ? Does this round
Of gaudy pomps—this glare of glitt'ring nothings—
Does it ne'er pall upon you ? To my eyes
'Tis as the earth would be if turf'd with scarlet,
Without one spot of green.
Lau.   We all feel thus
Until we are used to it. Art has grown *my* nature,
And if I see green fields, or ill-dress'd people,
I cry " How artificial!" With me, " *Nature* "
Is " Paris and Versailles." The word, " a man,"
Means something noble, that one sees at court.
Woman's the thing Heaven made for wearing trinkets
And talking scandal. That's my state of nature !
You'll like it soon ; you have that temper which
Makes courts its element.
Mme. de Mon.   And how ?—define, sir.
Lau. First, then—but shall I not offend ?
Mme. de Mon.   Be candid.
I'd know my faults, to make them look like virtues.
Lau. First, then, Athenè, you've an outward frankness.

Deceit in you looks honester than truth.
Thoughts, at court, like faces on the stage,
Require some rouge. You rogue your thoughts so well,
That one would deem their only fault, that nature
Gave them too bright a bloom !

MME. DE MON.   Proceed !

LAU.   Your wit
Is of the true court breed—it plays with nothings ;
Just bright enough to warm, but never burn—
Excites the dull, but ne'er offends the vain.
You have much energy ; it looks like feeling !
Your cold ambition seems an easy impulse ;
Your head most ably counterfeits the heart,
But never, like the heart, betrays itself !
Oh ! you'll succeed at court—you see I know you !
Not so this new-made duchess—young La Vallière.

MME. DE MON. The weak, fond fool !

LAU.   Yes, weak—*she* has a heart ;
Yet *you*, too, love the king !

MME. DE MON.   And she does *not* !
She loves but *Louis !*—I but love the *king ;*
Pomp, riches, state, and power—these, who would love not ?

LAU.   Bravo ! well said !   Oh, you'll succeed at court !   .
I knew it well ! it was for this I chose you—
Induced your sapient lord to waste no more
Your beauty in the shade—for this prepared
The duchess to receive you to her bosom,
Her dearest friend ; for this have duly fed
The king's ear with your praise, and clear'd your way
To rule a sovereign and to share a throne.

MME. DE MON. I know thou hast been my architect of power ;
And when the pile is built—

LAU. (*with a smile*).   Could still o'erthrow it,
If thou couldst play the ingrate !

MME. DE MON.   I !—nay !

LAU.   Hear me !
Each must have need of each. Long live the king !
Still let his temples ache beneath the crown.
But all that kings can give—wealth, rank, and power—
Must be for *us*—the king's friend and his favorite.

MME. DE MON. But is it easy to supplant the duchess ?
All love La Vallière !   Her meek nature shrinks
E'en from our homage ; and she wears her state
As if she pray'd the world to pardon greatness.

LAU.   And thus destroys herself !   At court, Athené,
Vice, to win followers, takes the front of virtue,
And looks the dull plebeian things called *moral*
To scorn, until they blush to be unlike her.
Why is De Lauzun not her friend ?   Why plotting
For a new rival ?   Why ?—Because De Lauzun
Wins not the power he look'd for from her friendship !
She keeps not old friends—and she makes no new ones !
For who would be a friend to one who deems it
A crime to ask his Majesty a favor ?
" *Friends* " is a phrase at court that means *promotion !*

MME. DE MON. Her folly, I confess, would not be mine,
But grant her faults—the king still loves the duchess !

LAU.   Since none are by, I'll venture on a treason,
And say, the king's a man—and men will change !
I have his ear, and you shall win his eye.
'Gainst a new face, and an experienced courtier,
What chance hath this poor, loving, simple woman ?
Besides, she has too much conscience for a king !
He likes not to look up, and feel how low,
E'en on the throne that overlooks the world,
His royal greatness dwarfs beside that heart
That never stoop'd to sin, save when it loved him !

MME. DE MON. You're eloquent, my lord !

LAU.   Ah ! of such natures
You and I know but little ! (aside) This must cease,
Or I shall all disclose my real aims !
(aloud) The king is with the duchess ?

MME. DE MON.   Yes.

LAU.   As yet
She doth suspect you not ?

MME. DE MON.   Suspect !—the puppet !
No ; but full oft, her head upon my bosom,
Calls me her truest friend—invites me ever
To amuse the king with my enlivening sallies—
And still breaks off, in sighing o'er the past,
To wish her spirit were as blithe as mine,
And fears her Louis wearies of her sadness.

LAU.   So, the plot ripens—ere the king came hither,
I had prepared his royal pride to chafe
At that sad face, whose honest sorrow wears
Reproach unconsciously ! You'll hear the issue !
Now then, farewell !—We understand each other !
                            [Exit LAUZUN, R. 1 E.

MME. DE MON. And once I loved this man—and still might love him,
But that I love ambition ! Yes, my steps
Now need a guide ; but once upon the height,
And I will have no partner ! Thou, lord duke,
With all thine insolent air of proud protection,
Thou shalt wait trembling on my nod, and bind
Thy fortune to my wheels ! O man !—vain man !
Well sung the poet—when this power of beauty
Heaven gave our sex, it gave the only sceptre
Which makes the world a slave ! And I will wield it '—
                    [Exit MADAME DE MONTESPAN, L. 1 E.

SCENE II.—The Scene opens and discovers the KING, and the DUCHESS DE
            LA VALLIERE at chess.

LOUIS (R.). But one move more !

DUCH. DE LA V. (L.).   Not so ! I check the king.

LOUIS. A vain attempt—the king is too well guarded !
            There, check again ! Your game is lost !

DUCH. DE LA V.   As usual,
E'en from this mimic stage of war you rise
Ever the victor. (they leave the table and advance.)

LOUIS   'Twere a fairer fortune,
My own Louise, to reconcile the vanquish'd !

DUCH. DE LA V. (sadly). My best loved Louis !

LOUIS (C.).   Why so sad a tone ?

Nay, smile, Louise!—Love thinks himself aggrieved
If Care casts shadows o'er the heart it seeks,
To fill with cloudless sunshine! Smile, Louise!
E'en unkind words were kinder than sad looks.
There—*now* thou gladd'st me!

DUCH. DE LA V. (L. C.). Yet, e'en thou, methought,
Didst wear, this morn, a brow on which the light
Shone less serenely than its wont!

LOUIS.   This morn!
Ay, it is true!—this morn I heard that France
Hath lost a subject monarchs well might mourn!
Oh! little know the world how much a king,
Whose life is past in *purchasing* devotion,
Loses in one who merited all favor
And scorned to ask the least! A king, Louise,
Sees but the lackeys of mankind. The true
Lords of our race—the high chivalric hearts—
Nature's nobility—alas, are proud,
And stand aloof, lest slaves should say they flatter!
Of such a mould was he whom France deplores.

DUCH. DE LA V. Tell me his name, that I, with thee, may mourn him.

LOUIS. A noble name, but a more noble bearer;
Not to be made by, but to make, a lineage.
Once, too, at Dunkirk, 'twix me and the foe,
He thrust his gallant breast, already seamed
With warrior wounds, and *his* blood flow'd for mine.
Dead—his just merits all unrecompensed!
Obscured, like sun-light, by the suppliant clouds!
He should have died a marshal! Death did wrong
To strike so soon! Alas, brave Bragelone!

DUCH. DE LA V. (*starting*). Ha!—did I hear aright, my liege—my Louis?
That name—that name!—thou saidst not " Bragelone?"

LOUIS. Such was his name, not often heard at court.
Thou didst not know him? What! thou art pale! thou weep'st.
Thou art ill! Louise, look up! (*supporting her.*)

DUCH. LE LA V. (*aside*). Be still, O Conscience!
I did not slay him! (*aloud*) Died *too soon!* Alas!
He should have died with all his hopes unblighted,
Ere I was—what I am!

LOUIS.   What mean these words?

DUCH. DE'LA V. How did death strike him? What disease?

LOUIS.   •   I know not.
He had retired from service; and in peace
Breathed out his soul to some remoter sky!
France only guards his fame! What was he to thee
That thou shouldst weep for him?

DUCH. DE LA V.   Hast thou ne'er heard
We were betrothed in youth?

LOUIS (*agitated and aside*).   Lauzun speaks truth!
I'd not her virgin heart—she loved another!
(*aloud*) Betrothed! You mourn him deeply!

DUCH. DE LA V.   Sire, I do
That broken heart—I was its dream—its idol!
And with regret is mingled—what repentance?

LOUIS (*coldly*). Repentance, madam! Well, the word is gracious!

DUCH. DE LA V. Pardon! oh, pardon! But the blow was sudden;
How can the heart play courtier with remorse?

LOUIS. Remorse!—again. Why be at once all honest,
And say you love me not !
DUCH. DE LA V.   Not love you, Louis ?
LOUIS. Not if you feel repentance to have loved !
DUCH. DE LA V. What ! think'st thou, Louis, I should love thee more
Did I love virtue less, or less regret it ?
LOUIS. I pray you truce with these heroic speeches ;
They please us in romance—in life they weary.
DUCH. DE LA V. Louis, do I deserve this ?
LOUIS.   Rather, lady,
Do I deserve the mute reproach of sorrow ?
Still less these constant, and never-soothed complaints,
This waiting-woman jargon of " *lost virtue*."
DUCH. DE LA V. Sire, this from you !
LOUIS   Why, oft, could others hear thee,
Well might they deem thee some poor village Phœbe,
Whom her false Lubin had deceived, and left,
Robb'd of her only dower ! and not the great
Duchess La Vallière, in our realm of France,
Second to none but our anointed race ;
The envy of the beauty and the birth
Of Europe's court—our city of the world !
Is it so great disgrace, Louise La Vallière,
To wear, unrivall'd, in thy breast, the heart
Of Bourbon's latest, nor her least of kings ?
DUCH. DE LA V. Sire, when you deigned to love me, I had hoped
You knew the sunshine of your royal favor
Had fallen on a lowly flower. Let others
Deem that the splendor consecrates the sin !
I'd love thee with as pure and proud a love,
If thou hadst been the poorest cavalier
That ever served a king. Thou know'st it, Louis !
LOUIS. I would not have it so! my fame, my glory,
The purple and the orb, are part of me ;
And thou shouldst love them for my sake, and feel
I were not Louis were I less the king.
Still weeping ! Fie ! I tell thee tears freeze back
The very love I still would bear thee !
DUCH. DE LA V. " Would *still* !"—didst thou say " *still* ?"
LOUIS.   Come, lady !
Woman, to keep her empire o'er the heart,
Must learn its nature—mould into its bias—
And rule by never differing from our humors.
DUCH. DE LA V. I'll school my features, teach my lips to smile,
Be all thou wilt ; but say not " *still*," dear Louis !
LOUIS. Well, well ! no further words ; let peace be with us. (*crosses to* L.)
(*aside*) By Heaven, she weeps with yet intenser passion !
It must be that she loved this Bragelone,
And mourns the loftier fate that made her mine !
(*aloud*) This gallant soldier, madam, your betrothed,
Hath some share in your tears ?
DUCH. DE LA V, (R. C.).   Oh, name him not ;
My tears are all unworthy dews to fall
Upon a tomb so honored !
LOUIS.   Grant me patience !
These scenes are very tedious, fair La Vallière.
In truth, we kings have, in the council-chamber,

Enough to make us tearful—in the bower
We would have livelier subjects to divert us.

Duch. de la V. Again forgive me ! I am sick at heart ;
I pray your pardon ;—these sad news have marr'd
The music of your presence, and have made me
Fit but for solitude. I pray you, Sire,
Let me retire ; and when again I greet you,
I'll wear the mien you'd have me !

Louis.   Be it so !
Let me no more disturb you from your thoughts ;
They must be sad. So brave—and your betrothed !
Your grief becomes you !

Duch. de la V.   You forgive me, Louis ?
We do not part unkindly ?

Louis.   Fair one, no !
                    [*Exit* La Vallière, l. d.

She was my first love, and my fondest. *Was !*
Alas, the word must come—I love her yet,
But love wanes glimmering to that twilight—friendship !
Grant that she never loved this Bragelone ;
Still, tears and sighs make up dull interludes
In passion's short-lived drama ! She is good,
Gentle, and meek—and I do think she loves me,
(A truth no king is sure of!)—But, in fine,
I have begun to feel the hours are long
Pass'd in her presence ! What I hotly sought,
Coldly I weary of. I'll seek De Lauzun ;
I like his wit—I almost like his knavery ;
It never makes us yawn, like high-flown virtues.
Thirst, hunger, rest—these are the wants of peasants ;
A courtier's wants are titles, place, and gold ;
But a poor king, who has these wants so sated,
Has only one want left—to be amused !   [*Exit* Louis, r. d.

Re-enter the Duchess de la Vallière.

Duch. de la V. Louis ! dear Louis ! Gone ! alas ! and left me
Half in displeasure—I was wrong, methinks,
To—no !—I was not wrong to *feel* remorse,
But wrong to give it utterance !

Enter Madame de Montespan, c. l.

Mme. de Mon. (*looking round, then advancing*). What ! alone,
Fair friend ? I thought the king——

Duch de la V.   Has gone, in anger ;
Cold, and in anger.

Mme. de Mon.   What, with *thee*, dear lady ?
On the smooth surface of that angel meekness
I should have thought no angry breath could linger.
But men and kings are——

Duch. de la V.   Hush ! I was to blame.
The king's all goodness. Shall I write to him ?
Letters have not our looks—and, oh, one look !
How many hardest hearts one look hath won,
A life consumed in words had woo'd in vain !

MME. DE MON. To-night there is high revel at the court ,
  There you may meet your truant king.
DUCH. DE LA V.   To-night !
  An age !   How many hours to-night ?
MME. DE MON.   You know
  My office makes my home the royal palace ;
  I serve the queen, and thus shall see your Louis
  Ere the sun set.
DUCH. DE LA V.   You !—happy *you !*
MME. DE MON.   Perchance
  (The king is ever gracious to your friends,
  And knows me of the nearest), I might whisper,
  Though with less sweet a tone, your message to him,
  And be your dove, and bear you back the olive !
DUCH. DE LA V. My kind Athenè !
MME. DE MON.   Nay, 'tis yours the kindness,
  To wear my love so near your heart.   But, tell me,
  Since you accept my heraldy, the cause
  Of strife between you in this court of love.
DUCH. DE LA V. Alas !   I know not, save that I offended !
  The wherefore boots the heart that loves to know ?
MME. DE MON. Not much, I own, the poor defendant—woman,
  But much the advocate ;   I need the brief.
DUCH. DE LA V. Methinks his kingly nature chafes to see
  It cannot rule the conscience as the heart ;
  But tell him, ever henceforth I will keep
  Sad thoughts for lonely hours—Athenè, tell him,
  That if he smile once more upon Louise,
  The smile shall never pass from that it shines on ;
  Say—but I'll write myself. (*sits down to table and writes.*)
MME. DE MON. (*aside*).   What need of schemes—
  Lauzun's keen wit—Athenè's plotting spirit ?
  She weaves herself the web that shall ensnare her !
DUCH. DE LA V. (*rises, advances and gives letter*). There; back these feeble
    words with all thy beauty,
  Thy conquering eyes, and thy bewitching smile.
  Sure never suit can fail with such a pleader !
  And now a little while to holier sadness,
  And thine accusing memory, Bragelone !
MME. DE MON. Whom speak you of ?—the hero of the Fronde ?
  Who seem'd the last of the old Norman race,
  And half preserved to this degenerated age
  The lordly shape the ancient Bayards wore !
DUCH. DE LA V. You praise him well !   He was my father's friend,
  And should have been his son.   We were affianced,
  And—but no more !   Ah ! cruel, cruel Louis !
  You mourn'd for him—how much more cause have *I !*
MME DE MON. (*quickly*). What ! he is dead ? your grief the king
    resented ?
  Knew he your troth had thus been plighted ?
DUCH. DE LA V.   Yes ;
  And still he seem'd to deem it sin to mourn him !
MME. DE MON. (*aside*). A clue—another clue—that I will fo'low,
  Until it lead me to the throne ! (*aloud*) Well, cheer thee ;
  Trust your true friend ; rely on my persuasion.
  Methinks I never task'd its powers till now.
  Farewell, and fear not !   Oh ! I'll plead your cause,

As if myself the client. *(aside)* Thou art sentenced i
[*Exit* MADAME DE MONTESPAN, R. D.
DUCH. DE LA V. 'Tis a sweet solace still to have a friend—
A friend in *woman !* Oh, to what a reed
We bind our destinies, when man we love !
Peace, honor, conscience lost—if I lose him,
What have I left ? How sinks my heart within me !
I'll to my chamber ; there the day of tears
Lends night its smile ! *And I'm the thing they envy !*
[*Exit* DUCHESS DE LA VALLIÈRE, L. D.

SCENE III.—*The gardens of Versailles.*

LAUZUN, GRAMMONT, *and* COURTIERS *enter*, L. 1 E

LAU. 'Tis now the hour in which our royal master
Honors the ground of his rejoicing gardens
By his illustrious footsteps—there, my lords,
That is the true style-courtier !
GRAM.   Out upon you !
Your phrase would suit some little German prince,
Of fifteen hundred quarterings and five acres,
And not the world's great Louis ! 'Tis the hour
When Phœbus shrinks abash'd, and all the stars
Envy the day that it beholds the king !

Enter LOUIS, R. 1 E.

LOUIS.   My lords,
Pray you be cover'd. Hark ye, dear De Lauzun.
[*Exeunt the* COURTIERS, R. 2 E., *as the* KING *takes* LAUZUN *aside.*
The fair De Montespan ?
LAU.   Is worth the loving ;
And, by mine honor, while we speak she comes!
A happy fortune. Sire, may I withdraw ?   [*Exit*, R. 2 E.

Enter MADAME DE MONTESPAN, R. 1 E.   *Salutes the* KING *and passes on.*

LOUIS. Fair madam, we had hoped you with you brought
Some bright excuse to grace our cheerless presence
With a less short-lived light ! You dawn upon us
Only to make us more regret your setting.
MME. DE MON. Sire, if I dared, I would most gladly hail
A few short moments to arrest your presence,
And rid me of a soft, yet painful duty.
LOUIS. 'Tis the first time, be sure, so sweet a voice
E'er craved a sanction for delighting silence.
Speak on, we pray thee !
MME. DE MON.   Gracious Sire, the duchess,
Whom you have lately left, she fears, in anger,
Besought me to present this letter to you.
LOUIS (*takes the letter, and aside*). She blushes while she speaks ! 'Tis
passing strange,
I ne'er remark'd those darkly-dreaming eyes,
That melt in their own light ! (*reads, and carelessly puts up the let-
ter*) It scarcely suits
Her dignity, and ours, to choose a witness

To what hath chanced between us. She is good,
But her youth, spent in some old country castle,
Knows not the delicate spirit of a court.
MME. DE MON. She bade me back her suit. Alas! my liege,
Who can succeed, if fair La Vallière fail ?
LOUIS. She bade thee ?—she was prudent! Were *I* woman,
And loved, I'd not have chosen such a herald.
MME. DE MON. Love varies in its colors with all tempers ;
The duchess is too proud to fear a rival,
Too beautiful to find one. May I take
Some word of comfort back to cheer her sadness,
Made doubly deep by thoughts of your displeasure,
And grief for a dear friend ?
LOUIS.   Ay, *that's* the sadness!
MME. DE MON. He was a gallant lord, this Bragelone,
And her betrothed. Perchance in youth she loved him,
Ere the great sun had quenched the morning star !
LOUIS. She loved him—think'st thou so ?
MME. DE MON. (*dissimulating*).   Indeed I know not ;
But I have heard her eloquent in praise.
And seen her lost in woe. You will forgive her ?
LOUIS Forgive her—there's no cause !
MME. DE MON.   Now, bless you, Sire,
For that one word. My task is done.
LOUIS.   Already ?
MME. DE MON. What can I more ? Oh, let me hasten back !
What rapture must be hers who can but fill
An atom of the heart of godlike Louis !
How much more the whole soul !—To lose thy love
Must be, not grief, but some sublime despair,
Like that the Roman felt who lost a world !
LOUIS (*aside*). By Heaven, she fires me !—a brave, royal spirit,
Worthy to love a king !
MME. DE MON.   To know thee hers,
What pride—what glory ! Though all earth cried " Shame !"
Earth could not still the trumpet at her heart,
That, with its swelling and exultant voice,
Told her the earth was but the slave of Louis,
And *she* the partner ! And O, hour of dread !
When (for the hour must come), some fairer form
Shall win thee from her—still, methinks, 'twould be
A boast to far posterity to point
To all the trophies piled about thy throne,
And say—" He loved me once !"—O, sire, your pardon ;
I am too bold.
LOUIS. (*aside*).   Why, this were love, indeed,
Could we but hope to win it. And such love
Would weave the laurel in its wreaths of myrtle.
(*aloud*) Beautiful lady! while thou speak'st I dream
What love should be—and feel where love is not !
Thou com'st the suitor, to remain the judge ;
And I could kneel to thee for hope and mercy.
MME. DE MON. Ah, no—ah, no—she is my friend. And if
She loves not as I love—I mean, I *might* love—
Still she *believes* she loves thee. Tempt me not.
Who could resist thee ! Sire, farewell !
                              [*Exit* MADAME DE MONTESPAN, R. 1 E.

Louis.   Her voice
      Is husb'd ; but still its queen-like music lingers
      In my rapt ears.   I dreamt Louise had loved me ;
      She who felt love disgrace !   Before the true,
      How the tame counterfeit grows pale and lifeless.
      By the sad brow of yon devout La Vallière
      I feel a man, and fear myself a culprit !
      But this high spirit wakes in mine the sense
      Of what it is—I am that Louis whom
      The world has called " The Great !"—and in her pride
      Mirror mine own.   This jaded life assumes
      The zest, the youth, the glory of *excitement* !
      To-night we meet again—speed fast, dull hours !
                                            [*Exit* Louis, R. 1 E.

SCENE IV.—*Grand saloon in the Palace of Versailles—in the background the
      suite of apartments is seen in perspective—the* QUEEN, DUCHESS DE LA
      VALLIÈRE, *and* MADAME DE MONTESPAN *are discovered together with*
      COURTIERS, LADIES, *etc.*

FIRST COOK. (*approaching the* DUCHESS DE LA VALLIÈRE, *as she is advanc-
            ing*). Madam, your goodness is to France a proverb !
      If I might dare request, this slight memorial
      You would convey to our most gracious master ?
      The rank of colonel in the royal guard
      Is just now vacant.   True, I have not served ;
      But I do trust my valor is well-known ;
      I've killed three noted swordsmen in a duel—
      And for the rest, a word from you were more
      Than all the laurels Holland gave to others.
DUCH. DE LA V. My lord, forgive me !   I might ill-deserve
      The friendship of a monarch, if, forgetting
      That honors are the attributes of merit ;
      And they who sell the service of the public
      For the false coin, soft smiles and honey'd words
      Forged in the antechambers of a palace,
      Defraud a people to degrade a king !
      If you have merits, let *them* plead for you ;
      Nor ask in whispers what you claim for justice. (*retires towards* L.)
MME. DE MON. (*advancing* R , *to* COURTIER, *as the* DUCHESS DE LA VAL-
            LIÈRE *turns away*). Give me the paper.   Hush ! the king
      shall see it ! (*takes the paper, places it in her bosom and retires
      towards* R.   *Music.*)

Enter the KING, C., *with* GRAMMONT, LAUZUN, *and other* COURTIERS.   *He
      pauses by the* QUEEN, *and accosts her respectfully in dumb show.*

GRAM. (L., *aside*). With what a stately and sublime decorum
      His majesty throws grandeur o'er his foibles ;
      He not disguises vice ; but makes vice kingly—
      Most gorgeous of all sensualists !
LAU. (*aside*).   How different
      His royal rival in the chase of pleasure,
      The spendthrift, sauntering Second Charles of England !
GRAM. (*aside*). Aye, Jove to Comus !
LAU. (*aside*).   Silence ! Jove approaches !

The crowd breaks up into groups; the KING *passes slowly from each till he joins the* DUCHESS DE LA VALLIÈRE; *the* COURTIERS *retire.*

LOUIS. Why, this is well. I thank you.
DUCH. DE LA V.   And forgive me ?
LOUIS. Forgive you! You mistake me; wounded feeling
     Is not displeasure. Let this pass, Louise.
     Your lovely friend has a most heavenly smile !
DUCH. DE LA V. And a warm heart. In truth, my liege, I'm glad
     You see her with my eyes.
LOUIS.   You have no friend
     Whose face it glads me more to look upon. (*aside, and gazing on*
           MADAME DE MONTESPAN)
     What thrilling eyes! (*aloud*) My thanks are due to her
     For, with the oil of her mellifluous voice,
     Smoothing the waves the passing breeze had ruffled. (*crosses to* R,
           joins MADAME DE MONTESPAN, *and leads her through the
           crowd to the back of the stage, where they enter into conversation,
           and afterwards she shows him the paper.*)
LAU. (*advances to the* DUCHESS). Your grace resolves no more to be
     content
     Eclipsing others. You eclipse yourself.
DUCH. DE LA V. I thought you were a friend, and not a flatterer.
LAU. Friendship would lose its dearest privilege
     If friendship were forbidden to admire !
     Why, e'en the king admires your grace's friend—
     Told me to-day she was the loveliest lady
     The court could boast. Nay, see how, while they speak,
     He gazes on her. How his breathing fans
     The locks that shade the roses of her cheek !
DUCH. DE LA V. Ha ! (*aside*) Nay, be still, my heart
LAU.   It is but friendship ;
     But it looks wondrous warm !
DUCH. DE LA V. (*aside*).   He cannot mean it !
     And yet—and yet—he lingers on her hand—
     He whispers !
LAU.   How the gossips gaze and smile !
     There'll be much scandal.
DUCH. DE LA V. Lauzun—what—thou thinkst not—
     No, no, thou canst not think——
LAU.   That courts know treachery,
     That women are ambitious or men false ;
     I will not think it. Pshaw !
DUCH DE LA V. (*aside*).   My brain swims round !
     Louis, of late, hath been so changed. How fair
     She looks to-night—and oh, *she* has not fallen !
     (*aloud*) He comes—he nears us—he has left her. Fie !
     My foolish fancies wronged him !
LAU. (*aside*).   The spell works.
MME. DE MON. (*as the* KING *quits her, to* FIRST COURTIER, *giving him
     back the paper*). My lord, your suit is granted.
FIRST COUR. Blessings, madame ! (*the other* COURTIERS *come round him.*)
SECOND COUR. Her influence must be great. I know three dukes
     Most pressing for the post.
THIRD COUR.   A rising sun,
     Worthier of worship than that cold La Vallière.
     The king as well, methinks, might have no mistress,

As one by whom no courtier grew the richer. (*the* Courtiers
group round MADAME DE MONTESPAN)

LOUIS (*advancing*). My lords, you do remember the bright lists
Which, in the place termed thenceforth " *The Carrousel*," *
We sometime held ?—a knightly tournament,
That brought us back to the age of the First Francis !

LAU. Of all your glorious festivals, the greatest !
Who but remembers ?

DUCH. DE LA V. (*aside*). *Then* he wore my colors.
How kind to bring back to my yearning heart
That golden spring-time of our early loves ?

LOUIS. Next week we will revive the heroic pageant.
Proud plumes shall wave, and levell'd spears be shiver'd ;
Ourself will take the lists, and do defy
The chivalry of our renowned France,
In honor of that lady of our court
For whom we wear the colors, and the motto
Which suits her best—" *Most bright where all are brilliant !*"

GRAM. Oh, a most kingly notion !

LOUIS.   Ere we part,
Let each knight choose his colors and his lady.
Ourself have set the example. (*the* COURTIERS *mingle with the*
LADIES, *&c., many* LADIES *give their colors.*)

DUCH. DE LA V. (*timidly*). Oh, my Louis !
I read thy heart ; thou hast chosen this device
To learn thy poor La Vallière to be proud.
Nay, turn not from my blessings. Once before
You wore my colors, though I gave them not.
To-night I give them !—Louis loves me still ! (*takes one of the
knots from her breast, and presents it.*)

LOUIS. Lady, the noblest hearts in France would beat
More high beneath your badge. Alas ! my service
Is vow'd already *here*. (*turning to* MADAME DE MONTESPAN, *and
placing a knot of her colors over his order of Saint Esprit.*)

DUCH. DE LA V. How ! How ! (*the* KING *converses apart with* MADAME
DE MONTESPAN.)

LAU. (*aside, to the* DUCHESS DE LA VALLIÈRE). Be calm, your grace ; a
thousand eyes
Are on you. Give the envious crowd no triumph.
Ah ! had *my* fortune won so soft a heart
I would have——

DUCH. DE LA V. (*aside, to* LAUZUN). Peace !—away ! Betray'd ! Undone ! (*sinks almost exhausted, but* LAUZUN *catches and sup-
ports her.*)

---

* The *Place du Carrousel* was so named from a splendid festival given by Louis.
On the second day, devoted to knightly games, the king, who appeared in the character of *Roger*, carried off four prizes. All the crown jewels were prodigalized on
his arms and the trappings of his horse.

ACT IV.

SCENE I.—*The gardens at Versailles.*

Enter LAUZUN, R. 1 E.

LAU. So far, so prosperous. From the breast of Louis,
The blooming love it bore so long a summer
Falls like a fruit o'er-ripe ; and, in the court,
And o'er the king, this glittering Montespan
Queens it without a rival—awes all foes,
And therefore makes all friends.   State, office, honors,
Reflect her smile, or fade before her frown.
So far, so well !   Enough for Montespan.
Poor Lauzun now—I love this fair La Vallière,
As well, at least, as woman's worth the loving ;
And if the jewel has one trifling flaw,
The gold 'tis set in will redeem the blemish.
The king's no niggard lover ; and her wealth
Is vast.   I have the total in my tablets—
(Besides estates in Picardy and Provence.)
I'm very poor—my creditors very pressing.
I've robb'd the duchess of a faithless lover,
To give myself a wife, and her a husband.
Wedlock's a holy thing—and wealth a good one !

Enter LOUIS, L. 1 E., *and crosses towards* R., *whilst speaking.*

LOUIS. The day is long—I have not seen Athenè.
Pleasure is never stagnant in her presence ;
But every breeze of woman's changeful skies
Ripples the stream, and freshens e'en the sunshine.
LAU. (L. C.). 'Tis said, your Majesty, "that contrast's sweet,"
And she you speak of well contrasts another,
Whom once——
LOUIS (R. C).   I loved ;· and still devoutly honor.
This poor La Vallière !—could we will affection.
I would have never changed.   And even now
I feel Athenè has but charm'd my senses,
And my void heart still murmurs for Louise !
I would we could be friends, since now not lovers,
Nor dare be happy while I know her wretched.
LAU. Wearies she still your Majesty with prayers,
Tender laments, and passionate reproaches ?
LOUIS. Her love outlives its hopes.
LAU.   An irksome task
To witness tears we cannot kiss away,
And with cold friendship freeze the ears of love !
LOUIS. Most irksome and most bootless !
LAU.   Haply, Sire,
In one so pure, the charm of wedded life
Might lull keen griefs to rest, and curb the love
Thou fliest from to the friendship that thou seekest ?
LOUIS. I've thought of this.   The Duke de Longueville loves her,
And hath besought before her feet to lay
His princely fortunes.

LAU. (*quickly*).   Ha !—and she—
LOUIS.   Rejects him.
LAU. Sire, if love's sun, once set, bequeaths a twilight,
'Twould only hover o'er some form whom chance
Had link'd with Louis—some one (though unworthy)
Whose presence took a charm from brighter thoughts
That knit it with the past.
LOUIS.   Why, how now, duke !—
Thou speak'st not of thyself ?
LAU.   I dare not, Sire !
LOUIS. Ha, ha !—poor Lauzun—what ! the soft La Vallière
Transfer her sorrowing heart to thee ! Ha. ha !
LAU. My name is not less noble than De Longueville's ;
My glory greater, since the world has said
Louis esteems me more.
LOUIS.   *Esteems !—No—favors !*
And thou dost think that she, who shrunk from love,
Lest love were vice, would wed the wildest lord
That ever laugh'd at virtue ? (*crosses.*)
LAU.   Sire, you wrong me,
Or else you (pardon me) condemn yourself.
Is it too much for one the king calls fr'end
To aspire to one the king has call'd——
LOUIS (L. C., *sharply*).   Sir, hold !
I never so malign'd that hapless lady
As to give *her* the title only due
To such as Montespan, who glories in it—
The *last* my *mistress ;* but the first my *victim ;*
A nice distinction, taught not in your logic,
Which, but just now, confused esteem and favor.
Go to ! we kings are not the dupes you deem us. (*crosses.*)
LAU. (*aside*). So high ? I'll win La Vallière to avenge me,
And humble this imperial vanity.
(*aloud*) Sire, I offend ! Permit me to retire,
And mourn your anger ; nor presume to guess
Whence came the cause. And, since it seems your *favor*
Made me aspire too high, in that I loved
Where you, Sire, made love noble, and half dream'd
*Might be—*nay, am not—wholly there disdain'd—
LOUIS. How, duke ?
LAU.   I do renounce at once
The haughty vision. Sire, permit my absence.
LOUIS. Lauzun, thou hintest that, were suit allow'd thee,
La Vallière might not scorn it—is it so ?
LAU. I crave your pardon, Sire.
LOUIS.   Must I ask twice ?
LAU. I do believe, then, Sire, with time and patience,
The duchess might be won to—*not reject me !*
LOUIS. Go, then, and prove thy fortune. We permit thee.
And, if thou prosperest, why then love's a riddle,
And woman is—no matter ! Go, my lord !
We did not mean to wound thee. So, forget it !
Woo when thou wilt—and wear what thou canst win.
LAU. My gracious liege, Lauzun commends him to thee ;
And if one word, he merit not, may wound him,
He'll th'nk of favors words can never cancel.
Memory shall med'cine to his present pain.

God save you, Sire—(*aside*) to *be* the dupe I deem you !
[*Exit* LAUZUN, L. 1 E.

LOUIS. I love her not; and yet methinks, am jealous !
Lauzun is wise and witty—knows the sex ;
What if she do ? No ! I will not believe it.
And what is she to me ?—a friend—a friend !
And I would have her wed. "Twere best for both—
A balm for conscience—an excuse for change !
'Twere best—I marvel much if she'll accept him !
[*Exit* LOUIS, R. 1 E.

SCENE II.—*A private apartment in the Palace of the* DUCHESS DE LA VAL-
LIÈRE. *The* DUCHESS *discovered seated,* R.

DUCH. DE LA V. He loves me, then, no longer! All the words
Earth knows shape but one thought—" He loves no longer!"
Where shall I turn ? My mother—my poor mother !
Sleeps the long sleep ! 'Tis better so ! Her life
Ran to its lees. I will not mourn for her.
But it is hard to be alone on earth !
This love, for which I gave so much, is dead,
Save in my heart ; and love, surviving love,
Changes its nature, and becomes despair !
Ah, me !—ah me ! how hateful is this world !

Enter GENTLEMAN OF THE CHAMBER, L. D.

GENT. The Duke de Lauzun !
DUCH. DE LA V. (*rising*). News, sweet news of Louis!
Exit GENTLEMAN, L. D.
Enter LAUZUN, L. D.

LAU. Dare I disturb your thoughts ?
DUCH. DE LA V.   My lord, you're welcome !
Came you from court to-day ? (*they advance.*)
LAU. (L. C.).   I left the king
But just now, in the gardens.
DUCH. DE LA V. (*eagerly*).   Well !
LAU.   He bore him
With his accustom'd health !
DUCH. DE LA V.   Proceed.
LAU   Dear lady,
I have no more to tell.
DUCH. DE LA V. (*aside*). Alas ! (*aloud*) *No message !*
LAU. We did converse, 'tis true, upon a subject
Most dear to one of us. Your grace divines it ?
DUCH. DE LA V. (*joyfully*). Was it of *me* he spoke ?
LAU.   Of you
I spoke, and *he* replied. I praised your beauty—
DUCH. DE LA V.   *You* praised !
LAU. Your form, your face—that wealth of mind
Which play'd you not the miser and conceal'd it,
Would buy up all the coins that pass for wit.
The king, assenting, wish'd he might behold you
As happy—as your virtues should have made you.
DUCH. DE LA V. 'Twas said in mockery !
LAU.   Lady, no !—in kindness.

Nay, more (he added), would you yet your will
Mould to his wish——
DUCH. DE LA V.   *His* wish!—the lightest!
LAU.   Ah!
You know not how my heart throbs while you speak!
Be not so rash to promise; or, at least,
Be faithful to perform!
DUCH. DE LA V.   You speak in riddles.
LAU.   Of your lone state and beautiful affections,
Form'd to make Home an Eden, our good king,
Tenderly mindful, fain would see you link
Your lot to one whose love might be your shelter.
He spake, and all my long-conceal'd emotions
Gush'd into words, and I confess'd—O lady,
Hear me confess once more—how well I love thee!
DUCH. DE DA V. You dared?—and *he*—the king——
LAU.   Upon me smiled,
And bade me prosper.
DUCH. DE LA V.   Ah! (*trembles, and covers her face with hands.*)
LAU.   Nay, nay, look up!
The heart that could forsake a love like thine
Doth not deserve regret.   Look up, dear lady!
DUCH. DE LA V. He bade thee prosper!
LAU.   Pardon!   My wild hope
Outran discretion.
DUCH. DE LA V.   Louis bade thee prosper!
LAU.   Ah, if this thankless—this remorseless love
Thou couldst forget!   Oh, give me but thy friendship,
And take respect, faith, worship, all, in Lauzun!
DUCH. DE LA V. Consign me to another!   Well, 'tis well!
Earth's latest tie is broke—earth's hopes are over!
LAU.   Speak to me, sweet Louise!
DUCH. DE LA V.   So, thou art he
To whom this shatter'd heart should be surrender'd?
And thou, the high-born, glittering, scornful Lauzun
Wouldst take the cast-off leman of a king,
Nor think thyself disgraced!   Fie!—fie! thou'rt shameless!
        (*crosses, in an agony of grief.*)
LAU. (R. C.). You were betray'd by love, and not by sin,
Nor low ambition.   Your disgrace is honor
By the false side of dames the world calls spotless.
DUCH. DE LA V. (L. C.). Go, sir, nor make me scorn you. If I've err'd,
I know, at least, the majesty of virtue,
And feel—what you forget.
LAU.   Yet hear me, madame!
DUCH. DE LA V. Go, go! You are the king's friend—you were mine;
I would not have you thus debased—refused
By one at once the fallen and forsaken!
His friend shall not be shamed so!
                [*Exit the* DUCHESS DE LA VALLIÈRE, R. D.
LAU.   (*passing his hand over his eyes*).   I do swear
These eyes are moist!   And he who own'd this gem
Casts it away, and cries "divine" to tinsel!
So falls my hope!   My fortunes call me back
To surer schemes.   Before that ray of goodness
How many plots shrunk, blinded, into shadow!
Lauzun forgot himself, and dreamt of virtue! [*Exit* LAUZUN, L. D.

GENTLEMAN OF THE CHAMBER *enters*, D. F., *followed by* BRAGELONE *as a Franciscan friar.*

GENT. The duchess gone ! I fear me that, to-day,
    You are too late for audience, reverend father.
BRAGE. (c.). Audience !—a royal phrase !—it suits the duchess.
    Go, son ; announce me.
GENT.   By what name, my father ?
BRAGE. I've done with names. Announce a nameless monk,
    Whose prayers have risen o'er some graves she honors.
GENT. (*aside*). My lady is too lavish of her bounty
    To these proud shavelings ; yet, methinks, this friar
    Hath less of priest than warrior in his bearing.
    He awes me with his stern and thrilling voice,
    His stately gesture, and imperious eye.
    And yet, I swear, he comes for alms !—the varlet !
    Why should I heed him ?
BRAGE.   Didst thou hear ? Begone !
                  [*Exit* GENTLEMAN, R. D.
    Yes, she will know me not. My leatest soldier,
    One who had march'd, bare-breasted. on the steel,
    If I had bid him cast away the treasure
    Of the o'er-valued life; the nurse that rear'd me,
    Or mine own mother, in these shroudlike robes,
    And in the immature and rapid age
    Which, from my numb'd and withering heart, hath crept
    Unto my features, now might gaze upon me,
    And pass the stranger by. Why should she know me,
    If they who loved me know not ? Hark ! I hear her :
    That silver footfall !—still it hath to me
    Its own peculiar and most spiritual music,
    Trembling along the pulses of the air,
    And dying on the heart that makes its echo !
    'Tis she ! How lovely yet !

Re-enter the DUCHESS DE LA VALLIÈRE.

DUCH. DE LA V. (*bending*).   Your blessing, father.
BRAGE. Let courts and courtiers bless the favor'd duchess :
    Courts bless the proud ; Heaven's ministers, the humble.
DUCH. DE LA V. (*aside*). He taunts me, this poor friar ! (*aloud*) Well, my
        father,
    I have obey'd your summons. Do you seek
    Masses for souls departed ?—or the debt
    The wealthy owe the poor ? say on !
BRAGE. (*aside*).   Her heart
    Is not yet harden'd ! (*aloud*) Daughter, such a mission
    Were sweeter than the task which urged me hither :
    You had a lover once—a plain, bold soldier ;
    He loved you well !
DUCH. DE LA V.   Ah, Heaven !
BRAGE.   And you forsook him.
    Your choice was natural—some might call it noble !
    And this blunt soldier pardon'd the *desertion*,
    But sunk at what his folly term'd *dishonor*.
DUCH. DE LA V. O father, spare me !—if dishonor were,
    It rested but with me.

BRAGE.   So deem'd the world,
But not that foolish soldier!—he had learn'd
To blend his thoughts, his fame, *himself*, with thee;
Thou wert a purer, a diviner self;
He loved thee as a warrior worships glory;
He loved thee as a Roman honor'd virtue;
He loved thee as thy sex adore ambition;
And when Pollution breathed upon his idol,
It blasted glory, virtue, and ambition,
Fill'd up each crevice in the world of thought,
And poison'd earth with thy contagious shame!

DUCH. DE LA V. Spare me! in mercy, spare me!

BRAGE.   .   This poor fool,
This shadow, living only on thy light,
When thou wert darken'd, could but choose to die.
He left the wars;—no fame, since *thine* was dim;
He left his land;—what home without Louise?
It broke—that stubborn, stern, unbending heart—
It broke! and, breaking, its last sigh—forgave thee!

DUCH. DE LA V. And I live on!

BRAGE.   One eve, methinks, he told me,
Thy hand around his hauberk wound a scarf;
And thy voice bade him "Wear it for the sake
Of one who honor'd worth!" Were those the words?

DUCH. DE LA V. They were. Alas! alas!

BRAGE.   He wore it, lady,
Till memory ceased. It was to him the token   .
Of a sweet dream; and, from his quiet grave,
He sends it now to thee. (*produces faded scarf from beneath his
robe*) Its hues are faded.

DUCH. DE LA V. Give it me!—let me bathe it with my tears!
Memorial of my guilt—

BRAGE. (*in a soft and tender accent*). And *his* forgiveness!

DUCH. DE LA V. That tone! ha! while thou speakest, in thy voice,
And in thy presence, there is something kindred
To him we jointly mourn; thou art——

BRAGE.   His brother;
Of whom, perchance, in ancient years he told thee;
Who, early wearied of this garish world,
Fled to the convent shade, and found repose.

DUCH. DE LA V. (*approaching*). Ay, is it so?—thou'rt Bragelone's brother?
Why, then, thou art what *he* would be, if living—
A friend to one most friendless!

BRAGE.   Friendless—Ah,
Thou hast learnt, betimes, the truth, that man's wild passion .
Makes but its sport of virtue, peace, affection;
And breaks the plaything when the game is done!
Friendless!—I pity thee!

DUCH. DE LA V. (*clasping him, appealingly*) Oh! holy father,
Stay with me!—succor me!—reprove, but guide me;
Teach me to wean my thoughts from earth to heaven,
And be what God ordain'd His chosen priests—
Foes to our sin, but friends to our despair!

BRAGE. Daughter, a heavenly and a welcome duty,
But one most rigid and austere; there is
No composition with our debts of sin.
God claims thy soul; and, lo! his creature there!

Thy choice must be between them—God or man,
Virtue or guilt ; a Louis or——
DUCH. LE LA V.   A Louis !
Not mine the poor atonement of the choice ;
I am, myself, the Abandon'd One !
BRAGE.   I know it ;
Therefore my mission and my ministry.
When he who loved thee died, he bade me wait
The season when the sicklied blight of change
Creeps o'er the bloom of Passion, when the way
Is half prepared by sorrow to repentance,
And seek you then—*he* trusted not in vain ;
Perchance an idle hope, but it consoled him.
DUCH. DE LA V. No, no !—not idle—in my happiest hours,
When the world smiled, a void was in this heart
The world could never fill ; thy brother knew me ! .
BRAGE. I do believe thee, daughter. Hear me yet ;
My mission is not ended. When thy mother
Lay on the bed of death (she went before
The sterner heart the same blow broke more slowly)—
As thus she lay, around the swimming walls
Her dim eyes wander'd, searching through the shadows,
As if the spirit, half-redeem'd from clay,
Could force its will to shape, and, from the darkness,
Body a daughter's image—(nay, be still ')
Thou wert not there—alas ! thy shame had murder'd
Even the blessed sadness of that duty !
But o'er that pillow watch'd a sleepless eye,
And by that couch moved one untiring step,
And o'er that suffering rose a ceaseless prayer ;
And still thy mother's voice, when'er it call'd
Upon a daughter—found a son !
DUCH. DE LA V. (*overcome with emotion, she buries her face in her hands and sinks upon her knees before him*). O, Heaven !
Have mercy on me !
BRAGE.   Coldly through the lattice
Gleam'd the slow dawn, and from their latest sleep,
Woke the sad eyes it was not *thine* to close !
And the thin hairs—grown gray, but not by Time—
Of that lone watcher—while upon her heart
Gush'd all the memories of the mighty wrecks
Thy guilt had made of what were once the shrines
For Honor, Peace, and God !—that aged woman
(She was a hero's wife) upraised her voice
To curse her child !
DUCH. DE LA V.   Go on !—be kind, and kill me !
BRAGE. Then he, whom thoughts of what he *was* to *thee*
Had made her son, arrested on her lips
The awful doom, and, from the earlier past,
Invoked a tender spell—a holier image !
Painted thy gentle, soft, obedient childhood—
Thy guileless youth, lone state, and strong temptation ;
Thy very sin the overflow of thoughts
From wells whose source was innocence ; and thus
Sought, with the sunshine of thy maiden spring,
To melt the ice that lay upon her heart,
Till all the mother flow'd again !

Duch. de la V. And she!
Brage. Spoke only once again!—she died—and *bless'd* thee
Duch. de la V. (*vehemently, springing up*). No more! I *can* no more!—
    my heart is breaking! (*rushes off*, R. D.)
Brage. The angel hath not left her!—if the plumes
    Have lost the whiteness of their younger glory,
    The wings have still the instinct of the skies,
    And yet shall bear her up!
Louis (*without*, L). We need you not, sir;
    Ourself will seek the duchess!
Brage. (*takes the stage* L.). The king's voice!
    How my flesh creeps!—my foe, and her destroyer!
    The ruthless, heartless—(*his hand seeks rapidly and mechanically for
    his sword-hilt*) Why, why!—where's my sword?
    O, Lord! I do forget myself to dotage;
    The soldier, now, is a poor helpless monk,
    That hath not even curses. Satan, hence!
    Get thee behind me, Tempter!—there, I'm calm. (*crosses to* R.)

Enter Louis, C. D., *and advancing.*

Louis. I can no more hold parley with impatience,
    But long to learn how Lauzun's courtship prospers.
    She is not here. At prayers, perhaps. The duchess
    Hath grown devout. (*observing* Bragelone) A friar!—Save you,
        father!
Brage. I thank thee, son.
Louis (C., *aside*). He knows me not. (*aloud*) Well, monk,
    Are you her grace's almoner?
Brage. Sire, no! (*the* King *starts.*)
Louis. So short, yet know us?
Brage. (*advances to* R. C.). Sire, I do. You are *
    The man——
Louis. (*indignantly*). How, priest!—the *man!*
Brage. The word offends you?
    The king, who raised a maiden to a duchess.
    That maiden's father was a gallant subject;
    Kingly reward—you made his daughter duchess.
    That maiden's mother was a stainless matron;
    Her heart you broke, though mother to a duchess!
    That maiden was affianced from her youth
    To one who served you well—nay, saved your life;
    His life you robb'd of all that gave life value;
    And yet—you made his fair betroth'd a duchess!
    You are that king. The world proclaims you "Great;"
    A million warriors bled to buy your laurels;
    A million peasants starved to build Versailles:
    Your people famish; but your court is splendid!
    Priests from the pulpit bless your glorious reign;
    Poets have sung you greater than Augustus;
    And painters placed you on immortal canvas,
    Limn'd as the Jove whose thunders awe the world;
    But to the humble servant of Heaven
    You are the king who has betray'd his trust—
    Beggar'd a nation but to bloat a court,
    Seen in men's lives the pastime to ambition,
    Look'd but on virtue as the toy for vice;

And, for the first time, from a subject's lips,
Now learns he the name he leaves to Time and God!
LOUIS. Add to the bead-roll of that king's offences,
That when a foul-mouth'd monk assumed the rebel,
The monster-king forgave him. Hast thou done?
BRAGE. Your changing hues belie your royal mien;
Ill the high monarch veils the trembling man!
LOUIS. Well, you are privileged! It ne'er was said
The Fourteenth Louis, i.. his proudest hour,
B ow'd not his sceptre to the Church's crozier.
BRAGE. Alas! *the Church!* 'Tis true, this garb of serge
Dares speech that daunts the ermine, and walks free
Where stout hearts tremble in the triple mail.
But wherefore?—Lies the virtue in the robe,
Which the moth eats? or in these senseless beads?
Or in the name of Priest? The Pharisees
H ad priests that gave their Saviour to the cross!
No! we have high immunity and sanction,
That Truth may teach humanity to Power,
Glide through the dungeon pierce the armed throng,
Awaken Luxury on her Sybarite couch,
And, startling souls that slumber on a throne,
Bow kings before that priest of priests—THE CONSCIENCE! (*they
cross.*)
LOUIS (R. C.—*aside*). An awful man!—unlike the reverend crew
Who praise my royal virtues in the pulpit,
And—ask for bishoprics when church is over!
BRAGE. (L. C.). This makes us sacred. The profane are they
Honoring the herald while they scorn the mission.
The king who serves the Church, yet clings to Mammon;
Who fears the pastor, but forgets the flock;
Who bows before the monitor, and yet
Will ne'er forego the sin, may sink, when age
Palsies the lust and deadens the temptation,
To the priest-ridden, not repentant, dotard,—
For pious hopes hail superstitious terrors,
An I seek some sleek Iscariot of the *Church,*
To sell salvation for the thirty pieces!
LOUIS (*aside*). He speaks as one inspired!
BRAGE. (*crosses*). Awake!—awake!
Great though thou art, awake thee from the dream
That earth was made for kings--mankind for slaughter—
Woman for lust—the people for the palace!
Dark warnings have gone forth; along the air
Lingers the crash of the first Charles's throne!
Behold the young, the fair, the haughty king!
The kneeling courtiers, and the flattering priests;
Lo! where the palace rose, behold the scaffold—
The crowd—the axe—the headsman—and the victim!
Lord of the silver lilies, canst thou tell
If the same fate await not thy descendant!
If some meek son of thine imperial line
May make no brother to yon headless spectre!
And when the sage who saddens o'er the end
Tracks back the causes, tremble, lest he find
The seeds, thy wars, thy pomp, and thy profusion
Sow'd in a heartless court and breadless people,

Grew to the tree from which men shaped the scaffold—
And the long glare of thy funeral glories
Light unborn monarchs to a ghastly grave !
Beware, proud king ! the Present cries aloud, (*moves up the stage
whilst speaking*)
A prophet to the future ! Wake !—beware !

[*Exit* BRAGELONE c. D

LOUIS. (*uneasily*). Gone ! Most ill-omen'd voice and fearful shape !
Scarce seem'd it of the earth ; a thing that breathed
But to fulfill some dark and dire behest ;
To appal us, and to vanish.—The quick blood
Halts in my veins. Oh ! never till this hour
Heard I the voice that awed the soul of Louis,
Or met one brow that did not quail before
My kingly gaze ! (*pacing to and fro*) And this unmitred monk !
I'm glad that none were by.—It was a dream ;
So let its memory like a dream depart.
I am no tyrant—nay, I love my people.
My wars were made but for the fame of France ;
My pomp ! why, tush !—what king can play the hermit ?
My conscience smites me not ; and but last eve
I did confess, and was absolved ! A bigot ;
And half, methinks, a heretic ! I wish
The Jesuits had the probing of his doctrines.
Well, well, 'tis o'er !—What ho, there !

Enter GENTLEMAN OF THE CHAMBER, L. D.

Wine ! Apprise
Once more the duchess of our presence—Stay !
Yon monk, what doth he here ?
GENT.   I know not, Sire,
Nor saw him till this day.
LOUIS.   Strange !—Wine !

[*Exit* GENTLEMAN, R. D.

Re-enter the DUCHESS DE LA VALLIÈRE.

(C.)   Well, madam,
We've tarried long your coming, and meanwhile
Have found your proxy in a madman monk,
Whom, for the future, we would pray you spare us.

Re-enter GENTLEMAN, *with goblet of wine on salver, the* KING *drinks.*
GENTLEMAN, R. D.

So, so ! the draught restores us. Fair La Vallière,
Make not yon holy man your confessor ;
You'll find small comfort in his lectures.
DUCH DE LA V. (R. C.).   Sire,
His meaning is more kindly than his manner.
I pray you, pardon him.
LOUIS.   Ay, ay ! No more ;
Let's think of him no more. You had, this morn,
A courtlier visitant, methinks—De Lauzun ?
DUCH. DE LA V.   Yes, Sire.
LOUIS. A smooth and gallant gentleman.

You're silent.   Silence is assent! 'tis well!

DUCH. DE LA V. (*aside*), Down, my full heart! (*aloud*) The duke declares
your wish
Is that—that I should bind this broken heart
And—no! I cannot speak! (*with great and sudden energy*) You
wish me wed, Sire?

LOUIS. 'Twere best that you should wed; and yet, De Lauzun
Is scarce the happiest choice.—But as thou wilt.

DUCH. DE LA V. "'Twere best that I should wed?"—thou saidst it,
Louis;
Say it once more!

LOUIS.   In honesty, I think so.

DUCH. DE LA V. My choice is made, then—I obey the fiat,
And will become a bride!

LOUIS.   The duke has sped!
I trust he loves thyself, and not thy dower.

DUCH DE LA V. The duke! what, hast thou read so ill this soul
That thou couldst deem thus meanly of that book
Whose every page was bared to thee? A bitter
Lot has been mine—and this sums up the measure.
Go, Louis! go!—All glorious as thou art—
Earth's Agamemnon—the great king of men—
Thou wert not worthy of this woman's heart!

LOUIS (*aside*). Her passion moves me! (*aloud*) Then your choice has
fallen
Upon a nobler bridegroom?

DUCH. DE LA V.   Sire, it hath!

LOUIS. May I demand that choice.

DUCH. DE LA V.   Too soon thou'lt learn it.
Not yet! Ah, me!

LOUIS.   Nay, sigh not, my sweet duchess.
Speak not sadly. What though love hath past,
Friendship remains; and still my fondest hope
Is to behold thee happy. Come!—thy hand;
Let us be friends! We are so!

DUCH. DE LA V.   *Friends!*—no more!
So it hath come to this! I am contented!
Yes—we are friends!

LOUIS.   And when your choice is made,
You will permit your friend to hail your bridals?

DUCH. DE LA V. Ay, when my choice is made!

LOUIS.   This poor de Lauzun?
Hath then no chance? I'm glad of it, and thus
Seal our new bond of friendship on your hand. (*kisses her hand*)
Adieu!—and Heaven protect you!   [*Exit* LOUIS, L. D.

DUCH DE LA V. (*gazing after him*), Heaven hath *heard* thee;
And in this last most cruel, but most gracious
Proof of thy coldness, breaks the lingering chain
That bound my soul to earth.

Re-enter BRAGELONE, C. D.

O, holy father!
Brother to him whose grave my guilt prepared,
Witness my firm resolve, support my struggles,
And guide me back to Virtue through Repentance!

BRAGE. Pause, ere thou dost decide.

Ducn. DE LA V.   I've paused too long,
And now, impatient of this weary load,
Sigh for repose.
BRAGE.   O, Heaven, receive her back!
Through the wide earth, the sorrowing dove hath flown,
And found no haven; weary though her wing
And sullied with the dust of lengthen'd travail,
Now let her flee away and be at rest!
The peace that man has broken—Thou restore,
Whose holiest name is FATHER! (*soft music*)
Ducn. DE LA V. (*sinks on her knees, raising her hands in prayer whilst clasp-
ing* BRAGELONE'S *left hand, he standing with uplifted face,
and his right hand raised pointing upwards*).
                    Hear us, Heaven!

ACT V.

SCENE I.—*The Gardens at Versailles.*

Enter MADAME DE MONTESPAN, GRAMMONT, L. 1 E., *and* COURTIERS, R. 1 E.

MME. DE MON. So she has fled from court—the saintly duchess;
A convent's grate must shield this timorous virtue.
Methinks they're not so many to assail it!
Well, trust me, one short moon of fast and penance
Will bring us back the recreant novice——
GRAM.   And
End the eventful comedy by marriage.
Lauzun against the world were even odds;
But Lauzun *with* the world—what saint can stand it?
MME. DE MON. (*aside*) Lauzun!—the traitor! What! to give my rival
The triumph to reject the lawful love
Of him whose lawless passion first betray'd me!
GRAM. Talk of the devil! Humph—you know the proverb.

Enter LAUZUN, R. 1 E.

LAU. Good day, my friends. Your pardon, madame; I
Thought 'twas the sun that blinded me. (*aside*) Athenè,
Pray you, a word.
MME. DE MON. (*aloud, and turning away disdainfully*). We are not at lei-
sure, duke.
LAU. Ha! (*aside*) Nay, Athenè, spare your friend these graces.
Forget your state one moment; have you ask'd
The king the office that you undertook
To make my own? My creditors are urgent.
MME. DE MON. (*aloud*). No, my lord duke, I have not ask'd the king!
I grieve to hear your fortunes are so broken,
And that your honor'd and august device,
To mend them by your marriage, fail'd.
GRAM (*aside*).   She hits him
Hard on the hip. Ha, ha!—the poor De Lauzun!
LAU. Sir!—Nay, I'm calm!
MME. DE MON   Pray, may we dare to ask
How long you've loved the duchess?

LAU.   Ever since
You were her friend and confidante.
MME. DE MON.   You're bitter.
Perchance you deem your love a thing to boast of.
LAU. To boast of?—Yes! 'Tis something e'en to love
The only woman Louis ever *honor'd!*
MME. DE MON. (*laying her hand on* LAUZUN's *arm*). Insolent! You shall
rue this! If I speak
Your name to Louis, coupled with a favor,
The suit shall be your banishment!
                    [*Exit* MADAME DE MONTESPAN, R. 1 E.
FIRST COUR.   Let's follow.
Ha! ha!—Dear duke, your game, I fear, is lost!
You've play'd the knave, and thrown away the king.
COURTIERS. Ha! ha!—Adieu!   [*Exeunt*, R. 1 E.
LAU.   Ha! ha!—The devil take you!
So, she would ruin me! Fore-arm'd—fore-warn'd!
I have the king's ear yet, and know some secrets
That could destroy her! Since La Vallière's flight,
Louis grows sad and thoughtful, and looks cold
On her ruin rival, who too coarsely shows
The world the stuff court ladies' hearts are made of.
She will undo herself—and I will help her.
Weave on thy web, false Montespan, weave on;
The bigger spider shall devour the smaller.
The war's declared—'tis clear that one must fall;—
I'll be polite—the *lady* to the wall!   [*Exit* LAUZUN, L. 1 E.

SCENE II.—*Sunset—the old Chateau of La Vallière—the Convent of the
Carmelites at a distance—same scene as that with which the play opens.*

Enter the DUCHESS DE LA VALLIÈRE *and* BRAGELONE *from the Chateau.*

DUCH. DE LA V. Once more, ere yet I take farewell of earth,
I see mine old, familiar, maiden home!
All how unchanged!—The same, the hour, the scene,
The very season of the year!—the stillness
Of the smooth wave—the stillness of the trees,
Where the winds sleep like dreams! and, oh! the calm
Of the blue heavens around you holy spires,
Pointing, like gospel truths, through calm and storm,
To man's great home!
BRAGE. (*aside*).   Oh! how the years recede!
Upon this spot I spoke to her of love,
And dreamt of bliss for earth! (*the vesper bell tolls.*)
DUCH. DE LA V.   Hark! the deep sound,
That seems a voice from some invisible spirit,
Claiming the world for God.—When last I heard it
Hallow this air, here stood my mother, living;
And I—was then a mother's *pride!*—and yonder
Came thy brave brother in his glittering mail;
And—ah! these thoughts are bitter!—were he living,
How would he scorn them!
BRAGE. (*who has been greatly agitated*). No!—ah, no!—thou wrong'st him!
DUCH. DE LA V. Yet, were he living, could I but receive
From his own lips my pardon, and his blessing,
My soul would deem one dark memorial 'rased

Out of the page most blister'd with its tears!

BRAGE. Then have thy wish! and in these wrecks of man
Worn to decay, and rent by many a storm,
Survey the worm the world call'd Bragelone.

DUCH. DE LA V. Avaunt!—avaunt!—I dream!—the dead return'd
To earth to mock me!—No! this hand is warm!
I have one murther less upon my soul.
I thank thee, Heaven!—(*swoons.*)

BRAGE. (*supporting her*). The blow strikes home; and yet
What is my life to her? Louise!—She moves not!
She does not breathe; how still she sleeps! I saw her
Sleep in her mother's arms, and then, in sleep
She smiled. *There's no smile now!*—poor child! (*kissing her*) One
  kiss!
It is a brother's kiss—it has no guilt;
Kind Heaven, it has no guilt.—I have survived
All earthlier thoughts; her crime, my vows, effaced them.
A brother's kiss!—Away! I'm human still;
I thought I had been stronger; God forgive me!
Awake, Louise!—awake! She breathes once more;
The spell is broke; the marble warms to life!
And I—freeze back to stone!

DUCH. DE LA V. (*reviving*).   I heard a voice
That cried "Louise!"—Speak, speak!—my sense is dim,
And struggles darkly with a blessed ray
That shot from heaven.—My shame hath not destroy'd thee!

BRAGE. No!—life might yet serve *thee!*—and I lived on,
Dead to all else. I took the vows, and then,
Ere yet I laid me down, and bade the Past
Fade like a ghost before the dawn of heaven,
One sacred task was left.—If love was dust,
Love, like ourselves, hath an immortal soul,
That doth survive whate'er it takes from clay;
And that—the holier part of love became
A thing to watch thy steps—a guardian spirit
To hover round, disguised, unknown, undream'd of,
To soothe the sorrow, to redeem the sin,
And lead thy soul to peace!

DUCH. DE LA V.   O bright revenge!
Love strong as death, and nobler far than woman's!

BRAGE. To *peace*—ah, let me deem so!—the mute cloister,
The spoken ritual, and the solemn veil,
Are naught themselves—the Huguenot abjures
The monkish cell, but breathes, perchance the prayer
That speeds as quick to the Eternal Throne!
In our own souls must be the solitude;
In our own thoughts the sanctity!—'Tis *then*
The feeling that our vows have built the wall
Passion can storm not, nor temptation sap,
Gives calm its charter, roots out wild regret,
And makes the heart the world-disdaining cloister.
This—*this* is peace! but pause! if in thy breast
Linger the wish of earth. Alas! all oaths
Are vain, if nature shudders to record them—
The subtle spirit 'scapes the sealed vessel!
The false devotion is the true despair!

DUCH. DE LA V. Fear not!—I feel 'tis not the walls of stone,

Told beads, nor murmur'd hymns, that bind the heart,
Or exorcise the world ; the spell's the thought
That where most weak we've banish'd the temptation,
And reconciled, what earth would still divide,
The human memories and the immortal conscience.
BRAGE. Doubt fades before thine accents. On the day
That gives thee to the veil we'll meet once more.
Let mine be man's last blessing in this world.
Oh ! tell me then, thou'rt happier than thou hast been ;
And when we part, I'll seek some hermit cell
Beside the walls that compass thee, and prayer,
Morning and night, shall join our souls in heaven.
DUCH. DE LA V. Yes, generous spirit ! think not that my future
Shall be repining as the past. Thou livest,
And conscience smiles again. The shatter'd bark
Glides to its haven. Joy ! the land is near !
          [*Exit into the chateau, dropping her glove as she goes.*
BRAGE. So, it is past !—the secret is disclosed !
  ⁻The band she did reject on earth has led her
To holier ties.⸱ I have not lived in vain !
Yet who had dream'd, when through the ranks of war
Went the loud shout of " France and Bragelone !"
That the monk's cowl would close on all my laurels ?
A never-heard philosopher is life!
Our happiest hours are sleep's—and sleep proclaims,
Did we but listen to its warning voice,
That *rest* is earth's elixir. Why, then, pine
That, ere our years grow feverish with their toil,
Too weary-worn to find the rest they sigh for,
We learn betimes *the moral of repose ?*
I will lie down, and sleep away this world.
The pause of care, the slumber of tired passion,
Why. why defer till night is well-nigh spent ?
When the brief sun that gilt the landscape sets,
When o'er the music on the leaves of life
Chill silence falls, and every fluttering hope
That voiced the world with song has gone to rest,
Then let thy soul, from the poor laborer, learn
" Sleep's sweetest taken soonest !" (*as he moves away, his eye falls*
          upon the glove ; he takes it up)
And this hath touch'd her hand—it were a comfort
To hoard a single relic ! (*kisses the glove, and then suddenly throws*
          it away) No !—'Tis sinful ! [*Exit* BRAGELONE *into chateau.*

SCENE III,—*The exterior of the Gothic Convent of the Carmelites —The*
windows illumined—Music heard from within. Enter COURTIERS.
LADIES, PRIESTS, *etc.* R. 1 E.. *and* L. 1 E , *and pass through the door of*
the chapel, in the centre of the building.

          Enter LAUZUN, L. 1 E., GRAMMONT, R. 1 E.

LAU. Where hast thou left the king ?
GRAM.   Not one league hence.
LAU. Ere the clock strikes, La Vallière takes the veil.
GRAM. Great Heaven !—so soon !—and Louis sent me on
          To learn how thou hadst prosper'd with the duchess.
He is so sanguine—this imperious king,

Who never heard a " No " from living lips !
How did she take his letter ?

LAU.   In sad silence ;
Then mused a little while, and some few tears
Stole down her cheeks, as, with a trembling hand,
She gave me back the scroll.

GRAM.   You mean her answer.

LAU.   No ; the king's letter.   " Tell him that I thank him ; "
(Such were her words ;)   "but that my choice is made ;
And e'en this last assurance of his love
I dare not keep ; 'tis only when I pray,
That I may think of him.   This is my answer."

GRAM.   No more ?—no written word ?

LAU.   None, Grammont.   Then
She rose and left me ; and I heard the bell
Calling the world to see a woman scorn it.

GRAM.   The king will never brook it.   He will grasp her
Back from this yawning tomb of living souls.
The news came on him with such sudden shock ;
The long noviciate thus abridged ! and she—
Ever so waxen to his wayward will !—
She cannot yet be marble.

LAU.   ⌠Wrong'd affection
Makes many a Niobe from tears.⌡ Haste, Grammont,
Back to the king, and bid him fly to save,
Or nerve his heart to lose, her.   I will follow,—
My *second* charge fulfill'd.

GRAM.   And what is that ?

LAU.   Revenge and justice!—Go!   [*Exit* GRAMMONT, R. 1 E.
(*looking through the doors*)   I hear her laugh—
I catch the glitter of her festive robe !
Athenè comes to triumph—and to tremble !

MADAME DE MONTESPAN *and* COURTIERS *enter*, L. 1 E.   *The* COURTIERS
                    go into the convent.

MME. DE MON. (*aside*).   Now for the crowning cup of sparkling fortune !
A rarer pearl than Egypt's queen dissolved
I have immersed in that delicious draught,
A woman's triumph o'er a fairer rival ! (*as she turns to enter the
convent she perceives* LAUZUN)
What ! you here, duke !

LAU.   Ay, madame ; I've not yet
To thank you for—my banishment !

MME. DE MON.   The Ides
Of March are come—not over !

LAU.   ·   Are they not ?
For some they may be !   You are here to witness——

MME. DE MON.   My triumph !

LAU.   And to take a *friend's* condolence.
I bear this letter from the king ! (*produces letter*.)

MME. DE MON. (*taking it*).   The king ! (*reads the letter*)
"We do not blame you ; blame belongs to love,
And love had naught with you."—What ! what !   I tremble !
"The Duke de Lauzun, of these lines the bearer,
Confirms their purport : from our royal court
We do excuse your presence."   Banish'd, duke ?

Is that the word ?—What, banish'd !
LAU.   Hush !—you mar
The holy silence of the place.   'Tis true ;
You read aright.   Our gracious king permits you
To quit Versailles.   Versailles is not the world.
MME. DE MON. Perdition !—banish'd !
LAU.   You can take the veil.
Meanwhile, enjoy *your triumph !*
MME. DE MON.   Triumph !—Ah !
She triumphs o'er me to the last.   My soul
Finds hell on earth—and hers makes earth a heaven !
LAU.   Hist !—will you walk within ?
MME. DE MON.   O, hateful world !
What !—hath it come to this ?
LAU.   You spoil your triumph !
MME. DE MON   Lauzun, I thank thee—thank thee—thank—and curse
          thee.   [*Exit* MADAME DE MONTESPAN, R. 1 E.
LAU.   (*looking after her, with a subdued laugh*).   Ha, ha !—the *broken* heart
          can know no pang
Like that which racks the *bad* heart when its sting
Poisons itself   Now, then, away to Louis.
The bell still tolls ; there's time.   This soft La Vallière !
The only thing that ever baffled Lauzun,
And felt not his revenge !—revenge, poor soul !
Revenge upon a dove !—she shall be saved
From the pale mummies of yon Memphian vault,
Or the great Louis will be less than man—
Or that fond sinner will be more than woman.
                              *   [*Exit* LAUZUN, R. 1 E.

SCENE IV.—*The interior of the Chapel of the Carmelite Convent.   On the
foreground,* COURTIERS, LADIES, *etc.* (*all kneeling except the officials*).   *At
the back of the stage the altar, only partially seen through the surrounding
throng.   Kneeling at the altar the* DUCHESS DE LA VALLIÈRE, *attended
by the* LADY ABBESS *and* SISTERS, *etc.   The officials pass to and fro,
swinging the censers – The stage darkened—Lights suspended along the
aisle, and tapers by the altar.   As the scene opens, solemn music, to which
is chaunted the following*

            HYMN:

Come from the world, O weary soul,
For run the race and near the goal !
Flee from the net, O lonely dove,
Thy nest is built the clouds above !
Turn, wild and worn with panting fear,
And slake thy thirst, thou wounded deer,
     In Jordan's holy springs !

Arise ! O fearful soul, arise !
For broke the chain and calm the skies !
As moth fly upwards to the star,
The light allures thee from afar.
Though earth is lost, and space is wide,
The smile of God shall be thy guide,
     And Faith and Hope thy wings !

As the Hymn ends, BRAGELONE *enters,* L. U. E., *and stands apart in the back-
              ground.   All rise.*

FIRST COUR.   Three minutes more, and earth has lost La Vallière !

SECOND COUR. So young!—so fair!

THIRD COUR.   'Twas whisper'd that the king
Would save her yet!

FIRST COUR.   What! snatch her from the altar?
He durst not, man!

Enter LOUIS, GRAMMONT, *and* LAUZUN, R. 1 E.

LOUIS.   Hold! we forbid the rites!

All fall back R. *and* L. *As the* KING *advances hastily up the aisle,* BRAGE-
LONE *advances and places himself before him.*

Back, monk! revere the presence of the king!

BRAGE. And thou the palace of the King of kings!

LOUIS. Dotard! we claim our subject.

BRAGE.   She hath pass'd
The limit of your realm. Ye priests of Heaven,
Complete your solemn task!—The church's curse
Hangs on the air. Descendant of Saint Louis,
Move—and the avalanche falls!

The DUCHESS DE LA VALLIÈRE, *dressed in the bridal and gorgeous attire
assumed before the taking of the veil, descends from the altar, and
advances.*

DUCH. DE LA V.   No, holy friend!
I need it not; my soul is my protector.
Nay, thou mayst trust me.

BRAGE. (*after a pause*). Thou art right.—I trust thee!

LOUIS (*leading the* DUCHESS DE LA VALLIÈRE *to the front of the stage*). Thou
hast not ta'en the veil!—E'en Time had mercy.
Thou art saved!—thou art saved!—to love—to life!

DUCH. DE LA V. (C.).   Ah, Sire!

LOUIS (L. C.). Call me not Sire!—forget that dreary time
When thou wert duchess, and myself the king.
Fly back, fly back, to those delicious hours
When *I* was but thy lover and thy Louis!
And thou my dream—my bird—my fairy flower—
My violet, shrinking in the modest shade
Until transplanted to this breast—to haunt
The common air with odors! Oh, Louise!
Hear me!—the fickle lust of change allured me,
The pride thy virtues wounded arm'd against thee,
Until I dream'd I loved thyself no longer;
But now this dread resolve, this awe of parting,
Re-binds me to thee—bares my soul before me—
Dispels the lying mists that veil'd thine image,
And tells me that I never loved but thee!

DUCH. DE LA V. I am not then despised!—thou lov'st me still!
And when I pray for thee, my heart may feel
That it hath nothing to forgive!

LOUIS.   Louise!
Thou dost renounce this gloomy purpose?

DUCH. DE LA V.   Never!
It is not gloomy!—think'st thou it is gloom
To feel that, as my soul becomes more pure,

Heaven will more kindly listen to the prayers
That rise for *thee ?*—is that thought *gloom*, my Louis ?
Louis. Oh ! slay me not with tenderness ! Return !
And if thy conscience startle at my love,
Be still my friend—my angel !
Duch. DE LA V.   I a n weak,
But in the knowledge of my weakness, strong !
I could not breathe the air that's sweet with thee,
Nor cease to love !—in flight my only safety ;
And were that flight not made by solemn vows
Eternal, it were bootless; for the wings
Of my wild soul know but two bournes to speed to—
Louis and heaven ! And, oh ! in heaven at last
My soul, unsinning, may unite with Louis !
Louis. I do implore thee !
Duch. DE LA V.   No ; thou canst not tempt me !
My *heart* already is the nun.
Louis.   Thou know'st not
I have dismiss'd thy rival from the court.
Return !—though mine no more, at least thy Louis
Shall know no second love !
Duch. DE LA V.   What ! wilt thou, Louis,
Renounce for me eternally my rival,
And live alone for——
Louis.   Thee ! Louise, I swear it !
Duch. DE LA V. (*raising her arms to heaven*). Father ! at length, I dare
to hope for pardon,
For now remorse may prove itself sincere !
Bear witness, Heaven ! I never loved this man
So well as now ! and never seem'd *his* love
Built on so sure a rock ! Upon thine altar
I lay the offering. I revoke the past ;
For Louis, heaven was left—and now I leave
Louis, when tenfold more beloved, for heaven !
Ah ! pray with me ! Be this our latest token—
This memory of sweet moments—sweet, though sinless!
Ah ! pray with me ! that I may live till death
The thought—"we pray'd together for forgiveness !"
Louis. Oh ! wherefore never knew I till this hour
The treasure I shall lose ! I dare not call thee
Back from the heaven where thou art half already !
Thy soul demands celestial destinies,
And stoops no more to earth. Be thine the peace,
And mine the penance ! Yet these awful walls,
The rigid laws of this severest order,
Yon spectral shapes, this human sepulchre—
And thou, the soft, the delicate, the highborn,
The adored delight of Europe's mightiest king—
Thou canst not bear it !
Duch. DE LA V.   I have borne much worse—
Thy change and thy desertion !—Let it pass !
There is no terror in the things without ;
Our souls alone the palace or the prison ;
And the one thought that I have fled from sin
Will fill the cell with images more glorious,
And haunt its silence with a mightier music,
Than ever throng'd illumined halls, or broke

From harps by mortal strung!

LOUIS.   I will not hear thee !
I cannot brave these thoughts. Thy angel voice
But tells me what a sun of heavenly beauty
Glides from the earth, and leaves my soul to darkness.
This is *my* work!—'twas I for whom that soul
Forsook its native element ; for me,
Sorrow consumed thy youth, and conscience gnawed
That patient, tender, unreproachful heart.
And now this crowns the whole ! the priest—the altar—
The sacrifice—the victim ! Touch me not !
Speak not! I am unmann'd enough already.
I—I—I choke ! These tears—let them speak for me.
Now ! now thy hand—farewell ! farewell, forever !
                                    [*Exit* LOUIS, R. 1 E.
DUCH. DE LA V. Be firm, my heart, be firm ! (*after a pause, turning to*
      BRAGELONE, *who advances,* C., *with a slight smile*)
                              'Tis past ! we've conquer'd !

The DUCHESS *re-ascends the altar,* BRAGELONE *with head bent down walking
part of the way by her side, then pausing,* L.—*the crowd close around and
shut her out ; during which she puts on the convent dress. Music.*

CHORUS.

Hark ! to the nuptial train are open'd wide
The Eternal Gates. Hosanna to the bride !

GRAM. She has ta'en the veil—the last dread rite is done.
ABBESS (*from the altar*). Sister Louise ! before the eternal grate
Becomes thy barrier from the living world,
It is allow'd thee once more to behold
The face of men, and bid farewell to friendship.
BRAGE. (*aside*). Why do I shudder ? why shrinks back my being
From our last gaze, like Nature from the Grave ?
One moment, and one look, and o'er her image
Thick darkness falls, till Death, that morning star,
Heralds immortal day. I hear her steps
Treading the mournful silence ; o'er my soul
Pauses the freezing time. O Lord, support me !
One effort more—one effort!—Wake, my soul !
Tis thy last trial ; wilt thou play the craven ? (*crosses towards* L.)

The crowd give way ; the DUCHESS DE LA VALLIÈRE, *in the habit of the
Carmelite nuns, passes down the steps of the altar, led by the* ABBESS. *As
she pauses to address those whom she recognizes in the crowd, the chorus
chaunts :—*

Sister, look and speak thy last,
From the world thou'rt dying fast ;
While farewell to life thou'rt giving,
Dead already to the living.

DUCH. DE LA V. (*coming to the front of the stage, sees* LAUZUN, R.). Lauzun !
thou serv'st a king, whate'er his fault,
Who merits all thy homage ; honor—love him.
His glory needs no friendship ; but in sickness
Or sorrow *kings* need love. Be faithful, Lauzun !
And, far from thy loud world, one lowly voice
Shall not forget thee.

BRAGE. (C. L.—*aside*).   All the strife is hush'd !
My heart's wild sea lies mute !
DUCH. DE LA V. (*approaching* BRAGELONE, *and kneeling to him*). Now!
friend and father,
Bless the poor nun !
BRAGE. As Duchess of La Vallière
Thou wert not happy ; as the Carmelite Sister,'
Say—*art* thou happy ?
DUCH. DE LA V.   Yes!
BRAGE. (*laying his hand on her head*). O Father, bless her !

CHORUS.

Hark ! in heaven is mirth !
                    Jubilate !
Grief leaves guilt on earth !
                    Jubilate !
Joy for sin forgiven !
                    Jubilate !
Come, O Bride of Heaven !
                    Jubilate !

(*Curtain falls slowly.*)

EXPLANATION OF THE STAGE DIRECTIONS,

The Actor is supposed to face the Audience.

L.	Left.	C.	Centre.
L. C.	Left Centre.	R.	Right.
L. 1 E.	Left First Entrance.	R. 1 E.	Right First Entrance.
L. 2 E.	Left Second Entrance.	R. 2 E.	Right Second Entrance.
L. 3 E.	Left Third Entrance.	R. 3 E.	Right Third Entrance.
L. U. E.	Left Upper Entrance	R. U. E.	Right Upper Entrance.
	(wherever this Scene may be.)	D. R. C.	Door Right Centre.
D. L. C.	Door Left Centre.		